DEDICATION

This book is dedicated to the Marines I served with and especially to the ones who gave all they had and to the love of my life, Martha, without whose support, dedication, love and editing skills these books would have never been published.

Other books by Noble Callaway

Marine Top Sergeant

Marine Gunner

Noble Callaway

ISBN:979-8-6756-9032-9

CONTENTS

Chapter 1 Sergeant Major

I heard the soft footsteps outside my tent coming nearer. Instinctively, I unsnapped the K-bar fighting knife with my right hand from its scabbard lying by my side on the cot, which I held with my left hand. As I slipped it out of the scabbard, I heard the flap to my tent being pulled back and a voice saying, "Sergeant Major, the time on deck is zero five."

"Thank you, Lance Corporal," I said to the fire watch as I pushed the K-bar back into its scabbard. Old habits die hard I thought.

I rolled on my back and stretched my legs and arms out straight feeling the cool morning air on my bare arms. I was surprised how unusually cold it was in the middle of July 1978 at Camp Lejeune, North Carolina.

I must be crazy. After fourteen years in the Marine Corps I still love this shit. I threw my blanket back and sat up on the side of the cot shivering. I reached down into my sea bag and pulled out my red shorts, hooded sweatshirt and running shoes.

As I dressed, I smiled to myself thinking I've only been the sergeant major of this battalion a little over a month and already the Battalion Commander, LtCol Skipper had agreed to several of my recommendations. The one I felt the best about was my PT (Physical training) program. When I had joined the battalion, PT had been left up to the individual discretion of the company commanders or platoon leaders. I recommended that when we were in the rear and whenever possible in the field the whole battalion should PT together. At first everyone from the lieutenant colonel on down ran with their troops. But after the first week LtCol Skipper, the major and several captains began missing the PT sessions. But when a couple of the 1st Sergeants skipped a morning run, I called all four of them to my office. I told the 1st Sergeants, "I know that the senior officers are beginning to slack off on PT. I have spoken to LtCol Skipper about it. But I will not stand for my senior Staff NCOs failing to PT with their companies unless they were over forty-six years old." (At this time in the Corps no one over forty-six had to take the Marine Corps Physical Fitness test.) "And no one here is of that age. Every enlisted man will PT unless sick in bed or standing duty." I could tell they weren't very happy. Especially with the fact that I was thirty years old and they all were thirty-six to forty-two years old. But I ended it by saying, "Any morning you don't see me fall out for PT you'll know you don't have to."

Dressed now, I ran out to the portajohn to relieve myself. Usually in the field we didn't have time for PT. But this time, we had been in the field a week and a half and we'd PT'd every morning at sunup.

By the time I stepped out of the portajohn the battalion was forming up by companies. I joined a different company each morning as the company gunnery sergeants put their companies through their daily seven exercises. When these where done, the battalion fell in by companies for the four-mile run. I love early morning runs. But I especially enjoyed the runs of the last week and a half. Our tent city was only two miles from the beach. So, like each morning since we'd been here, we ran down to the beach using the dirt roads. Although the companies like to race each other I made it clear from the beginning that a company could only run as fast as its slowest man. No man was to be left behind. Because I believe that if you allow men to drop back, the gap between your fast runners and the slower just gets wider. But when everyone runs as one the gap closes and the unit will grow even tighter.

The first day we ran down to the ocean, I dropped down at the water's edge and did thirty pushups in the ocean. The company I was with loved it and did the same.

So today as we reached the ocean the four companies quickly spread out in a long line along the ocean's edge. Soon there were a thousand Marines doing pushups in the breaking waves. Many of the men then jumped up and ran out into the cold ocean up to their necks. I stood up laughing feeling great as a jeep with a lieutenant and his driver stopped nearby.

"Good morning Lieutenant," I said walking over to them.

"Good morning sir," he said, not sure what rank I was in my PT shorts and sweatshirt. Then he asked, "Is this a special kind of unit like recon or something?"

"No sir, it's just a regular Marine Infantry battalion. I like to think it's the best battalion in the Corps," I answered smiling.

"Well they sure look motivated. But I better be going," said the lieutenant pointing forward. As the driver put the jeep in gear I said, "Good day sir." I turned back to the battalion who were now being reformed up into companies by their company gunnery sergeants for the run back.

Later in the afternoon, LtCol Skipper sent me to the rear to check on the mail and messages.

Driving the colonel's jeep back, I first picked up the mail for the companies. Then I drove to our battalion headquarters and parked in my parking space. I walked into LtCol Skipper's office and looked through his in basket. I pulled out what I felt couldn't wait until the end of the week and carried them with me down the hall to my office. As I looked through my in basket, I found a hand written note for me to call Major Hester. I smiled thinking of my old friend Major Dana Hester. I first met him in Vietnam when he was a new butter bar second lieutenant. I was a young sergeant then and watched him grow to become our company commander and make captain. Under his leadership we fought through some of the worst fighting in the war. In fact, he promoted me to staff sergeant right after Hue City when many thought I was too young for the rank. Again in 1972 when he was a major, we served together as advisors to the Vietnamese Marine Corps. Later as a company First Sergeant I served under him again when he was my battalion XO (executive officer). But I still wondered what he could want.

I put the note aside looking through the rest of my paperwork. The easy stuff I took care of and placed in my out basket. What could wait until the end of the week I put back in my in basket. The rest I placed next to LtCol Skipper's papers.

Then I picked up the phone and dialed Maj Hester's number. The phone didn't ring three times before it was picked up and I heard, "Second Battalion XO. Major Hester speaking sir."

"Sir this is Sergeant Major Cord."

"Nathan, congratulations," said Maj Hester.

"For what sir?"

"You haven't seen the list yet?"

"What list sir?" I asked.

"The warrant officer list. We just got a copy today and you're on it."

I was so shocked I couldn't speak. I had wanted to be an officer for fourteen years. But with my limited education (I was a high school drop out) I hadn't had a high enough IQ to get a regular commission. And to be a warrant officer or a limited duty officer you had to be at least a staff sergeant with ten years in the Corps to even apply for either of them. The staff sergeant part had come easy for me because of the war. But by the time I had ten years in, the war was over and the Corps was cutting back in total strength, which meant a reduction in officers also. So, I applied for Infantry warrant officer and after being passed over the last three years, I had all but given up hope. And this year for the fourth time I felt I was now just going through the motions when I applied. Of course, some people would say I was crazy to want to be an officer of any kind now that I was a sergeant major. Starting out warrant officers don't make as much money as first sergeants. It could take me six or more years as a warrant officer to make as much as I did now. But I missed being a small unit leader.

"Nathan are you still there?" asked Maj Hester after I hadn't answered.

"Yeah, yes sir. Are you sure?"

"Yes, I have the message right in front of me."

"I can't believe it, sir. What's the MOS (military occupation specialty) does it have me in?" I asked wondering if I would have a new job and career path I would have to learn to get these bars.

"You're going to be that special kind of warrant officer, a Marine Gunner with the MOS of 0302, small unit leader. You made it, what you wanted."

"Marine Gunner! The Corps hasn't made any of them in at least four years. How many others made gunner?"

"Sixty-two were selected for warrant officer, but only you were selected for Marine Gunner."

"How can this be sir? I just can't believe it."

"Do you remember our battalion commander we had when I first met you in 67?"

"Yes sir. He's the one that promised to get me a commission to lieutenant. I'm still waiting."

"He's a general now. He called me last month about you. He wanted to know what kind of an officer I thought you'd make now. I told him you would make an excellent officer, but it would be a waste of talent to make you anything but an infantry officer."

"Thank you, sir."

"No problem."

"Well sir, I better get back to my colonel."

"Take care, Nathan."

"Good day sir," I said hanging up the phone. I then gathered up the papers and walked out to the jeep. I got in and drove to regimental headquarters.

Once there I went to see the regimental sergeant major. I knocked on his door. He looked up from his desk and waved me in saying, "Come in Sergeant Major Cord."

I walked in saying, "How you doing sergeant major. Anything new from regiment we should know about before I head back out to the field?"

"Nothing hot except this," he said pushing a message across his desk toward me. I picked up the paper and saw it was the warrant officer selection list from the office of the Marine Corps Commandant.

"Have you seen this?" he asked.

"No but I just heard I was on the list."

"Then it's true, that's really you and it's not a mistake?"

"No, it's not."

"But why would you want to give up being the youngest sergeant major in the Corps to be just another middle-aged warrant officer?" He protested.

"I'm going to be a Marine Gunner, a small unit leader doing what I like best."

"But you could have my job in four years. In eight years, you could be a division sergeant major. You could be the youngest sergeant major of the Corps. Instead ten years from now you'll still be a platoon leader and you'll be in your forties."

"I'd be proud to be the Sergeant Major of the Corps. But I would rather be a small unit leader."

"Do you realize that your free meals and uniforms will be over? Because as an officer you have to pay for your mess hall meals and all those new officer uniforms?"

"I know. But I've waited fourteen years for this chance and I'm going to take it."

"I see. I think your crazy. But I wish you luck."

"Thank you. I better be going," I said. We shook hands and I walked out to the jeep. I then drove to a pay phone and called my wife Marty who was staying with her mother up in Georgetown, Delaware. We had decided it was best she stay up there until I was either passed over again for warrant officer or was promoted.

Because if I was promoted, I would attend the warrant officer school at Quantico VA. Once that was over and I found out where my new duty station would be, hopefully she, our daughter Samantha and stepson Kyle could join me there. We had been married for three years and not only still in love with each other, but happier than ever. Although she is my second wife, she is the one I should've waited for. This marriage is the way I thought love and marriage was supposed to be.

Then finally I heard a voice come on the line saying, "Hello."

"Marty this is Nathan."

"Nathan, I didn't expect to hear from you until Friday. Is everything okay?"

"Yes, everything is fine. But guess what?"

"What?"

"I just found out I've been selected for promotion to warrant officer."

"Great, but what does this mean for us?"

"Well it means I'll put the bars on October first. Then after some leave, I'll report to Quantico for the warrant officer basic school."

"How long will that last?"

"I'm not sure. Maybe nine months."

"Then will we be able to be together?"

"Unless I'm ordered overseas, we will be together."

"Oh, I'm looking forward to that."

"Me too."

"Do you think you'll get home this weekend?"

"As far as I know I'll be there by Saturday. If not, I'll call you."

"Okay. I love you."

"I love you, too. I'll see ya."

"See ya."

"See ya," I said again hanging up.

I then drove back out to the tent area. I put the colonel's paper work in his tent. Then I walked over to my own tent and placed my paper work on top of my cot.

I then drove out to the training area. It took me half an hour to find LtCol Skipper who was observing one of his companies. I drove up next to him and stopped. As I got out, he looked over at me and then looked back at the troops as he asked, "Anything hot going on at regiment?"

"No sir. All's quiet."

"No news?"

"No sir. Just the usual stuff. But sir I do have some personal news you need to know."

He looked at me saying, "What's that?"

I smiled saying, "Sir, I've been selected for warrant officer."

He gave me a funny look asking, "Are you sure?"

"I've seen the message sir."

"Well you have a big decision to make."

"I've already made it sir."

"Shit. When do you put the bars on?"

"October first, sir."

"God, I hate to lose you. This battalion's spirit has improved just since you've been here."

"Thank you, sir."

In August the staff NCOs of our battalion threw a party for me at the staff NCO club on Tuesday night.

I hadn't drunk much since I met Marty. But this night I let myself go, drinking black Russians. I knew that soon my career would take a turn from which my life would never be the same. Although I was looking forward to it, I knew that my relationship with the enlisted ranks would never be the same. And I would miss that.

Sometime after midnight I lost tract of time. I remember a staff sergeant helping me walk back to my room. I managed to set my alarm clock for 0500 and got undressed before I passed out on the bed.

The next thing I knew I felt a hand on my foot. I jumped and the movements made my head feel like it was going to split open. I rolled over on my back opening my eyes. First, I was surprised it was daylight, but then I was shocked to see LtCol Skipper standing at the foot of my bed.

"Yes sir." I moaned sitting up slowly holding my head in my hands.

Then I asked, "What time is it sir?"

"1000," answered LtCol Skipper smiling.

"Oh, shit I can't believe this," I said.

"I heard you really tied one on last night. I knew you weren't at morning PT or chow. But when I hadn't heard from you by 0945, I figured I'd better check on you."

"I'm sorry, sir," I said standing up on wobbly legs.

"Did you hear your serenade?"

Picking up my towel and razor I looked back at him and asked puzzled, "Serenade?"

"Yes. When you didn't show up for morning PT the battalion ran down here and stopped long enough to sing you the Marine Corps hymn."

"I never heard a thing. Not even my alarm clock. Shit!" I said embarrassed and added, "Sir, I'll be in the area within half an hour."

"I'll see you in your office then."

"Sir, if it's Okay I'd like to visit the companies first."

"That's fine sergeant major. But I expect to see you at noon chow."

"I'll be there colonel," I said entering the head.

I heard him walk out the door as I started to shave. After I shaved, I washed my burning eyes with cold water. Then I put on a clean set of cammies. I took two aspirins and walked outside. The bright sunlight seemed to slap me in the forehead. But I drove over to the battalion area in my GMC truck. As I visited each company there were a lot of smiles and kidding from the staff NCOs and each company gunnery sergeant or 1st Sergeant gave me at least one cup of coffee.

The first of September our battalion was preparing for two weeks in the field when I received a phone call in my office.

"Sergeant Major Cord speaking sir." I answered.

"Sergeant Major this is Gunny Hennessey."

I had served with GySgt Hennessey the first time back in the 70's when we were both advisors to the Vietnamese Marine Corps. Later we served together on the USS Hampton and last time in an Infantry company.

"Gunny Hennessey, how are you?"

"Just fine."

"You still with Mike Company, Second Battalion?"

"Yes, and that's why I'm calling. You put your bars on the first of October, right?"

"Yes," I answered.

"Well the men of Mighty Mike (the last company I was 1st Sergeant of before making sergeant major) would like to give you a party on your last night as an enlisted man. That would be September

30th. Is that a good time for you?"

"Yes, we get back from the field that day so I can make it that night. Where at?"

"We'll get a place off base. We'll have buses to take us there and back. So, we can drink all we want and won't have to worry about driving. I'll let you know where and when."

"Sounds good, Gunny. I'm looking forward to seeing you guys again."

"Well, good day, Sergeant Major."

"Good day, Gunny." I said hanging up thinking of my last duty station with the men of Mike Company when I was a First Sergeant. As much as I like being a battalion sergeant major, I like being at the company and platoon level better. Which was why I looked forward to being a warrant officer.

I got up and walked down to the hall and knocked on LTCol Skipper's office. "Come in Sergeant Major."

I went in and explained to him about the party my last unit was going to give to me on the day we returned from the field.

"Is your wife coming down to the promotion ceremony?"

"Yes, sir and there maybe a couple car loads coming down too."

"That's great. We're planning a little get together for you afterwards with cold cuts, beer and sodas."

"Thank you, sir," I said smiling.

"By the way is there someone special you'd like to have promote you?"

I was surprised he asked this, but right away I said, "Well sir if you don't mind, I would like to have Major Hester from Second Battalion."

"Major Hester. He was the XO from the battalion you came from, right?"

"Yes, sir, we go way back. He was my platoon leader in Nam and as a captain he promoted me to staff sergeant after Hue City in 68. And in 1972 as a major we were advisors to the Vietnamese Marine Corps together."

"Then I can understand you two being close. I'll call him today."

"Thank you, sir.

The night before the battalion was due to leave for the field, I called Marty. When she answered I said, "Hi."

"Nathan it's good to hear your voice. I can't wait to see you."

"Just two more weeks."

"I can't wait."

"Me neither. Who's all coming down with you?"

"Well let's see. Me and Samantha, Phil and Donna (Marty's twin sister) and their boys, Mom, your Uncle Clark and Aunt Del, your cousins Charles and Pauline and your father."

"My father. Are you sure?"

"He says he is. He seems excited. He's planning the route. He wants us to leave a day early and get a hotel about halfway. We don't have to be there until 2PM, right?"

"Yes 1400. I just can't believe he's coming all this way. What about Kyle?"

"I asked him if he wanted to go. But he wants to visit with his father. Did you call Bunny (my ex-wife) about your boys?"

"Yes, I did. She said no. I even told her if she didn't want them to ride with you, they could ride with my aunt and uncle or my cousins. But she still said no. Then she wanted to know how a high school dropout could become an officer?"

"She does love to put you down doesn't she? What did you say?"

"I just said I worked hard and my war record didn't hurt either." I answered laughing.

"I love you."

"I love you too," I said.

The two weeks in the field passed quickly. At times it was hard to keep my mind on the field problems as I kept thinking about the fact that on October 1st, I'd be a warrant officer and then go on fifteen days leave with Marty.

On September 30th we were back from the field. That evening I dressed in civilian clothes and stood outside of the Staff NCO barracks until the camouflaged school bus pulled up out front. As I walked out to the bus, the door opened and Lt Scotto waved me in saying, "Come on in Sergeant Major."

"Thank you, sir," I said stepping up into the bus and took a seat next to him up front behind the driver. Across from me sat my old friend big GySgt Hennessey. We had been advisors together in Vietnam in 1972. Next to him was another friend SSgt Knight. Behind them I was happy to see other men I recognized from my last unit. There was SSgts Taper, Vance and Manuel, Sgts Schwartz, Williams, Reilly and Campbell. Further back in the bus was PFCs

Wynne, West and Coston and many others. Soon we arrived at a bar, which Mike Company had rented for the night. Inside there were Marine Corps stickers and posters all over the walls. In the center of the bar was a table big enough for Lt Scotto, his Staff NCOs and me. Soon the drinks were flowing freely. But I kept sipping mine knowing it was going to be a long night and that my family would be here tomorrow. Soon we were telling sea stories (war stories and lies). First, we talked about our times together in Mike Company. Then SSgt Knight talked about serving with me on sea duty on the USS Hampton. GySgt Hennessey told them about our days of being advisors to the Vietnamese Marine Corps during the Easter Offensive in 1972. The younger Marines wanted to know more and more about Vietnam, especially Hue City.

Finally, at 2300 I said I had to go because my battalion morning PT would come early. As if ordered and somehow it probably was almost 200 Marines stood up and got in line one behind the other with Lt Scotto at the front who said, "Sergeant Major you can't leave without having a drink with each one of us."

Knowing I'd been had, I just answered, "Yes sir, one for the road, right?"

"Yes, one for us and about two hundred for you," said Lt Scotto.

Then GySgt Hennessey stepped up with a bottle and two shot glasses. He filled both glasses and handed one to Lt Scotto and the other to me. We touched glasses and drank them down. As Lt Scotto stepped out of the way GySgt Hennessey refilled the glasses. This time he and I touched glasses and drank them down. Then up stepped SSgt Knight smiling as GySgt Hennessey refilled the glasses. And so, it went with one man after another stepping up to have a drink with me. I don't remember getting to the end of the line although later I was told I did. But I do remember sitting on the floor in the corner and talking to an older civilian couple who somehow had wondered into the bar. Later yet, I remember riding in the back of the bus back to the base singing the Marine Corps Hymn as a PFC stood up pissing out the bus window.

The next thing I knew for sure was when I noticed the sun was up. I looked over at my clock and picked it up. I hadn't even set it. I knew the battalion had already done their PT, once again without me and were now at chow. With a splitting head, I slowly got up, shaved, dressed and took two aspirin and drove over to the mess hall. I went in and started through the chow line. Looking at the eggs made my stomach turn over. So, I just got toast, orange juice and coffee. As I sat down at a table across from the regimental Sergeant Major, who was smiling and asked, "Another rough night Sergeant Major?"

"Yes, I'm afraid so. If I don't get promoted soon these promotion parties are going to be the end of me."

After chow, I went to my office. There I finished up the last of my paper work. My replacement would have to take care of the rest. I then packed up the last of my things and put them in the cab of my truck. I then drove around to the Staff NCO Barracks. There I put my uniform bags in the cab of my truck and sea bag and footlocker wrapped in plastic in the back of my truck. Then I checked out of my room. I spent the rest of the morning visiting the four companies of my battalion. I also stopped at the base bank and exchanged a ten-dollar bill for ten silver dollars.

As I left the chow hall at 1257 a runner from battalion headquarters found me and reported that my family was waiting for me in my office. I drove over and parked in my parking space. As I got out, I noticed there was a row of chairs already set up for my family on the edge of the parade deck and behind them rows of tables and chairs for them to eat on later.

I walked into our battalion headquarters building and started down the hallway past LtCol Skipper's office when I saw Samantha walk out of my office. She was wearing a white long sleeve shirt, a skirt with strawberries, long red stockings and black shoes. Her bright red hair was just getting long enough that if she were a boy she'd need a haircut. But what really surprised me was she was walking without holding on to anything. I hadn't seen her do that.

I smiled as she looked around. When she first saw me, she started backing up. She had never seen me in cammies before. But then she smiled and came running yelling, "Daddy! Daddy!"

Out the door behind her came Marty hurrying. I kneeled down on one knee and caught her as she leaped into my arms. I stood up hugging her gently as she squeezed my neck. Marty was dressed in a dark blue skirt, white shirt with what I called a Wyatt Earp style string tie and a blue jacket. She came and put her arms around me as I held Samantha with one arm and put my left arm around Marty and kissed her.

"I heard one of the Marines here say you weren't feeling too good. Have you been sick?" Marty asked.

"No, I'm fine. I just had too much to drink last night," I answered embarrassed. There was a time I took pride in how much I could drink. But now I knew it was not a good example to set for the younger troops. You can't tell how good a Marine is by how much he drinks. To get drunk is to lose control and a good Marine should never allow himself to lose control. Something I still had to work on.

"Shame on you. Well, everybody is here."

Together we walked into my office where I found my couch and chair full with my family. Someone had even brought in some extra fold up chairs. Chad and Josh, the children of Marty's twin sister Donna, were both sitting in my chair behind my desk. I put Samantha down and stood as she held my hand looking up at me as we talked about farming, the Corps and kids. About 1330 Maj Hester knocked on my door and I waved him in and introduced him to everyone. They had all heard about him, but this was the first time any of them had met him.

At 1345, I told them we better go outside because I had to form up the battalion. As we walked outside, I showed them to the row of chairs set up for them. I also found the four companies of the battalion already formed up with their first sergeants out front.

I marched out and centered myself in the front center of the battalion formation. From the corner of my eye I could see Donna's husband Phil sitting all the way to the left. Next to him were Donna, then Chad and Josh with both their hands behind their heads. Next was Samantha, Marty and Mrs. Pieper, then my father with one leg crossed over the other, then was uncle Clark, cousins Charles and Pauline and Aunt Del.

Then I yelled the order, "Battalion! Atten-sun!" A thousand Marines snapped to attention as one. "Report!" I yelled.

One after another each first sergeant saluted me and yelled, "All present or accounted for!" And I in turn saluted each of them.

After all four first sergeants had reported, I did an about face. I looked over to my left where LtCol Skipper stood with Maj Hester. I nodded my head to LtCol Skipper and he stepped off marching toward me. He stopped directly in front of me and did a right face to face me.

I snapped a salute saying, "Sir, the battalion is formed and is all present or accounted for!"

He returned my salute saying, "Thank you Sergeant Major. Take your post."

I did a left face, took one step and did a right face, took two steps, which placed me at his right rear. From here I did a right face, took two more steps, which placed me to his left rear. From here I did another right face facing the battalion.

"Post!" yelled LtCol Skipper.

As one, the four 1st sergeants did a left face and marched to the rear of their companies as four Captains as one replaced them.

Then LtCol Skipper said, "As you all know we are holding this formation today to promote our Sergeant Major to the exalted officer rank of Warrant Officer. Sergeant Major Cord has requested that Major Dana Hester promote him. The Major and Sergeant Major have served three tours together. They first met in Vietnam in 1967 when the major was a young lieutenant and the sergeant major was a young buck sergeant. Again in 1972 the then major served with then Gunnery Sergeant Cord. During their last tour together right here at Camp Lejeune, Cord was promoted to sergeant major." Then he yelled looking to his right, "Major Hester! Front and center!"

Major Hester marched out carrying a red folder in his left hand. He stopped in front of LtCol Skipper and did a left face to face him. Then he saluted saying, "Major Hester reporting as ordered sir."

LtCol Skipper returned his salute saying, "Carry on Major."

"Aye, Aye sir," answered Major Hester who then did an about face facing the battalion. He then did one side step to his right and yelled, "Sergeant Major Cord! Front and center!"

I marched straight out four steps, did a right face, took some more steps and did another right face facing Maj Hester. I saluted him saying, "Sir, Sergeant Major Cord reporting as ordered."

He returned my salute and then opened up the red folder and began reading my promotion warrant. As he read it, my mind drifted to my future as an officer. The thought of the Basic Warrant Officer School was a little frightening to me at my age. I was afraid I wouldn't be able to control my temper for six months of being treating like a boot Marine again.

But soon he was finished reading and he said, "Mrs. Cord would you like to help me pin these new bars on?"

This was a surprise to me and in about two seconds it seemed Marty was standing next to Maj Hester as he dug out of his pocket one warrant officer bar (a red bar with a gold box in the middle) and one black bursting bomb emblem.

"Gunner (the nick name for Infantry Warrant Officers in the Marine Corps) I hope you know how these go on?" said Maj Hester smiling.

I smiled too feeling funny being called Gunner. But I answered, "Yes sir. The bar goes on the right collar and the bursting bomb on the left collar."

"Well Mrs. Cord you get the bursting bomb," said Maj Hester handing it to her. Together they stepped forward and reached up to my collars unfastening the sergeant major strips and taking them off. Then as they pinned on my bar and bursting bomb Marty asked, "How does this bomb go? Flame toward your neck or down toward the collar point?"

"Toward my neck," I answered.

Then they both stepped back. Maj Hester snapped to attention and handed me the red folder holding my promotion warrant with his left hand saying, "Congratulations, Gunner."

"Thank you, sir," I said taking the red folder with my left hand as we shook hands with our right hands.

As Marty turned to walk back to her chair, LtCol Skipper spoke up, "Mrs. Cord don't you think the new Gunner deserves a kiss?"

Marty spun around smiling saying, "I sure do." But as she walked toward me, I noticed her face turning red. I stepped out to meet her and we kissed quickly. Then as I stepped back to attention and Marty again turned back toward her chair LtCol Skipper smiling said, "You two can finish that later."

Marty spun around again smiling at LtCol Skipper, her face turning even redder. Then she walked back to her chair.

Then I saluted both officers who in turn saluted me. I did an about face and marched off to the rear of the battalion. Standing back there where nobody could see, I looked at my right collar pulling it out so I could see the bar. I still couldn't believe it. Then I pulled the left collar up and looked down at the bursting bomb. This I'm the proudest of all because it shows the world, I am a Marine Infantry Warrant Officer.

Then I heard someone yell, "Gunner Cord! Front and center!"

I looked through the ranks and saw all four company first sergeants standing at attention side by side in front of LtCol Skipper and Major Hester facing the battalion. Realizing what was up, I was glad there where only four of them as I marched out and centered myself in front of the four of them.

"We felt we should be the first enlisted men to salute you sir," said one of them as all four 1st sergeants saluted me as one.

I returned their salute, holding it too long forgetting that as an officer they can't lower their salutes until after I do. Suddenly, I realized they were waiting for me and I dropped my right hand down like a karate chop to the seam of my trousers.

Then as I stepped forward to the 1st sergeant to my left and digging in my pocket with my right hand I said, "And as by tradition the first enlisted men to salute a new officer will receive a silver dollar," I gave him a silver dollar and then side stepped from one first sergeant to the other handing out their silver dollars to them. Then I stepped back. The four first sergeants again saluted me. I returned their salute, did an about face and marched again to the rear of the battalion.

Then LtCol Skipper yelled, "Company commanders dismiss your companies and let's eat!"

The four captains saluted him and then did an about face facing their companies. Then each captain yelled, "Company dismissed!"

As the battalion broke ranks many of the troops ran to put the food on the table while captains, lieutenants, gunnery sergeants, staff sergeants, and some sergeants and corporals gathered around me shaking my hand and slapping my back congratulating me. After I had spoken to the last one, I walked over to my family who were still sitting in their chairs. I handed the red folder to Marty who opened it up. Samantha reached up to me with her right hand and I held her hand with my left hand.

Donna, sitting three chairs down from Samantha said, "Nathan, Chad says he wants to be a Marine when he grows up."

I looked over at her smiling as I said, "That's good. Somebody will have to take my place someday. But when he's seventeen send him to talk to me first, though."

LtCol Skipper walked up to me and said, "Gunner would you and your family like to get your chow first?"

"Yes sir. Thank you," I said and then opening my arms to my

family I added, "Let's eat." I swung Samantha up onto one hip and led the family to the table filled with cold cuts, salad, potato chips, pretzels, pies, cupcakes, cookies, sodas and a keg of beer. My family alone took up one table except for a couple of seats. And here to my surprise sat LtCol Skipper and Major Hester. I was again surprised to learn that LtCol Skipper had come from a farm family. So very quickly the talk between him and Uncle Clark, Cousin Charles and my father turned to farming. But Aunt Del, Cousin Pauline and Donna seemed more interested in Major Hester, I guess because of the three tours we had served together. And as usual when Marines talked to people who aren't Marines, he talked only of the funny things that happened. Our eyes met once and I could feel the pain of the stories it would hurt too much to tell.

Later we all got into our cars and my truck. I hung my uniform bag in my father's car so Marty and Samantha could ride with me. Then we headed north toward Delaware. Near Norfolk Virginia we stopped at a motel for the night. It felt good to hold Marty in my arms again.

The next day, we drove the rest of the way to Georgetown, DE where we would stay with Mrs. Pieper. Every day I got up at 0630 and did 100 pushups, 80 sit-ups and ran 3 miles out of town past the college and back, then finished up with my karate routine. I knew I had better be in shape when I arrived at the Basic School. I was worried about going through this officer type boot camp so much I even dreamed about it. The worse dream I had was when I dreamed I was called into the colonel's office. He told me the only way I could stay in the Corps was if I went through Parris Island boot camp again. And then I was there at boot camp, a 30-year-old private being trained with teenagers by DI's who were in high school when I was fighting in Hue City. They were giving me hell and I already knew what they were trying to teach the others.

Marty had shaken me awake asking, "You all right Nathan?"

"Yes," I answered.

"You were moaning in your sleep."

"I was having a nightmare. I guess I'm getting uptight about the Basic School."

"I know you'll do fine dear."

"I hope so."

"You will."

"I love you Marty."
"And I love you.

Chapter 2 Warrant Officer One

On October 13th, I finished packing up my footlocker and was checking the expert rifle and pistol badges just above the left breast pocket on my dress green blouse. Above them were my six rows of ribbons. I measured the warrant officer bar and bursting bomb on the shoulders of the green blouse and the collars of the tan shirt.

Marty woke up behind me asking, “Everything all right?”

“Yes,” I said pulling the plastic down over the uniform. “It’s just this uniform looks kind ’a bare. There’re no chevrons, rockers and hash marks on the sleeves.”

“I think it looks good on you.”

I turned looking at her saying. “It still feels funny knowing I’m an officer.”

“You do still want to be an officer?”

“Of course.”

“Good because you deserve these bars.”

I smiled saying, “I love you.”

“I’m glad you don’t have that uniform on right now.”

“Why?” I asked.

“It might get wrinkled,” said Marty pulling her blouse over her head she added, “Well don’t look so surprised. Marine officers turn me on.”

Pulling her into my arms I said, “How come you never told me before?”

“I didn’t know it myself until a few days ago,” she said smiling before we kissed.

I didn’t have to report to Quantico until midnight of the 15th. But on the morning of October 15th, I put the footlocker in the back of my truck and hung the uniforms in the cab of my truck.

After a big dinner at noon, I left giving myself plenty of time to drive the three hours across the bay and down to Quantico, VA.

At a McDonalds just outside the main gate of Quantico, I stopped for supper. Afterwards, I went out and got my dress green uniform and went into the restroom and changed. Soon I found the Basic School was just a part of the vast Quantico base in the Virginia pinewoods near Fredericksburg.

I found the building I was looking for and parked in the main parking lot. With my orders in hand I walked inside. In a big hallway were several tables with a lieutenant colonel and several majors standing around.

"Step right up, Gunner," said the lieutenant colonel walking toward the nearest table. But his smile suddenly left his face as he asked, "What are you doing with those bursting bombs on?"

After fourteen years in the Corps and serving as a sergeant major, I no longer stood in awe of the commissioned rank structure except for full bird colonels and generals. I'm as yet not sure how mortal men get to wear eagles or stars. But I did know I could be a good officer if I could just put up with the bullshit of basic school and here it was starting already. I looked hard at the lieutenant colonel before I said, "Sir, I rate these bursting bombs."

"And just how do you figure that?"

"Sir, because I am a real Marine Gunner."

"Bull shit, the Corps hasn't made any real gunners in four years."

"These orders say I'm a Marine Infantry Warrant Officer," I said handing him my orders.

He almost ripped my orders out of my hand as he tore them open. He pulled them out and started reading through them. His face turned red as he looked up at me, "Son-of-a-bitch you are an Infantry Warrant Officer."

"Yes sir."

"I'm sorry gunner. I'll check you in and give you a room number myself. You're on your own until morning."

"Thank you, sir."

A little later I found my room that I would share with three others. I changed into civilian cloths and went out to my truck and carried in my footlocker. Then I went out and brought in my uniforms.

By midnight my three roommates had checked in. There was big strong Gunner Boni an ex-gunnery sergeant. Then there was medium built Gunner Callaway an ex-master sergeant from the bulk fuel field and Gunner Chionsini an ex-staff sergeant of MP's. They were surprised and seemed awed that not only was I an ex-sergeant major, but I had been promoted to Infantry Warrant Officer. In their careers in today's Corps they would likely be called gunners, but only the bursting bomb that I wore made me a true Gunner. The next morning at 0345 I woke up with a start with the sounds of pounding on our door. As I sat up the door opened. A hand reached in turning on the light. Then through the door walked a young captain in dress greens, who yelled, "All right, drop your cocks and grab your socks. Shit, shower and shave, make your racks and the uniform of the day is cammies. Be outside at 0430!"

Then he was gone to the next room down the hall. We were left standing at attention looking at each other when Gunner Boni started laughing and said, "And now let the fun begin."

At 0430 over a hundred new Warrant Officers were standing in our first formation. Standing in front of us was a major; the same captain who had woke us, a lieutenant and an old warrant officer in his forties.

We were standing in one mass formation of four ranks when the old warrant officer came forward and marched us the short distance to chow.

After a breakfast of scrambled eggs, bacon, fried potatoes, a piece of bread which I cleaned my plate with, we again formed up in one mass four ranked formation. Then the old warrant officer marched us to a theatre. There we were marched in by columns and took seats up front.

The major walked up on the stage and stood looking down on us and said, "I'm Major Kelly and on behalf of the Commanding General, US Marine Corps School welcome to Quantico and I wish you well during your course of instruction. Here at the Basic School you will be introduced to officer life. Just like the young second lieutenants, you will serve your apprenticeship here before you're sent out to your first unit as an officer. The only difference is the lieutenants are in their early twenties and have more hair." He then introduced Captain Rose, the lieutenant and the old warrant officer. Later I would learn this warrant officer had been a lieutenant colonel. But he had been passed over for promotion twice. Facing forced retirement much earlier than he wanted from his beloved Corps he requested to stay in as a warrant officer and it was granted. Some people would say he was crazy. But I can understand not wanting to retire as long as you can serve Corps and country and be productive.

Then Major Kelly went on, "I have gone over your record books and I have selected certain individuals to be the student company commander, platoon leaders and first sergeant."

As the highest-ranking ex-enlisted man, I knew my name would be called to command the company.

But instead I heard Maj Kelly say, "Mr. Willis will be the company commander. Come on up here."

I felt hurt as Gunner Willis walked up to the stage. Well I figured I'd be a platoon leader. Then the student 1st Sergeant was called up.

Then Maj Kelly said, "Mr. Escamillo you'll be the first platoon leader. Go on outside and I'll call out your platoon." Then in alphabetical order he called out the names as they got up and walked out. Soon I heard the names Boni, Callaway, Chionsini and Cord called and I got up with the other thirty odd men of the student 1st Platoon and walked out. Inside I felt rage at not being selected for one of the senior billets in the student company. If they had really looked at my record book, they would have seen I had been an acting company commander several times. Was someone trying to put me in my place? But for once in many years I was not the youngest Marine in my rank. And there were older men in this class and it seemed they were getting the senior billets. Was it because I was the only Infantry warrant officer in the class? Was somebody trying to make me quit? "No way!" I thought. "I would keep my mouth shut and I wouldn't quit. I would finish this bullshit and then I'll take my place as a platoon leader and do what I do best, train and lead Infantry Marines."

Soon the company was organized into platoons and squads. Then we were marched to the company supply room where we were issued our 782 gear, made up of an Alice pack, war belt, magazine pouches, two canteens, two canteen pouches, one canteen cup and a first aid pouch. After we put it all together and put it on, we were marched to the armory. There we were issued M-16 rifles, a sling and a cleaning kit consisting of a chamber brush, folding screwdriver, patches and cleaning rod.

Capt Rose stood in front of us saying, "These weapons will be inspected at 1300 tomorrow and you are to know the serial number of your weapon as well as the nipples on your favorite girl's breast."

Then he doubled timed us to the mess hall for noon chow.

While eating chow Gunner Boni said, "Can you believe Captain Rose? Who the fuck does he think he is, a DI?"

"As if the first thing we learned at boot camp was to learn your rifle's serial number," said Gunner Chionsini.

"As if we don't know how to clean weapons," said Gunner

Callaway.

"He must think we're boot butter bar lieutenants," I said.

Soon we were standing outside waiting for Capt Rose and Gunner Escamillo when Gunner Boni said, "I haven't been here a week and I'm already so horny I could fuck a snake in a rock pile." We all laughed and of course from then on, we nicknamed him rock pile.

When Capt Rose came out he marched us to the classroom where we had classes the rest of the afternoon.

After evening chow Capt Rose gave us a class at 1800 on how to take the M-16 rifle apart and clean it. As he did this, I thought to myself, "I was fighting a war with this weapon when he was in high school. This is pure chicken shit. They're proving to us that they have absolute control over us. There is no point in this rifle cleaning class except to make us all miserable. Alter all we aren't young college boys, we've all been in the Corps at least ten years."

When he was finished, he said, "At 2100 tonight I will inspect these rifles. I know you all want to pass your first real inspection tomorrow by Major Kelly. Good Marines pride themselves on having clean pieces."

After he was gone and we were cleaning our weapons, Gunner Boni said, "Who does he think he's talking to? I know for a fact that 90% of us served in Nam. 75% of us are ground combat veterans!"

"That's the idea to let us Infantry guys know we're no better than the Air Wing, Admin or Bulk Fuel guys," said Gunner Chionsini.

"I know you're right. But it still pisses me off," I said laughing.

"But this is what we asked for," said Gunner Callaway laughing.

The inspection went at 2100 and I was in my rack by 2200. It seemed I had no more then settled in when my alarm went off at 0400. Again, we started the routine that did not vary much for the next six months. After reveille came PT followed by a run around the area. We then showered, had chow and walked to classes. Classes lasted about 45 minutes each, followed by 10-minute breaks.

The first six weeks were spent deep in the forest. I loved the rigorous training from dawn until night. We marched and drilled, learned and relearned drill regulations, ran and climbed over obstacle courses and went on conditioning hikes. But I didn't like being shouted at, kicked, humiliated and harassed constantly.

Field days (room cleaning) where held every Thursday night in preparation for Friday morning inspections. Our rooms had to be scrubbed and polished. First, we had to pass Capt Rose's inspection on Thursdays and sometimes to meet his high standards took us well into the night.

Then Friday morning at 0400 he would inspect the rooms again to see if we had messed anything up. If we had we would clean it up instead of going to morning chow. But I was not concerned. For I knew that once it was clean, it's out of our hands. For the final inspection was conducted by Maj Kelly. And if Maj Kelly wanted to find something wrong, he would.

By evening chow on Fridays, we were released for the weekend. I was luckier than most with my wife living close enough by I could visit her each weekend except for the weekend of November 10th. That weekend I had reserved a room at a nearby Motel. At 1800, I was already in the Motel room when Marty drove up in her car. Although we were both hungry, without talking except with our fingers we began undressing each other. Over an hour later we decided we needed food in order to go on. Saturday night was the Marine Corp Birthday Ball. Marty wore a low-cut dark blue dress to the ball, which I couldn't wait to get my hands inside afterward. I wore my new officer dress blues for the first time.

Maj Kelly and a colonel I didn't know, were in their mess dress uniforms with shoulder boards. At the bar was a brigadier general wearing a blue cape. During the ceremony Commandant Wilson made a speech, which drew to my surprise only a polite applause. After this and the meal we danced to music played by a Marine band who sat in rows dressed in red uniforms.

Three more weeks passed by. At Parris Island fourteen years ago, I had had to prove I was man enough to be a Marine. Now here at Quantico I had to prove I was good enough to be an officer of Marines. And I was driven by the all, overwhelming desire to be a Marine Gunner.

There was more close order drill, bayonet practice and hand-to-hand, pugil stick fighting and the running of the obstacle course. We ran in formation at times chanting, "One, two, three, four, we love the Marine Corps!" Twice a week wearing full pack and equipment we ran the Hill Trail, which actually crossed seven steep hills. At first many men softened by years of desk jobs fell out along the way.

Capt Rose would grab these men by the collar yelling, "You want to be an officer in my Corps do ya! On your feet chicken shit!"

But by mid-December, everyone was keeping up.

Each day in the mess hall I would read the red and gold sign which said, "Since 1775 the Marine Corps has been the most invincible fighting force in the history of man." And by God I believe it.

We were lectured on the officer code we were expected to live by. Never leave your wounded on the battlefield. Never retreat; never surrender so long as you have the means to resist. One instructor said, "The only time an officer doesn't have the means to resist is when he's dead."

We also got classes on Marine Corps history.

I began to realize that the Warrant Officer Basic School was little more than a rehash of boot camp, but on a higher level. The training was surely no snap, but it was no real problem either.

By now the training had become almost fairly pleasant compared to what I figured it would be. The harassment from Maj Kelly wasn't even as bad.

I enjoyed the classes in the large lecture rooms and the gymnasium named in the honor of an officer medal-of-honor winner killed in Korea.

On December 22nd we were released for the holidays and I drove home.

Christmas morning, we opened presents at Mrs. Pieper's house. Then we dropped Kyle off at his father's and went on to have breakfast at Marty's Aunt Bernice's house. In the afternoon we had a big supper at Mrs. Pieper's where the Pieper clan exchanged gifts. Then in the evening we picked up my sons Nat and Lance and brought them back to Mrs. Pieper's where we watched them open their gifts.

New Year's Eve, Marty and I went to a New Year's dance at the Seaford Fire Hall. I was surprised to run into my cousin John and his blond wife. I hadn't seen him since he was sixteen and I was seventeen. We all sat together and talked of our mothers who were sisters and other family members. His hair was longer than I remember and of course my hair was a lot shorter and grayer. After we danced in the New Year of 1979, we all went out for breakfast at a truck stop in Laurel.

But much too soon I was back at Quantico.

The winter of 1979 was turning unusually bad and we spent much of it in the wet deep snow-filled forest of Virginia.

But still, the next six weeks passed quickly. At times it reminded me of a cold Parris Island. If Capt Rose didn't think we fell out in the company street fast enough, we would go back and do it again and again. If you dropped your rifle you had to double time around the area with it held at arm's length above your head while yelling, "My rifle is my best friend and I'm a shit head for dropping it!"

And we still did an hour of PT every morning before morning chow and an hour of close order drill afterwards.

Like the young lieutenants, we older warrant officers were being turned into professional Marine officers. The course emphasized Infantry tactics and weapons training. Like ITR in 1965 we were taught in the how-to-do-it fashion, how to take a hill by frontal assault or envelopment, how to defend it once you had it, how to deliver searching and traversing fire with the machine gun. We also did chopper assaults. Half our training was in the field and half in the classroom.

We composed five paragraph attack orders. We trained in squad rushes, platoon envelopments and company frontal assaults.

The young lieutenants in their basic classes stared at our balding or graying hair and our colorful chest full of combat ribbons while their chests were naked except for rifle badges as they met us in the hallways between classes.

I still enjoyed the fieldwork and firing the weapons, but the classes were boring for me. I could've taught these classes because I'd lived it for eight years in Vietnam. The training schedule was still a demanding one. Now we were being instructed in the subjects of tactics as well as engineering, military law, naval gunfire, close air support, communications, scouting, patrolling, compass, map reading, care and the use of equipment and how to handle troops, guard duty, security, small arms firing regulations, administration and the unit organization of a US Marine Division, Air Wing and support group.

Many of my fellow warrant officer students had at least some college. A few of them had been sergeants, many had been staff sergeants, a few gunnery sergeants, a very few had been master sergeants and 1st Sergeants and I the only sergeant major. I came to know the NCOs and staff sergeants in my platoon and made friends with some, but there was always a tendency for the senior Staff NCOs to draw together.

On February 18th, the company stood in formation with our rifles. Suddenly Gunner Willis yelled, "Standby, Company attention!"

As one the company snapped to attention, our feet at a 45-degree angle, the fingers of our left hands along the seam of our trousers, our right hand holding our rifles just below the front sight.

I stared straight ahead as I watched the inspection party made up of Maj Kelly and Gunner Willis march over to Capt Rose who stood in front of 1st platoon. After saluting each other they marched to the first squad and started the inspection.

I listened to the clatter of the rifles as one by one, first Gunner Boni, then Gunner Callaway followed by Gunner Chionsini came from order arms up to inspection arms as the sounds moved closer to me. From the corner of my eye I saw Maj Kelly approaching followed by Capt Rose, Gunner Willis and Gunner Escamilla.

Then Maj Kelly stepped in front of me. As he did a left face to face me, I sapped my rifle up to port arms across my chest, pulled the bolt lever to the rear and looked down into the chamber to make sure that the rifle was unloaded and safe for the inspecting officer. Then I looked back up and straight ahead waiting for it to be snatched from my hands. Suddenly Maj Kelly snatched my rifle from my hands, looked into the open chamber, and then raised the butt in the air so he could look down the barrel.

"Looks good Gunner," he said before he threw it back at me so hard it stung my hands. As he moved to the next man to my left, I let the bolt slide home and returned the rifle down to my side, wondering what the hell was the major's problem?

The next day I listened to a senior captain teach us counter guerrilla operations. I could tell he was nervous because he had only served three months in Vietnam as an advisor before his group was pulled out in 1973. As he gave the class, he was looking at men older than him with balding and gray hair and he knew many of us had seen several years of guerrilla fighting.

I couldn't help smiling to myself as he lectured us on the tactic of the hammer and anvil movement, the ambush, how to trap the enemy in a constricting cordon and to defeat their attacks by being in a 360-defense cycle.

Then for days we practiced these tactics, ambushed each other's squads and raided each other's camps.

We went on forced marches; a double file of cammy-clad men bent under heavy packs walking down muddy and snow-covered roads. The snow and mud caked to our boots. The snow clung to our uniforms and ran in streaks down our faces. As always rifle slings and scabbards rattled. And always there's the cry, "Close it up, keep your interval!" echoing up and down the column.

I knew that even among the best of troops, a unit gets gaps in it during a forced march as it stretches and contracts because different size men take different size steps. During the ten-minute breaks on the march we would step off the trails and slip our packs off and lay down on the cold ground with our backs against them or just sit exhausted with our backs against a tree drinking cold water from our canteens.

Then Maj Kelly would yell, "Saddle up! Prepare to move out!" Soon we were on our feet. And as in all force marches it was just putting one foot in front of the other. After almost fifteen years of this, it was like I had never been a child or went to high school. It seemed my whole life had been carrying a pack too heavy beneath a sun too hot or like now when I wished I could have felt more heat from the sun as I walked down a trail that was too long.

Late that afternoon we marched back toward main side as dusk fell. As we marched over a hill in a firebreak, I looked back at the column on each side of the road. Looking back to the front I saw Maj Kelly leading the company on one side of the road. On the other side of the road the company right guide was carrying the red and gold guide-on. I watched the guide-on flapping in the breeze as we followed in two columns through the cold pine trees. Main side came into view and the company knowing young lieutenants would watch us seemed to pick up speed as backs and shoulders straightened. A few Marines near the front started singing the Marine Hymn.

Soon the whole company began singing with a feeling of defiance that we the older ex-enlisted men, had just forced marched twenty miles through forest trails in intense cold with 40-pound packs, and we were coming in singing with pride in our Corps and ourselves and no one was more proud then I was to earn the title of

Marine Gunner.

We spent the last week of February at Little Creek VA, going through amphibious warfare training. We made a landing at Damn Neck, VA. Then we returned to Quantico for house-to-house fighting in combat town, then night attack training under the glow of illumination flares. Day after day we relearned our trade in the leadership of Marines.

We practiced ceremonies, how to put on reviews, the proper way to draw a sword, how to behave at social functions such as Mess Nights which date back to the British Royal Marines. We held a Mess Night and dressed in dress whites, we filed into the mess to a drum roll. Around us were silver trophies from the Royal Marines and other British regiments in glass cases. All of them had been presented to us because of battles the British Royal Marines and US Marines had fought together as allies.

Finally by April, the weather was warming up. On April 5th, we had a dress green uniform and weapons inspection in the afternoon. We had cleaned our weapons in the morning, then showered and shaved. We then put on our uniforms and inspected each other before Gunner Willis yelled, “Fall out!”

We rushed out to the company street with our rifles, where we formed up by platoons standing at attention. Then Gunner Willis shouted, “Open ranks!” And we did so, so Maj Kelly could more easily inspect our shaves, the press of our uniforms and the cleanliness of our rifles. As usual Capt Rose checked us, making sure we were all squared away in the few minutes we had left, before Maj Kelly came out.

And as usual he found nothing wrong with my appearance and didn’t bother inspecting my rifle.

A little later Maj Kelly walked out and Gunner Willis ordered the company to attention. After his inspection was done Maj Kelly marched back out front. There he spoke with Gunner Willis. Then he saluted Maj Kelly who returned the salute, then did an about face and marched away.

Then Gunner Willis yelled, “Company dismissed!”

As we walked back in Gunner Boni muttered, “Just another big to do about nothing!”

Our last week of training went by quickly. There were lectures on the manners and life style expected of Marine officers. There were also lectures on personal finance management, insurance and the regulations involved in the travel and transfer of officers. On April 13th in the afternoon, we had our final inspection in the dress green uniform we would wear during graduation.

The next morning, we rehearsed the graduation. Afterward, back in our rooms we were changing uniforms when Gunner Chionsini yelled, "Attention on deck!"

"Stand at ease," said Capt Rose as he walked into our room and handed each of us our orders.

"Thank you, sir," I said tearing open the big brown envelope and pulled the orders out. I read through them quickly and found out I had orders back to the 2nd Marine Division at Camp Lejeune, North Carolina. I had made some good friends here, but I didn't regret the coming graduation tomorrow and especially my return to Camp Lejeune.

The next morning before chow we fell in for our last formation run. We ran all around the Basic School area. The rest of the morning we spent packing up and saying our goodbyes to each other before our orders would scatter our class to the winds.

At 1245 on Friday, we fell in for the very last time at the Basic School. Then Gunner Willis marched us to the base theater.

As we filed into the theater, I saw Capt Rose and the other three staff platoon leaders sitting on the stage. To their right sat Maj Kelly. On his right was a tall old white-haired man. And next to him was a Marine major general.

Then Maj Kelly stepped forward and introduced retired Col 'Iron Man' Lee as our guest speaker. I will never forget that tall, but thin, stooped white haired man as he stood in the middle of the stage. He held us spell bound, his voice, even in his advancing age was still full of power as he talked of being Chesty Puller's (LtGen Puller, probably the most famous Marine in our history and the most decorated Marine in history with five Navy Crosses) gunny in South America, his years as a Chief Marine Gunner (Marine Infantry Warrant Officers in the old Corps), the years he spent as a prisoner of war after he was captured by the Japanese in China at the outbreak of WWII. He talked of the greatness of our country, of his belief in it, of his faith in it. Of patriotism, love and loyalty, his words were like a banner of glory for all of us to see. But especially to me because I was the only Infantry warrant officer in this class.

Then the major general got up and said a few words, which I can't even remember now. When he was finished Col Lee and Maj Kelly stood up to his left. Then one by one Maj Kelly called us up to the stage. I followed Gunner Boni, Gunner Callaway, and Gunner Chionsini up to the stage.

I halted in front of Major Kelly and did a right face facing him.

"Congratulations, Gunner," said Major Kelly shaking my hand.

"Thank you, sir," I answered. I then did a left face and stepped in front of Col Lee, halted and did a right face toward him.

At seeing the bursting bomb on my left shirt collar and left shoulder of my green blouse he smiled saying, "Congratulations, Gunner. I'm glad to see the Corps is still making a few good enlisted men Marine Gunners."

"Thank you, Colonel Lee. I've heard and read a lot about you and I'm proud to get to meet you."

"I'm the one honored," he said with a handshake that was firm for a man in his eighties. Then I did a left face and stepped in front of the major general and did a right face.

"Congratulations and welcome to the officer corps," he said. I shook his right hand as he handed me a rolled-up tube of paper, which contained my Warrant Officer Basic School diploma with his left hand.

Then we walked off the stage and took our seat watching the rest of the company go up across the stage.

When the last man had returned to his seat the major general said, "Major you may dismiss these gentlemen."

"Aye, Aye sir," answered Major Kelly. Then he yelled, "Company Attention!" and we all snapped to our feet.

"Company! Dismissed!" Major Kelly yelled.

We stood there for a moment, not willing to believe it was actually over. Suddenly as one we growled the recon yell and started shaking hands and slapping each other on the back. Within the hour I was driving home for ten days leave. Three hours later I was holding Marty in my arms in her mother's living room.

"You had a phone call a few days ago from Colonel Hester and he left his number for you to call him."

"Colonel Hester? Are you sure it wasn't Major Hester?" I asked.

"No, he said Colonel I'm sure."

"Well I better call and see what's up. He probably wants to

congratulate me on finishing the basic school and I need to congratulate him on making lieutenant colonel," I said walking to the phone holding her hand.

I dialed the number she had written down. As the phone rang, I knew it wasn't the same number I had for Hester.

But then I heard his voice, "Second Battalion Eighth Marines, Lieutenant Colonel Hester speaking sir."

"Colonel Hester this is Gunner Cord."

"Hello Nathan. Congratulations."

"Congratulations to you sir. It's about time the Corps promoted you to light colonel."

"Thank you, Nathan. The reason I called is to tell you I pulled some strings to get you ordered back to the Second Mar Div."

"Thank you, sir."

"I know it's highly unusual for a new warrant officer to go back to a unit to serve with the enlisted men he had once served with. But I would like to have you in my battalion. But it's up to you. I'll understand if you'd rather not."

"No sir, I wouldn't mind that at all."

"Now wait a minute Nathan. We're due to go out on a four-month cruise starting in July and that's only three months away."

I looked at Marty as I said, "Well sir I'd be back for Christmas and it'll probably be August before we can get base housing anyway."

"No matter what you decide to do you'll have base housing the day you get here."

"How can that be sir?"

"I pulled some strings Nathan. Bring Marty and the kids. You can get a house after you check in."

"Well thank you sir. I'd be proud to serve in your command again even if I had to wait for base housing."

"Good. Have a good leave and I'll see you on the twenty fifth."

"Yes sir. Good day sir."

"Goodbye Nathan."

"What is going on?" asked Marty with worried eyes.

"Hester made lieutenant colonel. I'm going to report to his battalion at Camp Lejeune. And he's cut red tape so we have base housing waiting for us when I report in."

"You mean we can go with you when you go back?"

"Yes."

"But what did you mean about being back by Christmas? From where?"

"The battalion is going on a cruise for four months."

"When do you leave?"

"July."

"Well, we'll be together for three months and that's the longest we've ever been together before."

"I know. I love you lady."

"I love you Nathan."

"How long will you be home after the cruise?"

"Should be at least a year. But you know I can be anywhere in the world in seventeen hours."

"Yes, I know. We'll make the best of the time we have together."

"I love you Marty."

The rest of my leave passed quickly. I visited with my sons on both weekends. But it was probably worse on Kyle who not only would have to change schools, but who wouldn't be able to see his father every other weekend except in the summer.

During the evening of April 25th, we checked into a Motel just off base for two days. I then checked in at the 2nd Marine Division headquarters and they, of course, told me to report back in the morning.

First thing the next morning I reported back to the 2nd Marine Division. From there I was sent to the 8th Marine Regiment. And from there I was ordered to the 2nd Battalion. As I drove my truck to battalion headquarters, I passed along the street by Mike Company's barracks where I had served before.

I pulled up to battalion headquarters and parked in a visitor's spot. I walked into the building and knocked on the battalion CO's door.

LtCol Hester looked up saying, "Come in," and then smiled at seeing me.

I marched in to the front of his desk and snapped to attention saying, "Sir, Gunner Cord, reporting as ordered."

He stood up and shook my hand saying, "Welcome aboard Nathan. Where's Marty and the kids?"

"At a motel off base."

"Here are the papers you need to get your house on base," he said handing me the papers. Then he added, "Take the rest of the day off. Go out to the base housing. Get Marty and the kids settled in and report back here tomorrow at 0800 ready to work."

"Yes sir. Thank you, sir."

By nightfall we were in our base house. There was a stove, refrigerator, washer and dryer and little else. What furniture we had wouldn't get down here for probably a month. We had brought with us in our truck and car our clothes, dishes, sheets, blankets, pillows, pillowcases, a TV and a kitchen table and four chairs. But our new neighbors, warrant officers, lieutenants and their wives loaned us beds and a couch.

At 0730 the next morning, I returned to LtCol Hester's office. I waited out in the hallway as he talked with his company commanders. With the door open, I peeked inside to see if I knew any of them. I could see Butler who I had known as a captain had made major and was now the battalion XO. I also recognized Capt Bird and Capt Graham. I didn't know the other two officers or the sergeant major.

A little later when the meeting broke up Capt Bird walked out and said, "How you doing, Gunner?"

"Fine, sir." I answered as he walked by. As an unknown officer passed by, Capt Graham stopped to shake my hand saying, "Welcome aboard Gunner. It's good to have you with us again."

"Thank you, sir."

Then I heard LtCol Hester yell as he waved me in, "Come in Gunner."

"Yes sir," I answered walking into his office.

"This is my Sergeant Major, Hanson."

"Glad to meet you Sergeant Major," I said shaking the red-haired man's hand.

"It's an honor to meet you. It's good to have a real Marine Gunner aboard," said SgtMaj Hanson.

"And this is your company commander, Captain Hays."

Capt Hays stuck out his hand saying, "Hello Gunner. I've heard a lot about you."

"Don't believe all you hear sir," I said shaking his hand.

"It was all good Gunner," said Capt Hays.

"Oh well, in that case it must be God's truth," I said smiling.

"Colonel if you have nothing else, we'll get back to Mike

Company," said Capt Hays.

"No, go right ahead captain," said LtCol Hester.

I followed Capt Hays outside where he climbed into a jeep. I got in my truck and followed him to Mike Company. Together we walked into his office. Inside I was surprised to see Lt Scotto who I had served with last year and even more so to see Lt Jones who had been wounded with me in 1975 on an island off of Cambodia and also 1st Sergeant Burns who had relieved me as 1st Sergeant a few years ago on Sea Duty.

"I believe you know these three men?" asked Capt Hays.

"Yes, sir I sure do."

Then to the two Marines I didn't know Capt Hays said, "My gunny is Gunny Fisher and this is Lieutenant Messenger."

I shook hands with GySgt Fisher who reminded me of a short Fonzie from the TV show 'Happy Days'. Then I shook hands with the tall thin lieutenant.

"Gunner, you'll take over the weapons platoon," said Capt Hays. He must have seen the look on my face and he asked, "Any problems Gunner?"

"Well sir, I'd hoped to get a line platoon."

"Afraid not. I already have officers in place there."

"Yes sir."

"Gunner, I know you and the colonel go way back. But in this company, I am boss. Do you understand?"

I looked at him hard before I spoke, "Sir I've been in this Corps almost fifteen years. I know how to take orders."

"Very good," he said, then looking at GySgt Fisher he said, "Gunny would you show the Gunner to his platoon."

"Yes, sir Capt'n," answered GySgt Fisher and then to me, "Come with me sir." We found the platoon cleaning their weapons sitting under a tree. Seeing us coming, SSgt Manuel who I remembered ran this platoon when I was in Mike Company before, called the platoon to attention.

"At ease. Carry on men," I said surprised and pleased to see Sgt's Reed, Rienbold, Simon and Cpl Cochran and L/Cpl West who I had served with before were still here.

"Well Gunner, I better be checking on the rest of the company," said GySgt Fisher saluting me.

I returned the salute saying, "Thank you, Gunny." Then I looked back at the platoon and said, "Staff Sergeant Manuel I want to talk to you and your section leaders."

"Yes sir," answered SSgt Manuel and then said, "Section leaders up!" I walked away to another tree and sat down as the four of them followed.

"Sit down men," I said smiling at old friends.

"Welcome aboard sir," said Sgt Reed.

"Yes sir, glad to have you sir," said Sgt Simon.

"It just proves there's a God getting you as our platoon leader," said Sgt Rienbold.

"Thank you, men. I'm happy and proud to serve with you again. You all know me. So, you know what to expect."

"Yes sir," they all said smiling.

"Well men, is there anything I can do to help you do your job better?" I asked looking at Sgt Rienbold.

"Not really sir. The guns are in good shape. And we don't have the racial problems we had a few years ago," answered Sgt Rienbold.

Then I looked at Sgt Simon who said, "It's the same story with the tubes (60 MM mortars) and we all get to fire the weapons quite often on the ranges."

"Sounds good. Now how's Captain Hays?"

At first, they all looked at each other and then Sgt Rienbold said, "He's a dick head."

Laughing Sgt Reed said, "Sir, at first he was hard to take. He's hard-nosed and his word is law. But he's fair. If you do a good job, he'll back you all the way."

"That sounds good," I said.

"I still say he's a dick head," said Sgt Rienbold again.

Smiling, I said as I stood up, "Okay men carry on."

All four of them stood up saluting me. I returned their salutes and they returned to their men.

That evening I drove off base to the karate school I had trained at before and signed up to take classes again hoping I would be able to take my 2nd degree black belt test sometime next year.

The next morning, I arrived early for the CO's briefing. Capt Hays saw me waiting outside in the hallway by myself and said, "Good morning Gunner, come on in."

"Good morning sir," I said walking into his office.

"How did you find weapons platoon?"

"Sir, from what I saw yesterday I was very impressed."

"Good, this is a fine unit Gunner. But how can weapons platoon operate better?"

"Well sir, I understand they get to fire live ammo quite a bit. But sir, any extra range time you can get for us the better we'll be able to support the rifle platoons."

"I see. I'll keep that in mind and I'll do all I can."

"Thank you, sir."

On May 5th, I took my platoon to the machine gun and mortar range for the day. I spent the morning with Sgts Reinhold's and Reed's gun teams as they fired live ammo at old tanks and trucks while SSgt Manuel stayed on the mortar range.

In the afternoon, SSgt Manuel and I traded places. I enjoyed watching Sgt Simon put his mortar teams through their paces. He could bring a target under fire the quickest of any man I ever knew. Like LtCol Hester and me, he had also survived Hue City in 1968, although we didn't know him then. But whatever company he was supporting then was surely lucky. And if I have to go into combat anytime soon, I sure hope he's still with us. The next day we returned to the machine gun range. I had the mortar men cross train on the machineguns. In the afternoon, my platoon went to the mortar range and the machine gunners were trained on the mortars.

The rest of May passed quickly as the whole Battalion trained hard for the upcoming float. I felt the tension between Capt Hays and I over my long friendship with LtCol Hester fade away.

And as far as my job as weapons platoon leader, it seemed too easy. Because with section leaders like Sgts Reed, Rienbold and Simon the platoon all but ran itself.

God, I loved this life, especially with Marty, Kyle and Samantha finally able to live with me. And the karate classes were going well and I have become an assistant instructor.

In June, Lt Scotto was promoted to captain and left 2nd platoon and took command of Kilo Company.

By July 17th, the battalion was on ships starting our four-month float to the Caribbean. During these days on ship I thought back over my almost fifteen years in the Corps. My first time onboard ship as a seventeen-year-old private, I lived in a troop compartment stuffed in with over a hundred other men. We had to stand in long lines to eat in the mess hall. Then eleven years later as a gunnery sergeant, I shared a small compartment aboard ship with only about a dozen senior staff NCOs. Next to us was a small mess hall and lounge just for us with a TV. All we had to do was go in and order something to eat anytime we wanted.

And now as an officer, I'm sharing a small room with Lt Jones, which has a fold down desk, a mirror and vanity between us. And anytime we wanted something to eat we walked down to the Wardroom where the officers ate. There was also a lounge with a TV and VCR with a library of movies to watch.

On July 21st our ship docked at Panama City. After two days of liberty we passed through the canal on July 24th.

On the evening of July 26th there was a knock on our hatch. "Enter!" Lt Jones and I both shouted.

The hatch opened and SgtMaj Hanson stuck his head in and looked at me saying, "Gunner, the colonel wants to see you in his room."

Lt Jones and I looked at each other as I asked, "Does Captain Hays know about this or is this a social call?"

"It's business and Captain Hays is already there."

"Okay sergeant major, I'll be right there," I said as I started pulling my boots on. After lacing my boots up, I left my room and walked down the passageway to LtCol Hester's room. I knocked on the hatch and from inside LtCol Hester said, "Come in." I opened the metal hatch and stepped through seeing LtCol Hester and Capt Hays sitting in chairs. Once inside I snapped to attention saying, "Sir, Gunner Cord reporting as ordered."

"Close the hatch Nathan and take a seat," said LtCol Hester.

"Yes sir," I answered closing the hatch and sitting across from the two senior officers. LtCol Hester had a look on his face I hadn't seen since Vietnam as he said, "Gunner, I need an officer for a special mission. You can only take twelve men with you. It could turn out to be only a couple weeks or months of clean guard duty for your men. But it could turn into a shit sandwich in a hurry. And if it goes bad you may be on your own. I can't promise you we'll even get ordered in to help you."

I was shocked and I believe my mouth dropped open before I asked, "What is going on sir and where are we talking about?"

"First, I want to know if you want to do this."

"Do I have a choice sir?"

"Yes, you do. I can send any number of officers from this battalion. But I need a cool head for this job as well as a combat veteran. Of all the junior officers I have to pick from for an important mission like this it's you I want. But it's your choice."

"Of course, sir, I'll do it."

"Capt Hays knows all about the mission. In fact, he wants to go. But I'm authorized to send only one officer and I need him to run Mike Company."

"Okay sir, but where and when am I going?"

"First light tomorrow morning, you will be choppered to the airport at San Salvador, El Salvador. From there you will be trucked to the American Embassy. You will report to the Ambassador. You will be there to reinforce the Marine Security Guard Detachment there. You will help them protect the embassy from ground assault. The political situation has become explosive since January of last year with violent demonstrations and physical assaults on embassy personnel. The embassy has received reports that there may be a full out armed attack against the embassy."

"Sir, it sounds like to me they need at least a rifle platoon with a couple gun teams and a mortar team. Not a weapons platoon leader and twelve men," I said.

"I agree, but the ambassador wants to keep this as low key as possible."

"Can I pick my own men sir?"

"Yes, sure."

"Which sergeant do you think you'll take Gunner?" asked Capt Hays.

"Sergeants Reed, Rienbold and Simon," I answered.

"Why all three when you only need one?" asked Capt Hays.

"Well sir if the shit hits the fan with this few men, I want the best with me. That is if I'm allowed to take two gun teams and a mortar team? Besides you'll still have Staff Sergeant Manuel to run the rest of weapons platoon and I have good corporals which could use the experience as acting section leaders while we're gone."

"But why a mortar team?" asked Capt Hays.

"Sir I don't know if I'll be able to deploy the mortar or not. But if I could, they could make the difference. And if I can't, they've been crossed trained with the guns or I could use them as riflemen."

"I think you can do it with just one sergeant," said Capt Hays.

"I would agree with you Skipper if we were all going into combat. But as it stands now Nathan is more likely to see action then we are," said LtCol Hester as Capt Hays looked at him. Then he went on to say, "Nathan, pick your men and have them on the helo deck fully armed and packed by 0600 in the morning."

"Yes sir," I said standing up.

"Gunner, I'll get Gunny Fisher to draw the ammo," said Capt Hays.

"Thank you sir and I also want a dozen grenades per man," I said.

Capt Hays looked at LtCol Hester who nodded his head in agreement.

"And so, it will be, Gunner," said Capt Hays.

"Thank you again, sir," I said as I walked out.

I went to the Staff NCO's room and walked in through the hatch.

At seeing me, 1st Sgt Burns jumped up from his rack yelling, "Attention on deck!"

As the rest of the Staff NCOs started to stand, I waved them back down saying, "At ease men." I looked around until I found SSgt Manuel and said, "Staff Sergeant Manuel get the section leaders and bring them to my room."

"Right now, sir?" asked SSgt Manuel.

"Right now," I said as I started to turn to leave.

"Anything up Gunner?" asked SSgt Knight another old friend I'd served with before.

I looked back at him knowing he had been with recon in Vietnam and I wished I could take him with me now, but I could only say, "Nothing I can talk about." Then I stepped through the hatch and walked to my room. Inside, Lt Jones watched me pull my sea bag out of my locker and start packing.

"Gunner you going somewhere?"

"Yes sir."

"Anything I should know about."

"No sir, not yet anyway."

"Everything okay at home I hope."

"Yes sir."

"I take it you're not going to tell me where you're going?"

"No sir," I answered smiling back at him.

About fifteen minutes later there was a knock at our hatch. "Enter!" I yelled. The hatch opened and in stepped SSgt Manuel followed by Sgts Reed, Rienbold and Simon.

Lt Jones looked at me, at them and then back to me.

"Lieutenant would you mind leaving us alone for about fifteen minutes?" I asked.

"Sure thing, Gunner," said Lt Jones as he stood up looking concerned.

After he had walked out closing the hatch behind him, I sat down on my rack saying, "Take a seat, men."

SSgt Manuel sat down beside me. Sgt Simon sat in the chair while Sgts Reed and Rienbold sat on the floor.

"Men, I've been ordered to take twelve men on a special mission. We may be gone a few days, weeks or the rest of the float. We will not be in the field. We may be bored out of our suck. Then again, we may find ourselves in a sudden shit sandwich. I need at least one of you sergeants to go with me. Captain Hays has agreed to let me take all three of you if you want to go. I'll understand if you don't want 'a go, especially you two who have seen combat before."

"If you're going Gunner I'll go," said Sgt Rienbold smiling.

"Me too," said Sgt Reed.

Sgt Simon looked at them and then at me.

"Sergeant Simon it's up to you," I said.

"Sir where are we going?" asked Sgt Simon.

"Those who go with me will find out when we land."

"Will the landing be hot?" asked Sgt Simon.

"No, but we will be taking live ammo."

"Mortars sir?" asked Sgt Simon.

"Yes," I answered smiling.

"Well hell, I'm in," said Sgt Simon smiling now.

"How about me sir?" asked SSgt Manuel.

"I wish I could. But I need my second in command to run this platoon while I'm gone," I said.

"Yes sir," said SSgt Manuel clearly disappointed.

"Okay. Sergeants Reed and Rienbold, each of you pick your best gun team. Sergeant Simon you pick your best mortar team with one tube. Get them and all their gear up on the fantail in one hour. We will sleep up there. This mission is a secret. So, tell your men to keep it quiet. Do you understand?"

"Yes sir," they all said together.

"Then carry on," I said.

All four men stood up and walked out.

I finished packing my sea bag and was strapping on my shoulder holster when Lt Jones opened the hatch and stepped in. He seemed shocked at the sight of me pulling my pistol out of my locker and pushing it into the holster on my left side.

I picked up my sea bag with my left hand and started around him. We looked at each other and I could see in his eyes that he knew I was on a real mission of some kind.

"Gunner," he said touching my right arm and added, "I wish I was going with you."

"I wish you and your whole platoon was going. But do you remember what happened the last time you and I went on a real mission?"

"Yeah you almost got me killed," said Lt Jones joking.

"That's funny I remember it as just the opposite."

"Be careful and keep your head down. We need you."

"Sir, you just keep your powder dry and train your men well. I may need you all to save me," I said as I slipped past him and out the hatch. I walked down the passageways and up the ladder well to the outer skin of the ship. At the fantail, I laid down my sea bag and sat down leaning back against it looking up at the stars. I thought, "It's been four years since I've been shot at." I felt calm and yet uneasy that maybe I may have lost my nerve. I prayed that I would do my duty and keep my men safe from harm. But I was glad I had two Vietnam veterans going with me I could trust. I must have drifted off for when I heard the footsteps, I was startled awake.

Sgt Reed was leading, followed by Cpl Sieple another Vietnam veteran carrying a M-60 machinegun, behind him L/Cpl West carrying the extra barrel bag and another Marine. Then came the other gun team made up of Sgt Rienbold, Cpl Johnson and two privates. Following them was Sgt Simon, Cpl Cochran carrying the mortar tube, Cpl Manese carrying the tripod and a private.

They had been smiling and laughing. But at seeing me their expressions changed to a look of worry.

"Gunner! What's going on?" asked Cpl Johnson.

"Johnson, I told you you'd find out in the morning," spat Sgt

Rienbold.

I had to smile saying, “Make yourself comfortable while you can men. Try to get some sleep."

At 0400 we were awakened by GySgt Fisher and a small working party with boxes of ammo, grenades and a crate of LAAWs (Light Anti-Armored Weapon) that I hadn’t even asked for. Cpl Johnson jumped up looking closely at the crates.

“Thanks Gunny,” I said standing up.

“No problem Gunner,” said GySgt Fisher pulling a M-16 rifle off his shoulder and handing it toward me.

“What’s this Gunny?”

“The colonel thought you might want to carry this along sir.”

I took the rifle, smiling because I knew that LtCol Hester knew I liked carrying a rifle in combat even though it’s not authorized for officers.

“Gunny, have you been briefed on where we’re going?”

“No sir. But I can tell this is no training exercise you’re going on.”

“It’s hard to fool an old war horse like you. Gunny, tell Colonel Hester I said thanks.”

“Good luck sir,” said GySgt Fisher saluting me.

“Take care Gunny,” I said returning his salute.

Then the gunny and his working party turned walking away.

Cpl Johnson turned back looking at me saying, “Gunner this stuff is real, not blanks.”

“Yes, it is corporal,” I said as the others stood up looking at the crates.

“Sir, then we’re going into combat. Some kind of secret mission?” asked Cpl Johnson.

“Secret mission, yes. But combat only a maybe,” I answered.

“But maybe,” smiled Cpl Johnson.

Looking around I noticed he was the only one smiling.

“Can you tell us where we’re going now sir?” asked Sgt Simon.

“No sergeant. I want everyone to load their magazines now. Bust open two of the gun ammo boxes, but leave the ammo inside. And leave the grenades boxed up. Do not insert any magazines in your weapons. Once that is done get some rest while you can. A chopper will pick us up at 0600.”

Near 0600 I heard the Ch-46 chopper coming in the distance.

"Okay men saddle up," I said.

Quickly the men jumped up picking up their weapons and crates of ammo. Nearby I noticed LtCol Hester and Capt Hays standing. I walked over saluting them and asked, "Any last orders sirs?"

"No Nathan. We just came to see you off," said LtCol Hester.

"Good luck, Gunner," said Capt Hays shaking my hand.

"Thank you, captain," I said.

"Nathan, you be careful," said LtCol Hester.

"Thank you, sir," I said saluting them. Then I turned as the chopper landed.

The ramp in the rear of the chopper lowered and the crew chief jumped out waving to us to get on.

The men looked at me and I waved them forward as I led them across the deck and up the ramp into the chopper. Sgt Reed brought up the rear making sure everyone and everything got onboard the chopper. Once inside we sat down, placed our weapons between our legs with the muzzles pointed down and buckled up our safety belts. Then the chopper lifted off heading for El Salvador.

It wasn't long before we landed at an airport. As we walked off the chopper, I noticed a truck parked nearby with two Marines in cammies standing beside it. I led my Marines toward the truck as one of the two Marines near the truck walked toward us. As he neared me, I noticed by his collar that he was a gunnery sergeant. He saluted saying, "Good morning sir. I'm Gunnery Sergeant Stevenson."

I returned the salute saying, "Good morning Gunny. I'm Gunner Cord."

"Sir, if you would have your men get in the truck. I'll drive you to the embassy."

"Very good, gunny," I said looking back at Sgt Reed and said, "Sergeant Reed get the men and gear on the truck."

"Yes sir. All right, you heard him, on the truck," he yelled.

"Gunner, where are we?" asked Cpl Johnson.

"San Salvador, El Salvador, corporal," I said.

"Where the fuck is that?" Cpl Johnson said more to himself.

"Shut the fuck up and get on the damn truck," ordered Sgt Rienbold.

As we walked toward the truck GySgt Stevenson waved to his Marine to get in the back of the truck also.

I noticed the Marine turn and reach in the cab and pull out a M-16 with magazine inserted.

"Gunny should my men lock and load their weapons?" I asked.

"Sir, there shouldn't be any problem. I would rather you didn't until you speak to the ambassador."

"Okay, gunny," I said throwing my sea bag into the back of the truck. Then I walked around and stepped up into the right-hand side of the cab. The embassy Marine in the back closed the tarp so nobody would see who or what was in the back of the truck when we left the airport. GySgt Stevenson climbed into the left side and soon we were driving through the streets of San Salvador.

Finally, we turned a corner and up ahead was a group of young people dressed in different types of clothes. Some of them wore white shirts and cowboy hats. All of them were walking in a circle. Some carried signs, some in English and some in Spanish. Some of the signs in English said, 'Gringo's Go Home! Beyond them was the three-story American embassy building ringed with a wall topped with barbed wire and shredded glass.

I looked at GySgt Stevenson as he slowed the truck down to a crawl inching through the crowd. The people moved slowly away from the front of the truck, but swarmed around the sides and back and began pounding on the truck hitting it with the signs and their fists. Several people spit at the truck.

At the main gate the truck stopped. Two Salvadoran policemen pushed people out of the way as the Marine embassy guard swung the iron-gate open. Then GySgt Stevenson drove the truck slowly through as the crowd moved in behind the policemen and the Marine guard swung the gate shut. I noticed several other embassy Marines standing along the wall out of sight of the crowd with shotguns to reinforce the guard if need be. As we started getting out of the truck a man in the crowd pulled out an American flag. The demonstrators nearby yelled, "Americans go home!" Another man yelled in Spanish as he set fire to the flag.

Cpl Johnson made a move for the gate, but Sgt Rienbold stopped him holding him back, but looking at me as if for guidance.

I shook my head no as the demonstrators cheered the burning flag. As the charred cloth fell to the ground they stomped on the ashes.

As I stood there watching, feeling the rage inside me, GySgt

Stevenson walked over to me.

"I'd like to lead these men out that gate," I spat.

"I know how you feel, sir. But we can't legally do anything outside of this compound," he said.

I felt my jaw muscles pop as I gritted my teeth and turned following him into the embassy.

He took me to an office I could use to live in. Down the hall was a small conference room set up with cots and wall lockers for my men to live in.

Later my sergeants and I met with the senior members of the Marine Security Guard in a large conference room around a table.

The door opened and a man in his fifties with gray hair, long nose, cold eyes and pointed chin dressed in a dark black three-piece suit, white shirt and blue tie walked in. GySgt Stevenson stood up saying, "Mr. Ambassador, this is Gunner Cord."

I jumped up, but he waved me to sit back down. He sat down at the head of the table saying, "I'm Ambassador Turley. The situation here is tense, as you have probably guessed. I asked for more Marines just as a backup. You will stay within this compound at all times and keep a low profile. Have you seen any combat Mr. Cord?"

"A little sir. Two of my sergeants and one corporal have seen combat too."

Then the ambassador went on as if he wasn't listening, "I'll leave it up to you and Gunny how you want to use your men. We have to be careful. I don't want an international incident if I can help it. Because it'll be my ass. I think that'll be all gentlemen unless Mr. Cord has any questions"

"Yes sir. I would like to build two sandbagged machinegun positions and dig a mortar pit out in the compound and a lookout on the roof"

"You can put a man on the roof as a lookout. But nothing in the compound."

"But sir we need fighting positions to better protect ourselves as well as the embassy from armed attack."

"No way, Mr. Cord. You're here to react to a threat or attack. Not to make us look like an armed camp and a threat to the capital of El Salvador."

"Yes sir."

"Sergeant Stevenson, do you have anything?" asked

Ambassador Turley.

"Well sir, if you and the Gunner would agree I'd like my men to keep on handling all the guard duties as before. Then Gunner Cord would drill his men in quick reaction and be ready twenty-four hours a day to assist us."

"Any problems with that Mr. Cord?" asked Ambassador Turley.

"No sir, I can live with that. But I would like to position a machinegun and mortar team on the roof," I said.

"The machinegun is fine as long as it's kept out of sight. But no mortar."

"But sir if this compound is all out attacked, we could sure use the mortar to back us all up."

"No way. In this small area it would be too easy for the mortars to fall outside of the compound. I don't want that."

"Not even if the incoming rounds are coming from outside the compound."

"No."

"Sir, Sergeant Simon here can drop a mortar shell in your hip pocket. That's why I brought him."

"No mortar, Mr. Cord."

"Yes sir. How about LAAWs on the roof?"

Ambassador Turley seemed confused and GySgt Stevenson said, "They're like little bazookas."

Ambassador Turley thought a minute and finally answered, "Okay." Then he got up and walked out of one door and we Marines walked out of another door past a young dark-haired secretary at her desk. She looked up smiling at me. Down the hallway, we passed a Navy officer standing as he talked to a woman in a light blue dress.

When we were away from everybody Sgt Simon said, "He definitely don't want any fucking mortars."

GySgt Stevenson looked back at him as Sgt Reed and I looked at each other and we all laughed.

Back in the men's living quarters I explained the situation to the men. Then GySgt Stevenson gave the three sergeants and me a tour of the building, the compound grounds and the walls. Afterwards we sat down with him. I briefed him on what I decided to do. Sgt Simon would be in charge of the LAAW team and look-outs on the roof. Sgt Reed would be in charge of the machinegun team on the roof. Sgt Rienbold would be in charge of the machinegun team on the ground floor. Two men would be on watch on the roof twenty-four hours a day standing two-hour watches.

Later when I briefed Ambassador Turley, I also requested that a radio be set up on the roof so the roof watches could contact me in my office, the troops living quarters and the gym in the basement. He did one better the very next day by having new phones put in just for us.

The first few days passed quickly as I drilled the teams in quick reaction to help the embassy Marines.

By August, the excitement wore off and boredom became a problem. As well as doing PT and running in the gym every morning, the sergeants and I gave Marine Corps classes. In the afternoon, I taught them a three-hour Tae Kwon Do karate class. At night I allowed each man two beers in their quarters as they watched movies on a VCR.

When GySgt Stevenson's men were off duty, he had them train with us and a few of them took my karate classes.

By mid-September it was growing difficult to keep moral up. They wanted to get out of this compound. They actually longed to be back with the battalion. As Sgt Simon said, "Even with the field duty in the rain and mud and being eaten by insects they would've gotten liberty."

With October came the word we would rejoin our battalion in November as it headed back to the states. None of us could hardly wait.

October 30th started like all the rest. But at 1312 L/Cpl West and Sgt Simon were on watch on the roof when they watched a man crossing the street in front of the embassy gate when suddenly he was hit by a car flipping him in the air into the middle of the street.

"Damn! Some guy just got run down," said Sgt Simon.

One of the Salvadoran policemen guarding the embassy main gate ran toward the man lying in the street as L/Cpl West shifted his position to see better.

"Do ya think he's hurt bad?" asked L/Cpl West as the policeman kneeled down next to the man.

Suddenly from under him the man lying in the street pulled a pistol and pushed it into the policeman's face and fired. The policeman flipped back as his head exploded.

"Oh shit! Westy, guns up," said Sgt Simon as he ran to the

phone. The other policeman ran away down the street.

In my office I heard the sound like a car backfiring, but knew it wasn't. As L/Cpl West broke open the M-60 ammo box a truck appeared around the corner scattering people as it raced toward the embassy gate.

My phone rang and I picked it up on the first ring.

On the roof L/Cpl West placed the ammo belt in the machinegun as the embassy Marine at the gate opened fire with his pistol at the truck.

"Gunner Cord here," I said hearing the pistol shots.

"This is it Gunner! Front gate!" yelled Sgt Simon.

"Anyone else on the line?" I asked hoping someone in the troops' quarters had also picked up the phone.

"Yes sir," said Cpl Manese.

"Corporal, pass the word. This is not a drill. Lock and load and repel a front gate assault!" I yelled.

"Yes sir," said Cpl Manese hanging the phone up.

Meanwhile the truck rammed through the gate. Once inside rebel troops jumped from the back, firing AK-47 rifles.

In my office I swung my flak jacket on, then my war belt with extra magazines and grabbed my rifle slamming a loaded magazine in it as I ran into the hallway joining my men also rushing up the hallway. Up ahead I could see Sgt Reed, Cpl Sieple and two Marines turning right rushing up to the roof with rifles, boxes of machinegun ammo and LAAWs.

Running straight ahead past them was Cpl Johnson leading the way carrying a machinegun. Behind him were Sgt Rienbold, Cpls Cochran, Manese and two other Marines.

Men and women office workers were running down the hallway toward us screaming and scattering out of our way for cover.

On the roof, Sgt Simon dropped down next to L/Cpl West as he opened fire with the machinegun. As Sgt Simon started feeding the belt, he saw the embassy Marine gate guard in dress blues get shot down by rebel fire.

The sound of the M-60 firing from the roof was music to my ears as we raced through the front office.

Outside, a rebel running from the truck started to raise his rifle, but machinegun bullets stitched themselves across his chest and he spun around to the ground, blood spreading under him. He tried to sit up, but fell over on his side.

From somewhere, GySgt Stevenson joined us with his rifle as we scattered toward the front door and windows. Bullets were already bursting through the windows and door ricocheting off the walls and furniture. GySgt Stevenson fired a burst from the hip through a window. I dived and rolled behind a desk as Cpl Johnson squeezed off a burst of machinegun fire out another window.

The first truckload of rebels was already against the outer wall as a second truck entered the compound filled with rebels.

On the roof, L/Cpl West fired at a rebel leaning out of the passenger door of the second truck. The bullets struck him in the face. He dropped his rifle and fell out the open door and hit the ground rolling.

There was a sound to my right like a big rock bouncing around off the floor, desk and wall. I turned away yelling, "Grenade!" It exploded as the rebels began spraying bullets through the windows.

I pulled the men back across the room toward the main hallway. GySgt Stevenson ran backwards firing wildly. I crawled to the left as Cpl Johnson rolled over behind a desk and then fired over the top.

A rebel came through the doorway as GySgt Stevenson fired and the force of his bullets lifted the rebel back outside. Behind me a civilian woman who was hiding under her desk screamed as she jumped up running. She slipped on the empty shell casings and fell, but kept crawling around the corner and down the hallway.

Several more rebels came through the door as GySgt Stevenson fired from the hip shooting the rifle out of one rebel's hands.

Seeing this, Sgt Rienbold spun firing striking the other rebel in the face, which seemed to explode. His hands started to go up as he fell forward.

GySgt Stevenson fired another burst at the weaponless rebel that hit him from belly up to his neck.

Two other rebels rushed through the door as Sgt Rienbold fired a burst. Bullets hit one rebel in the side and he fell back against the wall moaning slipping to the floor. He then swung the rifle to the left still firing as bullets hit the other rebel in the chest who staggered backwards and fell as a flow of blood stained his shirt.

Then I moved back down the hallway following Cpls Cochran, Manese and two other Marines. Sgt Rienbold and Cpl Johnson followed me in, but stopped at the entrance. GySgt Stevenson ran back between them. Sgt Rienbold pulled a pin to a grenade as more rebels rushed in. I heard the ping of the spoon fly off as he tossed it into the room. A few seconds later came the loud explosion. Cpl Manese pulled the pin to a grenade as he moved back up glancing around the corner of the hallway. He saw a rebel trying to stand up, but kept falling down. Then Cpl Manese tossed his grenade into the room. This grenade exploded in a flash of light throwing wood splinters into the hallway. Another rebel hit in the chest by shrapnel was slammed across the top of a desk. Meanwhile, Sgt Reed, Cpl Sieple and two Marines reached the roof and added their fire at the rebels in the courtyard below. Bullets hit one rebel in the chest blowing out his back. Meanwhile, inside Cpl Johnson fired his machinegun around the corner of the hallway as bullets ripped through rebels, furniture and walls.

When the belt went dry, Cpl Johnson moved back down the hallway as Cpl Cochran handed him another belt. GySgt Stevenson moved forward firing his M-16 on full automatic. From the corner he saw a rebel leap through a window escaping to the outside. One of his bursts hit a rebel in the chest flipping him back against the wall. When he had emptied the magazine, he stepped back as Cpl Johnson moved forward.

On the roof, Sgt Reed could hear the firing and explosions from inside the building as he looked over the rebel bodies lying in the courtyard below.

Inside, we moved back into the main lobby jumping over broken chairs, tables and desks. Suddenly, two rebels rose up behind an overturned desk, one of which aimed a pistol. GySgt Stevenson dropped to one knee firing. A bullet hit the man in the face, which exploded in blood. The other rebel turned to run, but another burst of fire smashed him to the wall. He slid in his own blood to the floor.

"Spread out and check this room!" I yelled. The Marines fanned out across the room and found the rest of the rebels either dead or dying as they lay among the furniture in pools of blood.

Sgt Rienbold jumped next to the shattered door and tossed a grenade outside. After the explosion GySgt Stevenson ran out the door into the cloud of dust and smoke firing to the right. Sgt Rienbold followed him outside firing to the left. He could see a rebel running away close to the building. Sgt Rienbold fired hitting the man in the middle of the back lifting him off his feet and smashing him to the ground. Sgt Rienbold moved up slowly and made sure the rebel was dead.

I ran up to the door and as I looked out a sudden burst of fire came from the main gate as bullets ripped the wall near me. I spun around back into the building.

I heard the machinegun team on the roof suddenly come alive again as they opened up.

As I sat up with my back to the wall the other Marines around me returned fire from the door and windows.

Another burst of fire hit the doorframe above me spattering me with splinters of wood. I rolled flat on the floor and fired out the door. I emptied the magazine, rolled back against the wall, let the empty magazine drop to the floor and pushed in a full one, rolled back flat and fired again. I could see Sgt Rienbold crawling along the wall toward the gate. Suddenly an RPG (rocket propelled grenade) rushed across the yard exploding against the wall. The blast blew a large hole in the wall rolling me over as part of the ceiling dropped and plaster and dust filled the air. The blast broke windows on the second and third floors shaking the building. I looked over at Cpl Cochran lying in the rubble. I crawled over lifting shattered boards off of him. As I pulled him out, I saw his left hand, wrist, elbow and shoulder was bleeding. I bandaged him up as smoke drifted across the room. Nearby Cpl Manese sat in a daze as blood ran down from a head wound.

I crawled over next to him saying, “Let me bandage up that wound.”

“What wound?” asked Cpl Manese touching his head. Then he looked at the blood on his hand.

I took him by the elbow and gently lay him down as I waved over another Marine to help him.

As I crawled back to the door, a group of rebels rushed through the gate. Bullets hit them from the roof, from along both walls and from the embassy door and windows. I saw one rebel, hit in the neck stagger, blood pouring down his chest and sides, fall.

But the rebels kept coming on firing in every direction.

On the roof, Sgt Reed fired his rifle at a big rebel running across the yard as bullets kicked up dirt all around him before he was shot down.

Then bullets hit the edge of the roof. Sgt Reed dropped flat hugging the roof. As he rolled to the right rebel tracers flew over his head.

Then from the doorway I heard the rush of a LAAW being fired from the roof. A few seconds later the anti-armored shell exploded in the yard in a shower of sparks and shrapnel. One rebel was blasted from his feet toward the embassy building. Another rebel badly wounded staggered through the smoke and fell sideways.

On the roof, Sgt Reed lifted his head up peeking down. Again, he fired his rifle in short bursts while Sgt Simon fired another LAAW down toward the yard.

More rebels rushed into the yard only to be cut down. From the doorway I saw a rebel running toward me with his head down as if he didn't want to see the bullets hitting around him. I squeezed off a burst and watched the bullets slam him to the ground. Another rebel ran through the gate as GySgt Stevenson fired at him from along the wall and missed. He fired again and the rebel seemed to lose his balance and fall rolling. GySgt Stevenson fired another burst into him just to make sure he was dead. Another rebel rushed through the gate and I fired a burst hitting him from the groin up to the chest driving him back out the gate.

By now all the Marines were pouring fire at the gate entrance shattering windows and splintering wood across the street. The rebels return fire, now seemed halfhearted and not well aimed.

Another Marine and I ran out the door firing from the hip. A rebel appeared around the corner of the truck aiming at me. But GySgt Stevenson fired a burst hitting the rebel in the chest knocking him off his feet back against the side of the truck and then to the ground.

Another rebel ran around from the back of the truck and GySgt Stevenson shot him in the stomach. He fell back as if sitting down holding his ripped belly moaning. GySgt Stevenson fired another burst into him. Looking back at me GySgt Stevenson said, "These people ain't shit."

Around us the firing was slowing up with only a few rifle shots and a burst of machinegun fire from the roof. More Marines now moved out into the yard, got on line and began sweeping across the yard checking the scattered rebel bodies which lay across the yard.

Then a grenade came over the wall.

"Hit the deck!" I yelled as the grenade landed near several

Marines. The grenade exploded spraying shrapnel around us hitting the wall, truck and men. One Marine moaned quietly as he struggled to sit up. GySgt Stevenson himself wounded, kneeled down next to the wounded Marine whose face was smeared with dirt and blood. It was suddenly quiet as I looked around at the death and destruction. Sgt Rienbold walked across the yard toward me smiling. I looked up at the roof and Sgt Reed was waving his black hand giving me the thumbs up sign. My eyes searched the flagpole where our flag was still waving and I thought, "And our flag was still there."

Then I had the Marines pick up all rebel weapons. They loaded the dead rebels on the trucks, which would be turned over to the local police. Our wounded were checked over at the local hospital. The worst, like Cpls Cochran and Manese were later flown back to the states by a US Air Force medical plane, which also carried the one Marine killed, the embassy guard at the front gate.

A few days later we were withdrawn by chopper back to the ship as it passed heading back to the states. So, we returned to the battalion and were treated like heroes. But Sgts Rienbold, Simon, Cpl Sieple and I didn't feel like heroes. Sgt Reed felt better about himself after finally getting a small taste of combat. L/Cpl West was quieter than usual, but I felt he would be fine. Cpl Johnson was louder then before telling everyone within hearing about his acts of bravery under fire, which grew with each telling.

In November, the ship docked and we off loaded and went by bus convoy back to Camp Lejeune. It was late Sunday night before Mike Company had put their weapons and gear away.

It was after 2200 when I pulled into my driveway. I got out of my truck and pulled my sea bag out of the back. As I walked up to the house, I noticed Marty standing at the doorway looking through the screen door. I smiled at her, feeling the need for her grow. She in turn smiled a half smile; a smile I had come to realize meant something wasn't just right.

A chill went up my spine. I had worried how she'd really make out with me being gone four months on deployment for the first time and her so far away from home. At the same time, I hoped something hadn't happened to one of our kids, my father or her family. She opened the door for me and I said, "Hey girl." As I started to step past her to put my sea bag down in the living room, she threw both arms around me almost crying saying, "I was afraid they wouldn't let you come home!"

I kissed her and then laughed saying. "I know it's late, but I wanted to get everything done so when I came home, I could stay with you for the next ninety-six hours."

She seemed shocked saying, "You have four days off with what's happened?"

"What's happened?"

"You don't know?"

"Know what?"

"The American Embassy in Iran has been overrun and all the American civilians and military personnel have been taken hostage."

I was shocked, almost stunned with disbelief especially with what I had just been through last month as I asked, "Are you sure?"

"Yes, there's been news flashes on TV for hours."

"What about casualties?"

"Iran is saying no Americans have been killed."

"Christ this means war," I said dropping the sea bag to the floor.

"What do you think is going to happen?"

"Well we should invade Iran. But with the way President Carter has cut the throat of the military since he was elected it'll be awhile before we can get ready."

"That's why I'm surprised your home."

"Me too. I better call Captain Hays and see if he knows anything." I walked to the phone and dialed his home number.

"Captain Hays residence," a female voice answered.

"Mrs. Hays is the captain in?"

"No, he's not. Who is calling?"

"Gunner Cord."

"Oh, hi Gunner."

"Have you talked to the captain?"

"Yes a few hours ago."

"Did he say anything about the Iran thing?"

"No, in fact he didn't even know anything about it until I told him."

"Well I just wondered if there'd be a recall or not?"

"Jim said as far as he knew he'd be home late tonight after he got caught up on his paperwork. He said he'd call me if there was a change."

"Well, thank you ma'am. I'll try him at his office. Good night." I hung up and then dialed his office number.

"Mike Company, Captain Hays speaking."

"Yes sir, this is Gunner Cord."

"Gunner Cord what's up?"

"Sir I'm hoping you could tell me."

"You've heard about the embassy in Iran."

"Yes sir, what's our status?"

"I called Colonel Hester to ask the same thing. He tells me that the rest of the division is on full alert. But for us it's all quiet. I guess because we just got back from float."

"So, our ninety-six (96 hours of liberty) is still on?"

"Yes, if there is a change we'll be recalled. So, if you want to visit your family up north, you'd better do it now. Even if we get the next weekend off, we probably won't be allowed to leave the area. If we invade Iran, we'll be gone a long time."

"Okay Capt'n. See ya Friday."

"Sure thing, Gunner. Thanks for calling."

"Good evening, sir."

"Good evening, Gunner."

I hung up the phone smiling and as I turned to Marty who asked, "Well?"

"We have four days."

"Then what?"

"Then we just have to take it one day at a time. But he said we might have next weekend off."

"Then you won't have to go?"

"Yes, I'm sure we will be going, but nobody knows when," I said putting my arms around her. We walked arm in arm to Kyle's room and looked in on him. Then we looked in on Samantha in her room. I leaned over her small body and kissed the red curls on her forehead. Then we walked toward our bedroom.

"I love you Nathan."

"I love you," I said looking down at her.

"I want you."

"I'm glad," I said running my hand down her back and rubbing her behind. The next four days passed quickly and I enjoyed myself except when I watched the evening news. Then I felt rage toward Iran and President Carter who seemed to be doing nothing but talk while fellow US Marines were being held captive. I tried to be careful what I said in front of Marty, but she knew I wanted to be in the first wave to land in Iran.

Friday morning, we had a battalion formation at 0800. The Marines of Mike Company were buzzing with talk about Iran and the coming invasion. I noticed that some of the brave talkers a few weeks ago who had wished they had been with us in El Salvador were now shaking in fear. While others who a week ago had said they didn't want to fight in a war, now wanted to go kick some Iranian ass. But the quietest of all were the Vietnam veterans. For we knew too well what going to war really meant. And as much as I wanted to go, there was a fear growing in me that surprised me. Am I getting old, have I been away from combat too long? Or was it the fact this wouldn't be jungle type warfare of small units, but instead massed units, massed tanks and massed artillery, massed air support all out in the open in the desert.

LtCol Hester told us that so far, we were still not on alert. Today would be an admin day. We would have the weekend off. But no one would be allowed to go further then 200 miles away. But come Monday be back and be ready to go to the field for the week. We would be training harder and longer in the field until this Iran thing is over.

The rest of Friday we spent cleaning weapons and equipment and inspecting them. In the afternoon 1stSgt Burns walked up to me, shook my hand and said, "Congratulations."

"For what?" I asked.

"You don't know?"

"Know what?"

"You're on the promotion list for Chief Warrant Officer Two."

"I can't be. I've barely got over a year in grade as a W-1."

"I can't help that. You're on the list. Don't forget to get your physical even though it may be next year before you actually get promoted. Hell, you'll be making more money than me again."

The rest of November we trained night and day and listened to the news waiting for something to happen. During this time, I heard the least complaining and had the fewest people reporting to sick call than I had ever seen in years. It seemed everybody from privates to lieutenant colonels wanted to make sure they were ready when our time came. We were all surprised when we got a ninety-six-hour pass for Thanksgiving.

The first of December I made Sgt Reed my platoon guide.

I did my best to prepare Marty and the kids that I probably wouldn't be home for Christmas. But as Christmas neared and we didn't go on alert I requested two weeks leave and it was granted. So, a few days before Christmas we packed up our cloths and presents and headed north to Delaware. Once there, we stayed with Mom Piper in Georgetown. For twelve days, Kyle visited with his father as Nat and Lance visited with us.

The day after Christmas we visited my father on the farm. Father and I took a walk up through the old farmyard. We talked about crops, hogs and the past November deer season. From out of nowhere he said, "I guess you guys are going to have to go over and slap that jerk in Iran aren't you."

"Yes, I think we should."

"Do you think you will?"

"I don't know what Carter's waiting for."

"Do you think today's military is up to it?"

Shocked I looked at him saying, "Well the Marines are and we want to go."

"You may not be as lucky as you were in Vietnam."

"I know Dad. But this is what I do."

"I know. But be careful."

"I will."

The day after New Year's day 1980 we headed south back to the base. I was returning with dread in my heart for I felt for sure that by years end we would be in a bloody war in Iran. I had felt sure I would see two more real wars in my career. I had just returned from Vietnam seven years ago and I wasn't ready for another war so soon. And yet I knew I was still lucky. The guys from WWII only had five years of peace before Korea. I knew we were ready to go, its just I knew we would lose a lot of our best young men. Again, we went back to training for the invasion that many began to wonder would ever come.

In March L/Cpl West, who was already an acting machinegun team leader, was promoted to corporal.

The first of April, I went to the morning CO's meeting in Capt Hays office as usual on Monday. He told us platoon leaders of his plans for the company in the field this week. Then he ended by announcing command changes, "As of now Lieutenant Messenger will take over second platoon and Gunner Cord will take over third platoon."

I was surprised, but happy because I had wanted to command a rifle platoon again ever since becoming an officer. Of course, I had already been an acting rifle platoon leader many times in Vietnam as a corporal, sergeant and staff sergeant.

When the meeting broke up, I hung back as the other platoon leaders walked out and asked, "Capt'n can I ask you a question?"

"Sure Gunner."

"Sir did Colonel Hester have anything to do with this change?"

"No, Gunner he didn't."

"Well, thank you, sir," I said starting to leave.

"Gunner, I liked what I saw you do with weapons platoon and when we invade Iran, I want you leading a platoon for me."

"Thank you, sir."

I first went and gathered weapons platoon together and told them as of now SSgt Manuel was their platoon leader again.

Sgts Reed and Simon both said they hated to see me go.

Sgt Rienbold said, "As much as I hate to lose you, I know it's what you really want. I just can't understand what took Captain Hays so long to realize you should be in charge of a rifle platoon."

"Well, there's one good thing. From time to time some of your gun and mortar teams maybe attached to third platoon," I said.

Then I went over to the 3rd platoon. SSgt Knight, the platoon sergeant, had already gathered the platoon together. I had served with him before and felt he was the best platoon sergeant in Mike Company. He introduced me to the troops and I told them what I expected from them.

As the week in the field went on, I was more impressed with black Cpl Coston who was my 3rd squad leader than I was with either of the two sergeants running the other two squads. I was also impressed with PFCs Harris, Bower, Pvt Blandon and especially Pvt Street who was a full-blooded Indian.

Later in April, Marty and I were sitting on our couch watching TV when suddenly there was a newsbreak. There had been a rescue attempt made by the American military to rescue the hostages in Iran and it had failed with American deaths. I was shocked, but saddened at the loss of American lives. But at least we had finally tried something after all these months. I felt it was too little too late.

"What now?" asked Marty?

"Well if they start killing hostages because of this it'll definitely be war."

The next few days, Mike Company again buzzed with the failed rescue attempt and what could happen. For the first time our battalion went on alert.

Months later, I would run into a Marine chopper pilot who was in the rescue attempt and he told me what happened. It was called Operation Blue Light. It was a joint operation made up of ninety Green Berets, Marine chopper crews and Air Force C-130's aircraft and ninety crewmen.

Preparations had started a few days after the hostages had been taken. Desert One was an area where they were all supposed to meet in the desert of Iran. The Green Berets and Air Force troops flew 250 miles from Egypt to Desert One. Eight Marine Ch-53 choppers lifted off the USS Nimitz in the Arabian Sea and flew 530 miles in the dark to Desert One.

They had to fly low to escape radar detection, which caused them to fly through a sandstorm. The sand was so thick the Marines were shoveling sand out the back of the choppers. One chopper broke down and had to be destroyed on the ground. Another chopper developed problems and was forced to return to the Nimitz.

Six choppers made it to Desert One with one of them left inoperable. If they lost one more chopper it would mean leaving forty-three men in Iran.

An Iranian bus drove right up to the planes forcing the troops to stop it and unload the driver and passenger.

Then a tank truck driving by was shot at and stopped, but the driver escaped in a small pickup following the truck.

The senior commander at Desert One, Col Beckwith US Army then ordered the operation aborted.

One of the Ch-53's lifted twenty feet into the air to go around a C-13 transport plane to a tanker plane on the other side to refuel. As the chopper banked in the dark, one of its rotor blades slashed the transport just behind the crew compartment. The C-130 burst into flames killing five Air Force crewmen and four Marines.

With the dangers of spreading fire and explosions, Col Beckwith ordered the four remaining choppers to take off right away. And they did so, abandoning eight US bodies left behind.

It angered me that for an operation this small they used three military services. They were asking for trouble. Of course, I believed the best group to use should have been Marine recon units with Marine choppers. If not us, why didn't they go with the Green Berets and Army choppers that they usually trained with or Navy Seals with Navy choppers. But instead of using men of the same service who had trained together for months, they used men from three services who didn't even get to train together. Then met together in the middle of the desert of an enemy country with three colonels from three different services wondering who was in charge. President Carter could've done better than this. We hadn't learned a thing from the joint service Cambodian operation in 1975.

In May LtCol Hester received transfer orders and I hated to see him go. This was the third time I had served with him. I felt he was not only the best officer I had served with, but also my best friend. He stopped by my house after the change of command ceremony to say, "I just wanted to thank you for your support Nathan."

"Thank you for your leadership, sir."

"Keep up the good work Nathan and you'll be a Lieutenant yet."

"I'm not sure how I'll make out with Major Butler as acting battalion CO. You know I had a run in with him a few years ago when he was a captain and I was a first sergeant."

"I don't think you'll have to worry about that. He knows a good officer when he sees one. Besides Captain Hays tells me you're the best officer he's got."

"Well sir, we did get off to a rough start, but he seems to respect me now and I think he is a good officer. One of the best. In fact, he reminds me of you when you were a captain."

"That's good. I guess."

"Sir, do you ever think we'll invade Iran?"

"No, I don't. We'd 've done it by now."

"Well sir, I hope to get the chance to serve with you again."

"Me too, Nathan."

The 1st of June, Hays was promoted to major and Jones was promoted to captain. Maj Hays became our battalion XO and Capt Jones took command of Mike Company. On June 5th, 2nd Battalion packed up for a month and a half of training in California. We flew out there and landed at San Diego Airport. We spent the first two weeks at Coronado Navy Base where we took classes on raids and infiltration, both by day and night. We climbed dry nets with full packs down into fake landing craft and then climbed back up. The one thing new for me was when they took us out to sea almost a mile and we were ordered to jump overboard and swim ashore.

Into the second week we boarded amtracks and trained hitting the beach.

On June 19th, 2nd Battalion had packed up to leave Coronado. We marched down to the beach to wait to be picked up by the amtracks, which would take us out to amphibious ships.

As most of the men took their packs off to sit on in the sand, I stood with mine on, looking around. In the distance I saw red haired SgtMaj Hanson, the oldest Marine in the battalion, standing like a rock with his pack also on, but unlike me he was wearing his soft cammy cover, smoking a cigarette looking out to sea. I couldn't help but wonder how many real and practice landings he has made since 1950 in Korea.

Closer, I watched 1stSgt Bums standing talking with GySgt Fisher. Near them Capt Jones stood talking with SSgt Knight.

Then we all watched the amtracks come roaring to shore on line and then spin around pointing back out to sea and drop their back ramps down as GySgt Fisher yelled, "Okay Mighty Mike, on your feet and put it on your back."

We boarded the amtracks by companies. I followed Cpl Coston's squad into an amtrack. After we sat down, the ramp rose up and shut sealing us inside. A little later I felt the amtrack jerk forward as it ran down the beach and into the ocean. I could feel the coldness of the ocean through the metal against my back.

Once we were aboard the ship, we climbed out of the amtracks and formed up by platoons. We waited as Maj Hays who had gone out on the advance party, now took GySgt Fisher to show him where the troop compartment was and where the Staff NCO's quarters was. When they returned, Maj Hays took the officers to our rooms. Lt Messenger and I shared a room. After we put our gear away, we walked up on deck to look around. We looked across the ocean at a ship carrying the rest of our battalion. The amtracks were back in the water now and we watched their formations of circling and then coming on line.

In the afternoon, Capt Jones briefed us platoon leaders and

platoon sergeants on our objectives when we hit the beach in the morning at Camp Pendleton. After our briefing, SSgt Knight and I gathered 3rd platoon together and briefed them.

The next morning, we were up at 0400, at chow by 0500 and were sitting in our assigned amtracks by 0600 as they sat inside the ship. It still seemed funny to me when we climbed down into the huge bay area where the amtracks were parked, to see the whole back of this ship which was just a big ramp which was now lowered into the water on which the amtrack would drive down into the ocean.

Then I felt the amtrack jerk forward as it raced toward the ramp and to sea. I didn't show it, but I always had a fear that when the amtrack ran off the ramp and dropped into the ocean it would just keep going down and wouldn't come back up.

I felt the amtrack run off the ramp and nose dive down; again, I felt the coldness of the ocean through the steel hull against my back. Slowly I felt the amtrack start to move back up to the surface.

Soon we hit the beach and I felt the amtrack climbing up and over the sand dunes. Then the amtracks stopped suddenly and the ramp lowered. I led Cpl Coston's squad out down the ramp screaming. We ran around both sides to the front of the amtrack and took cover in the sand on line. Lt Messenger's 2nd platoon was doing the same to our left as I ran to the right to get to the rear center of my platoon where SSgt Knight joined me. Ahead of us was a group of twenty some Marines in civilian clothes acting like anti-war demonstrators.

My radioman handed me his handset saying, "Gunner, it's the Capt'n."

Over the radio Capt Jones told me Mike Company had been ordered to take the point for the battalion and he wanted 3rd platoon to be the point platoon for Mike Company and start by clearing a hole through those demonstrators.

I looked over to SSgt Knight saying, "Okay we have the point. First have the men fix bayonets. Then form up into a tight riot control wedge."

"You got it, Gunner," said SSgt Knight rolling away. Quickly, he formed the platoon up and they started stepping forward as one. With each step they thrust their bayonets forward and screamed. SSgt Knight walked just behind the point of the wedge giving directions. I walked just behind him with my radioman behind me. Behind us came Capt Jones with the rest of Mike Company in two columns, one anchored to each of our wedge ends.

As we neared the demonstrators they split apart and we stepped through them. With the demonstrators behind us, SSgt Knight quickly fanned the platoon out with 3rd squad still out front. Behind us the 1st platoon spread out to our right as Lt Messenger's 2nd platoon spread out to our left. Then Capt Graham's Lima Company moved up to our left and Capt Scotto's Kilo Company moved to our right. Behind us now was Maj Butler's battalion CP group, three tanks and behind them Capt Bird's India Company. Then Maj Butler ordered the battalion into a column as we walked under the civilian dual highway bridge. For the next two weeks we trained in the hills of Camp Pendleton, mostly in the rain.

On July 3rd, our battalion was carried by buses and cattle cars to El Toro Marine Air Base. Mike Company was lucky because we got to travel in the green military type school buses. At El Toro, we off loaded and formed up by platoons in a field next to the air field and staged our packs and gear as we waited for the planes which would take us to 29 Palms Marine Base in the California desert.

No more had the buses got out of sight then I heard SSgt Manuel yell, "I can't believe this shit!"

I turned to see SSgt Manuel striding toward Capt Jones with Sgt Simon following. Capt Jones had also turned at the outburst.

As SSgt Manuel neared him, he said, "Capt'n, one of the mortar teams left it's mortar base plate on the bus."

"Are you shit'n me staff sergeant? Are you sure Sergeant Simon?" asked Capt Jones.

"Yes sir. I've checked three times. They slid it behind the back seat on the bus and forgot it," answered Sgt Simon.

"I can't believe this. Shit, wait till Major Butler hears this," said Capt Jones as he turned and walked toward the Battalion CP group.

I felt bad for them and guilty because my first thought was, I was glad I wasn't still in charge of weapons platoon. But still the company gunny, GySgt Fisher should have checked the buses before they left.

I watched Capt Jones talking to Maj Butler. I couldn't hear what he said, but I sure heard Maj Butler shout back, "Just fucking great captain. Because of your incompetence, if your company was flying into a hot LZ (landing zone under enemy fire) that mortar tube would be absolutely useless. Good Marines would die for lack of mortar support. You tell that shitbird team I hope they've saved up some money because they're going to pay the Marine Corps for that base plate."

I felt sorry for Capt Jones as he returned to us. I think he was one of the best officers in the Corps. But I've seen things like this hurt good Marines' careers.

Two hours later we were still waiting in the open field leaning against our packs with the rest of our battalion.

Suddenly up the road next to us we heard a horn blowing. It seemed the whole battalion sat up, turning their heads to see a green bus speeding toward us. The bus slid to a stop next to Mike Company. Many men stood up as the bus door opened and out stepped the bus driver with the missing mortar base plate. Already Sgt Simon was throwing and kicking the team members toward their missing base plate.

We all laughed and SSgt Knight, sitting next to me said, "I've never seen Sergeant Simon so mad."

"One thing you don't do is misuse one of his mortars," I said, still laughing.

Then the big planes came in and landed. Soon our whole company moved across the pavement following Capt Jones up the ramp into the back of the biggest military plane I'd ever been in.

Soon we were in the air. We flew over the desert and I was surprised to find mountains in the desert. The planes flew tactically which meant they flew down low in the valleys, then up skimming over the top of the mountains and then back into the valleys. Finally, we landed at the airfield at Camp Wilson on 29 Palms base. As we walked off the plane, the heat hit us in the face. I hadn't felt heat like that since Vietnam. Although this heat was different, it was a dry heat, but there was no shade out here except for a little man-made shade.

In two columns, Capt Jones led Mike Company off the air strip which had no buildings at all, across the hot sand through Camp Wilson. Camp Wilson was little more then a tent city. Each platoon was assigned to a tent. All the companies' Staff NCOs were in one tent. Mike Company's admin and supply sections shared a tent. Another tent was split in half. We platoon leaders had one half and

Capt Jones and 1stSgt Burns had the other half. Each company had a six-sitter outhouse. And nearby was a piss tube stuck into the ground. In almost sixteen years in the Corps this was the first time I had ever seen piss tubes. And for the first time in my career we were ordered to wear sunglasses to protect our eyes from the sun.

Also, for the first time, I heard of over drinking. Maj Butler ordered everyman to drink a half a canteen of water every half hour during daylight hours. Each company had a truck assigned to it, which pulled a water buffalo behind it to keep us in water. It seemed the Israelis had discovered that even a man who had never been in the desert before, if he drank a glass full of water every half hour, he could survive in the desert without heat stroke or heat exhaustion in a combat situation. After all these years of training to conserve water, this was a complete turnaround. But in the next two weeks, I would find it worked because Mike Company only suffered one heat exhaustion case even though we spent most of that time in the desert or in the back of the amtracks. The amtracks left their rear hatch doors open and the tops open to cut down on the heat inside. But it was still hot and this let in the desert sand and dust which covered us.

When we set up positions, we put up ponchos and camouflage poncho liners on poles to give us a little shade. This was the best training I had ever seen. A lot of it was live fire. At times we had tanks and artillery firing over our heads. Company Commanders called in live mortar and air strikes. We were involved in two companies attacking on line, firing live rounds and LAAWs. In the open desert I could see it all, both companies on line doing team, squad, and platoon rushes, unlike being in the jungle or forest. I loved it. I also knew for sure if we invaded Iran our 2nd Battalion 8th Marine Regiment would go. We were as ready as any battalion in the Corps.

On July 17th, it was all over and we stood in a Battalion formation as Maj Butler spoke to us over a loud speaker. "Well men, we've finished another successful training mission. We all will long remember this training mission. Once again, the second battalion has proved itself the most outstanding unit in the eighth regiment. Once again, we have proved that we are ready to respond to any mission assigned to us even in temperatures in excess of over 110 degrees, and still perform in an outstanding and professional way.

This battalion has been exposed through different phases of amphibious training from the beaches of Coronado and Camp Pendleton to the desert sands of 29 Palms. The fact that there were no major accidents nor heat casualties proves that every Marine in this battalion is well informed and could very well take care of himself. Every Marine will return to Camp Lejeune with memories, new knowledge and experience of shipboard and desert life. Well done to all of you and congratulations as well as my deep appreciation to all of you. Regiment will be well pleased by the professional way you performed out here. Thank you."

We flew back to the east coast the same day. When I finally got home that night, Marty met me at the door and we kissed and held each other. Over her shoulder I noticed a homemade card sitting on the kitchen table. I walked over and picked it up and read the front, "Welcome Home to My Marine. I missed you so much!"

I opened it up, and on the inside, it said, 'Nathan. Once again, these long days since you've been gone, have made me realize even more that life for me is you. I LOVE you. I NEED you. WELCOME HOME!'

She signed it, "Me."

I smiled at that and she said, "I'm sorry I couldn't find a real card for you."

I kissed her and said, "This means more to me than any store-bought card. I love you."

Four days later, Messenger was promoted to captain. Maj Butler assigned him to take command of India Company replacing Capt Bird who had been selected for promotion to major and was assigned to the 2nd battalion staff as the S-4 (Logistic officer.)

The 1st of August, Sieple was promoted to sergeant. This made too many sergeants in weapons platoon. Even though I requested him for my platoon Capt Jones felt he was needed more in 1st platoon.

Ever since the hostages had been taken in Iran last year our battalion had been on and off alert more times than I could count. I had never been in a unit that had been on alert so much that didn't go somewhere. So, when 2nd Battalion went on alert again on August 18th, none of us even got excited anymore. But this time our training schedule was changed overnight. We were ordered by regiment to train by companies in combat town. Maj Butler ordered

Mike Company to start first the next morning. Capt Jones asked me to teach the company what I had learned in Hue City. I asked to have Sgt Simon to help me because he had also been there in a mortar team. Sgt Simon and I drove out to combat town. We walked the streets and inside the buildings floor by floor. We were up until midnight planning how we would take this town street-by-street and room-by-room. I worked out the squad and platoon tactics while he looked for places to set up the mortar teams to support the company.

The next day, I gave classes on fire team tactics in clearing rooms, alleys and streets. Sgt Simon gave classes in calling in supporting fire from mortars, artillery, tanks and aircraft. We walked the company through the town showing them the danger areas. In the afternoon, the company trained by fire teams in the town. The next morning, we ran the company through the town in squads. In the afternoon, we were running the company by platoons through the town when Majors Butler and Hays drove up. I kept on running the training as Capt Jones walked back to speak to them.

When Capt Jones returned, he sent GySgt Fisher to get SSgt Manuel and me. We arrived together and I asked, "What's up, skipper?"

Capt Jones looked worried as he asked, "Gunner, which is your best squad?"

"Third squad, sir." I answered puzzled.

"Corporal Coston's squad?"

"Yes sir."

"Go get 'em and bring them back here with all their gear. Your gear too, and tell Staff Sergeant Knight he'll run third platoon for the next few days."

"What's going on Capt'n?" I asked.

"Just go get 'em, Gunner."

"Yes sir," I said saluting him.

When I returned leading my fourteen Marines I asked, "Is this it, sir?"

"This is it."

Then I noticed Sgt Faust walking up leading Cpl West's machinegun team. "They're going with you, Gunner," said Capt Jones.

As I looked at them, I was thinking, "I have no problem with Sgt Faust or Cpl West, but I'd rather have the experience of Sgt

Rienbold."

"What the hell Capt'n. Are we the advance party for the company or battalion?" I asked. "Gunner the battalion is staying on alert, but as of now only twenty-one are going on a special mission."

"Capt'n, do you mean to tell me they're sending twenty-one Marines into the heart of Iran to rescue forty some hostages."

"I don't know that it is Iran."

"Do you know where we're going?"

"No."

"But this is real, sir?"

"As far as I know, yes. There is a truck waiting down the road to pick you up. Another truck with it has your ammo. You'll be driven to Cherry Point where you will fly out tonight. You and your men will not make contact with anyone including family members. I will report to your wives after you leave tonight that you're on special assignment for several weeks."

"This is real, sir. Well, we better be going."

"Gunner."

"Yes sir," I said looking back.

"You were requested by name."

"By whom?"

"I have no idea except it came from higher up than division."

That night after dark we walked up the ramp of a Marine plane loaded down with ammo and weapons. We still didn't know where we were going.

Once we were in the air, I waved the crew chief over to me and asked, "Where are we going?"

He looked at me in disbelief, "You don't know sir?"

"No."

"San Salvador, El Salvador."

"El Salvador! What's happened there now?"

"Beats me, sir. We were alerted early this morning for this flight. In fact, we expected a lot more of you guys then just twenty-one."

I shook my head wishing I had my whole platoon or at least knew what I was getting into.

Several hours later, we landed at the San Salvador airport. As we walked off the plane, I could make out two 6 by 6 trucks sitting off the airfield. Next to the trucks stood someone blinking a red light toward us. I led my men toward him. As I neared him, I thought I recognized the man's stance and I asked, "Gunny Stevenson is that you?"

"Yes sir. Gunner Cord?"

"Gunny, I'm glad you're here. I hope you know what we're here for?"

"I sure do. But let me get you and your men to the embassy first." I turned around and said, "Sergeant Faust get the men on the trucks."

"Yes sir," said Sgt Faust to me and then said, "Okay Corporal Coston put two of your teams on the left truck and the other team on the right truck with the gun team."

Later, after arriving in the embassy, GySgt Stevenson showed the men to two conference rooms, which had already been set up with cots for their use. Then I took Sgt Faust and Cpl Coston with me to a meeting with GySgt Stevenson.

We entered the same room I had met Ambassador Turley in last year. But it was not Ambassador Turley that was waiting for us.

GySgt Stevenson said, "Mr. Randle this is Gunner Cord."

The man stood up holding his hand out to me saying, "Glad to meet you, Gunner."

"Same here, Mr. Randle," I said shaking his hand.

"Please, you and your men take a seat," said Mr. Randle.

As we sat down Mr. Randle said, "A little over forty-eight hours ago Ambassador Turley was taken hostage on his way to work. How do you feel about that Gunner?"

"I feel whatever the cost we should get the ambassador back."

"I agree," said Mr. Randle smiling. Then he said, "The terrorists are demanding the release of whom they call five political prisoners being held by the El Salvadorian government. The local Police and military are feeding us information on his possible where-abouts. If we pin his location down, you will be in charge of the rescue attempt.

"Yes sir," I said.

"But Sergeant Stevenson has requested that he and some of his men would be the point section and would actually bring the ambassador out and I agree," said Mr. Randle.

"Sir, if this is to be my operation, I want my own men on the point. I know Gunny Stevenson's men are good Marines. But my men have been training for this sort of thing," I said.

"Gunner, you may not realize it. But your orders read that you are to support Sergeant Stevenson's men. You are in charge of helping him get the ambassador back."

"I have yet to see orders to that effect."

"You'll have them in the morning," said Mr. Randle.

"I'll take no more than Gunny Stevenson and three of his best men," I said.

"Mr. Cord, you'll take as many of Sergeant Stevenson's men as he wants."

"I can live with four Mr. Randle. We the embassy guards feel we should get our ambassador back. But we can't do it alone. We'll take the Gunner's orders as long as we can lead the way," said GySgt Stevenson.

"Very well, Gunny. Pick your men tonight and take them off the guard roster. We'll rest during the day and train in room-to-room fighting and clearing tactics at night," I said.

For the next week we trained and waited as more reports came in. By now, we knew what house he was being held in on what street and in what village. Six terrorists were known to be holding him with two on guard at all times.

I planned for the rescue for about 0130. I still felt our casualties could be very high. GySgt Stevenson and I both agreed that we really had a slim chance of getting the ambassador out alive. But intelligence reports stated that the Ambassador might be executed soon if the terrorist's demands were not met.

The rescue would either be a great success or a terrible failure. But the probability of the ambassador's execution definitely was putting added pressure on us.

I planned the rescue for tomorrow morning and as the final hours passed, I became haunted with the fear of hitting the house only to find the ambassador gone. With discreet contacts made with the police, we had found out at least one of the terrorists was a woman. I told my men that if they came upon this woman, not to think of her as a girl, but as a cold-blooded killer who will kill them if they give her the chance. We now knew the location of the doors in the old house, the room the ambassador was held in and how the windows opened.

Everyman had studied the lay out of the building. I had run rehearsals with the squad divided into fire team s GySgt Stevenson's team and the machinegun team. The machinegun team would support the other teams as they cleared the different rooms. After dark, I talked to all the men. They all felt confident they would complete the mission. I had them run one last rehearsal. I thought we could rescue the ambassador within sixty seconds of entering the building.

Again, I studied the layout of the house with the latest intelligence showing where the guards should be found.

I was impressed that none of the men felt there was anything impossible about my plan, even though they didn't understand the problems or the dangers we faced. They were confident that secrecy, speed and surprise would be our key to victory. Bottom line, I believe they trusted me. And I prayed to God not to allow me to let them down. Finally, the time came and we walked out into the embassy compound were a truck and a black armored car waited.

No one talked as Cpl Coston and two of his fire teams and Sgt Faust machinegun team climbed into the truck. Meanwhile GySgt Stevenson climbed into the car behind the steering wheel as two of his men slid in beside him and PFC Bower stuffed himself in on their right. In the backseat, another of GySgt Stevenson's men slid in flanked on one side by PFC Harris and the other side by Pvts Street and Blandon. I looked into the car at their expressionless faces. GySgt Stevenson gave me the thumbs up sign as he rolled up the bulletproof window and I turned and walked jumping into the open cab of the truck next to the driver. From the car, I had smelled that special sweet smell of fear of the unknown of coming danger. But yet, the atmosphere was relaxed.

As we followed the car into the street, I thought about the ambassador. He or we, could be caught in a murderous crossfire. GySgt Stevenson's group who would enter the house first, knew that their first shots at the terrorist must be fatal. There won't be any second chances.

The long ride through the streets, and then out into the countryside, seemed endless. But finally, we entered a small town. The streets here seemed too quiet; it was almost a deathly silence that frightened me. Then we were one street corner away as the truck rolled to a stop. I jumped out, waving Cpl Coston's two fire teams to go around the corner as the car went out of sight. As the Marines ran past me, I fell in behind Cpl Coston's men and in front of Sgt Faust's machinegun team.

Ahead of us around the corner, the car nearing the house sped up and then suddenly turned left smashing right through the front door. Once inside, the Marines hurled themselves out of the car. GySgt Stevenson moved so fast, Pvt Blandon couldn't believe it. A man standing next to a window spun around with rifle in hand, but with a bewildered look on his face. There was a long burst of fire from someone Pvt Blanton wasn't sure had fired, as he saw the man twist and fall. GySgt Stevenson jumped over the man's body as he ran toward the stairs. PFC Bower kicked the body over and shot him again in the head. On the other side of the car, PFC Harris stopped when he noticed a woman moving in the shadows along the wall, holding a rifle in one hand and a grenade in the other. She seemed confused, as he squeezed the trigger firing a burst into her body. With a sickening feeling he stepped over her body and burst into the next room. Meanwhile, GySgt Stevenson raced to the top of the stairs breaking into the first room to the right. Seeing Ambassador Turley lying on the floor he yelled, "Down! Stay down!" Two men in the room opened fire, one with a rifle and the other with a pistol. GySgt Stevenson poured bullets back at their directions. The man with the rifle, shot at the ambassador before he himself was killed. Bullets spattered pieces of plaster around in the air. Then the man with the pistol fell bleeding.

GySgt Stevenson grabbed Ambassador Turley and pulled him up and out into the hallway. The house seemed to fill up with smoke as he helped the ambassador down the stairs.

By now the rest of Cpl Coston's squad was bursting through the door and windows into the house. As I entered through the door, the shooting lasting no more than two minutes had stopped.

GySgt Stevenson and his men pushed the ambassador into the car and began backing out of the house as Cpl Coston's squad hunted through the other rooms looking for the remaining terrorists. In one room, PFC Bower found a terrorist hiding under a bed and he killed him where he lay. PFC Harris's team killed the last terrorist found in the house. I felt good, six terrorists dead, Ambassador Hurley alive and only four Marines wounded including GySgt Stevenson, and all of them able to walk. I yelled, "Okay fall back!" Outside, Sgt Faust's machinegun team, covered us as we withdrew from the house. Suddenly, we were fired at from the next house. Cpl West returned fire with his machinegun instantly. I dropped down next to him as Cpl Coston moved his squad by fire teams back around the corner to the truck.

Then Cpl West shouted, "Sarge is hit! Faust's wounded!"

I looked over and saw Sgt Faust hit in the chest roll on his side bleeding heavily. He tried to get up, but fell back.

At the corner, Pvt Street's fire team stopped to fire to cover the machinegun team as they prepared to fall back. Another Marine and I picked up Sgt Faust, carrying him down the street as the rest of the machinegun team walked backwards behind us in a skirmish line with Cpl West firing his machinegun from the hip.

Around the corner, the truck was backing up as we ran around to meet it. Quickly we lifted up Sgt Faust to Pvt Street and another Marine. Then I climbed up inside followed by the machinegun team. Cpl Coston, with one of his fire teams was firing around the corner covering us. From inside the truck I yelled, "Let's go!" as the truck slowly started moving forward.

Cpl Coston and the fire team turned running and jumped up as we pulled them into the back of the truck as it speeded up. I turned around looked at Sgt Faust as Cpl West worked over him patching him up the best he could. I was worried because I knew he was hit badly. When Cpl West had done all he could do, he held the blond-headed sergeant in his small skinny black arms. Finally, we arrived in the embassy compound, and before the truck had stopped, Cpl Coston and PFC Bower had jumped out. Cpl West and Pvt Street lowered Sgt Faust into their arms. They quickly carried him into the embassy to the dispensary where the embassy doctor was working on GySgt Stevenson.

At seeing the pale face of Sgt Faust, GySgt Stevenson said, "Oh shit doc. Take care of him. I can wait."

The rest of us waited outside with the walking wounded until finally the doctor walked out and said, "He's gonna make it."

Tears rolled down my face as I fought not to cry as I thought of another young blond-haired Marine buddy of mine who years ago in Vietnam didn't make.

All of us but Sgt Faust flew home the same day. He flew back to a military hospital in Maryland a week later. There, I'm sorry to say, the Corps medically discharged him after his recovery.

Late that night after Maj Butler debriefed me, I went home. Marty met me at the door crying, "Why didn't you call me and let me know you were back?"

I pulled her close to me saying, "I'm sorry I've had one meeting after another behind closed doors."

"Oh, I heard about the embassy Marines getting their ambassador back and I was afraid you were there."

"I was."

"Oh, are you all right?"

"Yes."

"Your men?"

"One slightly wounded and one badly wounded."

"Anyone I know?"

"Sergeant Faust."

"The blond-haired young sergeant from weapons platoon?"

"Yes, machine gunner, the one you said looked too young to be a sergeant."

The next few months passed as we trained for the Iranian invasion that even I had begun to believe wouldn't happen unless Reagan got elected President in November.

In October, Mike Company got a new Lieutenant named Evans who Capt Jones assigned to 1st platoon.

I had now been in the Corps sixteen years. It was hard to believe I was thirty-three years old and only had four more years to go to rate retirement. For the first time, I really thought about retirement or life after the Corps. I wasn't sure I would be ready to retire in four years. I would be pinning on my W-2 bars soon. In three years, I should be about to pin on my W-3 bars. And if that happens, I know I'll want to stay past twenty to try to make W-4.

In November Harris and Bower were promoted to lance corporal.

As usual Marty and I went to the officers Marine Corps Birthday Ball on November 10th. But of course, the best thing that happened in this month for our Corps, country and the hostages in Iran was that Reagan was elected President. Almost right away, Iran started talking about releasing the hostages about the same time President elect Reagan would take office the first of the year.

In December, again, I took two weeks leave and we went up to Delaware to spend time with our families, my sons and let Kyle spend time with his father over Christmas and the New Year of 1981.

By the end of January, Reagan was President and the hostages were home free from Iran. There were many young Marines like Cpl Johnson and Pvt Street who hoped that once the hostages were free, we still would invade Iran just to kick their ass and to pay them back. But by now most of us realized it was not to be. As for me and the other combat veterans of Vietnam, we definitely sighed in relief even though I think we should have invaded over a year ago.

In April, the newly promoted Maj Bird was transferred out of our battalion.

In May standing in front of Mike Company, Capt Jones promoted me to Chief Warrant Officer Two. Again, Marty was called forward to pin on my new bar (red bar with two gold boxes.) I was glad to see the warrant was backdated to October 1st of last year, which meant I would also get the back pay.

In June, Harris was promoted to corporal and Blandon was promoted to PFC.

In July, my platoon sergeant, SSgt Knight was promoted to gunnery sergeant. As much as I hated losing the best platoon sergeant in our company, I also hated the fact he might have to leave our company. But Capt Jones, knowing that GySgt Fisher was due to be transferred next year, put GySgt Knight in charge of weapons platoon.

Because I now had no sergeants left in my platoon, Capt Jones transferred a newly promoted Sgt Ward from 1st platoon to be my platoon sergeant. I would much rather have had one of the older sergeants like Sieple, Rienbold, Simon, Reed or Reilly. But I knew that Capt Jones wanted me to break in Sgt Ward.

The same month, SgtMaj Hanson left our battalion to be a regimental sergeant major in another regiment.

The 1st of August, Bowers was promoted to corporal and Street was promoted to PFC.

On August 6th our battalion was bussed up to Little Creek, VA.

The next day Mike Company was marched out to an area where they had wooden structures the size and shape of Ch-46 choppers. We were broken down by platoons. Then I broke down my platoon by squads and they trained, boarding a chopper and how to get off under fire. In the afternoon the real choppers came in and landed. By platoons, we loaded a squad on a chopper. Then they took off, circled and came in and landed as the Marines rushed out and set up a 360-degree perimeter.

The next morning, August 8th, Mike Company marched to the obstacle course and ran it with the officers and Staff NCOs going first. We crawled through pipes in the ground, climbed over chest high logs, crawled under barbed wire, climbed by rope up a wall and through a second story window and then jumped down including many other obstacles.

Then we marched down to the docks and went aboard a troop ship. There, after a class on the correct way to climb up and down a cargo net, we climbed down by four-man teams abreast into a landing craft. Then, with Mike Company in one craft and Capt Scotto's Kilo Company in the landing craft loaded on the other side of the ship, the two crafts backed out into the bay and turned around. Side by side, we raced to the other side of the bay until we hit the beach. The ramps dropped and 200 Marines from each craft ran screaming and set up a 180-degree perimeter on the beach with our backs to the sea. Mike Company was on the right and Kilo Company on the left. My platoon was on the far right of Mike Company with Lt Evans platoon on my left, Cpl Coston's squad to my right and with PFC Street lying partly in the water.

Then after lunch, we marched to the amtrack compound. There, each squad was assigned to an amtrack and they practiced boarding an amtrack and getting out under fire. We rode them down to the beach and into the bay. Then the amtracks carrying Mike Company turned around and came roaring to the beach on line. I felt the jolt as our amtrack hit the beach and climbed up off the beach. As the ramp went down, I rushed out with Cpl Coston's squad taking cover in the sand behind the line of amtracks, linking up with the rest of my platoon on my left and right as well as the rest of Mike Company off to my left. Then Capt Jones advanced the company in platoon rushes with one platoon moving as the other two covered. I in turn moved my platoon in squad rushes as we advanced past the amtracks across the sand and up into a hilly tree line.

The morning of August 9th, our battalion fell out in formation to march to the obstacle course to run it again, but this time as a battalion. After a few words by Maj Butler, over a 1,000 Marines marched off with company red and gold guide-ons flapping in the morning breeze with Maj Butler and Maj Hays leading the way followed by India Company, Lima Company, Kilo Company and Mike Company bringing up the rear.

Once at the obstacle course, Maj Butler told us each company would run as a team. The clock would start as the first man crossed the starting line and would stop when the last man from that company crossed the finish line. We waited as the other three companies ran it one after the other. By the time we stood up to run the course the best time was held by India Company followed by Kilo and Lima.

As before, the officers and Staff NCOs lined up at the front. Soon after we started, I was ahead of all the staff and officers. Of course, by the time I was half way through about a dozen of the seventeen, eighteen and nineteen-year-olds had passed me. But of the NCOs only Sgt Reilly and Cpl Coston were ahead of me.

Then came the rope climb up the two-story wall. Running, I jumped at the rope, caught it and pulled and walked my way up the wall and through the second story window. I then jumped down to the sand. I landed with my knees bent, but my left ankle popped with sounds as if I had cracked all my knuckles at once. Thinking nothing of it I started to run, but when I came down on my left foot it gave way and I fell rolling in the sand. I got back up trying to walk to the finish line, which was in sight. But with the pain of the next step, I again went down.

Cpl West jumped down from the wall and saw me sitting holding my ankle and ran over to me asking, "You all right Gunner?"

"I think I broke my damn ankle," I grumbled.

"Let me help you sir," he said bending over me. I put my left arm around his neck as he put his arm around my waist helping me to my feet.

Embarrassed, as I hopped along on one foot I said, "I can't believe this shit."

"Sir don't try to do it by yourself. Put some weight on me," he said.

Then Cpl Johnson ran up and together they picked me up in a firemen's carry, carrying me toward a jeep where a corpsman was getting out.

"Just like old times, sir. The machine gunner's taking care of you," said Cpl Johnson laughing.

Once they sat me in the jeep, the corpsman took my left boot off and felt of my ankle. Then he drove me to the base hospital. There a doctor looked at my ankle and took x-rays. A little later I was told my ankle wasn't broken, but it was very badly sprained. The doctor wrapped it up and said he was sorry, but they had no crutches for me because all the ones they had, had been given out had never been brought back. Then he filled out a light duty chit. It said for the next 24 hours I was to have bed rest. Then for the next five days I was to do no prolonged standing greater than 10 minutes.

No marching.

No PT.

No excessive walking.

No running.

Walking limited with the aid of crutches.

The corpsman that had brought me, then drove me back to my barracks and helped me to my room and into my rack where he placed a pillow under my left foot.

At noon a Marine from the mess hall brought me my meal, which surprised me and did it again in the evening.

That night when Lt Evans, who shared the room with me, showed up he said, "Gunner you'd do anything to get out of the field."

"Sir you know better than that," I said.

Later, Maj Hays and Capt Jones stopped in to see me. At seeing them, I started to get up, but Maj Hays waved me back down.

After they left Sgts Reed, Rienbold and Simon showed up with a big stick they had found and shaped for me to use as a crutch. They will never know how much that meant to me.

Five days later, I was limping around still unable to put my full weight on my left foot so Capt Jones wouldn't let me join the company as they went aboard a troop ship for the beach landing at Camp Geiger, NC. Instead four other sick and lame Marines from our battalion and I were put in charge of the bus that was sent up from Camp Lejeune to pick up the extra baggage.

So, as our battalion followed the coast in troop ships, we rode in a green bus. We only stopped once to get gas and cold cut sandwiches at a little country store that reminded me of Anna Hall's little store back home at Atlanta crossroads. Late in the evening, we finally arrived at Camp Lejeune. I helped the four enlisted men unload the baggage in a storage area at our battalion. Then I called Marty to come pick me up because my ankle wasn't up to driving a stick shift.

The next few days Marty drove me to the Mike Company office and dropped me off until I called her around 1630. All day I hung around the office wishing I was in the field with my platoon even though it had rained the past three days.

Late in the afternoon of August 17th, I heard a truck pull up outside the company office. Looking out the window, I saw 1stSgt Burns, unshaven, cammies muddy and wet, climb out of the green pickup truck and walk toward the company office.

As he entered the office I asked, "First Sergeant how is it out there?"

"Wet, hot and the jiggers are eating us alive sir. How's your ankle?"

"Getting better every day. I hope to be back to full duty by next week."

"Gunner, why aren't you home with your wife?"

"I guess I have a problem being home taking it easy when my men are in the field. How are they doing?"

"Sergeant Ward is doing you proud."

"Good, good," I said smiling.

"Sir would you like to visit them for awhile?"

"Sure. When?"

"Soon as I check the COs incoming box and mine. Then I'm going to take what can't wait back out to the skipper. When he's done, I'll bring you back."

A half hour later, we climbed into the pickup and drove out to the field.

A little later, we passed through our battalion lines to Mike Company, which was in the battalion reserve.

1stSgt Burns stopped next to 3rd platoon and I got out. Then he drove on to Mike Company's CP.

Sgt Ward and Cpl Coston got up and walked toward me smiling through dirty unshaven faces with cammies muddy and torn. I felt bad limping toward them with a clean body and cammies.

"How's it going Sergeant Ward?"

"Pretty good Gunner. It's good to have you back."

"I'm afraid I just came out for a visit. But I hope to be back next week."

Then from behind me I heard Sgt Rienbold say, "Hey Gunner what did you decide to do visit us field Marines?"

I turned around smiling saying, "What are you doing?"

"Why, me and climbing Simon are supporting this platoon of hogs of yours."

"Well good, you might learn something."

"Hell, sir you know a grunt can't teach a machine gunner nothing."

"Pretty bad I hear," I said.

"Well sir, we got rain, mud, heat, insects and little sleep, but the bullets ain't real, so how bad can it be."

"Roger that," I said looking around watching Sgt Reed walk by in the distance waving at me.

It wasn't long before I heard the pickup pull up nearby. As I said goodbye to my men and started limping toward the truck a captain I didn't know ran up to the truck.

"Top are you going to main side?" asked the captain.

"Yes sir," answered 1stSgt Burns.

"Good I need a ride."

"Fine sir, climb in the back."

"I'll ride up front."

"My Gunner rides up front."

As I limped up to the passenger door the captain again said, "I'll ride up front."

"Sir, my Gunner rides up front," said 1stSgt Burns as I opened the door and climbed in.

The captain stood there looking at us, his face turning red. But he turned and walked to the rear of the truck and climbed in. As we drove away, I noticed GySgt Knight laughing. Friday morning our battalion came in from the field and after cleaning their weapons and equipment, went on liberty for the weekend.

Monday, even though my ankle still bothered me some, I was returned to full duty.

In October, our battalion was MCCRES (Marine Corps Combat Readiness System) tested.

We were to start the test with an early morning chopper assault to kick off an operation. But because of bad weather the chopper assault was canceled. Still the assault had to go on, so our battalion, by companies, climbed on trucks and raced to the jumping off point, near the LZ.

Our mission was to rescue an American ambassador and his family and American civilians being held hostage by insurgent forces.

To add realism, Marines from another regiment acted as aggressors and harassed us whenever they could.

The men of my platoon liked the realism of contact with an enemy which added to their excitement of the test even though we were surprised by them using tear gas. But even that didn't slow down our advance. I was proud to see Mike Company's morale didn't drop even though we were on the move from 0600 in the morning until midnight in the rain and without chow since 0530.

On October 5th, the last day of the test, the weather was cold without rain. At noon, Capt Jones halted our company for noon chow. As Sgt Ward set the platoon in a defensive position before we ate, I dropped my pack next to a tree and sat alone. I pulled out a couple C-ration cans and sat down on my pack with my back to the tree. Knowing I would get chilled now that I wasn't moving, I zipped my green field jacket all the way up. As I opened a C-ration can I heard a voice say, "Gunner."

I looked up to see Sgt Simon aiming a camera at me.

Hearing the camera go off I asked, "Sergeant Simon what are you doing sliming through my platoon area?"

"Well sir, your boys are a little slack today. They're just letting anyone walk through their perimeter."

"So, what's up sarge?"

"Nothing sir, I just wanted to get a picture of a real Infantry Warrant Officer."

"Shit sarge, you better get back to the CP before I get Gunny Knight to inspect your mortar tubes for rust," I kidded.

"Sir, I inspected them myself this morning and you could drink beer out 'a 'em."

"I hear ya."

"Well I'll see ya sir," he said turning to leave.

"Take care," I said.

We passed the test with flying colors and worked late into the night cleaning our weapons and equipment.

The next morning each company had their own rifle, equipment and personnel inspection. After that was done, Maj Butler gave our battalion a four-day weekend.

By October 13th our battalion was back in the field. First, Maj Butler called the company commanders together for a briefing at the battalion CP. After their briefing, they returned to brief their companies. To do this, Capt Jones called us platoon leaders together. As I walked up to our company CP, the rest of the platoon leaders were already there. It was still cold and we all wore green field jackets over our cammies. Capt Jones' face and hands were camouflaged up, but his helmet had no branches stuck in it like GySgt Knight's and mine. Lt Evans' face and hands were camouflaged, but he had his green soft cover on backwards which surprised me and I could tell it irritated Capt Jones. I was surprised he didn't say something to him about it as he opened his map case, which also held his notes. As he briefed us, we took notes on the mission for our platoons.

When I had my orders, I started to return to brief my platoon. I passed Sgt Simon kneeling down putting small branches on his helmet, which was sitting on his pack.

As I walked on, I felt the pride of our battalion's readiness for combat. We trained hard no matter what, in mud, sand, snow or ice. There was a large amount of combat experience in this battalion. Many of the officers and Staff NCOs and some NCOs had fought in Vietnam.

In November, five days after the Marine Corps Birthday Ball, Mike Company flew up to Fort Drum, New York, an Army base, to train in cold weather in snow on skies. There was no snow when we got there, but the weather report was calling for 17 inches. This was the first time I had ever been issued real cold weather clothes. We wore thick green trousers, thick green coats with fur hoods, hats that went down around our necks under our chins, big thick mittens with liners and big thick rubber boots we called Mickey Mouse boots. We had classes on how to fight on skis, snow shoes and how to survive in snow. The only thing missing was the snow. The whole time we were there the only snow we got was snow flurries at midnight.

But no matter, as before, the orders were passed out and the training went on. My squads worked well together with the machinegun teams attached to us.

I sometimes wondered why these young men joined the Corps. After all there was no draft now and these boys could get fairly good paying jobs on the outside. So, it sure wasn't for the pay. But then again why did I join seventeen years ago, there wasn't a war on then. I guess it was for the adventure, to get away from the day after day routine of high school. Like me back then, they joined to prove their manhood, sleep on the ground, crawl in the mud, eat food out of a can and tell war stories around a campfire. Maybe to feel important, to wear the uniform, to be Marines.

Leatherneck magazine came up and did a story on us. They too waited for the snow, which never came. But they took pictures and did the story anyway. I only got in one picture. It was taken during a company briefing. Capt Jones was kneeling over a big map board talking with his hands. To his left was Lt Evans, bent over studying the map. Next to him was GySgt Knight with his heavy cold weather coat unzipped all the way down. Next to him was 1stSgt Burns eating raisins and nuts out of a plastic sandwich bag. Next was GySgt Fisher with a jaw full of chewing tobacco. Then there was me holding my own plastic bag of raisins, nuts and coconut.

Three months later, I would see the picture in Leatherneck, but I was disappointed that our names weren't under the picture. I guess I would have liked my old friends from the war to see how far I had come.

By November 22nd we had rejoined our battalion. The same day, I was glad to see Johnson get promoted to sergeant and take command of his own machinegun section.

The day before Thanksgiving, Maj Butler transferred out leaving Maj Hays in command of our battalion. We felt better with Maj Hays in charge.

On December 3rd at a morning briefing in Capt Jones office, he announced command changes. He said, "Gunner Cord you will take command of second platoon. Staff Sergeant Cain, you will take over third platoon."

SSgt Cain and I both looked at each other as I answered, "Yes sir."

SSgt Cain looked back at Capt Jones saying, "Sir, I request to stay with second platoon if at all possible."

Capt Jones stared hard back at him as if thinking before he spoke, "If I let you stay it will be as Gunner Cord's platoon sergeant."

"That's fine sir. I just want to stay with second platoon."

Then Capt Jones looked over to me saying, "Gunner can Sergeant Ward handle being a platoon leader?"

"Yes sir, I believe he has already proven he can," I answered.

"Then so be it. The command changes are in effect as of now," said Capt Jones.

When the meeting was over, I went to 3rd platoon and said my goodbyes to Sgt Ward, Cpls Coston, Harris, Bower and PFCs Street and Blandon.

Sgt Ward was concerned about being a platoon leader again, but I told him he would do fine.

Then I walked over to the 2nd platoon area and found SSgt Cain. I had served with him before. He was a tall big-armed man.

Although he had been in during the last years of Vietnam, he had never seen combat. But he had learned the Infantry trade very well and seemed to be a natural. He had already gathered the men together and told them that I was taking over. I was glad they didn't seem to mind as they welcomed me aboard. He introduced me to Sgts Wise, Reilly and Cpls Mitchell, McGerk, Poplos, Crew and McAllister.

The next couple of weeks I got to know the men of 2nd platoon and found out SSgt Cain ruled with an iron fist, but was fair and he had done an outstanding job training this platoon and I could understand why he didn't want to leave it.

Near the end of the month, I took two weeks leave and Marty and I drove up to Delaware to visit our families for Christmas, especially my sons and let Kyle visit with his father. We returned to Camp Lejeune on January 4th, 1982.

Now our battalion began planning and training for our six-month Mediterranean cruise coming up in May.

On January 6th, our whole regiment went to the field for three weeks. The first week our battalion was on its own training in small unit fire and maneuver tactics with supporting arms.

The second week, all three battalions joined together and trained as a regiment until January 27th when we returned to main side.

The rest of the winter and early spring passed quickly as we trained for our cruise. As usual, when a battalion nears its cruise date, division starts beefing it up to full strength. Mike Company alone got three lieutenants. Lt Wright replaced Lt Evans of 1st platoon and he became our company XO. Lt Cregar took command of 3rd platoon. Lt Littleton took command of weapons platoon bumping GySgt Knight back to platoon sergeant and SSgt Manuel back to platoon guide and Sgt Reed was transferred to 3rd platoon as a squad leader. A new staff sergeant named Spidden checked in and became the 3rd platoon sergeant. But when LtCol Kersher took command of our battalion it really bothered us. It was like it was fine for a major to command the battalion for over a year, but because we were going on a med cruise, we all of a sudden had to have a lieutenant colonel. But at least Maj Hays was staying on as our battalion XO.

I was glad to see Street of 3rd platoon get promoted to lance corporal.

The first Saturday in May at 1030, I took my karate test for 2nd Degree Black Belt. The Master, an 8th Degree Black Belt, had me do two forms out of the 18 I knew. I had to do a combination of red and blue belt defenses, eight knife defenses and kneeling defenses. He asked me about six questions which I knew from studying for two years. Then I had to fight a 2nd Degree Black Belt. After about five minutes he stopped us. I was pleased with how I, at thirty-four years old, had held my own against a twenty-two-year-old. But then he sent in another man in his early twenties and I had to fight both of them at the same time. But again, after five minutes, I was pleased I was still on my feet having only been hit once. I thought I would have to write a paper. But the Master said that because I had scored so high on the test and the fact I was going on a med cruise soon that I wouldn't have to write the usual six-page paper.

On May 25th, our battalion, as part of a larger MAU (Marine Amphibious Unit), embarked on five ships at Moorehead City, NC. We would be the landing force of the 6th Fleet. We would be in the Mediterranean for six months to train in amphibious landings in Portugal, Italy, Turkey and Somalia.

I was looking forward to training with the troops from each of these different countries.

During the Atlantic crossing, we planned and prepared for our first joint amphibious landing in Portugal to begin on June 21st.

But first at 0930 on June 6th, our MAU arrived off of Rota Spain. We would get 10 days of liberty ashore while the crews of the five transport ships resupplied and did necessary maintenance.

While most of the Marines went on liberty right away, I was in no hurry. I stopped by the wardroom to get a cup of coffee. As I walked through the hatch, I noticed Navy and Marine officers gathered around the TV. I walked over to see what was going on and noticed Col Studt, our MAU commander, standing among them.

As I neared the group, I heard the newsman talking about Israeli forces attacking into southern Lebanon trying to destroy the PLO (Palestine Liberation Organization) there.

"All right, Israel," I said.

Most of the faces looked at me, some in surprise and others seemed upset.

"Instead of ten days we'll be lucky to finish out the day here," said Col Studt.

From that statement the rumors spread that we might be sent into Lebanon to protect the American Embassy as well as other American property and lives.

I went back to my room, which I shared with Lt Evans to tell him. But he wasn't there and I should have known he would've been one of the first off the ship on liberty.

So, I decided to stay aboard ship to listen to the news of the Israeli invasion of Lebanon.

By noon, in anticipating orders to Lebanon, Marines still on the ships were put on working parties to rearrange the cargo holds of the five ships in order to support evacuation operations.

After only ten hours of liberty instead of ten days, the MAU was placed on immediate alert. Marine MPs (military police) and Navy SPs (shore patrol) went out to recall everyone back to their ships.

In the early hours of June 7th, the MAU was ordered to head straight to a point 100 miles off the coast of Lebanon, to stand by to support possible operations on shore.

At 0600 the ships pulled anchor and headed at maximum speed to the Eastern Mediterranean.

By now, everyone was listening to the reports of Israeli progress through southern Lebanon. No one knew what to expect. Most of my young Marines hoped we would go in to rescue somebody. They were bored with months or years of preparing for combat and they wanted to test their combat skills.

When I thought about it, I'm surprised at how few of my forty-five-man platoon had never seen real action even though it had only been nine years since the last Marines were pulled out of Vietnam. Only Sgt Reilly and Cpl Crew and myself had seen combat. I heard out of our whole battalion there was only 10% with combat experience.

For the next week the ships steamed in circles as the war in Lebanon went on. While underway, our battalion staff conducted extensive planning and training in preparations for the evacuations of American citizens and foreign nationals from Lebanon.

Because Maj Hays knew I had been part of the evacuation of civilians and military personnel from Phnom Penh and Saigon in 1975, LtCol Kersher had me brief his staff on what I saw and did during Operation Eagle Pull and Frequent Wind.

On June 15th, the MAU was placed on a three-hour alert to prepare for an evacuation operation.

But then we waited for nine days before we finally received the order to go in.

Capt Jones gathered us platoon leaders in his room for a briefing and said, "The runways at Beirut International Airport are being heavily shelled which makes it unusable and the road from Beirut to Damascus runs through the area of heavy fighting. It has been determined that the civilians should be evacuated from the port of Juniyah which is about five miles northeast of Beirut. The reports have the number of evacuees will be over 5,000 men, women and children. Even as we speak, Marine choppers are transporting the Department of State negotiators. Already, it's being called the Cammie Cab Service as the state people try to mediate a peace settlement.

Only Mike Company is going in for now. Captain Scotto's Kilo Company will be in a landing craft as our reserve if we find ourselves in a shit sandwich."

The next day at 0800, June 24th, Lt Wright's 1st platoon was the first to land at the dock in Juniyah. He led his platoon off the landing craft and found no evacuees in sight. Capt Jones CP group and 3rd platoon landed next. My platoon landed last. GySgt Fisher was standing just off the dock next to Mike Company's guide-on flapping in the wind. He waved me to the area my platoon was to set in as part of our company's 180-degree defensive perimeter. Quickly, SSgt Cain set our platoon in as I walked over to Capt Jones.

"Where are the evacuees sir?" I asked.

"I have no idea. But we'll wait here."

Later we would learn that they didn't assemble in Beirut on time and when they did show up, they had too much luggage. There were not enough busses to carry both the evacuees and their luggage. It ended up taking all day to get 580 evacuees onto the ships.

As we returned to our ship, I noticed the Navy Catholic chaplain had changed from his cammies into civilian clothes with his clerical collar on because it seemed to calm the evacuees. Many Marines gave up their sleeping spaces to the civilians for the overnight trip to Larnaca Cyprus.

After dropping the civilians off at Larnaca, our ship returned to Lebanon. My platoon morale was high with the satisfaction of helping remove men, women and children from the danger of the intense fighting in Lebanon.

Meanwhile, it was becoming evident that the situation in Lebanon wasn't going to end quickly and the MAU would be on station off of Lebanon for some time.

Finally, on July 19th, to give us some relief from boredom the 6th Fleet commander sent our ship and another to Naples for R & R.

When we landed in Naples, we were promised 15 days of rotating liberty. But just as before it would be cut short to only four days.

By July 26th, the political upheaval in Lebanon had gotten worse.

Meanwhile in Naples, liberty came to an end and we returned to the ships and again trained and prepared for a Lebanon deployment. Our battalion staff gave classes on fire support coordination and emergency evacuation procedures. Each company took turns doing PT trying to stay in shape.

In the wardroom I heard on the news that Israeli casualties were rising as they were forced to use massive air and artillery fire to destroy the PLO, leaving whole neighborhoods of West Beirut in heaps of stone and concrete.

As Lt Evans and I ate chow in the wardroom, several Navy officers sitting nearby were discussing President Reagan's announcement of his willingness to provide American troops to escort the PLO safely out of Beirut.

"Why in the hell would we want to help the PLO escape?" I said.

"Why not?" asked Lt Evans?

"Sir they're nothing but terrorists. Let the Israelis wipe 'm out."

"So were the Israelis in the early 50's. They blew up a hotel killing 300 British soldiers."

I looked across the table at him hard.

"It's true. Besides if the Israelis could destroy the PLO, they would. I think they have found the PLO harder to crack than they thought. They're losing too many troops and their own people are starting to demonstrate against the invasion. They're losing their guts to finish the job. So, they want an easy way out."

"Well sir, I think if we help the PLO escape, we're helping the wrong people."

By August 1st, PLO leader Arafat was asking that any evacuation of his PLO fighters be handled by the UN. But the Israelis refused to allow the UN to intervene. So, the US, Italy and France agreed to form a Multinational Force to move in between the warring factions and see to the safe evacuation of Arafat's PLO forces.

Meanwhile promotions came out and Crew from my platoon made sergeant. Also, Blandon from 3rd platoon was promoted to lance corporal.

Capt Jones transferred me over to 1st platoon and Lt Wright over to 2nd platoon. Both of us requested to stay where we were because of the chance we may be going into combat again at any time. But the orders stood.

Although I hated leaving the men of 2nd platoon, I knew the 1st platoon had some very good men, too. SSgt Tapper, the platoon sergeant was a Vietnam veteran, as well as all three squad leaders, Sgts Sieple, Schwartz and Williams. Even one of the fire team leaders, Cpl Meadows had been in Vietnam.

On August 16th, the 6th Fleet Commander ordered the MAU to be on alert to a possible landing to take place maybe as early as August 20th as part of the Multinational Force.

It seemed now the Lebanon governmental cabinet had requested help in evacuating the PLO.

The 6th Fleet Commander briefed Col Studt. Then he returned and briefed LtCol Kersher and the battalion staff, the Air Wingers staff and the Service Support Group staff. From this meeting, LtCol Kersher called the company commanders together. Then Capt Jones called for a staff meeting of our platoon leaders, platoon sergeants, 1stSgt Burns and GySgt Fisher.

He began by saying, "Well here it is men. Out of an 1,800-man MAU force the colonel can only allow 800 of us go in."

"Shit, every Marine wants to go to shore just to get off this stinking ship," said Lt Wright.

"Well don't worry lieutenant, all of Mike Company is going whether we want to or not," said Capt Jones.

"Outstanding," said Lt Evans smiling.

"Now the colonel said that if we have anybody who doesn't want to go ashore, to send him to him and he'll have him sent home. He doesn't want him here," said Capt Jones looking around at us.

"Sir, that's the dumbest thing I ever heard. These are Marines, they don't get a choice. They asked for this," I argued.

Capt Jones looked at me hard and then went on, "Once on shore, we'll help 800 French Foreign Legionnaires and 530 elite Italian troops. Together we will help evacuate the PLO. At first, we were to land without offensive weapons, which meant no machineguns or mortars. But lucky for us the colonel got the higher ups to listen to common sense. So now we're taking machineguns, mortars and antitank weapons so we can defend ourselves if need be. And the colonel orders that every swinging dick will wear his helmet on shore at all times. The French will go in first, followed by us and a day later the Italians will land. We and the Lebanese Army will be placed together at points between the Syrians and PLO forces in West Beirut and the Israeli and Lebanese Christian forces deployed in East Beirut. Now because of peacetime rules of engagement we will carry our weapons unloaded. I know this is bullshit. But it doesn't take long to insert a magazine into a weapon and chamber a round."

"Just long enough to die if the bad guys already have a round chambered sir," I muttered.

Capt Jones looked at me hard saying, "That's the way it will be Gunner, like it or not."

I didn't like, but I said nothing more.

"Is the whole battalion going in?" asked Lt Evans.

"No, only three companies are going in, Kilo, Lima and Mike. India Company will be held back as a reserve," answered Capt Jones.

When the meeting was over, I told SSgt Tapper to get the squad leaders together as well as Cpl Meadows and bring them to my room.

It wasn't long before I heard a knock at my door and I yelled, "Enter!"

SSgt Tapper opened the hatch asking, "Ready sir?"

"Yes come in."

Through the hatch he stepped followed by Sgts Sieple, Schwartz, Williams and Cpl Meadows.

As they sat down on the floor, I carefully briefed them on what I knew of the coming operation. When I had finished and answered their questions I added, "You all probably wondered why I asked Corporal Meadows here. Well because he like the rest of us in this room was in Vietnam. We know what combat is. I know we're not supposed to fight here. But it's hard to say what may happen. Among the PLO there are maybe 1,000 other radicals from all over the world including the January Red Army terrorist group and some Americans fighting with them. Our young Marines are good, but they're going to be looking toward us, the older veterans to show them the way. We have to keep calm to keep them calm."

Soon, we got the word that H-hour and L-day was set for 0500 August 25th. Our battalion began its final intensive training in field sanitation, crowd control and relations with the media. We were told that in 1958 when the Marines had landed here, there had been a large number of dysentery cases.

On August 21st, the French landed and began evacuating the PLO fighters.

On August 24th, LtCol Kersher, Capts Scotto, Graham and Jones flew into the port to recon the area and meet with the French we would relieve.

Over the ship's loudspeaker, two messages were read to us. The first one was from our Marine Commandant, Gen Barrow:

"You will soon be engaged in carrying out an extremely important mission in Beirut. Clearly it is also a most different and delicate one. Your soldierly virtues, especially discipline, will in all likelihood be severely tested. At this critical hour, you will serve as the primary instrument of our national will to further the course of peace in that troubled region. As Marines, you will meet the challenge and conduct yourselves, not only honorably, but also with distinction. The eyes of your countrymen will be on you as surely as their hearts are with you. Beyond that, speaking for myself and your fellow Marines, be assured we have every confidence that as professionals you will superbly represent our Corps and country."

The second message was from President Reagan.

"You're about to embark on a mission of great importance to our nation and the free world. The conditions under which you carry out your vital assignment are, I know, demanding and potentially dangerous. You are tasked to be once again what Marines have been for more than 200 years, peacekeepers. Your role in the Multinational Force, along with that of your French and Italian counterparts is crucial to achieving the peace that is so desperately needed in this long-tortured city. I expect that you will perform with the traditional expertise and discipline for which the Marine Corps is renowned. Godspeed."

Meanwhile, the ships circled through the night as we ate our last meal of steak and eggs and packed up. Then we carried our packs and weapons up to the port side of the ship from where we would climb down cargo nets into the landing craft below.

At 0100 August 25th, our ship moved to within 1,000 meters of the breakwaters of the port.

Once again, like seventeen years ago, the Corps was landing me into God only knows what. Of course, then I was a seventeen-year-old rifleman in a fire team. Now I'm a thirty-four-year-old platoon leader. Back then, I had no idea what war was. Now I did and I didn't know which was worse, the knowing or the not knowing.

I spent the long hours waiting on the open deck with the other platoon leaders of Mike Company. The night was cool and clear. There wasn't much talk among us. I guess we were all too deep in our own thoughts. Nearby, my platoon was laying back against their packs trying to catch whatever sleep they could get in the cool night.

Standing among us, Capt Jones broke the silence saying, "You know you can tell where the so-called Green Line is."

"What the hell is that?" asked Lt Cregar.

"It's the border between the Muslim West Beirut and the Christian East Beirut," answered Capt Jones.

"How can you tell in the dark?" asked Lt Littleton.

"The Christian side is brightly lighted. But the Muslim side is dark," answered Capt Jones.

"Yeah except for the burst of tracers," said Lt Evans laughing. The rest of us didn't laugh.

We watched Col Studt, his staff and Capt Scotto's Kilo Company climbed down into their landing craft first and headed in toward the shore.

Dawn broke at precisely 0500 on a clear morning, as the first landing craft dropped its ramp at the port of Beirut. Capt Scotto marched off first with a lance corporal carrying Kilo Company's guide-on flying in the breeze. The lance corporal slipped on the wet concrete deck, almost falling, as flash bulbs flashed along the shore and they were met by a large press contingent as well as Ambassador Hobib, US Ambassador to Lebanon, Dellon, the French and Italian ambassadors, the Lebanon Armed Forces Commander Lt Gen

Khoury and other dignitaries, greeted the tense, but relieved Marines of Kilo Company at the water's edge.

A few seconds later, the other landing craft landed and Col Studt stepped ashore through the mass of almost 100 news reporters.

Twenty-two minutes later, Mike Company landed. It sure felt good to be on solid ground again.

Maj Hays stood near LtCol Kersher and waved us on to quickly relieve the French forces on the perimeter in our assigned area.

The relief in place went well because of the recon that LtCol Kersher and the company commanders had done the day before. We began taking over French Foreign Legion positions right away. Capt Jones led Mike Company into a line of shattered buildings. Once he showed me where my platoon area was, SSgt Tapper quickly set the platoon in, not knowing what awaited us.

The houses were covered with human and animal shit. SSgt Tapper ordered each squad leader to put two men to work with entrenching tools to clean the place up as best they could.

As this was going on, I heard Sgt Sieple yell, "Gunner we got people coming our way!"

I ran to a broken window and looked out as men and women walked toward us from their smashed homes.

"Should we lock and load sir?" asked Cpl Andrews.

"No, they're not carrying weapons. But stand ready," I said.

The civilians slowly picked their way into our bombed out three-walled stone house. The women cried as they welcomed us. An old woman threw her arms around SSgt Tapper saying in English, "It's just like 1958 all over again. When the Marines come it means peace."

SSgt Tapper didn't have the heart to tell her that we'd probably only be here about two weeks, just long enough to get the PLO forces safely out. Our mission here this time, we were told, was just to provide a symbolic presence, whatever the hell that meant.

Capt Jones came back through checking his company positions and then radioed LtCol Kersher that Mike Company had secured their objectives.

Meanwhile, the French forces we had relieved had moved on to new positions south of our battalion near the gutted racetrack.

At 0600, French Brig Gen Granger officially turned the port area over to Col Studt. Col Studt had noticed the French flag was still flying from a nine-story grain elevator, the tallest building in the port area. As soon as the relief was done, he ordered Capt Scotto to lower the French flag and replace it with the Lebanese flag. When the civilians saw their flag being raised, they cheered. He hoped this would prove we were here to support the Lebanese government.

At 0730, Capt Jones ordered me to take my platoon and move up and take over a French Foreign Legion checkpoint and the positions around it.

The rest of Mike Company moved up setting up blocking positions and other checkpoints as far as the wire fence topped with barbed wire, which surrounded the port.

I didn't like the fact that we weren't allowed to take the high ground ahead of us. Capt Jones came by again checking the company lines and checkpoints finding my platoon settled in. He pointed to a large yellow office building the French had used and that GySgt Fisher had picked to be Mike Company's CP. Of course, the troops soon nicknamed it the yellow submarine.

At 0915, the first evacuation ship, a Greek ship arrived and docked at the port. Capt Jones radioed me and said the evacuation would get underway right away. To be ready.

At 1000, Col Studt and LtCol Kersher drove up to my checkpoint in a jeep and stopped, waiting.

As we waited, I looked around. I was surprised at the amount of destruction I saw in the port area and on the city streets ahead of our checkpoint. It reminded me of Hue City in 1968.

"This reminds me of pictures I've seen of Berlin during WWII," said Sgt Williams.

Up the street we could see PLO troops standing around a Syrian tank with its big gun pointed right at us. With the colonels here I whispered to SSgt Tapper to go around and make sure our men had their helmets and flak jackets on.

First came cars filled with PLO supporters. Behind them, down the street we heard scattered small arms and automatic weapons firing which quickly increased in frequency and fierceness. Then came Lebanese Army trucks carrying the first group of PLO fighters to my checkpoint. Coming down the street they fired pistols, rifles, machineguns and RPG's in the air. With the gunfire always in the background, RPG rounds would suddenly explode about 200 feet overhead. It seemed as if everyone was firing, the PLO fighters in the truck, the people lining the sides of the street and in the buildings nearby.

The Lebanese soldiers at our sandbagged checkpoint halted the trucks and then waved the trucks forward one at a time. In these trucks were men, women and children as young as twelve or thirteen, dressed in camouflaged uniforms carrying automatic weapons. There were also a few younger children, some as young as two being carried. A Lebanese official in civilian clothes inspected each truck while uniformed Lebanese soldiers and my platoon watched.

Capt Jones walked up near the lead truck. Behind him stood Sgt Sieple's squad in a line blocking the street to control the traffic. The rest of my platoon was in positions in and on the roofs of nearby buildings overlooking the checkpoint.

The Lebanese official allowed the PLO to keep only light personnel weapons such as rifles and pistols. Machineguns and RPG's were thrown in a pill. Still the PLO were celebrating, for what I didn't understand, by firing into the air as their spent bullets fell back to earth like rain.

When the Lebanese official was satisfied, he waved to Capt Jones and he in turn looked over to me shaking his head.

"Okay Sergeant Sieple, let that truck pass," I ordered.

"Yes sir. You heard the man, make a hole," said Sgt Sieple.

The squad then split in half, moving to each side of the road with Sgt Sieple with one half of the squad on one side and Cpl Meadows with the rest on the other.

The first truck moved slowly through the squad who closed ranks behind it, as the truck drove around the corner and then halted to wait until all five trucks had been checked. After all five trucks had been inspected and lined up together again, LtCol Kersher stepped up on the runner of the lead truck and led the first convoy to the processing area 300 meters away to the dockside next to the Greek ship.

Once at the pier, the PLO fighters were offloaded from the trucks and began being processed through one of eight stations manned by Lebanese soldiers. Each evacuee had to give his name and turn over their weapons and ammo and then they were allowed to walk up the ramp to the ship.

After the next five trucks had been inspected, Col Studt led this convoy.

By 1015, 564 PLO fighters had been processed through our battalion and Lebanese checkpoints and had boarded the ships.

The first ship was full and left disappearing over the horizon.

My platoon settled down as our duty evolved into a routine.

A PLO lieutenant colonel showed up and stayed at our checkpoint just in case there was any problem.

And a Lebanese Brigadier General started accompanying each truck convoy that brought the PLO fighters to our checkpoint. Although I was in charge of this checkpoint, Capt Jones was usually here, too. Both of us wanted to get as many of these people through here as quickly as possible before something went wrong.

Meanwhile, LtCol Kersher would stand at the ramp of each ship to make sure that no weapons were taken on the ships.

Overhead, I looked up to watch a dog fight between an Israeli and Syrian jet. I saw two missiles fired, but neither jet was hit.

So far for us, the worst danger was from the thousands of spent bullets that constantly rained down around us, fired as victory salutes by the departing PLO.

By now we had begun to see a pattern. We could tell when a convoy was nearing our checkpoint because women standing nearby would start to chant and a few men would fire weapons into the air. Then as the mass of firing increased, the Lebanese trucks would come into sight covered with banners and pictures of PLO leader Arafat and so-called martyrs.

Standing next to me, Maj Hays said, “You know Gunner, I have to admire the PLO’s effort to go out of here looking victorious. Instead of bringing their wounded out first for all the world to see. They’ll bring them out last when most of the news people won’t be here to record them.”

“Sir have you noticed that every PLO fighter that has passed through here so far is wearing brand new camouflaged utilities?” I asked.

“Yes, I have.”

“Sir there’s something about that, that bothers me.”

As we talked, the PLO lieutenant colonel walked over to us and asked, “Major what would you call these troops of mine? Regular or irregulars?”

“I’m not sure sir,” answered Maj Hays.

"Well, major, I can tell you they are much more than just a band of guerrillas," said the PLO lieutenant colonel.

I was surprised at how disciplined the PLO were. I just wished the crowd outside our checkpoint had been as well disciplined. Several times live grenades had been rolled out of this crowd toward the sandbags in front of our checkpoint. But these explosions hurt no one, so I held my men back from reacting. They may have been testing our discipline. But after the first one, I had SSgt Tapper go and tell Sgt Johnson, whose machinegun team was attached to my platoon and was positioned on a nearby roof, to lock and load his guns. But not to fire except on my command.

Most of the time, the PLO didn't fire their weapons once they had passed through my checkpoint. But if they did, whomever the Marine officer was leading their convoy would stop the trucks until they stopped. Then the convoy would move on.

By 1530, 488 more PLO had passed through our battalion's checkpoints and boarded ships.

After dark, Capt Jones ordered me to pull my platoon back to several houses, but to keep a fire team on guard at the checkpoint. SSgt Tapper rotated fire teams at the checkpoint throughout the night.

Our interpreter told me that the house I had set up my platoon CP in had been damaged six years ago in the civil fighting in 1976. There was no electricity, running water and the sewer lines were broken. The whole area was infested with rats as big as I had seen in Vietnam and they were the size of cats. During the day, the flies came in hordes. At night they left only to be replaced by mosquitoes. Soon we were all covered with red itching welts. GySgt Fisher, with a working party, came around with fresh water, fruit and sandwiches that had been made by the sailors on board the ships. This was a welcome break from C-rations.

At dawn the next morning, I moved my whole platoon back up to our checkpoint. It wasn't long before the convoys of trucks loaded with PLO started arriving. Again, the potential for danger was constant. Again, there were weapons of all kinds being fired just twenty feet away from our lines. I could see AK-47's, SKS rifles, RPG's grenade launchers, Uzi's, 9-MM, 38's and 45cal pistols. Again, the spent bullets fell like rain around us. Grenades exploded just on the other side of our waist high sandbagged wall.

A PLO driving a jeep with a mounted 106 recoilless rifle, kept racing down the winding street toward us and then come to a screeching stop just short of our sandbags, where he would fire a round over our heads out to sea. From time to time, artillery shells would burst over our heads. I was proud of my men for standing their ground through it all even though we all ducked at one time or another. Only discipline could cause men to stand up to this.

One truck was so packed with PLO fighters that the Lebanese official had them all get off. Then he checked them one by one as they climbed back on. An older PLO man and woman walked up to SSgt Tapper and asked him to watch their four-year-old son and three older sisters until they got their luggage checked.

Fearing the kid could be booby-trapped somehow, he walked away from us closer to the PLO truck holding the little boy's hand. Near the truck, hard looking young PLO fighters waiting to be inspected stole sidelong glances at him. They were plainly nervous and avoided the eyes of the flak jacketed, camouflaged helmeted and uniformed SSgt Tapper.

But soon, they were all back on the truck and this convoy had passed through our checkpoint.

I turned to look at my radioman as he spoke our call signs into his radio handset and then listened and answered, "I copy that and out." Then he turned toward me with a funny look on his face saying, "Sir it's the gunny. Captain Jones just got a call that a truck filled with PLO just drove right through the French road block up ahead and is heading toward us. He says to stop that truck. The Capt'n is on his way."

"First platoon lock and load," I yelled.

My men who were scattered in houses on both sides of the road and the squad standing at parade rest across the road quickly pulled loaded magazines out of their magazine pouches on their sides and inserted them into their rifles and chambered a round.

With this done, I yelled to the squad standing across the street, "Sergeant Sieple have your squad return to sling arms and at parade rest."

The rest of my platoon on both sides of the street stood at the ready in windows, doors and rooftops.

I walked out in front of Sgt Sieple's squad and turned facing them and yelled, "No one will take aim or fire unless I give the order.

If anything happens to me, only Staff Sergeant Tapper will give the command to fire."

Behind me now, I heard the PLO firing their weapons as the truck raced toward us. Behind my platoon, I saw Capt Jones driving up in his jeep. I smiled at him for some reason, as I did an about face, to face the rushing truck. I then snapped to a parade rest position with my hands behind my back at belt level. It suddenly crossed my mind that after eight years in Vietnam that I might die here without firing a shot in self-defense. My mind pictured Marty and the kids. But I had to stand tall. That truck would have to run over me first, before it hit any of my men. This was so damn stupid. To be killed by the very assholes we're here to help escape.

Meanwhile, the truck came roaring down at us with the PLO in the back, firing weapons into air. I stood there staring, I hoped without expression, from beneath the lip of my camouflaged helmet. I hoped no one in front or behind me could see my knees shaking in fear.

Suddenly, the truck driver hit the brakes and skidded to a stop, only feet away from me. The truck driver was smiling down at me, but I wasn't smiling back. I stood there like a statue until the Lebanese official had inspected the truck. When he waved to me, I did a left face and marched off to the side of the street as Sgt Sieple gave his squad the order to open up so the truck could pass through. I walked over to SSgt Tapper and said, "Have everyone but the machine gunners unload their weapons. I want the squad leaders to check each of their men to make sure there are no rounds in any chambers."

"Aye, Aye sir," said SSgt Tapper and then walked away yelling, "Squad leaders up!"

As Capt Jones walked up to me I said, "Good morning Capt'n."

"Gunner who authorized these men to lock and load?" he asked.

"I did sir. Your orders, as passed by the gunny was to stop that truck, was it not?"

"Yes, yes it was. But I don't want one of my men to fire the first shot."

"And I agree except if that truck had run me down my platoon had orders to shoot to kill to defend themselves."

"Jesus gunner!"

"Capt'n, you and I have been in a shit sandwich together before and we lost some damn good men. But they died like Marines. And if my men are going to die here, they too are going to die fighting, like Marines sir."

"Shit! If Colonel Studt heard you talking like this he'd probably relieve us both."

"Sir if they don't want us to act like Marines then we should be replaced by a bunch of dog soldiers. They make better occupation troops than we do anyway."

"Gunner just keep the lid on here!"

"Sir, have I ever let you down?"

He smiled saying, "No gunner, no. But just remember we're not here to fight."

"That's just why we should be replaced by the Army."

"But Gunner, President Reagan wants an elite disciplined military force here."

"Well, you're right sir. If he wants a military force here, then he doesn't want any dog soldiers," I said smiling.

"Well I better get back to the CP," said Capt Jones as he turned away.

"Don't worry sir, I'll take care of you just like the old days," I said, still smiling.

I looked around at my camouflaged men with pride. Beyond our checkpoint I saw young boys playing at war as I had done when I was a kid. But instead of watching war movies as I had as a child, these kids had watched the real thing. They stopped playing to watch PLO fighters drive by standing up in the back of trucks.

One of the PLO fighters lifted his AK-47 and fired a whole magazine into the air yelling something about Allah. The rest of the PLO in the back of the truck started yelling and firing their weapons into the air also. They smiled as some of my young Marines ducked. In doing so Cpl Wynne dropped his helmet and scrambled to pick it back up.

"Better keep that helmet on your head!" yelled GySgt Fisher with his thumbs stuck inside of his cartridge belt as he walked around checking Mike Companies lines.

Cpl Wynne wiped the sweat from his forehead as he put his helmet back on his head saying, "I wish they'd stop that fucking bullshit!"

"What a bunch of assholes. These rag heads are crazy. They got no fire discipline at all," added Sgt Schwartz.

GySgt Fisher walked up to me saying, "Just a bunch of Ethiopian sand nigger showoffs if you ask me."

I looked at him to see if he was speaking to me. But he had turned walking off through the rubble-piled street. As he walked, he yelled over his shoulder, "Keep them helmets on! Remember what goes up, will come down."

I could now tell another convoy was coming from the firing like hell up the street. As if they had something to celebrate, as if we weren't escorting them safely out of Beirut away from the Israelis.

As the gunfire came closer, mixed with the sounds of truck engines, Sgt Sieple shouted, "All right first squad standby!"

Behind us, I now heard the sound of a jeep coming again. I turned and saw Col Studt drive up. The jeep stopped and he stepped out. Walking up to me he said, "It sure ain't the Nam is it gunner?"

"No sir, it surely ain't."

Both of us flinched instinctively as tracer rounds flew overhead. He shook his head in disgust saying, "Ain't these assholes something? They act like they just won a war instead of getting their asses kicked."

"Sir it's just like the Nam in one way. It just don't mean nothing."

He laughed saying, "I haven't heard that expression in a while."

"There's not many of us old Nam vets still in sir. We're like a fading breed."

"Yes, I'm afraid you're right. Well, the sooner we get these people out 'a here, the sooner we get back to our Med cruise and liberty call in Naples."

"There it is sir," I said smiling.

He turned around walking back to his jeep, stepped in and sat back next to his driver and said, "Take care Gunner, the Corps still needs war horses like us."

"Yes sir," I said smiling.

Rifle fire split the air again and I turned back to the front watching Sgt Sieple walking along behind his squad, steadying them as they stood at parade rest across the street.

Then I saw the next convoy come in view, full of shouting and shooting PLO.

As they stopped, I thought of our instructions not to deal directly with the Israelis, who were nearby. I hadn't seen one yet. I heard they were trying to disrupt the evacuation by blocking the port entrance, refusing entry to commercial ships. Israeli gunboats kept holding up ships trying to leave port. This was starting to back up the PLO convoys. And of course, as the trucks sat waiting the PLO kept shooting wildly in the air. And the longer they sat still, the greater was the chance of trouble.

When night came, I again pulled most of my platoon back into our houses. SSgt Tapper set up the fire team watch schedule for the checkpoint through the night.

The morning of August 27th began like all the rest with gunfire and exploding artillery shells growing in intensity until the PLO convoys started coming toward us.

By noon, the 90-degree heat had been made worse by our helmets and flak jackets, which no one dared take off with all the falling spent rounds.

Today would be a little different when the PLO high command group moved through the port.

In the afternoon, GySgt Fisher drove up in a jeep pulling a trailer. From the trailer he issued us mosquito netting. At least tonight we would be able to sleep a little more comfortably.

On August 28th, Col Studt ordered LtCol Kersher to have our battalion prepare to escort PLO leader Yasir Arafat safely through the port area, which was due to happen on the 30th.

There was fear that some Palestinian faction might try to assassinate him. Col Studt ordered immediate beefing up of security measures. Arafat wouldn't be our problem until he passed through one of our checkpoints. But once inside our perimeter, he would be our responsibility from then on until his ship cleared the harbor.

That night after another hectic day of watching truckloads of PLO moving through our checkpoint, we bedded down in our houses under mosquito nets. Exhausted, I was drifting off to sleep when suddenly I heard someone humming the Marine Hymn. Then several Marines started singing it. I sat up singing too. And it seemed my whole platoon began to sing as tears rolled down my face. God, I love being an officer of Marines.

August 29th was passing like the rest, except Capt Jones radioed and called me back to his CP. There with the other platoon leaders he informed us that Yasir Arafat would be coming through tomorrow.

The next morning at dawn, our battalion made a security sweep of the port area. At 0500, the whole battalion went on full alert even though we didn't expect him to arrive before 1100. His arrival time was supposed to be a secret, but by 1000 a large crowd of news reporters, well-wishers and hundreds of PLO family members had gathered at my checkpoint. Among the women and children and news reporters with their bulky cameras, were armed Palestinian guards and armed Lebanese soldiers.

Also, with my platoon this morning was Col Studt, LtCol Kersher, Maj Hays and Capt Jones.

At 1100 Arafat came into view in a Mercedes ringed by his own armed honor guard.

I hoped we would be able to quickly pass him through this checkpoint and on his way.

As he neared our checkpoint, the crowd cheered as they pushed in close to touch him. The car stopped in front of our sandbagged checkpoint as Arafat got out. His honor guard spread out accepting flags from several PLO units, which had accompanied him this far. They in turn formally presented these flags to Arafat.

Col Studt sat quietly in his jeep watching Arafat, who was clearly enjoying this day at the center of worldwide attention.

Col Studt shook his head muttering, "Jesus, he's one ugly little shit."

Maj Hays stood nearby next to LtCol Kersher, chewing tobacco and spitting the juice off to the side.

I smiled looking at the thin rawboned major. He was the picture poster Marine officer. The battalion had come to love him in a way they just could never love LtCol Kersher, maybe because they understood the major loved them.

Col Studt leaned out of his jeep toward LtCol Kersher and said, "Colonel your battalion has done well."

"Thank you, sir," said LtCol Kersher looking over at Col Studt.

Meanwhile Arafat was waving to the crowd and stepped back into his car.

But then Arafat's honor guard moved out ahead of his car and tried to push their way through Sgt Sieple's squad, who pushed back.

"Third squad up!" I yelled and Sgt William's squad ran out

across the street closing ranks across the street behind the 1st squad. I walked out behind the two squads as the PLO guards threatened us with their weapons, but my twenty-eight Marines not only stood up to them, but also slowly pushed them back.

Then from behind Arafat, a French convoy drove up led by the French Ambassador Henri. With him was a French General followed by four armored carloads of about fifty French Legionnaires in full battle uniform. As the Ambassador's car pulled to a stop next to Arafat's car, the French Legionnaires ran out of the armored cars to protect him.

Col Studt jumped out of his jeep and quickly walked out in front of our checkpoint and stopped them saying, "Can I help you Mr. Ambassador?"

Ambassador Henri said, "Colonel I plan to personally lead the march to the dock to see Arafat off with a French guard of honor."

"Mr. Ambassador, why does he need French troops when I have 800 Marines who are perfectly capable of looking after Arafat and seeing him to his ship. The last thing I need is any political grandstanding."

Meanwhile LtCol Kersher jumped into the colonel's jeep and had the driver drive him out onto the street and stop crossways in the street behind my two Marine squads adding to our blocking force.

Then Ambassador Henri said, "This has been agreed to by your American Ambassador Draper."

"Well it hasn't been communicated to me," answered Col Studt. He put his walkie-talkie to his mouth and to my surprise called Ambassador Draper.

Then Col Studt looked hard at Ambassador Henri saying, "Mr. Draper knows nothing of this agreement. And I feel the excessive number of French forces is creating a problem in the middle of a highly combustible situation already. And a guard of honor ceremony with political overtones are outside the bounds of a peacekeeping mission."

At this point several French Legionnaires tried to push their way through our ranks.

LtCol Kersher, Maj Hays, Capt Jones, SSgt Tapper and I ran up and helped my two squads to physically push the Legionnaires back.

"Mr. Ambassador, I will allow only your car and Arafat's car to enter through my checkpoint," said Col Studt.

Ambassador Henri and the French General spun around and stormed back to their car.

Col Studt returned to his jeep and backed it up so as to lead the two cars through.

I waved to SSgt Tapper and my two squads opened up to allow the cars through. I noticed the Lebanese soldiers had suddenly disappeared leaving us to fend for ourselves.

As Arafat's car started to enter our lines, his twenty-five bodyguards started slapping their rifles as they made threatening gestures at us trying to push their way through. Before I could give the order, both Marine squads quickly pushed the PLO bodyguards back.

Suddenly a rifle shot cracked overhead and echoed through the crowded street adding to the tension.

A hush fell over the crowd as the French, PLO and Marines braced for an attack. But then from among the French forces armored cars a Frenchmen yelled in English, "Sorry. It was only an accidental discharge."

That could have caused a bloodbath, but maybe because of the rounds fired into the air for days, all sides had held their fire.

Still once again, my platoon had handled themselves with the kind of coolness and professionalism that I had seldom seen in my seventeen years in the Corps. They kept calm under the pressure during a situation that could have been disastrous.

Even the air seemed still with tension, but nothing else happened and Arafat's car led by Col Studt's jeep drove away toward the evacuation ship.

Next to me SSgt Tapper said, "You know sir, that hawked-nosed colonel is starting to grow on me."

"He's definitely got a big set of balls," I said.

The evacuation operation went on smoothly the rest of the day.

By noon the next day August 31st, the last of the PLO had been evacuated.

The 1st of September was the first quiet day we had had and we enjoyed only scattered gunfire.

The next day, Col Studt passed the word we could take our helmets and flak jackets off if we weren't standing guard along the perimeter even though we still heard both gunfire and artillery bursts in the distance.

By September 3rd, I had begun to notice a change in the atmosphere. Lights were left on at night. There was increased traffic in the streets, shops were reopening and I watched Lebanese civilians repairing damaged buildings and cleaning up the rubble in the streets. LtCol Kersher even allowed the companies to exercise one at a time.

Mike Company exercised in formation wearing only red shorts and combat boots. We ran in company formation with headquarters platoon up front, followed by my platoon, then Lt Wright's 2nd platoon, Lt Cregar's 3rd platoon and Lt Littleton's weapons platoon bringing up the rear. Of course, Capt Jones and 1st Sergeant Burns set the pace up front. As usual I enjoyed the run. We passed Italian troops standing with rifles in hand at the ready. We saw the tin roofed sheds that some men of Capt Scotto's Kilo Company slept under because of the spent bullets that still fell from time to time in their area. We passed Col Studt's MAU headquarters in the old, but air-conditioned building and ground maintenance building. LtCol Kersher's battalion headquarters was in a warehouse near the docks. We then passed LZ Barrow named after our Commandant.

After our company run, we all lined up to get the gamma globulin shot because of the chance of disease from the large number of rats.

Just like in Vietnam the young Marines here began to fight the rats. But here they started by catching cats and bringing them into the houses with us. But the rats ran the cats out. Then they set large traps and the rats just ran around them. At night you could hear the rats breathing.

Each morning, Lebanese civilians brought us thick Lebanese coffee (which in later years I would know as Turkish coffee), fruit and vegetables. We combined our C-rations with the vegetables that Cpl Meadows somehow always seemed to find and mixed it all in a pot to make stew. I didn't dare ask him where he got them. At least these Lebanese seemed to love us being here. They knew we didn't want their land. One old lady everyday kept telling us, "Whenever Marines come, they bring peace."

Cpl Meadows even rigged a hose and a big plastic bottle with holes in it so we could take a cold shower.

On Sunday, Protestant and Catholic services were held in a

warehouse. I went to the protestant service and saw Sgt Wise, Cpl McAllister, GySgt Knight and Cpl West there. When it was over, we walked out and met Sgt Reilly going in for the Catholic service. With jeeps in short supply, we saw the Catholic Chaplain driving up on a forklift. As he got off, he laughed saying, "I call it my Sweet Chariot because it swings so slow."

On September 9th with our mission finished, our battalion began loading onto our ships.

But it was September 10th before Mike Company returned to our ship. As we sailed from Beirut, heading for Naples, I could tell the men of my platoon were filled with self-satisfaction for the job they had done so well, even under the pressure of international attention. I was proud in the way they had performed and even happier that no one in the whole battalion had even gotten a scratch.

But even as we headed for liberty call in Italy, we now started preparing for a training exercise called Operating Display Determination 82, which would be in Saros Bay Turkey scheduled to begin on September 25th. I really enjoyed my first hot shower in days. We started holding personnel, weapons, uniform and 782 gear inspections getting ready for a visit from Commandant Barrow.

On September 14th, we were a day away from Italy when I was shocked to see the news on the TV in the wardroom of the assassination of Lebanese President-Elect Bashir Gemayel. With sinking hearts, we knew we might have to return to Beirut already.

Four days later returning to the ship from liberty, I heard of the Israeli push into Muslim West Beirut and then of the massacres of 800 Palestinian refugees by Christian militiamen at the Sabra and Shatila camps in West Beirut.

A few days later, the new President Amin Gemayel, the brother of the slain ex-President requested the return of the Multinational Forces to ensure the safety of the population of West Beirut until the Lebanese Army would be able to undertake this mission on their own.

On September 20th, our MAU was ordered again to return to the Eastern Mediterranean to await further orders. All maintenance and liberty were suspended. Again, the MP's and SP's went out herding the Marines and sailors back to their ships.

Lt Evans came back drunk and in a rage. He stormed through the hatch into our room saying, "It's just not fucking meant for us to pull liberty in Italy!"

I just lay back in my rack and laughed which made him even worse.

Finally, after sitting in port two more days, our five ships left Naples in the early morning of September 22nd to deploy off of the coast of Beirut.

As we neared Beirut, Capt Jones gathered us platoon leaders together and told us that again we were being ordered back into Lebanon with the French, Italian and this time British Forces. Our mission would be to establish a presence in Beirut that would in turn help establish the stability necessary for the Lebanese government to regain control of their capital and to enable the withdrawal of foreign military forces from Lebanon. We would occupy positions in the vicinity of the Beirut International Airport, establish and maintain close continuous liaison with the French, Italians, British and Lebanese forces. Once ashore we would establish hasty defenses at the airport, which was in the midst of the area densely populated by Shiite Muslims who had close religious ties with Iran. 1,200 US Marines would land, knowing we could face the threat of individual acts of terrorism and a lot of unexploded munitions from the heavy fighting around the airport area. The operation was intended to be a short one. I suddenly remembered my uncle Clark telling me in 1965 that this Vietnam thing wouldn't last six months. The thought sent a shudder through me.

Maj Hays flew into Beirut to coordinate our upcoming deployment.

During September 26th and 27th, Vice Admiral Rowden and Commandant Barrow visited our battalion. The Commandant presented the Navy Unit Commendation medal to our battalion for our performance during the PLO evacuation.

Capt Jones gathered us platoon leaders together in his room and briefed us on the document that established the US peacekeeping mission. Most important to us was the statement concerning the rules of engagement. We were told that if units other than the Lebanese soldiers infiltrated our assigned area or perimeter, the intruders are to be warned that they are in an unauthorized area and can proceed no further. If the intruders fail to withdraw, Colonel Studt will be informed of the incident and he will decide what further action will be taken. Only if Marines or Lebanese soldiers are fired on can we return fire, only to ensure our safety and that of the Lebanese.

At 1158 on September 29th, Capt Scotto's Kilo Company walked off landing craft onto Beirut's shore making sure the area was secure. At 1340, trucks rolled off the landing craft. These trucks began carrying the Marines of Kilo Company to the Beirut airport where they started setting in a defensive perimeter around the airport. At 1400, Capt Messenger's India Company was choppered to the airport. Mike Company was choppered in next. Lt Cregon's 3rd platoon landed first, followed by Lt Wright's 2nd platoon and Capt Jones, Lt Evans and the Company CP with my platoon landing last.

I was shocked by the thousands of unexploded ordnances I saw littering the airport area around us. I had never seen anything like this even in Vietnam. LtCol Kersher radioed Capt Jones with the order for us to stay on the hard surface of the runways until the bomb disposal teams could clear the area. They had started at the beach moving toward the airport clearing and marking paths and then clearing the areas in between.

During the day the disposal teams found 125 different types of explosives laying on the ground left over from the past eight years of heavy fighting. They found everything from WWII artillery rounds to modern multiple-warhead munitions. Col Studt would soon request extra mine clearing teams to be flown in from Camp Lejeune NC.

Meanwhile we waited, sitting on our packs on the airstrip watching the teams work. The explosive devices were so thick that the Marines who handled the mine detectors were being relieved every ten minutes so they could stay sharp.

The runway surfaces grew hot as the day wore on. There was nothing for us to do but sit and wait. We left the runways only to go to the head or piss tubes following the cleared paths.

By 1700 Capt Graham's Lima Company had landed, joining us. We slept on the pavement that night.

By the next day, the bigger munitions were being blown in place or were being carried off to dump sites. But still, the mine clearing went slowly. Marine communicators followed the cleared paths setting up communications wire and sentries began working carefully setting up checkpoints.

Lt Wright of 2nd platoon, ordered Sgt Reilly to send one of his fire teams to provide security for one of the disposal teams. He picked Cpl McGurk's team.

By now they were finding mostly smaller and harder to find munitions. This made Cpl McGurk nervous because he knew that stuff could be set off by stepping on it. He was wishing Sgt Reilly hadn't picked his team for this detail when he noticed the demolition Marine stop to look at something on the ground. The fire team also stopped as Cpl McGurk said, "Stay on your feet men. Don't even kneel down." He then looked at each of his three men making sure his order was heard. He wondered what they had found this time. He took his helmet off wiping his forehead with a camouflage handkerchief. He put his helmet back on, and then lit a cigarette as he looked over at the nearby Muslim village. Then he looked forward, ahead of his fire team as the demolition man squatting down probed the dirt with his K-bar. Between the man's feet Cpl McGurk saw something that looked like a black golf ball partly buried in the ground.

"Back up fire team. It could be a cluster bomb," ordered Cpl McGurk. As he too backed up, he felt the hair stubble stand up on the back of his neck.

Meanwhile the demolition man probed the K-bar closer to the small object.

"Fuck this shit!" muttered Cpl McGurk as he took another step back.

The demolition man slowly lifted the little black object out of the ground. He stood up turning around facing the fire team smiling holding the object in one hand as he replaced the K-bar into its scabbard saying, "More than likely it's a dud."

I was sitting on my pack when I heard a tiny crack of an explosion. I looked around to where I had last seen Cpl McGurk's fire team, a corpsman and the two-man demolition men. Four Marines were lying on the ground.

Cpl McGurk ran to the side of his two wounded men. The corpsman ran past him to the Marine who had been holding the cluster bomb. His chest, stomach and face were shredded.

Even from a distance I could see blood spreading around the man as the corpsman worked over him.

Seeing that his two wounded men weren't that bad, Cpl McGurk ran to the side of the corpsman and started wiping blood from the shattered face as the corpsman gave him mouth to mouth.

A jeep filled with Marines raced past my platoon to the wounded men. Together they picked up the bloody Marine that the corpsman and Cpl McGurk had been working on and placed him in the jeep. Then the jeep raced back by us. We could plainly see his bloody stomach, chest and face.

"Holy shit, look at 'em," cried Cpl Andrews.

Then another jeep came out and picked up the rest of the wounded.

Later I was still sitting on my pack on the airfield with my platoon. I had been thinking about our first blood loss. I had quit smoking cigarettes seven years ago, but I had a sudden strong desire for one when GySgt Fisher walked up to me.

Sitting near me, Cpl Wynne asked, "Gunny how are those wounded guys?"

GySgt Fisher looked down at him saying, "The first one out died at the battalion aid station. The other three have been medivaced out to the Guam."

Nearby, I noticed Col Studt and LtCol Kersher standing as they studied a map and looked up into the mountains.

LtCol Kersher rubbed his knee asking, "What d' ya think Colonel, is the shit about to hit the fan?"

"I don't know. Shit I'm ready to retire. Two tours in the Nam was enough," answered Col Studt.

"Shit Colonel, we could kick some ass here, take names and be home by Christmas. This could mean a star for you and eagles for me," said LtCol Kersher smiling.

Col Studt shot a hard stare at LtCol Kersher who just kept smiling.

I looked up at GySgt Fisher who just shook his head as I thought to myself, a man should be careful what he asked for, or he just might get it.

Again, we spent all day on the hot airfield and slept there at night.

Finally, the next day September 31st, LtCol Kersher assigned each company to their areas. All four companies began moving into their assigned positions to the south and east of the airport runways with checkpoints as far east as the railroad line. The Marines in the northernmost areas linked up with the Italians. All forward observation, listening posts and checkpoints were to be located near posts manned by Lebanese forces.

Mike Company's area covered a big area, which was isolated from the rest of our battalion. And each platoon was in turn also isolated. I looked out over a Shiite Muslim village that was mostly a refugee camp, which surrounded the main routes to and from the airport and near the Israeli forces. Capt Jones ordered us to dig fighting holes just in case we were attacked by hostile forces whoever they may be. SSgt Tapper saw to it that our platoon dug their fighting holes chest deep. Then he had them fill sandbags and build overhead covers to protect them from small arms fire and overhead fragmentation shells.

I was glad to get away from our battalion CP. They were occupying a bombed-out, fire-damaged four-story reinforced concrete administration building offered to LtCol Kersher from the management of the airport. This was the strongest looking building within the MAU lines. The Lebanese government's Aviation Administration Bureau had used it, and then the PLO and the Syrians had used it as an Army headquarters and hospital before and during the Israeli invasion. It had withstood heavy caliber artillery rounds and at least twice had been hit by Israeli bombers. Even though there were many pockmarks and broken windows, the building had never been penetrated. Even the Israelis had used it for a time as a major headquarters.

LtCol Kersher thought it was great, but Maj Hays didn't like any of this. The bunching up of 200 Marines in one building bothered him. He also didn't like having our backs to the sea and we weren't allowed to advance far enough to take the high ground.

We had started being issued some of the new MRE's (Meals Ready to Eat) foil packed rations. I liked these new meals except for the fact that a lot of the meals you needed to add water to eat it to keep from being thirsty. I wondered what would happen when there was a shortage of water. With the old C-rations if you didn't have water you could sip on the fruit juice as you ate the meal and eat the fruit last without using water.

That night LtCol Kersher called for a battalion officer's call and invited all officers, not just the company commanders. A jeep came and picked up the six of us from Mike Company and carried us to the battalion CP. We seemed to be the last ones to enter the noisy conference room.

Maj Hays called us to attention. Everyone stood up as the room went instantly quiet.

LtCol Kersher then stood up saying, "At ease men. Now I don't want to hear about how this place sucks. I know that. But we have our orders. And I don't want to hear any more about Diem Bien Phu. We're not the French and this isn't Vietnam." As he made this statement he looked right across at Maj Hays, who's face suddenly turned red.

Mostly the meeting ended up being another talk on the rules of engagement. The two most important things were:

1. In every possible case, local civil or military authority will be used.
2. We will use only the degree of military force necessary to accomplish the mission or reduce the threat.

On October 1st, Capt Jones ordered my platoon to run squad-sized patrols through the streets nearby. I gave the first patrol to Sgt Sieple. I wanted to go with him but Capt Jones refused to let me go. I kept in radio contact with him while he was gone and had another squad armed and ready to go in case they got into trouble. But when they returned, I was surprised when Sgt Sieple reported how friendly the Lebanese civilians were and these were mainly Shiite Muslims, after they found out we were Americans and not Israelis. Soon we would be allowed to put American flags on our vehicles and arms, which seemed to relieve the uneasiness of the civilians.

Our presence seemed to be creating an environment of stability. It seemed order had been quickly restored and the confidant civilians had begun new construction of homes and businesses throughout the battered city. Civilian bathers again crowded the beaches and the restaurant business picked up. It seemed for the first time in years it was relatively peaceful again in Beirut. Muslims waved at Marine patrols, slapping hands with every Marine they came in contact with. Some civilians smiled while others cried.

Other squad leaders who came back from patrols reported how ruthless the Israelis were dealing with even minor acts against their convoys. It seemed if a single sniper round hit anywhere near an Israeli, they would all return fire from their amtracks and tanks in every direction. Any vehicle parked along the road they traveled, would be blown up by the lead Israeli tank.

The Marines soon nicknamed the Shiite town they routinely patrolled through Hooterville. As one Marine put it, it seemed all the women had big noses and big breasts.

To fight boredom, SSgt Tapper kept our men who were not on patrol working, filling sandbags with which they continued improving our positions.

On October 2nd, our battalion posted the promotion list. Cain made gunnery sergeant. With too many gunnery sergeants in Mike Company, GySgt Fisher was transferred to Lima Company. GySgt Knight became our company gunny and GySgt Cain became Weapons platoon sergeant.

Sieple, Reed and Simon made staff sergeant. SSgt Simon would stay where he was in charge of the company's mortar section. SSgt Sieple left my platoon to be the platoon sergeant of 2nd platoon. SSgt Spidden from 3rd platoon was transferred to India Company. And SSgt Reed took his place as the 3rd platoon sergeant.

Meadows from my 1st squad made sergeant and moved up from fire team leader to squad leader.

On October 12th, the Deputy Secretary of Defense, Carlucci and his staff flew into the airport and toured our battalion's positions.

The next day, FMF Lant Commander LtGen Miller USMC visited our battalion.

On October 17th, Congressman Wilson from Texas was given a tour of our battalion area.

On October 20th, Vice Adm Hays the CinCusNavEur and Vice Adm Rowden the 6th Fleet Commander visited our MAU CP.

By now, I was thirty-five years old and had gone over eighteen years in the Corps, two years to go to rate a retirement. It was hard to believe.

Around us the atmosphere still seemed peaceful in this ravaged capital. For the most part the Lebanese still seemed happy with our presence here as they started rebuilding their city.

Near our battalion CP, Marine amtracks had now been dug in deep into fortified defensive positions. They stood at the ready with their 50cal machineguns pointing up toward the hills ringing Beirut. They were ready to support us infantry types if need be. They could also be part of a reaction force if one of our patrols got into trouble.

Everywhere Marines were constantly fortifying their positions and struggling to keep weapons and equipment clean in the mud as the rainy season started.

The Lebanese kids, just like the kids in Vietnam, seemed fascinated with us Marines. Where the Vietnamese kids sold us cokes with dirty ice these kids sold us coffee and mosquito repellant coils to help support their families.

Out checking Mike Company's line, GySgt Knight walked up to me as he watched some of my men filling sandbags with the red dirt and said, "Sir, ain't this weather unique? We have the bugs of Lejeune, the rains of Nam and the sands of 29 Palms."

"Yeah gunny and we get paid for all this too," I answered smiling.

The morning of October 30th, Sgt Meadows squad went out on patrol in three jeeps. They drove carefully on the streets where traffic signals, signs and laws were nonexistent.

He soon learned it was survival of the fastest. He learned to blow the horn and speed through, or sit in traffic for hours.

Later he described it like a free-for-all. But he was glad he hadn't had the patrol yesterday that had taken along a news reporter and congressmen around the bombed-out city. They returned wide-eyed and holding on to their seats.

Suddenly, a civilian car ran into a taxi. The taxi driver jumped out yelling and shaking his fist at the other driver. The civilian driver stepped out of his car with a pistol and began firing.

From around the next corner a young civilian boy ran out into the street frantically waving for the Marines to stop and asked if they had a doctor. The three jeeps stopped as the corpsman looked back at Sgt Meadows.

"Okay Doc go ahead," said Sgt Meadows.

As the corpsman grabbed his bag, Sgt Meadows said to his radioman, "Call the gunner. Tell him I'm taking a team with me to check this out." Then to his squad, "First team you're on me. The rest of you spread out and take cover. Let's go."

Then Sgt Meadows and four Marines followed the corpsman and kid. As they went Sgt Meadows said, "You guys stay spread out and keep your eyes open for trouble. If you see anything out of the way let me know."

The kid led them to a house. Once inside they found a woman lying on a bed rolling around. Her face was blue.

"She's choking," yelled the corpsman as he ran to the bed quickly and slapped her twice on the back. Then he lifted her up and did the Heimlich maneuver. Suddenly with a loud cough and a gasp she spit up a big ball of food. As they returned to their jeeps, she followed them thanking the corpsman again and again for saving her life.

The next day, Sgt Schwartz's squad was returning from a patrol when they passed a car sitting off to the right side of the road. His jeep was the second of three jeeps when suddenly the car exploded. The blast turned Sgt Schwartz's jeep over wounding the Marine sitting behind him. This was the first blood from my platoon and the third for Mike Company.

Capt Jones still felt these patrols into Hooterville were a good thing to keep the troops busy, it also showed our concerns for the people of Beirut and it was good real-world experience for fire team and squad leaders.

On November 1st, our MAU's mission was expanded when President Reagan approved the conduct of daily daylight motorized and foot patrols to begin in East Beirut. Our jeeps would now fly American flags from their 15-foot antennas so there was no way anybody could mistake us for Israelis. We also now had orders to fire if fired upon.

At 1115, a car bomb exploded near one of Capt Graham's Lima Company checkpoints. But no one was hurt.

The next day the Assistant Secretary of Defense Frances West, a former Marine toured the MAU area.

On November 4th, the battalion ran its first patrol into Christian East Beirut. The first patrol came out of Capt Graham's Lima Company. It was made up of a Lebanese liaison officer and 15 Marines spread across four jeeps. Two of the jeeps went out first. After five minutes the other two jeeps followed.

They drove carefully through the war battered sections. As before, the Marines carried unloaded weapons, but with loaded magazines in magazine pouches on their sides. They encountered mostly friendly smiles from the civilians who waved and called out, "Hello."

Patrols were under orders to report any sighting of armed militiamen or Israeli soldiers. They were surprised to find Christian Beirut was mostly untouched by the war. This first patrol returned in the afternoon after 2 ½ hours.

The next morning the second patrol made up of Sgt Meadows' squad to East Beirut went out for 2 hours.

Congressmen John Murtha, Robert Levingston, Nick Rohall and Vice Adm Rowden showed up to see the patrol return.

On November 10th, Ambassador Dillon was our battalion's honored guest at our battalion CP for the Corps' 207th birthday celebration. Cake and ice cream were sent out to us Marines on the line. In Vietnam we would have gotten beer too.

On November 20th, the staffs of Senators Paul Laxalt and Howard Baker visited us. Three days later US Ambassador to Cyprus Raymond Ewing toured the MAU.

On November 25th, Adm Rowden brought the JCS (Joint Chiefs of the Services) Chairman Gen Vessey US Army to tour the MAU.

By the end of November, our patrol area had been expanded again to now cover Northeast Beirut.

In early December, MajGen Gray our 2nd Marine Division Commanding General and Cardinal Cook the Military Vicar of the US Armed Forces toured our MAU. The tobacco chewing MajGen Gray went out of his way to speak to the lance corporals and PFCs. He was the only one to do that here. The young Marines knew he really cared about them and they loved him for it. He's probably the closest thing we have to Chesty Puller in the Corps today.

Also, two senatorial groups visited us, one headed by Senator Dan Quayle.

In late November and early December, Israeli vehicles making a resupply run to their troops on a road near us had been fired on by Muslims. This seemed to cause confrontations between Marines and the Israelis.

On Christmas Day, an Israeli patrol moving along the road near us was suddenly ambushed. The Israelis returned fire in all directions, even toward the Marine lines, but no Marines were hit.

Capt Scotto of Kilo Company whose men were closest to the ambush, felt the Israelis were undisciplined. Some of Capt Scotto's men who had felt threatened made threatening gestures with their unloaded weapons after the ambush was over. Israeli and Marines alike gave each other the finger.

Near the end of December, a high-ranking Israeli officer was killed in an ambush.

Once again, I spent another Christmas and New Year's overseas.

New Year's Day 1983 an Israeli command vehicle in a convoy was destroyed with several men killed. The Israelis suspected that the attacks were coming from PLO who were slipping back through our lines.

Also, incidents of incoming small arms fire into our area had increased with some very close calls for the men of my platoon.

The next day Cpl Harris, a fire team leader in 3rd platoon, watched two Israeli tanks heavily sandbagged to protect them from anti-tank shells and an amtrack moving across a field running over small trees. Then the lead tank turned toward a jointly manned Lebanese and Marine checkpoint. They had done this sort of thing before just to turn away before they hit the gate. But to be on the safe side Cpl Harris called for Lt Cregar on the radio.

The tank stopped just short of the gate as the tank commander yelled down at them, "I demand to be allowed to enter!"

Nearby Lebanese soldiers jumped into their bunkers leaving small Cpl Harris and his four-man fire team standing their ground alone.

"I'm sorry sir, but I can't allow that," answered Cpl Harris.

Suddenly the tank engine roared and the tank lurched forward crashing through the gate.

Cpl Harris grabbed the handset to the radio to call Lt Cregar. SSgt Reed rushed past him toward the tank coming at them.

The lead tank stopped halfway through the gate as the small white Cpl Harris ran up and stood next to the medium built black SSgt Reed holding his M-16 rifle at port arms across his chest in the tanks path. As the rest of Cpl Harris' fire team moved up closer to back him up SSgt Reed looked up and yelled at the bearded Israeli, "Halt! You're in the US Marine perimeter. Now back out 'a here!"

The bearded Israeli yelled down, "Step aside. I'm an Israeli officer."

"Listen Moses, I don't give a shit who you are. My orders are no one passes through here. If you want to enter our perimeter you have to go to the main gate and ask permission like everyone else. Now back this shit can out 'a here!"

The tanks and amtrack backed up and started off back along the road the way they had come.

But within minutes the tanks turned and crashed through the

perimeter fence and roared off across the airfield.

Meanwhile, Lt Cregar had radioed Capt Jones who in turn notified LtCol Kersher what was going on. Now from our battalion CP, raced a jeep carrying Col Studt and LtCol Kersher. The jeep skidded to a stop in front of the lead tank. The tank stopped as Col Studt and LtCol Kersher jumped out of the jeep. Col Studt walked up to the tank staring up at the Israeli officer and asked, "What's going on here?"

An Israeli lieutenant colonel climbed off the lead tank and answered, "Sir I'm lost and I'm trying to take a shortcut back to our lines."

Col Studt's jaws popped in anger as he yelled over the roar of the tank engines, "The rules of the game as you must know are, we are to have no contact. Your column just entered an area controlled by the Lebanese Armed Forces and US Marines of the Multinational Force. You must return the way you have come."

The bearded lieutenant colonel took his helmet off smiling and said, "We're looking for terrorists."

Col Studt placed his hands on his hips bending forward just a little saying, "Do you expect me to believe that you really think there are terrorists in my compound. Now back these vehicles out of my area."

The Israeli lieutenant colonel still smiling put his helmet back on his head and said, "If we could this once continue on my way."

"No way. You Israelis need to coordinate your movements through here with the proper authorities and you know that is the Lebanese airport security force," said Col Studt.

The Israeli lieutenant colonel turned and climbed back up and into his tank. He spoke on his radio and the amtrack and tanks began backing up. The Israeli lieutenant colonel looked back at the tank behind him and then looked forward at Col Studt. Saying, "Sorry about the gate and fence. But somebody has got to kill these terrorist dogs. Shalom."

Col Studt answered, "Shalom." As he stood watching the tanks and amtrack back out of his area.

A few days later, an Israeli jeep patrol drove up to a jointly manned checkpoint of Lebanese and Marines of India Company. The Israeli officer in charge said, "I want to speak directly with the senior American officer."

When SSgt Spidden showed up the Israeli officer asked, "Are you an officer?"

"No sir, I'm a staff sergeant," he answered.

"Then I demand to speak to an American officer."

"Sir, I'm the senior Marine here. So, what do you want?"

With this the Israeli jeeps turned around and drove away.

Again, on January 8th the Israelis attempted to enter our battalion perimeter through India Company positions and again were stopped.

The next day Israeli patrols started a reconnaissance by fire, which amounted to firing their small arms and tanks intermittently at vacant buildings, open fields and treetops. Their patrols were made up of about four armored vehicles or tanks followed by five to fourteen walking troops. To us, these patrols had become predictable and routine, but some of the firing was dangerous to our Marine positions.

On January 10th, the Israelis tried to enter our perimeter again this time through Capt Scott's Kilo Company and again they were not allowed to pass.

On January 17th, two jeep loads of Israeli soldiers drove up to a joint checkpoint manned by Marines of Capt Graham's Lima Company. This time the Israeli officer in charge demanded, "Let us through your lines. We are following terrorist and I want to sweep your area."

Capt Graham was radioed from the checkpoint and he and the Lebanese sector CO rushed to the checkpoint.

Again, the Israeli officer repeated his demand. Capt Graham answered, "No one has passed through here all day."

"You cannot pass here," added the Lebanese officer and the Israelis drove away.

During the next three days, the Israeli patrols made up of tanks and amtracks tried four times to pass through our battalion lines. In one instant, Capt Scotto of Kilo Company ordered his men already in their fighting positions to prepare to repel an Israeli attack.

Another time, Israeli soldiers in a jeep drove up to a 2nd platoon checkpoint manned by Cpl McGurk's fire team.

Again, the Israeli officer in charge said, "I want to go through this checkpoint."

"I can't allow that sir," answered Cpl McGurk.

Meanwhile, seeing what was happening, Lt Wright yelled,

"Reaction force up!"

As the rest of the squad ran up to support Cpl McGurk, Sgt Reilly yelled, "This is not a drill!"

And behind them Capt Jones drove up in his jeep.

The Israeli officer looked at Capt Jones and again said, "We need to pass through here!"

"You can't pass," answered Capt Jones.

The Israeli just sat there staring at the Marines who stared back for a good ten minutes. Then the jeeps turned around driving away.

"Boy these jerk faces are either slow learners or they're just probing our lines to test our reaction," said Sgt Reilly.

On January 20th, an Israeli patrol including tanks and amtracks tried to pass through a checkpoint manned by 3rd platoon. Cpl Harris's squad stopped them reminding them that their orders were to allow no armed men to pass through except Lebanese soldiers or police.

On January 28th, Maj Hays was fired at by an Israeli machinegun, but was unhurt. He reported this to LtCol Kersher. Two days later Maj Hays riding in a jeep clearly marked with a UN flag was again fired on by Israeli forces. This time he complained straight to Col Studt. And on the way out of his office, Maj Hays was overheard saying, "It's just a damn good thing these Jews can't shoot straight!"

We were still taking some small arms fire. Our orders were to keep our weapons unloaded, but to keep loaded magazines ready. This country was like Vietnam in so many ways, it was beautiful, but deadly. The Lebanese custom of men blowing other men kisses shocked us just as the sight of Vietnamese men holding hands as they walked did eighteen years ago.

At night, we could hear shooting up in the mountains between the Christians and the Druse.

Marines on patrol were still followed by kids yelling, "Allo, chocolate, American." Kids had now switched from coffee to selling us cokes. The young Marines had nicknamed the kids, 'Hi Joes'.

Each night I tried to send a few of my men back to the battalion CP to watch a movie and drink two beers. The young Marines had wanted to go swimming in the brilliant blue sea. But our medical doctors had ruled that out because the water was so polluted.

The first of February, Capt Graham was driving through

Hooterville when he was stopped by Israeli troops at gunpoint.

"What's the problem?" he asked.

"If you drive any further you will be killed," came the answer.

"Payback is a bitch isn't it," said Capt Graham laughing. But the Israelis didn't laugh.

"Okay, okay," he said as he turned his jeep around returning the way he had come.

The same day Sgt Williams from my platoon and SSgt Sieple from 2nd platoon were appointed warrant officers and were transferred up to battalion until they would leave for the warrant officer basic school at Quantico Va. Also, Coston from 3rd platoon was promoted to sergeant.

Evans was promoted to captain and took command of India Company. Lt Littleton moved up to be Mike Company's XO. At hearing this, Gunner Sieple requested to return to Mike Company to be our weapons platoon leader until his stateside orders came in and LtCol Kersher granted his wish.

And Street of 3rd platoon was promoted to corporal.

At 0800 February 2nd, Capt Jones was at his company CP looking through field glasses at three Israeli tanks racing along the road at battle speed coming up from the south until they went out of sight.

Half an hour later, he spotted the same patrol coming back from the north.

"Gunny Knight, call the platoons and tell them to take cover with helmets and flak jackets on," ordered Capt Jones.

"What's up skipper?" asked GySgt Knight.

"With three tanks these guys could make one hell of a recon by fire," said Capt Jones as he watched the Israeli officer in the lead tank with his head and shoulders showing from the turret.

After my radioman passed the order on to me, I passed it to my platoon. SSgt Tapper asked, "What's going on sir?"

"Don't know, but the skipper must think something is not right," I answered as I now saw the tanks moving along the road. Suddenly, they abruptly turned off the road driving through a small Muslim orchard toward us. I felt something was up. I grabbed the radio handset out of my radioman's hand and called Capt Jones' CP and GySgt Knight answered.

"I got three Israeli tanks heading toward our perimeter! Do you copy! Over!" I yelled into the handset.

"Copy that. The six already knows and is on his way to your pause. Over," answered GySgt Knight.

"Out," I answered tossing the handset back to my radioman.

The three tanks came on, in a column smashing through our perimeter fence advancing toward my platoon positions.

Behind us, Capt Jones with his jeep driver drove up quickly and around to the front of my platoon position skidding to a stop in the area the tanks were approaching. I couldn't believe these asshole Israelis were actually going to try again to force their way through our combined Lebanese and Marine checkpoint. The Lebanese had quickly locked and loaded their weapons. I knew if a firefight started, we would have to support the Lebanese. I wasn't worried about the fire discipline of my men, but the Lebanese soldiers were another thing.

As the tanks neared running at battle speed, I was surprised to see Capt Jones jump out of his jeep jogging toward the lead tank to place himself between the tanks and the Lebanese soldiers. Then he stopped and stood with his hands on his hips facing the tank.

With the tank roaring down on him less then twenty-five meters away the Israeli lieutenant colonel yelled, "Get out of my way!"

All along Mike Company lines, Marines without orders jammed magazines into weapons and chambered rounds. SSgt Tapper looked at me as if asking what to do? I just nodded my head. Also, GySgt Knight had sent dragon tank killer teams forward from the company CP and they arrived and set up taking aim.

"No one fires unless I do!" I yelled. Then I moved to the right and laid my rifle across the top of the sandbagged wall and took aim at the Israeli lieutenant colonel's chest fearing he was about to run down this young captain and my old friend of the last eight years.

Just as I flipped the safety off, suddenly the lead tank stopped rocking back and forth about six inches in front of Capt Jones.

Capt Jones took a deep breath as he looked up at the smiling face of the Israeli lieutenant colonel and asked, "Sir are you in charge of this patrol?"

The Israeli lieutenant colonel looked down from the turret at him and then slowly around at the Marines aiming at his tanks before he spoke, "I'm going through here!"

As politely as he could through gritted teeth Capt Jones said,

"Sir, you are heading directly at a Lebanese checkpoint, beyond which you are not allowed and I request you leave the way you came."

"I'm a colonel in the Israeli Army and I'm going through."

"Not through my Marine lines you're not."

After a short pause the Israeli lieutenant colonel dismounted climbing down off his tank and stood toe to toe in front of Capt Jones. With a sneer he said, "I'm going to pass through this checkpoint!"

Now unable to take a clear shot I raised the rifle up in the air and flipped the safety back on. Capt Jones bent forward almost touching nose to nose and said through gritted teeth, "Sir, that you will do only over my dead body."

The lieutenant colonel spun around and climbed back up into his tank. Then the tanks engine revved up. Capt Jones reached down unsnapping his black holster flap and pulled his 45 cal pistol out with his right hand. With his left hand he pulled a loaded magazine out of his cargo trouser leg pocket and pushed it into the pistol, then pulled the slide to the rear chambering a round and held the weapon at the ready position, pointing skyward.

"This whole area is an Israeli patrol zone!" yelled the lieutenant colonel.

"Sir that's bull shit and you know it."

The lieutenant colonel spoke Hebrew into the microphone on his helmet. When he finished, he stared down at Capt Jones and said, "If you want another war, we can start it right here!"

The lieutenant colonel studied Capt Jones face, which suddenly broke into a smile.

There was another long pause, the lieutenant colonel spoke Hebrew rapidly into his microphone and the lead tank suddenly started backing up as Capt Jones walked alongside the tank's track.

But just as suddenly the second and third tanks revved up their engines and whipped forward roaring around the lead tank and Capt Jones, bearing down on the Lebanese checkpoint. Capt Jones leaped up on the lead tank, climbing up to the turret and grabbed the lieutenant colonel by the collar pulling him forward and yelled in his face, "You had better stop those damn tanks! Now!" as he pushed the cold 45 cal pistol barrel against his left temple.

Ever so slowly the lieutenant colonel touched the microphone speaking Hebrew and both tanks stopped, rocking on their tracks.

Then the lieutenant colonel said, "One thing we don't want to do is kill each other."

"Yes sir, but if you people keep doing shit like this, it's going to happen," answered Capt Jones.

Within seconds all three tanks started backing up out of our perimeter.

From Mike Company lines, there was total silence as Capt Jones climbed down from the tank and walked back toward his jeep as he cleared his weapon putting the magazine back inside his left trouser cargo pocket. His jeep driver drove up to meet him. Capt Jones climbed in and as the jeep turned around heading toward my position the whole company erupted cheering and growling the Marine yell "Ooorah!"

I walked out and saluted him saying, "Capt'n, I'd follow you anywhere."

"Yeah and when Colonel Kersher hears about this my career will probably be over," said Capt Jones.

"Skipper, those assholes are deliberately testing us and I'd say you passed in flying colors. And these young Marines know it and they are the ones that really count."

As we talked, LtCol Kersher drove up beside us and demanded, "Captain I want a full report on what happened here."

"Yes sir," answered Capt Jones. For twenty minutes he walked the ground with LtCol Kersher telling him what happened. Then LtCol Kersher took Capt Jones back to the MAU headquarters. Later, Col Studt drove back out here with Capt Jones and they walked the area. When they were through, Col Studt said, "I'm going to report this up through the chain of command requesting the Israelis and we mark our boundary lines more clearly so there will be no more misunderstandings like this in the future."

"Thank you, sir. That sure would help. If this keeps on someone is going to get killed," answered Capt Jones.

At 1600, a tank shell ricocheted into Capt Evans India Company's area and exploded. But no one was hurt.

The routine of daily jeep patrols went on in East and West Beirut. Finally, LtCol Kersher allowed Marines on patrol to keep loaded magazines in their weapons, but no rounds in the chambers. By now the squads knew the terrain and areas well. Still SSgt Tapper kept the Marines not on patrol busy improving our positions. This kept the young men from being too idle or bored as well as keeping them in physical shape.

And as the cold weather grew worse, we were issued cold weather clothing.

On February 5th, an Israeli amtrack fired its 50 cal machinegun at a Lebanese civilian hunting birds with an ancient muzzleloader. Some of these machinegun rounds hit within Capt Scotto's Kilo Company lines.

On February 13th, Sgt Meadows squad, manning our platoon's checkpoint stopped a convoy of three Israeli tanks and an amtrack. The Israeli officer in the lead tank said, "We're coming through this checkpoint."

"Not through my checkpoint you're not," answered Sgt Meadows.

Then from the amtrack, a squad of Israeli soldiers jumped out and formed into a skirmish line facing the Marine squad. Sgt Meadows squad locked and loaded their weapons.

From my position, I saw what was going on and radioed both Sgts Johnson and Rienbold and ordered them to have their machinegun teams to stand ready to support the first squad. GySgt Knight listening to the radio reported the situation to Capt Jones who in turn radioed LtCol Kersher.

The Israeli officer again said, "We will pass through this checkpoint!"

"I'm sorry but you can't," Sgt Meadows answered again.

Troops on both sides prepared to fight taking aim at each other. I was thinking that I never dreamed that someday I would be in a firefight with Israeli soldiers who I have always respected so much.

Over the radio, Capt Jones told me that Col Studt was coming from MAU headquarters with Marine TOW wire guided antitank missiles teams.

Suddenly the Israeli officer waved his troops back. But as they climbed back into the amtrack the Israeli officer said, "We're coming back."

"Yeah, yeah sure and we'll be right here waiting on ya," muttered Sgt Meadows.

Again, I had aimed in on an Israeli officer and now lowered my rifle, relieved that we hadn't exchanged fire with people I think of as allies. But I knew all it's going to take is a nervous trigger finger on either side to start a real firefight if this kind of shit keeps on happening.

On February 17th, Senator Roger Jepsen, Congressmen Jack Edwards, Anthony Beilenson, Carroll Campbell, Bernard Dwyer, Clarence Miller, George O'Brien, Neal Smith and Jack Hightower landed at the Beirut airport to visit the MAU.

The MAU had received intelligence reports of a growing threat of a terrorist attack against the Marines, so we reinforced our positions and our number of patrols increased.

During February 20th, it snowed heavy in the mountains in the distant front of us and a number of villages became isolated and civilian travelers became stranded. President Gemayel requested Marine help in rescuing 200 Lebanese who were trapped about twenty miles east of Beirut.

The next day, Col Studt sent choppers and an amtrack convoy in the rescue effort after the Lebanese officials had obtained Syrian clearance for the Marines to move through and behind their lines.

But the choppers were forced to turn back because of the heavy icing conditions.

On February 22nd, a column of nine amtracks headed out with Lebanese Red Cross personnel to help people stranded 40 miles away. A Marine Ch-53 chopper landed on a mile-high mountain and was given coffee by poorly dressed Syrian soldiers.

Meanwhile, the amtracks had to burst through deep snow and blocked roads. At times the mountain road was so narrow that only part of one tread was on the road with the rest hanging over the edge, sometimes it was over 300-foot drop down into deep gulleys. But in the end these Marines saved many people stranded in their cars, but also found several people frozen to death.

By February 24th, the rescue mission had been called off after winning the gratitude of many Lebanese people.

Again, our battalion's patrol area was widened to the northeast of Beirut. The Israelis immediately challenged these new patrols and threatened to obstruct them.

By February 28th a mess hall had been set up and was open. So now I could send my platoon by squads to get at least one hot meal per day.

I had heard this winter was the worst in forty years with the temperatures dropping into the low 40's. And this was supposed to last until early April.

But even worse than the weather was the changing political situation. It seemed that various factions in Lebanon had begun choosing sides and terrorist threats against us had increased. Our patrol routes and times were varied to keep terrorists from finding a pattern.

In March, Col Studt ordered our battalion to start foot patrols north of Beirut airport even as terrorist groups threatened to attack our patrols.

On the morning of March 7th, Sgt Meadows squad was on a foot patrol when it was stopped at an Israeli checkpoint. An Israeli soldier said, "You Marines are not supposed to be in this area."

Sgt Meadows pulled his squad back a block and halted them as he double-checked his map. Seeing that he was right, he moved his squad around the Israeli checkpoint on the next block and continued his patrol.

That afternoon, Sgt Crew's squad from 2nd platoon was returning from a patrol and was challenged by an Israeli patrol that stood in their way as they neared their platoon lines. Sgt Crew signaled Cpl Poplas whose fire team was on point to maneuver around them. As they did so, the Israeli soldiers verbally harassed them with things like, "You Marines have gotten soft since Vietnam." Or, "It's been a long time since Iwo Jima."

Sgt Crew, a Vietnam veteran returned red faced with anger and reported to Lt Wright what had happened and what was said. This was reported up the chain of command to Col Studt who in anger said, "I'll personally lead the next patrol through the Israeli checkpoint the next time they try and stop one of my patrols from executing their duties.

Meanwhile, the Russians had by now re-equipped the Syrians who had been battered by the Israelis during the fighting before we came with better and more modern weapons. The Syrian troops had been retrained and reinforced. Also, we had reports PLO fighters had infiltrated back into Beirut. Individual Lebanese units, organizations and religious sects in and around Beirut had been set up to protect their own vested interest and areas.

It now seemed the Lebanese reaction to our presence ranged from total acceptance to relative indifference.

On the night of March 9th, unknown persons ambushed an Italian jeep patrol. One Italian soldier was killed and nine wounded.

The next day, Sgt Wise's squad from 2nd platoon was out on foot patrol with Sgt Rienbold's machinegun team. Moving through a Palestinian neighborhood, Sgt Rienbold didn't like these patrols down these narrow streets past many alleys with two story building on both sides of the street, which he knew was the perfect place for an ambush, a sniper or anyone who just wanted to drop a grenade down from a window. This was the first time he had ever wished he was back in the jungles of Vietnam. But it was a good sign when friendly young children still yelled, "Hi Joe."

Sgt Wise gave the hand signal for the squad to close it up.

Near the front of the column, Cpl Mitchell with the point fire team turned walking backward watching the rooftops.

The squad entered a dusty Muslim shantytown. Near the rear of the column, Sgt Rienbold breathed deep as he looked back at his machinegun team behind him. Meanwhile, at the front, Cpl Mitchell was moving along the street with his fire team past a broken window of a shell damaged house when he heard a click above him. He looked up in time to see a single arm flash out from a second-floor balcony landing above them, and then he saw the Russian type grenade falling.

"Grenade! Hit the deck!" he yelled diving for cover into the mud.

"Lord I don't wanna die," thought Sgt Rienbold as he spun to the ground.

Sgt Wise heard the grenade splash in a mud puddle off to his left. The blast caught him in the back, but his flak jacket took all the shrapnel as other shrapnel zinged over him and off his helmet.

With ringing ears, Sgt Rienbold looked up and around. He quickly came up on one knee shaking as he picked up his M-16 out of the mud. Suddenly, a burst of fire sent bullets across the street in front of him splattering him with mud and water. He fired a burst back as Sgt Wise looked around saying, "Shit!" Seeing a stonewall nearby he pointed yelling, "Back over that wall!"

Cpl McAllister ran and dived over the wall and landed hard on his left shoulder and rolled up on his hands and knees. An AK-47 assault rifle opened up with a long Kak! Kak! Kak! Bullets hit the top of the wall sending pieces of stone against Cpl Mitchell's helmet and face as he came across the top of the wall. Rolling next to the wall he wiped blood away with the back of his hand as he peeked over the top as another burst hit the stone house behind him. Sgt Wise came over the wall next with a group of Marines.

Then Sgt Rienbold dived across the wall with another group of Marines and all of them hit in a pile. As they rolled and crawled for cover Sgt Rienbold yelled, “Wise, we’re caught in a cross fire from the top floors!”

Sgt Wise had counted his men and now looked up and down the wall realizing he still had five men missing as another burst of fire hit around them followed by another grenade explosion. He crawled to his radioman and grabbed the handset calling Lt Wright asking for help. Then he tossed the handset back to the radioman.

“What’d he say, Wise?” asked Sgt Rienbold as he fired his rifle over the wall.

Sgt Wise shook his head saying, “He said a Lebanese patrol is on the way to help us. We’re ordered to stay under cover and hold our fire.”

“Don’t shoot! What fucking shit is this!” yelled back Sgt Rienbold.

“Fuck that!” said Cpl McAllister as he rose up to return fire only to have a burst of bullets shatter his M-16 right out of his hands.

Then they heard the sounds of an amtrack coming toward them. Then the Lebanese Army amtrack came into sight swinging around the corner and its 50 cal machinegun opened fire on the second story houses on both sides of the street. As the amtrack moved past the Marines spraying fire, the Marines jumped up following behind it as the enemy fire stopped.

As they moved, Sgt Wise could hear Capt Jones’ voice over the radio of the man behind him, but he couldn’t understand what he was saying over the sound of the Lebanese 50 cal machinegun firing from side to side shooting big chunks of concrete and wood splinters out of the houses. The enemy forces quickly disappeared and Sgt Wise began searching for his missing men. Meanwhile, Lt Wright raced out with Sgt Reilly’s squad in jeeps. When they found them, Lt Wright jumped out saying, “Everybody okay?”

“Four men wounded sir, mostly in the legs from shrapnel and bullets and one man missing,” answered Sgt Wise.

“Okay, spread out and look for him again,” said Lt Wright.

Sgt Wise felt sick deep down as what was left of his squad swept back up the street on line. By now the street was filled with armed men, Marines, Italians, Lebanese soldiers, Lebanese security police and members of the UN peacekeeping force.

It was Cpl McAllister who found the missing man lying face down in the mud. There were shrapnel wounds in the back of his neck. The corpsman rolled him over. His eyes were open with a look of surprise on his face.

Back with my platoon, I listened to my radio as Lt Wright's voice choked up as he told Capt Jones, "Be advised we have one KIA and four WIA."

Unlike my years in Vietnam my world was not only my platoon anymore. I had many close friends in all the platoons of Mike Company as well as throughout our battalion. I walked over to 2nd platoon's positions and waited for Lt Wright to bring his men back. I didn't know the young Marine that had been killed. I had been worried he might be Sgt's Wise, Rienbold or Cpls Poplos or McAllister.

At seeing me, Sgt Rienbold walked up to me saying, "Why Gunner you weren't worried about me were you?"

"Yeah, I was old friend," I said.

"Yeah for a few seconds I thought I'd survived Nam just to die in these stupid streets."

"How did Sergeant Wise do?"

"He's young sir, but he did fine. He proved himself this day."

"Good."

Capt Jones also drove over to check on the dead and wounded. After he had seen them, he too walked up to me and said, "I take it you never get used to losing a man?"

"No sir. Each time is like the first time."

A little later the dead Marine and the wounded were flown out to the USS Guadalcanal.

The same day two grenades were thrown at an outpost manned by the French.

Later, a group I had never heard of calling themselves Jihad Islami which means "Islamic Holy War" had placed a call to the local news agency claiming it had ordered grenade attacks on the American Occupation Army and warned the Americans to leave Lebanon.

On March 11th, the Italian CP was hit by small arms fire. It seemed the French, Italians, and British, like us were now all facing an increased threat.

On March 12th, LtGen Miller, Commanding General of FMF Lant, visited Beirut while MajGen Trainer visited our battalion. At the same time Representative Lyle Williams visited Col Studt.

On March 13th, Geraldine Ferraro and Barbara Milkulski toured the MAU.

On March 15th, Patricia Schroeder visited our battalion.

The next morning started unusually quiet as Col Studt hosted and provided orientation briefings for Congressmen Louis Stokes and Gen Smith. But within hours, terrorists attacked the French and Italian forces killing an Italian soldier.

In the afternoon, Capt Jones ordered me to report to his CP with one squad for a patrol. I picked Cpl Andrews' squad because they were the most rested and we entered the company CP. I was happy to see Sgt Johnson's machinegun team had already reported in.

Cpl Andrews, Sgt Johnson and I all got out our maps as Capt Jones briefed us on the patrol that had been ordered by LtCol Kersher. This would be the longest foot patrol so far into East Beirut. It would cover nine miles. We marked our route and circled checkpoints in grease pencil on our maps. We would be passing through a disputed part of the city, which contains token elements of Israeli defense forces. Capt Jones said he would be going along and said I could too if I wanted to.

"Yes sir," I answered, shocked because I had requested to go out with my squad's patrol before and had been refused.

The weather was crisp outside as we left the CP to get extra ammo and gear.

A little later, Cpl Andrews checked his squad over, then looked over at Sgt Johnson and asked, "Sarge, your gun team ready?"

"You bet," answered Sgt Johnson.

Then Cpl Andrews looked at me and then to Capt Jones and asked, "Ready sir?"

"It's your show corporal. The Gunner and I are just going along for the walk," answered Capt Jones.

Taking a deep breath, Cpl Andrews shouted, "Move out!"

Once again, a Marine patrol was extending its presence outside of our perimeter and into the factionally divided eastern part of the city.

A little US flag fluttered from the top of the radioman's antenna as the patrol moved uphill.

Soon, we passed through the first roadblock, then across a main road used by the Israeli defense forces to support troops remaining in Lebanon. Nearby, Christian militiamen glared at us as we passed.

As we moved, Cpl West carrying the machinegun was impressed with the militia's bearing saying, "Man these guys look like they know what they're doing."

"Yeah if anything's going to happen on this patrol it should've been then," muttered Sgt Johnson.

Cpl Andrews stepped to the middle of the muddy shell-cratered road and waved for the squad to spread out.

Two miles later, we passed our first checkpoint and the radioman called it in to our company CP where Lt Littleton was monitoring our progress. Then we started the climb up into the mountains. Cpl Andrews stayed near his point fire team constantly checking his map as they led the patrol through the twisting narrow side streets. I could tell he was excited. The civilians we had met seemed friendly enough. But every time the point man rounded a corner, I could see Cpl Andrews tense up. Sweat ran in streams down my face as we moved upward. None of us knew what to expect.

Further back, Cpl West cautiously scanned the buildings and alleyways.

At our next checkpoint we passed a five-man Lebanese Army squad manning a 50 cal machinegun mounted on an armored personnel carrier. They waved smiling happily at us.

At the top of the mountain was another checkpoint. Here Cpl Andrews halted the patrol for chow. I sat down next to Capt Jones and asked, "Skipper what are you doing out here on a squad size patrol?"

"Colonel Kersher ordered me to go so I could brief the other company commanders what's up here when they send their patrols," answered Capt Jones.

"And why couldn't Corporal Andrews brief your company commanders when he returned?"

He just looked at me with a disgusted look and I smiled saying, "Sorry sir, I lost my head. So how come you let me come along?"

"Well after refusing to let you go out earlier, I knew you'd have a fit if you couldn't go on this one," said Capt Jones smiling.

Nearby, Cpl West slowly stretched to massage his aching feet through dusty combat boots with his black hands and said, "Most of these people are a lot friendlier than I thought they'd be."

"Yeah," said Sgt Johnson as he waved at a carload of children passing by.

After Cpl West had changed his socks, he leaned back on a pile of rocks and said, "These can't be my feet. At least they don't feel like the ones I started out with."

"They're yours all right. Ain't nobody got feet that ugly but you," said Sgt Johnson laughing.

After half an hour, Cpl Andrews yelled, "Saddle up!" Soon the patrol had turned around and started back toward the airport.

As we moved down the opposite side of the mountain, Sgt Johnson laughed saying, "Look at the bright side Corporal West, the rest of the patrol is all downhill."

I was tired by the time we passed through the Christian roadblock. But I noticed a change in their attitudes. This time the green uniformed militiamen smiled and one of them even waved saying, "Hello."

"Shit, them dudes don't seem half as bad as they did the first time," said Cpl West.

After we had passed into my platoon area, Capt Jones said, "Corporal Andrews you ran this patrol in fine style."

Then we walked to the shower tents at the old airport parking lot among the trucks and jeeps. As we neared the two shower tents, I was glad to see steam rising from them, which meant there was still hot water. In the hot shower we washed away the Beirut dust and sweat. Then the squad and machinegun team returned to their tents to rest as I went to check on the rest of my platoon.

The night of March 17th, Cpl Bower of 3rd platoon was checking a Marine sentry when a sniper fired on him. The bullet ripped off the left leg cargo pocket of his camouflaged trousers. Thinking his fire team leader had been wounded, the sentry returned fire in the direction of the muzzle flash with unknown results. This was the first time a sentry had done this.

At 1300 the next day, I heard a low distant sound like thunder. But after eighteen years in the Corps I knew it wasn't. But with all the artillery rounds exploding daily in the hills and mountains above

Beirut I still didn't think anything of it.

Within half an hour, I heard the report that the American embassy had been bombed by a terrorist driving a van into it. Later I would hear the van had been stolen from the embassy a year ago and was carrying 2,000 pounds of explosives, which had driven past the sleeping Lebanese guard crashing into the embassy stopping in the lobby where it exploded. The blast tore through the front portion of the seven-story embassy causing the eight-story building to fall like a house of cards. Sixty-three occupants were killed of which one was Lebanese and the rest Americans. Another 130 people were wounded. A Marine embassy guard corporal standing duty behind a bulletproof glass booth in the main lobby was among the dead. It would be two days before his body would be dug out. His fellow Marine embassy guards draped him in an American flag and carried him away on a stretcher. Capt Graham's Lima Company was rushed to the embassy grounds in full combat gear. They searched the area for classified documents. Later GySgt Fisher would tell GySgt Knight his Marines found legs and chunks of flesh in the rubble.

A symbol of our determination to stay, became the US flag flying outside the bombed-out embassy on a makeshift metal flagpole set up by the Marine embassy guards.

The initial reaction from the men of my platoon was great anger. As SSgt Tapper said, "How dare anyone strike our embassy!"

I also felt the frustration because it seemed we weren't being allowed to do anything about it. I felt we should bring in a second battalion and go out and take the high ground.

After this, my young Marines seemed to begin to realize they could die here. They suddenly had to deal with their own mortality and it seemed overnight they grew older.

We all realized just how much the political and military situation had deteriorated.

On March 19th, Lebanese soldiers at a checkpoint near Capt Scotto's Kilo Company opened fire at a civilian car that had failed to stop at their order. Marines nearby dived for cover with rifles, machineguns and grenade launchers at the ready as the car spun around in the middle of the road and returned the way it had come.

The next morning at our battalion officers call, LtCol Kersher told us of the new change to the rules of engagement. As of now we could open fire if we even perceived the threat of hostile intent.

At 0220 in the early morning of March 21st, Sgt Meadows squad was manning my platoon's checkpoint when he noticed a car turn toward our barbed wire barrier in front of our checkpoint. As the car speeded up, he yelled, "Halt or I'll shoot!"

Still the car came on. He fired three warning shots just over the top of the car, one of which was a tracer. When this didn't slow the car down, he lowered his aim and fired three bullets into the hood forcing the car off the road. At this, Lebanese soldiers ran out from their checkpoint and pulled two plainly drunken men from the car and turned them over to the Lebanese police. Later I would learn that one of the drunks was a Syrian with a fake Lebanese identification card.

As the Beirut environment worsened, Col Studt ordered more barriers built, sentries doubled at all posts and all vehicles were to be detail-searched before they were permitted to enter our lines. I sure felt better when he ordered our battalion's tanks and artillery to come ashore to support us line troops.

By now the fighting between the Christian Lebanese, the Lebanese Army and the Muslim Druze had spilled over into Beirut in the form of artillery bombardments and rocket attacks.

On March 23rd, when French positions were attacked, Col Studt put our artillery, mortars, cobra gunships on alert and requested possible naval gunfire support. As Col Studt flew back from a ship in a Huey command chopper, it was hit by a three-round burst from a machinegun.

Artillery shells hit the French positions until around 1330. After 1430 Col Studt called off the alert.

There were intelligence reports that Druze artillery would hit us the next day. Early the next morning Col Studt put all MAU artillery, mortars and naval guns on alert. During the morning, enemy artillery and rockets did hit in the French and Italian sectors. At 1450, five artillery rounds flew over our head exploding out in the ocean, followed by two rounds exploding near the beach.

It seemed we were becoming less and less welcome to many of Beirut's poorer residents, especially the Shiite Muslims who lived close to the airport. Even my squad leaders returning from their patrols reported they could feel the change.

Cpl Andrew's squad was up for a mobile patrol again and SSgt Tapper assigned Sgt Johnson's machinegun team to go along. I requested to Capt Jones to go with them and I was surprised he agreed to let me go.

We were well into town when suddenly we were forced to stop in a large, formless traffic jam. I looked around for an exit our four jeeps could take when the street suddenly filled with heavily armed Christian gunmen. Slowly, I moved the bolt back on my M-16 rifle chambering a round. At hearing or seeing what I had done the other three Marines in my jeep with me did the same.

I was truly relieved when the Christian gunmen in khaki tiger-striped uniforms passed along side of our column of jeeps without paying any attention to us.

Then a Christian gunman walked up to me and said in English, "I will clear a path through for you."

"Thank you," I said.

Then with a lot of yelling, waving of his arms and pointing his pistol, he helped us move on passed the accident, a head on collision, which had caused the traffic jam.

We had no more than gotten clear when Cpl Andrews stopped the patrol and yelled back to me, "Sir the captain just called on the radio. It seems an Israeli tank and APC has crossed into the battalion boundary and is heading directly for the battalion lines. We're ordered to go on full alert and to head back and try and cut them off."

"Shit! Okay corporal, have your squad and the gun team lock and load," I answered. I then had my driver drive around to the front of the squad and led the way back.

We caught up with the Israeli tank and armored personnel carrier just a block away from our battalion lines. My driver raced around the personnel carrier and tank and skidded to a stop in front of the tank. The tank stopped as I jumped out of my jeep and looked up at the Israeli tank commander and said, "Don't you know you're not supposed to be here?"

The Israeli tank commander said, "I know about the agreement. I just wanted to take a picture of an American Marine."

Surprised I looked hard at him. When he didn't smile, I said, "Okay take my picture and get back where you belong."

He pulled a camera up out of the turret and snapped my picture. Then the tank turned around and the personnel carrier followed.

I climbed back into my jeep shaking my head and said, "I don't believe this place!"

Then I turned the patrol back over to Cpl Andrews and we returned to our patrol route.

Almost each night Marines on watch at the checkpoints watched Israeli patrols pass nearby. But one night, the call went out from Cpl Mitchell at 2nd platoon's checkpoint, "Sergeant of the guard!"

Sgt Wise ran out toward him.

Lt Wright was sound asleep in his tent when Cpl McAllister shook him saying, "Sir, sir, they're up there with weapons and they're laughing. Sir, it don't sound good!"

Lt Wright sat up rubbing his eyes asking, "Who's laughing. What the shit is going on?"

"The Israelis, sir. They're at the checkpoint."

Lt Wright quickly pulled his boots on without tying them, grabbed his 45-cal pistol and ran out of the tent. As he neared the checkpoint, he could see Sgt Wise with his M-16 rifle at the ready with Cpl Mitchell's fire team confronting eleven Israeli soldiers.

"What's going on here?" asked Lt Wright as he ran up.

Sgt Wise explained saying, "These here Israelis are demanding to enter our lines."

At seeing Lt Wright, the Israeli leader stepped closer saying, "I'm certain we are well within our patrol area."

"This is not your area and you can't go through here," said Lt Wright.

"And why not?"

"Because this is the US Marine perimeter and you don't belong here. Now take your men and get out of here before somebody gets hurt."

"Okay I have to agree," said the Israeli leader and he turned his patrol around and left.

Lt Wright returned to his tent and had no more than sat down on his cot when he heard, "Halt! Who goes there?"

Again, Lt Wright swung on his flak jacket, grabbing his pistol and ran back out. He heard Cpl Mitchell yell, "You fucking guys better stop fucking with me or I'm going to fuck you up!"

The laughing Israeli leader saw Lt Wright and said, "We became lost. Can we please pass through your sector to take a short cut back to our lines?"

"Get the fuck out 'a my sight before I forget you're an ally!"

yelled Lt Wright. He then placed his whole platoon on full alert. After the Israelis left and didn't return, he relaxed the alert at 0240 the next morning.

But scattered small arms fire continued through the early morning as stray bullets hit within our battalion positions.

That afternoon as Lt Wright's platoon placed more trip flares and noisemakers along their front, they stopped to watch an Israeli mechanized patrol shoot up cars and buildings near the road. And still, bullets, rockets and mortar rounds fired at the Israelis, hit within our battalion perimeter.

At 1447 a bullet hit inside Capt Evans India Company within SSgt Spidden's platoon positions. A few minutes later several bullets hit behind the positions of Capt Graham's Lima Company.

At 1455 Col Studt put our artillery and mortars on alert when our battalion began taking scattered artillery shells and rockets. This shelling and rocketing continued on into March 26th with the majority of the shelling landing close to our battalion lines.

The next day the governments of Lebanon and Israel signed a withdrawal agreement at the urging of the US Government. But Syria rejected the withdrawal plan.

On March 28th, Commandant Barrow made a farewell visit prior to his announced retirement coming up in July. He visited every position within the MAU and presented Purple Hearts.

The next day Congressmen William Gray and Stephen Solorz visited our battalion.

By now the battalion had received reports of stepped up activity within the Syrian controlled Bekaa Valley. There was even reports of Libyan military units moving into the valley.

Meanwhile, the different factions in Beirut were shooting at each other with us having a ringside seat. We prepared for anything, as the firing got heavy at times. A lot of artillery rounds passed overhead.

Attacks on the Israeli defense forces increased as the anniversary of the Israeli invasion neared. As our patrols moved through the streets of Beirut, the Marines began to feel like moving targets. But still they liked the patrols because most of the people were friendly. The little kids, even the Shiite kids, would run up waving and smiling when they saw the American flag on the Marine shoulders. Even the eyes of the older Lebanese seemed to light up with pleasure.

But the squad leaders had to keep their men on their toes. They just didn't know what might happen or when. They were always worried about a terrorist attack by rifle fire, grenade, booby trap or car bomb.

We heard shelling in the distance as stray small arms rounds often fell within our perimeter.

On the 1st of April, Cpl Andrews squad was out on patrol when a Lebanese lady ran up to him and asked him to kiss her baby. Red faced he did so and the patrol moved on.

The next day Col Studt hosted and briefed Congressmen Thomas Faglietta, Peter Kostmayer and Theodore Weiss.

I had become sick of all these constant dog and pony shows we had to put on because of all the VIPs visiting our battalion. Lord help me if one of my men were caught scratching his ass, picking his nose or if a piece of trash should be found by a VIP within a hundred meters of my platoon positions.

We began noticing that young men seemed to be returning to Hooterville. But with their arrival we began seeing pictures of Ayatollah Khomeini plastered on nearby buildings.

On April 4th Assistant Secretary of the Navy Chapmen Cox visited our battalion.

Meanwhile, Cpl Andrew's squad was on patrol again with Sgt Johnson's machinegun team in support. The patrol went well until they passed half a dozen teenagers standing on a corner. One of these Lebanese teens said, "Look Americans." Then he finished the sentence in Arabic. Then the teen ran up and grabbed Cpl West's arm. Sgt Johnson stepped forward grabbing the teen with his left hand and spun him around. With his right fist he knocked the kid down.

About the same time, Capt Scotto was with one of his squads from Kilo Company on a mobile patrol through Hooterville. Suddenly, he realized a young boy standing in the shadows of a narrow street had tossed something into his jeep. Capt Scotto and the other three Marines instantly dived out of the jeep to the street rolling for cover. The jeep slowed down and bumped off the street into a stonewall of a house. As a Marine slowly walked over to the jeep he found the object was an empty coke can and he held it up smiling. Around the patrol the Lebanese civilians burst into laughter too. Red-faced, Capt Scotto climbed back into the jeep and the patrol went on.

In the afternoon, Lt Wright of 2nd platoon went along on a jeep patrol with Sgt Crew's squad and Sgt Rienbold's machinegun team as support. Suddenly they saw a crowd of civilians running toward them up the street yelling and crying.

Fearing danger, Sgt Crew yelled over the squad radio, "Out 'a the jeeps and take cover!"

Immediately the squad jumped clear of their jeeps running behind a knee-high stonewall next to the road. Quickly Sgt Rienbold's machinegun team set up the gun as the squad's rifles and grenade launchers were aimed across the top of the wall. As the civilian mass ran up closer the air seemed to grow thick with tension. Suddenly the mob stopped. A white dressed Lebanese lady slowly stepped out front and yelled, "No shoot! No shoot! Is only wedding. Me bride with new husband and wedding party and neighbors."

Sgt Crew had been kneeling and now stood up smiling as he said, "Okay you can pass on."

Although looking sheepish, the Marines still stayed at the ready as the wedding party passed, still fearful of some kind of an ambush.

As the jeep patrol moved on, kids thirteen or younger ran along following. Some of them tried to sell the Marines sodas. While other kids seemed to be testing the Marines reflexes by tossing rocks or soda cans into the jeeps as well as food.

"These little shits remind me of a bunch of rock apes in Nam," muttered Sgt Crew.

Then Cpl Poplas was hit on the helmet by a stone thrown by a kid standing in a group of kids as the jeep passed by. He jumped out of the moving jeep and chased the kid until he caught him. He grabbed the kid by the throat with one hand and drew back his other fist to hit him. But from behind him Lt Wright ran up and grabbed Cpl Poplas up raised fist saying, "He's just a kid corporal."

Cpl Poplas looked back at Lt Wright and let the kid go. As they walked back to their jeeps the rest of the patrol had locked and loaded their weapons as they covered them watching the rooftops and windows along the narrow street.

As they walked up to Sgt Crew, Lt Wright said, "Just a dumb kid having fun."

"Sir, in Nam kids younger than him killed Marines," said Sgt

Crew.

Another kid standing nearby yelled, "Khomeini good! America no good!"

As the three returned to their jeeps, a kid ran up and punched Cpl Poplas in the back. Then a teenager ran out of the crowd and stood between Sgt Crew and his jeep. Sgt Crew walked right up to the teen, and then hit him in the face knocking him down. He then stepped over the teen and climbed into his jeep.

A little later, a young boy pointed a real looking cap pistol at the passing patrol. Almost the whole squad took aim at the boy, as Sgt Crew yelled, "Don't fire! It's just a toy."

Lt Wright thanked God for the older Vietnam veteran who quickly realized the toy wasn't real. He still worried that some jumpy Marine might end up killing a kid because of their childish actions.

Sgt Crew also noticed that the local civilians were giving them less and less fruit, cakes and cool drinks as they passed.

As the area outside our lines became increasingly hostile our battalion was now sending out four to seven patrols a day.

On April 5th at 0030 Cpl Poplas' fire team of 2nd platoon had been on watch for half an hour. The morning was deathly quiet when suddenly a RPG was fired at a passing Israeli patrol.

At the sound of the explosion the rest of Mike Company rolled off their cots and headed for their fighting positions. Within minutes, a second RPG was fired which drew Israeli 50-cal machinegun fire in a 360-degree circle. Several of the large bullets ripped through Mike Company sandbags behind which we crouched in a cold sweat. This gunfire went on for ten minutes. Then the Israelis fired illumination rounds, some of which landed within 75 meters of our company positions. The next morning SSgt Tapper had the Marines of my platoon again work hard on improving our fighting positions. On April 8th, Lebanese Army fire teams started going out on some of the patrols with the Marines.

The next day the Israelis responding to hostile small arms fire again caused rounds to land within Capt Evans' India Company.

There were rumors going around of a possible expansion of Marine operations after the Israelis withdraw. Rumor had it the MAU might expand to brigade size, which would mean our whole regiment would come in with a full Air Group.

By April 10th, Marine volunteers working in their free time had built a playground for the local Shiite school children using donated materials.

The next few days were quiet days for us. But it was the quiet before the storm.

On April 13th, the Beirut area suffered bombardments as anti-government forces protested Lebanese President Amin Gemayel's visit to the US. It seemed only a matter of time before we got drawn into the conflict erupting around us.

The next day the Israeli cabinet authorized a partial withdrawal of their forces to the Awali River south of Beirut.

The same day a car bomb exploded next to a seaside resort hotel. A RPG knocked out the Lebanese satellite receiving station, which stopped the live coverage of President Gemayel's visit to the US. Midmorning of April 17th started a ten-hour bombardment of a Lebanese Army camp and Christian neighborhoods as Christian and Druse fought in the hills overlooking Beirut.

At 2130, I was checking my men as they watched the hills toward the east light up and then we heard the crash of artillery shells start to hit closer to us. It seemed to be spill over, intended for the Israelis as shells hit within Capt Evans' India Company. I ran back to my platoon CP where I found my radioman listening to the battalion net hoping to find out what was going on.

"Shit! Somebody is telling Capt'n Evans he has three men wounded," said the radioman.

Rockets and mortars exploded inside our battalion lines within Capt Graham's Lima Company.

"Capt'n Graham says a rocket just blew up a civilian grocery truck delivering goods to the battalion," said the radioman.

"Staff Sergeant Tapper, go back to the houses and make sure the whole platoon is on line with helmets, flak jackets and weapons loaded," I ordered.

"Yes sir," answered SSgt Tapper as he ran out.

More rockets exploded in Capt Evans company area.

In 15 minutes, eleven rockets and mortars had hit within the MAU compound. For the first time, Col Studt put the whole MAU on Condition One alert which is our highest state of alert which means the battalion should be prepared to defend against an all-out attack.

"All right! Colonel Kersher just ordered the battalion arty to return fire," said my radioman.

"Get some, arty!" yelled Cpl West.

My platoon watched anxiously as more rounds exploded within Capt Graham's Lima Company lines.

"Shit! Damn. Colonel Studt just radioed Colonel Kersher ordering him not to return fire with arty," said my radioman. Then he adds, "Colonel Kersher is cursing over the radio. He says the rules of engagement clearly state we can defend ourselves. Colonel Studt says his hands are tied. Colonel Kersher wants to know how the hell he can protect his men? Colonel Studt is telling him to fire illume up there instead. At least they'll know we have their range and we can hit them if we want to."

The area around the Marine artillery flashed as they opened fire. The Marines along the line cheered as they waited for the explosions up in the hills after the outgoing shells roared overhead.

But then instead of explosions, they heard the whoop, whoop, whoop sound of illumination canisters falling to the ground as the flares burst into light hanging from parachutes.

Up on the line Sgt Schwartz yelled, "What the fuck is this shit?" Cpl Wynne hit the sandbag wall with his fist saying, "What the fuck is going on here. If we can't fight back, then let's get the fuck out 'a here."

"Yeah if they don't want us to fight, then they should replace us with the Army," muttered Sgt Schwartz.

Finally, the artillery shells and rockets suddenly stopped hitting our battalion area. It was deathly silent except for the barking of a frightened dog. Cpl Andrews yelled, "Shut up!" The rest of the night passed quietly.

But the next day the airport was hit by rockets for ten hours.

The same day, Sgt Wise from 2nd platoon went out on patrol with his squad supported by Sgt Johnson's machinegun team. Most of the civilians still waved hello, but a few gave them the finger. Increasingly they were being harassed by civilians. One such civilian walked up to Sgt Wise and hit him in the chest. Controlling his anger, he just pushed the man away from him. A little later, Cpl McAllister's point fire team turned a corner as three armed Muslims stood on the next corner. At seeing the Marines, all three Muslims swung their rifles firing short burst at the Marines as they dived for cover. Then they disappeared around the corner as the Marines returned fire.

It seemed the situation in Lebanon was deteriorating quickly. Not taking any chances, I now slept with a full magazine in my rifle. But being an officer of Marines and being over here serving my country still gave me a sense of pride. I guess some people just can't understand that.

On April 19th, Adm Martin and Army Gen Vessey visited our battalion.

By now, the fierce fighting between the Lebanese Army and Muslim militiamen had turned Beirut into exploding shells, machinegun and sniper fire. Artillery shells fired from the mountains to the east exploded throughout both the Christian and Muslim sections of the city as the Lebanese Army units met stiff resistance in trying to gain control of the Shiite Muslim neighborhoods in South Beirut.

Hostile fire against our battalion had also picked up in the form of car bombs and sniper fire.

Marine foot patrols still went out and as before they were long and hot, usually following roads and sometimes into parts of downtown Beirut. Marine squads were now allowed to carry LAAW's. To me these patrols were more dangerous than the patrols I went on in Vietnam because these were in the close confines of a city. The biggest problem, just like Vietnam, was the boredom of the patrols. Squad leaders had to keep their men alert to stay alive. And there was always fighting going on around them. The worst thing was the fact that almost everyone in Beirut was armed, unlike the civilians in Vietnam. The fighting around us increased and at times bullets passed close over our heads.

I was proud of my platoon. They knew why we were here, they, like me, believe we are doing the right thing and they want to be here. But that was the way I had felt in Vietnam also.

On April 21st, Senator Robert Kosten seemed to just appear from nowhere when he visited my platoon. We hadn't been told he was even in the area.

That night two rockets hit the airport.

At 0525 on April 23rd, SSgt Tapper was walking back from our battalion CP when he heard two explosions near the Lebanese grenade range north of the battalion compound. He ignored the explosions as he walked past Mike Company's CP, when he heard two more explosions, he thought they were grenades on the grenade range. He was thinking, "Man the Leb's have started early today." But as he reached my platoon CP, we distinctly heard rockets being fired from the hills beyond the battalion lines.

Suddenly, Capt Evans' India Company was caught in a crossfire of mortar and rocket fire wounding a lieutenant sitting in a six-hole shitter.

Meanwhile, at Mike Company, Capt Jones was at the company mortar pit talking with SSgt Simon when a rocket exploded less than 200 meters away.

At 0630, the MAU headquarters came under rocket attack.

As usual the Marines of my platoon showed courage and calmness mixed with a sense of humor under bombardment. But like me, they were frustrated at not being allowed to return fire because of our so-called non-combative peacekeeping role. Then I got a radio call from Capt Jones telling me that LtCol Kersher had put the battalion on Condition One, the highest state of alert. And that all hands were ordered to get into bunkers with overhead protection. As if any of us on the line had to be told to take cover. We were ready and waiting.

Within the next half hour, twenty-seven rockets exploded within our MAU compound. One rocket made a direct hit on our battalion CP control tower.

By 0725, battalion had located the rocket launching sites. Listening over the radio, I heard Maj Hays order the first fire mission to the mortar sections. In Mike Company's mortar pits, SSgt Simon watched his mortar crews break out the illumination shells and start dropping them down the mortar tubes.

"I can't fucking believe we're still ordered to only fire illume. Big fucking deal, we're giving those assholes a warning. We know where you are and if you don't cease fire, we have the power to take you out," grumbled SSgt Simon.

But after firing only four illumination shells over their heads, the enemy firing stopped. SSgt Simon, as did I, wondered just how long this would work.

Even this was still a big boost to moral for my Marines who for the most part had been forced to stay in their bunkers and take the so-called random shelling of our positions.

A sign was put up at the battalion club, which said, "Can't Shoot Back Saloon." But it would soon be changed to, "Can Shoot Back Saloon."

Still the seriousness of the situation had not registered on some of the young Marines despite several of their buddies suffering wounds. And still the order of the day was visibility, as Marine squads went on foot and mobile patrols.

On Sundays, our battalion still had barbecues back at LtCol Kersher's CP. Although we had stopped exercising as units you could still see individuals running in the rear areas in PT uniforms. But it now was a common occurrence to have Sunday afternoons interrupted by gunfire.

The Israeli forces had started turning over a number of their checkpoints in East Beirut to the Lebanese Army. But local warlords were moving their militia forces into this power vacuum created by these Israeli withdrawals. And with anticipating the main Israeli withdrawal, the fighting escalated between the Druze and Christians and also between the Druze and the Lebanese Army who was also fighting with Pro-Khomeini Amal militia.

I knew that not all these rounds hitting within our battalion lines were accidents, but were on purpose. Also, spill-over fire landed on our Marine squadron terminal wounding one Marine.
Fighting in the hills and within the city grew worse, as isolated shells landed in our battalion area. By now the French, British and Italian forces were all taking small arms and mortar fire.

On April 25th, our new Marine Corps Commandant Kelly and new Sergeant Major of the Marine Corps, SgtMaj Cleary visited our MAU. Gen Kelly talked of his pride in the good things that he was hearing about our performance here. I remembered him from Vietnam. Back then he was a colonel commanding a regiment. He was known as the Good Humor Man because he used to bring ice cream out to his troops in the jungle.

The next day Congressmen Clarence Lang, Lawrence Coughlin, Williams Lehman, Marty Russo, John Porter, Richard Lehman and Secretary of the Navy John Lehman visited our battalion. Secretary Lehman told us that the world expected our presence here to be a factor in resolving Lebanon's conflict. That we were making a meaningful contribution toward peace in the Middle East.
But still, the fighting in Beirut continued to escalate as the roar of

heavy fighting grew between the Lebanese Army and the militia. The fighting was becoming very bad near the airport. The small arms fire was like rapid fire on the rifle range with mortars and rockets landing just beyond our positions. A Marine checkpoint in Capt Scotto's Kilo Company and another in Lt Cregar's platoon was fired on. Marines from both units returned fire until the enemy fire stopped.

It had become easy for the young Marines to tell deliberate attacks on us from stray rounds that were just passing overhead. Before sunup on Sunday April 28th, street fighting started in Beirut's southern suburbs between rival religious factions and grew until it spilled over into our battalion compound.

In the afternoon, I went out on patrol with Sgt Schwartz's squad, supported by Sgt Johnson's machinegun team. As we moved through the streets, I noticed that the city was too quiet. Even the traffic was unusually light for a Sunday, which is a Muslim workday. There wasn't even the usual number of civilians on the streets. Some of the civilians walked close to us warning, "There's going to be a fight." At times civilians seemed to run in all directions along the narrow streets, including young men carrying rifles, machineguns and RPG's. The farther our patrol went, the more frantic the civilians seemed to be. When we turned around heading back, the hair stubble on the back of my neck stood up just as it had in Vietnam when I felt danger was near.

Finally, at 1600, the patrol left the town crossing the open field back to Mike Company's lines. Then we heard nine mortar rounds pass overhead toward a Lebanese position near the airport.

Without orders, the squad instinctively spread out across the field as Sgt Johnson's machinegun team set up waiting to see what was going to happen. When nothing happened near us, Sgt Schwartz quickly moved the patrol back into our platoon's positions.

Down the company line, Lt Wright and Lt Cregar had stood watching my patrol re-enter our lines. They were still talking when they heard several bullets crack overhead.

"I think someone is shooting at us," said Lt Wright.

"No way," said Lt Cregar laughing.

Then they heard several more bullets crack overhead and Lt Wright said, "Damn it I know they're shooting at us."

"No, it's nothing. No problem GI," said Lt Cregar still laughing.

Lt Wright looked over to 2nd platoon and they had all taken cover.

Two bullets hit the sandbagged wall in front of both lieutenants and they dropped, as one, behind it.

"Christ they are shooting at us!" shouted Lt Cregar.

"No shit Sherlock!" muttered Lt Wright.

Then I heard bullets popping just over our heads. Quickly, the rest of the platoon ran from our houses up to the line putting on helmets and flak jackets. Over the radio, Capt Jones ordered Mike Company into their bunkers and on full alert.

At 1705, bullets even slammed into the dirt near the press bunker just outside of our MAU headquarters. A little later, we heard the siren sound the Condition I alert.

My men and I laid low for half an hour as the intensity of the incoming fire grew. Over the radio, my radioman heard Lt Cregar of 3rd platoon call Capt Jones saying, "Sir we have to return fire.

You can no longer deny it.'

There was a long pause before Capt Jones answered, "Return fire."

Before he could tell us what was said, we heard 3rd platoon open up with a roar. Even with this, the firefight still lasted into the night. Mortar, rockets and rifle fire passed over our heads. Many bullets hit our dirt berms and sandbags. The disciplined Marines took it for hours as the volume of unanswered fire rose, except for 3rd platoon. Then one after the other we platoon leaders requested permission to return fire. At my request, Capt Jones granted permission for me to pick designated men to return fire only if we had clear targets that were actually initiating or shooting at us. Our return fire was not to spill over into civilian targets.

When I explained this to SSgt Tapper he asked, "How in the hell can we stop that?"

"The squad leaders, you and I will have to closely supervise. We have to prove we have the will and the ability to dominate this battlefield. I want each squad leader to have several men fire at each confirmed target," I answered.

But it became very hard to spot the Muslim fighters who had survived eight years of fighting already. They fired through open windows two or three houses back from the line of houses facing us. It became extremely hard for the squad leaders to confirm even the sighting of clear targets and only the close supervision by SSgt Tapper and I held the platoon from returning fire wholesale just from pure frustration.

Only SSgt Tapper, Sgts Meadows, Schwartz and I out of 1st platoon had ever fired at a live target before. And like us years before these young Marines were surprised at the rush of power, danger and fear of firing at armed men and having them fire back. Luckily, the Muslim militiamen's marksmanship wasn't very good. Finally, after 0200 the next morning, the firing slowed up and stopped altogether. Soon after, the Condition I alert was lifted and I let three men out of each fire team get some sleep.

But at 0400, light gunfire started up again waking everybody up. The fighting increased at 0700 as a Lebanese Army unit landed by choppers at the airport. A Lebanese officer walked over to Capt Jones' bunker. Meanwhile, artillery shells, mortars, 106 recoilless rifle shells and rockets started to land on the battalion lines and at the Lebanese unit behind us. The enemy fire even got worse as the Lebanese company moved through our lines toward Hooterville on their way to reinforce the Lebanese unit already fighting with the Shiite militia.

At 0730, the level of small arms fire steadily increased as Lt Littleton radioed each platoon ordering us to bring all our troops into the bunkers and trenches. The incoming fire throughout Mike Company suddenly intensified at around 0800. Still my squad leaders kept leaving cover to check on their men.

At Mike Company's CP, every time Capt Jones or Lt Littleton tried to look over their sandbag wall, they drew fire.

"It's a good thing these assholes are shooting high," said Lt Littleton.

"Keep your head down anyway," said Capt Jones.

"I can't believe this shit," said Lt Littleton.

Since we weren't allowed to fire at gunman who were not actually firing their weapons at us, we had to watch groups of Muslim fighters walk with weapons slung over their shoulders into houses or bunkers in front of our positions. We knew these men would fire at us later until they ran out of ammo or just get bored. Then they would just sling their weapons over their shoulders and walk out in plain view and leave. Sometimes the Muslim militiamen in the open would laugh pointing his finger at us yelling, "Bang,

bang!" The only answer we were allowed to give them was our middle finger.

The gunfire grew at 0900 even with the whole battalion returning fire. In Lima Company Capt Graham and GySgt Fisher left their CP and split up checking their company trenches and bunkers.

Capt Graham ran up to his forward positions to get a closer view of Hooterville. He saw a militiaman stand up on top of a house in full view and fire a RPG round that exploded in the road in front of Lima Company positions. He radioed LtCol Kersher requesting permission to call in artillery fire on the house. As he waited for the answer a mortar shell exploded about 100 meters in front of him. Capt Graham also requested artillery fire on the Shiite gunmen in Hooterville. At 0915, a mortar shell exploded behind his position. He ducked down as shock waves passed over him. Another shell exploded in the open field between his 2nd and 1st platoons. The next shell hit farther east and closer to his 3rd platoon. He radioed battalion telling LtCol Kersher that mortars were being walked straight toward his CP. With his many years as an Infantryman, an enlisted man and officer he held his breath watching the mortar shells walk across his area as he waited for an answer.

Meanwhile, GySgt Fisher checked Lima Company lines during a hailstorm of rocket and mortar fire.

At 0940, LtCol Kersher again ordered the battalion mortar crews to fire illumination shells over the heads of the Shiite militiamen as a warning.

Just minutes later several shells landed on Lima Companies 1st platoon killing one Marine and wounding four others.

When Capt Graham, enraged, reported this, LtCol Kersher ordered the battalion artillery to return fire with HE (high explosives). Shells were hitting all along the battalion lines by now. Suddenly, Marine artillery opened up on the Shiite batteries. But by 0945 shells were still hitting the airport area at a rate of six to eight a minute.

Capt Graham watched his men crouching low behind their waist high sandbag walls, returning fire with M-16 rifles, machineguns and grenade launchers.

GySgt Fisher was checking on 1st platoon's casualties when he also found that their radio batteries were running low. He ran to the platoon CP tent to get fresh ones.

Capt Graham looked back in time to see GySgt Fisher enter the 1st platoon CP tent followed by Gunner Williams from battalion. He wondered what the gunner was doing up here. Suddenly, two rockets roared in. One rocket exploded just to the left outside of the sandbagged wall surrounding the 1st platoon CP tent. The next rocket made a direct hit in the center of the tent.

"Corpsman up!" yelled Capt Graham running toward the shredded tent.

Outside the tent he saw a young corporal sitting with blood running down his head and left arm. As Capt Graham passed him, he heard other Marines moaning in pain. A corpsman ran up and dropped down next to the corporal quickly checking him over and opening his first aid pouch. First, he patched up the cut on his head saying, "You're not badly hit. You'll be fine." The corporal sighed with relief.

Another Corpsman found five bleeding Marines lying in the open, patching each other's wounds. He checked them quickly, but found none of them were bad.

Meanwhile, Capt Graham stepped through a large rip in the shredded tent finding Gunner Williams and GySgt Fisher lying on the ground. He found the smell of blood to be just as awful as he had remembered from Vietnam. He knew GySgt Fisher was dead from the bloody head and neck wounds. A corpsman ran past him to Gunner Williams who was alive, but also had many head wounds and a deep cut in his right leg. Quickly, he checked the wounds of the unconscious gunner. Capt Graham helped the corpsman carry him to the aid bunker.

LtCol Kersher knew mortars and rockets had been hitting Lima Company especially hard. He had wanted to know about the casualties. After having trouble with the radios, he had sent Gunner Williams to find out what was going on. Finally, Maj Hays had managed to get through to Lima Company over the radio and had asked to speak to Whiskey Oscar Whiskey (Warrant Officer Williams).

SSgt Campbell came on the radio saying, "Be advised that Whiskey Oscar Whiskey is a WIA and Echo Seven Foxtrot (GySgt Fisher) is KIA."

When my radioman passed this news on to me, I just shook my

head. I felt like my heart was in my throat. GySgt Fisher had survived three tours in Vietnam just to die here. "And for what?" I thought, fighting back tears of rage.

Meanwhile, in disbelief Maj Hays grabbed a corpsman and driver and drove his jeep toward Lima Company bouncing at top speed as mortars still hit nearby. Within minutes, he saw the destroyed tent and drove up to it. Jumping out of the jeep, he ran into the shattered tent and found the body of GySgt Fisher. Learning Gunner Williams was at the aid bunker, they put GySgt Fisher's body in the back of the jeep and drove to the aid bunker as more wounded were being brought in. Maj Hays walked in finding Marines patching up each other as two corpsmen worked over Gunner Williams. The corpsman with Maj Hays started working on the other Marines.

Outside three amtracks roared up to the aid bunker in a column.

Gunner Williams was carried onto the first amtrack as the corporal and the other wounded went on the second. Two Marines carried GySgt Fisher's body on a stretcher covered with a green blanket onto the third amtrack.

I watched the amtracks moving back across the area toward our battalion CP building. My men around me were tense and quiet. It was like this suddenly had changed their whole perspective. They forgot about home and only wanted to attack up into them damn mountains and do what they had been trained to do. By now there was no doubt left in anybody's mind just how serious this mission had become.

Later over the radio, my radioman heard that Gunner Williams had been flown out to the USS Iwo Jima.

Meanwhile, the overhead and direct small arms fire came in waves, rising and falling.

I looked at Cpl Wynne who looking at me said, "This shit's for real sir."

Much of the enemy fire in Mike Companies area seemed to be hitting Lt Wright's 2nd platoon. Cpl McGurk's fire team returned fire at a house fifty meters away from which the incoming seemed to be coming. The militiamen's fire grew as the whole platoon opened fire. A Muslim gunman with a rifle tried to run and was shot down. Then our artillery opened up and Cobra gunships flew in firing for the first time.

SSgt Tapper smiled saying, "Boy, it sure feels good to let these mothers get a taste of it."

Meanwhile, at the same time the French, British and Italian troops were all being fired on and five Frenchmen were killed. Still the incoming fire was as intense as anything I had ever seen in Vietnam. But around me, Marines cheered as Marine artillery fired salvo after salvo at the enemy above the big Shiite and Palestinian slums to the east of us.

"This is good. This proves at last that if they're going to get at us, they're going to have to pay a heavy price," said SSgt Tapper. The young Marines were proud to have been bloodied and survived combat whether Washington classified it as combat or not. Like the other Marines before them, they had proven themselves. This life-threatening situation had given them a certain amount of confidence. It had made my platoon, as well as all of Mike Company, even tighter.

At 1000, Druze rockets began hitting Lebanese Army positions outside of our battalion lines. Then the rockets began hitting us again. And again, Marine mortars fired in return at the Druze battery that was firing a rocket every fifteen seconds at us.

At 1045, an armored personnel carrier opened fire with 50-cal machineguns on the checkpoint manned by Lebanese soldiers and my platoon. I grabbed the radio handset and requested that mortars be fired in support of my platoon. But then out of nowhere, a Marine Cobra gun ship flew over our heads as tracers came from the APC up toward it. The Cobra stopped in midair dropping its nose down lining up on the APC and fired a rocket blowing up the APC as we all cheered. "You just don't fuck with the Marine Corps team!" I yelled.

At 1150, US ships fired illumination rounds over the heads of Druze positions followed by Marine artillery fire, which silenced the Druze rocket positions.

One thing for sure, we weren't seeing any Muslim gunman walking around this day as they so often had before.

But then over the radio, my radioman heard that Gunner Williams had died in the chopper on the way to the ship.

Then a mortar shell exploded in a tree fifteen meters to the left of Capt Scotto's Kilo Company CP. The blast wounded his XO and radioman in the legs and hip. Capt Scotto had his map case blown out of his hands.

Again, Marine artillery fired six illumination shells directly overhead of the Druze rocket battery position as a warning. But the shelling of our battalion continued.

At 1155, Marine artillery fired HE and as we saw the shells explode on target, my platoon erupted into screams, rebel yells, cheers and whistles.

"Pay back is a mother fucker!" yelled SSgt Tapper.

I shook my fist yelling, "That's for Gunner Williams!"

Still, we took fire from other Druze areas, and then suddenly it stopped. Capt Scotto watched an Amal officer with several bodyguards walk right up to one of his Kilo Company checkpoints and asked to see their unit commander. Quickly, Capt Scotto drove his jeep up to the checkpoint. He jumped out of the jeep, walking up behind his troops and said, "I'm the commanding officer here."

"Why are your men shooting at us?" asked the Amal officer.

"My Marines are only returning fire."

The Amal officer waved his arms yelling, "We not shoot! You shoot us!"

"Well, if you don't shoot at us, we won't shoot back."

The Amal officer replied, "Good. We not shoot." Then he spun around and walked back toward Hooterville.

Ten minutes later, two battle hardened Druze lieutenants walked up to Capt Graham's Lima Company lines. SSgt Campbell radioed Capt Graham saying, "Be advised we have a couple Muslim Lieutenants here, demanding that I surrender this checkpoint and turn over all our weapons to them or face annihilation in a direct assault."

"You tell them to get the hell away from your checkpoint. Then you call the Lebanese checkpoint and tell them we have no intention of abandoning them," answered Capt Graham.

A little later, SSgt Campbell radioed Capt Graham again saying, "Be advised the Lebanese echo five (sergeant) in charge of their post says he wants to leave because there are too many enemy out there."

"Tell him if he's attacked, I'll call in arty, if we can't handle them with what we have. With arty we can stop any Shiite or Druze attack," said Capt Graham.

Again, a little later, SSgt Campbell radioed Capt Graham saying, "Be advised the Lebanese echo five says he will stay."

Suddenly at 1220, gunfire erupted and quickly built as Shiites added machinegun and RPG fire. Soon, Druze artillery and rockets began exploding in the field next to a Lebanese checkpoint in front of Capt Evans' India Company positions. Marines choked and coughed from within the dust thrown into the air from all the explosions.

One of the Lebanese soldiers ran away from his checkpoint throwing down his rifle.

Back home, the American public was being told we were just being caught in crossfires. Bullshit, we were in the middle of a full fledge war.

Meanwhile over the radio, my radioman heard that Sgt Wise's squad from 2nd platoon while on patrol in the village had been caught in crossfire's between Shiite fighters and Lebanese soldiers. It seemed the whole squad was pinned down in a street.

SSgt Tapper, Cpl Andrews and I gathered around the radio listening to what was going on.

A Shiite officer had walked out into the open and asked Sgt Wise to leave the area before any of his men got hurt. Sgt Wise's squad slowly eased their way out by crawling backwards the way they had come. Then they returned to our lines as gunfire throughout Hooterville grew.

As the afternoon wore on, more and more stray rounds cracked across the battalion lines as we watched Muslim fighters move through the town toward us.

As two Marine Cobra gunships flew overhead, they took 50-cal machinegun fire from a Druze bunker about 200 meters from the positions of Capt Graham's Lima Company. The second Cobra flew directly over the Marines heads at treetop level and stopped dropping its nose.

The Marines heard the roar and saw the flash as a stream of smoke shot from under the Cobra as it fired a rocket at the enemy bunker destroying it.

Old gray-haired Capt Graham cried tears of pride.

The Cobras circled overhead drawing more heavy fire from other Druze machineguns which hit one cobra as both headed back out to the ships.

At 1400, a burst of bullets hit around the Lebanese checkpoint near Capt Evans India Company lines. Bullets cracked over his CP position nearly tearing off his left ear lobe. It was clear to him these were no stray rounds, but aimed shots.

For the next two hours, the gunfire from Hooterville grew steadily worse.

At 1600, civilians harvesting mint leaves, suddenly ran from the field. At 1610, a Shiite machinegun across this field opened fire. The Lebanese checkpoint near Mike Company became the target of RPG, mortar, 106 recoilless rifle fire and AK-47 rifles on full-automatic.

In 2nd platoon, Sgt Wise begged Lt Wright to be allowed to return fire. Lt Wright radioed Capt Jones requesting permission to return fire. As he talked a bullet ripped off the top of his radio antenna. But still he managed to tell Capt Jones that his platoon was taking direct fire.

Capt Jones answered, “If so and you have clear targets open fire.”

So, Lt Wright carefully selected targets and picked certain riflemen to fire at the houses from where most of the enemy fire was coming. He fired the first shot after aiming at a Shiite gunman. Then he went along his platoon line picking out targets for his men to fire at. As his Marines shot to kill, the firing from the windows and doorways soon slowed.

With his machine gunners begging to fight, Lt Wright told them to open fire.

Cpl West placed his machinegun on top of the bunker in full view of the Muslims and squeezed off a burst, but then the gun jammed.

“Shit,” groaned Lt Wright as Cpl West pulled back the bolt extracting the jammed round, then he fired again. But the machinegun only fired two rounds before it jammed again. Again, the jam was quickly cleared. Cpl West squeezed the trigger and the gun only fired once this time. Frustrated, Cpl West pulled the gun back down behind the sandbags and started stripping the gun apart looking for the problem. Sgt Johnson ran over and looking over the parts said, “I think the bolts defective.”

Suddenly, a Muslim stepped out in the open and fired at the 2nd platoon nearly hitting Cpl McAllister.

“Take him out!” yelled Lt Wright.

Sgt Johnson, grabbing up another machinegun, opened fire and saw blood and bone burst from the man as he fell in a heap and laid still. He held fire as other Muslims ran out and dragged the body around the corner of the house.

Later, fifteen Shiite fighters walked out in the open in front of my platoon and one of them yelled to us over a bullhorn, "Marines leave peacefully. We have no quarrel with Americans. We leave while you talk with higher headquarters."

I radioed Capt Jones and reported what had been said. He just laughed.

As we waited, we watched teenagers carrying RPG's and AK-47 rifles run back and forth across the streets between houses. It was like they were daring us to fire on them. I knew they were probably reconning our positions. Sometimes these armed men would stop and wave to us. Muslim women also walked near the Lebanese Army checkpoint in front of my platoon. One fat woman kept walking back and forth across the street. Suddenly, without orders SSgt Tapper fired one shot. The fat women fell revealing a Shiite gunman duck walking on the other side of her out of sight. Now he jumped up running out of sight behind a house.

"How did you know?" I demanded.

"I didn't sir. But I knew she was sneaking something across there," answered SSgt Tapper.

Then a little boy stepped out in the open and fired a RPG hitting the Lebanese Army checkpoint bunker. He ran back around the corner of the house. After this, anytime anyone appeared in the open the Lebanese soldiers and my platoon opened fire. Four more RPG's were fired, but all of them hit behind our positions. Then a RPG exploded in the air above my platoon, but none of us was hurt. Another RPG exploded against our bunker. The Marines of my platoon were suddenly happy SSgt Tapper had made them dig in so deep and build up so many sandbags.

At 1745, there were scattered and at times heavy firefights and artillery shelling in Beirut. And still our battalion came under random fire.

At dusk two machineguns opened up on Capt Evans' India Company. A Marine machinegun team with SSgt Spidden's platoon returned fire at one enemy machinegun position and then at the other silencing both.

After dark, SSgt Tapper moved among my platoon and reported

back to me that most of the men had fired over twenty bullets and about ten grenades from grenade launchers during the day.

Like the other platoon sergeants, SSgt Tapper requested a resupply of ammo from GySgt Knight.

Later, GySgt Knight drove a truck out to each platoon bringing us ammo, MRE's, water and warm cokes. But just like Vietnam we didn't care that the cokes were warm, we were just glad to get them.

He even brought out a new bolt for Cpl West's defective M-60 machinegun.

Meanwhile, Gunner Sieple went to see Capt Jones and told him that SSgt Manuel had requested a transfer from weapons platoon to be the platoon sergeant of 2nd platoon. Capt Jones agreed saying he should have thought of it sooner.

During the morning of April 30th, Capt Evans was awakened by 50-cal machinegun fire. The Lebanese Army had moved up two brigades and where firing into Hooterville. He watched the Lebanese gunners on APC's (armored personnel carriers) calmly change overheated barrels and reload empty ammo drums. In the town, he watched bricks and chunks of cement explode from the half-inch bullets.

Suddenly, there was a loud BOOM nearby. Capt Evans ducked and then peeked up to see a Lebanese tank which had just fired a shell into a house from which Shiite snipers had fired at India Company yesterday. The tank fired another shell and then moved into the town with the Lebanese soldiers walking behind it. Once in the town the Lebanese soldiers kicked open doors firing rifles inside as they moved down the streets.

As more Lebanese soldiers walked past, several of them asked the Marines of SSgt Spidden's platoon for water, which they gladly gave.

The Marines listened to the heavy fighting as the two Lebanese brigades tried to sweep West Beirut clean of the enemy.

Later, a Lebanese APC came back by Capt Evans India Company carrying many wounded soldiers. At this time our battalion came under scattered artillery fire.

SSgt Spidden saw where the enemy artillery fire was coming from and radioed the information to Capt Evans. He in turn radioed LtCol Kersher requesting authority to use his company's 60-MM mortar section to return fire.

"Negative," came LtCol Kersher's answer.

Then Capt Evans asked for support from battalion's 81-MM mortars.

"Negative," answered LtCol Kersher.

Capt Evans then asked for artillery support.

"Request denied."

"I demand to know why I'm not allowed to take out these Druse arty positions that are firing toward my company," shouted Capt Evans over the radio.

"The answer is simple Captain. I don't have the authority to fire in defense of the Lebanese Army."

Listening to this over the radio, I knew Capt Evans didn't care about supporting the Lebanese Army. But India Company was being shot at, even if it was high, even if no one had been hit so far today.

The firing seemed to be intentional and his men wanted to return fire.

Then Marine artillery fired illumination shells over each of the enemy emplacements, which quieted them for about an hour.

Sgt Rienbold approached me complaining, "Sir, we got a sniper shooting at us that you have to do something about before he kills someone."

Knowing I had to do something, I looked at the Lebanese Army checkpoint ahead of us. I could see the Lebanese sergeant sitting in the rear of his bunker. "Sergeant Rienbold go tell that Lebanese sergeant you need his help," I said.

"Yes sir," said Sgt Rienbold, as he looked at me funny. Then he turned and ran out to the Lebanese checkpoint. I watched as the two sergeants spoke. Then the Lebanese sergeant stepped into the bunker and returned with a rocket launcher. Sgt Rienbold pointed at the sniper's window. The Lebanese sergeant took aim and fired. The rocket went right through the window exploding inside. The Lebanese sergeant put the launcher down smiling as he gave Sgt Rienbold the thumbs up sign. Sgt Rienbold ran back over to me also smiling and said, "Gunner the sniper's gone."

In the afternoon, a Muslim machinegun started hitting the sandbagged wall of Lt Cregar's 3rd platoon tearing them up. He asked L/Cpl Blandon, "Could you hit that MG in that window with your grenade launcher?"

L/Cpl Blandon answered, "I'll try sir."

Lt Cregar knew the range was about 150 meters away as L/Cpl Blandon aimed and fired. But to everybody's surprise the grenade went right through the open window destroying the shack and enemy machinegun crew. The Marines of 3rd platoon cheered around L/Cpl Blandon who just smiled saying, "Shit guys, it's only my job."

Wednesday May 1st before sunup, GySgt Knight drove a truck around to each platoon with our requested resupply of ammo, water and MRE's.

At 1000, a Shiite officer walked up to Capt Evans India Company lines and asked to speak to the commanding officer. Capt Evans went forward knowing this was probably a waste of time.

"Your brave Marines have killed a baby girl in our town. Maybe you stop shooting now?" spat the Shiite officer.

Capt Evans looked at him hard asking, "How many Shiite fighters have we killed?"

"None!"

"You're a lying ass," sneered Capt Evans.

The Shiite officer spun around and stormed away.

Meanwhile, Sgt Rienbold's machinegun team was firing on targets along the edge of Hooterville.

Then, a 50-cal machinegun opened up on 3rd platoon with supporting fire from nearby buildings. The half-inch bullets were shredding the top row of sandbags as the Marines flattened themselves against the wall. Trying to see where the firing was coming from, Sgt Coston had his helmet shot off.

Lt Cregar and L/Cpl Blandon each grabbed a LAAW and positioned themselves trying to get a clear shot at the distant enemy machinegun. But the machinegun fire stopped before they could pin point it. Quickly, Lt Cregar checked his men and was amazed to find no one had been hit.

But still the 50-cal machinegun kept firing from time to time hitting so close to them that they were unable to get a clear shot.

Finally, it disappeared leaving Lt Cregar and 3rd platoon shaken, but still unhurt. With that, the other enemy firing slowed down and stopped at 1500.

During the lull Lt Cregar had 3rd platoon eat a very late lunch.

Suddenly, Cpl Harris yelled, "Watch out!"

Sgt Coston's squad looked up to see a man dressed in US Marine camouflage walking toward them.

"No shoot! Marines! No shoot. I Lebanese Army!" yelled the man covered with belts of ammo and grenades hanging everywhere.

Lt Cregar stood up waving him forward.

The camouflaged-uniformed man waved his arm and a whole squad walked out of the town, all dressed in Marine camouflage.

"Could we have water please?" the Lebanese leader asked.

"Sure, give us your canteens," answered Lt Cregar.

Cpl Harris's fire team gathered up the canteens and left to fill them at the company water buffalo.

"Who are you with? What kind of a unit?" asked Lt Cregar.

"I'm a lieutenant and we are with an assault battalion. I was trained in America and went through your Army Ranger School."

By the time they left with full canteens, Lt Cregar was very impressed with the way this Lebanese Army officer handled his men. He just wished the rest of the Lebanese Army were as good.

By radio, Lt Wright of 2nd platoon was ordered to report with Cpl McGurk to Capt Jones' CP. Once there, Capt Jones promoted McGurk to sergeant. With the 2nd platoon having too many sergeants he was transferred to my platoon and I put him in charge of my 3rd squad.

In late afternoon, the Druse and Shiite started firing and kept firing until dusk. As night fell, we quickly began spotting the muzzle flashes of the enemy machineguns. Cpl West silenced an enemy machinegun with only one burst of return machinegun fire. He went on to knock out several more enemy machineguns.

In the afternoon of May 2nd, Muslim artillery shells again hit the US Embassy residence endangering American lives. Two Marine artillery guns fired high explosive shells at the enemy positions and the shelling stopped.

By now, the Lebanese Army was locked in combat for the control of the high ground overlooking the airport as US naval gunfire was being used in their support for the first time.

The next day a Shiite officer walked toward Capt Scotto's Kilo Company. Capt Scotto and a Lebanese sergeant walked out and met him. Before the Shiite officer could say anything, the Lebanese sergeant said, "If you fire at us, we shoot back and kill plenty!"

Without a word the Shiite officer turned and walked away.

The rest of the day our battalion received only scattered sniper fire.

The next day, SSgt Tapper requested a resupply of 5,000 rounds of rifle ammo, 5,000 machinegun rounds and 150 grenades. But the day was quiet.

And May 5th was too quiet until around 1900 when Syrian backed forces quickly captured the Chouf Mountains of Bhamdun.

This became another ruined Sunday afternoon as Druse and Shiite gunman fired on Lebanese units near us. Many shells landed within Capt Graham's Lima Company. Although some shells were short or long rounds, it was soon apparent that Lima Company was being fired at.

My platoon, like the rest of Mike Company was in bad need of a shower and hot chow. With it quiet in our sector, I sent one squad at a time back to the battalion CP building to get a shower and a hot meal.

My men seemed charged up by the experience of combat of the past months. They had come to know that level of excitement of physical pleasure of living on the edge. Now after killing men, they knew what it's like to feel the Marine brotherhood.

But for me, I felt let down because of the lack of support at times by LtCol Kersher. My platoon had been in serious trouble at times without the support we should have received, the kind I'd had come to expect while in Vietnam.

I went up to our battalion CP building with my last squad to get a shower. After the hot shower, I walked into the chow hall. While I was sitting down eating, LtCol Kersher walked over to me. At seeing him I started to stand up, but he waved me back down saying, "Sit down Gunner and eat. I just wanted to congratulate you for a job well done. I will back your decisions because you are the man on the spot."

"Thank you, sir," I answered surprised.

At 0240 on May 6th, I heard the thunder of jets overhead, west of us and out across the sea. Minutes later over the radio my radioman heard that finally the Israelis had begun redeploying its troops back from Beirut without notifying the Lebanese government or the Multi-National Forces or any of the embassies. LtCol Kersher put our whole battalion on 100% alert. As my platoon manned our positions for hours, the excitement of what might happen helped them stay awake.

But I remembered their last partial pullout and how it started an explosion of fighting between the different Lebanese factions. Meanwhile, Israeli jets roared all across Beirut protecting the columns of retreating Israeli vehicles from attack.

At dawn, SSgt Tapper put the platoon to work filling more sandbags to strengthen our bunkers. And as usual the men bitched and moaned, even though they now knew it was for their own good.

But as the Israelis pulled back, there was no one ready to fill this sudden vacuum.

As the Lebanese Army tried to assemble its troops to move into the area, our battalion came under fire, which increased with the growing number of Lebanese troops massing nearby. Christian militia units began trying to move in and take over as Muslims fought back fiercely using Syrian supplied heavy mortars, tanks and artillery.

When SSgt Spidden of India Company complained to Capt Evans about the incoming fire he said, “Battalion says the shells coming in are either long or short rounds.”

“Sir, does battalion think we’re stupid up here? Do they expect us to believe that all these rounds we’re taking are just accidents?

All this old Nam vet knows is, these Druse gunmen are shooting the hell out of us. I already have one man wounded and battalion won’t fire in our support,” grumbled SSgt Spidden.

Meanwhile, Capt Scotto’s Kilo Company returned fire with their small arms and machineguns at eleven identifiable targets.

Still, the withdrawal went on without incident for the Israelis as the Druse clashed with the Christians up in the mountains.

The fighting grew worse near noon, as a 106 recoilless rifle began firing at Lebanese armored vehicles and Capt Scotto’s Kilo Company bunkers. At the same time, mortar rounds began hitting all over Kilo Company positions. Then a Marine tank moved up into Kilo Company lines.

Firing at the airport stopped when sixty Lebanese Army mechanized vehicles moved into the attack.

At noon, Capt Graham noticed Lebanese sentries at their checkpoint were sleeping. He shook his head saying, “Just like a bunch of soldiers. Even their lieutenant is asleep. These guys remind me of ARVN soldiers (South Vietnamese soldiers).”

At 1230, Druse Artillery hit close to Capt Scotto’s Kilo

Company. Over the radio we heard the Lebanese Army was forming up another armored formation nearby. A little later, Lebanese tanks, armored cars and jeeps mounted with 106 recoilless rifles rolled out.

Capt Scotto was glad to see the Lebanese Army out in force making an effort to fill the gap left by the Israelis.

Suddenly, the convoy was hit by 50-cal machinegun fire from several directions, followed by artillery air bursts exploding overhead as mortar shells fell in volleys around Kilo Company. Shells exploding on the road sent shrapnel slamming into Kilo Company bunkers and ricocheting off the vehicles.

The convoy stopped right in front of Kilo Company, as the fire grew worse. Capt Scotto couldn't even hear what was being said over the radio. He hoped the lead vehicle hadn't been knocked out because the longer this convoy sat here the longer the incoming would last. Finally, after four minutes, the convoy started moving again and the incoming shifted with it.

At 1250, four mortar shells exploded near Capt Graham's Lima Company as other shells hit across the airport followed by rockets and artillery.

Capt Graham radioed LtCol Kersher and in a calm voice reported that Lima Company was being hit by 50-cal machinegun and heavy rifle fire and requested permission to return fire. Right away LtCol Kersher said over the radio, "Captain you take appropriate action as long as you remain within the guidelines of the rules of engagement."

By now, Lima Company was taking fire from RPG's aimed at Lima bunkers and 106-recoilless rifle fire aimed at Capt Graham's Company CP.

Meanwhile, in Mike Company, heavy fire was falling around Lt Cregar's 3rd platoon as SSgt Reed begged him to let them return fire. 2nd platoon, without orders had already returned fire and Lt Wright had tried to stop them when Capt Jones gave permission to fire.

Mike Company Marines returned fire and ducked the fierce incoming enemy fire.

But I was still bitter because we weren't getting the artillery, gunship, tank, mortar or naval gunfire support we requested. What the hell is the use to have all this stuff if we weren't allowed to use it?

And a half hour later in the middle of this fierce combat, LtCol

Kersher ordered Capt Jones to ceasefire because our fire was hitting near a Lebanese Army column attacking in the town.

Meanwhile, Sgt Schwartz had one of his fire teams crawl under Muslim fire to get more ammo for his squad. As we held our fire waiting, I plotted an enemy 106-recoilless rifle position on my map, as Capt Jones requested artillery fire. LtCol Kersher denied it. Capt Jones requested 81-MM mortar fire. It was then a Lieutenant from Kilo Company broke in over the radio to report that Capt Scotto had been killed. Still, LtCol Kersher denied Capt Jones request for mortar support.

My platoon was now having trouble from snipers in a nearby house. I radioed Capt Jones again requesting tank support to fire its 50-cal machinegun at the snipers. As I waited for an answer, a 106-round passed overhead. Still no answer as three more 106 rounds passed us. Finally, LtCol Kersher gave permission to fire. A Marine tank roared up behind us, but instead of firing at the snipers it fired its 105-MM gun and the shell hit just behind the enemy 106 position. The tank's second round hit short. But the third round was a beehive round and its thousands of steel darts destroyed the enemy 106 and crew. Then the tank turret slowly moved left toward the sniper position. But then a Muslim fired a RPG from the top of a house at the tank forcing it to back up.

I yelled, "Sergeant McGurk take out the snipers!"

Three of Sgt McGurks men with grenade launchers fired at the house and silenced the snipers.

SSgt Tapper was standing watching them fire when a RPG round exploded knocking him down.

Sgt Meadows yelled, "Staff Sergeant Tapper's hit!"

Then a second RPG exploded a few meters away. SSgt Tapper sat up feeling himself all over surprised to find no wounds and stood back up. A third RPG exploded about three meters behind our bunker. The blast again knocked SSgt Tapper down. Then our bunker took a direct hit as heavy rifle fire also hit it.

Cpl Andrews suddenly pointed yelling, "It's coming from that cement building right there!" I looked at the house about twenty meters away. My whole platoon opened up with M-16 rifles, but the enemy fire still was hitting our bunker.

SSgt Tapper again finding himself unhurt yelled, "Give me a LAAW!"

Sgt Meadows handed one to him and he opened the rocket launcher to full length, aimed in and fired. The shell exploded in the concrete house and the enemy fire stopped. A little later, my platoon took fire from another house.

Over the radio, my radioman heard Lt Littleton report to LtCol Kersher that Capt Jones had been killed. When I heard this, I dropped down fighting back bitter tears. First Capt Scotto, who I had known since he was a second lieutenant and now Jones. We had served together on and off since 1975 when we both were wounded together on an island near Cambodia.

"Damn it!" muttered SSgt Tapper as he fired another LAAW into that house silencing it.

And still, the Muslim gunners fired rounds at my platoon bunkers followed by mortar attacks. Around me, the Marines of my platoon bitched about not being able to counterattack into the town to get at the enemy.

Bullets ripped through the firing hole next to Cpl Wynne, hitting the sandbags behind him spilling sand to the floor. I ducked as more bullets rattled off the metal matting that formed the roof of our bunker.

At our company CP, GySgt Knight had just sat down, leaning back against the bunker wall in his helmet and flak jacket, when artillery shells exploded within our company area. Then rockets started whistling in.

Lt Littleton radioed LtCol Kersher requesting artillery support, which again was denied.

"The fucking Druse arty crews must be laughing at us," grumbled 1stSgt Burns.

Meanwhile, two men in civilian clothes carrying AK-47 rifles ran across an open field in front of Capt Evans India Company.

SSgt Spidden said, "I don't believe this shit!"

A Marine machine-gunner swung his gun and fired one long burst cutting them in half. Still, five Muslims kept snap shooting at India Company from behind a wall. The same Marine machine-gunner again swung his gun at them and with two bursts of fire, he blew four of them apart. A Marine aimed his M-16 and shot the fifth man as he fired over the wall.

Capt Evans was watching India Company return fire from his CP. He noticed seven Muslim with weapons climb the upper stories of an unfinished building about 200 meters north of him. Knowing these militia fighters could fire down at the airport he radioed SSgt Spidden and ordered his platoon to fire on that building. The whole platoon opened up at the steel-girded building. The nearby Lebanese checkpoint, seeing this, also opened fire on the same house. Capt Evans could see Muslims falling out of the building.

During this time, LtCol Kersher radioed Capt Graham to put his XO in command of Lima Company and report to battalion. I was concerned why he had been relieved of his command. I would learn later the reason was worse than I feared. He was to become our battalion XO because Maj Hays had been killed. Again, I felt sick with grief at the loss of another good officer.

At 1426, the incoming fire finally stopped.

But still, the Marines left on watch were tense as evening came.

As usual the Muslim gunners could be heard shouting and shooting to keep us awake.

With night, many Marines said screw the rules of engagement as they fired at muzzle flashes in the town trading fire with armed bands. The worst was an hour-long exchange of grenades and small arms fire from a reinforced squad hitting Lt Cregar's 3rd platoon with RPG's.

At 2000, four rockets landed at the end of Capt Evan's India Company. This began a night long shelling of the airport. Three of his men were wounded.

Our battalion CP was hit by incoming shells smacking into sandbagged walls. LtCol Kersher, his radiomen, corpsmen and Capt Graham ducked down as bullets burst through a window and ricocheted around the room. They could hear a machinegun firing short bursts as RPGs roared in.

In India Company, SSgt Spidden radioed Capt Evans saying, "Sir, they're coming up the road. At least twenty of them in cammies!"

Several AK rifle bullets cracked over his head as SSgt Spidden added, "They're fucking Syrians!"

Capt Evans ducked as another burst of incoming fire ripped over his head. He yelled back over the radio, "Fire!"

SSgt Spidden's whole platoon opened fire as one. Riflemen fired thirty-round magazines as fast as they could change them. Rifled grenades were being fired as machineguns chewed up the streets of the town butchering the Syrians. Slowly the enemy fire slacked off.

On May7[th] around 0345, twenty-one rockets hit Mike Company. One of them exploded in the trench line among Lt Wright's 2nd platoon killing Sgt Wise and Cpl Poplas and wounding two others. At hearing this report from Lt Wright, over the radio Lt Littleton begged LtCol Kersher for artillery support against the enemy's mortars, rockets and artillery that was constantly exploding up and down Mike Company's line. But again, he only allowed the artillery to fire illumination rounds back over the enemy positions until 0400 when eleven rockets hit Capt Evan's India Company wounding two Marines. He also complained over the radio to LtCol Kersher about his company taking artillery, rocket and small arms fire. Meanwhile, in Lima Company, three more Marines were wounded, one in the neck, who had to be evacuated by chopper out to the USS Iwo Jima. Lima Company area tents looked more like camouflaged netting because of all the battle damage. Capt Graham argued face to face to LtCol Kersher on behalf of the whole battalion. And still he would only allow the artillery to fire more illumination shells over the enemy's head.

"Whoopee!" yelled Capt Graham as he turned hitting his fist against the wall.

But he did move M-60 tanks forward to fire on the battalion's attackers.

The incoming fire finally stopped around 0500. I was surprised we had lost so few men.

And yet the news people back home were still telling the world we were just receiving spill over or stray rounds.

Through the day, the Lebanese Army was unable to capture the high ground from the Druse, which overlooked both the city of Beirut and our battalion positions.

At 0300 on May 8th, incoming rockets and artillery shells hitting around our company awakened me.

About 0420, SSgt Manuel was checking his 2nd platoon lines when he ran into Cpl McAllister walking back in the open from making a head call. Together they ran toward Cpl McAllister's bunker. They were within sight of it in the dark, when a barrage hit near them fired by Druse positions up in the Chouf Mountains.

Minutes later, Lt Wright heard someone shouting "Help!"

The rockets and artillery shells were exploding so close that the ground shook as Cpl Mitchell yelled, “Someone has been hit!” He and Sgt Reilly leaned over against the sandbagged wall of the trench as more rockets and artillery shells exploded in the fields around Mike company.

Cpl Mitchell crawled over the wall yelling, “Someone’s been hit between us and the company CP!” Once on the other side, he ran toward the company CP. He dived for cover as a rocket hit between him and the company CP. He jumped up running again and found Cpl McAllister’s burned and shattered body. Nearby, SSgt Manual was bleeding from deep holes in his neck, face, legs and arms. Quickly, Cpl Mitchell put the pressure bandages he had and the ones SSgt Manuel had on SSgt Manuel. Then he picked him up over his shoulder and carried him and ran back to 2nd platoon’s CP bunker. As he entered the bunker, he laid SSgt Manual down as a corpsman ran over breaking open more bandages. A pool of blood was forming as Cpl Mitchell and the corpsman knelt down working on him.

SSgt Manual opened his eyes and asked, “How…is…Corporal Mac…?”

“He’s okay,” lied Cpl Mitchell as he thought, “Staff doesn’t know how bad he’s hurt.”

“I’m…okay too. Go take care of Mac!” argued SSgt Manual.

“Staff Sergeant Manual, you’re okay and he’s all right. Don’t worry.” Cpl Mitchell again lied as the corpsman rolled him over on his side trying to keep him from drowning on his own blood.

As Lt Wright looked on, he thought, “Not again. Not this platoon again.” He was angered, but trying to stay calm and professional. He wanted to go out there and kick some ass. But he knew we weren’t here to fight. We had been picked for this mission because Marines are the most disciplined troops in the nation. We’re expected to take everything here in stride as we try to give the Lebanese people time to get their government back together.

Then, Lt Littleton ran through the bunker hatch and kneeled down beside SSgt Manual who had slipped into unconsciousness.

Outside, a Marine tank rolled up beside the bunker shielding them from Hooterville.

Cpl Mitchell and another Marine ran back to Cpl McAllister’s body with a poncho. They picked up the remains of the black Marine with the Irish name and placed it on the poncho. As they carried it back to the 2nd platoon CP bunker, it seemed the weight was much too light for the man McAllister had been.

A Marine amtrack rolled up next to the bunker as SSgt Manual was carried on it. But when Cpl Mitchell and a Marine placed the poncho on the amtrack a crewman yelled, "We're not carrying your fucking trash back!"

Cpl Mitchell spun around yelling, "You dumb shit, this is a Corporal of Marines!"

The amtrack crewman's mouth dropped open and then he burst into tears. The corpsman climbed in to stay with SSgt Manual as the amtrack's ramp slowly lifted up and it roared off in a cloud of dust. Lt Wright tried to hide his own grief in busy work. But the wide-open eyes of the wounded he had seen in the last twenty-four hours had shocked him.

At hearing the news myself, I felt like crying in frustration, but through past experiences I kept it inside.

Worse yet, we would hear later that SSgt Manual died at the aid station in the basement of the battalion CP.

As the sun came up, my platoon began taking sniper fire as we tried to pinpoint their locations.

Finally, Cpl Wynne spotted a Muslim rifleman wearing a green uniform and a helmet, run in the open and enter a house. From inside the house, the green-uniformed man kept shooting from a window. Cpl Wynne carefully laid his rifle across the top of the sandbag wall, aiming at the window. The Muslim quickly fired a burst at him. Cpl Wynne quickly ducked down, but rose back up sighting again across the top of the sandbags. But again, he had to duck as the Muslim sprayed bullets around him. Again, Cpl Wynne aimed in, but ducked as another burst of bullets hit nearby.

"This time you're mine," muttered Cpl Wynne, aiming in as the Muslim rose up in the window. The rifle jumped in Cpl Wynne's shoulder and the green-uniformed man fell through the window to the ground. Sgt Schwartz laughed, as the rest of the 2nd squad cheered hitting him on the back.

Through the day until 1600, more than 120 artillery shells, mortars and rockets exploded in our battalion area wounding another Marine. The French too suffered one killed and three wounded.

LtCol Kersher finally allowed Marine artillery and mortars to fire on some enemy positions.

The rest of the night passed relatively quiet, although shells continued to fall in our battalion lines as well as the French positions.

The next day at 1815, three shells landed within Capt Evan's India Company perimeter, as several hit just outside of his lines. Six more shells landed in our battalion chopper landing area and the MAU headquarters wounding a Marine. Our battalion returned fire with six high-explosive artillery shells on a suspected Druse fire direction center. The Druse artillery position ceased firing.

On May 10th, Gen Miller (CG FMF Lant) and MajGen Gray our division CG visited our MAU. As soon as he could, MajGen Gray broke away to visit us in the trenches. The troops loved his usual rough and gruff style. In over 18 years in the Corps, he's the first general I liked and respected as much as I did Gen Walt who commanded the Marines in Vietnam. My young Marines loved him because they could see he really enjoyed being with the enlisted men. He had fought in Korea as a sergeant receiving a battlefield commission. He had served three tours in Vietnam. I am one of the few Marines that served there longer than he. He was short, white-haired and wore goggles on his helmet.

At 1130, he visited Mike Company along with his staff of brass, all spit-shined boots and starched camouflaged uniforms. He slapped SSgt Tapper hard on the shoulder and asked, "What's your biggest problem over here?"

"General, there ain't no chewing tobacco," he answered.

With tobacco juice running down his own chin, MajGen Gray pulled a bag of Red Man from his side trouser cargo pocket and put it in SSgt Tapper's hand.

Then he walked up to me and shook my right hand as he punched me hard with his left in my shoulder asking, "How's it going Gunner?"

"General, it would sure help if battalion could use more of that arty to support us," I answered looking him in the eyes with shaking knees.

His smile vanished, as did the smiles on his staff's faces who to a man turned looking at me hard.

Then three rockets roared in exploding 200 meters from where we were standing. MajGen Gray and I remained standing, as his whole staff moved as if in confusion, their faces now suddenly white from fear. To me, I had never seen a short man stand so tall. He turned and stood several minutes looking at the town, and then he looked back at me still not smiling and said, "I will see about this."

"Thank you General," I said.

"Thank you, Gunner," he said and walked tall back toward our battalion CP as his staff followed bent over as if in a heavy wind.

"My kind of General," said SSgt Tapper standing nearby.

"You better believe it. I didn't think we had any like him left," I said smiling.

"Just think what this Corps would be like if he were Commandant," said Sgt Meadows.

"It'll never happen. He's got no college. He's self-educated. I'm amazed he's gotten this far," I said sadly.

"Make's ya believe there's a God," said Sgt Rienbold.

"Shit, he hasn't done bad. Private to sergeant and then up to Major General. I could handle that," I said still hoping.

"You'll do it Gunner," said Sgt Meadows.

"Bull shit," I answered.

And maybe, just maybe because of what MajGen Gray saw and heard of what we were up against, Marine artillery opened fire on Druse positions. And for the first time US Naval guns fired and hit Druse batteries in our support, silencing the hostile fire. Of course, this also changed the MAU mission from one of a peacekeeping presence to one of an active participation.

Later Cpl Mitchell saw a Muslim with a RPG aiming up at a Marine chopper as it came in for a landing at the airport.

Cpl Mitchell yelled, "Lieutenant I have a raghead aiming a RPG at choppers. Can I take him out?"

Lt Wright yelled back, "Waste him!"

Cpl Mitchell aimed in as the Muslim again, put the RPG on his shoulder. The rifle cracked and the Muslim fell. "Scratch one raghead," said Cpl Mitchell.

My platoon also had good clear targets in the houses in front of us as sniper bullets and RPGs hit and ripped across our bunkers.

Cpl West fired his machinegun, killing one Muslim firing from a window. Also, Lebanese soldiers at the checkpoint near Lt Wright's 2nd platoon fired 50-cal bullets down the road at Druse gunmen. A Lebanese tank rolled up firing its big gun, as other Lebanese soldiers followed firing rifles, machineguns and RPG's. A

Lebanese jeep, mounted with a 106-recoilless rifle, also rolled up. But before it could fire, it was hit by Druse fire and burst into flames.

The firefight went on for hours. At dusk, the Druse brought up an antiaircraft gun and fired shells at the Lebanese checkpoint near Capt Evans India Company. Several shells burst right over his company CP bunker wounding one Marine.

Finally, after midnight the firing stopped.

But the next morning, before light, twenty mortar shells exploded near Lt Wright's 2nd platoon. After dawn, we could see ambulances around the Druse positions. So, we knew we had drawn quite a lot of blood during the night. But the Lebanese soldiers at the checkpoint near Lt Wright's 2nd platoon had lost six killed and two wounded.

As the Lebanese forces moved further into the mountains, they placed themselves into a better position to be supported directly by us. And as the Lebanese Army advanced, the firing into our battalion's lines slowed.

I heard the Lebanese LtGen Tannous had formally asked our Special Ambassador Robert McFarlane to provide direct US support for his forces, which were facing a powerful enemy force made up of Syrian backed Palestine Liberation Army with some Druse, PLO, and Iranians who had massed in the hills overlooking the town. Druse artillery had stopped a Lebanese Army unit from reinforcing a Lebanese Brigade which was low on ammo and was in danger of being overrun. I was concerned with the emergence of Syrian forces starting to openly fight against the Lebanese Army.

Meanwhile, the moral of my platoon was still high, but it was hard for these young Marines to fully understand the complexities of our changing mission. All they knew was they were here to bring peace. None of them were satisfied with sitting in their fixed positions and firing back when fired at. They wanted to attack with the Lebanese Army as they had been trained to do and kick some Muslim ass. They reminded me of myself years ago in Vietnam when I wanted to take the war to the enemy and invade North Vietnam.

But even with the shift of the fighting in the hills, the Druse didn't forget us. Suddenly, a 50-cal machinegun opened up on my platoon sending us diving for cover. Sgt McGurk and Cpl Andrew located the enemy machinegun on a rooftop about 200 meters away.

As the big bullets hit the top of our bunker Cpl Andrews raised a grenade launcher and fired four grenades silencing the Muslim gun crewmen. A Lebanese Army patrol searched the roof and threw off the dead gun crew.

After dark, three rockets hit around SSgt Spidden's platoon bunker in India Company. Severely shaken, he checked his platoon and was surprised that no one was hurt even when another rocket hit nearby.

Several bullets hit Lt Cregar's 3rd platoon bunkers. He observed the muzzle flashes coming from a second story window about 300 meters in town. A minute later, he saw another burst of fire from the same house. He reported this by radio to Lt Littleton and he was told to fire illumination grenades over the militia position to warn them we had spotted them.

"Damn," said Lt Cregar turning to Sgt Higgins saying, "Third squad, have one of your grenadier's fire illume over that house."

Sgt Higgins turned looking down his squad and said, "Blandon, you're up."

L/Cpl Blandon fired an illumination round which was answered by a burst of fire from the same building as well as from another three-story building.

Lt Cregar again radioed Lt Littleton saying, "We fired illume and the incoming got worse."

"Go ahead return fire, but stay within the rules of engagement," answered Lt Littleton.

"Riflemen and guns (machineguns) open fire!" yelled Lt Cregar.

Sgt Rienbold fired his M-60 machinegun at the two-story house while the riflemen fired at it and the three-story house. But the incoming fire increased. Again, Lt Cregar reported the results to Lt Littleton.

"Okay use grenade launchers," said Lt Littleton over the radio.

L/Cpl Blandon and two other Marines fired grenades hitting the houses, which only silenced the incoming for about a minute.

Over the radio, Lt Littleton again suggested that 3rd platoon fire only illumination rounds from the grenade launchers. When L/Cpl Blandon fired the grenade launcher with a loud POP, the incoming stopped as the Muslims ducked expecting a HE round to hit them. But as soon as the illumination round burst into nothing more than a flare the incoming started again. Again, L/Cpl Blandon fired an illumination round and the Muslims stopped firing. And when the illumination flare faded, the incoming fire grew even heavier as a third Muslim position joined in from a small chicken hut.

Now, without orders, Lt Cregar over the radio assigned each of his squads a separate target. They opened fire with rifles and grenade launchers. Sgt Rienbold took turns firing his machinegun on all three targets. After about ten minutes of this, the incoming fire stopped.

Lt Cregar then ordered 3rd platoon to cease fire and then said, "Lance Corporal Blandon fire an illume round over each target."

After L/Cpl Blandon fired his third illumination round, 3rd platoon was immediately fired at from the two-story house.

"Hit 'm with grenades Blandon," ordered Lt Cregar.

L/Cpl Blandon aimed, firing his grenade launcher five times quickly. Every grenade went right through a different window exploding inside. There was no return fire.

Lt Cregar proudly radioed Lt Littleton saying, "We got the bastards."

As I listened to all this over the radio, I still couldn't understand this high-level decision to fire illumination rounds at an enemy firing at us. I know this is supposed to be a peaceful way to show our enemy what we can do if they don't stop firing. But to me and I'm afraid the Muslims here, force met with less than equal force is a sign of weakness.

Each day, we watched close to 6,000 artillery shells fired by Lebanese soldiers and Christian Phalange forces against Druse and Shiite positions who in turn fired back mortars, rockets and artillery of their own. I sometimes wonder what purpose we serve just sitting here in one spot. This is not what we have been trained to do.

At 0100 on May 12th, Shiite forces attacked a joint checkpoint manned by Lebanese soldiers and Marines of Lt Wright's 2nd platoon. But the attack was beaten back without any Marine or Lebanese Army casualties.

Throughout the day, our battalion received small amounts of small arms, rockets, artillery, mortar and RPG fire. All four-line companies and checkpoints were fired upon wounding five Marines. Lt Littleton reported to us that President Reagan had authorized US ships to fire in support of the Lebanese forces only if they were in imminent danger of being overrun.

The next day, the Lebanese Presidential Palace, The Lebanese Ministry of Defense, the American ambassador's residence and the US embassy in West Beirut were shelled heavily.

At 1000, two US Naval ships fired six gunfire missions firing seventy rounds on six Druse battery positions silencing the attackers.

But still, rockets began landing closer and closer to Capt Evans India Company. Then a few shells landed just beyond the perimeter and the shrapnel blasted back toward his CP bunker. He heard shrapnel splattering on the ground behind them and whizzing overhead.

Another shell slammed nearby, setting a tree and bush on fire. BOOM! All of a sudden, a rocket exploded twelve meters away blowing a large hole in the perimeter wire. Shrapnel went zinging by them hitting Capt Evans helmet. He hit the deck shaking with fear. He lay there on the ground next to one of his men, their legs shaking against each other. They both looked at each other and laughed.

"That was close," said Capt Evans.

Then two more shells hit near them after which it got really quiet. SSgt Spidden went out with one of his squads to check the big hole in the wire. They carried out more concertina wire and repaired the hole. Then they moved back to their bunker.

Capt Evans saw flashes, and then he heard the noise BLOOP…BLOOP…BLOOP. Then he saw more flashes coming from the mountains looking like flares as the rockets headed toward the Presidential Palace.

Then a shell hit on the north side of India Company, and then a shell hit on the eastside, then on the westside and one on the south side. Then another shell blew another hole in the wire. Capt Evans felt it was the Muslims saying we know where you are and here are just a few rounds, just to let you know we can hit you anytime we want to. He was amazed at the accuracy of their fire. He couldn't believe this was just a rag-tag militia firing like that; this had to be the work of Syrians with possibly Russian advisors.

Then, the USS John Rodgers and the USS Bower fired and we watched the shells hit up in the hills followed by secondary explosions. Their deadly accurate fire had destroyed multiple rocket launchers.

Afterward, the Lebanese Air Force flew air strikes against the ridgelines above the town destroying many Druse positions and several Russian made Syrian supplied tanks.

Again, the next day, Lebanese Jets flew air strikes as our ships fired at Druse batteries, which had fired at the airport.

On May 15th, Col Studt gave LtCol Kersher permission to call in Naval air strikes against hostile enemy targets.

The next day, PLO units also attacked Lebanese soldiers in the mountains. Throughout the morning, the fighting grew heavy as we listened to gunfire of all calibers. As the Lebanese Army artillery ammo began to run low, the Lebanese Ministry of Defense requested US naval gunfire to support Lebanese soldiers who were under attack by two Muslim battalions made up of tanks and Infantry supported by heavy artillery. The Lebanese soldiers were in danger of breaking under this pressure.

Also, artillery shells hit Mike Company positions and the airport.

At 1004, in response to the Lebanese request, four US ships fired 360 shells in the support of the Lebanese Army for over five hours, hitting Druse gun emplacements in the hills to the southeast of Beirut, which turned the tide of battle.

Once again, this instant of combat support by us of the Lebanese Army ended the perception of us being neutral in the eyes of the anti-government factions. We were more and more becoming legitimate targets by the anti-government forces.

Again, the Ambassador's residence and the Ministry of Defense came under heavy shelling causing fires. And again, two US ships fired thirty shells at the enemy battery.

I heard that President Reagan had phoned Col Studt and said, "I'm determined to see to it that we provide whatever support it takes to stop the attacks on your positions. Tell your Marines the entire nation is proud of you and the outstanding job they are doing against difficult odds."

But still our battalion came under rocket and artillery fire three times within the hour.

On May 17th, a Navy carrier reconnaissance plane was attacked by a surface to air missile, but missed the plane by two miles.

The next day the US Congress authorized President Reagan to keep up to 1,200 Marines on the ground in Lebanon for up to eighteen months. The same day we heard that our Commandant PX Kelly had told reporters that he thought a ceasefire in Lebanon was imminent.

"What 'a ya think about that Gunner?" asked Cpl Andrews.

"I wonder if he is talking about the same Lebanon we're in," I answered.

As the day wore on, it seemed the Muslim artillery had doubled its shelling of Beirut and its suburbs. A Druse rocket had destroyed the main Italian ammo dump. Four French soldiers had been wounded by artillery shells and two more by a hand grenade.

During the night, three of our ships fired ninety shells at two Muslim targets. It felt good that they were being killed and wounded too.

Early on May 19th, I heard the world's only battle ship, the USS New Jersey had passed Gibraltar on its way to Beirut.

The fighting around the airport intensified once again. In India Company, SSgt Spidden's platoon came under heavy attack including fire from anti-aircraft guns.

In Mike Company, Sgt Coston was using the piss tube ten meters behind the 3rd platoon's bunker when small arms fire hit across the sandbagged positions. He turned running back toward his bunker trying to button up his trousers when a shell exploded nearby filling the air with steel shrapnel which shredded his face and neck killing him.

At about the same time in my platoon, Cpl Andrews was returning from battalion across an open field when a rocket landed on top of him blowing him to pieces.

Lt Littleton had seen it and radioed me and added it was like the rocket had come out of nowhere as if it was aimed just at him.

At the same time, both the French and Italian lines were caught in a crossfire. A French lieutenant colonel and his driver were killed and one wounded. Up to now they had lost sixteen killed and forty-four wounded.

We and the French responded with a show of force, by sending two French fighter bombers from their French aircraft carrier Foch, and two F-14 Tomcats from the USS aircraft carrier Eisenhower, making low-level reconnaissance passes over the Lebanese capital and the hills to the east.

Still, by 1325, the fighting between the Lebanese Army and

Muslim militia had also become heavy. Two hours later, the spillover fire began to endanger my platoon. SSgt Simon's mortar crews fired twelve high explosive shells at a Druse position silencing it.

A little after 1600, SSgt Simon's mortars fired another twenty-eight shells after Sgt Schwartz's squad at the checkpoint was hit by intense small arms and RPG fire.

Just before sundown, we watched fifteen Muslims walking down the street carrying weapons and ammo. I couldn't let my men fire first. But the Lebanese soldiers at our checkpoint opened fire on them with a 50-cal machinegun and M-16 rifles knocking ten of them down. A half hour later, two Ford Pinto station wagons flying Red flags drove up and picked up the dead and wounded Muslims.

During the evening, eighteen rockets hit around Lt Wright's 2nd platoon. Marine artillery and Naval gunfire engaged Druse artillery positions that were firing on the airport.

Later, Col Studt's MAU-CP came under fire and Marine mortars and Naval gunfire fired back. Meanwhile, the French were using air strikes against enemy positions firing at them.

On the morning of May 20th, French jets hit Muslim batteries behind the Syrian lines.

At 1300, Muslim fire hit the Lebanese Army checkpoint in front of my platoon. I ordered SSgt Tapper to have our whole platoon move into their fighting positions. I could see Muslim militiamen moving up into their own prepared bunkers and fighting holes, aiming their weapons at us. But we were under orders to do nothing until the Muslims opened fire on us first, even though I knew we were about to be attacked.

At 1345, the first RPG flew over our bunker, followed by a mass of small arms fire raking our perimeter, followed by 50-cal machinegun fire and rounds from a 106-recoilless rifle.

Sgt Rienbold and his machinegun team hit the deck along with the rest of us.

"Remember only a minimal careful response!" I yelled through gritted teeth hating this stupid order.

Sgt Rienbold yelled back, "Okay gun teams return fire!" He kept running back and forth along the trench between his machinegun teams pointing out enemy machinegun positions for them to knock out. He was worried about keeping control of his men. But the well-trained machinegun teams were firing at clear targets just as they had been trained, watching their tracers going into windows killing and wounding Muslim militiamen.

Suddenly, Sgt McGurk was hit in the chest and flipped backwards on his back. Cpl Wynne the nearest man to him yelled, "Corpsman up!" He then crawled over beside him and opened his flak jacket as the stain of blood spread across his chest. The corpsman ran to his side and started cutting Sgt McGurk's T-shirt with scissors. Small chunks of flesh fell away with his shirt. Then the corpsman shook his head saying, "He's gone." Then he and Cpl Wynne rolled the body onto a poncho and carried him into my platoon CP bunker.

The fighting had definitely changed from what it had been in the early months. The enemy now was well-armed and it seemed with an endless supply of ammo. The incoming was fierce as bullets splintered the old olive trees behind us and caused the sandbags in front of us to leak. RPG rounds were skipping across the compound exploding.

SSgt Tapper bent over Sgt McGurk's body with tears in his eyes and then looked up at me. I shook my head and yelled, "Staff Sergeant Tapper pass the word to the men to take whatever action they have to, to survive!"

He ran out of the bunker and along the trench. I heard him yell, "Wax the mothers!" as well as other things.

A rocket exploded just behind my CP bunker.

Afterwards I could hear Lt Littleton yelling over the radio, "Gunner! Gunner!"

My radioman reached out the handset to me. I grabbed it saying, "Six this is Mike one actual. Over."

I could hear the relief in his voice as he said, "Oh, oh...Mike one actual this is the Six. How's it going up there? Over."

"Six this is Mike one actual. Be advised I have one echo five (sergeant) KIA. The rest of us are okay. Over."

"Mike one this is the Six. Sorry to hear that. Well, keep it up. Out."

"Six this is Mike one. Out," I said feeling that old rush again like the old days, that incredible feeling of excitement of battle when time passes quickly and yet things seem to move in slow motion around me.

The Muslim militia had prepared their bunkers better than before making them harder to see. Sgt Rienbold stood up firing a machinegun as incoming fire hit all around him. Sgt Schwartz was firing over the sandbagged wall when he was hit in the throat and he dropped behind the wall. I found his body as I made my rounds checking the line. Beside him Sgt Rienbold knelt over him. He had turned the machinegun back over to the gun team. He looked up at me with blood running down his own neck.

"You all right?" I asked this old Vietnam veteran as I touched his shoulder.

"I just got my ear nicked, sir. Another purple heart," he said smiling.

"You take care of yourself," I said forcing him to sit down. I took his helmet off and broke open a bandage and placed it over his ear.

"Yes sir," he said, still smiling as he put his helmet back on, lopsided because of the bandage, and stood back up and went back to directing the fire of his gun teams. There is truth in the old saying; there is nothing better than a good sergeant.

I radioed Lt Littleton to request help from battalion for 81-MM mortar support, but it was denied. Around me, my men looked at me in fear. In front of us were hundreds of Muslim fighters moving toward us in fire team rushes.

But then from behind us, a Marine Dragon team rushed up to us.

"I don't know who sent you guys, but I'm glad to see you," I said smiling.

"Captain Graham ordered us up," answered the Dragon leader.

"Thank God," I said as I pointed at their first target, a Muslim militia bunker in a two-story house. They fired six shells making direct hits through four windows before the front of the house collapsed.

Then I pointed out another enemy bunker. This time it took four direct hits to put it out of action.

Then the Dragon team fired their last two shells at two heavy machinegun positions.

I tried to stay constantly on the move checking on each of my men. Sometimes I would stop and fire my rifle over the sandbagged wall with them.

I saw a group of militiamen in a building about sixty meters away and yelled, "I need a LAAW over here!"

Sgt Rienbold picked up one of the disposable light anti-armored weapons. As he ran along the trench line toward me, he extended the plastic launcher. I pointed to the target as he reached my side. He took aim and fired. The rocket rose leaving a smoky trail behind and exploded on top of the house.

At this point, my radioman yelled to me that Lt Littleton had called and said he had just got the authority to return fire with our companies 60-MM mortars.

I knew that behind us at our company CP, SSgt Simon's mortar crews were already swinging into action.

Gunner Sieple the weapons platoon leader was surprised when the first shells hit 300 meters off target. Before he could say anything, SSgt Simon jumped into the mortar pit taking over one mortar himself. And within two more shells the fire was adjusted on target and the enemy firing stopped.

At 1600, SSgt Spidden of India Company radioed Capt Evans and reported, "They're getting on line and coming at us."

Capt Evans instantly radioed LtCol Kersher requesting immediate 81-MM mortar support and was surprised to hear him say, "Request approved."

Capt Evans then radioed SSgt Spidden asking for grid coordinates. SSgt Spidden already had the grid numbers figured out and quickly gave them to him.

A few minutes later, Capt Evans heard the explosions, but couldn't see them. Then SSgt Spidden radioed him with the correction. Capt Evans radioed the mortar crews saying, "Drop 150."

The next mortar shell exploded about 60 meters from SSgt Spidden's platoon's barbed wire.

Again, he radioed Capt Evans saying, "Lift 400, add 50, fire for effect." Capt Evans passed the adjustments on. This time the mortar shells fell in a militia trench system dug through olive trees. The mortar shells exploded throwing up tree splinters and human flesh stopping the line of advancing militia. SSgt Spidden saw the Muslim militia running back through the shattered trees.

SSgt Spidden radioed again saying, "Left 50, add 50, repeat."

The Marine mortar crews shifted their fire as the shells dropped in a field across six Muslim bunkers, which had been giving India

Company a hard time. Several direct hits quieted these Muslims down.

Meanwhile, the fire to the east and north of our battalion was still heavy, but the incoming had slowed to the battalion front.

The night was still filled with the flash of exploding rockets and the never-ending crack of small arms fire as the militia crawled forward probing Mike Company lines. Lt Littleton requested and our battalion 81-MM mortar crews fired illumination to help us see.

In Lt Wright's 2nd platoon, Sgt Reilly, using a starlight scope, shot several Muslim fighters who crawled too close to their positions. Nearby Cpl Mitchell fired at movement in the dark in front of his squad's position.

From the darkness to our front, voices yelled, "Marines you die in the morning." None of us along the lines slept until 2300 when it finally got pretty quiet.

The next day, the battleship USS New Jersey with her 16-inch guns able to hurl one-ton shells twenty-seven miles and level a 1,000-meter grid square, arrived off the coast of Beirut. My men talked about what she could do to these Muslim gunners even as far away as Damascus.

Meanwhile, the Lebanese Army battled Muslim and Druse militia with artillery and machineguns.

During the day, a Marine CH-46 chopper came under ground fire while flying over the fighting in the slums and returned fire with its 50-cal machinegun.

Strangely, just like Vietnam, I found myself loving this country. Like Vietnam it was beautiful even at night with rockets and artillery fire lighting up the hills like July 4th back home. And just like the Viet Cong and North Vietnamese Army, the Druse and Shiite here didn't care about the casual slaughter of civilians. But here, they left the bodies lying unburied in the streets and fields for days.

On May 22nd, Col Studt hosted a large congressional delegation led by Congressmen Sam Stratton made up of Representative William Dickinson, William Nickols, Larry Hopkins, Bob Stump, Beverly Bryon, Richard Ray, John Spratt, Solomon Ortiz, Duncan Hunter. Also with them was Gen Mead.

By now, the Druse had been armed by Syria and the PLO had returned to fight with them and the Shiites. Russian advisers were working with the Syrian troops.

Druse artillery in the mountains continued to hit the airport wounding two Marines in Capt Evan's India Company. For the first time, LtCol Kersher was allowed to call in air strikes and artillery without going through the chain of command all the way back to Washington, and he could even call in support for the Lebanese Army if an attack on them posed any danger to his battalion.

The bombardment around our battalion on this day was the biggest so far. Enemy artillery shells had hit the US Ambassador's residence, the Lebanese Defense Ministry, which had offices for the American advisers and airport personnel. Because of this, Col Studt determined that our battalion, as well as the other multinational peacekeeping force was in danger and called in Naval gunfire.

The Navy ships opened fire on targets located ten to twelve miles inland within Syrian controlled territory, from which enemy gunfire had come from.

The USS New Jersey was ordered to fire in support of an embattled Lebanese Army unit near the mountain resort town of Souk el Gharb. This 16-inch gun barrage lasted for over an hour. When it was over the incoming fire from the targeted area had very much diminished.

But snipers, car bombs and harassing fire were still directed against us.

The next day, Ambassador McFarlane, who I had just found out was a retired Marine lieutenant colonel, toured Mike Company's positions. As his chopper made an aerial recon it was hit by a bullet.

As May 24th dawned, scattered fighting started in the suburbs with some spill over fire hitting my platoon's positions.

When Druse militia attacked the French forces, the French in return launched air strikes against enemy artillery positions in the hills.

It was reported that small units of Libyan and Iranian troops had now joined the fighting against the Lebanese government.

A 1,700 Lebanese Army force, fighting in the mountaintop town outpost had come under a fierce artillery attack from Druse militiamen. Behind this barrage came five waves of Druse infantrymen. The Lebanese soldiers drove them back at first with their own artillery.

But later, the Lebanese CO telephoned the Lebanese Defense Ministry and reported that his unit was nearly out of ammo. An

American colonel serving as the chief of US advisory team called Col Studt and explained the situation and added, "Without help they will be overrun."

Col Studt ordered naval gunfire. US Navy ships fired on the Druse forces around the mountain and at enemy artillery positions farther east in Syrian controlled territory.

Happy with the Naval gunfire, Sgt Meadows said, "I'm glad something's being done about these assholes."

SSgt Tapper still kept teams of men filling sandbags against the times the incoming fire pinned our platoon down.

"I bet every Marine left in the states wants to get over here," said Cpl Wynne.

"Yeah, and every Marine here wants to get back to the states," grumbled Sgt Meadows.

"It was the same way in the Nam at first," I answered.

During this day, four French soldiers were wounded when a rocket landed in their compound near the Beirut racetrack and two more were wounded when someone threw a grenade at one of their trucks. The French quickly retaliated by sending eight jet fighters from the aircraft carrier Foch and attacked artillery positions behind Syrian lines.

Three Marines from Lima Company were wounded from a grenade attack while on patrol in Khomeiniville.

Meanwhile, enemy rockets hit the Beirut schoolhouse that the Italians were using as an ammo dump setting off a huge explosion.

Lt Wright's 2nd platoon was hit by small arms fire from the nearby Druse and Shiite Muslim neighborhoods. Four of his men were wounded as they returned fire with small arms. Then they were hit by artillery fire from the Druse mountain area. Lt Littleton radioed for and got naval gunfire fired on the Druse mountains again. By now, Lt Wright had suffered three more wounded men.

Meanwhile, the Lebanese Army had become involved in an artillery duel with militiamen in the Druse and Shiite neighborhoods, which meant the hard-pressed Lebanese Army was engaged in a battle on two fronts.

A Syria-backed militia group calling itself the Lebanese National Resistance was warning that it would attack European interests in Beirut as well as US, French, Italian and British civilians if US ships kept shelling the Druse positions.

The morning of May 25th, Cpl Wynne from my platoon took out a patrol made up of his squad and Cpl West's machinegun team. They left our sandbagged positions heading for the Shiite Muslim area of town, the Marines had started calling Khomeiniville. He kept his men well spread out along the slightly populated road, which led them to the narrow streets of Beirut. They were armed to the teeth with M-16 rifles, M-60 machineguns, LAAWs and grenade launchers. A shepherd crossed their path with his sheep and a robed man leading a donkey passed them in the other direction alongside of the road.

The buildings rose up just as abruptly as the streets grew narrow. These streets were winding, cluttered passageways where vehicles and humans struggled for what available room there was and everybody tried to anticipate what the other fellow was going to do. People in cars blew their horns at each other.

In Khomeiniville, there were posters of Ayatollah Khomeini plastered on the walls and strung across the streets.

Within these heavily populated areas, Cpl Wynne pulled his squad closer together so they could better keep an eye on each other. Children were still all around them shaking the Marines hands as they greeted them asking for cocoa and gum.

Cpl West yelled to them, "Marhabla!" which means hello in Arabic. The response was usually good from the civilians, which were everywhere. Pretty girls waved at the Marines from balconies and the Marines waved back.

Cpl Wynne knew that even though most of these people were friendly, there were terrorists in the area. But these patrols, with loaded weapons were still a chance to get out of the compound even knowing terrorists could do anything at any time they wished. Everything was so tightly closed in here. He still smiled thinking of the time a kid threw firecrackers off a roof at his squad. The men had dived for cover thinking they were under fire. They looked up to see a Lebanese adult slapping the kid on the head.

By now he knew the danger signs, such as no kids on the street or people suddenly running into their homes at the sight of a coming patrol.

Today, Cpl West was concerned when he noticed two teenagers counting the Marines as they passed by.

Cpl Wynne heard a man yell, "Marine!" He looked to see the

man give them the thumbs down sign. One young Marine stopped, staring at the man.

"Keep moving Marine!" yelled Cpl Wynne.

Then a Lebanese man walked right up and bumped into Cpl West and then looked at him like he was crazy, glaring at him. Cpl West pushed him to the side with his rifle and walked on.

Later a kid walked up and down the column saying, "Americans no good! Marines go home!" Suddenly the kid pulled a pistol out from inside his shirt. Several Marines swung their rifles toward him.

"Stop! Stop!" yelled Cpl West, "It's a water pistol!"

Cpl Wynne snatched the water pistol out of his hand, threw it on the ground and smashed it to pieces with his foot. Then he kicked the kid in the ass yelling, "Get out 'a here you stupid little shit!"

Later, when Cpl Wynne reported this to me, I suddenly thought back to when I almost shot a little Vietnamese kid in 1970 when he ran at me pointing a toy pistol.

Even with all the dangers of patrolling, my men seemed to feel a purpose in what they were doing and believed we were welcomed by the majority of the Lebanese.

The next day our battalion was hit only by scattered sniper fire. But that night a rifled grenade exploded in India Company next to SSgt Spidden's platoon bunker. He ordered a flare shot up into the night. At seeing three militiamen running across a field, every Marine in his platoon opened fire cutting them down.

On May 27th, the Chief of Naval Operations, Adm Watkins and the 6th Fleet Commander Adm Martin visited our battalion.

Several of our choppers were hit by small arms fire during the day, but all landed safely. It seemed more PLO had infiltrated back into Beirut. Fighting between the PLO and the Lebanese Army caused more stray rounds to land in our battalion lines. Three RPG rounds hit behind Lt Wright's 2nd platoon positions and machinegun fire raked their bunkers. Then, snipers began firing at his platoon from buildings close to their lines after armed men had been spotted entering it earlier.

May 28th saw heavy fighting between the Lebanese Army and the militia. Enemy fire spilled over into our battalion positions most of the day, wounding a Marine in Lima Company.

Around 0900, Capt Evans' India Company came under sniper fire. One Marine was hit in the shoulder.

A little after 1000, twice, bullets hit a Marine chopper. By now the sniper fire had spread throughout the whole battalion as we returned fire whenever targets were identifiable.

SSgt Spidden of India Company spotted an enemy sniper and pointed the man out to a Marine sniper team who fired one shot killing him.

The next morning a ceasefire was reached. Nearby, a Lebanese lieutenant played music on an old abandoned piano. Meanwhile his men played paddleball in the street or rode bicycles, maneuvering around the shell holes.

Col Studt lowered the alert status down to Condition Three. At first, we eased out of our bunkers without flak jackets and helmets taking no chances. Still when no one shot at us, I told my platoon to keep their guard up because nobody could tell how long this truce would last. So, SSgt Tapper kept our men who were not on duty filling sandbags as we waited.

We began seeing professional-looking soldiers wearing the Russian rust and brown colored camouflaged uniforms. Another new group we saw were wearing white headbands with red Arabic letters written on them. I heard these were Iranians. Along with these new troops, we watched the quality and numbers of enemy bunkers increase. In the afternoon, the sniper fire started up again.

We noticed large numbers of civilians had begun leaving Hooterville. We watched flag covered buses picking up whole families. I could tell the fighting was about to start up again. Just like the communist in Vietnam, the Muslims here were using the ceasefire to resupply and bring up more troops.

On May30th, our Commandant, Gen Kelly visited our MAU for the second time and awarded twelve purple hearts.

The next day, a Marine sentry at the American Embassy was wounded by a grenade thrown from a car speeding by.

Meanwhile, we watched two young men near the perimeter carrying rifles and wearing red head and armbands.

At 2130, Marine choppers at the northern end of the airport came under heavy small arms and RPG fire. A short while later enemy fire hit my platoon positions.

The morning of June 1st, Sgt Higgins of 3rd platoon took his squad out on patrol supported by Sgt Johnson's machinegun team. At 1030, they were in sight of our company's line, returning from their patrol when sniper fire hit the rear point man in both legs. As the squad dived for cover, Cpl West spun around swinging his machinegun from the hip and was hit in the chest and fell. The rest of the squad opened fire, as did Marines on the perimeter with unknown results. Sgt Johnson crying, picked up black Cpl West in his arms and ran carrying him through the perimeter wire. Behind him, two Marines from Sgt Higgins squad carried in the other wounded man. Both men were patched up within the 3rd platoon's bunker and were medivaced out to the USS Iwo Jima. Later we would hear that Cpl West had died.

In the afternoon, we watched militia clearly building sandbagged positions in the ruined buildings across from my platoon lines, stocking them with weapons and ammo. After dark, snipers began firing into my platoon positions. This sniper fire continued all night and into the next morning. I radioed Lt Littleton requesting a sniper team to deal with them. Soon, the Marine sniper team arrived carrying modified high-powered hunting rifles with telescopic sights. They first surveyed the area with their sniper scopes for several hours, pinpointing the enemy snipers actually firing at us. Then they opened fire with eighteen shots on fourteen selected enemy positions. They recorded four kills, one probable kill and ten wounded Shiite gunmen. Their success was evident by the sudden silence from each hostile position.

Later, the Shiite gunman tried to say the Marine snipers had killed women and children. But reporters discounted these claims after they were escorted to our firing positions and were permitted to sight through the sniper scopes. Then representatives from the Shiite community asked us not to use snipers. Col Studt answered that no snipers would be necessary if the Shiite gunman would leave or not fire on his Marines.

Then, Lt Cregar's 3rd platoon started being hit by Syrian artillery. Iranian fighters wounded a Marine in the arm.

At 1000, Sgt Ward of 3rd platoon yelled, "I've been hit!" then slumped down holding his chest beside the sandbagged wall. SSgt Reed fired his rifle at the enemy in a nearby tree line. The rest of 3rd platoon joined in pouring rifle and machinegun fire at the Muslim positions, as heavy return fire whipped past over their heads.

Meanwhile, Cpl Bower and a corpsman rushed to Sgt Ward's side. From nowhere, LtCol Kersher appeared next to the fallen sergeant. Cpl Bower helped the corpsman put bandages on the lung wound. Sgt Ward was coughing up blood through blue lips. His eyes began rolling back into his head as the blood on his lips turned pink. The corpsman began giving him mouth to mouth.

An amtrack rumbled up to pick up the wounded man. Behind it rolled up a Marine tank firing to cover them. Cpl Bower, the corpsman and two other Marines lifted Sgt Ward up carrying him up the ramp into the amtrack.

As the rest of 3rd platoon fired at the Muslims with everything they had, the amtrack turned around heading back to the battalion aid station. Later we would hear Sgt Ward died on the operating table.

Many of the men in our battalion at hearing about Sgt Ward's death, had had enough and decided, as SSgt Spidden of India Company did and said, "Let's get some!"

The 3rd platoon began firing grenade rounds just behind the walls where the Muslim snipers were hiding. Some of the better Marine grenadiers even bounced grenades off buildings to get at the Muslim snipers. Marine machine gunners silenced the Muslim militia's automatic weapons.

The next morning, I watched armed gunmen move through the streets wearing red tinted camouflage uniforms like the Russians wore. Some of them wore red head and armbands. A few wore Russian helmets. I could see machinegun positions being set up, but of course under our rules of engagement there was nothing we could do unless we were attacked.

Meanwhile, a few stray rounds hit SSgt Spidden's platoon in India Company. Then the Muslim militia opened up with accurate fire on the whole company. Capt Evans ordered India Company to return fire with the same type of weapons. Gradually the firefight grew. Marine snipers reported to him of helmeted men carrying RPG's through the streets.

Upon hearing this, SSgt Spidden said, "Yeah they're getting ready to come. That's why there wasn't any women and children on the streets this morning." Then he ordered his grenadiers to open fire. The grenadiers dropped three rounds into a house forcing three Muslim gunmen carrying weapons to run out into the street. A Marine machinegun team shot them down.

In Mike Company, a Marine was shot in the shoulder as Sgt

Johnson fired his machinegun at the hole in the wall of the house where the shot had come from.

Lt Littleton and GySgt Knight watched the firefight from our company CP bunker.

At 1615, Marine snipers were ordered to join the fight and they fired for the next two hours.

At 1830 near dark, Cpl Street of Lt Cregar's 3rd platoon saw a light in the distance like that of a mortar being fired near a Muslim bunker. Then mortars started exploding around 3rd platoon's positions.

Lt Littleton still watching from the company CP bunker requested a fire mission of 81-MM mortars. Soon mortar rounds were rocking the Muslim bunker with explosions.

A RPG round passed over our company CP bunker exploding behind it. Suddenly, the bunker was hit by RPGs, rifle and machinegun fire from two directions. All of Mike Company returned fire into Hooterville. It was clear to me that our company CP was the main target of the enemy fire. SSgt Simon's three 60-MM mortars fired illumination shells over the areas from where the heaviest incoming fire was coming. A Marine 50-cal machinegun ripped at the enemy positions with its ½ inch bullets, as rifle grenades scattered Muslim machinegun teams.

Sgt Rienbold then heard the POP, POP, POP of incoming 50-cal bullets as he fired his M-60 machinegun.

An illumination shell flashed into light over a known Muslim position about 320 meters away from 3rd platoon. L/Cpl Blandon, sighting down his rifle saw someone aiming right at him. He fired three quick rounds and ducked down behind the sandbagged wall.

Cpl Bower saw a man stand up in the field in front of him and fire a RPG. "Hit the deck!" he yelled dropping flat. Nearby someone else yelled, "Duck!"

The RPG exploded with a crack. Cpl Bower found himself lying on his back and felt blood running down his face. To his right he watched unbelievingly as a Marine rocked back and forth with pieces of bone and blood stuck all over his face. The man's hands were just bloody stumps. Cpl Bowers then looked to his left at an unconscious Marine. Beyond him another Marine kept trying to push himself up, but kept falling back down.

Cpl Bower then rolled over to help the wounded and screamed,

"Corpsman up! Corpsman up!"

Lt Littleton heard his screams above the noise of battle back at the company CP bunker.

Meanwhile, Lt Cregar, L/Cpl Blandon and a corpsman ran to the smoking bunker. The first Marine they met was standing covered with puncture wounds of the head, neck and upper left arm. The front of his flak jacket was ripped to pieces.

Cpl Bower found the blood on him wasn't his as he helped the corpsman move the wounded men near a candle so they could better work on them.

Then, more RPGs came in and another hit just outside the bunker wounding two more Marines who had run over to help, one in the wrist and the other in the left hand.

Lt Littleton ran up with more corpsmen to help.

With the enemy fire too heavy for a medivac, Lt Littleton ordered the Dragon teams to open fire to cover them. The first Dragon round knocked out an enemy 50-cal machinegun position. The second Dragon round destroyed a Muslim bunker, which had fired a RPG as the five wounded Marines were hand carried in ponchos to the battalion aid station.

When Lt Littleton returned to our company CP, he found the enemy fire was even fiercer. Even with our whole company firing all its weapons it was hard keeping fire superiority.

At 1915, the volume of enemy fire increased even more. Two more Marines were wounded when a RPG exploded among the positions of India Company. It seemed our whole battalion was returning fire with rifles and machineguns. Again, the heavy enemy fire kept the medivac choppers from landing. At this point, a Marine amtrack rumbled up and picked up the wounded. Still the enemy fire increased as the Dragon team with Mike Company fired two rounds silencing a machinegun bunker.

At 1930, a Marine Dragon gunner sighted the big wire-guided antitank launcher on his right shoulder. With the amount of incoming fire hitting around them, they missed their target. It took them five minutes to get set again before they fired destroying the target. Still the incoming fire went on without let up.

Enemy RPGs kept exploding around our company CP bunker.

In the 2nd platoon, Cpl Mitchell was trying to pinpoint the enemy position firing the RPGs. But it was Sgt Johnson nearby that found it. He called Lt Wright over as he fired machinegun tracers into the enemy bunker to mark it.

Lt Wright looked through field glasses. He started to speak when a burst of enemy machinegun fire came over the top of the waist high sandbagged wall. One of these bullets hit Sgt Johnson just under the helmet hitting him in the right eye.

Cpl Mitchell was sprayed with blood. Thinking he had been wounded he spun away to the left dropping to the ground.

Lt Wright dropped to one knee looking at a Marine nearby who was looking at his wounded hand. Hearing a sigh, Lt Wright looked up to see Sgt Johnson slowly drop the machinegun as he fell to his hands and knees. Lt Wright crawled to Sgt Johnson's side and found him dead.

Sgt Reilly was firing his rifle, aiming through a starlight scope. He looked around to see why Sgt Johnson had stopped firing the machinegun and saw him on the ground and asked, "Johnson! You okay?" He bent down smelling the raw blood and realized he was dead.

Two corpsmen ran up, as Cpl Mitchell pointed to Sgt Johnson's body. Quickly, the corpsmen checked him and then told them what they already knew, but had hoped somehow they were wrong. They wrapped the body in a poncho.

At our company CP, Lt Littleton was talking to GySgt Knight when a RPG exploded against a beam over their heads knocking both of them down. They checked each other over for wounds and found each other unhurt.

The volume of incoming fire was so bad, neither Sgt Johnson's body nor the wounded man could be evacuated until after midnight when it began to taper off and finally ended.

GySgt Knight came around to each platoon with a working party handing out more ammo and hot coffee.

As I took a cup he grumbled, "You know Gunner, it upsets me that all these Muslims have to do is tell a reporter that Marines are killing women and children and that lie appears in the papers around the world. Why aren't they telling our story?"

"Just like the Nam, ain't it. Besides, Reagan doesn't want the American people back home to really know just how heavy our daily combat is here," I answered.

In the afternoon of June 5th, Col Studt and a Naval officer rode in a supply convoy as they went to visit the Italian zone.

At 1622, after the visit, they rejoined the convoy as it returned.

Col Studt's driver shifted gears as the convoy started up the long slope toward the airport. They watched the point jeep pass a white Mercedes sitting along the road. They were following a slow moving amtrack when Col Studt ordered his driver to pass it. He heard the truck behind them downshifting as the jeep pulled around the amtrack. The amtrack was passing the white car as Col Studt's jeep came abreast of the left side of the amtrack. Suddenly, the white Mercedes exploded with a BAM! The truck now following the amtrack took most of the blast slamming it sideways against a telephone pole wounding the Navy officer and two Marines.

A corpsman jumped out of another jeep, ran up and started checking the wounded. A Marine squad rushed out of the perimeter to cover the convoy. Nearby, Italian soldiers also helped treat the wounded and evacuated the most serious to the Italian field hospital. Later intelligence would report what we all figured, that Col Studt was the intended target of a Pro-Iranian Islamic fundamentalist sect.

The next two days were quiet with only the checkpoint in front of India Company taking incoming fire.

Finally, Col Studt had ordered our MAU to prepare for our upcoming scheduled relief by another MAU.

On June 8th, our battalion began back-loading our nonessential equipment on ships. This was welcome news to most of my Marines because we were well beyond our planned six months' deployment.

The next day, the colonel from the incoming MAU and a small liaison team came ashore to be briefed by Col Studt.

On June 10th, a 50-cal machinegun duel started between the Lebanese Army and the Druze militia. Several artillery shells landed along Lt Wright's 2nd platoon perimeter.

I had written Marty and told her not to expect me home until this was over. Remembering how Bunny would have taken such news I wasn't sure how she would take it. But she had written me back and said for me to do what I thought was right even though she would rather I come home. She went on to say everything at home was fine. She loved and missed me.

So, after thinking about it most of the night and all the next morning I walked up to our company CP bunker. As I walked in, 1stSgt Burns said, "Good morning Sir."

"Good morning, Top," I answered.

Lt Littleton looked up from studying a map and asked, "What's up Gunner?"

"Can I speak to you sir?"

"Sure," answered Lt Littleton as he stood up and walked over to me.

"Sir I have three men in first platoon and myself who want to request an extension here to help the green troops coming in."

"Request denied. No double pumps this trip in Mike Company."

"Just like that sir?" I said shocked.

"You're not the first man I've had request to stay on and for good reason. And Colonel Kersher is authorizing people to stay on. But I'm not. When I get home, Mike Company will lose a lot of these men due to transfer or discharge. Our turnaround in the states instead of being a year this time may only be six months and we'll be coming right back here. I'll need men like you to help me rebuild Mike Company and train the new men we get in."

"Aye, Aye sir."

"Gunner you can still request mast over my head to battalion you know."

"No sir," I said. As I walked back to my platoon, part of me was glad. Back in my bunker, I sat down and wrote Marty a letter telling her I would be returning with 2nd Battalion after all.

The next day, the incoming MAU's advance party flew in to work out the relief plan. As 2nd Battalion began loading equipment on ships, the company commanders from the incoming battalion came around reconning our positions.

Beginning at 0700 on June 12th, the relieving companies moved ashore to take up their assigned positions. The relief of Mike Company was completed by 1300 and we started re-embarking on our ship.

At midnight, the ships carrying our MAU steamed from Beirut heading for Rota Spain.

On June 16th, our MAU landed and Marine working parties washed down the wheeled vehicles, heavy equipment, tanks, and amtracks. Although my young Marines grumbled about this wash down in Spain, it was required by the US Department of Agriculture in order to remove snails from all stateside-bound equipment. It seemed several years ago, a snail infestation in North Carolina resulted in massive crop damage.

Two days later, we sailed for the states with a feeling of a difficult job well done. I was proud of my young Marines who had dealt with patrols, security, terrorist attacks and rescue operations. While underway we prepared for the unloading at Moorehead City, NC, on June 26th.

While crossing the Atlantic Ocean, we were lectured and had literature handed out to us about safe driving from a Virginia state highway representative who had boarded our ship in Rota Spain. This must have been for the sailors because we the Marines were going to North Carolina.

During the same time, the chaplain held classes for all hands trying to prepare the young Marines for the homecoming and reunion with their families. This was something new for me. I had never seen this done during Vietnam. It would have helped.

Although we had gotten used to the press coverage in Beirut, we were unprepared, especially us Vietnam veterans for the reception waiting for us when we returned to the states.

As we docked at Moorehead City, I was standing with Lt Littleton on the hanger deck when L/Cpl Blandon of 3rd platoon ran up to Sgt Higgins and said, “Sarge you won’t believe it. Go look out there!”

We followed Sgt Higgins to see what was going on. On the pier, we saw two high school bands with cheerleaders and people all over the area waving up at us. I felt cold chills and tears roll down my face. The 2nd Marine Division band was also there playing Semper Fidelis. When they played the Marine Hymn, 1,000 Marines stood at attention.

Our Division commanding general, MajGen Gray was there to shake our hands as we stepped off the ship. There were network and local TV crews and even some family members there.

We boarded buses for the trip back to Camp Lejeune. All along the route there were people lining the road cheering and waving, some holding signs reading, “Welcome back Marines. Good job.”

Finally, back at Camp Lejeune, as the buses pulled to a stop in our battalion area, we were met again by MajGen Gray and our families. This was surely different from the times I came home from Vietnam. Nothing had compared to this.

As we stood in battalion formation, MajGen Gray told us how

proud he was to have this battalion of warriors in his division.

Then LtCol Kersher got up and spoke of his pride in commanding 2nd Battalion. Then he asked for a moment of silence for the good men we lost in the last ten months. Finally, he turned the companies over to their company commanders.

Lt Littleton did an about face and yelled, "Platoon commanders of Mighty Mike Company, when you finish with your platoons, dismiss them!"

As one, the four of us platoon leaders saluted him and did an about face to face our platoons.

"Staff Sergeant Tapper! Front and center!" I ordered.

SSgt Tapper marched from the back of the platoon to the front and did a right face in front of me and saluted saying, "Staff Sergeant Tapper reporting as ordered."

I returned his salute saying, "Staff Sergeant Tapper have the men turn in their weapons and 782 gear and get 'm on liberty."

"Aye, Aye sir," he answered.

I did a right face and marched off.

In the distance I saw Marty, holding Samantha back as she struggled to reach me.

As I walked toward them smiling, Marty let go of her and she ran to me with her red hair flying behind her yelling, "Daddy! Daddy!" She jumped into my open arms as I knelt down. I kissed her and asked, "Well how was first grade, Sam?"

"It was fun at first, but I like vacation better."

"Vacation! Already? It must be nice," I said, then looked at Marty as she walked up to me with her arms out. I stood up shifting Samantha to my left arm as I reached out with my right arm and pulled her to me saying, "How are you lady?"

"Fine now that you're back. It sure feels good to be in your arms."

"You feel pretty good yourself girl." Looking around I asked, "Where's Kyle?"

"His father came down and got him for the summer."

"Oh, I forgot," I said feeling jealous that her first husband had been at our home while I was so far away when I knew I shouldn't feel this way. I had forgotten I had missed a whole school year.

"Are you getting any leave?"

"Fifteen days."

"When?"

"Even as we speak, I'm on leave."

"You can leave right now?"

"Yes, but first I want to say goodbye to Gunner Sieple."

"Where is he going?"

"The Warrant Officer Basic School at Quantico."

"And he doesn't know where he's going after that?"

"No."

Together, we walked over to him and his wife for a few minutes. Then we walked over to our car and drove home.

As we turned into base housing Marty said, "A few weeks ago Bunny called. She wanted you to call her as soon as you got back."

"Oh, shit what's she want, more money?"

"I don't know. She wouldn't say."

"Well, I wanted to call her anyway to see if I could visit with the boys during my leave."

A little later, we pulled into our driveway. I got out and got my sea bag out of the trunk and followed Marty and Samantha into our house. I unpacked my dirty clothes next to the washer and dryer. Then I looked from the pile of dirty clothes to Marty and asked, "Still glad I'm home?"

"It's worth it," she said putting her arms around me as she kissed me. I kissed her back feeling her breast even through my camouflaged jacket.

"I need you," I whispered into her ear.

"I can't wait till tonight," she whispered back.

"I don't know if I can keep my hands off you that long."

"So, what are we going to do?"

"Well we could take a shower."

"I knew you were going to say that," she said smiling.

"You know me too well," I answered also smiling.

"I should after seven and a half years."

"Well?"

"Why not?"

Together we walked into the bathroom. Marty locked the door as I turned the shower on. After we had finished, I unlocked the door and stepped into the shower behind Marty.

After the shower, I got dressed and walked over to the phone, dreading the call to Bunny. But I had put it off long enough and dialed the number. It rang three times before I heard Bunny's voice on the other end say, "Hello."

"Bunny, this is Nathan."

She said, "Today." And then there was silence on the other end. So, I asked, "You wanted me to call?"

"Yes. I think it's time Nat came to live with you. He's getting a little big for me to handle."

I was almost speechless with surprise. This was the last thing I had expected to hear.

"Nathan, are you still there?"

"Yes, I'm just surprised. How about Lance?"

"No, he's not ready."

"How soon can I pick Nat up?"

"Do you know when you'll be coming up for a visit?"

"I have fifteen days leave. We plan on leaving the first thing in the morning. We'll probably only visit the families a few days now instead of the whole two weeks. I think I should get him down here at least a week before I have to report back to duty."

"I think that's a good idea. Do you mind if he stays here until you're ready to go back?" Bunny asked.

"No that's fine. We'll pick him up three mornings from now at 0700, I mean 7 in the morning."

"I know what 0700 hundred means."

"I'm sorry."

"Do you have any idea how long you'll be in the states this time?"

"Should be here a year. But you know how it goes."

"Yes, I remember too well how you are."

"Okay then. Thank you. Goodbye," I said.

"Goodbye."

I hung the phone up smiling and raising my fist yelling, "All right!"

Marty stood looking at me with a mixture of shock and fear and asked, "What in the world?"

"Nat's coming back with us."

"For how long," she asked smiling.

"To live."

"What's going on? What happened?"

"I don't know and I am not going to ask."

"Do you want to leave now?"

"No, I'm too beat, for a nine-hour drive. We'll pack up tonight and leave at sunup tomorrow."

We went to bed early. We made love again and afterward I couldn't get to sleep. I kept thinking of bringing Nat home with us. It was a dream come true. A dream I had given up on.

At 0700 on June 29th, Marty, Samantha, Lance and I drove up into Bunny's yard. I had picked up Lance three days ago to visit with him. Lance and I got out and he walked into the house. Meanwhile, I opened the back door to the station wagon. Then I walked up to the front door and knocked.

From inside Bunny said, "Come in."

I opened the door finding Nat standing with his bags in his hands. I stepped up to him and hugged him smiling, finding it hard to speak.

But he wasn't smiling as he said, "I don't want to live with you!"

I pulled back shocked, looking at him and then back at Bunny who was sitting at the kitchen table.

"Put your stuff in the car Nat," said Bunny.

Nat pushed past me in a huff walking out the door.

I turned toward Bunny asking, "I thought he wanted to come."

Bunny dropped her head in her hands saying, "He's getting to be more than I can handle. He's as big as you are. For the last six months whenever I got on him about something, he got so he threatened to go live with you. I think it's time he does."

"I see," I said.

"You still want him?"

"Yes sure. I think it'll be good for both of us."

Bunny was silent for almost a full minute before she said, "Do you have room for Lance and his things."

My mouth dropped open again before I said, "You said only Nat."

"Yes, I know. But he wants to go too."

"Sure," I said almost laughing.

"Lance!" yelled Bunny.

I looked back toward the hallway and Lance was already coming into the living room smiling and carrying his bags.

Bunny got up and walked over and hugged and kissed him.

Then Bunny turned to me saying, "Should you speak to Marty

about Lance first?"

"No. We've both wanted them from the beginning."

Then we walked out the door toward the car finding Nat already sitting in the back seat looking mad.

At seeing Lance carrying his bags, Marty looked surprised, but smiled her understanding way.

Soon, we were driving south down route 13 with little five-year-old red headed Samantha sitting between her oldest brothers. All we needed was Kyle now to have our whole family complete. But that would have to wait until September.

By the time we got below Salisbury, Maryland, I noticed in the mirror Nat had started to smile some as the family talked.

We stopped on the Chesapeake Bay Bridge and Tunnel and walked out on the pier. We took pictures of each other and laughed. I felt whole and complete at last.

We stopped again in Norfolk, Virginia visiting the Naval base, which had been home port for the ship I had been assigned to when I was a 1st Sergeant. Then we drove by the house we had lived in.

We arrived at home on Camp Lejeune, NC, after midnight. We carried everything into the living room and dropped them there. I carried the sleeping Samantha into her room to her bed. Then Nat took Kyle's bed. Lance took the living room couch for the night.

The next morning, we all slept in late. Then Marty fixed breakfast. Then the boys went out to find old friends they had met on past visits and to make new ones.

As usual my leave passed too quickly, especially now that the boys were living with us. By July 10th, I was back with 1st platoon training and snapping in the new men who had joined us because of the big turnover that always happens after a unit returns from an extended deployment.

But at least for now, I'm able to get home most days by 1800 and have most weekends off.

The rest of July quickly passed. I lost Tapper when he was promoted to Gunnery sergeant and transferred to Lima Company

On Aug 2nd in the middle of the afternoon, Lt Littleton sent GySgt Knight to round up the platoon leaders for a staff meeting.

"What's up Gunny?" I asked.

"No idea Gunner. But Colonel Kersher called a company commanders' meeting at 1300. I guess the Skipper wants to brief us on that meeting,"

Soon Lt Littleton's office was filled with Lts Wright and Cregar, Me, 1stSgt Burns, GySgt's Knight and Cain, SSgt's Simon and Reed and acting platoon sergeants, Sgts Reilly and Meadows.

Lt Littleton slowly looked around the room before he spoke, "The battalion has received deployment orders."

"Deployment orders. Sir, we haven't been back two months," said SSgt Simon.

"Where are we going sir?" asked GySgt Cain.

"Back to the Root," answered Lt Littleton.

"Sir with all the battalions in this division why are we going back so soon. Usually we get a year between deployments," said SSgt Simon.

"The word I get is the division is stretched thin because of our commitment to Beirut. We still have to keep a battalion in Cuba, the Med and the Caribbean. Everybody's turnaround time has been shortened," said Lt Littleton.

"When do we leave?" asked GySgt Cain.

"Sometime in October," answered Lt Littleton.

"How soon do we start pre-deployment training and exercises?" I asked.

"The battalion leaves for a month-long exercise at 29 Palms in six days."

"Man, my wife is going to be pissed," said SSgt Simon.

"Your wife should be used to the Corps," said 1stSgt Burns.

"The Colonel did say if this quick turnaround would cause anybody any real hardship, he will listen to any request mast on a case by case basis. But they have to be turned in to me no later than 1630 today. If there's no more questions, return to your platoons," said Lt Littleton.

"Mine will be in, sir," said SSgt Simon.

"I probably will too, sir," said GySgt Cain getting up to leave.

As we all started to file out the door Lt Littleton said, "Gunner wait a minute."

I turned around as the rest walked out and said, "Yes sir."

"Gunner I've already talked to Colonel Kersher about you. So much as I hate to lose you. I know that after eight years of trying to get custody of your sons, you finally got them two months ago. The Colonel said just submit a request for transfer and he would approve it," said Lt Littleton.

Even though I felt torn I said, "Thank you sir. I do hate to leave this soon after finally getting them. But sir, I can't let my men go in harm's way without me. I couldn't look them in the face."

"How about your kids?"

"They have to realize what it means to have a Marine as a father."

"How about your wife?"

"She knows how I am. I am concerned whether she can handle a son that's bigger than she is. But it's time we find out. And if they won't listen to her while I'm gone, they'll have to go back to their mother until I get back."

"Why don't you take the afternoon off and go home and talk this over with your wife."

"Thank you, sir. I was thinking about asking for a few hours off."

"If you decide to change your mind just call me before 1630. If I don't hear from you, I'll know you're going with us."

I smiled saying, "Thank you, sir."

"I'll have Gunny Knight go over to First platoon and tell Sergeant Meadows he'll have the platoon the rest of the afternoon," said Lt Littleton.

"Thank you again, sir."

I walked out of the company headquarters building to my truck. I drove to base housing and parked in my driveway. I opened the front door and stepped through as Marty walked in the living room smiling, "You're home early."

"The Skipper gave me the afternoon off."

Her expression changed to one of worry as she asked, "Is everything all right?"

"We need to talk."

She took my hand and led me back to our bedroom and closed the door and again asked, "What's wrong?"

"The battalion has received heads up orders back to Beirut."

Her mouth dropped open, then she said," What about the year stateside?"

"No unit is getting the usual year stateside because of Beirut."

"How soon?"

"Sometime in October. But we leave in six days for thirty days of desert training at 29 Palms California."

"Oh great," she said putting her hands on her hips in a way I wasn't used to seeing her.

"But I don't have to go."

"What do you mean?" she said smiling.

"Lieutenant Littleton talked to colonel Kersher about my boys, just coming to live with us. He said if I ask for a transfer, he would approve it."

"Praise the Lord," she said coming toward me.

I stopped her, holding her at arm's length and said, "Marty I can't."

"Can't what?"

"I can't ask for a transfer."

"Why not?"

"Because I'm a Marine officer and my platoon is going back to war. I couldn't look them in the face."

"Nathan your boys need you. Kyle needs you. Samantha needs you."

"I know Marty. But our kids will be safe. I can help keep some of these young Marines alive."

"Nathan you have done enough for Corps and country. Eight years in Vietnam, not to mention San Salvador and one tour already in Beirut."

I looked down at the floor thinking; I thought she understood me and how I felt. Especially after seven-and-a-half-years of marriage to me. Then I looked back up into her eyes and said, "Do you remember eight years ago on our first date. We took a long walk on the beach and I told you how I was and what it would mean to share your life with a career Marine."

Then she looked down saying, "Yes I remember." She then looked up into my eyes saying, "Just how would you feel if I didn't try to talk you out of it?"

I had to smile as I said, "I guess I would think you didn't care."

"See?"

"Yes, I understand."

"And I understand too. You do what you feel is right and I'll stand by you. Because I love you."

"I love you too," I said pulling her close and then asked, "But what about Nat and Lance. Do you want me to see if Bunny will take them back while I'm in Beirut?"

"No. Finally our whole family is a real family. We will all have to learn to live together while you're gone."

"Good. But are you sure you'll be all right?" I asked.

"I'll be fine. But you should explain this to the boys."

That night after supper I sat Nat, Lance and Samantha down in the living room and explained what was going to happen and why I felt I had to go. When I was done, I asked, "Do any of you have anything to say? Do you have any questions?"

"I wish you would retire," blurted Nat.

"Nat I can't retire until October of next year and get a pension for all these years I have put in."

"Are you going to retire next year?" asked Nat.

"Nat, I haven't even thought about retirement. But I might. But I can't say now what I'll do when the time comes. I hope that someday you boys will have a job that you love as much as I do."

"I don't want to be a Marine," said Lance.

"You don't have to be a Marine. I have never told you boys that you had to go into the service unless you're drafted."

"I don't want you to get shot," said Lance.

"I don't either. I've been shot enough," I said laughing and then added, "I love you guys." I held my arms out to all three of them. Nat jumped up and hugged me saying, "I love you too." Followed by Lance and Samantha.

The afternoon of Aug 8th, our battalion was bussed to Cherry Point NC. We could see the big plane on the airfield that would take us all to 29 Palms.

After the buses stopped, company gunnies started yelling for their companies to form up.

Soon, GySgt Knight had Mike Company lined up by platoons and their sea bags stacked in front of them. Off to the side, stood Lt Littleton, 1stSgt Burns and us, platoon leaders.

Across from us, GySgt Tapper had Lima Company lined up. On the other side of the plane stood Kilo Company and Capt Evans' India Company.

Our battalion sergeant major had each company, one at a time load their gear on the plane. Mike Company was the last company to load our equipment. By the time we were done it was dark. LtCol Kersher, Capt Graham and the rest of the battalion staff boarded the plane first. Then the company commanders climbed on, followed by us, platoon leaders, and 1st Sergeants. Then company by company the rest of the battalion boarded.

The next day, in the desert of 29 Palms, the company gunnery sergeants supervised their men in setting up squad tents for the enlisted men, as us officers moved into our wooden A-frame barracks. Then LtCol Kersher, Capt Graham, the company commanders and us platoon leaders walked up to the airfield. When we landed, I had been surprised at how much bigger the airfield was since the last time I was here. The first time I landed here it had been nothing but a landing strip without buildings, in the middle of nowhere. Now it had buildings and a control tower. We got on Ch-46 choppers and flew over the area where our battalion would be training.

By the time we had gotten back to the battalion, tent city was all set up. As we walked down Mike Company's street, we saw GySgt Cain, SSgt Simon and Sgt Rienbold standing in front of Weapons platoon tent. In front of them was a red and gold sign which said, 'Harlem Plaza, Weapons platoon, Mighty Mike Co, 2/8.

Lt Littleton looked at the sign and then at GySgt Cain. GySgt Cain just shook his head looking over at Sgt Rienbold who just smiled.

Starting the next day, we were miles away in the desert training.

As always, I found the desert of 29 Palms to be harsh and bare, a place unforgiving of weakness or error, but yet a place of strange beauty.

Yet, this desert is the one Marine base where a Marine battalion or regiment can test their fighting skills in realistic training exercises with live ammo and supported by live artillery and air power.

As the days passed, the battalion staff had to coordinate the combined arms fire as the companies moved around the desert. And the young Marines had to put up with the unrelenting heat and sharp winds, which stirred the sand around them.

The training went on at a quick pace as the battalion and individual companies had objectives to take.

Tanks, amtracks, TOW's, engineers and the Infantry companies moved as one, each with the same mission, but with different roles to play. Artillery and air power meshed together when we called for it. And behind us were the men and women in supply, support and maintenance, without whom, no vehicle moved, no plane flew, no bullet fired and no war is possible.

The first week we had used many of the ranges, firing machineguns, TOW's, LAAW's, Dragons, mortars, rifles and setting off demolition charges.

Then on Aug 17th, Mike Company moved into the southern end of the Delta Corridor and took up positions around a rocky hill. From here, Lt Littleton and GySgt Knight had an eagle's eye view of the assault area. From behind us, Lt Littleton called in artillery. Then Marine A-4 jets screamed in overhead and dropped napalm and bombs ahead of us.

Then in amtracks, we lunged ahead with tank support. On our flanks were jeeps darting around with teams of TOW gunners.

Our assaults were following combat tested patterns. Air and artillery prepped the targets. Tanks lumbered in for direct fire as we ran out the back of our amtracks moving in platoon formations to capture our objectives.

For two weeks more, our battalion moved as a team, accomplishing objective after objective.

When we took our final objectives on Aug 24th, we were tired and strained. We were looking forward to the tent city with its cots and warm showers.

The 1st of Sept, as we prepared to return to Camp Lejeune, I could feel my newer Marines' greater knowledge of the warrior's art, their confidence had increased in their ability to perform when we get to Beirut. If only we could be allowed to fight this way there, instead of being forced to stay in place in the bunkers and trenches.

On the plane home I thought back to the desert. I remembered SSgt Simon sitting in the shade of his poncho, which he had tied to tent poles and sticks, as he ate a can of civilian franks and beans.

Then, there was the day GySgt Cain had burst the seat out of his camouflaged trousers. I could see him sitting in the desert sand pulling off his trousers while his white underwear stuck out like a sore thumb. He had laughed with the rest of us as he pulled his other camouflaged trousers out of his pack, while SSgt Simon took his picture.

"Come on gunny, cover up them white underwear before you give our position away," kidded Sgt Rienbold.

By the time we landed at Cherry Point, NC, unloaded our gear, loaded it on the buses, rode back to Camp Lejeune, unloaded the buses and put everything away, it was after midnight before I got home.

As I unlocked the front door and stepped into the living room, Marty sat up from the couch.

"I guess I fell asleep," said Marty getting up.

I walked over as she rushed into my arms.

"How did it go?" I asked.

"Fine, just fine."

"No problems?"

"Nothing I couldn't handle."

"Good."

"Do you know when in October you're leaving?"

"Yes, not until the 17th."

"Well that's better than I thought. I figured it would be the first."

"No, you'll have to put up with me a little bit longer."

"I can handle that. I'm glad you're home."

"I'm glad. How's Kyle making out with his older brothers around all the time?"

"He loves it."

"How are they doing in school?"

"Lance and Samantha are off to a good start. But Nat and Kyle are struggling."

"Let's go to bed."

"I'm ready," said Marty.

The morning of Sept 18th, Mike Company was lined up by platoons with the platoon sergeants out in front facing 1stSgt Burns. He did an about face as Lt Littleton marched out and faced him.

They saluted each other and 1stSgt Burns took his place to the left rear of Lt Littleton.

"Post!" yelled Lt Littleton.

Sgt Meadows marched around to the rear of the platoon, as I, like the other platoon leaders marched around to the front of our platoons and snapped to attention.

"I have here an article that was in the Moscow Red Star back in August of this year. In it, the Russian Defense Ministry condemns President Reagan for sending US Marines to Lebanon," said Lt Littleton. Then he went on to say, "It says the Marines are willing to murder, knife and rape, casting aside honor and conscience and forgetting everything that makes man different from an animal. This latest Marine Corps deployment is forceful proof of the hegemonistic course and aggressive schemes of US imperialism and it's striving to bend other nations to its will by force of arms. The traditional role of the Marine Corps has been paving with fire and sword the way for American capitalism, and as having wrought havoc and practiced brute arbitrariness everywhere."

Lt Littleton looked up at our company and then said, "I wonder what they call their military venture in Afghanistan. I realize Jane Fonda wouldn't invite one of my platoons to one of her cocktail parties. It's plain to me that we scare the hell out of the commies. For they know we have esprit de Corps. We are proud of the fact that our Corps is a profession of arms that means more than just a paycheck. I read this to you so we can laugh at the commies and also get our martial juices flowing,"

My chest swelled with pride as Lt Littleton looked over Mike Company. Then he ordered, "Platoon leaders carry out the training schedule!"

"Aye, Aye, sir!" the four of us platoon leaders said as one, saluting him.

Lt Littleton returned our salute. Then he and 1stSgt Burns did a right face and marched off.

And another day in the Corps began.

In the early morning of Oct 17th, I said goodbye to Marty and the children with hugs and kisses. With just five days short of being in the Corps 19 years, I'm leaving again for war. Once again, I won't be home for Christmas. I've long ago lost count of how many Christmases I've missed.

Marty had vowed not to watch the nightly news until I got back home. Especially when last nights' news had said that heavy fighting had erupted around the Marine Battalion positions at Beirut.

Our battalion was bussed to Moorehead City where we boarded two ships. Mike and India Companies went on the USS Guam. For many of my platoon, it was their first time at sea and they found the quarters too tight. Col Studt had bragged to us that 40% of our battalion had been together for two years or more. But my platoon only had three of us that had even been in Lebanon together and the new men didn't seem worried about heading toward a combat zone. We had trained hard for it and most of them were looking forward to the experience.

The next day we left the port city of Moorehead. We joined up with the rest of the Amphibious task force made up of two amphibious assault ships, USS Trenton, USS Fort Snelling, USS Manitowoc and USS Barnstable County. There was 1,900 Marines in this MAU. First, we were heading to Spain to do an amphibious exercise.

Late in the afternoon GySgt Knight came to my room and told me Lt Littleton wanted to see me. When I entered his room, he handed me my promotion warrant to Chief Warrant Officer Three, saying battalion had just gotten it in the mail this morning. I walked back to my room disappointed that it hadn't been given to me in a company formation. If it had arrived a few days ago, all my children could have seen me get promoted for the first time together. Back in my room, I took my blouse off, hanging it on a hanger. I took the old bars off and pinned on my new bar (a red bar with one silver box in the center)

Chapter 4 Chief Warrant Officer Three

About midnight Oct 20th, our task force passed north of Bermuda heading for the Mediterranean. We were fifty miles past Bermuda when suddenly, the task force was ordered to turn south 500 miles and then sail in a holding position northeast of the Island of Grenada for something more than a peaceful exercise. This news swept through the ship even though it was the middle of the night. Tension on the ship got heavy as we wondered what was going to happen.

The night was cool and the day broke hot as Lt Wright and I stood at the rail looking out at the ocean. We were surprised to see a sailboat out in the middle of nowhere with two pretty blonds on it.

Later as I ate breakfast in the wardroom, I watched the news on TV, especially the stories about the civil upheaval in Grenada.

The hot subject at the table between Capt Evans, India Company officers and us from Mike Company was what we might do in Grenada. Most felt we would probably help evacuate US citizens. So far, we had no specific mission, no idea of the number or locations of the US civilians who might have to be evacuated and so far, there are no maps of Grenada except for a nautical chart of the island based on a 1936 British chart. From looking at that, Capt Evans figured we might make a landing on the southwest peninsula. We had trained for evacuation type operations and had begun planning and preparing our companies for it.

We were told the ships would hold our present position until midnight Oct 23rd. Then, if without further instructions, our task force would continue on to Beirut.

By the afternoon of Oct 22nd, thirty-six hours had passed and we hadn't received any word. My fellow officers began to feel the likelihood of us landing in Grenada wasn't very good.

I was lying in my rack at 2200 when I heard a knock on my hatch.

"Enter!" yelled Lt Wright in the rack below me.

GySgt Knight opened the door, sticking his head in saying, "Excuse me gentlemen, but Capt Graham wants all officers in the wardroom asap."

"Oh shit," I said sitting up.

"What's up gunny?" asked Lt Wright.

"Don't know sir. I figure it's either a go at Grenada or we're being told we're heading on to the Root," answered GySgt Knight.

Quickly, we climbed into our camouflage utilities and pulled on our boots. Then we hurried to the wardroom. Soon, all the officers of India and Mike Companies were there.

Capt Graham stood in front of us as he spoke. "We just received the message from Colonel Studt, which directs us to turn toward Grenada. We will be responding to an urgent request from the Organization of Eastern Caribbean States. Our task is to evacuate 1,000 American students and other US Nationals. The Grenadian prime minister, Bishop and three cabinet members have been shot down in the streets and killed by Cuban backed rebels."

As I listened, I knew this could be serious.

Capt Graham went on to say, "Our mission is called Operation Urgent Fury and the mission will be to stop political unrest that is threatening the lives of other US civilians."

As He spoke, the sergeant major stepped in with a second message with orders of battle and information about the Grenadian forces.

Then Capt Graham said, "Well. It seems the US Army is going to conduct an airborne assault on Grenada with us. We will be there Sunday October twenty-third. We may end up serving as their reserve."

"Are you shittin' me!" roared Capt Evans of India Company.

"That's all I have for now," answered Capt Graham.

"If there's fighting to be done, we should be the obvious choice," said Capt Evans. "I agree. But we'll just have to wait and see," said Capt Graham.

I returned to my rack, but couldn't sleep. After breakfast, I gathered my platoon together and told them what little I knew. We all spent a frustrating day and evening wondering what the hell was going to happen. In my room, I prayed this wouldn't end up like the Iran crisis.

In the middle of my prayer, Lt Wright opened the hatch saying, "Gunner! Capt Graham wants all officers in the wardroom. There's a problem in the Root."

"Now what are we doing?" I asked

We rushed to the wardroom and found the TV on. The rest of the officers started arriving, but nobody seemed to know anything.

Just as Capt Graham stood up, the sergeant major opened the

door saying, "Excuse me Captain Graham, but the ship's captain wants you to report to him for a further brief."

"Okay, sergeant major. I'll be right there." Then he turned back to us and said, "All I know right now is the Colonel in charge of the MAU in the Root has requested reinforcements, consisting of a complete battalion headquarters with attachments, most of a weapons company and a rifle company.

"Has the battalion staff in Beirut been wiped out?" asked Capt Evans.

"I don't know. But it sure doesn't sound good to me. I've got to go," said Capt Graham leaving.

As we sat there looking around the room at each other wondering what had happened, suddenly there was a news flash. As all heads turned toward the TV, we heard there had been an explosion at the battalion headquarters in Beirut.

A few minutes later, we heard it had been a large explosion at the battalion headquarters destroying the battalion building.

Two and a half hours later, I watched news films showing the battalion building had collapsed completely. I was horrified at the large numbers of Marines that must have been killed and wounded.

The French also reported one of their buildings in their sectors had also been bombed.

When Capt Graham finally returned to brief us, we learned more details of the damage and the loss of Marine lives, our shock deepened as the count of casualties continued to mount.

As I walked around the ship, I saw Marines of all ages wiping tears away. All the Marines of India and Mike Companies seemed to be in mourning as old and young wept bitter tears of rage, frustration and sorrow.

Now that our battalion had been diverted to Grenada indefinitely, postponing our tour in Beirut, we felt even more frustrated. We all wanted to get back to Beirut and invade Hooterville and take the high ground.

At 2200 Sunday Oct 23rd, a chopper landed on our ship with Col Studt, LtCol Kersher, the CO's of Kilo and Lima Companies and liaison officers from Atlantic Command carrying new orders for us. Col Studt called for Capts Graham and Evans and Lt Littleton to join them in the wardroom. They had just thirty hours to plan their mission to take Pearls airfield and Grenville town and neutralize any opposition in the north end of the island.

The southern part of the island would belong to the US Army. Our MAU would provide support, as they required.

Maps of Grenada and radio frequencies were handed out to the company and squadron commanders. The island was 133 square miles with a population of 110,000 people. The American students and staff members were still at St George's University School of Medicine.

Grenada has about 800 regular soldiers. The size of the militia is unknown.

It was difficult to verify the condition of the foreigners in Grenada because the government had banned foreign journalists and closed the airport.

A ham radio operator in New Jersey who had been in contact with two Americans on Grenada, including a medical student, said they were scared to death to move around.

President Reagan had signed the order for an assault landing by dawn on Tuesday. The US Army units would seize the Point Salines airfield at the southwestern corner of the island.

With this little bit of guidance, Col Studt's staff began planning for the operation. Their plan was for Mike Company to be choppered in and Capt Evan's India Company would land by amtrack.

By midnight, Capt Evans and Lt Littleton were working on exactly how their companies would take their objectives.

They both wanted to take these objectives by surprise, during the early hours of darkness of Tuesday Oct 25th. But Col Studt had been ordered that no landing could take place before 0400. Capt Evans complained to LtCol Kersher that this didn't give us much time before sunup. He agreed, but said orders were orders. So, the chopper and amtrack landing would both go in at 0400. By dawn or very soon after he wanted all objectives to be taken.

At 0100 Oct 24th, Lt Littleton called us platoon leaders together in his room and briefed us saying, "Well men, we are going to contribute to Marine Corps history by landing on Grenada." He went on to tell us of our mission and objectives. "Seal teams will land late tonight by rubber raft. Also, two battalions of US Rangers will parachute the same morning we go in." Then he carefully briefed us on the rules of engagement. Heavy weapons would not be used indiscriminately, but only if essential to accomplish the mission.

Our objectives were to liberate, not attack Grenadians. There is to be no search and destroy operations.

There was little intelligence so far. Lt Littleton seemed to feel lucky to have naval charts of the island, even though they didn't have grids on them. "So, let your troops sleep. Get some sleep yourselves and brief them in the morning."

As I lay in my rack, I couldn't get to sleep thinking about us going in tomorrow in the first wave of choppers. I found myself scared and afraid for the young Marines of my platoon. I prayed as I had done so often, for God to help me make the right decisions to keep them alive.

In the morning, as I ate breakfast of steak and eggs in the wardroom, the TV news reported that it had been a truck bomb which had blown up the MAU headquarters in Beirut. Again, names and faces of captains and 1st Sergeants I knew there, came to mind. Were they okay? The truck had been packed with explosives equivalent to over 12,000 pounds of TNT, which not only completely destroyed the building, but also left a crater thirty feet deep and forty feet across.

Then, I went to Sgt Meadows and had him gather my platoon together. First, I briefed them on our mission tomorrow and then told them the latest update on Beirut.

Again, they became angry and talked of revenge. I couldn't blame them because I felt the same way. But I said, "Men, first we have this mission. Remember an angry Marine doesn't think. And I'm going to need thinkers tomorrow."

Later, Capt Graham was choppered to the USS Trenton for another briefing about our contingency plans. As usual, when he returned, there was a high state of urgency as the officers of India and Mike Companies gathered in the wardroom for his briefing. He began by saying, "Well I have bad news. Colonel Studt has been ordered to change H hour up to 0500 which will only give us at best a half hour of dusk."

"So much for surprise," grumbled Capt Evans.

"Also, our chopper landing site has been moved eighty miles southeast. And the Seals have reported six-foot-high surf and coral obstacles, which means the amtrack landing is canceled," said Capt Graham.

"So, what about India Company?" asked Capt Evans.

"They will land by helo, too," answered Capt Graham.

Again, Sgt Meadows gathered our platoon together and I briefed them on the changes.

My young Marines were clearly thrilled to be going ashore, but at the same time they naturally felt some anxiety.

Through the day, I supervised the training of Mike Company for house-to-house fighting, by using the compartments of the ship.

As night came, I felt a grim determination set in through my platoon to see this mission through, regardless of our losses, and then get on to Beirut. My men were eager to get on with it, for this kind of operation was what they had really been trained for.

As the ships steamed through the night with no lights on, I tried to get some sleep, but couldn't because of fear and excitement. I knew I was heading for the largest combat action since Vietnam.

At 0100 Oct 25th, I went to the wardroom with the rest of the officers of India and Mike Companies and listened to Capt Graham's final briefing. He told us the Seals were on the beach and had little resistance so far. But four of them had drowned in the rough seas caused by the intermittent rainsqualls.

When I left the wardroom, I found that Sgt Meadows had my squad leaders waiting for me. I briefed them on the latest news. Then we discussed what we would do if different circumstances ensued.

I knew LtCol Kersher and his staff were getting little sleep as they revised their plans. The biggest problem was the weather. It was dark with high winds and rain. Our ship had to be headed into the wind for the choppers to take off. And with the heavy seas this would cause the choppers lift-offs to be slower. Instead of four choppers taking off at once, only one would take off at a time. There couldn't be a two-company landing at the same time, which meant Pearls must be taken first.

At 0200, I finished briefing my platoon and the squad leaders gathered their squads together and briefed them and made final equipment checks

Cpl Wynne and his squad had watched the John Wayne movie Iwo Jima. "Somehow, it seemed the proper thing to do", he told Sgt Meadows as our platoon ate a hurried last meal of steak and eggs. Then Sgt Meadows passed out the live ammo.

Then I sat with my platoon, waiting to board the choppers which would fly us into battle.

The first chopper had been scheduled to lift off at 0300. But because of the poor weather it was delayed until 0315.

It was 0500 before all of Mike Company was in the air and heading for shore. Again, Sgt Meadows and I, the only Vietnam veterans left in our platoon, tried to steady the others as we flew the ten miles to shore. It was still dark as we flew without lights.

By the time the choppers crossed the beach flying low, the rain had stopped. I could make out some terrain features in the dawn. All was quiet as we neared landing zone Buzzard just south of Pearls. This LZ had been marked on our maps as an unused racetrack, but all I could see was tall palm trees and high scrub brush everywhere.

Then we were greeted by antiaircraft fire from a lone hill north of the LZ, as we started to land. I saw the tracers and noticed Sgt Meadows face become grim. First the tracers went by above us, and then below us and I knew the next burst should go right through us. I could see the enemy firing at us, dressed in T-shirts and jeans and a few in uniforms. One was a woman firing a machinegun. But two Marine Cobra gunships quickly fired rockets in the direction of the tracers, silencing the enemy fire as the Grenadian gun crew fled.

Later, Cpl Wynne's squad would find two anti-aircraft positions knocked out with eight dead enemy soldiers.

Then, our chopper landed and I was proud to see my men run out of the chopper and fan out like I had trained them to do from day one. My God, they were Marines and just as good as we were in Vietnam eleven years ago. They're going to kick some ass. I felt like my heart would burst with pride.

It was now 0536, and I knew that down south the two US Ranger battalions were parachuting in.

Meanwhile, Lt Littleton ordered Mike Company to advance toward the airfield. As we moved, the Cobra gunships flew overhead covering us.

We neared the airfield and cut through a chain link fence. As we neared the terminal, a machinegun fired several short bursts at Lt Wright's 2nd platoon. Sgt Reilly's squad returned fire and they saw Grenadians running toward the western end of the runway.

As the 2nd platoon moved on, the Grenadians seemed to concentrate their fire at the choppers instead of the Marines on the ground.

Capt Graham called in airstrikes on the enemy positions.

I was relieved that so far, the enemies fire hadn't been effective.

By 0730, Mike Company had captured the airfield at Pearls.

In so doing, my platoon had captured two Cuban aircraft and twelve crewmembers.

Lt Littleton radioed Capt Graham the news, who in turn reported this to LtCol Kersher and added, "The Marines of Mike Company have executed their mission perfectly."

We also heard the Rangers had met heavy resistance in the south and had been unable to take their objectives, the airfield or get to the Medical School Campus. They were calling in Naval gunfire.

Meanwhile, Lt Littleton ordered my platoon to take a hill from which an anti-aircraft gun had been spotted. So, with heavy packs, weapons and flak jackets, we struggled up the steep hill expecting to take heavy fire at any time. But not a shot was fired. Instead, as we reached the top, the Grenadian soldiers dressed in T-shirts and shorts threw down their weapons and ran down the other side of the hill. We didn't fire, but Cpl Wynne's squad tried to catch them. The Marines carrying their packs, flak jackets and weapons couldn't catch the frightened Grenadians running for their lives. But we did capture two 12.7-cal machineguns, rifles and stacks of ammo.

Just as a Marine antitank team caught up to us on the hill, LtCol Kersher radioed Lt Littleton and ordered Mike Company to advance toward the west.

As we moved out, we heard mortars being fired in the hills west of the runway.

"Spread out some more!" I yelled to my platoon as I bent low walking. But the shells exploded behind us around the LZ area.

Grenadian civilians began coming out to wave their welcome to us.

By 1028, the Rangers had finally captured their airfield, the medical school campus and the high ground around that airfield. Also, two battalions of the US Army 82nd Airborne Division had landed at Point Salines in Air Force CH-11s.

Meanwhile, with the help of the Grenadian civilians, we of Mike Company captured Grenadian soldiers and caches of weapons and equipment.

By midmorning, our battalion had suffered only two injuries.

When Mike Company neared a village and took fire, Lt Littleton ordered Lt Cregar's 3rd platoon and my platoon to attack. Sgt

Rienbold's machinegun team laid down a base of fire for us as SSgt Simon's mortar team fired mortars over our heads as both platoons advanced toward the village. As I moved my platoon in squad rushes, the enemy firing increased.

L/Cpl Blandon grabbed his neck and stumbled, but found he had only been creased by a bullet.

Cpl Wynne, leading his squad, crouched low as he entered the first house finding only an abandoned enemy machinegun.

In the distance, I saw our jets diving and strafing enemy targets.

But enemy firing still came from other houses. I suddenly felt like I was having a flash back from Hue City as my men returned fire, smashing through windows and slamming against walls as they fought in fire teams from room to room, house to house, street by street and the enemy troops retreated north.

Both platoons pushed on receiving heavy fire.

L/Cpl Blandon jumped over a dead Grenadian soldier as an enemy machinegun opened up from across the street.

Behind us, Lt Wright's 2nd platoon saw Grenadians setting up mortars on top of a hill. Sgt Crew's squad opened fire on them scattering the enemy mortar crews.

But then, Mike Company started taking recoilless rifle fire. As the whole company dived to ground, Lt Littleton radioed for air support.

As usual, when I needed him most, Sgt Rienbold came diving through a doorway into the room with his machinegun team.

"Just thought you could use a hand sir," he said smiling, rolling to his feet, as two Marine Cobra's flew overhead.

"Yes! Get that gun over here and fire at that house," I said pointing down the street.

Sgt Rienbold crawled across the floor like a crab, laid the M-60 machinegun across the windowsill and opened up sending tracers into the house holding the enemy recoilless rifle.

Then, the first Cobra banked in firing a burst from its 20-MM cannons. Following the first, the second Cobra circled in, firing a rocket through the window of the house destroying it. Then three Grenadian soldiers ran from the ruble. The first Cobra spun around, dropping its nose and fired a burst knocking all of them down. Their job done; the Cobras flew away.

Again, we came under heavy fire as 3rd platoon and my platoon fought on house to house. In room after room, my platoon found abandoned rifles and one recoilless rifle.

As our two platoons captured Grenadian soldiers, we held them for Lt Wright's 2nd platoon to escort them to the rear. At one time, seven Grenadian soldiers with a recoilless rifle surrendered to Cpl Harris's squad, when the Marine Cobras returned overhead.

With the Cobras back and firing at enemy positions within the town, the enemy fell back.

By noon, we heard that resistance against the US Army in the south had been unexpectedly strong. They were up against Cubans and there were enemy units not yet accounted for. We heard the Seal team had been thrown back from their objective at the Beausejour transmitting station. Also, the Delta Force and a company of Rangers had been badly chewed up in their attack on the prison. And the Rangers had not reached the Grand Anse Campus where it was feared US hostages could be taken. Another Seal team that was supposed to rescue the governor-general, was now pinned down with him inside his house.

So far, the only Marine deaths had been from Cobras that were shot down by anti-aircraft fire.

As Mike Company pushed on, Marine jets roared in overhead, strafing and bombing enemy positions ahead of us.

About this time, Col Studt was ordered to use some of his Marines to relieve the pressure on the Ranger units and rescue the Seal team and the governor-general.

At 1300, LtCol Kersher ordered Lt Littleton to be ready to be choppered to a new area at 1630. We heard the Seal teams had suffered heavy casualties and were getting low on ammo.

Meanwhile, Mike Company was fighting on against the poorly trained Grenadian soldiers who seemed to have little motivation. So far for us, the enemy resistance usually hadn't lasted long. Although a few did fight hard, but then surrendered or retreated.

At 1400, we heard that the US paratroopers were pinned down now and taking heavy casualties.

At 1430, Capt Evans' India Company had returned to the beach and boarded amtracks to make a landing down south to help the Seals at the governor's house near the middle of the island. We heard armored personnel carriers were supporting the enemy force surrounding them.

At 1500, LtCol Kersher radioed Lt Littleton that Mike Company would land by chopper near Grand Mal as India Company landed across the beach. Our final objective would still be the governor-general's house. We heard rumors there was a Cuban battalion north of there.

As Lt Littleton moved our company toward the LZ site, LtCol Kersher radioed that the landing would be delayed until 1830.

Later as Mike Company gathered around the LZ, Lt Littleton gave us the word the chopper lift of our company had been delayed yet again.

Mike Company settled down in a 360-degree defense perimeter to wait. It had been a long day, but we were amazed and happy because Mike Company had suffered no casualties bad enough to be medivaced. We all knew our luck couldn't last through tomorrow.

At 1930, Capt Evans' India Company with five tanks, landed by amtracks on the west coast at Gravel Mall Bay and finding no resistance, advanced west toward the governor's house.

The weather was still very warm even at 2100. We heard Col Studt thought we would have control of the island by tomorrow night.

As we waited, I wondered what the people back home were thinking about this. I wondered if my family knew I was here. I felt we were doing the right thing here. I was very proud of my platoon and I hoped the American people understood what was happening down here.

Up north, we heard Lima Company had captured an Agriculture Experimental Station. In so doing, GySgt Tapper saw three Cubans running away. He ordered them to halt. When they didn't his Marines opened fire killing one and wounding another. The third Cuban then stopped and surrendered.

Finally, in the early hours of Oct 26th, Mike Company boarded choppers. A little later, we landed in a LZ, covered by SSgt Spidden's platoon from India Company. The rest of India Company was moving toward St George's. Quickly forming up, Mike Company followed SSgt Spidden's platoon, moving in single file along a road.

Up ahead of us I heard the rattling of amtracks and M-60 tanks in the night.

Then we heard small arms fire start up. But under heavy Marine fire, the enemy resistance faded away as we moved through the night. A little later, we heard Capt Evans' India Company had taken Queens Park. Here, LtCol Kersher set up his battalion CP.

After fighting through the night, Capt Evans' India Company took up defensive positions north of Grenada's capital, St George. Col Studt was now ordered to minimize civilian casualties. So, he in turn ordered LtCol Kersher not to have his Marines launch a full-scale ground assault. Instead, India Company was ordered to attack in small units supported by heavy air power. I was afraid this would cause India Company to have a fierce battle.

Meanwhile, Lt Littleton was ordered to push on toward the Government House. As Mike Company neared the Government House, we advanced carefully up a steep hill. Sgt Higgins squad from 3rd platoon checked out a house, while the rest of the company moved through the trees and brush to the grounds of Government House. I looked at my watch. It was 0715 and I wondered where the enemy forces were that had kept the Seals pinned down for the last twenty-four hours.

At 0730, Cpl Wynne's squad from my platoon made contact with the Seals inside. I went in with my two corpsmen to check on their casualties and was surprised to find that they had none. With the Seals was British Sir Paul who had requested asylum.

Lt Littleton decided it was too risky to chopper Sir Paul, his wife and the other civilians with him out from here. So LtCol Kersher sent up a heavy guard, which took them by foot back to Queens Park where later they were evacuated out to our ship.

Then LtCol Kersher ordered Mike Company to move south and help the Rangers capture the second half of the Medical School campus.

Later, as Mike Company neared the campus, we moved carefully through thick brush and trees covering a ridge area.

Sgt Rienbold's machinegun teams covered my platoon as we moved from some high ground about 300 meters north of the campus. I saw it consisted of five barracks-style dorms, a cafeteria and basketball court.

As Mike Company advanced toward a wall, we came under withering AK-47 rifle and machinegun fire from Cuban forces well-armed and well-trained.

As we dove for cover, Lt Littleton and Sgt Rienbold were both nicked by bullets. Lt Littleton radioed LtCol Kersher for air support. Soon, Marine jets raced in to strafe the Cuban positions.

Then Lt Wright's 2nd platoon rushed forward. As they climbed over the wall, they saw Cubans running around behind one of the dorms. Without firing another shot, we captured 250 Cuban prisoners and had secured our part of the campus by 1600. Six Marine choppers then evacuated the American students.

Then LtCol Kersher ordered Mike Company to push on in the direction of Fort Frederick.

Again, we found ourselves advancing carefully through high grass and thick brush covering a ridge.

Suddenly, my platoon in the lead, we bumped into Grenadian forces. We took cover, firing as we were hit by machinegun and rifle fire from both our flanks. A bullet passed through Lt Littleton's trouser side cargo pocket.

Lt Cregar's 3rd platoon crawled forward firing on my left flank. With their support I was able to move my platoon in squad rushes driving the Grenadians back. But still as the whole company advanced, we came under fierce small arms fire from enemy positions that we found hard to find in the thick grass and bushes. Fearing heavy casualties, Lt Littleton ordered SSgt Simon's mortar teams to fire over our heads. He also called in naval gunfire as our company halted.

After the naval gunfire, Mike Company moved forward. My platoon found sixteen dead enemy soldiers as we inched forward. We spent the rest of the evening collecting enemy weapons. What Grenadian civilians we ran into seemed delighted that we were there.

At 2300, the enemy resistance still could be called light and for us the fighting for today seemed over. Again, Mike Company's casualty report to battalion was none.

At daylight, Mike Company left our overnight positions. As we advanced on Fort Frederick, enemy anti-aircraft emplacements lined a ridge manned by Cubans, fired at Marine Jets. They were protecting the command center for the Grenadian People's Revolutionary Army. But as Mike Company, led by my platoon, fought our way over the wall, the Cubans were climbing over the wall across from us to escape.

Cpl Wynne's squad entered a building, which had been used by the Cuban high command. In it were rows of beds with briefcases stuffed with classified documents, official documents, and food from Cuba, East Europe and dishes from Bulgaria. Later we would learn that these papers belonged to forty-nine Russians, twenty-four North Koreans, sixteen East Germans, fourteen Bulgarians and three Libyans.

Lt Wright's 2nd platoon found heaps of crumpled uniforms with many weapons and ammo including three 82-MM mortars.

Meanwhile, Capt Evans India Company had fought a tough battle for Fort Rupert. From behind limestone walls of a French built 18th century fortress, Cuban and Grenadian defenders showered small arms fire on the Marine squads. Grenadian soldiers even fired their AK-47's straight up at American dive-bombers and Cobra's. Two Marine Cobras were shot down. Finally, it took Capt Evans calling in air strikes to reduce Fort Rupert to smoldering rubble, leaving only one wall left standing. SSgt Spidden's platoon moved in finding dead Grenadian soldiers sprawled on the ground near Russian antiaircraft guns. Then India Company swept through a Cuban complex of barracks and warehouses. They ran into sharp firefights at the Cuban workers shelter, a supply dump and headquarters finding weapons caches.

Meanwhile, Mike Company pushed on as the temperature rose and we sweated. The Grenadian civilians we meet often helped us, pointing out the hiding places of the enemy as we swept the island.

At 0920, we slowly passed the burned-out remains of a building.

Lt Wright's 2nd platoon, now in the lead, advanced, stopping and starting from occasional sniper fire.

By 0930, our worst resistance was from the heat and the steep hills.

At 1345, my platoon, back on point, neared a crossroad when suddenly we came under heavy fire from behind and to our left.

I dived for cover as I saw a house where the firing was coming from. When I reported to Lt Littleton by radio what I had, he in turn called in an airstrike. I gave him the grid numbers of the house on my map; also adding it had a red roof. As the Marine jet came in low, Sgt Rienbold's machinegun team fired tracers into the window of the house marking the target. The jet fired its cannons as shells ripped into the house destroying it.

Then LtCol Kersher and our battalion CP group drove up in two command amtracks. LtCol Kersher ordered Lt Littleton to establish security around a nearby crossroad. He sent Lt Cregar's 3rd platoon up to the high ground. He ordered Lt Wright's 2nd platoon to secure the crossroads itself. My platoon was sent to secure the high ground to the north.

We found our high ground steep with dense brush. I placed two squads on two peaks along the high ridgeline. I started rotating one squad on patrol around our hill as the other two rested on watch.

Lt Wright's 2nd platoon stayed busy at the crossroads, stopping and searching vehicles, checking papers for identification and confiscating weapons. Again, the civilians seemed very happy to see us and were eager to point out members of the militia who had participated in the coup or had terrorized them.

At 1600, a car with two men tried to run through the checkpoint. Cpl Mitchell fired his M-16 once, shattering the windshield. The car stopped and the Marines of Cpl Mitchell's squad pulled the two men out. When they were found carrying several weapons, they were marched back to a small lumber yard with a warehouse and fenced in area our battalion was using as a POW compound.

Then the US forces were ordered to move toward the one remaining important Cuban stronghold, a hill top communications site.

India and Mike Companies, advancing carefully, came back together again as we moved toward Fort Adolphus. India Company was on the left side of a road, which followed the Morne Jaloux Ridge southward with Mike Company on the right.

The 2nd platoon was the point unit for Mike Company. Lt Wright reported by radio he could see that the fort was occupied. But he couldn't recognize the flag that was flying from it.

Lt Littleton reported this to LtCol Kersher. He in turn called for airstrikes and naval gunfire to be on standby if we should need the fort softened up.

As the rest of us covered them, 3rd platoon moved up to the fort. Lt Cregar radioed back that the fort was the home of the Venezuelan embassy.

We all sighed with relief.

Then both companies moved into St George. We found the city to be silent with nobody on the streets and all the cars parked.

Lima Company entered the city behind us to search for weapons or hidden enemy troops.

Meanwhile, LtCol Kersher with India and Mike Companies moved out of the city southward. Our new mission was to evacuate 400 US, British and Canadian citizens from the Ross Point Inn.

2nd platoon, leading the way quickly, got there after dark, but Lt Wright found only 20 Canadians who were happy to see US Marines, but really didn't mind staying were they were.

Both companies dug in here for the night in a 360 circle.

Again, Mike Company's casualty report to battalion was none. I wondered just how much luck we could have.

The next morning was Friday and both companies were up at dusk and moved into the mountains. Quickly, we began running into Cuban and Grenadian ambushes, taking RPG and small arms fire.

SSgt Spidden's platoon from India Company took sniper fire from the roof of a house.

Both Capt Evans and Lt Littleton, from time to time, called in artillery fire pounding Cuban and Grenadian positions in these hills.

SSgt Spidden's platoon captured Russian and Cuban weapons.

There was by now 2,800 Marines, US Army Rangers, Paratroopers and 300 troops from the six Caribbean nations of Antigua, St Lucia, St Vincent, Dominica, Jamaica and Barbados here.

The fighting for Capt Evans' India Company at times became intense enough for him to call in jets to make strafing runs.

Once a Grenadian civilian came to speak to him and said he knew where a senior Grenadian Communist General was hiding in a house.

SSgt Spidden's platoon followed the civilian to the house and surrounded it. Then a Marine squad moved forward and broke in capturing the general, his wife and his aide. They were marched back to our battalion. From there, LtCol Kersher had them choppered out to the USS Guam to be placed in protective custody.

Then Capt Evan's India Company captured six warehouses. In two of them, they found a large cache of Cuban and Russian weapons, AK-47 rifles, 120-MM mortars, machineguns, anti-aircraft guns, rocket launchers, and pistols all jammed in boxes stacked to the ceiling. Some of these boxes had been clearly disguised as ordinary Cuban imports with markings stating, "Cuban Economic Office."

Meanwhile, Lt Cregar's 3rd platoon, acting on a tip from another friendly Grenadian civilian, surrounded a house. Cpl Bower's squad broke through the back door and captured six young Cubans armed with AK-47 rifles.

Over at India Company, LtCol Kersher's amtrack rolled up to Capt Evans CP group, when sniper rounds hit around the feet of Capt Evans.

"They came from that burned out building!" yelled SSgt Spidden pointing.

"Let's go clear this up captain!" barked LtCol Kersher.

Capt Evans waved to SSgt Spidden to advance his platoon. After a twenty-minute firefight, the Grenadians threw their AK-47 rifles and uniforms out the windows. When the Marines stopped firing, they walked out with their hands up.

Then both companies advanced to the outskirts of a town.

SSgt Spidden's platoon was met by Grenadian civilians who directed them to a cave that they said was an arms cache. SSgt Spidden had his platoon surround the cave. Then he sent a fire team in, but they found it empty. But he decided to have his men search the area around a hospital nearby on the top of a ridge. As his platoon neared the top of the ridge, the heavy brush turned into a banana plantation. As the point man walked over the top, he stopped suddenly dropping to one knee as he pointed silently with his rifle at three Cubans standing next to a land rover. Then he yelled, "Freeze!"

The Cubans first looked at each other, spoke among themselves and then ran. The Marine point man opened fire knocking two of them down.

Then SSgt Spidden's rear squad came under fire. The rear squad spun around returning fire and within minutes all was quiet.

SSgt Spidden had ordered the other two squads to fall back to help his rear guard. But as they started to fall back, they too came under fire from the ridgeline. Both squads returned fire with rifles, machineguns and LAAW's. SSgt Spidden ordered these two squads back up the ridge. They did so in fire team rushes killing and capturing eight Grenadian soldiers.

Then LtCol Kersher, by radio, ordered both India and Mike Companies to halt where we were.

Lt Wright's 2nd platoon set up a roadblock. At 0800, suddenly down the road, Sgt Crew saw troops heading toward them.

"Lieutenant! We got company coming!" yelled Sgt Crew. Then he realized they were US troops. Then quickly added, "They're American troops!" He hesitated and then waved to them yelling, "Come on! We're Americans, too."

As they walked up to 2nd platoon, Lt Wright saw that they were troops of the 82nd Airborne. An Army lieutenant colonel walked up to Lt Littleton and said, "I'm surprised to find you Marines here. I was told this was a free fire zone with no friendlies in the area."

"Well colonel, I guess you didn't get the word about the change in boundaries," answered Lt Littleton.

By now we were hearing rumors we might be here for a month.

"I hope so," said Sgt Meadows.

"This is sure better than going to the Root. At least here we're allowed to do what we've been trained to do," said Cpl Wynne.

But we also heard we might invade Nicaragua and we all knew that would be a harder nut to crack.

LtCol Kersher came around talking to us. He said by now all the key political figures had been captured and most resistance had ceased. He said he was very proud of our efforts and how well we had performed our task.

Even I was amazed that we did this without any casualties in Mike Company.

In the afternoon, Lt Littleton was ordered by LtCol Kersher to be ready to be choppered to another area early in the morning.

At 0330 on Oct 29th, Mike Company boarded choppers, which flew us to the west coast.

At 0515, we had landed and had moved into a town along deserted streets. As before, we found the civilians cooperative, especially after some of the men gave the hungry people some of their MRE's. They in turn pointed out enemy soldiers who had changed into civilian clothes. Cpl Wynne's squad captured a Grenadian Major that was pointed out to him.

LtCol Kersher came riding up in his jeep among my platoon when a civilian lady waved him down and asked, "Are things all right now?"

"Everything is under control," he said.

"How can I be sure of that?" she asked.

"My Marines are here aren't they?"

We kept hearing the US Army was still having problems down south. Later I would read what the Joint Chiefs of Staff Gen Vessey USA had to say on this day, “I can’t believe that we have two Marine Companies running roughshod over the northern two thirds of that island and yet there are 6,000 paratroopers sitting on their asses in the south. Tell them to get going!”

But even so, despite the unexpected Cuban and Grenadian resistance, the combined forces had achieved their key objectives and evacuated 599 American citizens and eighty foreign nationals. So far US casualties had been only eighteen killed and 116 wounded.

By Sunday morning of Oct 30th, Capt Evans’ India Company had captured the town of Sauteurs on the north coast.

Meanwhile, Mike Company moved north on the west coast meeting no opposition.

It seemed Gen Vessey had arrived in Grenada because of his disappointment with the Army’s 82nd Airborne’s slowness against a few snipers. Again, he ordered them to get moving.

In the afternoon, amtracks landed for Mike Company to ride in. At 1530 we moved through small villages. Over our heads flew LtCol Kersher in a Huey. South of the town of Gouyave, the road ran between the sea and high cliffs. Here Lt Cregar’s 3rd platoon, on point, found a ditch had been dug across the road.

As Lt Cregar radioed back to Lt Littleton with the news. SSgt Reed noticed a bulldozer nearby.

Smiling SSgt Reed took Sgt Higgins’ squad with him to cover him. SSgt Reed climbed on top of the bulldozer and played with it until he got it started. Then he managed to get it turned around and filled the ditch in. As Mike Company moved on across the fresh dirt, SSgt Reed climbed down rejoining 3rd platoon still smiling and said, “I always wanted to drive a bulldozer.”

We passed through Gouyave and reached the town of Victoria at 1900.

Then Lt Littleton was told by LtCol Kersher to expect to be relieved by the Army today.

Later I heard choppers coming our way. Then I saw they were US Army Blackhawks. As the first two Army choppers landed, a platoon of combat ready soldiers charged out forming a circle around the choppers hitting the deck ready for action. LtCol Kersher walked pass Lt Cregar to meet them. Again, these were 82nd Airborne troops and they had been told they were landing in a hot LZ to relieve us.

Even after the Army had relieved our battalion, we still found ourselves spread thinly over two-thirds of the coastline of Grenada overnight.

On Oct 31st, our battalion began back-loading out to our ships. As Mike Company waited our turn, I noticed my men were smiling the smile of victory. Grenadian civilians came out to watch us and to say thank you.

It was dusk when Mike Company returned to our ship. Once aboard, Capt Graham sent for Capt Evans and Lt Littleton. Later Lt Littleton returned and gathered us platoon leaders together.

As we looked at him, he said, “Mike Company has a new mission. We are to prepare for a scouting mission on the tiny island of Carriacou, which is just fifteen miles northeast of Grenada. Intelligence has picked up radio signals from Cuban forces there requesting help from Cuba. Our aircraft have photographed sophisticated bunkers there. There are rumors there may also be North Korean soldiers with them preparing to make a last stand.

The combined surface and air assault are to go before dawn tomorrow.”

“Christ sir!” I said.

“No rest for the weary,” said Lt Wright.

“This sounds like another invasion, not a scouting mission,” said Lt Cregar.

“Be ready for anything. Your men have time for a hot shower and a hot meal,” answered Lt Littleton.

At 2000, the ship started sailing toward Carriacou Island.

I had Sgt Meadows gather our squad leaders together and I briefed them on what little I knew. At first, they thought I was kidding. So again, we spent a sleepless night planning and preparing for battle.

Mike Company would land by chopper and India Company would hit the beach in amtracks.

The next morning at 0430, we landed on Carriacou Island without a shot being fired. Lt Littleton formed our company up and we began sweeping the area looking for Grenadian, Cuban or North Korean soldiers.

At 0530, Capt Evans' India Company landed across the beach also unopposed.

The civilians we did run into were happy to see us and even asked Lt Littleton to raise the US flag to show the island now belonged to the US.

Seventeen Grenadian soldiers in civilian clothes surrendered without firing a shot to Cpl Wynne's squad.

A civilian gave Cpl Mitchell of 2nd platoon a key to a warehouse. When it was opened, he yelled, "Lieutenant Wright you better come look at this." Inside was a large cache of weapons. There were 700 rifles, 38 AK-47 assault rifles, 150 cases of ammo, two Cuban jeeps and a truck.

At 0820, LtCol Kersher declared the island secured.

Later in the day, Capt Evans India Company returned to the ship as Mike Company dug in for the night.

The next morning at 0700, elements of the 82nd Airborne began arriving to relieve us.

At 0900, Mike Company started withdrawing from the island back to our ship. With this, the Marines had successfully completed our role in Operation Urgent Fury.

The cost had been nineteen American dead and 115 wounded. Of these, the Marines had lost three dead and fifteen wounded. US forces had captured 691 prisoners of which thirty were Russian advisors. The Cubans had twenty-four dead and fifty-nine wounded, the Grenadian military had sixty-seven killed and 358 wounded. Our allies, the Caribbean Peacekeeping Force suffered no casualties.

At 1740 the ship carrying our MAU, steamed past St George's harbor with its battle flags flying as we again headed on our way to the Mediterranean to relieve the 24th MAU in Beirut. The ships then turned and headed north for Barbados where our MAU was resupplied by choppers from the beach.

I woke up on Nov 3rd feeling proud of what we had done. We had stopped the communist takeover and the construction of bases of operations in Grenada.

I took a walk at dawn on the outer deck of the ship and stopped to watch another beautiful sunrise as I had done so many times in Vietnam. This was just another day when it was good to be alive. It was time I wrote to Marty.

But once again my mind turned to Beirut, where it seemed the

Marines had become targets of opportunity in the ruthless struggle between the Israelis, Syrians and the different factions of Lebanon. Sometimes it seemed Israel and the US where being drawn toward a collision with Syria who was backed by Russia.

Later in the day, Capt Graham gathered all the officers together of Mike and India Companies in the wardroom. There he told us that BGen Joy, our Assistant Division Commander, was going to take command of all the Marines in Beirut because after we land a second MAU would soon be stationed afloat off shore in case we should need them. He would take command of our MAU even before we land. This was all great news for us.

On Nov 4th, Col Studt and LtCol Kersher choppered to our ship and promoted Graham to Major. Again, I was glad to see an old warrior get promoted. He had been doing the job of a Major as our battalion XO for months. I hoped this promotion would allow him to keep this billet for two or three more years.

On Nov 9th, we received mailbags filled with cards, letters and boxes of cookies and candy, from family, friends and strangers thanking us for what we had done in Grenada. It brought tears to my eyes. I had never received anything like this during my eight years in Vietnam.

On Nov10th, one day out of Rota Spain, we celebrated the 208th Birthday of our Corps. As before I loved listening to the reading of the Gen Lejeune birthday message. Of course, there was the tradition of cutting the birthday cake with the first piece handed to the oldest Marine present and the second piece going to the youngest.

As we neared Lebanon, Maj Graham again briefed the officers of Mike and India Companies on the rules of engagement. And we in turn briefed our platoons. Again, I briefed my men on the history of Lebanon, and its many religious factions, the reasons for limited contact with the Lebanese civilians. But the big change was, this time if we saw a man with a weapon pointed at us, don't wait to be shot at, shoot to kill first.

Our MAU arrived off the shore of Beirut on Nov 16th and we prepared to land the next morning. During the night as I walked with Lt Wright on the outer deck of the ship, we watched a fierce firefight going on between the Marines ashore and whoever. This seemed worse than anything I'd seen here before.

"Well Gunner, welcome back to the Root," said Lt Wright.

"It sure seems it's definitely gotten worse," I said.

"I just wish they'd cut us loose and let us take the war to the enemy like we're trained to do. Like we did in Grenada."

The next morning was fair and beautiful as Mike Company came ashore before dawn. As the sun came up, the Beirut airport now looked more like a prairie dog town covered with reinforced bunkers. Dirt revetments had been built to block the entrance to the compound of the airport.

"War is hell, but peacekeeping is a mother," I overheard 1stSgt Burns say to Lt Littleton.

As Mike Company settled into our part of the battalion perimeter, we found trench lines were now so deep we could walk erect inside of them.

The lieutenant in charge of the platoon my platoon relieved, told me that as of Nov 11th we were in an undeclared war with Syria after they started firing Sam-5 surface to air missiles at our Navy fighter-bombers conducting recon flights.

On Nov 18th, the other MAU began back-loading onto their ships.

As the company we had relieved was falling back, I watched a warrant officer place some plastic flowers near the site of the destroyed battalion headquarters next to a sign which said, "They came in peace."

Suddenly, a 122-MM rocket landed within Mike Company lines. As my men scrambled grabbing helmets and flak jackets, I heard the yell, "Corpsman up!" coming from 2nd platoon. I wondered who it was as we sat it out, ducking as more rockets and artillery rounds from the hills above Beirut flew overhead to their targets in nearby sections of the city.

As we sat in our bunkers waiting, everyone had his own thoughts. It's funny, but I was thinking of the experience that was being gained by these Marines. These are the newest generation of combat veterans. Not only do they know now how to act under hostile fire, but also more important, they know it and have confidence. I thought back to my own baptism of fire as a private in 1965 in Vietnam. The day when six of us called in artillery on a large NVA unit moving through a valley. Damn that had been eighteen years ago and yet it seemed like yesterday. I could still remember the names of the squad members. Especially blond-haired Gant, who we tried so hard to get to, the day he was wounded. And after we finally did, only to have him die on the operating table. Later there was Goins, like the brother I never had, who went home wounded and was smart enough to get out of the Corps and settle down. And there was Big Ben, the crazy man of Hue City. He also got out of the Corps as a sergeant, only to come back months later as a lance corporal. And then, there's Hester who like me never wanted to be anything else but a Marine and is now a lieutenant colonel.

Those Marines like these young Marines were dedicated Marines doing what their country asked them to do.

I guess I hadn't done bad, for a kid who quit school at sixteen and joined the Corps on my seventeenth birthday. I felt then the Marines were the best and I still believed it.

Now, I was leading a platoon of more than forty men. Once again, I was in center stage of world attention. Somehow, I still felt this was an honor. I guess I love the challenge everyday of keeping my platoon going in the right direction, keeping them pulling together. And I was proud of how my men had shouldered the responsibility of this peacekeeping role. I had young corporals making split second decisions like Cpl Wynne, which could mean the difference between life and death for their highly disciplined fire teams or squads. I could tell they're proud by the way they took care of their men. With grim determination, they were prepared to see the mission through regardless of their losses.

Then I heard it was Sgt Rienbold who had been wounded in the arm while he was attached to 2nd platoon. I felt sick. He was an old Vietnam veteran too. Here we just went through Grenada without a casualty in Mike Company and here we lose a good man our first day back in Beirut. But at least it's not too bad and he'll be safe on the ship in a clean bed with good food for a while.

After dark, Mike Company was attacked by anti-government forces. As the attack intensified, the Marines of Mike Company released their anger and frustration at all the friends we had lost here the last time. Marines who had never lived to see their babies, which had been born while they were here. Their names flooded over me as the weapons fire of my platoon erupted around me.

Some were old Vietnam veterans like me, good Marines, real

motivators. One had planned to retire in two months before he was killed.

The battle raged for hours as we returned fire, seeking revenge on our enemy firing everything we had at them.

After midnight a cold winter rain began to fall. Finally, the enemy weapons fell silent around 0300.

As dawn broke a bullet popped past Cpl Wynne's ear. As he ducked a whole burst cracked over his head.

It sure seemed the militias were welcoming Mike Company back to Beirut.

By the afternoon, Lt Wright of 2nd platoon had counted a hundred militia fighters moving into positions in front of Mike Company with heavy machineguns.

Cpl Mitchell watched several militiamen setting up a 50-cal machinegun. He yelled to Lt Wright, "Sir, this looks like trouble."

Then seeing a puff of smoke Cpl Mitchell yelled "Hit the dirt!"

Militia fighters all along Mike Company's front opened fire. Over the radio I heard Maj Graham yell, "Open fire!"

It seemed the whole battalion returned fire at the militia positions at the same time.

From Mike Companies CP, Lt Littleton could see the fight was spreading. He ordered SSgt Simon's mortar teams to open fire. The Muslim fighting positions close to us were firing RPGs at our platoon positions and our company CP bunker behind us as we returned fire with rifles, grenades and machineguns.

Cpl Wynne hid behind our chest high sandbag wall from which he kept popping up returning fire. A burst of bullets hit the top of our trench. A bullet ricocheted down into our trench across Cpl Wynne's left leg. He fell to the ground in pain. But then he bandaged his own wound and fought on.

As the hours passed, Mike Company's bunkers were ripped by RPGs and machinegun bullets until the sandbagged walls had been lowered from chest high level to knee level.

Cpl Wynne had fired eighteen grenade rounds and had hit eighteen targets. Then he fired two LAAWs destroying two enemy bunkers. But still the Amal fire was heavy coming in. One enemy bunker, 100 meters away from my platoon, was pouring heavy machinegun fire straight at us. As we covered him, Cpl Wynne stood up under incoming fire and fired two LAAWs and destroyed this bunker too.

Another enemy bunker opened up on my platoon. Sgt Meadows crawled up next to me and yelled, "Sir we're out of rifle grenades."

I got on the radio and called Lt Littleton for help. Within minutes enemy bunkers to our front were hit by SSgt Simon's 60-MM mortars, some HE and white phosphorus shells leaving them in a white fire. But still other enemy bunkers fired on us.

India Company was being hit hard too. Capt Evans wanted to move from his bunkers up to the front with his men, but was held back by the heavy volume of bullets. RPGs were exploding everywhere. The fight went on into the evening.

Meanwhile, the complete relief of the old MAU went smooth and was finished twelve hours ahead of schedule even with all the harassing fire from the enemy.

Finally, at 2200, most of the incoming fire stopped as a cold rain started falling.

In the following days to come, Sgt Meadows had the squads of our platoon improve and rebuild our fighting positions. Every morning our battalion went on 100% watch from 0445 to 0700. For several days there had been little sniping or incoming artillery fire.

The last of November, a rocket was fired at a Marine CH-46 chopper as it came in for a landing, but missed. The same day, Muslims using rifles and RPGs shot at another Marine chopper. Later, I would learn Maj Graham had been killed on this chopper as he was returning from visiting our wounded out on the ship. Just like our first tour in Beirut, we had lost our battalion XO. Capt Evans was ordered by LtCol Kersher to leave India Company and join the battalion staff as our battalion XO.

The 1st of December, Burns was promoted to sergeant major and moved up to be our battalion sergeant major. Spidden of India Company was promoted to gunnery sergeant. Reilly, the acting platoon sergeant of 2nd platoon, was promoted to staff sergeant. Blandon of 3rd platoon was promoted to corporal.

Dec 3rd was a day filled with violence between the Muslims and our battalion.

At 0700 on Dec 4th, BGen Joy ordered our battalion on maximum alert condition.

US Navy jet bombers flew from the Naval ships, flying major air strikes against Syrian positions in the Chouf area east of Beirut.

Two of the fighter-bombers were shot down. One Navy pilot was killed and another one captured.

During the day, our battalion was hit by occasional sniper and mortar fire, which we returned in force.

At 1935, an outpost of India Company was hit by small arms fire. The outpost manned by a squad, machinegun team, sniper team and a LAAW team returned fire with everything they had.

At 2204, Druse gunners fired rockets making a direct hit on top of a combat post of India Company killing eight Marines and wounding two. It seemed when the small arms fire had hit the other outpost, GySgt Spidden had left the company CP bunker to check the company positions and he was one of the eight killed. He was a good Gunny, out checking his men, doing what should be done as he always had done. But somehow, I wish he hadn't.

As the word of the deaths went out through our battalion, we returned fire with small arms, mortars and artillery. LtCol Kersher retaliated by calling on the USS New Jersey to fire its 14-inch guns into the Chouf area. This caused several secondary explosions in the hills in the night.

None of us believed the report that this attack on us had been so-called spillover fire. They were definitely shooting at us. After eight years of combat in Vietnam, I knew the difference.

The evening of Dec 6th, an Amal officer walked up to 3rd platoon positions and asked Lt Cregar to speak to the senior Marine. Lt Cregar radioed Lt Littleton who contacted LtCol Kersher. Soon, he and Capt Evans rode out to 3rd platoon in an amtrack. When they got out the Amal officer complained, "Your Marines are building their bunkers in my territory. They are too close to our positions. I want it stopped or I will order my men to shoot at your Marines."

"Colonel we aren't building any closer than before," ragged Lt Littleton as Capt Evans took notes.

"My Marines are only building defensive positions as well as clearing fields of fire. And it will continue!" answered LtCol Kersher.

The Amal officer spun around and stormed away. LtCol Kersher and Capt Evans walked back onto their amtrack and drove away.

The Amal officer had no more then disappeared when a short violent firefight erupted when Amal troops fired grenade launchers, small arms and machineguns at Mike Company from fortified bunkers. When Mike Company's small arms, machinegun fire and rifle grenades didn't silence the radical Amal, Lt Littleton requested tank and Dragon support. Within an hour, a Marine tank and a Dragon team had destroyed two enemy bunkers and the enemy fire stopped.

The afternoon of the next day, the same Amal officer walked up to 3rd platoon and repeated the same statements of the evening before to Lt Cregar.

Lt Littleton came forward and yelled, "Get the hell out 'a my area before I shoot you myself!"

"If you don't stop by tomorrow, we will attack," said the Amal officer before he turned walking back to his lines.

True to the Amal officer's word, the next day a bitter firefight started between Mike Company and the Amal positions, which had been fortified with firing slits directly facing us. This time using the tank and Dragon teams, we destroyed all of the Amal bunkers in front of Mike Company. The last time we were here we had returned fire proportionally to life threatening fire. But this time when fired upon, we destroyed positions causing many enemy casualties.

On Dec 9th, a Navy Seabee was wounded when a rocket destroyed the bulldozer he was driving. At the same time, a Marine in Lima Company was shot in the leg.

Our battalion continued to receive fire from small arms and mortar fire from time to time. When our battalion was obviously being fired at directly, and when we determined where the fire was coming from, we destroyed it.

Sgt Meadows continued to have my platoon upgrade their fighting positions.

And still we were continually visited like the last time by congressional delegations and high-ranking officers in our chain of command.

By the middle of Dec, the weather continued surprisingly to be fair, surely not like last year. Of course, Sgt Meadows said this gave the platoon extra time to work on improving our fields of fire, building berms and putting out more wire obstacles in front of our positions. Lt Littleton had each platoon build platoon size strongpoints, so if it came down to defending against a major attack each platoon strongpoint could fight and defend themselves. Each platoon strongpoint could be covered by fire and observed by other strong points.

By Dec 15th, we heard President Reagan was hinting about withdrawing us from Lebanon. I couldn't believe it. Will this end like Vietnam with us pulling out too soon before the job was finished?

Meanwhile, US Naval planes attacked Syrian positions in central Lebanon, knocking out a major radar complex that the Syrians were using to track our fleet and its aircraft.

At 1630, Lima and Mike Companies came under heavy attack from the Shiite Muslim neighborhood near the airport, as the firing between the Lebanese Army and the Shiite spilled over on us. About twenty mortars hit near or among Lima Company. Meanwhile my platoon was repeatedly fired on by a 50-cal machinegun. Our battalion responded with small arms, LAAWs, tank fire, 81-MM mortars, 155-MM artillery and naval gunfire. Soon the Shiites were waving white flags as they stopped firing at us. Even so BGen Joy ordered our battalion to continue firing for fifteen more minutes to make sure all enemy targets had been destroyed.

Later, a car crashed into the barrier in front of my platoon bunker. Cpl Wynne, taking no chances, quickly shot out its tires. One of his fire teams rushed out surrounding the car as I ran over. The civilian driver in his car said he was lost.

"Corporal Wynne, have your men search the car and driver," I ordered. They did, but found nothing.

"Okay Corporal Wynne, have your men help him change his tires and send him on his way. I just hope he realized he's lucky he wasn't killed."

As I returned to my platoon CP bunker I thought, "The caliber of young kids we're getting now is totally different from the guys we were getting in the 70's. These guys even like getting their haircut. There does seem to be a wave of patriotism returning to America. It sure does my heart good."

In 3rd platoon, Cpl Street grumbled, "Hell the only thing I've ever seen of Lebanon in two tours is this airport and this is too much for me." Then he yelled, "Muhammad's a queer!"

Rockets exploded in the distance and Cpl Blandon joked, "Them rockets are missing us by two first downs."

"Yeah, you missed again you fagget!" yelled Cpl Street.

"Here we are at the movies with peanuts and tracers," said Cpl

Blandon.

As Christmas neared, more high-ranking military and civilian personnel visited our battalion. Tons of letters arrived addressed only to "To a Marine, 22MAU." In mailbags, we found many fruit cakes, Christmas cards, pounds of cookies and candy. Pallets of live Christmas trees arrived decorated with ornaments. I never saw anything like this in Vietnam.

On Dec 21st, President Reagan said, "The Marines would remain in Beirut unless the Lebanese government decided it no longer wanted them there."

On Dec22nd, a sniper wounded a Marine in Cpl Blandon's fire team.

The next day LtCol Kersher allowed 400 men to fly out to the ships USS Guam and New Jersey to see the Bob Hope show. I could have gone, but I told Sgt Meadows to pick five men from our platoon to go. I ended up running Mike Company because all the other officers went along with GySgt Cain, SSgts Simon and Reilly, Sgts Meadows, Higgins, Cpl Bowers and eleven others to see the show. I was glad that GySgt Knight and SSgt Reed stayed behind to help me run things for the day.

I spent Christmas day like I had so many other Christmas days in a combat zone. But this time for the first time, Bob Hope flew in and walked around from position to position visiting those of us who had been unable to see his show. After all these years I not only got to see him, but to meet him. This visit meant more to me than any show could have.

Also, Chaplain Takesean, the Chaplain of the Marine Corps and Chaplain Libera the senior chaplain of the 2nd Marine Division visited us holding Christmas services which I attended with SSgt Reilly.

Later in the day, our battalion chaplain put on a Santa Claus suit and drove around in an ambulance to all of our battalion positions handing out Christmas presents to us line company Marines.

Still I thought of home and my children this Christmas morning and wondered how Marty and they were doing as they visited family back home in Delaware.

But I had to keep my mind on the business here. By now 95% of the tank ditch around our battalion perimeter had been dug and 70% of the Dragons teeth were now in place.

And even during Christmas, the attacks by fire on our battalion went on, but at a much-reduced level.

Surprisingly, by Dec 27th, the unseasonably good weather was still holding.

On Dec 29th, spillover fire and stray rounds hit Lt Wright's 2nd platoon.

Meanwhile, Lima Company from time to time was hit by mortars. GySgt Tapper began to call them the phantom mortar crew. I thought of that other phantom mortar crew in 1965 that almost killed me.

The next day, the Lebanese ambassador to the US said, "The government of Lebanon wished it had never invited the Marines into Lebanon. But my government probably would have fallen without the Marine presence."

I was sure now that we would be withdrawing soon whether the country fell or not, just like we did in Vietnam. The same day Cpl Mitchell of 2nd platoon was promoted to sergeant. Also, Wynne of my platoon was promoted to sergeant.

As New Year's Day 1984 broke, I awoke thinking this is the year I would go over twenty years in the Corps. I could retire in October at the age of thirty-seven. Maybe it's time to hang it up and return to the farm. I would like that and the boys would be closer to their other parents. I felt Nat wanted me to retire more than anyone.

Also, on this day Italy cut the size of its forces in Lebanon by half. The next day a booby-trapped bomb killed a French soldier and twenty-two Lebanese civilians.

On Jan 5th, President Reagan announced that early troop withdrawals were a distant possibility.

On Jan 8th, an RPG slammed into 3rd platoon killing Cpl Harris. When SSgt Reed reported this to Lt Cregar he cursed, "Damn it if we're going to pull out anyway, let's get the fuck out 'a here before I loose anymore good men."

The same day, Sgt Rienbold returned to Mike Company from the hospital ship and took back command of the machinegun squads.

The next day, we received the word President Reagan had decided to withdraw the Marines from Lebanon in stages.

On Jan 16th, Lima Company came under small arms, rockets and rifle grenade fire from spillover fire between the Druse militia and the Lebanese Army. GySgt Tapper was killed and four of his men were wounded.

On Jan 17th, I got a letter from Marty. It seemed the people back home were having second thoughts about us being in Lebanon as well as the nature of our mission. There seemed to be increasing pressure upon the American government to pull us out.

That evening a lone rifleman fired on Lt Wright's 2nd platoon. They returned rifle fire and rifled grenades, which blew the attacker away.

At about the same time, a rocket exploded near Sgt Crew's squad positions wounding two of his men. This, Lt Littleton felt, was spillover fire from the Lebanese Army and Druse fighting nearby.

On Jan 18th, Cpl Bower of 3rd platoon was killed. He was supervising his squad as they improved their positions when they were fired on from a building nearby. As 3rd platoon fired back with small arms, Lt Littleton called in mortars, tank and Dragon fire which destroyed the building stopping the hostile fire.

The evening of Jan 19th, our battalion perimeter came under small arms fire as well as some large caliber rounds. But after LtCol Kersher had artillery fire 155-MM illumination rounds over the suspected enemy firing positions, their firing ceased.

The next night our battalion perimeter came under a large volley of fire of all calibers from enemy firing positions running all along a ridgeline. A rocket hit our battalion bulk fuel farm inside our perimeter destroying large fuel bladders, which ignited 2,500 gallons of gas. Our battalion returned fire fiercely and LtCol Kersher called in naval gunfire. After the firing stopped, I learned there had been no Marine casualties.

By Jan 23rd, rumors again began to go around that we would soon be withdrawn, as a constant stream of Senators and Congressmen visited our battalion.

At 0830 on Jan 28th, a rocket was fired at a Marine CH-46 resupply chopper coming in from the ships and landing at the airport. The rocket missed landing in the sea.

The morning of Jan 30th started with small arms fire and RPG's coming from a house, hitting my platoon positions killing Sgt Wynne and wounding another man. My platoon returned fire with small arms, rifle grenades and LAAWs. I also requested and received tank fire, SSgt Simon's 60-MM mortars and 50-cal machinegun fire, killing three Amal fighters and wounding eleven.

But as before it didn't compare to the loss of an NCO like Sgt Wynne.

The firing continued throughout the day getting worse in midafternoon and finally ending.

But three hours later, twenty mortar shells hit around our battalion CP wounding one Marine.

Also, Mike Company was hit by seven mortars. During this, Lt Littleton's radioman handed the radio handset to GySgt Knight so he could receive a supply request from SSgt Reed of 3d platoon. The radio was breaking up and GySgt Knight stepped outside of the bunker trying to hear better. An enemy sniper shot him dead.

As his body was carried away, a badly shaken Lt Littleton radioed GySgt Cain of Weapons platoon and ordered him to report to the Company CP to take over the job of company gunnery sergeant. Before GySgt Cain left, he ran down to the mortar pit and grabbed SSgt Simon and told him he was now the acting Weapons platoon leader.

Meanwhile, Amal mortars were fired at us from a heavily populated area. I radioed Lt Littleton requesting artillery fire on these enemy mortar positions. He reminded me what LtCol Kersher had said the last time we took fire from there, that under the existing rules of engagement we aren't allowed to fire back.

"Mother fuck the rules of engagement!" I screamed as I tossed the radio handset back to my radioman.

The problem was that even my men who were well protected were still dying and being maimed. This was a very sobering thought to my young Marines to realize they could get hurt no matter how well they defended themselves.

On Jan 31st, Sgt Mitchell of 2nd platoon and two others were wounded during a daylong battle with Amal fighters around Hooterville. A week later, we would learn Sgt Mitchell died of his wounds in a hospital in Germany.

In the next few days, tensions rose between the Lebanese Army and the various militia factions. We heard rumors of an impending major government operation against the militia and all sides seemed to be preparing for heavier fighting.

The Amal and Shiites, probably hearing the same rumors, started their offensive first. The fighting was very heavy on the night of Feb 4th with some spillover fire hitting inside our battalion perimeter.

Especially heavy fighting broke out between Lebanese Army forces and Muslim elements on Feb 5th.

In late morning, Lt Wright's 2nd platoon positions were hit by direct and spillover fire without any Marine casualties.

That night I watched as a Lebanese Army Company east of us fought a particularly hard battle which lasted from dusk to about 2230 before it died down. Then at 2300, loud speakers in front of the Lebanese Company began blaring messages in Arabic.

By dawn, the Lebanese Company had few troops left. As they withdrew, the Lebanese captain warned Lt Cregar that the enemy was following them.

LtCol Kersher ordered Lt Littleton to have Mike Company ready for the coming attack. But it seemed at this time the Amal had no desire to fight us.

Meanwhile, the Shiite and Druze gunman were rampaging through West Beirut. Armed youth wore cloth masks, opening fire on Lebanese Army bases across the predominantly Muslim sector. Firefights raged up and down the central section of the city.

And once again, the Marine and other multinational peacekeepers were caught in the middle. A French soldier was killed and two others wounded by rockets in the northern sector of West Beirut. Eight Italian soldiers were wounded in grenade attacks. All day long, unidentified gunmen sniped at us.

At 1530, a heavy volume of large caliber and small arms fire hit the battalion from a Druze controlled area. Then shortly before sundown our battalion CP came under fierce attack from the eastern Chouf Mountains where Syrian and Druze forces were manning 130-MM artillery and rocket launchers. In retaliation, our battalion returned fire with all our organic weapons. Col Studt called in two A-6 fighter-bombers from the aircraft carrier USS John F Kennedy offshore. Also, we were supported by naval gunfire from the five-inch guns of the USS Garcia. At 2230, the enemy firing on our battalion stopped, leaving one Marine dead.

By Feb 7th, Muslim militiamen had taken complete control of West Beirut. I watched the deteriorated Lebanese Army units with their tanks, retreat north.

We listened to the 16-inch guns of the battleship USS New Jersey, as it fired 275 shells in nine hours at enemy artillery, anti-aircraft and other positions in the Syrian controlled territory fifteen miles east of Beirut.

Israeli warplanes swooped down on Bhamdoun, twelve miles east of the city, strafing artillery positions belonging to Syrian backed Palestinians. This attack came after three rockets fired from southern Lebanon landed in northern Israel.

At this time, we got the word that Secretary of Defense Weinberger had ordered a mild nonpunitive letter of instruction be issued to Col Geraghty, who had been the last MAU Commander, and LtCol Gerlach, who had been the last battalion commander at the time their battalion headquarters was destroyed by the truck bomb. We all felt that their reprimand was a personal insult to us all. Especially when we knew that for all those months our battalion had been here and then the last battalion before, all those congressmen, Admirals, Generals of all the services had visited them and us and not one complained about the battalions CP being held in a cement hotel.

At 1300, large caliber fire landed in the center of the MAU.

The same day, the MAU began the evacuation by choppers of non-combatants, 250 Seabees, 200 Marine combat engineers and 400 American civilian embassy employees and their dependents, and faculty from the American University of Beirut and their families out to the ships.

Also, 115 British soldiers were choppered out to the British Royal Fleet auxiliary ship Reliant which was offshore.

Italy by now had reduced its force from 2,000 down to 1,400.

Feb 8th, began with the USS New Jersey and Moosbrugger firing at the enemy artillery positions in the Syrian controlled area.

Rumor had it that BGen Joy was under orders again to reduce the number of Marines ashore.

GySgt Cain was listening to his civilian radio when the news came on and he heard President Reagan announce that the Marines would begin a phased withdrawal to the Navy ships, but would stay in the area off shore.

Later in the day, the British received its orders to leave immediately and they were completely withdrawn by the end of the day. Also, the Italian government announced their plans for a gradual withdrawal of the rest of their forces.

Meanwhile, the PX truck we all called the “Gunny’s Tavern”, came around. GySgt Cain was having a going out of business sale of such items as Lebanese and Syrian flags and T-shirts with the words, "The Druze Brothers" on them. He also passed the word that all mail delivery was being halted. The base television station was going off the air. Now I was sure we were leaving soon.

Later, I watched choppers take off from the airport with about 150 MAU and battalion headquarters Marines heading out to the ships.

I looked around at my platoon, which were just some of the 1,100 men left of our battalion ashore. I knew we could all be out including the tanks, trucks and artillery within twenty-four hours if BGen Joy gave us the order.

But to me this was too much like Vietnam. Again, I felt we were leaving too soon, before the job was done and screwing over the very people we had come here to help.

On Feb 9th, our battalion backloaded more support elements and equipment out to the ships.

Capt Evans was wounded when rockets hit our battalion CP and he was medivaced out to the ships. LtCol Kersher called in naval gunfire on the enemy rocket positions until the firing stopped.

LtCol Kersher ordered Lt Littleton up to our battalion CP to take a staff job and Lt Wright took over the command of Mike Company.

On Feb 10th, Lt Cregar's 3rd platoon positions received heavy mortar fire, which Lt Wright answered with SSgt Simon's 60-MM and 81-MM mortars until the enemy was silenced. But three shells exploded, severely damaging our battalion's counterbattery radar equipment, which limited our battalion's ability to determine where the enemy fire was coming from.

On Feb 14th, as the rest of the nonessential Marine personnel and equipment was being backloaded aboard ships, Lt Cregar's 3rd platoon was fired on again, but suffered no casualties.

The next day, Druze units swept down from the Chouf Mountains cutting through the Lebanese forces and capturing the Lebanese Army CP on the beach south of the airport perimeter.

Still, US ships fired in support of the Lebanese Army against anti-government forces if for no other reason than to get even.

On Feb 17th, Lebanon President Gemayel did just what Syria had wanted him to do from the beginning. He revoked the peace accord with Israel he had signed in May of last year.

We also heard that the Italian forces would be leaving on the 19th through the 21st.

On Feb 20th, BGen Joy ordered our MAU and battalion CP groups moved onboard the ships.

The same day, the Italian forces turned over their last checkpoints to Shiite militiamen and withdrew out to their ships.

Meanwhile, the Israeli Air Force launched strikes against targets all along the Beirut Damascus highway.

By Feb 21st with astonishing speed, Syrian backed forces took over almost all of Beirut routing the US trained Lebanese Army forces and encircling what was left of our battalion.

On Feb 25th, Kilo Company walked across Green Beach into amtracks as they headed out to their ships. Each company that was left behind had to shift positions, some to cover the gap left by Kilo.

Sunday morning dawned beautiful with birds singing. As Sgt Meadows went around preparing our platoon to leave, a young Marine asked, “Are we really leaving sarge?”

“Yes, we are really leaving Marine,” answered Sgt Meadows.

At 0400, I watched India Company climb on choppers and take off from the LZ.

I felt relief that we had finally reached the end of this frustrating mission. My young Marines called it weird and crazy. A place they said where it seemed every raghead enjoyed killing each other. All I knew was that I had lost too many good men here for nothing.

I watched our battalion’s artillery unit being trucked to Green Beach. From somewhere I heard the Marines Hymn being played from a tape recorder and tears ran down my face.

At 0630, the choppers returned to the LZ and picked up Lima Company.

Mike Company would leave from Green Beach in amtracks and landing craft. Lt Wright ordered the platoons to fall back to Green Beach. But only one platoon would move at a time while the other two covered them.

As my platoon fell back, young Lebanese kids moved into our old positions playing in the bunkers we had just left.

Off shore, US ships opened fire on Syrian and Druze positions beyond Beirut. I heard artillery and mortar fire in the hills.

Only the French were determined to stay on here now.

As another platoon pulled back from its positions, I stopped my platoon to cover them from the high ground where our battalion artillery unit had been emplaced.

We were departing with all that we had brought with us, leaving behind very little in the way of scrap materials.

As my platoon walked on a landing craft, I could see Amal gunmen moving carefully into our old battalion bunker complex.

At 1237, the landing craft slid out from Green Beach. I watched the Amal flag going up where the American flag had been. As the last of Mike Company left Green Beach in amtracks and was clear of the beach, the US ships including the USS New Jersey fired on targets again in the Chouf Mountains.

Soon the landing craft pulled up next to our troop ship. I sent Sgt Meadows up the cargo net with the first group of four. I waited as the rest of my platoon climbed up in groups of four. Then I climbed up with the last group. Once on board, Lt Littleton billeted me in a room with Lt Cregar. After a hot shower, I checked with Sgt Meadows to make sure our platoon was squared away in their troop compartments. Then I got some hot chow in the wardroom and went to bed early after I wrote a quick letter to Marty telling her I was safe on ship.

Our MAU would stay on as a reaction force to rescue the American ambassador if necessary or for other contingency operations in Lebanon or elsewhere in the Mediterranean.

By March, my men were as usual complaining that life at sea was more confining than duty in Beirut. But Sgt Meadows kept reminding them that they were at least free of sniper and artillery attack here.

On March 11th, Commandant Kelly visited us onboard our ships.

Our MAU remained off the coast of Lebanon until April 10th when it was relieved by the 24th MAU.

At 1600, I stood at the rail of our ship looking at the coast of Lebanon with Lt Cregar as our ships turned heading for Rota Spain.

Once at Rota, our battalion spent three days washing down all our equipment.

On April 19th, our MAU sailed for the good old USA or as we called it during Vietnam, returning to the world.

On May 1st, our troop ships pulled into Moorehead City and again bands, cheerleaders and well-wishers greeted us.

On our return to Camp Lejeune, many of our family members met us as the buses pulled to a stop within our battalion area.

I had just gotten off the bus when I saw little Samantha's red hair flying as she ran toward me. I caught her in my arms as she jumped yelling, "Dad! Dad!" I kissed her and swung her onto one hip as Marty put her arms around my neck kissing me saying, "I've missed you."

"I missed you, too," I said as Nat and Lance put their arms around all of us.

Looking around for our other child I asked, "Where's Kyle? Didn't he want to come?"

Marty looked up into my eyes as her eyes dimmed in sadness as she said, "He went to live with his father."

"What in the world happened?" I asked surprised.

"He just came to me one day and said he wanted to live with his father."

"When did this happen?" I demanded.

"About a month after you left."

"Why in hell didn't you tell me in all the letters you wrote me?" I yelled as my anger rose up within me.

She looked down and then back up into my eyes as tears filled her eyes saying, "I didn't want to worry you with my problems. You had enough to worry about there. I wanted you to be able to keep a clear head so you would return to me. I love you."

I felt the anger just as quickly drain out of me as I said, "I love you too. I can't believe this though. All these years I've prayed we would have all our children together. Instead we gain two and loose one."

"That's still a gain," she said smiling.

"Well how did you make out with these two hardheads?"

"We definitely had our moments of disagreements. But mostly I think the trouble came from all of us missing you. But I think we've all grown closer and understand each other better."

"Well, it sounds like you've made more headway with them in seven months than I did with Kyle in nine years," I said shaking my head realizing I could just never get through to Kyle I loved him too. Somehow, I had failed him.

"Well, we better go on home so you can get your gear put away. Nat drove your truck here so you'd have a way home."

"Good. Where's the keys?" I asked.

Nat smiled handing me the keys.

"I should be home in a couple of hours," I said.

"We'll be waiting. What do you want for supper?"

"Fried chicken," I said smiling.

"I should' a guessed," said Marty.

"I told ya," said Samantha.

I waved back at them as I walked through the crowd looking for Sgt Meadows.

Later that night after we had made love twice, we lay tangled in each other's arms and legs.

"Are you all right? You seem deep in thought," asked Marty.

"I'm sorry. But I'm feeling frustrated."

"About what?"

"I've just returned from my second undeclared war in almost twenty years as a Marine. Both times my nation said they would help a weaker nation. And both times, just when those nations needed us most my country decided it didn't want to play anymore. When I say I'll help somebody I help them. My country should do the same. I lost many of my best friends in Vietnam and too many good men in the Root. All for nothing. I wonder why I keep doing this."

"Well you can retire in October and move on to something else."

"I know."

"Do you have any ideas what you would like to do after retirement?"

"Return to the farm. If Father and Uncle Clark could use another partner or farmhand."

"Well we have to decide what to do with the kids."

"What about them."

"Well, if we're going back to Delaware to live, I think we should go up there near the end of the summer to find a place to live. That way, I can get the kids registered in school, so they won't have to change schools in the middle of the year. Then in October when you retire you can join us."

There was a long silence before Marty sat up looking at me and said, "What?"

Taking a deep breath, I said, "How would you feel if I decide to stay on for another ten years?"

"That's up to you. I just want to know what we're going to do before the next school year begins."

Now it was my turn to sit up in bed and look at her as I said,

"You mean you don't have a problem putting up with the Corps for another ten years?"

"Nathan, I love you. I want you to be happy. I can put up with the Corps as long as you can put up with me."

I pulled her naked body into my arms saying, "I love you. You're easy to put up with."

"Are you sure you want to do this ten more years?"

"Maybe not. But I made it to the top of the enlisted ranks. And I'd like to try to make it to the top of the warrant officer ranks."

"Ten years would do that?"

"Well, I figure I should make CWO-4 in eighty-six. Then I need to do two more years at that rank to retire with that rank."

"So, we're talking four more years at the least."

"Well, why don't we just take it one year at a time."

"That's fine. But you need to tell the boys. I think Nat is looking forward to you retiring in October."

"I'll talk to them tomorrow," I said pulling her down on top of me as we kissed.

The next morning as we ate breakfast, I tried to explain to the boys why I wasn't going to retire this year. Lance seemed to take it in stride, but Nat was plainly unhappy with my decision.

I spent the day with my platoon preparing for a possible inspection by the Secretary of the Navy and Commandant Kelly the next day when they would review our battalion.

The following day our battalion stood at attention by companies with LtCol Kersher standing out front.

Facing us was the Secretary of the Navy speaking to us. Next to him stood Commandant Kelly, BGen Joy and Col Studt.

When the Secretary of the Navy was finished, Commandant Kelly trooped the line by marching down each rank of every platoon in our battalion. Then he returned to the front of our battalion and faced LtCol Kersher and our battalion guide-on bearer. Then he honored our battalion by presenting us with the Armed Forces Expeditionary Medal by placing the AFEM streamer on our battalion guide-on with the rest of our battalion's battle colors. Then he stepped back and said, "You have returned victorious with your battle colors intact, with the love devotion and thanks of a grateful nation. You have proved once again the tremendous flexibility and potency of the Marine Air, Ground Task Force in Beirut and

Grenada. There is no Marine on God's earth that is prouder of the accomplishments of the men of this battalion than your Commandant. I salute you from the bottom of my heart." He saluted us and turned marching away.

During the rest of the month, our battalion received a large number of replacements for the casualties we took in Beirut and for those who were now transferring out.

Lt Littleton resigned his commission over his disgust over our Beirut mission and even more so over our withdrawal before the mission was finished. I believe the country and our Corps lost an outstanding lieutenant.

A Maj Sevenskie reported to our battalion and took over the XO billet.

Mike Company got a new first sergeant named Stall.

A big tall black staff sergeant named Samuels reported to me as my new platoon sergeant.

In June, the school year ended and I took a week leave. We drove up to Delaware to drop Nat and Lance off to spend the summer with their mother. Then we picked up Kyle to spend the summer with us.

After we returned to Camp Lejeune, Mike Company spent the rest of June working on forming the new and old members into a team. I found SSgt Samuels to be very good in the field after serving as an Infantry instructor for three years.

The first of July, LtCol Kersher transferred out and was replaced by LtCol Payne.

On July 9th, the warrant officer list came out and I was happy to see SSgt Reed of 3rd platoon had been selected for warrant officer. He would be due to put on his bars in October.

In late August, I took another week leave and we took Kyle back north to Delaware to his father. We visited with our families and then picked up my two boys and went back home in time for school to start.

In Sept Col Studt was transferred out.

On Oct 12th, I turned thirty-seven. Even though my hair was all but white I didn't feel that old. It was hard to believe. And still harder to believe that on Oct 22nd, I went over twenty years in the Corps. The same day Lt Wright transferred out. Lt Cregar moved up to take command of Mike Company. With no other officers left in Mike Company, he moved me up to the XO billet.

We were still waiting for SSgt Reeds promotion warrant to come in, when on Oct 23rd our regiment went to a Memorial ceremony honoring the nearly 300 Marines killed in Beirut. There were many guests, some of our wounded from the hospital, many families of the dead men, President Reagan and Commandant Kelly there.

When it was over, I stood next to Marty who asked, "Are you all right?"

"Yes."

"What are you thinking?"

"It's just like Nam. I am proud of what we did. My young Marines have that personal pride of weathering combat. I thought we were buying the Lebanese people more time. But in the end, it was for nothing. If we'd been allowed to fight in the Root like we did on Grenada we could've made a difference," I said as tears rolled down my cheeks.

"I'm proud of you," said Marty.

The 1st of November, SSgt Simon transferred out and Sgt Rienbold took command of Weapons platoon.

Months ago, when we were in Beirut, the staff and officers of Mike Company had talked about a company-size birthday ball. Every year the 2nd Marine Division had a big ball for officers, another for the staff NCOs, another for the NCOs and yet another for the nonrated men. Some of the staff, like me, had been to smaller unit balls and felt they were better. The best ball I had been to was when I was a seagoing Marine on a ship with a forty-four-man Marine detachment. So, we decided that on November 10th, after our return from Beirut we would have a company-size ball.

So, not long after our return home, GySgt Cain went to work and found a hotel ballroom off base that he reserved for Nov 10th.

Lt Cregar was planning to use SSgt Reed in the ball ceremony with his warrant officer bars on even though his warrant hadn't come in yet. His promotion warrant should have been here the 1st of October. So, we expected it to arrive any day.

The weekend before the ball, the staff and officers and senior NCOs practiced the ball ceremony. When we were done, Lt Cregar asked, "Staff Sergeant Reed do you have your officer uniform ready for the 10th?"

"Yes sir," smiled SSgt Reed and then added, "I also have my enlisted dress blues ready too just in case my warrant still hasn't come in."

"If your warrant's not here by the 10th, go ahead and put your bars on that evening," said Lt Cregar.

SSgt Reed and I both looked at Lt Cregar.

"Sir, we're going to have a frocking ceremony?" I asked liking the idea.

"No just put 'm on," said Lt Cregar.

"Are you sure sir?" asked SSgt Reed.

"Yeah sure. I'm your CO, right?" answered Lt Cregar.

On the afternoon of Nov 10th, I was in my living room with Marty when the doorbell rang. I got up and opened the door and I was surprised to see Lt Cregar standing there.

"Come in sir," I said.

"Thank you," he said as he walked in looking worried. Then at seeing Marty he added, "Mrs. Cord, how are you?"

"Fine," she answered.

As Lt Cregar sat down, I said, "I thought you'd be home with your wife resting up for tonight."

"I should be. But I was called to battalion."

"Are we on alert or something?" I asked.

"No. But I'm being transferred."

"When?" I asked.

"Two weeks."

"Will your replacement be here by then?"

"He's here now. I met him at battalion. He's a captain named Bread. I invited him to the ball to meet us."

"How about Staff Sergeant Reed putting on his bars?"

"No problem. I'll explain it to him tonight. Besides no one in the company deserves a promotion more than he."

"I agree," I said feeling uneasy for some reason.

Later at the ball, I felt the troops were having a great time. And yet, I felt also a somber mood because we were about to lose the last of the lieutenants we had served under in Beirut and trusted.

At the officers table, Gunner Reed and I tried to get to know Capt Bread. He had been an enlisted Navy corpsman for four years serving a tour in Vietnam with the Marines. After his discharge he went to college and was then commissioned in the Corps. As the night went on, I noticed that he talked freely with Lt Cregar and me. But he paid no attention at all to Gunner Reed, acting as if he wasn't even there.

As we danced Marty said, “You don’t care for the new captain?”

“I don’t know what it is about him I don’t like. But maybe it’s too soon to tell.”

Quickly the next two weeks passed and Lt Cregar was gone. I found Capt Bread hard to serve under. Although he treated me with respect, he never listened to my ideas or past experience. And he treated the Staff NCOs even worse.

I did like being a company XO. Because I was not tied to one platoon. I could roam from platoon to platoon checking on the men of the whole company and their training. I went out in charge of the advance parties to set up training areas. I was more involved in planning the company training. I just wished Capt Bread would listen to me. Of course, when he was away, I would run the company my way and I enjoyed that the best. I knew this was only a temporary assignment until a lieutenant reported in. It is not unusual for a Marine Corps warrant officer to command a platoon. But it is unusual for warrant officers to be company XO. Without getting a commission to lieutenant this would probably be the biggest command I would ever have.

In December, Mike Company went to the field for a week. It was unusually cold for North Carolina and the third day it even snowed. As Capt Bread trained the rifle platoons in one area he had Gunner Reed running the training of weapons platoon in another area, firing live ammo on the mortar and machinegun ranges.

On the fourth day, I drove a jeep over to the weapons platoon. As my driver stopped the jeep I stepped out. I could see the mortar section sitting in the snow as a sergeant taught a class. I could hear the machineguns firing off to the right. So, I walked in that direction. I could see the red tracers going down range. Soon, I could easily see the camouflaged trousers and helmets and green field-jacketed Marines lying in the snow behind their machineguns. Standing behind them stood Sgt Rienbold. Seeing me he snapped to attention saluting saying, “Good morning sir.”

I returned his salute smiling and said, “How ya doing?”

“Just fine Gunner. Red tracers in the snow and the sounds of mortars in the distance. It doesn’t get any better than this,” he said laughing.

“Damn right,” I said laughing too.

Nearby, Gunner Reed was on his knees with his left gloved hand on a machine gunner's shoulder as he talked to him. He then turned looking up at me, as did the machine gunner and assistant gunner. He smiled standing up to salute me saying, "Good morning Gunner."

I returned his salute saying, "And how are you Gunner?"

"I'd feel better if my promotion warrant would come in."

"I know. I'll drive back to the company office this afternoon and check on it."

"I don't know what's with the skipper. He won't even talk to me. Every time I try to talk to him he finds a reason to send me somewhere. That's why I'm here with weapons platoon instead of with my platoon."

"Well, we are short of officers and the rules say we must have an officer on each range."

"But you'd think he'd put you here and leave me with my platoon."

We then walked back to the mortar sections who had broken up into teams and were breaking open mortar shell boxes and laying the shells out in rows on ponchos.

Soon, they were dropping shells down the mortar tubes. They popped as they fired out of the tubes and exploded in the distant snow.

In the afternoon I drove back to where the rest of the company was training. As I drove up, I saw 1stSgt Stall had driven out from mainside with the mail and paper work that Capt Bread needed to sign.

He was walking back to his jeep as I was climbing out of mine.

"Good afternoon Gunner," he said saluting.

Returning his salute, I said, "Good afternoon Top. How's it going?"

He shook his head looking back at the company CP area and said, "This fucking guy is nuts."

"I know I haven't had an officer this hard to deal with since the Nam," I said.

"What happened, did he get fragged?"

"No, he was relieved of his command."

"Lucky."

"Yes, for us and maybe him too."

"If we could only be so lucky. And now he's getting on me about my weight."

"I guess you haven't heard anything about Reed's warrant?"

"No, not from battalion. But every day I hear it from the skipper."

"What's he say?"

"Gunner, it's like he hates him. He's even talked of court-martialing him for impersonating an officer."

"Christ! If he doesn't like him wearing his bars without his warrant why doesn't he tell him to take them off!" I spat.

"You tell me, sir."

"Shit!"

"Well Gunner I gotta go," he said climbing into his jeep.

I left him and walked straight to the CP area to find Capt Bread.

As I entered the CP area, Capt Bread walked out of his tent and at seeing me said, "Gunner you've returned. And how is weapons platoon?"

"They're outstanding. Captain can I speak to you?" I asked as GySgt Cain walked up to us.

"Sure, Gunner shoot."

"Sir, I know you don't like Reed wearing his bars."

"That's because on the Marine Corps roles he's still a staff sergeant."

"Sir you do know he has been selected for warrant officer?"

"That doesn't give him the right to wear his bars until the warrant comes in."

"Sir his warrant was supposed to have been here over two months ago. Because of Lieutenant Cregar's great respect for Reed and because he wanted him to take part in the ball as an officer, he told him to put his bars on."

"Lieutenant Cregar didn't have the authority to do that."

"But he did. If you don't like it why not tell Reed to take them off. He would do it."

"I shouldn't have to tell him."

"Sir, I've known Reed since he was a corporal. I served with him during two combat tours in the Root and on Grenada. He was one of the best squad leaders and platoon sergeants I have ever seen in my twenty years in the Corps."

Nearby GySgt Cain added, "Sir, he is a good Marine."

Capt Bread shot a hard look at him and then back at me saying, "I'll take both your opinions into account."

"Sir, Reed has always been a Marine that men of all races could look up to. He treated everybody equal and he took care of his troops," I said.

"As I said, I'll take into account your opinions. But now I have a company to train," said Capt Bread as he walked away.

GySgt Cain leaned over to me saying, "Sir what the fuck did he mean he'd take it into account?"

"I'll be fuck if I know Gunny."

Soon Christmas came and I took seven days leave. We drove up to Delaware to visit with our families and Kyle, and to let Nat and Lance visit with their mother.

A few days after our return to Camp Lejeune came the New Year of 1985.

In the middle of January, the rumor spread through Mike Company that Reed's promotion warrant had finally come in. At hearing this, I went to the company office and stuck my head in 1stSgt Stall's office. He looked up from his desk. Before I could say anything, he smiled saying, "It's in sir."

"Outstanding," I said and walked next door to Capt Bread's office. He saw me as I knocked on his door and said, "Yes Gunner. Come in."

I couldn't help smiling as I walked in saying, "I understand you have Reeds warrant."

"Yes, I do," he answered unsmiling.

"Well sir when do we have his promotion ceremony?"

"I'll let you know."

"Have you told Reed so he can plan his party?"

"All in good time" he said looking back down at his paperwork. Angered I turned and walked out.

The rest of the day, all of Mike Company waited to hear when the promotion ceremony would take place. Finally, at the end of the day Mike Company fell in formation for our final muster. I hoped maybe this would be a surprise promotion ceremony. But when Capt Beard dismissed the company, he hadn't even mentioned that Reed's warrant was in. The whole company seemed to stand in shock not understanding why Reed hadn't been promoted.

Disgusted, I drove home. As soon as I walked in Marty said,

"What's wrong?"

I stood in the middle of the dining room with my hands on my hips and said, "Guess?"

"What's Captain Bread done now?"

"Reed's warrant came in today and he didn't promote him. Christ he's only waited almost three months for it to come in and when it does, he sits on it."

"What are you gonna do?"

"What can I do? The guy doesn't listen to me. I don't know if I can deal with this guy much longer."

"What can you do then?"

"In October, I'll have two years in grade and I can retire at this rank."

"Are you thinking of retiring in October?"

"I just might if things don't change. If I can make it that long. Besides the way we bump heads he'll probably not give me a very good fitness report which would ruin my chance for further promotion. I would like to retire while I'm well thought of."

Marty walked up to me and put her arms around me saying, "I'll still want you."

"Good," I said kissing her.

A few hours later, after supper, I was sitting in the living room watching the news on TV when the phone rang. Nat raced through the house to get to the phone first. He answered it and then yelled, "Dad, it's for you."

I got up and went to the phone and answered, "Gunner Cord speaking sir."

"Sir this is Warrant Officer Reed."

"How are you Gunner?"

"Not good sir."

"What's happened?" I asked telling by his voice something was wrong.

"After the final muster, Captain Bread called me over and said he wanted to see me and First Sergeant Stall in his office. Once inside his office he had the First Sergeant close the door. Then he reads my promotion warrant."

"I can't believe this shit. It should've been done in front of the whole company," I said.

"I wish that was all. Then he hands me a copy of my fitness

report for changing grade. I wasn't marked once in the excellent or outstanding blocks. He wrote in the report that I had impersonated an officer for three months. That I was a disgrace to the Staff NCO ranks." His voice broke and I thought he was going to cry.

"I can't believe this shit!"

There was a silence as Gunner Reed cleared his throat and spoke, "Then he said he wanted me out of his company. He's going to have transfer orders sent to my house tomorrow. I told him I was going to request mast to battalion. He said that Colonel Payne already knows. I've called Sergeant Major Burns to see if regiment knew. He said Colonel Rice doesn't know and to send the request mast up through battalion to regiment and he would speak to the regimental sergeant major in my behalf. I'm calling you and some others who know the truth. I'm asking that you write a letter telling the truth. I'll understand if you don't because this could put your career on the line."

"No problem, I'll be glad to do it."

"Are you sure?"

"Reed, you were always there for me, and what can they do to me. Retire me."

"Thank you, sir."

"Good luck Gunner Reed."

After I hung up the phone, I sat down at the kitchen table. After telling Marty what happened I started writing on a yellow legal pad.

'To whom it may concern:

Subject: Conduct of WO Reed.

I first joined the Corps in 1964. In the last twenty years I have risen through the ranks to sergeant major and in the officer ranks to Chief Warrant Officer three.

In all those years I have seen many men come and go, both enlisted and officer, both good and bad.

When I first came to this company, we had a small racial problem in the Corps. I don't mean fights between whites and blacks as there were in some other units, but the problem existed. I could feel the undercurrent. I saw young black Marines who were highly motivated do fine until they made sergeant. It seemed at that rank many of their fellow black Marines would call them Uncle Toms. The peer pressure was against them to do well.

In the late seventies, Sergeant Reed served under me. At first, I considered him just another NCO. But slowly I realized that Sergeant Reed was anything but just another NCO. Sergeant Reed quietly and respectfully let his squad members, both white and black Marines know that he was not just a black Marine Corps sergeant, but a Sergeant USMC period.

He proved to be a true professional in every sense of the word making a deep impression upon his men and seniors alike. He showed a positive attitude toward his work and he always strived to improve himself and his squad.

When the platoon guide position became vacant, Sergeant Reed took over the position and I watched with pride and growing respect as the whole platoon improved under his guidance.

Later Reed was promoted to Staff Sergeant and he became the platoon sergeant.

Have always known Staff Sergeant Reed to be a strict disciplinarian, but as a platoon sergeant he also proved to be a caring father figure to his men. If one of his men had a personal or military problem, Staff Sergeant Reed always took the time to talk to the man and try his utmost to solve the problem. If a good man made a mistake Staff Sergeant Reed was the first to go to the commanding officer in the man's behalf. Sure, there were times when giving a man a second chance resulted in Staff Sergeant Reed being bitten in the back. But this never bothered Staff Sergeant Reed, because there were always the ones that given the second chance proved their worth time and time again.

I soon felt he was the best platoon sergeant in Mike Company.

During combat in Grenada and two tours in Beirut, Staff Sergeant Reed proved his leadership again and again.

When Reed was selected for warrant officer his troops and seniors all felt it was long overdue.

Warrant Officer Reed's warrant should have been in by October 1984. But because of red tape it didn't show up until late January 1985.

On the first of November 1984, our company commander 1st Lieutenant Cregar, who had served as Warrant Officer Reed's platoon leader and knew his worth and that he was respected by the entire unit, wanted Warrant Officer Reed to take part in the Marine Corps Birthday Ball as an officer. So, without a warrant, 1st Lieutenant Cregar ordered Warrant Officer Reed to put on his bars. 1st Lieutenant Cregar had thought he would be with us for at least another year. But just the day of the ball, he found out it would not be so. He had received transfer orders and we got a new commanding officer, Captain Bread.

The Monday after the ball I mentioned to Captain Bread the problem of Warrant Officer Reed's warrant and asked him to check into it to see what the holdup was with the promotion warrant.

Warrant Officer Reed was never asked, told, or ordered to take his bars off by Captain Bread and at least on one occasion that I know of, was asked to pay for his meal as an officer, which he did.

On December 10th, 1984, Warrant Officer Reed was ordered by Captain Bread to take the Essential Subjects test, which of course is only for Gunnery Sergeants and below. Warrant Officer Reed's answer was, "That's no problem, sir." And he took the test.

I talked to Captain Bread and pleaded my case for Warrant Officer Reed's past and future worth to Mike Company and the Corps. Captain Bread said that he would take my opinion into account.

The day that the warrant did arrive, we waited all day for a company formation to see Reed get his warrant.

After the final muster of the day I went home without knowing that Captain Bread had ordered Warrant Officer Reed to wait to see him.

After the company was dismissed, he called Warrant Officer Reed into his office. Then he gave him his warrant, then a bad fitness report for impersonating an officer for three months and then orders transferring him out of the unit even though we are short three officers.

It bothers me to no end that this could happen to a fine

Marine like Warrant Officer Reed. There was a time when this sort of thing could have led to a race riot. But of course, it didn't. And part of this fact is to be credited to Warrant Officer Reed, who trained his troops from the beginning as equals and focused on forming all races into one true band of brothers.

The men of third platoon had no idea what happened to him when he didn't show up the next morning. When the truth spread, they were stunned and shocked. How could this happen to a man that has proved to be the epitome of a Marine? How can a man who has given so much to this company alone, not to mention the Corps during peace and war, who gave hundreds of lesser men a second chance, get no second chance himself?

There is something very unfair and unjust here.

As the Executive Officer of Mike Company, I am duty bound to support and back Captain Bread. I believe I have done so and will try to do so in the future.

But on the other hand, I owe a great deal to Warrant Officer Reed for his professional performance, leadership and support through the past years of peace and war.

I have been in the Corps over twenty years and I had hoped for thirty years. And I realize that by writing this I may be ending my career short of my twenty first year. But this I hope must show my concern over the fate of Warrant Officer Reed. There are very few others that I would be willing to go to this extreme for.'

Sincerely
CWO-3 Nathan Cord
X.O. M Co 2/8

When I had finished, I asked Marty to type it up for me. When she was done, I drove into the company office. There I used the copy machine to make a copy of my letter. I then drove out to Warrant Officer Reed's house and gave him one copy to go with his request mass.

The 1st of February, Gunner Reed returned to the company area and handed Capt Beard his request mast as well as supporting letters like mine.

A few hours after Gunner Reed left, GySgt Cain came to get me saying, "Gunner the skipper wants to see you ASAP."

"What's up Gunny?" I asked.

"The Top tells me Captain Bread is pissed about all the letters of support written in Gunner Reed's behalf."

"Is that what he wants me for?"

"I can't be sure sir. But I suspect it is."

As I started across the parade field I said, "It's been nice serving with you gunny."

"Shit sir I suspect I'll be leaving with you. He wants to see me too."

I stopped, looking back at him as he said, "What's the matter Gunner? You surprised I wrote one too?"

"Why I didn't think you cared for officers," I answered smiling.

"I don't sir. But I like Captain Bread even worse," he said also smiling.

As I entered Mike Company office, I also saw SSgt Reilly and Sgt's Rienbold, Meadows, Crew and Higgins.

1stSgt Stall stood in the doorway of the CO's office and at seeing GySgt Cain and I, he looked back over his shoulder into the office and said, "Skipper they're all here."

From inside I heard Capt Bread say, "Have Gunner Cord come in first."

"Yes sir," said 1stSgt Stall still looking at Capt Bread. Then stepping back out of the way he said, "Gunner Cord report to the skipper."

I marched past him as he closed the door behind me. I marched on to the front of Capt Bread's desk and halted snapping to attention saying, "Sir Gunner Cord reporting as ordered."

"At ease Gunner," said Capt Bread looking up at me.

Instead of at ease I snapped to parade rest saying, "Thank you sir."

"Gunner you have a career which is the envy of any man I know. But fighting the wrong battle at the wrong time can lose the war."

"With all due respect sir, you should know us Nam veterans are used to that."

"Even though you should be careful of who you pick fights with. Especially when it's with a senior officer."

"Sir, I'm not picking a fight with you. I'm just telling the truth as I believe it is."

"I respect your support of a fellow Marine. But I disagree. I do not have to send these letters with Mr. Reeds request mast and I will not."

I looked at him hard flushed with anger. Trying to control myself I said, "Sir how can you not send them as part of Warrant Officer Reed's report in his defense."

"I don't see where these letters have any bearing to do with Mr. Reed's request mast. As far as I'm concerned, this matter is closed. And because of my respect for your tours of combat I will not record this disloyalty to me in your next fitness report. This time! Dismissed Gunner," he said smiling up at me.

"Aye, Aye sir," I said through gritted teeth taking a step backward, then did an about face. As I marched through the opening door, he said, "Top, have Gunnery Sergeant Cain report next."

That evening I phoned Gunner Reed and told him what had happened.

"I'm glad I made copies of all those letters," he said.

"Good. I was going to say I have a copy myself of mine if you needed it."

"I'm going to take copies to Sergeant Major Burns. I'm sure he'll see to it that Colonel Payne sees them. But maybe when they reach Colonel Rice at regiment, I'll get some justice. I just hope this doesn't hurt the careers of my friends like you who wrote these letters."

"We're big boys and we knew the chances we were taking. Good luck Gunner Reed."

"Thank you, sir."

"Thank you for always being where I needed you most."

A few nights later I returned home after a long day to find Nat sitting on the front step. As I pulled into the driveway, he got up walking over to me.

"What's up big guy?" I asked smiling as I got out of my truck.

"Can I talk to you Dad?"

"Sure. What 'a ya got?" I said standing still.

He stood before me looking down at his feet and then looking away said, "Dad I want to go back to Mom's."

"Nat in June after you graduate you can go anywhere you want."

"I want to go home now."

Feeling sick I said, “I had hoped that you had thought of my home as yours.”

“I do Dad. But I want to graduate with my friends back in Delaware.”

Now I looked down at my feet saying, “Does Lance know about this?”

“Yes, he does.”

“Does he want to go back to your mother’s too?”

“No.”

“Does Marty know?”

“No, I wanted to talk to you first.”

“I would like you to think about this for a while.”

“I have since Christmas.”

“I see. I’ll have Marty check with the base school tomorrow and get your records ready to be transferred back with you this weekend.”

“Thank you.”

I looked up at him as my eyes filled with tears. I turned to rush into the house. But Nat touched my shoulder. I turned back to him as he said, “I love you.”

“I love you, too,” I said as we hugged each other.

That night as I lay in bed Marty asked, “Are you all right?”

“No,” I said as tears ran down my cheeks in the dark and then added, “I don’t know if I can take much more between this shithead captain and now Nat leaving.”

“Well, you knew he would probably leave anyway in June.”

“I know but I thought I’d have him at least to then.”

The next day I went to see Capt Bread and requested a ninety-six-hour pass for the weekend. I was surprised that he agreed with a smile.

So, we packed Nat’s things up Thursday night and left at 0730 the next morning. At 2030 we arrived in Bunny’s yard. We carried Nat’s things in. Then Marty, Samantha and I left to visit our families for the weekend while Lance visited with his mother. We spent the night and Saturday night with Marty’s mother.

Sunday night I picked up Lance. Nat and I said goodbye with a hug and I love yous.

Monday morning, we again left at 0730 and arrived back on base at 2030.

In March, Col Rice ordered a Regimental Mess Night for the officers. A Mess Night is a very regimented affair. Everything is done upon order. You are told when you can eat, talk, drink, smoke or go to the head (bathroom). If you make a mistake you are fined. As the night wore on, I noticed some old friends from the past were there. Among them were Gunner Sieple, LtCols Hester and Al Genio.

I had to sit next to Capt Bread and I was surprised at how much he talked to me.

Near the end when we were allowed to get up and walk around to visit others, I walked over to speak to Gunner Sieple. I asked him how he had liked Warrant Officer Basic School.

Then he wanted to know what in the world had happened with Reed.

"So, you heard," I said.

"Hell, it's all over the division. What is the truth?" he asked.

So, I told him the truth, as I knew it to be.

He couldn't believe it either. As we were talking, LtCols Hester and Al Genio walked up. It sure was good to see them both, especially Hester. As we talked old times, I noticed Capt Bread across the room watching me.

Then LtCol Hester asked, "Just what did happen with Reed?"

Again, I told the story, as I knew it.

"And you wrote a letter in support of Reed," said LtCol Hester.

"Yes, sir I did."

"You must know you put your career on the line?" asked LtCol Hester.

"Yes sir. I had to do what I thought was right."

"You shouldn't fight battles you can't win," said LtCol Al Genio.

I was shocked at both of them. Both were known for backing up their men to the hilt, if they were right. And here they were, I felt telling me I should back off.

I left a little later, disgusted.

In early April, Mike Company went to the field as part of a battalion-size exercise, which lasted two weeks. It was the first time our battalion had trained together since returning from Beirut. With all the new men in the battalion, plus the new leadership we all needed this to prepare us for the thirty-day MAU training exercise coming up in June at 29 Palms California. The weather was unusually cold for this time of year in North Carolina. But the training went well even with the usual screw-ups.

At the end of the two weeks, we stood in battalion formation in the field. BGen Salesses spoke to us through a bullhorn telling us about the upcoming MAU exercise. Then LtCol Payne gave us the usual, I'm proud of you men and together we'll do great things speech.

A few days later as I walked into the company office, Capt Bread was talking to a black sergeant about being overweight. I was surprised because I didn't think the man was overweight. I stopped, looking at 1stSgt Stall who was standing to the left of the sitting captain. 1st Sgt Stall rolled his eyes toward Capt Bread.

"Sir, I just came off DI duty and my weight was fine," said the black sergeant.

"Well, it's your hips that are too big," said Capt Bread.

I turned walking out thinking, "I can't believe this shit."

The first of May, Mike Company went to the rifle range. The first week the men spent snapping in. The second week as the company fired on the range, I was in charge of the butt crew marking and taping the targets.

At the end of the day on Thursday after we had taken the targets down, locked them up and policed up the area, Capt Bread held a company formation. When it was over, I noticed the company break up into small groups talking instead of leaving. As I stood wondering what was going on, GySgt Cain standing with a group of Staff NCOs and NCOs waved me over.

"What the hell is going on Gunny?" I asked.

"You don't know, sir?" asked GySgt Cain.

"Know what?"

"About Corporal Thomas."

"What about Corporal Thomas?" I demanded looking around and seeing Cpl Thomas talking in another group.

"He's requesting mast to battalion," said GySgt Cain.

"Requesting mast about what?"

"Actions unbecoming an officer."

"Do what! Against who?"

"The Captain."

"What the hell happened?"

"Corporal Thomas was done firing for the day and got in line to get a sandwich when the meat wagon came around. Captain Bread was in line behind him. When Corporal Thomas had his hands full of food Captain Bread goosed him."

I waited for more and then said, "Well what else?"

"Sir, officers aren't supposed to do that."

"Gunny, hasn't Corporal Thomas ever been goosed before."

"Not by his commanding officer or any other officer of Marines. But Corporal Thomas says it's more than a goose. He touched his balls."

"He's saying it was a homosexual act."

"That's how he felt."

At hearing this, I looked over the group where Cpl Thomas stood and then GySgt Cain yelled, "Corporal Thomas come here."

As Cpl Thomas walked over I noticed Capt Bread looking at me as he stood with 1stSgt Stall.

"Yes Gunny," said Cpl Thomas.

"Tell the Gunner what happened," said GySgt Cain.

Cpl Thomas went on to tell me pretty much what GySgt Cain had told me.

"What did Captain Bread say when you requested mast?" I asked.

"He said he didn't mean anything by it. He said he was sorry."

"So, what else do you want?"

"Sir, I don't think a Marine officer should act like that and I want Colonel Payne to know what kind of officer we have running Mike Company."

"Are you sure you want to do this?" I asked

He stood looking at me.

"Gunner, you act like you don't want him to request mast," grumbled GySgt Cain.

I looked hard at GySgt Cain before I spoke, "I can't stop him from requesting mast or would I try. And you know I don't care that much for Captain Bread. But I do care about this company. Corporal Thomas is all but saying Captain Bread is a queer. Do you realize what will happen to this company if this should get out in the civilian papers? It'll not only hurt Mike Company, but the whole Second Marine Division. I just don't want the honor of this company hurt."

"Sir, why are you standing up for Captain Bread after what he did to Gunner Reed?" argued GySgt Cain.

"I backed Gunner Reed then and still do," I said to GySgt Cain. Then looking at Cpl Thomas I said, "Let me ask you this. Let's say Lieutenant Cregar or Littleton, Captain Evans or I had goosed you and touched your balls, and you had complained about it and they or I had said we were sorry, would you still request mast to battalion?"

Cpl Thomas took a deep breath before he said, "No sir I wouldn't. But I don't believe even by accident would you or them fondle my balls the way he did."

I looked around at the other Staff NCOs and NCOs. Only GySgt Cain was smiling. I turned walking to my truck. I drove home confused and sick at heart fearing what the outcome of this might be.

On May 19th, I was in Capt Bread's office when 1stSgt Stall knocked on the door saying, "Excuse me sir, but Staff Sergeant Samuels would like to speak to you."

"Have him come in Top," said Capt Bread.

The tall big black Marine marched in to the front of Capt Bread's desk.

"Yes, Staff Sergeant Samuels what can I do for you?" asked Capt Bread.

"Sir, I've been in this Corps for ten years now and I've never asked to get out of anything. But sir I'm asking to be allowed to stay behind during this thirty-day exercise in 29 Palms."

"Is there a reason?" asked Capt Bread.

"Yes sir, my mother is in the hospital; back in Virginia and she's not expected to live. When the end comes, I would rather not be three thousand miles away."

"Your mother is old. She wouldn't live forever anyway. She's lived her life and you have to live yours. You know we are short four officers in Mike Company. You're doing a Lieutenant's job. And you have corporals running squads. I need you on that exercise. Your platoon needs you. Your request is denied."

SSgt Samuels looked over at me stunned as his eyes filled with tears. Then he looked back at Capt Bread and said, "Aye, Aye sir." Then he did an about face and marched out.

I was surprised he didn't request mast. I would have. But then again being that Gunner Reed's and Cpl Thomas' request mast hadn't changed anything, why should he bother.

On May 25th, GySgt Cain walked into my office and closed the door behind him. He walked over and put both hands down on my desk leaning over it toward me.

"Yes Gunny?" I asked wondering what he was upset over.

"You remember what happened when Staff Sergeant Samuel's requested to stay behind during our 29 Palms exercise?"

"Yeah it was refused."

"You know I've been doing some carpentry work off base on my days off."

"Yes, I know."

"Well I just requested to stay behind because I've gotten behind in my carpentry work."

"Are you shittin me, Gunny?" I said laughing.

"No sir and you haven't heard nothing, yet. He granted my request."

I felt my mouth drop open as he went on to say, "And he told me no problem, Staff Sergeant Samuels could act as the company gunny during the exercise and Sergeant Meadows could run First Platoon."

"I don't believe this shit," I spat.

"You think about it, sir. This is the third good black Marine he has shit on big time in the last six months."

"Christ, this guy is screwing up my company."

"Gunner you've got to do something about this guy before there's real trouble."

"What can I do? He doesn't listen to me either and I have no old friends at the battalion level any more other than Sergeant Major Burns."

"Then I'm going to give Sergeant Major Burns a call."

"You have to do what you think is right Gunny. I'm at my wits end with the guy. I'm thinking about submitting my retirement papers after the exercise."

"I didn't think you're the kind to run away."

"This guy is going to ruin my career anyway and I'd rather retire while I'm still well thought of," I said.

GySgt Cain slowly stood up and then without a word walked out.

I threw my black ink pen on the desktop and spun around in my chair looking out the window as a squad of Marines marched by.

On May 28th, SgtMaj Burns was moved up to be our regimental sergeant major. Our new battalion sergeant major came out to the field to visit with the enlisted men of Mike Company. We were breaking for chow when 1stSgt Stall drove up in the new Hummer with the new sergeant major. As he got out, I thought he looked familiar. Capt Bread and I stood up walking over to meet him.

When I realized who he was I said, "When did you make sergeant major, Cacolone?"

He saluted us looking strangely at me and then said, "Is that you Cord? I mean sir."

"Sure is."

"Well, that explains why you didn't become the Sergeant Major of the Corps."

"I take it you two know each other. I'm Captain Bread."

"Glad to meet you sir. Did you know this guy was a seven-year gunnery sergeant?" said SgtMaj Cacolone.

"No, I didn't," said Capt Bread looking at me.

"It's been a long time," I said.

"Yeah it was in seventy-three when we left the Nam. Shit I was a staff sergeant then. The last I heard of you, you were a master sergeant. I didn't think the Corps was making anymore Infantry Warrant Officers."

"They haven't in the last seven years."

"Well Captain, I came to speak to the enlisted men," said SgtMaj Cacolone.

"Sure, sergeant major. First Sergeant Stall would you gather the men in a school circle?" said Capt Bread.

"Aye, Aye sir," answered 1stSgt Stall as he walked away.

"Well Gunner, it's good to be serving with you again," said SgtMaj Cacolone.

"Same here sergeant major," I said thinking that this was the first good news I had since Capt Bread took command of Mike Company.

On June 2nd, I walked into Capt Bread's office and handed him a list of the people I wanted to take with me on the advance party to 29 Palms.

He looked over the list slowly and then said, "Very good Gunner. But I'm going out with the advance party. You'll bring the main body out."

Surprised I said, "But sir it's the XO's job to go with the advance party."

"Maybe so. But this is my first battalion exercise at 29 Palms with Mike Company and I want to make sure everything gets off to the right start."

"Okay sir," I said flushing with anger. I turned and walked out.

About two weeks later, Capt Bread left on a Wednesday with the advance party and flew out to 29 Palms with Maj Sevenskie and the advance parties from the other companies.

Friday afternoon I drove home to have a quick supper with my family at 1630. Mike Company was packed up and we were due to leave by buses at 2230 to go to Cherry Point, from where we would fly to 29 Palms Ca.

I had just sat down at the table when the phone rang. Lance jumped up and grabbed the phone and said, "Hello. Oh yes he is."

As he handed me the phone I asked, "Who is it?"

"I don't know," said Lance shrugging his shoulders.

I put the phone to my ear and said, "Gunner Cord speaking sir."

"Gunner this is Colonel Payne."

"Yes sir," I said wondering what in the world had come up that couldn't wait six hours when our battalion was due to gather together to leave for 29 Palms.

"Gunner, you are now the commanding officer of Mike Company."

"What do you mean I'm the CO sir?"

"Just what I said. You are the CO until further word. At least until this exercise is over."

"Sir, what in the word has happened?"

"Corporal Thomas request mast reached General Salesses today at 29 Palms. He ordered Captain Bread to report to him and then relieved him of his command on the spot, subject to a court martial. Whatever happens he will not rejoin Mike Company."

I was lost for words as I struggled taking all this in.

"Gunner! You still there?"

"Yes sir. I'm just shocked."

"Well you have the ball. I'm afraid there will be a lot of eyes on you at 29 Palms."

"Yes sir, I can imagine. I'll do my best."

"I'm sure you will. I'll see you at Cherry Point."

"Yes sir. Thanks for the call."

I hung up the phone and just stood there as my mind raced.

"What is going on?" demanded Marty.

I looked at my family and all three of them were just sitting there looking at me and not eating.

As I sat back down, I said, "Captain Bread has been relieved."

"What does this mean?" asked Marty.

"It means I'm acting CO for at least the next month," I said smiling as I reached out to hold her hand.

At 1800, I drove to the company office. I found 1stSgt Stall in his office and said, "Top gather the staff for a meeting in Captain Bread's office."

"Sir you did say Captain Bread's office?" he asked looking at me funny.

"Yes, I did Top."

"Yes sir," he said smiling.

I then went to my old office and picked up my sea bag, pack, war belt and helmet and carried them into my new office and sat down at Capt Bread's old desk.

Soon, 1stSgt Stall walked in smiling again at seeing me behind the desk. Soon in walked SSgt's Samuels, Reilly and Sgts Crew, Higgins, Meadows and Rienbold. All of them seemed surprised that not only was this meeting in the CO's office, but that I was sitting at his desk.

"Gunner you look good behind that desk," said Sgt Meadows.

I smiled at him taking a deep breath before I spoke, "I have some word to pass to the company. But first I want to tell you. If you have any questions ask them now. You may have already heard rumors." I looked over at 1stSgt Stall who looked back at me strangely and shook his head as if saying he didn't have a clue what I was going to say.

Then I said, "A couple of hours ago Colonel Payne called me at home. It seems earlier today Captain Bread was relieved of his command by General Salesses."

"All right!" shouted SSgt Reilly smiling.

"We'll have none of that," I said looking hard at him. And then went on to say, "Whether we liked him or not, he is a Marine officer and it is a tragedy when any officer is relieved from command. As for Mike Company I am the acting CO until further word."

"Outstanding," said Sgt Rienbold.

"Because we are going on a battalion-size exercise, all eyes will be on us because not only am I now the only officer left in Mike Company, I'm a Warrant Officer commanding it. I'll need all your help in the next few weeks."

"No problem Gunner. We won't let you down," said 1stSgt Stall.

"Okay men, let's prepare the troops to get on the buses. But first I'll pass this word to the troops. Okay let's do it," I said getting up.

A few minutes later we held the company formation and I explained what had happened to Capt Bread. Then SSgt Samuels got the troops and their gear on the buses. The buses carried us to Cherry Point. Once there we climbed on a plane and flew across the country to 29 Palms.

At the landing field we were meet by SgtMaj Cacolone who saluted me and said, "Good morning sir and congratulations."

I returned his salute saying, "Thank you sergeant major."

"Sir have the company follow me and I'll show the troops to their tents and then I'll show you to the A frame hut for the battalion officers," he said.

I yelled for SSgt Samuels, "Company Gunny up!"

Big tall black SSgt Samuels walked up to me and said, "Yes sir."

"Is the company ready to move out?" I asked.

"Yes sir."

"Okay, have them follow me and the sergeant major," I said.

"Yes sir."

We followed SgtMaj Cacolone down the desert road and into the tent city. When he came to the row of tents, which had been set up for Mike Company, he first showed 1stSgt Stall the tent for the Staff NCOs. Then as SSgt Samuels assigned the four platoons to their tents SgtMaj Cacolone walked me to the A frame hut. As we stopped outside he said, "Officer call goes at 0730. Good luck sir."

"Thank you," I said. Then I tiptoed into the hut and used my flashlight to find an empty rack. I lay down trying to get some sleep in what few hours I had left until 0630.

At 0730, we company commanders gathered in LtCol Payne's hut he shared with Maj Sevenskie and SgtMaj Cacolone. I felt like all eyes were on me. I wondered if it was respect I saw in their eyes or jealousy because I was a warrant officer and not a captain or lieutenant. I looked around the room at the other company commanders. There was the tall thin Capt Anderson of India Company. Like me he was a former enlisted man, who unlike me left the Corps as a corporal, went to college and then was commissioned a lieutenant. Next was Capt Korhirst the short almost overweight CO of Kilo Company. Then there was Capt Rastis, the tall broad-shouldered long-distance runner of Lima Company.

LtCol Payne explained the plan of the day as well as what he expected from us over the next month. He never once mentioned Capt Bread or did he introduce me as the new or acting commanding officer of Mike Company. But of course, they all knew me. When he was done, we started to get up and leave when he said, “Gunner would you stay for a minute?”

“Yes sir,” I answered as the three captains looked back at me as they walked out.

LtCol Payne walked up to me and said, “Gunner, I want Major Sevenskie to spend the next few weeks with your company.”

“Yes sir,” I said feeling uneasy.

“He will not command Mike Company. You will still report directly to me. He will just observe.”

“Yes sir,” I said. But as I walked back toward Mike Company with Maj Sevenskie beside me, I was struggling to control my anger. I felt LtCol Payne didn’t trust my ability to command a company after twenty years in the Corps just because I wasn’t a college boy without railroad tracks on my collars.

As we neared the Staff NCOs tent, I stopped, turning toward Maj Sevenskie saying, “Sir, I would like to explain to my staff alone, why you will be spending the next month with us.”

“Sure Gunner. Go ahead. I understand.”

“Thank you, sir,” I said as I turned pulling the flap back to the tent. As I stepped in 1stSgt Stall saw me and yelled, “Attention on deck!”

As the men jumped up, I said, “At ease men.”

I walked over and sat down on a cot among them and said, “It seems while we’re here at the sticks Major Sevenskie will be staying with us to observe.”

“Why?” asked Sgt Rienbold.

“I’m not sure. Maybe they don’t trust a Warrant Officer commanding a company,” I answered.

“Bull shit sir,” said Sgt Crew.

"I will tell you this. I am commanding this company for as long as I am here or until I am relieved. You will report to me, not Major Sevenskie. And I in turn will report to Colonel Payne. Men I'm sorry I've put you all on the skyline. All eyes are on us. I understand Colonel Rice and General Salesses will be observing the battalion during the two-week war. We have to be the best. I need your help. Not for my sake, but for Mike Company," I said.

"No problem Gunner," said 1stSgt Stall.

"We'll take care of you sir," said Sgt Rienbold.

"Not for me. We have to work together for the reputation of Mike Company," I said.

Then I got up and asked Maj Sevenskie to come in. When he came in, he explained to my staff why he would be with us. I was happy that he had backed me up and then he sat down off to himself.

Then I briefed my staff on what I'd learned at the battalion briefing. When I was done, I said, "Okay let's do it."

For the next two weeks we started the day at 0400 with each company holding physical fitness training before breakfast while it was still cool. By the time the PT was over and we had showered and ate chow the sun would already be burning the desert sand. Then each company was trucked out to different training ranges to spend the day under the boiling sun.

I was surprised at how well everything went. I found Maj Sevenskie to be true to his word. He never tried to run things or tell me what to do. In fact, several times he praised my staff to their faces for their efforts as well as to LtCol Payne at the battalion meetings in front of the other company commanders.

The final two weeks we spent in the Delta corridor where we conducted the war game. Again, everything went well even during BGen Salesses visit.

Mike Company had just captured a big rocky hill and were busy digging in as I waited for further orders. Just then three white vans drove up to the rear of our positions.

Cpl Blandon and his fire team rose up with weapons raised ordering the vans to stop. As the vans stopped in a whirl of dust, Sgt Higgins ran down the hill to see what was going on.

From out of the dust stepped BGen Salesses and Col Rice and their staffs.

Sgt Higgins brought them through the positions of 3rd platoon up the hill to my CP.

As they approached, I didn't salute because we were under combat simulated conditions. I said, "Good afternoon General Salesses and Colonel Rice."

"How are you doing Gunner?" asked BGen Salesses.

"Fine General," I answered.

"Being a company commander isn't as easy as it sounds is it," said BGen Salesses.

"No sir it isn't, but General I think you would agree there's nothing else like it in the world," I said.

"Yes, I have to agree. But I've also enjoyed commanding battalions, regiments and now a MAU," said BGen Salesses.

"General, this is not the first time Gunner Cord had been an acting CO. The first time was under combat conditions and he was only a corporal. Later during stateside duty back at Lejeune as a first sergeant he again was put in command of this company," said Maj Sevenskie.

I looked back at Maj Sevenskie, shocked at just how much he had researched my military record to know all this.

"Yes, I've heard of Gunner Cord's distinguished service book. Now Gunner, I'd like a tour of Mike Company's positions," said BGen Salesses.

"Sure General," I said.

As we walked around the company positions, I introduced him to SSgt Samuels of 1st platoon, SSgt Reilly of 2nd platoon, Sgt Higgins of 3rd platoon and Sgt Rienbold of Weapons platoon. Then I walked them back down the hill to the waiting vans. Once in the vans, the General's van drove away first. As Col Rice's van started to move away, Col Rice in the back seat turned around and gave me the thumbs up sign through the back window.

As I turned to walk back up the hill, Sgt Rienbold stood there smiling and said, "I guess you did good sir."

"We all did good," I answered walking past him.

Returning to my CP, I found Maj Sevenskie there sitting on a boulder. I walked up to him and said, "Major, thank you for what you said."

He looked up smiling saying, "No problem Gunner. You're doing a good job."

"Thank you, sir. Major what do you think my chances are of

staying the CO of Mike Company?"

"Gunner if you were a Chief Warrant Officer-4 I think you would have a chance. So, don't get your hopes up."

Finally, the war game was over and we were packed up ready to return to Camp Lejeune.

At the end of the final battalion briefing I asked to speak to LtCol Payne as the rest left.

"Yes, Gunner what can I do for you?"

"Sir, I'd like to keep command of Mike Company."

"Gunner you know there're lots of captains out there that would give their left nut at the chance to command a line company."

"Yes sir. But I'm not just a Chief Warrant Officer. I'm an Infantry Warrant Officer. I realize you don't hear of Warrant officers commanding companies today, but it's not unheard of. This maybe the last chance I'll ever get to command a company again. Sir forgive me, but I believe I deserve this command."

"I see. You have done an outstanding job for me out here. I'll have to think about it. But Major Sevenskie had recommended you keep this command."

On July 18th, we returned to Camp Lejeune and our families.

The first of August, I promoted Blandon of 3rd platoon to sergeant during a morning company formation.

On Aug 12th, I was sitting at my desk looking over paper work when I heard a knock at my door. I looked up to see an old friend Gunner Sieple standing in the doorway.

"Gunner Sieple come in," I said, standing up to shake hands.

"How are you doing sir?" asked Gunner Sieple.

"Trying to keep my head above water and how are you?"

"I'm doing fine."

"What can I do for you?" I asked.

"Well sir you can accept these orders," said Gunner Sieple handing me a big brown envelope.

"Orders to report to Mike Company?"

"Yes sir."

"Well I don't know how this happened. But I'm glad you're here."

"I requested a transfer."

"I'm amazed it was approved. But God, I need a good XO. Welcome aboard."

"Thank you, sir."

"First Sergeant!" I yelled.

Seconds later 1stSgt Stall stuck his head in the doorway saying, "Yes sir?"

"Top, this is Gunner Sieple. He's just reporting in. He will be my XO. Show him to his office and have Gunny Cain show him around."

"Very good sir. Gunner Sieple would you follow me please?" said 1stSgt Stall.

As they walked out, I thought, "I hope this is a good sign that I'm going to be allowed to keep this command."

The first of September, I promoted Samuels to gunnery sergeant and put him in charge of Weapons platoon.

On Sept 2nd, I was returning to my office from chow with Gunner Sieple when 1stSgt Stall stopped us in the hallway saying, "Sir we just picked up another officer. I have him checked in. You need to assign him a platoon. He's waiting for you in your office," said 1stSgt Stall.

"What rank is he?" I asked.

"Warrant Officer sir. By the name of Reed," answered 1stSgt Stall smiling.

"Reed!" I said looking at Gunner Sieple. Then I walked on entering my office. Gunner Reed stood up sticking out his black hand saying, "Good afternoon sir."

"How are you?" I asked.

"Fine now. I didn't want to be assigned back here. But when I found out you were in command, I was more than happy to come back."

"Well I'm still only the acting CO. I take it you didn't request this assignment?"

"No sir. I received orders back to Lejeune after the basic school. But when I got here, I was surprised to be ordered back to the Infantry and then shocked to be sent back to Mike Company."

"Well Mike Company needs you. I'm glad you're back."

"Do you have a platoon I can run?"

"Yes, I have four."

"Then can I have third platoon?"

"No but you can have first platoon. Sergeant Meadows is a good platoon sergeant, but he's not quite ready to be a platoon leader. I can have Gunny Cain show you to your platoon unless you can still find your way."

"I'm sure I can find them. Thank you, sir."

"Well then, carry on Gunner Reed and welcome back."

On November 10th, I took Marty to the officers Marine Corps Birthday Ball. I wore my dress blues and Marty wore a dark blue dress with a red rose in her hair. We had our picture taken in front of the Marine Corps and American flag. We sat at a table with the other company commanders of our battalion. It was hot in the hall and the hair of the women drooped from the heat. But we still had a good time. I found Capts Anderson and Korhirst were easier to talk to now and get along with. But Capt Rastis was still distant and seemed like he felt he was superior to everyone. But as always, Marty made a big hit with all the Marine wives.

In December as usual I took a week leave and we went home to Delaware to visit our families. But we celebrated the New Year of 1986 back at Camp Lejeune at our home.

On Jan 3rd Col Rice was transferred out.

On Jan 8th as the morning battalion briefing ended, LtCol Payne asked me to stay behind. After the rest of the company commanders had left, he said, "Gunner I've taken eight months to decide on an officer to command Mike Company."

"Yes sir," I said feeling a lump build in my throat.

"At first I felt you had already been with Mike Company too long. I don't know how you have managed to stay with this same unit so long."

"Well sir I have wondered too. It's like CMC (Commandant Marine Corps) has forgotten about me. But I've been promoted twice since I joined this unit. So, somebody knows I'm here."

"I think it would be better for you if you did transfer."

I felt my heart skip a beat as he went on to say, "But I'm selfish. I have three captains who are trying to outdo you. You're good for Mike Company and for the battalion."

"Thank you, sir."

"And I agree with you. You do deserve this command, if for no other reason than saving the day for me out at 29 sticks. So, I'm giving you the command for a tour of two years. Then I think you should go."

"Yes, sir it will be time to leave. Thank you, sir," I said as I thought, "Mike Company was really mine. A dream come true."

I drove back to Mike Company area. As I walked in my company office, I knew the staff and officers were waiting for me in my office. So, I quickly ducked into 1stSgt Stall's office. I picked up his phone and called home.

"Hello," I heard Marty say.

"Hi," I said.

"Hi."

"Colonel Payne has picked an officer to command Mike Company."

"You got it," she said as if knowing.

"Yes. Did you know?"

"No, but you're too up to have not gotten it."

"Yeah you know me too well. But it's only for two years."

"Then what?"

"If I get my promotion this year, I'll still need close to another year after my tour is up here before I can retire at that rank. So, we'll see where I get transferred to. By then I'll have twenty-four years in the Corps."

"Yeah and then you'll say if you stay six more years you'll have thirty years in and would get 75% of your base pay when you retire."

"You do believe you know me, don't you?"

"I've known for a long time I married a career Marine. And being a Marine means more to you than pay or retirement."

"Do you think you can make it?" I asked.

"Like I've told you. You're not going to get rid of me."

"I love you girl."

"I love you."

Just then 1stSgt Stall stuck his head in his door and said, "Oh sir. I wondered who was on my phone."

"Be right there Top," I said to him and then to Marty, "Marty I've got to go and tell my staff the news."

"You haven't told them yet?"

"No. See ya later."

"Bye."

In March, LtCol Payne transferred out and I was glad to see Maj Sevenskie become the acting battalion commander.

On April 5th, Mike Company returned from four days of field training. As I dropped my pack, helmet and war belt down on the floor beside my desk, 1stSgt Stall stuck his head in my door saying, "Excuse me Gunner but your wife called earlier. Said there wasn't a problem, but asked if you could call her when you get a chance."

"Thanks Top," I said picking up the phone.

"Hello," I heard her say.

"What's up?" I asked.

"Oh hi. Last night I got a call from Kyle."

"He called?" I asked surprised.

"He called collect."

"What's happened?"

"He asked me if he could come home."

"Back here? With us?"

"Yes. I told him I would have to talk to you."

"Sure. When? After the end of the school year or the end of summer."

"Now he says."

"What's his father say?"

"If we want him, come get him."

"Okay this coming Friday as soon as the kids get home from school we'll leave."

"You sure?" asked Marty.

"Sure, I'm sure. See ya in a couple of hours."

"I love you."

"Love you too."

So, the weekend was spent mostly driving to and from Delaware.

As we tucked Kyle into bed late Sunday night I said, "Kyle I just have to ask why did you decide to live with us again?"

He looked at me kind of funny and answered, "I want to do better."

"I see. Well, I want you to know we love you. And we're happy and proud you've returned to us," I said feeling tears of happiness swell up in my eyes. And seeing tears in his eyes I hugged him.

Then I stood up and Marty and I walked out arm in arm toward our bedroom.

On April 10th, I promoted Street of 3rd platoon to sergeant.

In May I took Mike Company to the field for two weeks. It started raining the first day. But as always, I found the men of Mike Company performed brilliantly even in knee-deep mud, the cold wind and rain.

But soon June came and the end of the school year. I took a 96-hour pass and we drove Lance back to Delaware to spend the summer with his mother.

Then it was back to Mike Company training in the heat of summer with the sand fleas and jiggers.

In July the Chief Warrant Officer promotion list came out and I was on the list to be promoted to Chief Warrant Officer 4. I was overjoyed to know I would make it to the senior warrant officer rank. But at the same time, it seemed odd to think this would be my last promotion of my career.

Soon the summer was gone and Lance was back with us again and all three kids were back in school.

In October, Capt Korhirst of Kilo Company was transferred and Sgt Blandon of 3rd platoon was discharged from the Corps.

The first of November, Marty and I went to the retirement party of SgtMaj Cacolone after thirty years a Marine. 1stSgt Stall became our acting battalion sergeant major. GySgt Cain took over as my acting first sergeant. GySgt Samuels took over as my company gunnery sergeant. And Sgt Rienbold again became the platoon leader of weapons platoon.

The week before the Marine Corps Birthday Ball I again took Mike Company to the field. At first nothing had seemed to go right. My officers, staff and I had planned this for a week. The whole week before, the sun had shone and the temperature had been right around eighty. But then we went to the field Monday morning and it was pouring rain with dark gray skies and twenty mile an hour winds.

As we forced marched out to the field in the rain, I heard Sgt Crew of 2nd platoon say, “Once again we’re challenged by the weather of North Kaki-Lakie.”

But we had a lot of new men in the company now and we needed this time in the field to learn to work together.

The second day out, I looked out over the muddy training site. Nearby a six by truck was rocking back and forth, stuck in the mud.

“Well I don’t know whether Gunny Cain will get back to the rear today or not,” said GySgt Samuels.

Then I turned trying to walk in the knee-deep mud to check the platoons out as they trained.

“Just have to keep movin and grooving,” said GySgt Samuels following me.

I smiled pleased how well things had gone as I watched Sgt Crew moving with his squad from 2nd platoon. A little later I watched young Sgt Street with his squad teaching them squad tactics and formations. The whole week was muddy, windy and wet as it rained almost continually, but it never dampened the moral of Mike Company. And at the end I forced marched them back to our company area in the rain. They were dirty, wet and tired, but they were Marine Corps proud.

The next Saturday night Marty and I went to the officers Marine Corps Birthday Ball. We sat at a table with the other Battalion company commanders, Capt Anderson, Capt Rastis and Capt Hyndman the new commander of Kilo Company.

The birthday cake had a big eagle, globe and anchor in the middle. Below it was the words United States Marine Corps. On the upper left-hand corner was 1775 and on the upper right corner was 1986.

As usual we had a great time dancing and swiping sea stories. At times like this I felt old realizing I had not only been in the Corps twice as long as any of these captains, but I was the only company commander in this battalion which had been in Vietnam, Beirut and Grenada.

On November 16th, I stood waiting while standing at attention in front of Mike Company as the other three company commanders were doing the same in our battalion formation. At 1500, Maj Sevenskie and 1stSgt Stall marched out onto the parade field across the front of our battalion. To my front between Kilo and Lima Companies they did a left face as one behind a microphone.

"Report!" yelled Maj Sevenskie.

Capt Anderson saluted yelling, "India Company! All present and accounted for sir!"

Followed by Capt Hyndman yelling, "Kilo Company all present and accounted for sir!"

Then Capt Rastis yelled, "Lima Company all present and accounted for sir!"

Finally, I saluted yelling, "Mike Company all present and accounted for sir!"

As he had done with the others, Maj Sevenskie returned my salute. Then he yelled, "Gunner Cord! Front and center!"

I marched off across the parade field until I had centered myself in front of Maj Sevenskie. I halted snapping to attention, saluted and said, “Sir, Gunner Cord reporting as ordered.”

After Maj Sevenskie returned my salute, 1stSgt Stall handed him my promotion warrant to Chief Warrant Officer-4 in a red folder.

Thinking this would be my last promotion after twenty-two years in the Corps I had called my family in Delaware and invited them to come down to see it.

As Maj Sevenskie read the warrant, I looked over his left shoulder at Marty, Kyle, Lance and Samantha sitting in blue chairs watching. Next to them I was still surprised and happy to see my oldest son Nat and his girlfriend Donna had driven down yesterday and spent the night with us. This was the first time in my twenty-two-year career that all my children were together to see me promoted. Never was I prouder. Maybe because of this reason my eyes kept misting over and I had to keep blinking to clear them. And maybe it was from the pride and love of my family. As in the past, Marty was called forward to pin on my new Chief Warrant Officer-4 bar (red bar with two silver boxes) on the right collar of my tan shirt and the right shoulder of my green blouse.

Chapter 5 Chief Warrant Officer Four

The 1st of December I had the pleasure of promoting Gunner Reed to Chief Warrant Officer-2.

As usual I took a week's leave for Christmas and we drove home to Delaware to visit the family and let Lance visit his mother and Kyle visit his father.

By the 1st of the new year of 1987, we were back at Camp Lejeune.

On the 8th of January, I promoted Rienbold to staff sergeant. This was a promotion long overdue. His wife was so happy for him she cried.

On the 18th of January, I was glad to see Sevenskie be promoted to lieutenant colonel, which meant he would keep the command of our battalion.

The 1st of February, Reilly of 2nd platoon had already received his transfer orders when I promoted him to gunnery sergeant. I hated to see him go. There was getting to be fewer and fewer of the old Beirut veterans left in Mike Company.

On Feb 3rd, I was in my office when my phone rang. I picked it up saying, "Mike Company Gunner Cord speaking sir."

"Nathan can you come home?" asked Marty.

"What's wrong?"

"Lance is packing his bags."

"Packing his bags! Where is he going?"

"To his mother's."

"What the hell happened?"

"I don't know. I caught him packing and asked him where he was going."

"He didn't say why?"

"No."

"Okay I'm on my way," I said hanging up. I jumped up grabbing my camouflaged cover as I opened the side door to the first sergeant's office. As GySgt Cain looked up, I said, "Gunny find Gunner Sieple and tell him he's in charge the rest of the day. If he or the colonel needs me, I'll be at home the rest of the day."

"Is there a problem at home Gunner?"

"So it seems," I said hurrying out to my truck.

As I drove home, I tried to figure what had gone wrong. I thought he liked it here. Marty was a good mother to him, although lately I had felt coolness between them.

When I pulled into the driveway, Lance was putting his suitcases in the trunk of his car with Kyle helping him. Marty and Samantha were watching from the front steps.

As I stepped out of the truck, Kyle walked back toward Marty as Lance turned to face me.

"So, she called you, did she?" spat Lance.

Walking up to him I said, "Yes she did. Don't you feel you should say something to me?" I said trying to control my anger.

"Why?"

"You were just going to drive away without telling me why."

"Ask your wife."

"Oh, I intend to. But I want to hear your side right now. I've always told you that if you had a problem to let us know. You never complained to me. Did you say anything to Marty?"

"No," he said in a mumble.

Marty walked up beside me and said, "Lance what have I done? If this is about me, I'm sorry. But tell me what I did. Please."

"I can't believe it's her. Have you forgotten all the games she took you to? All of the baseball practices. Kyle's stepmother refused to do that for him when he lived with his father," I said.

"I know. I know." Lance said.

"Okay, tell us what is the problem," I said.

"Last Fall when Kyle and I were on the track team together. We went to an away game on a bus. On the way back, we stopped to get something to eat. Kyle pulled out ten dollars. I kidded him about he could buy my lunch. And he told me that Marty told him not to buy me anything to eat."

"I never told him that," said Marty.

"Well wait a minute. You did in a way," I said.

Marty and Lance both looked at me.

"Now Lance, I want you to think about it. I get paid twice a month. And Marty only gets so much money to give you guys for lunches, games and gas for her. There had been other times when Kyle had asked for a couple of dollars to buy a snack at the games. Well, several times she hadn't had any ones and she had to give him a five-dollar bill or a ten. Now she had expected to get change back.

But Kyle spent all of it buying his friends burgers and drinks. Do you remember that?" I said.

"Yes," answered Lance.

"I told him to buy only his food and to bring me back the change. But I never cared if he bought you something," cried Marty.

"So, this has been eating at you all these months?" I said.

"Yeah. I'm sorry," said Lance.

"Why didn't you say something then? It would've saved a lot of hard feelings," I said.

"I know," Lance said.

"So why don't we carry your stuff back in?" I said feeling better.

"I can't. I called Mom collect last night and told her I was driving up after school today."

"Well, we can call her back," I said.

"She didn't want me to drive up alone at night. She's flying down to ride up with me."

"I see," I said feeling my heart sink and then added, "I wish you'd have talked to us."

"I love you," said Marty-hugging Lance.

"I love you too. I'm sorry," said Lance hugging her back.

Then Lance and I hugged. Samantha ran up and hugged him too.

Lance then got in his car, started it up, backed out into the street and drove away.

As I watched him leave, I fought back tears.

"You all right?" asked Marty holding me.

"No, I'm not. We just can't seem to keep all of our kids under one roof no matter how hard we try," I said. And to myself I thought, "How can I be so good at being a Marine and be such a failure as a father?"

In March I promoted Higgins of 3rd platoon to staff sergeant.

In May, Marty, Kyle, Samantha and I drove up to Delaware for the weekend and watched Lance graduate from high school. Nat was there with his girlfriend Donna.

The 1st of June I promoted Crew of 2nd platoon to staff sergeant.

Later, I had Mike Company training in the field, going over company-size tactics in preparations for another thirty days training exercise in the desert of 29 Palms CA coming up next month. It was there that we learned the new commandant would be Gen Al Gray, our old division commanding general during 1983 and 1984 in

Beirut. I was surprised he got selected because he hadn't been a lieutenant general that long. But I couldn't think of a better man to lead our Corps.

The 1st of July, Meadows had received his transfer orders when I promoted him to staff sergeant.

On the 13th of July, our battalion was flown out to Palm Springs, CA. There, by buses, we rode through the desert to 29 Palms and then out to Camp Wilson.

Every time I came to Camp Wilson, I found the airfield bigger and more A-framed buildings had been built. Now there was even a firehouse out there.

1stSgt Stall, still our acting battalion sergeant major, showed GySgt Cain to Mike Company's tent area. Soon, GySgt Samuels had gathered the platoon sergeants together and they in turn had their men setting up squad tents and then covering it all with the new camouflaged netting.

Meanwhile, Gunners Sieple and Reed and I settled in to the A frame hut for the company commanders and platoon leaders of our battalion.

By the time we had finished with LtCol Sevenskie's briefing and walked down to our company area, they had already put up the big red and gold sign with the words, "Mighty Mike Company" along with a bulldog wearing camouflaged utilities and a DI cover.

For lunch I ate an MRE meal sitting on a bench outside of the A-frame.

Every morning our battalion was up at 0400 doing PT and running three miles before it got hot.

During the first week it did something I had never seen it do in the desert before. It poured rain so much that a small stream of water flowed past our A-frame down through the battalion tent city.

One evening, I walked with Gunner Reed through Mike Company's area. In 1st platoon's tent I found the sergeants had hung camouflaged screen between them and the rest of the platoon as both sides played cards.

Also, in the evenings, I would sit outside of the A-frame with the other officers dressed in shorts drinking beer. It always seemed the young lieutenants and captains wanted to talk to me about Vietnam.

Then, for two weeks, our battalion went to the field in the Delta corridor. For the first time, we trained with the new six wheeled LAVs (Light Armored Vehicles.)

On Aug 4th, our battalion returned to Camp Wilson covered with two weeks of dirt and sand. After getting showers, GySgt Samuels had Mike Company start cleaning their weapons and equipment.

On Aug 13th, we returned to Camp Lejeune. The same day, I promoted Cain to master sergeant. He requested to stay on as my acting 1st Sergeant until a 1st Sergeant transferred in or until he could be redesignated to the rank of 1st Sergeant. I agreed and requested he be allowed to stay and LtCol Sevenskie approved it.

On Aug 22nd, I went to the retirement party for 1stSgt Stall. He had decided to live in Jacksonville just off the base. I was always surprised when some of these guys retired and stayed near the base instead of returning to the place they were born and raised.

On Sept 10th, I was doing paper work at my desk when the phone rang. I picked it up saying, "Mike Company, Gunner Cord speaking sir."

"Dad."

"Nat is that you?"

"Yeah, how are you doing?"

"I'm fine. I'm surprised you remember my office number."

"I didn't. I called Marty."

"Oh. Is everyone all right?"

"Oh yeah. Um, you remember Donna?"

"Sure. The skinny blond."

"That's her. You know she has a baby girl."

"Yes, I remember."

There was a long silence, the he said, "We're getting married."

Then it was my turn to be silent with surprise before I said, "Are you sure?"

"Dad I've never been more sure of anything in my life. Mom and Lance are both against it."

"Why?"

"They both think I'm jumping into this too fast. What do you think?"

"Nat you're a twenty-year-old man now. I can't tell you what to do about this. Only you know your heart. How does Donna feel about marriage?"

"She's only seventeen. But she's been through a lot. It was her idea to keep her child. She went to work to support her. She's very mature for her age."

"But Nat you have to realize that if you marry a girl with a child you also marry the child. You don't marry one without the other."

"I understand Dad. But do you think I'm ready?"

"Son I can't answer that. Only you can answer that. But you're two years older than I was when I got married the first time."

"Dad would you come to the wedding?"

"If I can. When is it?"

"This coming Saturday."

"That's short notice," I blurted.

"That's the same thing Mom's saying."

"Well it is," I said laughing, but added, "And we'll be there."

"You will?"

"Yes. We'll leave Friday after the kids get out 'a school. I'll call you Saturday morning."

"Okay great. See ya Dad."

"See ya son."

"Dad I love you."

"I love you son."

So, Friday we took the long nine-hour drive up to Delaware.

And Saturday afternoon at a small church in Laurel Delaware we watched my oldest son get married with Lance standing up as his best man. When it was over, I hugged my new daughter-in-law, and kissed her cheek and said, "Welcome to the family."

Then Sunday we drove back to Camp Lejeune. It seemed funny to think that in just one day I had gained not only a daughter-in-law, but I had become the grandfather of a little blond headed granddaughter and I'm only thirty-nine. Well, until my birthday next month anyway.

On Sept 21st, GySgt Samuels transferred out. I picked SSgt Rienbold to be the acting company gunnery sergeant until a gunnery sergeant transferred in.

On Oct 6th, we were surprised when Nat, his family and Lance drove into our yard. Marty fried up some chicken for us. As we ate and talked, I looked around the table at our children. We didn't see all four of them together like this much anymore. Our children were growing up. I wondered where the years had gone. Here was Nat now twenty years old with his wife Donna. Next to her to my left was Lance now eighteen and out of school. To his left was Kyle now fifteen still struggling in school. To my right was Marty with gray and white showing in her dark brown hair to go along with my white hair. But on her it just added to her beauty. And to her right was little red-haired Samantha now ten.

Later, after supper, I went into the living room to read the paper while Marty and Donna did the dishes with Samantha's help. Kyle went over to a friend's house down the street. Nat had stepped outside to have a smoke. Lance walked in the room and sat down in a chair next to me. "Dad can I talk to you a minute?" he asked.

"Yeah sure," I said folding up the paper and putting it down on the coffee table.

"I went to see an Army recruiter."

Shocked and surprised and struggling to stay calm because it was just last year he had told me he didn't want to go in the military, I said, "I see."

"I know you don't think much about the Army."

"They're all right, but they're not Marines."

"How do you feel about one of your sons joining the Army?"

Taking a deep breath, I answered, "Lance I've always told you guys that you didn't have to join the Marines or go in the military services at all unless they brought the draft back and your number came up. You have to live your own life. I can't live it for you or you live mine. All I want is for you to be a good, honest hard-working man at whatever you do."

"You mean you wouldn't be upset?"

"If that's what you want, I'd be proud."

"Thank you, Dad."

"Let me know when you're leaving for boot camp and where it is."

Later that night as we lay in bed Marty asked, "How do you feel about your son going in the Army?"

Gritting my teeth, I said, "I'd rather see him in any service but the Army."

"Why didn't you tell him?"

"I couldn't. It's his decision. His life. I'll not talk him into going into any service. I'll support him in whatever he does."

"I hope he realizes that."

"I do too."

On Nov 10th, Marty and I went to Mike Company's Marine Corps Birthday Ball out in town. Marty's dress was red and white and of course I was in dress blues. We had our picture taken between the US and Marine Corps flags. During the ceremony Gunner Sieple and I marched up between the honor guards made up of SSgts Higgins and Crew, Sgts Street and another sergeant, two corporals, two lance corporals, two PFCs and two Privates. SSgt Rienbold marched in with the color guard.

As the commanding officer I gave a small speech. Then Gunner Sieple read Commandant Gray's message. Afterwards, Gunner Reed marched up and read the Gen Lejeune message.

I was happily surprised to see Col Hester who left the big ball on base early to come out to visit with us. As usual we drank a toast to our fallen brothers, especially those old friends from Vietnam and Beirut. But I was also sad to realize this was probably my last ball as the CO of Mike Company.

A few weeks later in the evening, the phone rang. Marty answered it and yelled from the kitchen, "Nathan it's for you."

"Who is it?"

"Lance."

I put the paper down and walked into the kitchen and took the phone from Marty and said, "Hello."

"Dad."

"Yes."

"I wanted to let you know I'm not going in the Army."

"I see," I answered relieved.

"Yes, I'm thinking about joining the Air Force."

After a long silence he said, "Well what do you think about it?"

"Like I said before it's your decision. You're boot camp is in Texas, right?"

"Yes. The recruiter said Air Force boot camp isn't near as tough as Marine boot camp."

"I'm sure. But let me know when you're leaving and write me when graduation day is. I'd like to be there if I can."

"Well it won't be til next year. So, we can talk more about it if you come up for Christmas."

"As far as I know now, we'll be up for Christmas and New Year's."

"Okay, see you then."

"Okay, bye," I said hanging up.

"Well, what's the news?" asked Marty.

"Lance is going in the Air Force now."

"How do you feel about that?"

"Anything's better than the Army. The Air Force has the best food and living conditions and for the most part the safest military jobs."

In December, I took fourteen days leave and we drove north to Delaware to stay with Marty's mother in Georgetown while Kyle visited with his father.

Christmas afternoon Lance stopped by as the family was eating homemade soup. Afterwards, Lance and I walked out to the back porch when I asked, "Do you know when you're leaving for boot camp?"

He looked at me kind of funny, and then said, "Oh I'm going into the Corps. I leave in May."

Looking at him hard I said, "Now we're going to talk." I went on to tell him just how hard Marine boot camp could be including the beatings. And if war comes, I don't care what your MOS might be, you could end up in the Infantry. And Marines are always sent in the worst places where the fighting is the worst. I could tell by his face that he was getting upset when he broke in saying, "You act like you don't want me in the Marines."

"No. I'd be proud to have you follow in my footsteps. But you're talking about joining my Corps now. And I want you to know just what you're getting into. I've seen too many kids come into the Corps and didn't know what they were getting into. It caused them trouble in the Corps. I don't want anybody joining my Corps and whining about how tough it is when it's too late."

"Don't you think I can take it?" he asked.

"Sure. But you've got to want to be a Marine. You've got to realize that if you're in the Corps and war comes, you're going to be sent to it."

"I understand that."

"Good," I said smiling.

By January 3rd, 1988, we were back at Camp Lejeune. As our battalion was getting ready for its six-month Mediterranean deployment, I was preparing to turn my company over to its new CO whoever that would turn out to be. It seemed strange I would not be going with Mike Company this time. But even so, I still had a lot to do to make sure Mike Company was ready. I had gotten up early so I could get an early start on all the paper work I knew had piled up while I was on leave.

I opened the door to my office and turned on the light. As I walked around my desk, I saw that my in-basket was overflowing, as I had feared. But in the middle of my desk was a big brown envelope. As I sat down, I saw that the envelope was addressed:

Commanding General
2nd Marine Division

Commanding Officer
Mike Company
2nd Bn 8th Marine Regiment

After twenty-three years in the Corps I knew what change of station orders felt like. I tore the envelope open wondering where I was being transferred. I pulled the papers out and began to read:

From: Commanding General 2nd Mar Div
To: Chief Warrant Officer- 4 Nathan Cord
Commanding Officer Mike Company 2nd Bn 8th Mar Reg

Subj: Transfer orders from 8th Mar Reg

You are relieved as Commanding Officer Mike Company 2nd Bn 8th Mar Reg effective 22 Feb 1988 and report to Commanding General 2nd Mar Div. for further assignment.

I was surprised my transfer wasn't even to another base and state. I had never heard of anybody doing back-to-back tours in the same division.

I picked up my phone and dialed my home number.

"Hello," said a sleepy voice.

"Hi."

"Nathan," said Marty waking up and added, "is everything all right?"

"Yes, but I've got my transfer orders."

"Oh my. How soon?"

"End of February."

After a yawn she asked, “What time is it?”

“About 0530.”

“Good grief. No wonder I can’t wake up.”

“Sorry,” I said laughing.

“Can we go with you?”

“You’ll have to stay here.”

“Where are you going?”

“Right here at Camp Lejeune.”

“Do what?”

“Yeah, it seems it’s just an inner division transfer.”

“This is good, isn’t it?”

“Sure, I don’t mind. The kids should have another three years before we have to move and they have to make new friends. And Kyle will be out ’a school then.”

“How about the Med Cruise.”

“I’ll be transferred before then.”

“But you want to go.”

“Sure, I’d like to go with my troops. But orders are orders. They’ll do fine. I better let you go.”

“Okay, I love you.”

“I love you too,” I said hanging up the phone.

At 0700, I was still doing paper work when MSgt Cain knocked on my door. Looking up I said, “Yes Top.”

“When are you leaving Gunner?”

“End of February. Gather the staff and officers together for a quick meeting before muster.”

“Yes sir,” he said spinning around.

At 0725, I looked around my office at my staff and officers. Among them were Gunners Sieple and Reed, MSgt Cain, SSgts Rienbold, Crew and Higgins. Some of these guys I’ve known for fourteen years. We had been in Beirut together twice. They were all outstanding Marines. I would miss them. Then I said, “Well as some of you have guessed I’m being transferred the end of February. I have no idea who your new CO will be. And it doesn’t matter. We have to make sure this company is ready for the Med Cruise. I wanted to tell you guys before I tell the troops at muster. Any questions?”

“Is there a chance you could make the Med Cruise with us?” asked SSgt Rienbold.

"At this time, I would say no," I answered. Then I said, "Okay let's hold the muster and start training Marines."

On Jan 9th, SSgt Higgins of 3rd platoon transferred out. I made Sgt Street the acting platoon leader of 3rd platoon.

When February came, it seemed funny to think this was my last month as the CO of Mike Company. I haven't felt this way about a unit since Vietnam. But maybe that was it, I had seen combat with these companies. My replacement still hadn't reported in yet.

On Feb 4th, I was at our battalion briefing about the upcoming Med Cruise. When it was over, LtCol Sevenskie asked me to stay a minute. As the others left, Capts Anderson, Hyndman and Ratis all wished me smooth sailing on my new assignment.

When they were gone, I said, "Sir you wanted to speak to me?"

"I still haven't gotten a replacement for you."

"Well sir if you want, I can extend until after the Med Cruise."

"No, no need for that. How has Gunner Sieple been as your XO?"

"Very well sir. Outstanding."

"Could he handle the CO job?"

"Why, yes sir, I believe he could," I said smiling.

"Good. I could replace you with a lieutenant, being there's no captain coming in. But you've done a fine job and I don't want Mike Company to change. It seems to set the pattern for the rest of the battalion."

"Thank you, sir."

"Would you like to be the one to tell Gunner Sieple he'll be your replacement?"

"Yes, sir I sure would."

"He'll have the orders by the end of the week."

"Thank you, sir."

I drove back to the company area. As I walked through the company office, I stopped by MSgt Cain's office and stuck my head in saying, "Top, find Gunner Sieple and have him report to my office."

"Yes sir," he answered getting up from behind his desk.

A few minutes later I was sitting at my desk when Gunner Sieple walked into my office and said, "You wanted to see me."

"Yes, I do. I just found out who my replacement is."

"It's about time. Anybody we know?"

"Yes."

"Well, who is it?"

"You are."

He looked at me in disbelief before he said, "Me?"

"Yes you."

"Are you sure?"

"Colonel Sevenskie just gave me the word. The orders should be here by the end of this week."

"I can't believe it."

"Well, believe it. Maybe you would like to tell Gunner Reed he will be the new XO."

"Yes, I would."

The morning of Feb 22nd, I looked at myself in the mirror checking my uniform as I always did just before I leave the house for the day. I watched Marty walk up behind me putting her right arm through my left arm and hugging it, asking, "You all right?"

"Yeah."

"You sure?"

"I do have mixed emotions. The only unit I served with longer than this was in Vietnam. In this company I've commanded each platoon, been the company XO and its CO. I don't know of any other officer that could say the same thing. I do hate to leave. But it's time to move on."

"So, you're okay with this?"

"Sure. Every officer that has commanded this company has received a plaque from the troops except Captain Bread. I just hope my troops think enough of me to do the same."

"But Colonel Sevenskie awarded you the Navy Commendation medal for the job you did as CO."

"I know. But that's just a star on a ribbon I already have. I have so many medals now I can't keep them straight. But a plaque from troops I have trained and led in combat would mean so much more to me."

"I love you," she said.

"I love you. I'll see you later. I'll be home early this afternoon," I said and then kissed her and walked out to my truck.

After morning muster, I went into my office and started packing up my things inside my walk-in closet. At hearing a knock at my door, I yelled, "Enter!"

"Gunner Cord," I heard a female voice say.

I laughed at myself saying, "Excuse me." As I walked out of the closet, I found Mrs. Rienbold, the wife of SSgt Rienbold standing in my doorway.

"Yes, can I help you Mrs. Rienbold?"

She stepped in through the doorway saying, "I have a gift for you." She handed me a big blue hardback book. Almost in shock, I took the book reading the title. It was a book I had been waiting to come out in soft cover, 'The New Breed,' the 7th of a series of books written by WEB Griffin. Before I knew what was happening, she kissed me on the cheek. I could feel my face turn red. I was speechless as she turned around and walked out.

Standing alone, I opened the cover and, on the inside, she had written:

To Gunner Cord
With Best Wishes
And much respect
You will be missed!

SSgt & Mrs. Rienbold

I closed the book and walked over to my desk and lay the book down on the corner. I patted the book looking out my window, fighting back tears. I may not get a plaque, but this will do.

Finally, I finished packing up and carried the last box out to my truck. I walked back to my office, which was now clear of my pictures and plaques from the wall. I walked into the walk-in closet and opened the locker. There were only two T-shirts left in it. One was red with gold letters, which said:
Commanding Officer
Mike Company 2/8

The other one was gold with red letters, which said the same thing.
Marty had them made up for me as a gift two years ago. I had been proud to wear them during company PT. But now they would be my gift to Gunner Sieple.

Later Gunner Sieple walked in my office and looked around and said, "Sure is bare in here."

I smiled saying, "It's time you started moving in. I left some things in the locker for you."

He walked into the walk-in closet. I walked in behind him as he touched the T-shirts. Then he looked over his shoulder at me saying, "These are for me?"

"Yes. As of 1500 this afternoon you will be the CO."

I walked out into my office and saw SSgt Rienbold standing out in the hallway talking to MSgt Cain.

"Staff Sergeant Rienbold," I said.

"Yes sir," he said turning around walking into my office.

"I just wanted to thank you for the book."

"Oh yes sir. She's given it to you already. You hadn't already got it, had you?"

"No, I was still waiting for it to come out in paperback. I was so surprised when she kissed me, I didn't even thank her."

With a surprised look he said, "She kissed you?"

"Yes, but on the cheek," I quickly added.

"Even though, she doesn't kiss me that much," he said laughing.

I laughed too saying, "Would you tell her thanks for me?"

"Sure, sir."

At 1500, I watched from my office window as SSgt Rienbold formed up the company for me for the last time. The platoon sergeants gave their reports. They were all younger sergeants, all fairly new to Mike Company. When he finished with the muster, he did an about face as MSgt Cain marched out.

I turned walking out of my office. As I walked through the hall, I pulled my camouflaged cover out of my right leg cargo pocket and placed it on my head squaring the top with both my hands. As I walked outside, I found Gunner Sieple waiting for me. By now SSgt Rienbold had marched off to take his post behind the company. MSgt Cain now stood at attention with his back to the company.

"They're ready sir," said Gunner Sieple as he fell in step with me, to my left.

"Yes, and they're ready for you Gunner Sieple."

Together we marched out and faced MSgt Cain who saluted saying, "Sir Mike Company is all present or accounted for."

I returned his salute saying, "Thank you Top. Take your post." As he marched around me to the left of Gunner Sieple, I yelled, "Post!"

As the platoon sergeants marched around the rear of their platoons the platoon leaders marched around to the front of their platoons. Three of them were old friends and old timers in Mike Company. There was Gunner Reed of 1st platoon who would be the company XO in a few minutes. In front of 2nd platoon was SSgt Crew. Then in charge of 3rd platoon was Sgt Street who I had raised from a private.

I took one step forward and yelled, "Company! At ease!"

I slowly looked over this company I loved standing in front of me before I spoke. "Men I have been proud to serve in this company, proud to command it and I am proud of you. As you know, it's unusual for a warrant officer to command a company in today's Marine Corps. But as we see, it can be done. There's nothing special about me. If I can do it so can you, whether you want to be a sergeant major or a company commander. All it takes is for you to do your best, spend the time in and get the promotions. And I didn't do this by myself. You and men like you helped me do these things. I salute you." I saluted them and then said, "Thank you and God bless you." Then I took one step backward and stood at parade rest.

To my left Gunner Sieple snapped to attention and took one-step forward and said, "I have served under Gunner Cord for years. We were even Staff NCOs together. So, I can truly say there's no better Marine than this officer. As much as I want to command this company, I hate to see him go. I just hope I can be half as good a CO as he was. And I hope I get to serve under him again." Then he took one step backwards and stood at parade rest.

"Stand by! Company Attention!" I yelled. As one, the company snapped to attention. Then I yelled, "Master Sergeant Cain present the guide-on."

MSgt Cain marched around and took the company guide-on from the company guide-on bearer. Then he marched in front of me and did a left face holding the guide-on out toward me. I grabbed the guide-on from him and did a left face as Gunner Sieple did a right face to face me. As he reached for the guide-on, I said in a low voice just for him to hear, "It's your company now, but never forget where you came from." Then I dropped my hands to my sides and did a side step to the left. Then I marched forward three steps as Gunner Sieple did the same. Then I did a right face as he did a left face handing the guide-on out to MSgt Cain. MSgt Cain took the guide-on and returned it to the guide-on bearer.

"At ease!" yelled Gunner Sieple and then added, Staff Sergeant Rienbold front and center."

As SSgt Rienbold marched out, I noticed something red folded up in his hand with a brown and black plaque. He marched up in front of Gunner Sieple. Gunner Sieple picked up the plaque and said, "Now I'm going to present this plaque to Gunner Cord. It says:

Presented To
Chief Warrant Officer-4 Nathan Cord
Commanding Officer
Mike Company 2/8
June 1985 to February 1988
Semper Fi

Then Gunner Sieple turned and handed it to me as we shook hands.

"Thank you," I said.

Then he turned back to SSgt Rienbold and said, "Every officer that has been the CO of Mike Company but one has received a plaque when they left. But we feel you've been more to us then our CO. So, a plaque just wasn't enough for you. To show you our appreciation we also got you this." He then unfolded a red jacket and turned showing it to me. On the back of the red jacket was big gold letters USMC. On the front left chest was gold letters: NATHAN CORD. On the right chest was gold letters: Semper Fi.

As I took the jacket, tears filled my eyes. Could it be that these troops think of me as I did about Hester when he was my company commander back in Vietnam in 68? Almost unable to speak, it was all I could do to say, "Thank you."

Then Gunner Sieple turned back to face the company as SSgt Rienbold marched off and yelled, "Company Attention!"

After the company snapped to attention Gunner Sieple yelled, "Company dismissed!"

It took almost an hour for me to leave as I said my goodbyes to old friends, as privates through Gunners came up to slap me on the back, shake my hand and wish me luck.

The next morning, I put on my dress green alpha uniform and drove my truck to 2nd Marine Division headquarters. From there I was ordered over to the 6th Marine Regiment commanded by an old friend Col Al Genio.

I drove over to the 6th Reg headquarters. When I handed my transfer orders to the admin chief, he looked at my name and said, "Oh yes Gunner Cord. Colonel Al Genio left word for you to report to him when you checked in." I followed his directions to the colonel's office and knocked on the hatch.

Looking up, Col Al Genio smiled at me and waved me in. I marched in to the front of his desk and snapped to attention saying, "Sir Gunner Cord reporting as ordered."

"At ease Gunner. Take a seat."

"Thank you, sir," I said sitting down.

"It's been a long time. How are you doing?"

"Yes, sir it has been. I'm doing okay."

"How much time you got in now."

"Twenty-three and a half years, sir."

"You're going for thirty."

"Well sir, at least two more years. Then after that maybe I'll just take it one year at a time. I feel lucky and honored to serve under you again."

"It's not luck. I requested you when I heard you were about to be transferred."

"How did you know?"

"You have been the talk of the division for years. First you command a company as a first sergeant. Then after becoming the youngest sergeant major in the Corps, you become one of the few Infantry Warrant Officers left in the Corps. And to top that off you command a company for almost three years."

"Yes, sir I have been lucky."

"Shit it wasn't luck. It was old-fashioned leadership. But you did make some enemies. Some officers hoped you would fail. And when the word got out you were about to be reassigned, some hope you will finally get your comeuppance."

"Well, sir there have been people jealous of me my whole career because of my fast promotions. First, I was told I was too young to be a sergeant, then too young to be a Staff NCO, especially a sergeant major. Then I was told I wouldn't have a chance to command a company as a warrant officer. But I did. I know I may never command a company again. And I've got my twenty years in. So, the worst they can do to me now is retire me. I figure this is my final promotion anyway."

"Maybe not. I've heard the Army is asking for a Master Chief Warrant Officer-5 rank."

"I hadn't heard anything about that."

"Well it seems the Army wants a warrant officer rank which could command troops."

"But the warrant officers in the Corps and Navy don't need the fifth rank because their warrant officers already command troops."

He laughed saying, "Yes I know, but you know if the Army gets it, the Navy and Corps will want it too. Plus, the Army says because their soldiers make warrant officer so early in their career they retire too soon and this rank would keep them in longer."

"Well maybe then I could command a battalion," I kidded laughing.

"Wouldn't that be something? I can't guarantee you a CO billet here. But no one will shit on you while I command this regiment."

"Thank you, sir. But I can take care of myself."

"I know you can. But anyway, I'm having you assigned to my first battalion, which is commanded at the present by Major Bird. I believe you know him?"

"Yes, sir we served together in the Root."

Later I drove over to 1st Battalion headquarters and reported to Maj Bird's office.

"I've been hearing great things about you Gunner."

"I've tried to do my best, sir."

"As always. I'm assigning you to Echo Company. Your CO is Captain Nelson. But you'll find two old friends there too."

"Who sir?"

"Gunnery Sergeant Simon and Staff Sergeant Reilly."

"Outstanding. Has Gunny Simon got the weapons platoon?"

"No, he's the company gunny."

"Good, good for him."

Later, I pulled into Echo Company's area and parked my truck. I asked a young Marine where I could find Gunny Simon. I found him observing a platoon doing close order drill.

"Gunny Simon!" I called.

He turned and at seeing me almost ran over toward me and saluted saying, "What are you doing here?"

I returned his salute and answered, "I'm reporting in."

"Here with Echo, sir?"

"Yes."

"You taking Captain Nelson's place?"

"No, I'm reporting to him."

"You haven't reported in yet?"

"No, I wanted to talk to you first about this unit."

"Well sir, it's a good unit in spite of Captain Nelson. Oh, he knows his job all right. He just worries too much about making major, for me. The Lieutenants are all young, but good. The XO is Lieutenant Norton. Lieutenant North has third platoon. Lieutenant Novak has weapons platoon. Lieutenant Vie has first platoon. He was born in Vietnam. He and his family escaped from Vietnam when he was eleven as part of the boat people. I never thought I'd serve under a Vietnamese in our Corps. But he's a good officer and he believes he owes this country something for taken his family in."

"Well, that's good. I hear Staff Sergeant Reilly is here, too."

"Yes sir. He acting, second platoon leader. You'll probably be his platoon leader."

"Well, I better report in."

"Yes sir. I'll show you where the skipper's office is."

"Thank you."

I followed him through the admin section to the CO's office, which was very much like the one I had had for almost three years. He knocked on the door as a blond-haired young captain looked up and said, "Yes gunny?"

"Captain sir, this is Chief Warrant Officer Four Cord. He's reporting in. He's the best sir. We were in the Root together."

"Thank you, gunny. Come on in gunner."

I marched in and snapped to attention in front of Capt Nelson's desk saying, "Reporting as ordered, sir." I handed him my orders and record book, as he looked me over. His eyes seemed to linger on my left chest where I wore almost seven rows of ribbons, rifle and pistol expert badges.

"Impressive," he said taking my record book and orders. "At ease," he said as he opened my record book. Then he asked, "How old are you?"

"Forty, sir."

"How'd you do on your last PT test?"

"Twenty pull-ups, eighty sit-ups and the run in twenty-one minutes and twenty-two seconds." At hearing this he's eyebrows lifted up as he looked up at me. Then he looked back down.

"Seven-year gunnery sergeant. Eight years in Vietnam. Thirteen-year sergeant major. Two special missions to San Salvador, then Grenada and two tours in Beirut. Well, you haven't missed anything."

"I did miss San Domingo, sir."

"When was that?" he asked looking up at me.

"Sixty-five, sir."

"Oh yes. Now I know where I've heard of you. You're the famous warrant officer that got a company command."

"Sir, I'm an Infantry Warrant Officer, not just a warrant officer."

"Oh yes, bursting bomb and all that. But there's so few of you people left." He said closing my record book and started looking over my orders. Then he said, "It must be a sudden take up to go from a company commander back to platoon leader."

"Well sir, I knew the CO's billet was a once in a life time chance for me."

"So, you won't have any problems leading a platoon again?"

"No sir."

"You'll be the oldest platoon leader I've ever seen. I probably should give you weapons platoon. But I like the job Lieutenant Novak's doing with them. So, you can have second platoon. They haven't had an officer in weeks."

"Thank you, sir."

"First Sergeant Bean!" he yelled.

From next door I heard, "Yes, sir." Then the short 1stSgt Bean walked through the door.

"Top, this is Gunner Cord. He's going to take over second platoon. Here's his record book and orders. Take care of the paper work and send for Staff Sergeant Reilly."

"Aye, Aye sir," said 1stSgt Bean. Then looking at me he said, "Welcome aboard gunner. Follow me."

After I was checked in, I found SSgt Reilly waiting for me. At seeing me he said, "Good to see ya, gunner."

"Good to see you, old friend. Did you know I was your new platoon leader?"

"Yes sir, Gunny Simon told me."

"I should've known. So, what kind of platoon do we have?"

"The platoon is under strength, but I have three good sergeants."

"Were any of them in Nam?"

"No sir."

"How about the Root."

"No sir, just you and me with real combat experience."

"Lordy, the Corps is really changing."

"Yes sir, peace is a real bitch ain't it."

"No not really," I said laughing.

"Yeah, I know sir, but I just felt better when there were more Nam veterans around."

"Yeah, we're a disappearing breed."

Over the next month I got to know my platoon well, after days in the field and main side. Sgt Ewing, the 3rd squad leader was the tallest of the three sergeants and chewed tobacco. Sgt Huebner was a little shorter with broader shoulders. Sgt Davis was the short young one with a baby face. As always, there were young Marines who caught my eye as being better than average. There were Pvts Morris and Conn of 3rd squad. Then, there was L/Cpl Cunningham of 2nd squad. He had started taking karate classes with SSgt Reilly off base. SSgt Reilly was a 3rd degree black belt. Of course, I hoped to be ready to take my 3rd degree black belt test next year.

On April 4th, I drove home after three days in the field. I walked in with camouflaged paint still on my face and needing a shower. As soon as I saw Marty's face, I knew something was wrong. "We need to talk," she said.

I followed her into our bedroom and closed the door behind us and I asked, "What's happened?"

"The day you left for the field, Kyle told me he wants to live with his father again."

Shaking my head, I said, "Have you tried to talk to him?"

"Yes. I've talked to him for three days."

"Okay, I'll put in for a ninety-six this weekend to take him up. Maybe you can talk some since into him tomorrow."

But the next day, Capt Nelson refused my request for a ninety-six-hour pass. Which gave Marty an extra day to talk to Kyle. Which didn't do any good. So, after I got home Friday afternoon the four of us drove nine hours through the night to Georgetown, Delaware to Marty's mother's house.

Saturday afternoon, Kyle's father came and picked him up. After shedding some tears, we went to visit Nat, Donna and our granddaughter. Donna was pregnant and due to have her second child in September. While there I called Lance. He asked if he could come down and spend some time with me before he left for boot camp at Parris Island.

So, early Sunday morning, Lance went back to Camp Lejeune with us. It was weird but it seemed we were always trading one child for another. But of course, Lance was no longer a child even though I wish he was. I was proud he was going in the Corps, but I dreaded it and worried about him.

It was good to have Lance with us for the month of April. Saturday mornings and Sundays after church Lance and I went running to help him get in shape for boot camp.

The first of May, Lance's Marine recruiter from Delaware mailed Lance's orders to boot camp to him at our house.

The closer it came to Lance leaving the more uneasy I felt. And the night before he left, I had trouble sleeping.

Early the next morning, we left Samantha with our neighbor so she could go to school. Then, after she and Lance hugged each other goodbye, we drove Lance to the bus station in Wilmington, NC. At the bus station Marty and he hugged each other, which did my heart good. Then, he and I hugged as I reminded him, "Remember, call everyone sir down there. And as soon as you get your rifle, look at its serial number and remember it. It'll save you a beating. And be careful."

"I will. I love you all," he said.

"I love you," I said.

"Me too," said Marty.

"Well, I'll see you when I see you," he said. Then, he turned and walked up into the bus. We watched him take a seat next to a window near the back and wave to us. We waved back. Soon, the bus pulled away and I watched it until it was out of sight. Now I knew for the first time how my father felt when I left for boot camp.

As we walked back to our car arm in arm I said, "This is the same station I left from twenty-three years ago after I finished ITR to go home on leave before I went to Okinawa."

"You all right?" asked Marty.

"Yeah."

"You sure?"

"It shouldn't bother me that one of my sons was going into the

Corps. My kids were no better than anybody else's. Somebody had to be willing to fight for this country. But I just hate to think of Lance going through some of the things I have been through."

"Like you, he made the decision."

"I know. But I don't want to lose him."

"Be glad we're at peace."

"I am and I pray the peace will last at least four more years."

"What if he decides to make the Corps a career?"

I laughed saying, "I'll cross that bridge if we come to it."

"I hope you have better luck then I do. I've prayed for peace for the twelve years I've known you. And yet you've been in action in San Salvador twice, Beirut twice and Grenada."

On May 17th, when I got home, I was surprised to find a letter from Lance. It was addressed to: CWO-4 Nathan Cord, followed by our base housing address. It was from:

Pvt Lance Cord
Plt 3055 I Co 3rd Bn
MCRD PI SC 29905

I opened the envelope and pulled the blue and white paper out. It had a gold Marine Corps emblem in the upper left-hand corner and a picture of the Iwo Jima flag raising in the left lower hand column.

At the top he had written, Sir Good afternoon sir!

Then he had written the date: May 14, 1988

Dad,

Well, I made it to Parris Island. The Marines got a hold of me before I reached the island. They caught me and others like me in Charleston airport and started giving us hell. The first night we stayed up all night and did paper work. The next day we went down to get a hearing test and every person that got in these booths, fell asleep one time or another and when you did, they would start hollering in the earphones and boy did we wake up.

When I wake up in the morning, I always try to fix my hair, but there's NONE there to fix.

Last night I pulled fire watch for my platoon. Being this, you have to observe everything that takes place. Well, I was checking locks on footlockers and seabags, when this guy wakes up and starts hollering, "No! No!" right in front of me. I about jumped out of my skin and I shined my red light in his face and he got worse. He thought I was a DI and I was going to take him away. Finally, I calmed him down. But man did he scare me.

I'm doing all right down here.

Well I better get going. I'm glad someone back home really knows what I'm going through.

Lance

Marty read the letter next and handed it to Samantha, then asked me, "Well what do you think?"

I smiled, breathing easier it seemed for the first time since he had left, and said, "So far so good. And from what I'm reading between the lines I think he'll do fine."

"Was there ever a doubt?" asked Marty.

"Sure, no one knows how they or anyone else will handle Marine Corps bootcamp."

On May 18th, our battalion got a new CO, LtCol Haring. He had served in Vietnam as a lieutenant in 1970-71. Although he was my age, I did believe he was the first battalion commander I had had that had less time in the Corps then I did. God, I was starting to feel old. But he was an easy officer to talk too and laughed easy. And he talked to me about my career and seemed impressed that I had commanded a company. I did believe Capt Nelson was jealous of the attention LtCol Haring always paid to me and not him.

On May 24th, SSgt Reilly transferred out. I hated to see an old friend go. Not only was he a damn good platoon sergeant, but we also worked out together on weekends going over karate forms and defensives. I made Sgt Ewing my acting platoon sergeant.

The same day we also got another letter from Lance. It was dated 880521 at 0930 and said:

Dear Dad,

How is everything? I'm doing fine. Today we went to church. This is the only day that a recruit looks forward to.

So far, I haven't messed up. They don't even know who I am except for my physical performance. Some guys get their ears chewed off it seems 4 times a day. The same stinking guys.

We had our first PFT test. I was considered 1st class because I ALMOST maxed it. I had 19 pullups, 82 sit-ups and ran a mile and a half in 9:36. Out of 4 platoons starting in a mob, I placed 6th in the run. On the pull-up bar they wouldn't let me pick my knees up at all. After my 19th pull up my arms weren't tired, but I couldn't pull up because my handgrip was tired. The bar is fatter than what I'm used to.

We also took a swimming test. I was good enough to be a 1st class swimmer. They call it an upgrade. They said I would have to teach other recruits how to swim.

Back to the PFT test, when I got off the pull-up bar I had to report to the Senior DI and tell him how many I did. When I told him, I walked past and he said in a low but stern voice, "Good job Cord." That made it easier for me to not get up tight when we did sit-ups.

The chow surprised me. It's really good. Although some things could be better. They have cantaloupe at breakfast, sometimes it tastes pretty good, but I know it could be a lot better after helping Poppop in his garden. It's not like home grown cantaloupe. Although some recruits don't even know what it is.

Tell Marty the sand flies aren't too bad all the time, but they are really bad most of the time.

The only thing I really don't like is the inspections at night, they take so long and they pick each and every person apart from head to toe.

Well, I have to get going. I'll try to write if I can find time. I love you all, take care. Don't worry and Semper Fidelis.

Love

Lance

As I handed the letter to Marty, I said smiling, "Some things never change."

The 1st of June we received another letter from Lance. It was dated 880528 at 2000 hours.

Dear Dad,

Well things are really starting to roll now. I never thought I could get completely dressed from boot to shirt in 2 minutes or less. Nor did I think I could eat a four-course meal in 5 minutes or make 2 bunks in 7 minutes. Well, all that and more is being done here at Parris Island.

The first couple of days running, my knee hurt bad because we had to run so slow with the platoon, but I started making myself run on the inside of my foot and it hasn't hurt since. I think that's why I kept spraining that same foot, because I run on the outer edge.

So far, we have had history, leadership and other different classes. Mostly we have been marching and marching with a weapon. Last week we briefly went over some bayonet slashes & jabs.

Next Monday we start the second phase, we spend two weeks on the rifle range. The following week we have mess and maintenance. The week following this, starts our 3rd phase; we spend 2 weeks in the woods (basic warrior training) after that we have 2 or 3 more weeks and we graduate.

I was selected with 6 other guys to go to guard mount. We are inspected by officers and asked pop questions, anywhere from general orders, history or enlisted rank structure. We are supposed to be representing our whole platoon in appearance and knowledge.

This Saturday we have a test on all the knowledge that has been passed to us. Everyone must get an 80% or above to move on to second phase. I don't think I should have a problem. I have been studying for this Guard Mount thing.

Today I went and had a personnel interview with the 1st Lt of my chain of command. That's something all recruits have to do. He asked me questions about Boot camp and my family and different stuff. He asked me who was coming to my graduation and I told him. Then he asked if anyone special or has achieved anything is coming. I told him that you were a CWO-IV. He acted kind of surprised. He asked if you served in Nam and I told him you did plus Beirut and Grenada. He said, "Well even if you don't have anything else you have a good line of blood." He also asked me how many pull-ups I could do and I told him I did 20 and he said I should try to be a squad leader. I kind of want to be one, but I just feel better right now laying low. So far, I haven't had to do any physical training punishment for messing up. Some guys have been up there 15-20 times already. They just won't learn to be disciplined. All the DI's ask is to do what we are told, fast and good. Most people just won't do it.

One guy this week refused to train, he got smart with officers and DI's and now he's on his way to the Brig. Some guys are failing their swim test to go home and others are limping around. I just don't understand these kinds of people. Why did they ever join?

Well, I better get going. Tell everyone to take good care of themselves. I miss you all.

Love ya
Lance

"They sure take a lot more tests down there now. In my day, they didn't send you home if you couldn't learn to swim. But of course, they were having trouble recruiting back then. And now they're recruiting 100%. In my day only about 75% were high school graduates. Now it's over 92%," I told Marty.

The next day, 1stSgt Bean found me observing my platoon. Saluting me he said, "Good morning gunner."

"Good morning, Top," I answered returning his salute.

"Sir, the skipper wants to see you in his office."

"What's up, Top?"

"We had a new staff sergeant check in this morning named O'Malley. The skipper is talking to him now. He's assigning him to your platoon."

"Thank you, Top."

1stSgt Bean saluted me saying, "Very well, sir."

I returned his salute and then turned back toward my platoon waving Sgt Ewing over to me. He quickly walked over saying, "Yes sir."

"First Sergeant Bean just told me we're getting a new staff sergeant," I said.

His smile disappeared as he realized he would be bumped back to a squad leader and said, "Yes sir, I knew it wouldn't last long."

"I wanted you to hear it from me first. But you have done a fine job the last week."

"Thank you, sir," he said smiling again.

"Well, I better go get 'm," I said turning around walking toward the company office.

I found SSgt O'Malley to be about six feet tall with broad shoulders and a scar on his chin. Checking his record book, I found he had been a machine gunner, a machinegun team leader, a machinegun squad leader, weapons platoon sergeant and weapons platoon leader. He had been in the corps nine years, but no combat tours, which surprised me. Although I could use him, I said to Capt Nelson, "Sir with all his experience wouldn't he be more useful in weapons platoon. There is an opening there."

Capt Nelson looked at me hard saying, "Because you need a platoon sergeant and he's it."

What could I say but, "Aye, Aye, sir?"

Late in the evening of June 5th, Marty and I were watching TV when the phone rang. Marty got up and walked into the kitchen and answered the phone. Then she yelled, "Nathan! It's for you."

I got up saying, "Who is it?"

With a puzzled look Marty answered, "I don't know."

"Is it a Marine?" I asked crossing the room.

"No, it's a woman."

Wondering myself I took the phone from her hand placing it to my ear saying, "Gunner Cord speaking."

"Nathan."

"Yes," I answered recognizing the voice of Bunnie's mother Dot.

"Have you heard from Lance?" she asked.

"Yes, I've been getting a letter about once a week, I guess. How about you?"

"I've gotten a few. I worry about him."

"Me too."

"Do you think he's telling us the truth?"

"About what?"

Well, from his letters, he seems to be doing all right."

"He probably wouldn't tell you or his mother if he wasn't."

"How about you?"

"Maybe."

"You don't think they're treating him as tough as when you went through do you?"

"I hope so."

"You know you don't mean that," she gasped.

"Yes, I do. Look, I didn't make him join the Corps. He wanted to. He asked for it. And I want him to be just as prepared for war as I was."

"But we're not in a war now."

"Dot, the time to train for war is not after war comes. But before it starts. Like you, I pray we won't get into a war in the next four years. But if we do, I damn sure want him to be ready."

"I don't know. I still don't like it."

"I don't like to think about it either. But he did ask for it."

"Well, goodbye Nathan."

"Goodbye," I said hanging up the phone.

The next day Samantha received a letter from Lance. It was dated June 3, 1988 and said

Dear Samantha,

How you doing up there on Camp Lejeune. I bet you're getting kind of bored without a bunch of brothers pestering you all the time.

Well I guess you're just about ready to go on summer vacation.

When Poppop brings down some Delaware watermelon, I want you to eat a big piece for me because I don't get any of that here.

It sounds like you did pretty good this year in school. Keep it up. Tell all your little school friends I said "Hi."

The next time you chew gum, drink Pepsi, or sleep in late, think of me. I'll see ya soon. I love you. Take care of Dad and Marty.

Love ya
Lance

On June 8th, we got another letter from Lance dated June 5, 1988 and said:

Dear Dad,

I'm still alive. Here on Hell island. Although I know it's not as bad as you had it. I know a lot of people that couldn't make it. Now I know what you meant when you said that it was an honored accomplishment JUST to graduate. I like the fact that we aren't Marines yet. We have to earn it the hard way.

Today we started 2nd phase of training; this is the rifle range phase. This week will be in classes and the following week we will be doing the actual firing.

Most of the hollering and all that is dying down, but we are still playing stupid games like dumping footlockers out. Now you have 2 minutes to get it all back together. Not fast enough. Do it again! Sometimes we get dressed and undressed 4 or 5 times in the morning. Also, we make racks 4 or 5 times in the morning, if we are not fast enough. We have lost about 15 people and gained some from other platoons. We have all of the wimps in here. We haven't won any competitions. Initial Drill- last place, 1st phase testing- last place, pugil sticks- last place, obstacle course- last place. It really frustrates me that we have such babies and wimps. Although we won first phase testing until the last two tests were graded. We had a 99-point average. Then the last 2 people failed. Do you believe that? They were lucky they got recycled before lights out, because the platoon had a blanket party planned for them.

I have had 3 inspections so far. One was a senior drill instructor's inspection and the other two was Guard mount inspection with an officer. During the inspection I got SOOOOO nervous and I can't think straight when they ask me questions, that I know like the back of my hand and I just can't think. So far, I haven't failed any. We do have a minor inspection every night (hygiene inspection.)

My swim test was pretty easy. We had to swim from one end of the pool to the other in a certain amount of time. Then to be an upgrade we had to put on cammies and stay in the water without ANYTHING coming above water except your head. Then we had to jump from the high platform.

Well, I got to go. I love you all. Take care.

Love Lance

As for me, I was busy as Echo Company trained hard getting ready for a month-long battalion training exercise coming up again at 29 Palms, CA.

Two days before we were due to leave, we got another letter from Lance. This one was undated and read:

Dear Dad,

I'm still alive. Sometimes it gets pretty tough, but they CAN'T break me. Last week was grass week on the rifle range. We just learned our positions and stuff. Thursday & Friday we shot from 15 meters. This was to zero our sights and windage. The best shooters were the ones with tight groups. The first I did about average, the second day mine was one of the best, every one improved. Tomorrow we start firing from the 200-yard line. I'm in the 6th relay. That's the last relay of the day. He said he put the better shooters in the last relay because by the end of the day the coaches are tired of helping recruits. All the classes we had have been like a refresher course for me because you taught me everything I needed to know, like trigger control, breath control, etc.

Yesterday we had the PFT. Well I didn't max it like I wanted to. My run time was 20 seconds short of max. I scored a 298 out of 300. There was 1 second subtracted for every 10 seconds up to a minute. I was so mad at myself, THAT CLOSE. I did the pull-ups and sit-ups with ease. I can do up in the mid 90's in sit-ups in two minutes now. But they only count for points up to 80. I had the highest score in my platoon and possibly in the series. Only five people came in ahead of me in the run and 3 of those didn't make it under 18 minutes. The guys in my platoon said I didn't look like the type that could score that high. I earned a lot of respect from most of the recruits, but there's that percent that are jealous especially the big muscular guys.

This Friday is qualification day. If I score a 230 or above, I will get one phone call and cross rifles. I hope I can do it. Wish me luck. I love you all!

Love

Lance

Early in the morning of June 17th, I looked in on sleeping Samantha and then kissed Marty goodbye for a month. I drove my truck to the company area. There, with the rest of Echo Company we boarded buses, which carried us to Cherry Point, NC. There, with the rest of the battalion we boarded a plane.

I found 29 Palms, CA just as hot as I remembered it. Camp Wilson was still growing with more A-frame buildings.

The first week, as usual, we spent on the ranges running squad, then platoon and company tactics and teaching the newer Marines how to live and survive in the desert.

By July, Maj Bird had laid out a large sand table of our area of operation in the Delta Corridor. Our battalion staff and company commanders studied it as LtCol Haring walked them through it, telling us of his plan of attack as he used a wooden pointer to point out high ground, company objectives and boundary lines.

The next day, Capt Nelson gathered us platoon leaders around the sand table showing us our platoon objectives. Later, I brought SSgt O'Malley and my squad leaders over and we discussed how we would take our objectives.

On July 11th, we were in the middle of the operation. Echo Company had taken a company size high ground objective at noon. So now, in the hottest time of the day, we were digging in. We had been told that BGen Trotter, our new assistant division commander and Col Al Genio were in the area observing our battalion's training.

Lt Norton was checking my platoon positions with me when he said, "Oh shit, here they come."

I looked back the way we had come to see three white blazers coming toward us.

"I better let the skipper know," said Lt Norton as he ran up the hill looking for Capt Nelson.

I watched the trucks drive up the hill past us. I could see BGen Trotter and Col Al Genio in the front truck. I watched them drive up over the top of the hill out of sight.

Minutes later, Lt Norton came running around the hill gathering up the platoon leaders. I arrived at our company CP about the same time, as did Lts Vie, North and Novak. Along with BGen Trotter and Col Al Genio was a dozen staff officers made up of lieutenant colonels, majors and captains.

Capt Nelson was all smiles as he bragged about his company and how he had taken his objectives. Then we all stood at attention as BGen Trotter promoted several of our Marines to lance corporal. I was unhappy that none of them were from my platoon. Capt Nelson hadn't even asked me for recommendations.

When it was finished, Capt Nelson said, "General, would you like to inspect the lines?"

"I'd like to, but I am on a tight schedule," he answered as Col Al Genio walked over to me asking, "How's it going Gunner Cord?"

"Fine, sir," I said, as BGen Trotter then turned and walked over toward me as Capt Nelson ran along beside him.

"Gunner Cord, isn't it?" asked BGen Trotter.

Before I could answer Capt Nelson broke in saying, "Yes sir, he's my second platoon leader."

"It must be a letdown after being a company commander," said BGen Trotter.

I smiled saying, "Well sir, I knew that was a once in a life time chance for me. And I think I can do some good as a platoon leader."

"I can vouch for that," added Col Al Genio.

"I'd like to see your positions," said BGen Trotter.

"Good. Follow me general," I said, leading him down the hill to my platoon. As he walked around talking to my men, this beer-bellied old general stood and walked like some of the older farmers I had known back home. He acted more like an elderly grandfather than a Marine general. But I knew he was quick to relieve company and battalion commanders who didn't perform the way he thought they should.

Soon, they were gone walking up and over the top of the hill. Soon, the white trucks came down the hill past us. As before, BGen Trotter was in the front truck. As the third truck came by, I saw Col Al Genio sitting in the back. He turned looking at me and smiled giving me the thumbs up sign.

"Well, sir, I guess we passed," said Sgt Ewing behind me.

I turned around smiling and said, "Yeah, I guess we did good."

It was July 16th when we got back to Camp Lejeune, NC. It was late that night when I finally got home. Marty was asleep on the couch when I walked in. On the stand next to her was a letter from Lance. I sat down in a chair next to her and opened it up. It was dated July 12, 1988 and said:

Dear Dad,

How is everything up at Camp Lejeune? Well 3 more weeks and Boot Camp will be history (Thank God!)

I'm all through Basic Warrior Training. I tell ya, before we went to BWT everyone was saying; I can't wait to go home. But…. when we got to BWT everyone was saying, I can't wait to get back to main side. It seemed like they forgot about home.

A lot of them at first bitched & moaned about the MRE's and in the beginning, I was getting food from other recruits because they didn't think that water added to it would make it look any better. But by middle way everyone was eating it all. I thought they tasted good; it's just that there wasn't enough.

You would have loved the things we did out there. We threw live grenades, crawled through infiltration courses while TNT went off all around us, we went through a booby trap course in day and night (that was pretty tough at night, but I didn't fail), we went through a compass course where we double-timed for a real long time, then we stopped and got in groups of 4s and had to find our way back (day & night), we did squad & fire team formations, we did night patrols until about 0130, then the next night we did the defenses and attacks, that night we slept in foxholes. We also went in the gas chamber, that was bad (I thought I had died and gone to hell). My drill instructor told us not to come out like wimps, he told us to come out marching. Well a couple of guys came out like wimps. When I came out, I was marching and I was singing, "From the halls of Montezuma…." I had snot hanging out of my nose and I couldn't see straight, but I wasn't gonna be a wimp. We also repelled from a 45-foot tower that was pretty fun, but those ropes pull tight on the crotch.

When I was in BWT I had 2 blisters that got infected. And I got an infection called cellulitis, which is like a blood poisoning that attacks glands. Both of my feet swelled and a gland in my left groin is sore but luckily, I went to sickbay after I took my BWT test. If I would have went before the test I would have been dropped back in training. (But I wasn't). I've had 48 hrs bed rest and I hope my feet hurry and heel so I don't get dropped. There was another guy who had this and he had bed rest for a week and he didn't get dropped.

Well, anyway, we have 3 major inspections to go through in the next 3 weeks and rifle inspections. I hope I do well on them. I get so nervous during inspections, my voice cracks and my hands sweat. Well, I better go I love you all.

Love ya
Lance

On July 22nd, we received another letter from Lance. There was no date on this one and it read:

Dear Dad,

Well, I'm still alive. I'm almost off this island. 2 more weeks and I'll be a Marine.

The promotions have already been chosen and no I wasn't one of them.

My foot is doing a little better. The sore is just about healed, but the swelling won't go down. I came so close to being dropped. I had my trash packed and ready to go and my senior DI came out and said he was going to keep me. I was so relieved.

When I was on bed rest one of the DI's tried to flip me & my rack over because he was mad that I didn't get dropped. He didn't succeed in doing that but in the process my letter writing gear fell out of my mattress and he picked it up and threw it across the squad bay and paper and stamps went everywhere

Monday, we get our pictures. Wednesday, we get our orders.

We have 2 major inspections then it's all over.

Well see ya soon. I love you all!

Love
Lance

The first Monday in August we packed up and headed down to

Parris Island SC.

Late in the afternoon we arrived at the main gate. As we passed through, I thought of the last two times I had been here. Over twenty-three years ago I had come here in the dark of early morning as a frightened seventeen-year-old kid recruit. Thirteen weeks later, I left in the dark of early morning as a seventeen-year-old Marine. Then I came back here eleven years later for First Sergeant school. Back then even after eight years in Vietnam, I still felt a tingle of fear returning here again. It had taken me probably three days to get used to the idea that no DI, no matter how mean was going to get in the face of, even an eleven-year first sergeant. Of course, like the second visit this one I came in daylight. This time for the first time Marty and eleven-year-old Samantha were with me, too. With them, I enjoyed the ride across the swampland to the main base. I was amazed at how the base had changed. All of the recruit barracks were brick now including the churches and mess halls. The old diner was now a Burger King. Being three days early we had plenty of time to look around. We visited the base museum. We walked to the Iron Mike statue of a WWI Marine caring a machinegun over his right shoulder and carrying a 45cal pistol in his left hand. Their comrades erected this in memory of the men of Parris Island who gave their lives in World War I. Then we had our pictures taken in front of the base Iwo Jima statue.

I knew Lance was in 3rd battalion, so every morning I'd run through the 3rd battalion area in PT gear. In the afternoons, Marty, Samantha and I would walk through 3rd battalion area looking for him as the different platoons marched by. I spotted him only once, marching by in his platoon.

The second day, I was surprised when they let him off four hours to be with his family which now included his mother Bunny and her mother Dot.

I couldn't wait to see him march by on the drill field on graduation day. But that morning it was raining and the graduation was held in the base theatre.

When we entered the theatre, the recruits were already there sitting in the middle rows like statues in their tan tropical short-sleeve shirts and green trousers looking straight ahead with their hands, palms down on their knees.

I was in the same uniform with the bursting bomb on my left

collar, and the red bar with two silver boxes on my right collar. On my left chest, was my rifle and pistol expert badges and above them was my almost seven rows of ribbons.

After we had sat down, I turned around searching the faces of the recruits for Lance. Like me in 1964, these recruits only had rifle badges on their left chest. Of course, by the next year of 1965 all recruits would wear the National Defense Medal because of the war in Vietnam.

I was surprised I actually found Lance in that mass of recruits and I took a picture of him.

Later the DI's, company officers and honor graduates marched on stage. The 3rd battalion CO marched out and gave a speech and at the end for the first time he called these recruits Marines.

Afterwards, we all went outside. Marty took pictures of Lance and I saluting each other and shaking hands as I congratulated him on becoming a Marine. I had mixed emotions; I was proud of him and honored, but concerned at what the future might hold for him in the next four years.

As we talked, I was surprised to learn he didn't have orders for the School of Infantry at Camp Lejeune. But instead had orders for the School of Infantry at Camp Pendleton Ca. After that he would go on to Mare Island Ca for FAST (Force Anti-Terrorist Security Team) training. But first he had fifteen days leave. I hoped he would spend it with me. But he said he was going with his mother back up to Delaware to visit with his friends. Maybe he had seen enough of the Corps for a while. He did ride with us around to his barracks. There he introduced us to his friends. Then I helped him load his gear in his mother's trunk. He rode with us off the base and then north up I95 until we got to Rt-17. There we stopped so he could get in with his mother and grandmother. Then they continued north up I95 as we drove northeast back to Camp Lejeune NC.

On Sept 6th, Maj Bird was transferred out and was replaced by Maj George as our battalion XO.

Meanwhile, I had other things on my mind. Nat's wife was due to have our second grandchild at any time.

Early in the morning of Sept 17th, the phone rang. I jumped up stumbling out to the kitchen in the dark and answered the phone, "Gunner Cord speaking."

"Dad."

"Nat?"

"Yes. I just brought Donna to the hospital. The doctor thinks this is it. But it'll be a few hours yet. I'll call when I have more news."

"You won't have to. We're coming up. It maybe an hour before I can get my ladies up and on the road."

"You're coming up?"

"Yes, we are. I've had a ninety-six-hour pass approved for when the baby is born. I was just waiting to hear from you. All I have to do is call my CO."

"Good, but I better get back. I love you and be careful driving."

"I love you, too," I said hanging up. Then I called Capt Nelson.

Afterward I woke up Marty and started putting our bags in the car trunk as she got Samantha up.

It was about 1700 when we pulled into the hospital parking lot in Seaford, De. We found Bunny in the waiting room. From her we found out the baby had already been born and was a boy.

Nat came in and took us to see our first grandson named Nathan Cord V. We hugged each other and a little later he took us in to see Donna.

We were talking about the baby when Donna said, "He is a pretty baby isn't he."

Everyone agreed and I added, "You guys do good work."

Donna smiled as her face turned red to match her hair.

By Sept 21st, we were back at Camp Lejeune, NC.

On Oct 11th, we had a change of command ceremony at Regimental headquarters. There, Col Al Genio was relieved by my oldest friend in the Corps Col Dana Hester. I couldn't think of a better officer to command our regiment. This was my fourth time serving under him, starting back in 1967 when he was a new second lieutenant in Vietnam, then again in 1972 as a major, then in the early 1980's as a lieutenant colonel. All three times, we saw combat together. Maybe this wasn't such a good idea after all. Then again, if I had to go into combat again who would be better to command our regiment.

Of course, when the ceremony was over, I walked over to Col Hester and congratulated him on his new assignment.

"How's Lance doing?" he asked.

"He's doing fine. He's at SOI at Camp Pendleton."

"Is Nat still a prison guard?"

"Yes, he is. He loves it. I don't know why. You know he's married with two kids."

Later, as I walked away with Capt Nelson beside me he said, "Gunner you must live a charmed life. Two old buddies commanding the regiment back to back."

"Well sir, if you stay in the Corps twenty-four years, you'll know a lot of people too," I answered smiling.

On Oct 26th, we received a letter from Lance. There were actually two letters in one. One of which was to Marty and one to me. Both were dated Oct 23, 1988:

Marty,

Hi how ya doing?

When I was younger, I didn't realize how much you did for me. Now that I've gotten older, I realize that you went out of your way a lot for me. Now I would like to thank you for all those times. I'm also sorry for acting like an ass when it came time for me to do something for you (as small as washing the dishes). I also want to thank you for your support and compliments as I was growing up.

I couldn't find a better stepmother.

I love and miss you.

Love

Lance

Marty cried even as I read this letter, it meant so much to her. Then I read my letter:

Dad,

Well, when I call you this weekend I'll finally be able to tell you if I'm honor man or not. One of the guys that were in the running was UA from the liberty formation today. So that probably limits his chances.

I think there's only one other guy, he beat me by 2 points on the first test, but I don't know how well he did on the rest of his tests. Man, I hope I get it. I never thought I would have a chance to be HONOR MAN. I just can't believe it.

I thought after boot camp all the challenges would be over. But the Corps never stops challenging a person who wants to be the best. Some of these guys just ease on through. They don't care how well they do or look. The Marine Corps would really suck if I were like that. Now I understand it's what you make of it.

We'll talk to ya this weekend.

I love & miss you.

Love
Lance

When he called, he was disappointed because he hadn't been selected for honor man. But I told him not to worry because I hadn't been selected for honor man out of boot camp or ITR either and I had done okay.

On Nov 10th, I took Marty to the Marine Corps Birthday Ball. The cake had the flag raising on Iwo Jima on it. In the upper left-hand corner, it said, 1775-1988. In the upper right-hand corner, it said, Happy 213th Birthday in red letters and gold numbers. Marty wore a red and black dress and of course I was in my dress blues with Sam brown belt. As we danced it did seem funny to think that Lance would be going to his first Marine Corps Birthday Ball himself in dress blues.

LtCol Haring gathered all the officers of our battalion together for a group picture. Later when I got my copy I was surprised when I checked the ribbons on the chest of the officers and found that there was only three of us, who had been in Vietnam, and they were LtCol Haring, Maj George and me.

Finally, on Nov 20th, I managed to get one of my men promoted. Morris in Sgt Ewing's squad was promoted to PFC.

On Dec 5th, Conn, another Marine from Sgt Ewing's squad was promoted to PFC.

I took a week's leave for Christmas and New Year's. We went home to Delaware to visit family, children and grandchildren. Lance even managed to get home on leave on his way to report to Norfolk Va. to the FAST Company there.

It was Jan 2nd, 1989, when we returned to Camp Lejeune. This would be my twenty-fifth year in the Corps. It was funny because in 1965 I didn't think I'd make it to the 70's and in no time, it was the 80's. Lordy, and next year it will be 1990. I didn't know where all the time had gone. There's been times I wanted to retire or had thought about retiring. I had given up my dream of being a general a long time ago. And now I had even given up hope of being a major. I knew I was as high as I would go unless congress should authorize the new rank of Chief Warrant Officer- 5, which I was still hearing rumors about. But even without another promotion I was still not ready to retire. More than ever I was glad I became a Marine Infantry Warrant Officer. If I had stayed a sergeant major, I would have been forced to retire in five years and I knew I wouldn't be ready then either. As it was then, I could stay in until I was sixty, which means by the book I would have sixteen more years to go. Maybe I would be ready to retire then.

As our battalion trained through the month of January, we began to listen to news and read about the trouble in Panama. Late last year, US re-enforcements including 400 Marines had been sent there in response to an organized harassment campaign against Americans ordered by their dictator Manuel Noriega.

By March, it began to seem sooner or later the trouble in Panama would force the US into military action. It seemed Manuel Noriega was determined to provoke us. He was causing a series of incidents directed at the US military, designed to probe the reaction of the US military. He seemed to think that American restraint was a sign of weakness. He was beginning to carry his campaign of harassment to the extreme.

On March 14th, I came home late from field training. As I took my field jacket off, Marty walked into the kitchen to put left overs in the microwave for me to eat and said, "We got a letter from Lance today."

"Did you read it?" I asked walking to the dining room table picking the letter up.

"No, I was waiting for you," she answered.

I tore the envelope as I sat down at the table. I unfolded the letter and began to read:

Dear Sir,

Dad, I don't have much time. But I wanted to get a quick note off to you and Mom. A few days ago, my FAST Company went on alert for possible deployment to Panama. I'm sure you know what's going on there. Well, this morning the balloon went up for us. 56 men from the company have been picked to deploy in 17 hours. I'm proud to say I am one.

I can't believe it. By the time you get this I will be where the action is. Maybe really get to do what I've been trained to do. I have to say I'm a little frightened. I just hope I measure up when the time comes. Of course, we weren't allowed to call anybody. Well I have to go. We have a lot to do. I'll write when I can.

I love you all

Take care of Marty and Sam

Lance

I dropped the letter to the table and hung my head in my hands fighting tears.

"What's the matter?" cried Marty seeing me as she brought my supper to the table.

"Lance is in Panama," I answered.

"Oh no."

"I wish it were me."

"I know. But we knew it could happen. He's your son."

"I know damn it. I know."

"It's not that bad in Panama."

"Not yet."

"We have to pray it all blows over," said Marty placing the meal in front of me and putting her arm around my neck. I turned putting my arms around her waist as a tear rolled down my cheek.

"If anything happens to him his mother will blame me."

"It won't be your fault. He's a grown man and you sure didn't make him join the Marines."

"I know. I know. But I'll blame myself, too."

The rest of the month the tempo of training picked up for our battalion as rumors spread that more Marines may be ordered to Panama. As I did my best to prepare my platoon for possible action, my mind was never far from Lance and I prayed for God to keep him safe.

The 1st of April, Echo Company was in the field training when Capt Nelson got a call over the radio to report to battalion headquarters. We wondered what was up when Maj George drove up to our company CP and picked him up in his jeep.

Lt Norton took command of the company and we continued training.

Less than an hour later, Maj George drove back and dropped off Capt Nelson. Capt Nelson got on the radio and ordered all platoon leaders to report to his CP as well as GySgt Simon. I walked up to the CP group with Lts Vie and North. We found Lts Novak and Norton were already there. We all sat down in a circle as GySgt Simon walked up.

Capt Nelson looked around from face to face before he said, "All right. Gunny have the company break for chow and then prepare to force march back to main side."

GySgt Simon's mouth dropped open and then he asked, "Do what sir?"

"What's going on, skipper?" asked Lt Norton.

"Gentlemen we are standing down to prepare for deployment to Panama," answered Capt Nelson.

We all looked at each other. No one was happier than I was although I knew it would add to Marty's worries.

"Sir, is the whole battalion going?" I asked.

"The whole battalion is on alert for possible deployment. But for right now only Echo Company is deploying. We'll be reinforcing the Marines already there reporting to a Colonel Doyle," answered Capt Nelson.

"Sir, how soon do we leave?" asked Lt North.

"Within the week is all I can say. So, return to your platoons and tell them what you know. We need to get our equipment checked and personal affairs in order," said Capt Nelson.

I returned to my platoon and had SSgt O'Malley gather Sgts Huebner, Davis and Ewing together. After I told them what I knew, I could see SSgt O'Malley wasn't too happy. Sgts Huebner and Davis didn't seem to care, but Sgt Ewing was thrilled with the news, which concerned me some.

"Okay, give the troops the word. You guys know the drill. Make sure the troops' wills, insurance and pay allotments are right before we deploy," I said.

On Apr 8th, Echo Company flew from Cherry Point, NC to Howard Air Force Base, Panama City and joined up with the US Southern Command.

After reporting to Col Doyle, Capt Nelson returned to tell us

Echo Company would be used as necessary to help with the worsening security situation there. So, in other words we were the colonel's reserve backup and quick reaction force.

The first of May, Col Doyle directed his staff to develop a contingency plan to prepare the Marine force to execute our assigned mission. The plan was to be called Spartan Gap.

On May 7th, elections were held in Panama. When Noriega lost the election the Pro-Noriega government tribunal annulled the election. This was followed by anti-government demonstrations. Anti-Noriega candidates were physically beaten on the streets. The Organization of American States condemned the tribunal's action.

By May 12th, Marine strength had risen to 484. Our mission now, with US Army support, was to provide reinforced security for American lives and property. For Echo Company, this usually meant guarding Bulk Fuel tank farms and ammo dumps.

Echo Company dug fixed fighting positions in our area of operations. During the day we sent out squad size patrols and at night we set up fire team size listening posts.

The morning of May 24th, Capt Nelson was ordered to Col Doyle's headquarters. When he returned, he gathered us platoon leaders together and he briefed us on possible objectives we may have to take within Panama City, if fighting should break out.

I then had SSgt O'Malley gather my squad leaders together and I briefed them.

Capt Nelson had Lt Norton and 1stSgt Bean set up sand table models of our objectives, which each platoon used to run rehearsals and make plans.

I told SSgt O'Malley, Sgts Huebner, Davis and Ewing, "We have to train this platoon harder than ever. They have to be ready for any emergency."

And train hard we did, throughout the day SSgt O'Malley would yell, "Faster, harder! Do it again and do it right!"

The sergeants picked up on it yelling, "Motivation, get harder, Go! Go! Go!"

Some of the young Marines grumbled, but Capt Nelson said it all when he said, "The most important thing is practice. A well-trained unit will function under the stress of combat just as if it is another exercise."

But even as we trained, we still conducted active patrols. Twice during the night, Marine listening posts had tipped off Lt Vie's 1st platoon that black clad intruders were moving toward them, which ended in firefights.

The few times Capt Nelson let me go out on patrol with one of my squads, I found life in the bush of Panama was like Vietnam, hot, dirty and exhausting. Moving through the jungle by day, carrying weapons and combat gear, the heat and humidity was just as brutal. Insects stung and bit the skin that was exposed. The young Marines of today joke just like we did in Vietnam and used the same insect repellant that seemed to help the bugs find us. And then there are the scorpions, tarantulas and poisonous snakes to watch out for. And not to mention the thorns, stickers and briars.

At night, Marines like L/Cpl Cunningham and PFCs Morris and Conn where out on our listening post and found the jungle canopy blocked out most of the moonlight. Still they took turns on watch and waited and listened trying to make sense of the odd crackles and cackles of the night of the jungle.

To Sgt Ewing, it felt good to be able to do what he'd been trained to do. This was real, not just another training exercise.

For this whole platoon except for SSgt O'Malley and I, this was the first time they had been in a situation where armed conflict was a real possibility.

Meanwhile Col Doyle announced Operation Nimrod Dancer had been launched to ensure the continued freedom of movement and adherence to the provision of the 1977 Panama Canal Treaty. To prove the point, Marines in Light Armored Vehicles started running patrols along Panama roads and even swimming across the canal.

One night during early June, I heard my radioman answer a call on his radio. Then he handed me the radio handset saying, "Here Gunner it's the skipper calling."

I reached over and took the handset out of his hand and placed it next to the right side of my face and spoke in a whisper, "Echo six this is Two actual. Over."

"Two actual this is Echo six. Be advised that Three Echo has confirmed movement in front of their positions. Place Two Echo on full alert," said Capt Nelson.

"Echo six this is Two actual. I copy that and will do. Out."

"Two actual this is Echo six. Good luck and out."

I handed the handset back to my radioman saying, "Call the

squad leaders and tell them to go on full alert until further word. Also tell Sgt Huebner to call his listening post and bring them back in at the first sign of trouble."

"Aye, Aye sir," he said.

I heard him whisper into the radio handset when suddenly I heard L/Cpl Cunningham of 2nd squad yell, "Halt! Who goes there!" in the distance in front of me. But no one answered him.

"Oh shit!" I heard my radioman gasp. Then he added, "Sir, Sergeant Davis says he has movement in front of him. He can hear them crawling toward them. And Sergeant Huebner's listening post won't talk back to him. But they are clicking their handset once for yes and twice for no. From what he can gather they have fifty some people around them heading our way."

"Christ," I muttered as someone in Sgt Huebner's squad popped an illumination star cluster. When it popped overhead in a flash of light floating downward, we saw nothing moving. But as soon as the star cluster burned out machinegun fire opened up on 1st squad. Sgt Huebner threw grenades back in return trying not to give his position away.

"Sir it's the skipper," my radioman said touching my arm.

I grabbed the handset saying, "Echo six this is Two actual. Over."

"Two Actual this is Echo six. What the Foxtrot is going on over there? Who authorized you to open fire?"

"Echo six this is Two Actual. I have movement along my whole front. I have a listening post cut off by possible five zero enemy troops. We ordered them to halt and we popped illume. They took cover and opened fire on us," I answered.

Just then a machinegun team from Sgt Davis' squad opened fire as the enemy's fire picked up."

"Two Actual this is Echo six. Is that or is that not an M-60 from your platoon firing as we speak?" yelled Capt Nelson.

"Echo six this is Two Actual. That's a positive sir. These assholes aren't throwing snowballs at us," I answered.

More of my men opened fire now as SSgt O'Malley was going from hole to hole checking on our men.

Then, over the radio I heard GySgt Simon's voice say, "Break, break this is Echo Seven Sierra with the eighty-one Mike Mikes. They are ready to support Echo One, two or three on your command sir."

As the enemy fire grew, my whole platoon opened up with rifles, machineguns, grenades and even a LAAW.

"Two Actual this is Echo six. All right. But this is on your head. If you feel the situation warrants it you have my authority to call in Mike support. Out," said Capt Nelson.

"Echo six this is Two Actual. I copy that and thank you. Out," I said. Then I added, "Whisky Echo this is Two Actual. Over."

"Two Actual this is Whisky Echo Actual," answered Lt Novak the weapons platoon leader.

"Whisky Echo Actual this is Two Echo Actual. Put Echo Seven Sierra on the hook!" I ordered.

It wasn't a second later when I heard GySgt Simon's voice saying, "Two Actual this is Echo Seven Sierra. Over."

"Echo seven Sierra this is Two Actual. I can use that support, but I have a listening post stuck out there. Over."

"Two Actual this is Echo Seven Sierra. I know that sir and I have them plotted on the map. These guys can drop them right around them clean as a whistle. Over."

"Echo seven Sierra this is Two Actual. You and I go back a long time. I knew you could do this. But can those kids do it without hurting my kids? Over," I begged.

"Two Actual this is Echo Seven Sierra. Sir these men can do it because I helped train them. I give you my word. Your men will be okay as long as they keep their heads down. Over," answered GySgt Simon sounding as if his feelings were hurt.

"Echo seven Sierra this is Two Actual. Fire a spotter round. Over," I ordered.

"Two Actual this is Echo Seven Sierra. Roger that. Out," said GySgt Simon.

I felt good that GySgt Simon had gone to the mortar team's positions when he didn't have too. But I was sure glad he did.

Then over the radio I heard Lt Novak's voice, "Two Actual this is Whisky Echo Actual. Shot out."

"Whisky Echo Actual this is Two Actual. Roger that," I answered waiting for the mortar to hit.

Then the mortar exploded right on target and I said, "Whisky Echo Actual this is Two Actual. Fire for effect."

"Two Actual this is Whisky Echo Actual. I copy that," answered

Lt Novak.

Soon, our whole front was filled with exploding shells. Slowly my platoon quit firing as the enemy fire suddenly stopped.

When the mortar barrage was over, we heard moaning and some screaming in front of us. Meanwhile, Sgt Huebner radioed to say that his listening post had called in to say they were fine, shaken, but fine. I ordered him to keep them in place and called for a repeat of the mortar barrage. Again, the area in front of us exploded in flames and smoke. I was amazed that we had suffered no casualties.

At daylight, a squad from Lt North's 3rd platoon swept our company's front. In front of my platoon they found parts of bodies, blood trails leading back into the jungle and bloody pieces of black clothing. It sounded almost like a flash back to Vietnam.

We also learned another Marine company was probed and a Marine was accidentally killed in a crossfire. I shuddered at the thought for two reasons. First, without GySgt Simon's expertise with mortars we could have lost a four-man fire team to friendly, mortar fire. Second, because the unit the Marine was killed from was the FAST Company Lance was in. I asked Capt Nelson to find out who the dead Marine was.

An hour later GySgt Simon walked up to me smiling and said, "Has the skipper found out about your son?"

"No, Gunny, not yet."

"It wasn't your son. He's fine," he said.

"Are you sure?" I asked feeling a load drop from my shoulders.

"Yes sir."

"How do you know?"

"I have a Staff NCO buddy in his unit."

"Thank God. And thank you Gunny. Again."

GySgt Simon looked down at his feet saying, "No problem sir. Us old Nam vets have to stick together."

"Thanks again, Gunny," I said placing my hand on his shoulder.

As the month wore on the Organization of American States tried to negotiate with Panama while Noriega worked to stabilize his grip on the government.

Meanwhile US forces were ordered to move US citizens out of Panama City.

In July, Gen Woerner the USA Commander in chief of the US Southern Command visited US forces. While he was there, Noriega got more aggressive when members of the Panama Dignity Battalion blocked the front gate of Fort Clayton, the Bridge of the Americas and surrounded the Papal Nuncio. Noriega also generated media attention by promoting anti-US activities by so-called disgruntled citizens.

During the month of August, a US soldier was detained by the PDF (Panama Defense Force), a US mail truck was held and PDF troops shot into student demonstrators.

In one of the letters I received from Marty, she told me that our old friend as well as my regimental CO Col Hester had been promoted to brigadier general and was being transferred to Okinawa to be the Assistant Division Commander of the 3rd Marine Division. His replacement was a colonel by the name of Beck. I was surprised we hadn't heard the news down here. But I guess that's what happens when your company is attached to another battalion in a foreign country.

I wrote a letter to BGen Hester congratulating him on his promotion to the general ranks. I told him I was truly sorry to see him go. I had always enjoyed serving under him off and on through the years. I always felt safer when he was in charge. I asked him if when we were fighting in Hue City in 1968, he would have believed he would be a general someday. He would probably say no. But I knew once he had survived, he would make it, if not Commandant someday. I finished by saying I hope to serve under him next as my division commanding general.

The first of September, Conn from Sgt Ewing's squad was promoted to lance corporal and Cunningham in Sgt Davis' squad was promoted to corporal.

Throughout the rest of the month tension mounted as Noriega had an opposition newspaperman arrested and exiled out of the country. A US Army patrol was fired on by the PDF.

On Oct 4th, there was a coup attempt against Noriega. Echo Company was put on full alert as other US forces moved out into blocking positions to stop Noriega's reinforcements' free movements, but even so the coup failed. Afterward, Noriega denied rights to government workers and teachers and had himself named Coordinator General by martial decree. His forces fired on a US helicopter and established roadblocks of their own.

By Oct 6th, after the failed coup, President Bush knew that some

Americans wanted him to use force to get rid of Noriega. For several weeks we heard rumors of more US troops getting ready to deploy to Panama.

After a meeting with Col Doyle, Capt Nelson gathered us platoon leaders together. He seemed pleased as he said, "The colonel says we have never been closer to going to war."

I looked around at the faces of those young lieutenants. Was it my age or the amount of real combat I had seen that caused me not to smile as they did?

He seemed to study the faces of these junior officers before he went on to say, "Plans are being studied right now, here and back home to rid this country of Noriega."

We began receiving classes on the Panamanian military. Our real enemy would be the regular Panamanian Defense Force troops and the Dignity Battalion soldiers, which are poorly trained local militia.

By Oct 26th, Echo Company had started running patrols through the streets off the base in LAV's (Light Armored Vehicles). On one such patrol, Lt North's 3rd platoon was on point followed by Capt Nelson's CP group, Lt Vie's 1st platoon and my platoon bringing up the rear. As we approached La Chorrera, Lt North halted the column reporting by radio to Capt Nelson of a hastily built roadblock of civilian vehicles.

Capt Nelson in turn radioed Col Doyle reporting the roadblock and asking for instructions.

Meanwhile, Lt North ordered his platoon to spread out into a skirmish line. At the rear of the column, I had Sgt Huebner's and Sgt Ewing's squads turn their vehicles around to cover our rear. Then I turned back and looked forward up the column of LAV's feeling Capt Nelson's frustration as he waited for permission to continue through the roadblock. The situation became more threatening as more armed civilians moved up behind the roadblocks.

Finally, Capt Nelson received orders to turn around and return to base.

Cursing among ourselves at being forced to back down, my platoon led Echo Company back to base.

A few days later, we learned that back home our Assistant Division commanding general BGen Trotter had retired. He was replaced by BGen Colyne.

On Oct 31st, during operation Chisum my platoon again was in the rear of the column of LAV's as we drove through La Chorrera. This time it was Lt Vie's 1st platoon leading Echo Company when it encountered a roadblock.

Again, Capt Nelson reported the situation to Col Doyle. And again, his answer was to withdraw. Although disappointed, the young Marines of my platoon maintained their strict discipline. Poor judgment by anyone of them could have resulted in a firefight, which would mean injury or death to Panamanian civilians, the PDF's or us.

The 1st of November, we were all surprised when Capt Nelson received transfer orders. Even though he called back to Camp Lejeune and asked LtCol Haring for an extension, it was turned down and he left. Lt Norton took command of Echo Company. He moved Lt North from 3rd platoon up to the XO billet and shifted Lt Novak from Weapons platoon to 3rd platoon.

By the middle of November, the situation in Panama was becoming unbearable.

During a visit of US congressional delegation, there was a bomb threat against Rodman Naval Station and a firefight on Galila Island. Col Doyle ordered an increase in security. Another Marine company patrolling in LAV's through an area that had been routinely traveled, ran into three roadblocks in a row. To reestablish freedom of movement rights, Col Doyle ordered the roadblocks breached.

So, back home while people were preparing for thanksgiving with turkey, cranberry jelly and stuffing, we Marines in Panama were exercising the US right to travel through the country as agreed to in the agreement of the 1977 Panama Canal Treaty.

"On Nov 22nd, Echo Company climbed into twelve LAVs as we prepared for a patrol which would take us through four major towns. Lt Novak's 3rd platoon would lead the way, followed by the Company CP, then Lt Vie's 1st platoon and my platoon bringing up the rear. When GySgt Simon had everybody loaded up, he gave Lt Norton the thumbs up sign as he climbed in the CP vehicle. Lt Norton radioed Lt Novak to move out.

Soon, the column was in the town of Nuevo Emperador where we received a warm reception with smiles and waves. Later in Nuevo Guarre, the column turned left on Thatcher highway leading directly back to Rodman Naval Station. As we approached Vista Allegre, Lt Novak radioed, "Echo six, Echo six this is Echo three actual. Over"

"Echo three this is Echo six. Over," answered Lt Norton.

"Echo six this is Echo three actual. People are gathering ahead of us waving a large Panamanian flag and several banners. Has the gunship reported this roadblock to you? Over," said Lt Novak.

"Echo three this is Echo six. Our air support has said nothing about roadblocks. Over," answered Lt Norton.

"Echo six this is Echo three actual. Well tell 'm to open their eyes up there. We have definitely got a deliberate roadblock ahead made up of a tow truck, ice truck and two cars."

"Echo three this is Echo six. Halt your platoon about seventy-five meters from the roadblock and set up a skirmish line. Break, break, Echo two actual do you copy?" said Lt Norton.

I'm sure Lt Vie like me had been listening to the radio as I answered, "Echo six this is Echo two actual. I copy. When the column halts I'll have my platoon set a rear defense. Over."

"Echo two this is Echo six. Roger that and keep your eyes open. Out."

Soon the column stopped and I ordered Sgt Davis's and Sgt Ewing's squads to spin their LAV's around to cover our rear.

Lt Norton and GySgt Simon climbed out of their LAV and walked forward to the edge of the roadblock. There, as GySgt Simon covered him Lt Norton said, "We are going to exercise our right to travel these roads under the treaty and it would be in your best interest to take down this roadblock."

The Panamanians refused and started shouting, exciting the crowd.

Lt Norton turned his back on them, walking back to his LAV as GySgt Simon walked backwards holding his M-16 level at his waist covering him.

Back in his LAV, Lt Norton radioed Col Doyle telling him of the situation and requested permission to give them five minutes to clear the roadblock. Col Doyle granted the request immediately.

Again, Lt Norton walked forward with GySgt Simon. For four minutes I watched as he tried to talk to them. Then he and GySgt Simon walked back to the command LAV as all the LAV drivers buttoned up and their gunners manned their weapons preparing for combat. The Panamanians realizing our intentions began throwing rocks at Lt Novak's point vehicles, yelling curses at them and giving us the finger.

Inside his LAV, Lt Norton grabbed the radio handset saying, "Echo three actual, Echo three actual this is Echo six. Over."

"Echo six this is Echo three actual. Over," answered Lt Novak.

"Echo three this is Echo six. Move out straight forward. Out."

Quickly, the column jumped forward. The point LAV rammed into the ice cream truck knocking it out of the way, making a lane through the blockade. As the 3rd platoon drove through the gap, a Panamanian rammed a LAV with a pickup truck, puncturing the right front tire. But the LAV kept on going. As the company CP LAVs passed through, a Panamanian girl tried to block the gap with her body. Lt Norton's LAV hit her flipping her backwards feet in the air over the hood of one of the cars in the roadblock. The Panamanians seemed in shock as Lt Vie's 1st platoon drove through. But as my platoon started through, they started beating on our vehicles with their fist, flag poles and rocks as they cursed at us and grabbed their crotches. But once we were through the roadblock there was another crowd of Panamanians cheering us for what we had done. Our column moved away until the roadblock was out of sight, then Lt Norton halted the column to change the flat tire and requested a damage assessment from us platoon leaders. Within five minutes our column was on the move again.

A little later, I listened to our radio as one of our Cobra gunships called Lt Norton and reported they had spotted another roadblock that had been set up ahead of us in the town of Arraijan. "No shit!" I thought.

Lt Norton radioed Col Doyle about this roadblock and he ordered us to take another route.

Lt Norton radioed Lt Novak with the route change and the column turned onto another two-lane highway.

But soon Lt Novak was on the radio calling, "Echo six, Echo six this is Echo three actual. Over."

"Echo three this is Echo six. Over," answered Lt Norton.

"Echo six this is Echo three actual. I have a hasty roadblock ahead of me made up of three electric trucks and several gas trucks. This one's manned by the Panama Defense Force," reported Lt Novak.

"Echo three this is Echo six. Halt your platoon twenty-five meters from the roadblock. Break, break, Echo two cover the rear. Out," ordered Lt Norton.

"Echo six this is Echo two. I copy your orders. Out," I answered.

Again, after our column halted, Lt Norton and GySgt Simon walked forward. Again, Lt Norton stated the US position concerning our right to travel the highways. These PDF, just like the civilian dressed Panamanians at the last roadblock, ignored him.

Lt Norton and GySgt Simon returned to their LAV. Once inside, Lt Norton radioed Lt Novak saying, "Echo three actual, Echo three actual this is Echo six. Over."

"Echo six this is Echo three actual. Over."

"Echo three this is Echo six. Since this roadblock is incomplete, I think there's enough room to go around the right side. Move out. Out," ordered Lt Norton.

Soon, Lt Novak's 3rd platoon was driving around the roadblock followed by the rest of our column. As my platoon drove around the roadblock, Sgt Huebner's LAV slid in the mud and crashed into the side of a white van which was part of the roadblock pushing it aside. The people inside the van jumped out unhurt as the last of my platoon made it around the roadblock leaving it behind.

Overhead, one of the Cobra gunships radioed Lt Norton reporting it looked like clear sailing back to the base. But later as our company neared the small farming community of Rio Petrero, even I in the rear of the column could see the PDF's had set up a deliberate roadblock across a bridge made up of a civilian dump truck and a white truck. This time there was no alternate route back to our base. At the head of our column Lt Novak could see that the PDF's had forced a farmer to place his truck in front of their roadblock while some of his neighbors were forced to stand around it.

Again, Lt Norton halted the column short of the roadblock. As he and GySgt Simon walked forward the farmers began nationalistic chants under the supervisions of the armed PDF soldiers.

Again, Lt Norton explained the US position on our freedom of movement to the PDF's. Then he explained to the farmers about the damage these LAV's had caused to the vehicles at the last two roadblocks and that his Marines would use force again if necessary. But in five minutes one way or the other his column would cross this bridge. Then Lt Norton and GySgt Simon began walking back to their LAV. But before they got there the farmers turned on the PDF's and they began removing the roadblock.

As we crossed the bridge returning to our base, I was impressed with the PDF's ability to figure out our route and the speed, which they could set up a roadblock at critical chokepoints. But I also felt good that we had helped reinforce President Bush's position of exercising the right of US forces to move freely throughout Panama.

During the rest of November, Echo Company ran more patrols. The PDFs began pre-staging old junk vehicles at key locations, which we just rammed out of our way as we went through. Sometimes they placed old tires in front of these roadblocks and set them on fire. We used grappling hooks to pull the burning tires out of the way.

By December, the heat and humidity at times still seemed to almost overwhelm the young Marines of my platoon. After months of hard training in the heat of Panama, these Marines had developed that hungry tired appearance of veterans with drawn faces, backs bent under heavy packs for long durations. I was able to visit with Lance twice since Thanksgiving and I could tell he and his buddies were like my own young Marines. We were all at that razors edge that troops reach when they need either combat or some sort of R & R to keep from losing our edge.

December 4th started like so many other training days before. At 0832, Lt Norton returned from a briefing with Col Doyle. As the Hummer rolled to a stop, he stepped out of the passenger side and yelled, "Gunner Cord I need to see you."

As I walked over to him, I wondered what he wanted with just me and not with all the other platoon leaders. "Yes sir," I said as I neared him seeing the seriousness in his face. "What in the world was going on? Have I fucked something up?" I wondered.

He reached out his hands toward my shoulders and without thinking I blocked both my arms up and out against his wrist blurting, "What the hell sir!"

"I'm sorry Gunner," he said in a whisper as he went on to gently place his hands on my shoulders. I let him turn me around and push me back against the Hummer. He shook his head as if struggling for words, "Gunner your son has been injured."

My mind raced, as my knees suddenly felt weak as I asked,

"Which one?" I have three."

"Is Lance Corporal Lance Cord your son?"

"Yes sir. What happened?"

Again, he shook his head before he spoke, "His Fast team was training to scale the walls of a building. He fell three stories."

"Oh my God!" I cried as my knees gave way as I slid to the ground, even with His support. In disbelief I held my face in my hands asking, "Just how bad is it?"

"Bad Gunner. Both arms broke and head injury that they know of," answered Lt Norton.

I looked up at him begging, "But he's alive?"

"For now. You better get over to the hospital. My driver will take you."

I still looked into his eyes in disbelief and shock hoping this was some kind of sick joke. I struggled with his help to stand up and sit in the hummer. As he closed the door he said, "I hope he makes it Gunner."

"Thank you, sir," I whispered as the hummer jerked into motion.

Soon we were speeding down the highway. I lay my head back trying to comprehend what had happened. Nothing had hit me this hard since my grandmother died back in 1971.

I entered the hospital as if in a dream, asking about Lance. A male nurse took me by the arm and led me down several hallways to a waiting room. At the waiting room doorway, I asked, "Can't you tell me how he is?"

"All I know is he is being operated on as we speak. But I'll get somebody in here as soon as I can," answered the male nurse.

"Thank you," I said as I entered the room where four young Marines from Lance's Fast team jumped up at attention.

"At ease," I said waving them back to their seats. One of the young Marines stepped forward saying, "I'm sorry Gunner Cord. I had just climbed through the third story window. I turned around and looked out at Lance Corporal Cord. He was smiling up at me when he reached for the windowsill. I saw a piece of the sill give way. I tried to grab his hand, but I missed." The young Marine started crying. I grabbed him and hugged him. Then he went on to say, "It's weird, but just before he fell, a hummer pulled up and parked right below us without seeing us above him. Lance Corporal Cord hit the hood breaking his fall, I think."

A little later I was sitting down when a female Navy lieutenant walked in and sat down next to me and asked, "Mr Cord?"

"Yes, mam how is Lance?"

She took a deep breath before she spoke, "I won't lie to you. He may not survive the operation. He's fighting for his life. What we know is, he has one arm broken and one arm shattered, one eye is injured, how bad we don't know. The damage to his head is the first problem. His brain is swelling. This alone may kill him."

I could feel myself turning white as she went on, "He may have brain damage. His neck is not broken. But from the chest down we just don't know yet, other than that we know his legs are not broken. Even if he survives the next seven hours it'll probably be seventeen hours before we know whether he'll be a vegetable or be paralyzed from the chest down."

I blew out a breath trying to take in all she had just said, fighting back tears.

"I'm sorry, Mr. Cord."

"I need to call home."

"Sure, I'll show you where," she said as she stood up and led me to an office and said, "Here you go. Call anywhere you want and talk as long as you want."

"Thank you, mam," I said sitting down behind the desk. She walked out closing the door behind her.

I picked up the phone trying to clear my mind of just what I had to say. I looked at my watch. It was 0934, Sunday. Hopefully I can reach Marty before she left for church. I wanted our Marine friends and their families at Camp Lejeune to pray for him.

The phone seemed to ring forever before I heard Marty's voice say, "Hello."

"It's me," I said.

"Nathan, are you in the states?"

"No."

"What's wrong?" she asked with worry in her voice.

"It's Lance," I answered as I went on to explain to her what I knew.

Her voice was breaking as she asked, "Do you want me to call Bunny?"

"No, I should be the one. But please ask the preacher and people in church to pray for him and call our families."

"Sure."

"I better let you go and call Bunny."

"Nathan, I love you."

"I love you too girl. Bye." I said hanging up the phone. Then I called Bunny, dreading this conversation. I knew somehow, she would blame me.

"Hello," answered Bunny.

"Bunny, this is Nathan."

"Nathan," she said in surprise and then, "Is Lance all right?"

"No, Bunny he's not," I answered as I again explained what I knew.

"I'm coming down there."

"Your what!" I said.

"You heard me."

"Bunny, this is not a good place for Americans to be right now especially a woman," I pleaded.

"I don't care. My son may die before tomorrow or before I can get there, but I'm coming somehow, someway."

"Okay, I'll let them know you're coming. Call me at this number," which I read off the phone, "Let me know the flight number and time of arrival and there'll be someone there to pick you up."

"Good. Thank you, Nathan. Let me get myself together and I'll get back to you. Bye."

I hung up the phone and dropped my head on the table crying, "Lord how could you let this happen. I've prayed every night for you to keep all my children safe from harm. But I guess he's still alive, isn't he? Dear Lord help him survive without brain damage or no permanent damage. In Jesus name, Amen."

Seemingly in a daze, I stood up and walked back to the waiting room.

It was 1634 when a doctor finally walked in asking, "Mr. Cord?"

"Yes sir," I said jumping up."

He smiled a tired smile saying, "The operation is over. I still can't promise you he'll survive the night. But the brain has stopped swelling. We had to drill holes into his skull to help relieve the pressure. I doubt if he'll ever see out of his left eye."

"How about his right eye?" I asked.

"We'll know tomorrow about everything else. Right now, we

have to wait to see if he survives to tomorrow. Then we'll find out what we have left of him. All we can do now is wait."

"Thank you, sir," I said shaking the doctor's hand. Then I went and called Marty and told her the news. She said, "Nathan I prayed for Lance after you called me this morning. He's going to be all right."

"How can you be so sure?" I asked feeling anger.

"I know you may think I'm crazy. But as I prayed, a calm feeling came over me. It was like God said Lance will be fine."

"God, I hope so," I said suddenly and for some reason I felt better myself for the first time that day.

"Oh, by the way Bunny called. She tried to reach you, but for some reason couldn't get through. Here is her flight number and time of arrival."

"Okay," I said as I wrote it down.

"Now you be good down there with her."

I laughed, saying, "Don't worry. I'll let you go. I'll call back when I hear more."

At 1850 in the evening, Lt Norton, GySgt Simon and SSgt O'Malley stopped by to see me and forced me to eat something.

At 1956, they all left except GySgt Simon. As he sat next to me, he said, "You know Gunner this really upset me. I wrote my honey back home and told her about it. I told her to lock up our three boys in the house and never let them out."

I looked over at him feeling the concern in his eyes and said, "You know that'll never work."

"I know sir. But we try so hard to keep our kids safe," answered GySgt Simon.

"Yes, we do, don't we?" I said thinking of Lance when he was a child following his big brother around. I had missed so much by staying in the Corps and being gone so much. And now the last sight I may have of him is that broken unrecognizable body I had been finally allowed to see hours ago.

At 0243 the next morning, GySgt Simon was asleep on the couch as I still sat awake unable to sleep. Suddenly the female Navy lieutenant walked in and sat down beside me smiling.

"What?" I asked.

"His spine isn't damaged at all. His right eye is fine. His left eye has some damage to it. He has no brain damage," she answered.

"Thank God," I cried almost cheering, waking up GySgt Simon.

"But he'll have to improve some before we can operate on that shattered left arm. He's going to be here for a while before we can get him back to the states. The one problem now is he is in a coma. He could wake up today, next month, six months from now or never."

"Thank you, mam, this is sure a lot better news than what I heard the last time."

"Well Mr. Cord, your son is a fighter and he's one lucky boy."

"Yes, mam I know."

After she left, I finally managed to drift off to sleep.

It was 0907 when Bunny shook me awake. I looked around finding GySgt Simon had left to rejoin Echo Company.

"Have you been in to see him?" I asked.

"Yes. I'd never recognize him."

"I know he's banged up quite a bit."

"But he's lived through the night and what they told me is a lot better than what it was."

"Yes, it surely is. Did you have any trouble getting here?"

"No. Although it did feel strange being picked up at the airport by an armed Marine escort and being driven here in a three-vehicle convoy. Are things really that dangerous down here?"

"Yes, I'm afraid so. It sure wasn't like this in the 70's when I was down here. Have you had breakfast yet?"

"No, I haven't been hungry until now."

I took her to get a pass from the hospital staff so she could eat in the mess hall and a place to stay nearby, for as long as she wanted. We spent the day together in the hospital waiting and going to see him when we could. That night we both slept on separate couches in the waiting room as Lance lay in his coma.

The next morning December 6th, I woke up early and went in to check on Lance. As he lay in his coma, I kissed his bruised forehead. As I walked out, I met Bunny going in. She smiled saying, "After I see him you wanna get some early breakfast."

I looked down then saying, "I need to get back to my men."

Her smile vanished as she said, "Your son is lying in a coma and all you can think about is your men!"

"Bunny. I love Lance. But I have a platoon of forty-five other people's sons that are depending on me. This place could explode into a shooting war any day. I can't let them down. I can't help Lance. I'll come to see him every night if I can."

"I will never understand you!"

"I know," I said turning and walking out.

While I was gone Morris of Sgt Ewing's 3rd squad was promoted to lance corporal. My platoon sergeant O'Malley was promoted to gunnery sergeant and Lt Norton put him in charge of the weapons platoon. Sgt Ewing was again my acting platoon sergeant and he had moved Cpl Cunningham over to take charge of 3rd squad.

I visited Lance every night through Dec 10th as he lay in a coma.

The evening of Dec 11th, I went to visit Lance and found Bunny crying.

"What's happened?" I asked sitting down beside her, dreading the answer.

"He's out of the coma."

"Well, that's great," I said sighing.

"But he doesn't act like he knows me. The doctor says it's normal that he is confused."

"But at least he's still improving," I said.

"I know, but it's so hard."

When I went in to see him, he looked at me as if he was looking right through me. I spoke to him, but he didn't answer. But his eyes tracked my every movement. I came out feeling good because I was happy to see him with his eyes open.

When I walked out, I told Bunny how he had acted.

"Yeah, the same with me," she said.

"You know for the first time I realize how my father, mother and grandparents felt the times I have been wounded," I said.

"And me," she blurted.

"I know. I'm sorry that I hurt you," I said feeling tears fill my eyes thinking of the love we once shared, that produced two fine boys. A love that didn't survive the Vietnam war or was it my love of Corps, country and my dedication to duty that killed her love for me.

"That was a long time ago," she said and turned and slowly walked away.

On Dec 12th, I took my platoon out on a daylight foot patrol in the jungle area bordering part of the base. It rained the whole time and we were soaked to the bone when we re-entered our lines with hard looks on our faces.

On Wednesday afternoon Dec 13th, Lt Norton reported to Col Doyle for a briefing. When he returned, he had GySgt Simon gather Lts North, Vie, Novak, GySgt O'Malley and me. Then he showed us on a map what our objectives would be and what was expected of us if war broke out. Then I went and had Sgt Ewing gather my squad leaders, Sgts Davis, Huebner and Cpl Cunningham, around me. After I briefed them and they in turn gathered their squads together it seemed the air around us was electrified with tension as we waited for a planned night patrol.

After dark the whole company entered the jungle with my platoon in the lead. Sgt Davis's 2nd squad was the point followed by Sgt Ewing, my radioman and me. This patrol like many I had endured over sixteen years ago in Vietnam was long, slow and miserable in the heat as birds screeched at us passing by.

And like Vietnam and the Marines before them, these young Marines of mine drifted silently through the jungle. In this thick jungle it took an hour to travel 200 meters correctly. Not since 1973 had I seen men move so quietly with cat like steps, eyes alert moving side to side, weapons held high, fingers on triggers. GySgt O'Malley and I had trained these men hard and each man knew his job. Heads turned at the slightest unusual sound or the sight of something in the dark that seemed to be unnatural. Of course, this caused a lot of halts as Sgt Davis's point man halted the column to check something out ahead. In this game it was still better to be safe then dead.

At the midway checkpoint, Lt Norton radioed me to halt for a break. I sat down with my back to a tree relaxing. I drank from my canteen as I looked at my watch. It was 1950. Ten minutes later, Lt Norton radioed me to move out. I touched Sgt Ewing on the shoulder. He got up without a word and walked forward through Sgt Davis's squad getting them up and the column headed back toward the base by a different route.

Soon, we were inching our way through a wall of thick elephant grass. Finally, after midnight we re-entered the base.

The next night I went to see Lance. This time he smiled when he saw me, but still didn't speak.

Outside Bunny asked, "Where were you last night?"

"Perimeter patrol."

"All night?" she demanded.

"Well until after midnight."

"More training?" she asked.

"No this was for real."

A concerned look came to her face as she spoke, "Is it getting worse?"

"Yes, by the day. The lid could blow off at any time. But you'll be safe here."

"If it happens, will you and your men stay here to protect the base?" she asked.

"No, our missions are off the base."

"I should have known. I guess Lance would've had a mission out there somewhere?" she asked.

"Yes," I answered sighing.

A look of concern again crossed her face as she said, "Nathan, you be careful out there, for Marty, Samantha and Nat's sake."

"As safe as I can be and get the mission done."

"God, I guess you'll never change, will you?" she said half smiling.

"Probably not," I answered smiling.

On Dec 15th, Noriega had himself officially named Panama's maximum leader and he declared that a state of war existed with the United States and said, "We the Panamanian people will sit along the banks of the canal to watch the dead bodies of our enemies float by."

At least to me this was the last straw and I knew we were going to war soon. There was by now 13,597 US forces in Panama of which 700 were Marines, against an enemy of 20,000 supposedly eager to take us on. But of these there were only 6,000 full-fledged military personnel. They had three battalions consisting of eight Infantry companies, one Special Forces Company and one Engineer Company. Some of these units did have fearsome reputations, like the black shirted and bearded mountain men. Most of the rest of the remaining armed Panamanians are police and paramilitaries organized into so called Dignity Battalions, which were formed and trained by Cubans, manned mainly by thugs and criminals.

Saturday night Dec 16th, four Marine lieutenants from Col Doyle's battalion left their base in a car to go to a restaurant in Panama City. Off duty, they were unarmed and wearing civilian clothes. On the way they got lost. They stopped at a Panama Defense

Force checkpoint. Suddenly the car was surrounded by a mob of about forty angry Panamanians including the six uniformed members of the PDF carrying AK-47's. When one of the PDF soldiers opened the front passenger door and tried to drag out one of the lieutenants, the driver stomped the gas pedal trying to make a getaway. As the car pulled away the PDF soldier opened fire wounding a lieutenant named Paz. The car raced to the base hospital, but soon after it got there Lt Paz died.

A US Navy lieutenant and his wife had witnessed this shooting. After the car had escaped, the PDF's grabbed the unarmed Americans, blind folded the couple and hauled them off to their headquarters. Once inside, a senior member of the PDF entered the room and without a word hit the lieutenant in the mouth and kicked him in the groin. Then the lieutenant was beaten and kicked for hours. Meanwhile his wife was brutalized with threats of rape. She was made to stand up against a wall until she collapsed. Then they slammed her head against the wall.

These two incidents would turn out to be the last straw that would lead us to war.

Back home on TV, President Bush would say, "General Noriega's reckless threats and attacks upon Americans in Panama have created an imminent danger to the 35,000 American citizens in Panama. And as President I have no higher obligation then to safeguard the lives of American citizens."

At 2205, the US Command ordered all US military installations in Panama to be put on Delta alert which restricted all personnel and their dependents to their bases.

At hearing this, Lt Norton sent GySgt Simon to pick up extra ammo and grenades for Echo Company.

At 2212, PDF troops in full battle gear began deploying combat vehicles outside the gates of American bases, blocking off the bridge of the Americas and setting up roadblocks throughout the city trying to intimidate us on the inside.

At 2235, the entire PDF forces nationwide were alerted and many of these units started deploying.

At 2259, the Dignity Battalion deployed as a guard force around the Panama Canal Commission building within the city.

But by Sunday morning, we all calmed down a little when our alert status was downgraded. There was still the rumor going around that we would retaliate in some way soon for the death of Lt Paz and the mistreatment of the Navy lieutenant and his wife. We knew for a fact that President Bush had refused to rule out military action against Noriega. He considered the incident involving Lt Paz an enormous outrage.

Again, Noriega had stated that Panama was in a state of war with the US.

We felt that some kind of action would happen soon. I looked around at the young faces of my platoon. It had been five years since Beirut and Grenada. Few of these young men had seen combat other than the few small firefights here. In all of Echo Company, only 1stSgt Bean, GySgt Simon and myself were Vietnam combat veterans. But I could tell from their faces that these young Marines of mine were like the young Marines from before them, full of determination.

Lt Norton trained Echo Company openly, as we prepared for the coming battle, we felt sure was coming. There was little talk of Christmas anymore.

Only the few Vietnam, Beirut and Grenada veterans seemed to take this training too seriously. At first the younger Marines were excited about going to war. But as the time drew near and reality set in their mood grew somber. A chaplain stopped by and handed out small camouflage Bibles just like the small black Bibles I received on Okinawa just before I went to Vietnam in 1965.

As we took a break for noon chow, Lt Norton sat down beside me. He opened his Bible and read out loud Psalms 91, "A thousand may fall at your side and ten-thousand at your right hand, but it shall not come near you."

I looked over at him feeling a chill race up my spine.

That evening the atmosphere grew tense as we listened to Pro-Noriega radio calling on the loyalists to defend their nation with yells of, "For Panama! Your life!"

I found it hard to sleep with my rifle at my side. So, I sat up and wrote letters home to Marty and each of my children including Lance here in the hospital. Then I re-read the last letter I had received from Marty.

At 0800 Dec 19th, Col Doyle ordered a complete maintenance stand-down of vehicles and equipment. Lt Norton had GySgt Simon gather his platoon leaders, Lts Vie, Novak, GySgt O'Malley and me together. He told us, "Until further notice all training has been canceled. Have your men clean their weapons and ammo, then inspect them as if their lives depended on it."

After I had inspected my platoon, Sgt Ewing asked, "Sir how do you feel about this platoon going to war?"

I looked at him feeling his unease before I answered, "Sergeant, I feel good that our hard work and training will see us through."

At 1800, Col Doyle ordered Lt Norton to report to his headquarters for a briefing. Three hours later at 2100 Lt Norton returned and gathered all the Staff NCOs and officers together in his tent.

Lt Norton looked around from face to face before he spoke, "Colonel Doyle as well as the senior Army officers here in Panama have been ordered to execute the planned operation."

As before the young Lts Vie, Novak and North smiled almost cheering while the older combat veterans, 1stSgt Bean, GySgt Simon and I sat silently in our somber moods.

"Echo Company is a part of Task Force Semper Fi in this operation called Operation Just Cause. The colonel emphasized that we are authorized only the minimum force necessary to counter a threat and to avoid as much collateral damage as possible," said Lt Norton.

"What does that mean?" I asked.

"It means Gunner, that other than the objectives that we are under orders to attack, we will not attack anyone or structure unless we feel threatened with death," he answered looking at me and then he went on to say, "H hour is set at 0100 tomorrow."

When he was done briefing us, I went back to my platoon and had Sgt Ewing gather our platoon together. I watched as these eighteen to twenty-two-year-old Marines assembled in front of me sitting on the ground.

"Gentlemen it's a go. In less than four hours we will help in the overthrow of Dictator Manuel Noriega's government."

I was shocked when there was no cheering as these young men watched, listening, hanging onto every word as I spoke. "I want each of you to remember that the Panamanian people are not the enemy. Even the Panama Defense Force will be given the chance to surrender. But our momentum of attack will be maintained. Marines, this is what we've been trained to do. This is the reason we joined the Corps. To fight our country's battles. And tonight, we will add to our Corps history."

I knew as I spoke that each man must have experienced that mixture of fear and excitement that came when you realized real combat was near. But I also knew they would execute their mission for which they had been preparing.

Later after rechecking my equipment I went to Lt Norton's tent to check his map against mine.

"Gunner you know we will lose men," he said.

"Yes, sir I know," I answered.

"This whole thing just doesn't seem real somehow," he said shaking his head feeling the heavy load of responsibility that comes with leadership.

"Sir, it's always the same. It comes down to us killing them before they kill us."

"What do I do about fear?"

"Well sir, you can't show fear in front of the troops because it's contagious. You must control your fear by leading by example. Too much fear can overwhelm you, too little can make you careless," I said patting him on the shoulder.

Then we went back to work going over again Echo Company's objectives on our maps.

By 2245, GySgt Simon had moved Echo Company into our jumping off positions. I watched with pride as L/Cpl Conn checked the equipment of the three men in his fire team one last time.

As we waited to go, I looked around at the other young faces of my platoon. They were grim with jaws set with determination. No one joked now as many of them smoked one last cigarette.

At 2300, Col Doyle radioed Lt Norton that we would not only capture the NDTT (National Department of Traffic and Transportation) number 2 station, but now we had to occupy it until relieved.

At 2320, we saw the first tracer rounds fired in Panama as an Air Force AC-130 fired rounds into Noriega's headquarters.

Shortly after midnight, we heard firing start up and it gradually moved closer and closer toward us as thousands of tracers split the darkness. We could also see flashes of bombardment behind the hills hiding Panama City. Added to this was the cough of mortars in the distance, which made it clearer than ever that this was war, not just a drill.

At 0015, Col Doyle radioed Lt Norton with three messages. He in turn sent GySgt Simon to round up the platoon leaders.

"The word isn't good. The enemy knows when H hour is. So, they know we're coming and they're moving toward us," said Lt Norton.

"Christ!" I muttered.

"I know it sucks, but it's too late. Pass the word to your troops and prepare to move out," he ordered.

Afterwards, I had Sgt Ewing gather our squad leaders together and I passed the word to them.

"This is fucking great," blurted Sgt Ewing.

"I know, but it's still a go," I said.

"Your shit 'n me sir!" argued Sgt Ewing.

"No. Get the platoon ready to load up," I answered.

Soon, Sgt Ewing split our platoon up between three Amtracks. I climbed into the Amtrack with Cpl Cunningham's squad feeling the adrenalin rush through me.

At 0055, I looked at my watch. In five more minutes, we would join the biggest US battle since Vietnam and the biggest night operation since WWII. I sat tensely in the front of my Amtrack with sweat pouring down my face, as I held my rifle with my right hand. Ahead of us, red and green tracers streaked through the night.

At 0100, Col Doyle radioed Lt Norton and gave him the order to attack. Then over the radio Lt Norton said, "Okay Echo Company this is it. Move out!"

I watched Lt Vie's 1st platoon move out leading our company followed by Lt Norton's CP group, then my platoon with Lt Novak's 3rd platoon bringing up the rear. As I sat in my Amtrack, I felt my knees shaking and my heart pounding as the hair stubble on the back of my neck stood up.

Ahead of us, Marine Cobra gunships were launching rockets streaking through the night, as suddenly the sound of explosions rippled across the city and the sky turned red from the blast of bombs and gunfire.

I was surprised that we hadn't taken any fire as our first objective the National Department of Traffic and Transportation station #2 came into sight.

As Lt Vie's 1st platoon neared the DNTT, the point vehicle, a

LAV made a hard-left turn in the driveway crashing through the locked barbed wire gate in front of the station. As two more LAV's followed the first one through the busted gate, they immediately came under automatic small arms fire. The three LAV's returned fire with their mounted M-60 machineguns. The LAV's drove to within five meters of the building. As they squealed to a halt the Amtracks carrying my platoon burst through the fence. The PDFs inside kept firing as the ramps on our Amtracks lowered. Then we ran out down the ramps for cover as the mounted machineguns laid down a base of fire as smoke filled our noses. The 3rd squad, led by Cpl Cunningham with their weapons blazing, rushed forward bent low in the shadows into a hail of gunfire from the building and threw themselves against its wall. Then Sgt Huebner's 1st squad rushed up to the left side of the building. Meanwhile Cpl Cunningham's squad slid along the wall and crouched down beside the doorway as gunfire suddenly sent tracers cracking around them. They dropped to the ground as tracers flew everywhere. Cpl Cunningham and L/Cpl Conn together tried to kick the door in, but were unable to break through. They fell back against the wall to each side of the door exhausted.

Still breathing hard, Cpl Cunningham yelled, "I'll cover you."

I watched L/Cpl Conn load his M-203 grenade launcher with a buck shot round.

This station had important radio equipment that can be used to monitor other PDF radio traffic once we had captured it. So, to keep it intact I had been ordered not to use grenades.

Then, they leapt back out from the wall as Cpl Cunningham fired up at the windows and tracers slammed into the ground around him. L/Cpl Conn fired the buckshot round blowing a hole where the door handle had been. He then hit the door with the butt of his rifle knocking it open. The 3rd squad then burst in through the doorway. Once inside the first room, they took various positions to better cover each other by fire. There was a hallway that ran through the whole building leading to a number of rooms including a kitchen and armory. Cpl Cunningham moved his squad by fire teams from room to room clearing the building as the enemy inside continued to fire as they withdrew. He followed a trail of blood to an outside door. Outside, he followed the blood trail across the grass where he found two PDF's sitting up against a tree with weapons at the ready. He threw himself to the ground firing his M-16 killing both men.

Back inside, at the end of the hallway, there was a larger room with a counter on the left side, there was a door that led outside on the right and another door that led into the last room of the building straight ahead. L/Cpl Conn knew that any remaining enemy troops most likely were in there.

L/Cpl Conn was the first to the doorway as he stepped around L/Cpl Morris who was changing magazines in his rifle, to take the point. Suddenly a hail of bullets came through the doorway from the PDFs hiding in the room. L/Cpl Conn pumped three buckshot rounds from his grenade launcher into the room. He then dived over a counter to clear the field of fire for Cpl Cunningham and L/Cpl Morris. L/Cpl Morris sprayed the room with his M-16 on full-automatic, as did another Marine in his team as their burst of fire vibrated through the building. Suddenly all firing stopped.

While L/Cpl Morris and Cpl Cunningham covered them from the hallway and L/Cpl Conn did the same from behind the counter, two other Marines entered the room and found a dead PDF officer and two enlisted men.

Meanwhile outside, I was watching as a corpsman worked on three bloody Marines, from Lt Vie's 1st platoon when Cpl Cunningham radioed me that the building was secured without any casualties from 3rd squad.

I thanked God for our luck so far as I radioed Lt Norton with my report.

The three wounded Marines were carried onto a LAV and were taken back to the aid station on base.

GySgt Simon came around dividing up the ammo within the Echo Company as we prepared to attack our second objective, the Arraijan Tank Farm. I looked at my map at this fuel storage area, which was within an 800-acre jungle area near Panama City.

Soon, Lt Norton passed the word by radio to move out. Lt Novak's 3rd platoon leapfrogged to the front of our column in their Amtracks behind the LAVs, followed by Lt Vie's platoon and then my platoon.

Later as our column moved up the top of a hill, we found an intersection blocked by a fuel tanker. Lt Novak halted our column. From a loudspeaker he warned the PDFs, "Attention! Attention! You have five minutes to move this blockade or I will open fire!"

The only answer from the PDF's was silence as the time passed. As we waited buttoned up inside of our Amtracks, the sweat dripped from our noses and ears soaking the collars of our camouflage jackets and flak jackets as our eyes blinked.

When the time ran out, Lt Norton ordered Lt Novak by radio to open fire. Suddenly the point LAV fired high explosive rounds from its 25MM bushmaster gun in three-round-bursts splitting the night with laser like darts of red and yellow flame. The PDFs fled from the blockade and our column pushed passed the oil tanker and quickly crossed a depression in the highway and drove to the top of the hill.

From here, Lt Novak saw the PDF troops entering a two-story fortress-like building with iron bars shielding the windows and doors. Lt Novak ordered his Amtracks to halt. As their ramps lowered, his 3rd platoon rushed out and opened fire on the building with small arms fire. Again, the LAVs fired their 25MM bushmasters causing gaping holes in the structure. Lt Novak led 3rd platoon in the assault into the building. Once inside they broke down into fire teams moving from room to room clearing out the small groups of PDFs.

With this building secured, Echo Company pushed on for three more miles to the town of Arraijan. Here, the PDF Station was a two-story building surrounded by a six-foot concrete wall with an iron-gate entrance. Quickly, Echo Company in our Amtracks surrounded the station as we ran down the ramps. My platoon took cover behind a low wall. A LAV pushed through the gate, as I ordered Cpl Cunningham's 3rd squad forward. They rushed through the destroyed gate behind the LAV. When they entered the station shooting began. As the firing continued, Lt Norton radioed Col Doyle reporting our location and situation. Meanwhile, muffled thuds of grenades added to the fury inside. Before the building was secured it caught on fire.

Again, Cpl Cunningham reported to me that he had no Marine casualties in 3rd squad as he brought them out of the burning building.

Our next objective was Peredes Headquarters, a one-story building. Each door and window were covered with locked iron bars. As before, Echo Company first surrounded the building. Lt Norton ordered Lt Vie to take this building. Lt Vie's point team tried to enter the door, but they had nothing to break the iron bars with. They used buckshot grenade rounds to bust the locks. A Marine speaking Spanish called inside warning the people to surrender. When he got no answer, he tossed in a concussion grenade. After it exploded, a Panamanian immediately stumbled out the door shaken from the blast. A fire team rushed past him through the doorway. They captured five more Panamanians inside.

Meanwhile outside, Lt Novak's 3rd platoon searched trailers near the building and captured more Panamanians hiding inside them. In all, seventeen prisoners were captured. Most of these turned out to be from the so-called Dignity Battalion.

With this building and the surrounding area secured, Lt Norton ordered Lt Novak's 3rd platoon and my platoon to blockade all access roads to Arraijan until further notice. We used Amtracks to block the roads.

Cpl Cunningham's 3rd squad had just set up their roadblock when a car approached them at a slow speed. When the driver noticed the Amtrack he speeded up toward the Marines. L/Cpls Conn and Morris opened fire. The car drove around the Amtrack as the volume of fire increased. The car was finally brought to a stop, hitting a building inside our perimeter. Although the driver had been killed, the other occupants tried to run, but were easily captured.

Sgt Ewing and I went around checking each squad as they continued to improve their positions.

Later, another car tried to drive through our perimeter, but was stopped by Sgt Huebner's 1st squad.

Col Doyle radioed Lt Norton and warned him that a large group of the Dignity Battalion troops were preparing to attack us. We finished digging in and waited, ready, but they never showed up.

By 0430, in less than four hours the Marine Forces had neutralized three major targets and secured a perimeter and controlled the main highway connecting North and South America.

As morning broke, the first rays of dawn climbed over the horizon shining on the debris-cluttered and deserted streets. Col Doyle ordered Lt Norton by radio to sweep the area and search the homes of Noriega's loyalists to look for arms caches.

Later, I halted Sgt Huebner's 1st squad and Cpl Cunningham's 3rd squad as Sgt Davis's 2nd squad moved up to secure an intersection. I looked around at my men's sunken eyes and hard faces after a sleepless night of fighting. Some smoked quietly as others talked in whispers while others just stared as if overwhelmed with it all.

Then suddenly from behind us, an old rusty truck came racing up the road filled with PDFs. Sgt Ewing ran out into the middle of the road waving his rifle yelling, "Halt! Halt!" But the truck speeded up. As he dived out of the way I fired a burst from my M-16 rifle. Both the 1st and 3rd squads opened fire including a M-60 machinegun. Tires screeched with the sounds of breaking glass as the truck was blown apart, turning over killing all the PDF troops in the cab as well as in the back.

As we moved on, two Marine Cobra gunships raced through the air overhead ahead of us. Suddenly, the low flying Cobras stopped in midair, then their noses dipped down as they fired into an office building.

I advanced my platoon in squad rushes firing toward the building. Sgt Ewing moved forward as tracers flew over his head from the doorway. He gritted his teeth, diving to the ground crawling over broken glass. Then he rolled and flattened himself against a wall.

Then there was the roar of a LAAW fired by L/Cpl Morris followed by the deafening explosion as the rocket hit the door. Sgt Huebner's 1st squad rushed through the destroyed smoking doorway firing.

Bullets flew down a hallway, as I rushed in with Cpl Cunningham's 3rd squad to help clear the building. L/Cpls Conn and Morris inched down the hallway tossing grenades into rooms as bullets cracked overhead. The 1st and 3rd squads pushed on through the building as they cleared the rooms killing fourteen PDF soldiers.

By 0700 the building was cleared and I had Sgt Ewing again divide up the ammo and grenades throughout our platoon.

Suddenly, Lt Novak's 3rd platoon received a volley of fire from the next building. Instantly I ordered Sgt Davis's and Cpl Cunningham's squads to maneuver toward this building as Sgt Huebner's 1st squad opened a base of fire pouring machinegun fire, M-203 grenade launchers firing grenades and rifle fire into the building. Meanwhile the corpsman in Lt Novak's 3rd platoon began working on four wounded Marines. As Sgt Davis's squad charged into the building the enemy escaped out the back, leaving blood trails everywhere from dragging their dead and wounded.

As Lt Vie's 1st platoon advanced toward the third house, they took fire as streams of tracers flew by them. Lt Norton moved Echo Company by platoons, leapfrogging each other as we fought on house-to-house killing PDF soldiers. It seemed like a flash back to Hue City for me as I maneuvered my platoon forward as I had done twenty-one years ago as a young sergeant. Except here our casualties weren't as high. These black shirted PDF's weren't near as good fighters as those NVA were back then. Echo Company pushed on as the PDF troops fired a few shots and then retreated only to hit us again in savage house-to-house fighting.

At times 122MM mortars hit us and Lt Norton in turn called in Cobra gunships to fire rockets, blasting the area ahead of us into fire and smoke.

As Lt Vie's 1st platoon lead our company up to an intersection, I realized we were all exhausted from the steady fighting. Lt North ran up through the column yelling for us to spread out more as the company moved in two columns on each side of the street.

Suddenly, there was an explosion to the front of 1st platoon from a booby-trap. A young Marine screamed, "I'm hit! I'm hit!" as the whole company halted.

"Corpsman up!" someone yelled.

As a corpsman moved up to the wounded man, the 1st platoon took fire from a house fifty meters up the street. The 1st platoon returned fire as the wounded man screamed. As I flattened myself in a doorway, I watched the corpsman drag the wounded Marine off the road. As he began working on the Marines leg he shuddered with fear.

With the 1st platoon pinned down by enemy fire, Lt Norton yelled, "Second platoon move up and flank them!"

I had Sgt Ewing move the platoon down an alley to the next street and then to the back of the enemy house.

Suddenly, L/Cpl Conn ran forward to the side of the house followed by L/Cpl Morris and the rest of the fire team. Marine machinegun fired into the house as pieces of steel and concrete flew everywhere.

As L/Cpl Conn's team inched forward L/Cpl Morris noticed another booby-trap and pointed to it.

"Be careful, there's more booby-traps in the area!" yelled Lt

North.

A grenadier from Sgt Huebner's 1st squad took careful aim and fired grenade rounds into the windows. Then L/Cpl Conn's fire team rushed into the house followed by the rest of Cpl Cunningham's 3rd squad to clear the house.

When the house was clear, Lt Norton halted Echo Company for chow at 1200. Lt North and I sat down in the cool grass and cut open MRE meals. We ate slowly in silence staring at the ground, too exhausted to think.

After we had finished eating, Lt Norton had GySgt Simon form Echo Company up and we moved forward again.

"Hey Gunny, this remind you of Hue City?" I yelled.

"Shit sir, these guys don't want to fight. This is a piece of cake," GySgt Simon answered smiling.

At about 1300, Col Doyle radioed Lt Norton and sent GySgt Simon to gather us platoon leaders together. Quickly Lts Vie, Novak, GySgt O'Malley and I followed GySgt Simon back into a house and found Lt Norton sitting at a kitchen table. As we sat down in chairs around the table Lt Norton said, "We have just been given a new mission. The capture of the 10th Military Zone headquarters in La Chorrera."

As we compared our maps with his, Lt Norton went on to say, "This headquarters is the central authority for all PDF substations located in the area. As you can see, it's about fifteen miles west of Panama City. We can expect to be outnumbered and outgunned. And we need to get there fast, so we'll be boarding our Amtracks again. Any questions?"

"No sir." We all said as I wondered if our luck was about to run out.

"Okay then. Gunny Simon prepare the company to reboard the Amtracks," ordered Lt Norton.

As always, the waiting was the worst part of any operation as we waited for the Amtracks to come up so we could climb in them.

But soon Echo Company was moving down the road toward La Chorrera with my platoon leading the way, followed by Lt Vie's 1st platoon, with Lt Novak's 3rd platoon bringing up the rear. In the distance, we heard the rip of 20MM gunfire from US Air Force A-7 attack jets, which to me was a comforting sound. I looked back at Sgt Huebner and his squad. Over the noise of the rumbling Amtrack

Sgt Huebner yelled, "Air support! Now we're in business!"

On the outskirts of La Chorrera, the LAVs leading us saw a roadblock being hastily set up by PDF forces. The PDFs were building the roadblock around a bus with vans and cars. The lead LAV, without stopping, opened fire with its machinegun ripping holes into the bus and the vans and cars near it.

Then the lead LAV hit the bus trying to shove it out of the way when it came under fire from PDF forces in La Chorrera. After the lead LAV had pushed a hole through the roadblock, the second LAV followed through the gap and the two LAV's rolled forward side by side at top speed firing their cannons as the PDF troops fled.

As we neared the 10th Military Zone headquarters, one of two Marine Cobra gunships flying overhead came under small arms fire from the headquarters building and trenches around it. As the two Cobras fired rockets at the enemy positions, Lt Norton ordered Echo Company to deploy from our Amtracks.

As we ran out of the Amtracks down the ramps taking cover, Lt Norton radioed Col Doyle requesting air strikes to help reduce the entrenchments of these determined enemy troops. My platoon took up fighting positions along the street and in a house, trying to move forward as the rest of the Echo Company moved up on our flanks. Soon the whole company was in the action, but unable to advance.

Soon a US Air Force OA-37 plane was circling overhead as Lt Norton gave him directions over the radio. This plane marked the target with white phosphorous rockets. Then two A-7 Jets rolled in above us guiding in on the white smoke firing their 20MM cannons with pinpoint accuracy.

As the air strike lifted, Lt Norton ordered Echo Company to move forward while the LAVs supported us. Leading the way, the two LAVs fired bursts through the iron gate of the large barracks complex. Again, from overhead, our Cobras fired rockets ripping through the six-inch concrete buildings leaving the headquarters building unrecognizable. As Echo Company moved forward under the LAV's cannon fire, Panamanian snipers from at least three locations fired at us. Once again, Lt Norton ordered my platoon to go inside to clear the building. Inside, Sgt Ewing broke our platoon down into squads and fire teams and they went to work clearing the rooms. As my men fought from room to room, the confined roar of grenades and the sharp shattering crash of glass were deafening. One by one they cleared the rooms. Cpl Cunningham's 3rd squad broke into the armory capturing boxes of new weapons. Soon, it was over as the PDFs fled. Again, I was surprised my platoon had suffered no casualties. I ordered Sgt Ewing to get our platoon out of the building as we all choked on the dust from grenade explosions.

As we came out, we saw and heard a cheering crowd shouting, "El Grand Liberador!" which I would later be told means, (The Great Liberator). It seemed the Panamanian civilians knew they were witnessing the rebirth of freedom in their nation.

Lt Norton radioed Col Doyle and reported the capture of the headquarters building. Then he gave Echo Company the mission to push on to search and clear this urban area and detain suspected Noriega loyalists.

At dusk, Lt Novak's 3rd platoon moved forward behind the protective fire of a LAV's 25MM gun against a suspected PDF stronghold. Kicking in doors, they moved from building to building, street to street throwing in concussion grenades. The point teams had taped small flashlights to the bottom of their rifle barrels so they could see better as they entered the pitch-black rooms. I was concerned with the lack of sleep and the high level of stress of the young Marines around me in this 100-degree heat and the fact they couldn't keep their fingers off their triggers as we kept taking fire.

Then Lt Norton halted Lt Novak's 3rd platoon and ordered Lt Vie's 1st platoon to move up and take the point.

Soon, Lt Vie's platoon was inching their way up to a small police station.

"Surrender!" yelled Lt Vie to the Panamanians inside. He was answered by a burst of fire wounding one of his Marines. Other Marines from 1st platoon returned fire killing an armed man standing in the doorway. Then a squad from 1st platoon burst into the station and captured three prisoners and a cache of AK-47 assault rifles.

Then, Lt Norton ordered my platoon to take the point as we headed toward a local ranch, which a known drug smuggler supposedly owned and which was supposed to be a staging area for the Dignity Battalion. I entered the ranch compound behind Cpl Cunningham's 3rd squad. The first thing I saw was about fifteen slaughtered hogs. Then I saw several hundred freshly gutted pigs. Nearby were several fires burning as if someone had prepared to have a giant barbecue.

"Sir I got PDFs over here!" yelled Sgt Davis.

I looked over to where several black shirted PDFs stood holding their arms up. But when two of Sgt Davis men moved up close to them, one of the PDFs dropped a grenade from between his legs. The explosion killed one PDF, wounded the others as well as both Marines. I helped Sgt Davis, who was crying as we worked with our corpsman on our wounded. Another corpsman ran up to work on the wounded PDFs. Luckily, neither Marine had critical wounds, but was still hurt bad enough to be medivaced back to the base.

At 1930, Echo Company got into a heavy firefight with PDF forces in several houses, which lasted for nearly an hour. I had two more Marines wounded from Sgt Huebner's 1st squad.

And still Col Doyle ordered Lt Norton to keep pushing Echo Company forward. I was tired and hot in my grimy camouflaged uniform; I moved my platoon on as they cleared more buildings liberating other small towns.

Finally, Echo Company climbed a hill in downtown Panama City overlooking another PDF headquarters. Here, Lt Norton ordered Echo Company to dig in and prepare to provide a base of fire for a US Army battalion who was preparing to maneuver against this headquarters. As we dug in on the hill overlooking a slum area of Chorrera, we began receiving heavy automatic weapons fire from the PDF garrison at Commandancia. The PDFs were firing from behind sandbagged barricades in a nearby housing project, as a US Army officer using a loudspeaker asked them to surrender. A PDF threw a grenade at him.

Then, Lt Norton ordered Echo Company to open fire. As the Marines fired, I ran from position to position checking the men of my platoon. As I passed along 2nd squad, Sgt Davis looked up at me with scared, almost pleading eyes. His two casualties earlier had really shaken him up. I patted him on the shoulder smiling as I yelled over the firing, "Don't panic sergeant. Just do your job and everything will be fine."

He then smiled, too, nodding his head yes.

As I moved on, I thought, "I'm glad that we don't have to run that gauntlet of fire, that Army battalion is fighting through." Down there were more narrow streets in front of the Commandancia where Noriega's men were staging their last-ditch stand. From what I could see from up here, this was the toughest nut to crack yet. All hell seemed to break loose down there as this turned into an all-out battle, becoming the fiercest fighting so far. And still, we took fire as bullets ricocheted off the LAVs and Amtracks behind us. The roar of gunfire was deafening as US Army tanks opened fire on snipers on the upper floors of the three-story white fortress. I could see at least four US soldiers shot down as well as a dozen civilians dead or wounded. The firing started fires that had the headquarters as well as much of the surrounding neighborhood blazing. The night sky was filled with tracers flying everywhere.

After two hours of steady gunfire, the PDFs melted away into the surrounding neighborhoods and began fighting in hit and run guerrilla tactics as the US Army battalion advanced, fighting in the main streets and side streets.

Echo Company had stopped firing when suddenly we heard the horrifying sounds of mortar shells shrieking in and exploding around us. This again shook up Sgt Davis pretty badly when another of his men was wounded.

At 2130, Echo Company was ordered to help the Army clear the streets. Soon, L/Cpl Conn's fire team was one of many in my platoon patrolling the streets searching homes for PDF holdouts or their weapons. To him, it still felt strange walking down these streets with basically no cover.

Because of a tip from a Panamanian civilian man, a squad from Lt Novak's 3rd platoon found 600 AK-47 rifles in one house. Most of the civilians seemed happy to see us. They even cheered and ran out and gave us food and sodas.

The merchants were also glad when we put a stop to the looting of their stores. Even the poor people living in the ghettos who had nothing, still found something to feed us as they cheered. Old women cried, happy to see us.

I had no idea what the people back home thought about this, but if they were here with us and could see the expressions of these people, they would have known we had done the right thing here.

More and more the civilians came to us and told us where we could find PDF hideouts and weapons stashes. So far, the tips had turned out to be 60% correct.

Like Vietnam, a hot climate was made even hotter by wearing a flak jacket, helmet and carrying a rifle, grenades and seven or eight magazines of ammo.

Finally, after fighting for twenty-four hours straight, Lt Norton received permission to halt Echo Company and dig in for the night. As we did so, we heard the crack of bullets and explosions in the distance. Once we were dug in, I ordered Sgt Ewing to pass the word that one man in each team would keep watch as the other three slept.

Dawn came too quickly and I ordered Sgt Ewing to have our platoon take turns cleaning, oiling their weapons and then eat chow.

Soon, we were back in our Amtracks and four tanks had joined us this morning as Echo Company moved through the blacked-out streets. Then firefights began breaking out, as we charged out of our Amtracks returning fire. Mortars were landing around us as Cobra gunships flew overhead firing. The PDFs were falling back trying to break contact with the US Army battalion and Echo Company. With pinpoint accuracy, my platoon returned fire at windows of one house for forty-five minutes. Then Lt Vie saw 150 men in civilian clothes walking up the street toward us with their hands up. Lt Norton ordered the men searched and taken to the rear.

Later, Echo Company was once again in our Amtracks with Lt Novak's 3rd platoon leading the way when we spotted PDF troops running into a building. Lt Norton ordered the rest of Echo Company to move up quickly and we surrounded the building. Then Lt Norton ordered Lt Vie's 1st platoon and Lt Novak's 3rd platoon to cover my platoon as we entered the building.

From room to room my fire teams searched, clearing the building. L/Cpl Conn and L/Cpl Morris covered from the sides of a doorway, as two other Marines burst through the open door firing, one going left while the other went right.

Two men in Sgt Huebner's 1st squad were wounded as we secured the first floor.

I waved for Cpl Cunningham to have his 3rd squad lead us up the stairs. As L/Cpl Conn's fire team climbed the stairs to the second floor, the smell of shit overwhelmed us. As I followed them, I found the second floor had been used as a head and was covered with human piles of shit and trash. I covered my mouth as some men threw up.

"What the hell is wrong with these people?" asked L/Cpl Conn disgustedly.

"Hell, at least they only used one floor," said Sgt Ewing

laughing.

I then had Sgt Huebner's 1st squad lead the way up to the 3rd floor where they killed five PDF soldiers.

When we left the building, I saw Amtracks had arrived with our resupplies. My platoon and I sat down with Lt North in the shade of a grove of trees.

Soon, GySgt Simon called men from each platoon to pick up their resupply of chow and ammo. My two wounded men were carried into the supply Amtracks to be taken back to the base.

Then the corpsman began treating blistered feet and handing out aspirins as we began eating chow.

Overhead, two Cobras were flying ahead of us when suddenly they were fired on from a building up the street. Both Cobras stopped as their noses dropped down firing rockets, filling the air ahead of us with fire and smoke hiding the building in a dark cloud.

"Damn look at that!" gasped L/Cpl Morris.

Everyone seemed to stop what they were doing and stared at the Cobras firing at the building.

Dusk was settling as Echo Company moved toward another building along a street that suddenly seemed too quiet.

Lt Norton waved Lt North over to his side and looked into his eyes saying, "Enemy troops have been spotted through the windows by one of the Cobras. When I halt the company, the Cobras are going to fire rockets. Then first and second platoons will attack the building while third platoon will lay down the base of fire. Have Gunny Simon pass this on to the platoon leaders."

"Aye, Aye sir," he answered, swallowing hard and blinking his eyes.

Echo Company was forty meters from the building as the sun slid below the horizon, when Lt Norton gave the order to halt as we ran for cover on both sides of the street. Around me lay civilian clothing, shoes and broken liquor bottles.

We pressed ourselves against walls as the Cobras came in roaring overhead. When they opened fire with their rockets, we felt the vibrations of the explosions followed by the shock waves and then the sounds of the blast.

Red-hot shrapnel and chunks of concrete rained down around us. Then enemy troops opened up on us from the building with AK-47 rifle fire.

When the Cobras ceased firing, Lt Norton yelled, "Let's go!"

Cpl Cunningham's 3rd squad led my platoon running toward a hole blown into the building as bullets flew around us. As we entered the building Sgt Ewing looked at me as the three squads without orders broke down into fire teams and started moving from room to room.

L/Cpl Conn yelled pointing, "You two go in and we'll cover you!" As he and L/Cpl Morris did so the other two Marines burst into the room firing, then yelled back, "All clear!"

"Roger that, let's move to the next room and you guys cover us!" yelled L/Cpl Conn.

Meanwhile, Lt Vie's 1st platoon moved upstairs. Once on the second floor, the Marines of 1st platoon moved along the walls when suddenly, bullets cracked by their heads splattering against the wall behind them. But soon we had secured the building and went outside and dug in for the night.

The next day, Dec 22nd, Echo Company was again searching houses as the civilians crowded the streets clapping their hands and cheering us. Marines from Lt Novak's 3rd platoon captured three of Noriega's loyalists in a car and in the car trunk they found a machinegun. This day would end up being the first day since the fighting had started that we hadn't been fired at. When night came, Lt Norton halted Echo Company and we dug in. Still he ordered us to stay at 75% alert, which meant only one in four men could sleep at a time.

The next morning the sun crept up over the horizon covering the dew-covered grass. Like so many other times in my twenty-five years in the Corps, I realized I would be away from home during Christmas.

Again, Echo Company found itself in Amtracks moving north. Col Doyle had radioed Lt Norton with a change of mission. We were now to conduct platoon size clearing operations up north.

Looters had again broken into stores and houses smashing windows leaving debris scattered throughout the streets.

Later when my platoon was on foot, the streets seemed to come alive with people, while other people stood in doorways or waved from windows, all of them cheering us like we were liberators.

"I thought this is an invasion. These people act like they love us," said Sgt Ewing smiling.

Men of Sgt Huebner's 1st squad nearby, laughed as they kept a close eye on the civilians around us. Turning their heads from side to side the weapons of my men moved in the direction of odd sounds. And I did feel like a liberator even among the smell of garbage and human shit in the streets.

We were also stopping civilian vehicles and searching them for weapons. Sgt Huebner's 1st squad stopped a car filled with men in civilian clothes. Stepping up to the car he noticed a grenade on the back seat and he ordered them to get out. But as the civilians opened the four doors, they suddenly pulled out pistols. Both the civilians and the 1st squad opened fire at point blank range at the same time. When it was over two Marines were wounded and all eight civilians lay dead in the street around the car.

Sgt Ewing and I ran over as a corpsman started working on the wounded Marines while a team of Marines checked the bodies of the civilians.

Meanwhile, a crowd of civilians surrounded us cheering us and jeering at their former oppressors lying in the street. Some of them even came up cursing and spitting on the dead men. "Viva Bush!" many of them shouted.

Sgt Ewing looked at me smiling saying, "I could get used to this."

My platoon joined the rest of Echo Company as we met up with the US Marine battalion for the first time since the fighting started. The Marine battalion had surrounded a large PDF garrison and was calling in air strikes to dislodge them. After the jets had made their bombing runs, Marines from the battalion moved into the PDF headquarters.

As Echo Company watched from a distance, again, civilians around us cheered, waving peace signs at us. Young girls kissed the dirty camouflage painted faces of my young Marines.

Down the street an effigy of Noriega hung from a stop sign burning.

Then Lt Norton moved Echo Company away from the Marine battalion as we went on searching houses. Even though the atmosphere seemed relaxed we were still tense from the occasional sniper fire.

Just before noon, Lt Vie's 1st platoon captured eight PDF soldiers in a house along with stacks of PDF documents and US money, weapons and ammo.

In the afternoon it began to rain drenching us all. Sgt Huebner's 1st squad caught a civilian looting a store. He captured him, forcing the looter face down in the mud as he searched him. Then he was placed in the Amtrack carrying the other PDF prisoners.

Christmas Eve day began like any other day since the invasion began, with Echo Company in Amtracks. This time we were operating with a US Army unit in their APCs (Armored Personnel Carriers). We arrived on the outskirts of a fishing village. Quickly, we surrounded the village and prepared to sweep through. This again brought back memories of Vietnam to me.

An Army officer using a loudspeaker, speaking in Spanish yelled, "You are surrounded by superior forces and you can't escape. Come out with your hands up. We have the firepower necessary to back it up. If you resist it will result in injuries and death. All civilians come out of the building. Now!"

Then we waited and when nothing happened and no one answered, Lt Norton was ordered to sweep through with his company. So, by platoons we charged in one building after another throwing grenades, as fire teams moved room to room. Once a platoon had secured a building, we popped a yellow smoke grenade to signal the US soldiers and other Marines that the building was all clear.

This village turned out to be larger than I had thought. Many of the houses were part of a big Cuban fishing operation. Overhead US Army Apache and Marine Cobra gunships were supporting us. Out along the water's edge were two Navy patrol boats with Seal teams.

By evening, Echo Company and the US Army unit had secured the village plus the harbor. Together we captured over 300 enemy suspects plus six weapons were found on a civilian boat.

At 1705, Col Doyle radioed Lt Norton with the word that Noriega had slipped into the Vatican Embassy in Panama City where he surrendered, asked for and was granted political asylum. As this news spread along the column, the young Marines cheered.

Then Col Doyle ordered Lt Norton to put Echo Company back on Amtracks and move to the Vatican Embassy.

Once we arrived at the Embassy, Echo Company ran out of our Amtracks and quickly set up a blockade position at the Parillo Plaza, which was just down the street from the Vatican Embassy compound. Lt Norton's orders were to block this approach to the embassy.

I was impressed with the friendliness of the majority of the Panamanian people who came up to our concertina wire just to talk to us.

Christmas morning, I was sitting next to GySgt Simon as we ate our MRE meal. As Lt North walked past us GySgt Simon grumbled, "Merry Christmas XO."

But Lt North smiled back answering, "Merry Christmas Gunny."

Nearby a group of kids were begging L/Cpl Conn's fire team for food.

Looking at the kids begging, GySgt Simon grumbled, "Just like Nam."

"Yeah it is. A little while ago a young girl was offering her body to Corporal Cunningham for food," I said.

As the morning passed, my Marines stayed by their weapons catnapping when they had the chance. The day was hot and steamy with the temperature rising over 100 degrees.

I had always found it tough being away from home during Christmas. But God knows I love the Corps. You would think a forty-two-year-old Marine with twenty-five years in wouldn't still love it like I do. But I can't imagine doing anything else or being a civilian watching this on TV.

Still, it helps when grateful Panamanians who consider us liberators bring us fried chicken, hamburgers, pizza, cakes, cookies, fresh fruit and cakes.

"Well, Gunny, the South Vietnamese never gave us fried chicken or pizza," I kidded GySgt Simon.

"Sir you're right about that," he said laughing.

Later Lt Norton ordered me to send out a patrol to check the streets near our position. I in turn gave the mission to Cpl Cunningham's 3rd squad. Out on the patrol, L/Cpl Conn's team led the way. Children watched them pass and cheered yelling, "Gringo! Gringo!"

Older people offered the Marines what food and drink they had, holding it out as they passed by. Still the men of 3rd squad held their weapons tight with fingers on triggers. They had heard of the US Army squad on patrol nearby who had one soldier stabbed and another soldier had his caller bone broken from a beating.

But on this patrol, some kids handed them Hallmark greeting cards. Some of them were Christmas cards, New Year's cards, mother, and father birthday cards.

But as Cpl Cunningham turned a corner, near the front of his squad he caught movement out of the corner of his eye. As he spun around, he saw a small boy pointing a pistol at him. He dived down to the hard street aiming at the kid who was smiling. He started squeezing the trigger when he suddenly realized the kid's pistol was a toy.

"Damn it!" mumbled Cpl Cunningham shaking all over in anger and fear at what he almost had done. He stood up and walked up to the boy, grabbed the toy and threw it down on the street and smashed it with his boot. The boy burst into tears and ran away down an alley.

As I watched my young Marines, I realized that just like in the past after I had taken young Marines in combat I could now feel and see a difference in them. I could see the change in their expressions on their faces that said they'd killed someone. It's that shocked look that means they, like me in 1965 would never be the same.

The next two days were quiet ones for my platoon as we waited at our block-aid position running two squad size patrols a day.

By Dec 28th, the Marine area of responsibility had been expanded to approximately fifty square miles. This area included a large coastal area west of the Pacific entrance to the Panama Canal opposite Balboa and Panama City. Our overall mission now, was to protect the western approaches to the Panama Canal and the US defense sites located in that area, to prevent PDF elements from moving out of Panama City, to provide security patrols and capture PDF and Dignity battalion personnel.

I was glad when our 1st Battalion 6th Marine Regiment commanding officer from Camp Lejeune, LtCol Haring arrived from the states with Hotel Company. From him we learned that my old friend SgtMaj Burns was now our division sergeant major.

After the days filled with excitement, the last days of December became boring and my squad leaders began having a hard time keeping their men from getting too loose. I began checking my platoon more often because I was afraid this thing wasn't over yet. I warned my men of the possibility that someone could drive by our positions and fire an automatic rifle at them or worse an RPG. I hadn't had a man killed yet and I wanted to keep it that way.

By New Year's Day 1990, my squad patrols were now being met by civilians who often argued among themselves over who would feed the Marines.

At hearing about this, Sgt Ewing said, "What the fuck, these people don't need us any longer."

At 2140 on Jan 3rd, President Bush appeared on TV and announced that Gen Noriega had given himself up to US authorities. At hearing this, my young Marines cheered.

The next day, Lt Norton came by checking on his company's positions. To each platoon he gave the same warning, "So far, we have been remarkably lucky, but keep your eyes sharp. We're not home yet."

I couldn't help but agree with him.

On Jan 5th, LtCol Haring was ordered by Col Doyle to take Echo and Hotel Companies back to our base to become part of a quick reaction force. There, I took my first shower in days and ate a hot meal. I requested five days leave in country to visit Lance and Lt Norton approved it.

By the time I got checked into visiting officer quarters near the hospital, it was almost midnight. Even though it was late, I called Bunny's room to find out how he was doing. When I didn't get an answer, I phoned the front desk to ask the corporal on duty to have Bunny call me when she got in no matter what the time. But I was surprised to find out she had left to fly back home earlier in the day. So, I put on a clean camouflaged uniform and walked over to the hospital. Once there I entered the front door and walked up to the sailor on duty at his desk. He was reading a book as he looked up at me and asked, "Yes sir can I help you?"

"Yes, I hope so. I'd like to check on my son's condition. Lance Corporal Cord," I answered.

"The Marine that fell."

"Yes, that's him."

"I think he's better. Sir do you know what floor he's on?"

"Yes, unless he's been moved to a regular room," I answered.

"Let me see sir," he said as he picked up a clipboard running his finger down a list of names and then said, "He is in a regular room on the third floor."

"Good, that means he's really improved."

"Yes sir. Why don't you go on up and speak to the senior nurse?"

"Thank you." I said as I turned walking toward the elevator. On the third floor I found a nurse sitting behind the main desk. She looked up at me and smiled saying, "I haven't seen you in a few days Mr. Cord."

"I've been a little busy," I answered smiling.

"Were you involved in the fighting sir?"

"Yes, I was. How's my son?"

"You'll find him a lot better. He's completely out of the coma now. But he doesn't remember the day he fell at all."

I fought back tears as I gasped, "Thank God."

"Why don't you go see him. I'll wake him."

"No, don't wake him. But I would like to see him," I said.

"Sure, follow me," she said getting up. I followed her down the hallway until she stopped in front of an open door and whispered, "Take your time, sir."

"Thank you," I said whispering as I stepped into the room walking around the bed to his left side. He seemed to be sleeping. He looked even thinner than before. He was lying on his back. I could see the surgical scars, which started on his forehead just behind his hairline and ran back across both temples and then ran down just behind both ears. His right arm was still in a cast from above the elbow down to his knuckles. His left arm still had those four shiny pins embedded in his arm, sticking out about six inches and bolted together to hold his shattered bones together so they could grow back straight. Tears filled my eyes as I realized again how close I came to losing him. I loved all four of my children, but he and I had shared a special proud bond when only he of my three sons chose to follow my footsteps into the Corps. And here he laid injured worse in training than I had ever been in combat.

Suddenly he opened his eyes and stared at me with a start. He reached for me with his left hand which surprised me asking, "Dad is it you?"

"Yes," I answered patting his left hand with my right hand and said, "I've taken five days leave to spend some time with you."

"You did?" he said smiling for the first time as if surprised at what I just said.

"I'm sorry I woke you. I know it's late. I just wanted to see you tonight."

"That's okay."

"Well, you go back to sleep. I'll be back, first thing in the morning."

"Okay," he said.

"Well good night."

"Okay Dad. Good night."

Early the next morning, I got up and ate breakfast in the hospital mess hall. When I entered Lance's room, he was sitting up in bed eating his breakfast. I was amazed he was feeding himself with his left hand.

"After you left last night, I wasn't sure if you had really been here. I was afraid I'd dreamed it," he said smiling.

I laughed in relief that he could talk so well and plain and seemed to have a good memory as I answered, "It was no dream, I was really here."

We spent the days talking about home, the family and yes, the Corps. He still didn't remember anything about the day he fell. And when he had finally come to, he didn't know where he was. After being around Marine green and camouflage uniforms for months, to wake up to see everyone dressed in white or Navy blue had him totally confused. And the treatments he was getting hurt so bad he began to think he was a prisoner of war and they were torturing him. He began having dreams about being a prisoner of war. But when his mother would come in, he was even more confused. For a while he thought his dreams were the real world and his mother's visits were his dreams.

Three times a day I would walk with him around the halls to give him exercise. Afraid he might fall, I would walk on his left side with my right hand under his left arm.

We were talking in his room on Jan 9th when I asked, "Have they said anything about you going home?"

"I've got to get therapy. I'll probably be here for at least six months."

"You could get that back in the states," I said.

"That's what they told me."

"Well it's up to you. I don't know if I can do anything about it or not? But I can find out if you can be transferred back to the states maybe at a hospital in Phila or somewhere in Maryland," I said as he looked at me with eyes getting big.

"Would you want to do that?" I asked making sure he understood what I was saying.

"Sure!" he blurted out smiling.

"Okay. But don't get your hopes up. I'll see what I can do," I said getting up and walking out.

After asking some questions and then directions to the office of a Navy Chief Petty Officer, I knocked on the open-door frame. Inside sitting behind his desk an old Chief Petty Officer looked up and at seeing me smiled saying, "Yes sir, come on in."

I walked in as he motioned me to one of two chairs to the right of his desk.

"Thank you, chief," I said sitting down.

"Now, what can I do for you sir?"

"Do you know Lance Corporal Cord's case?" I asked.

"I believe he's the young Marine with head trauma from a bad fall."

"Yes, that's him," I said.

"You his platoon leader, sir?"

"No, I'm his father," I answered smiling.

"I didn't know his father was in the service. Where did you fly in from sir?"

"Oh, I was ordered down here some time back with Echo Company, One, Six," I answered.

"Then you've seen some action down here."

"Yes, I did."

"I bet this wasn't your first."

"No, it wasn't," I answered.

"Okay sir, how can I help you?"

"My son tells me he may be down here for six months."

"Yes, I'm afraid it's going to be a long slow road for him with a head injury like he's had."

"I guess I don't understand why he can't get this closer to home where his family could visit with him on a regular basis."

He looked at me long and hard sitting back in his chair before he spoke carefully, "It is true that people do tend to recover quicker with family nearby. Where is his family?"

"Delaware," I answered.

"I could get him transferred to a military hospital near DC."

"That would be great," I said smiling and then said, "How soon?"

"Well with his kind of head injury it may be six months before he can fly. I can get him sent back by ship. But I'm sure it'll be February before the doctors will feel he's up to it."

"That will be fine."

"Well sir, consider it done unless something unforeseen happens. The doctors will have the final say, you understand?"

"Yes, of course. Thank you chief," I said standing up and shaking his hand.

"No problem, sir. Good luck to you and your son."

"Thank you, again," I said and then turned around and walked out of his office.

When I walked into Lance's room he asked, "What did 'ya find out?"

"They're going to send you back to the states in February on a ship unless you have a relapse."

"I can't believe it. That was quick. Mom had talked to the nurses and doctors about me going home and they kept saying six months."

"Well, you have to know who to talk to. Besides being a Marine Chief Warrant Officer ought to be good for something," I said laughing.

For the rest of my leave I was surprised every day at how quickly he was improving.

But too soon, on Jan 11th, I hugged him goodbye and returned to Echo Company. Once there, I learned that back in Camp Lejeune Col Beck, our regiment CO, had been transferred and replaced by a Col Gagush.

The rest of January was quiet for Echo Company. But because we were still the quick reaction force, we trained hard every day.

The first of February, Lance was carried on board a ship for his trip home.

Meanwhile, the people of Panama had started rebuilding their country. But it was reported that many troops of the Panama Defense Force had moved into the jungles planning to fight a guerrilla type war against the new Panamanian government and us. Because of these reports, LtCol Haring was ordered by Col Doyle to take Echo and Hotel Companies and begin long range patrols operating in an area covering 650 miles, stretching from the US Naval Station Panama Canal to beyond Santiago near the Costa Rican border. With most of our wounded men returned, Echo Company was almost back to full strength. To begin the operation, the three platoons of Echo Company were to be choppered out to three different areas. Our mission was to try to cut the trail of the PDF forces while Hotel Company would be our quick reaction force if we got into trouble.

On Feb 3rd, after moving down to the air field, I yelled to Sgt Ewing, "Separate the platoon by rifle squads and then attach the gun teams, mortar sections to different squads and make three lines."

In the distance I could hear the whump, whump, whump sounds of the approaching three CH-46 choppers and the two Cobra gunships.

As Sgt Ewing gave his orders, Sgts Huebner, Davis and Cpl Cunningham started shoving men into lines. As the 1st chopper settled to the ground, Sgt Huebner's 1st squad waiting in line, bent low holding onto their helmets against the blasting wind from the chopper and ran toward the lowered ramp. Sgt Ewing ran up the ramp with Sgt Huebner as the crew chief waved them all the way to the back of the chopper. They sat down in seats on opposite sides of the old CH-46 next to the two crewmen manning the M-60 machineguns, which can be fired out the big square holes on each side of the chopper. I entered the chopper last yelling, "Move up tight and sit down!"

As they slumped down, I walked up between them to the front next to one of the machine gunners. I had learned in Vietnam to watch the terrain below as we flew, so if anything happened and we had to land short of our objective I would have some idea of which direction we would need to go.

As the back ramp came up, the whump, whump, whump of the blades increased to a steady roar until my eardrums ached. Sgt Ewing looked at Sgt Huebner, but neither spoke because they wouldn't hear each other anyway above the whine of the engine.

I looked out as the other two CH-46s loaded up with the rest of my platoon and lifted up. I felt that old fear come over me. For all I knew we could be landing in a hot LZ. It's been a long time since I've been choppered into the middle of nowhere with just a platoon of Marines to search for an enemy force that once found could outnumber us. My mind raced back in time to the mountain jungles of Vietnam. Again, I was being flown into mountain country, which could be cold, wet or hot. At least I couldn't see any rice paddies below. But it was weird to think that many of these enemy troops were wearing black shirts, where the VC had worn black pajamas. I looked down at my Vietnam style jungle boots. Like me, they were old, but they felt good and were comfortable. Some things just didn't seem to change. I patted my old Cal-45 pistol in my shoulder holster.

I looked back over toward Sgt Huebner eating a chunk of MRE peaches. Then I looked out of the chopper at the jungle mountains below where somewhere there were black shirted PDF forces. They might be waiting at our LZ. Twenty years ago, I remember running off the chopper more than once as bullets hit the ramp. The stubble of hair on the back of my neck stood up as I checked the safety on my M-16 rifle.

I shuddered as I remembered a squad of men I knew ambushed in Vietnam. It was the next day when we found them. They had died fighting. But then the gooks had cut their heads off and placed them on sticks. Some had their balls cut off and stuffed into their mouths. Why was I thinking of this after all those years? I shook my head trying to clear my thoughts.

I looked at the tan and drawn faces of the men in Sgt Huebner's 1st squad. They in turn looked at me as well as each other, but not making eye contact.

Finally, the CH-46 choppers began to circle as the Cobras flew in low checking the LZ below. The machine gunners on both sides of me cocked their 50-cal machineguns as they searched the jungle for trouble.

Then the three Ch-46 choppers flew in and began to settle down. Sgt Huebner waved his squad up and they faced the rear, ready to run out. I felt the bump as the rear of the chopper touched the ground and the ramp began to drop. Suddenly, fire team leaders were pushing the back of their men to go. The 1st fire team ran out jumping even before the ramp was all the way down. I ran out last as all three squads were on the ground now heading off to my left. I watched a tree line as my platoon moved to a safe distance from the choppers and dropped for cover. I could almost feel bullets cutting through the elephant grass as I knelt down looking around. But as the choppers flew away, they left us in silence. The LZ was cold (no enemy contact) just like I like them. I quickly moved my platoon away from this area in case PDF forces had seen where we had landed. I wanted to get away from here before they had a chance to ambush us. I didn't want them to find us until we found them.

The next day, I moved my platoon parallel to an old dirt road that ran along the Panama and Costa Rican border. We crossed a hip deep river, and then a flat area covered with high bamboo and scattered elephant grass, then back into more mountains.

Sgt Ewing searched the area. I knew he didn't like being out here with only one platoon. As dusk settled in, I halted the platoon for the night on a small hill.

Sgt Ewing quickly threw his gear down and looked at me as I walked around studying the terrain, plotting where to place a squad and a machinegun position.

He walked over to me and asked, "What squads have the ambush patrols tonight?"

"First squad and a gun team will ambush and second squad by themselves," I answered. Then added, "Have Cpl Cunningham send out a listening post near those trees over there." As I pointed, I said, "I want the other gun team to dig in here to cover the listening post and those trees. Any questions sergeant?"

"No sir," he answered.

"Good, have them start digging in then," I said.

"Aye, Aye sir," he said.

I walked over to my pack and sat down. I opened the pack and pulled out a MRE meal and began cutting it open with my K-bar knife.

The next night as the platoon dug in, I walked back to my pack and sat down next to Sgt Ewing who spoke, "I just got off the hook with Lieutenant Norton sir."

"Any change in orders?" I asked.

"No sir, just more of the same."

I opened my pack and fished out a MRE meal. Soon I was spooning down my meal with a brown plastic spoon. Later, in the dark, I stood my turn as radio watch looking up at the stars. When my watch was up and I had woken up my relief I rolled up inside my poncho liner and poncho in my hole.

Near dawn it started to rain. It rained steadily for a while, but slowly grew heavier. First the ground became soaked and puddles began to form in the bottom of the foxholes. Then the wind picked up driving the rain in sheets. Sometimes the rain would slow up to a fine drizzle, almost stop, but not stop, just return in cycles, each time seemed the rain seemed to pour harder. Soon we were all wet, shivering in the cold.

Dawn broke in a gray mist. I knew that jets and choppers don't fly in weather like this. If the PDFs are in this area and they knew we were here and if they were like the VC and NVA of Vietnam, this is when they would like to fight us.

Then I heard the crackle of the radio nearby. I listened as my radioman answered it, sitting on his pack under his poncho. He looked over at me saying, "They want to talk to you Gunner. It's the CO." He then held the handset out toward me from under his poncho.

I shuffled over next to him taking the plastic wrapped radio handset and spoke into it, "Echo six, Echo six this is Echo two actual, over."

"Echo two this is Echo six. Be advised that all birds are grounded and weather reports rain for the next couple of days. Do you have enough chow and ammo for now? Over." asked Lt Norton. "Echo six this is Echo two. That is affirmative. Over," I answered.

"Echo two this is Echo six. That's great. Stay at your position until further orders. Echo six out," said Lt Norton.

"Echo six this is Echo two. I copy, out," I answered and handed the handset back to my radioman.

In the afternoon, I walked around the perimeter getting soaked as I checked my men and their positions. Sgt Ewing and I took turns doing this throughout the day. I could tell it was all he could do to force himself out of his hole and walk around in the rain.

Meanwhile, the water in my hole rose to four inches deep.

On Feb 7th, Sgt Ewing stood in the rain looking down the hill. Beside him was Sgt Huebner waiting for him to check his squad's fighting holes and men. Sgt Ewing seemed to be in a daze. But then he snapped out of it and together they moved from hole to hole talking to each man.

At first light on Feb 8th, I struggled out of my foxhole and walked around checking my platoon's perimeter. As I returned to my foxhole, I felt uneasy. We had been here too long. I picked up the radio handset and called, "Echo six, Echo six this is Echo two actual, over."

"Echo two this is Echo six," came the sleepy voice of Lt Norton.

"Echo six this is Echo two actual. I'm requesting permission to move to new position, over," I asked.

There was a long silence before he answered, "Echo two this is Echo six. Obviously, I don't have knowledge of your conditions or the terrain. I leave the decision up to you. But if you get into trouble on the move, I'll be unable to send re-enforcements to you. Over."

"Echo six this is Echo two actual. I understand that. But on the other hand, the longer we stay here the more dangerous it is. Over," I said.

"Echo two this is Echo six. I understand. But stay in contact with us, over."

"Echo six this is Echo two. Roger that. Out."

Quietly, I stood up looking around thinking, "Should I stay or should I move these men in this rain. It was still my decision to make."

But instantly, I knew it had nothing to do with rain. If the PDFs knew we were here, and after seeing the choppers that dropped us off, they would know our strength, the longer we stay in one spot the longer they had to not only build up their strength, but to figure our weak spots and plan their attack. I looked over at Sgt Ewing who seemed to be watching me and I said, "Sergeant Ewing prepare the platoon to move out."

He looked at me in disbelief and then grumbled, "Aye, Aye sir."

The next day I halted my platoon for a ten-minute break. As I sat down Sgt Ewing sat down next to me. As I looked over at him, he took off his helmet in the pouring rain. Instantly the rain ran down his forehead dripping off his nose. He looked over at me with eyes that seemed to bore right through me as he spoke, "Gunner I don't know about you, but I'm sick of this shit. We're getting short on chow. This rain could last for days, even weeks. If we get hit, how long can we last without air support or resupply of ammo?" The veins of his neck were beginning to stand out as he went on to say, "Gunner I'm telling you we gotta get out 'a here."

I looked at him hard and with a threatening voice said, "Sergeant, I've been through this before and we're going to stay out here and do our job until we're relieved."

"Gunner this is crazy," he said looking around and then added, "I'll tell you sir, the men want 'a get out 'a here, too."

Looking him in the eye I said, "Sergeant, it is our duty to stay out here and look for the PDF forces in this area. Doesn't that mean anything to you?"

He looked as if I had slapped him as his lips drew back into a snarl. Then he laughed and stood up, spun around in a rage and walked off.

On Feb 10th, I looked up ahead at Sgt Davis's 2nd squad leading my platoon on point. They entered a flat area with a forest of bamboo and tall grass which closed in over their heads. He halted his squad as he checked his compass, then waved his point team on. Soon, I was walking in pools of water in the rain as I also checked my own compass. As I walked on, the water rose to my ankles. I looked forward, but couldn't see Sgt Davis anymore because of the thick grass. I walked faster passing two of 2nd squad's fire teams until I was beside him and asked, "How you doing Sergeant Davis?"

Again, checking the contour lines on his map, he said, "Sir, it's slow going mostly by compass readings."

Together we sloshed through the tall grass and bamboo as I said, "You're doing fine sergeant. I know it's hard to see more than fifty meters in this grass, rain and mist."

I truly felt I was back in Vietnam.

Later, the point team halted the column while two Marines slipped forward to check out an area ahead.

Again, Sgt Davis and I checked our plastic-wrapped maps. The rain still came down steadily. But we had been wet for so long now it didn't matter or as we used to say in Vietnam, "It don't mean nothing."

My radio man walked up close behind me and said, "Sir it's the CO. He wants to know our location." He handed me the radio handset. Taking the handset from him I looked at the misty hills around us, then I checked the reading on my compass, then my map. Sgt Ewing walked up beside me, chewing tobacco, shifting it from one side of his jaw to the other.

Again, I sighted my compass studying my map. After double-checking myself, I radioed Lt Norton and gave him the grid coordinates off my map of our position.

"Sir, I don't know how you can be so sure where we're at in all this mist?" stated Sgt Ewing.

"You forgot, I learned well in eight years of finding my way through the jungles of Nam," I answered bluntly.

He shifted the tobacco in his mouth again, shrugged his

shoulders turning abruptly walking back down the column.

Then the point team waved Sgt Davis that it was okay to follow them again. So, through the rain we walked again.

The next day as we moved through the rain, I looked back at Sgt Ewing who was three men behind me. Then I looked forward at the men of the 2nd squad leading my platoon. Sgt Davis was just behind his point team. He shrugged his tired shoulders keeping his rifle pointed downward to keep the rain out of the barrel.

I pulled up my trouser waistline wishing I had a dry cigar. Then I thought, "Here I am with twenty-five and a half years in the Corps, and still searching for enemy troops in a rainy jungle. Eight years in Vietnam, from Red Beach up to the DMZ, Hue City west to Laos. All this walking for days in the rain kept taking me back to Vietnam. Then came El Salvador, two tours in Beirut and Grenada, and now the jungles of Panama. Still I thought of my father and uncle back home working their lives away on the family farm. But they're among their lifelong friends and family. It sure can't be a bad life. Still I hope to retire there myself someday. Of course, it was my choice to leave the farm. But I can't explain it to them. I love the Corps and it's been good to me. From private to the youngest sergeant major in the Corps and now I'm one of the senior Chief Warrant Officers in the Corps. I'm paid well; my family is well taken care of and retirement with medical benefits for life.

I shook my head to stop daydreaming. I pulled out my compass and sighted in on the hills around me. My platoon was functioning as one as never before. Maybe it was because they felt just how dangerous our situation could become at any moment, even though we hadn't seen a sign of PDF forces. Their moral was high. Still we were all looking forward to getting back to a rear area to get some dry clothes and hot chow.

Ahead of me, Sgt Davis shifted the weight of his pack higher on his shoulders. Then he looked down at his map. An hour later we moved through a mist as Sgt Davis again sighted in his compass.

On we moved. The rain continued to pour as I took my map out checking it again.

Ahead of me, Sgt Davis moved with his map constantly in his hands.

Again the next day, Sgt Davis's squad was leading the platoon. I was walking about four meters behind him as his squad moved over a little ridge. He walked around a bend in the thick brush and started down a steep slope just out of my sight.

I checked my watch as I rounded the bend and saw him looking back at me. I signaled to him to halt his squad to give them and the rest of the platoon a break.

I sat down in a bamboo patch. As my radioman sat down nearby, I reached out to him for the radio handset. I radioed Lt Norton and gave him our current location the best I could figure it on my map.

Sgt Ewing walked up and sat down nearby on another clump of grass. He leaned back against his pack, propping up his rifle against his shoulder. He looked down at his muddy boots. Then he leaned forward resting his head on his wet arm. He looked tired. He didn't look like the same gung-ho sergeant I had known back at Camp Lejeune. I looked around at what other Marines I could see. They were all exhausted and yet they were waiting for my command to move out again.

"Fuck this shit," I thought to myself. For several minutes I just stared at Sgt Ewing's drooped shoulders. We were out here because it was our duty. This was another dirty job that somebody had to do.

"Fuck it! It don't mean nothing," I said in a whisper, then, laughed out loud.

Tired faces looked at me. I looked back at Sgt Davis who quickly looked away, but smiled.

I stood up looking at the faces on both sides of me. I saw their fear and their exhaustion. But I also saw them waiting for whatever orders I was about to give them.

I looked behind me saying, "Pass the word for first squad to move up and take the point." Then I swung my pack on as Sgt Huebner's 1st squad scrambled to their feet behind me. Soon the 1st squad was walking past me. When they had passed by, I started following them as I splashed through the rain-soaked grass. I was hungry, but God I felt good, my mind and senses seemed as sharp as my K-bar knife. Why, I wondered after all these years? Maybe it was just that old feeling of being with armed men who move as one. I can see the pride in their eyes too. Behind me I looked and saw Sgt Ewing stand up and begin checking the men.

Later, Sgt Huebner's squad moved along the base of a hill. He looked back at me and I could see his confidence.

On Feb 13th, Sgt Davis's squad was on point when they

discovered a ring of fighting holes around a small hill. I moved up along the column with Sgt Davis, to his point fire team who were checking out the holes.

"What d' ya think, sir?" he asked.

I walked along, looking down carefully into the rain-filled holes and sniffing the air. In Vietnam, I had learned to smell that fishy smell that meant Vietnamese where either nearby or had been there. But of course, the rain had washed away any scent of the PDF forces that may have dug these holes. Then I answered, "These are definitely holes dug by a military unit. And if we are the only unit who's supposed to be in this area, I believe they are a PDF unit of platoon size." I looked around at the Marines of 2nd squad standing in the rain and I could see fear in their eyes. This was the first real signs we had found of actual enemy forces out here.

"Move out Sergeant Davis. Now we know the PDFs are out here."

As we began to move, I radioed Lt Norton and reported what we had found.

That evening as the platoon dug in for the night, I noticed, smilingly, that they were digging in a lot deeper than they had the night before. And I, too, was a little more careful as I plotted our position on my map just in case I needed to call in artillery fire.

Meanwhile, the rain continued to fall as we shared the last of our MRE meals. In their holes, the men took turns, huddled staring over their gun sights and waited.

The next evening after another long day patrolling in the rain, we had dug in for the night. But now they were not only tired, but also hungry after twenty-four hours without food.

I stood in my fighting hole as the rain poured down around me. With radio handset in hand, I radioed Lt Norton with my situation report telling him also my men were getting in bad shape and needed food.

Sgt Ewing walked up to my hole and squatted down in front of me. I paused looking into his eyes as he asked, "Gunner are we going to get chow tomorrow?"

"Not unless the rain stops. You should know that," I answered sharply.

"Well Gunner, it just don't make sense to keep us out here now."

I stared at him hard with anger and frustration saying, "Damn it sergeant, we're going to be out here until we're relieved. In the Nam I was with a platoon that went without chow for three days before the weather broke. So just shut the fuck up!" I felt bad instantly. I had lost my temper in front of the troops nearby.

Sgt Ewing looked down at the toes of his boots and said, "I'm sorry sir. Sometimes I guess I say things I shouldn't."

Relieved, I stared at him and said, "It's okay. We're all tired and hungry."

"Yes sir," he said as he stood up and walked away.

I sat down in my hole, troubled with worry myself. I handed the handset back to my radioman as I looked out through the mist.

Two days later the rain suddenly stopped and the sun came out. Three choppers came out and dropped off a platoon from Hotel Company and picked my platoon up and carried us back to our base. At the airfield, LtCol Haring and 1stSgt Bean were there to meet us. As my starved men walked off the choppers, they were smiling and yelled at everybody they saw.

"Hot damn, we're gonna get a hot shower!" yelled L/Cpl Conn.

"The hell with that, I want hot chow. Where's the mess hall," said Sgt Ewing smiling.

I walked up and saluted saying, "Good morning, Colonel."

As my filthy, muddy, ragged Marines yelled for joy around me LtCol Haring answered, "Good morning Gunner. How are you?"

"Well, sir, better now. But we could use some chow, a shower and a place to sleep and in that order."

Smiling he said, "I had the mess hall save breakfast for you, as well as the rest of Echo company as they come in. Have your platoon sergeant have the platoon stack their gear by the back door to the mess hall."

"Yes sir. Thank you," I said.

A little later, Sgt Ewing grinned as he led our platoon into the mess hall. The people serving us chow seemed shocked at our condition.

After we ate, we took showers, then Sgt Ewing had our platoon clean their weapons and gear and then we took showers again. Then I went to the officer's tent and went to sleep the rest of the afternoon, all night and into the next day.

It was Lt Vie who woke the rest of us up with news from Hotel Company. It seemed that one of their platoons patrolling through the

Vacomonte Peninsula twenty-five miles west of Panama City was checking out reports of weapons caches in the area. They were looking for anything suspicious when they discovered a hollowed-out cave beneath a cliff. It had been used as a bunker and cache site. The platoon leader had said he was glad there wasn't anybody there because it would have been tough for a full company to dig them out. Whoever built it knew what they were doing. From it they could have covered the entire area leading up to it.

On Feb 18th, another platoon from Hotel Company found a tunnel, which had been used for a weapons cache site. But all they found were several AK-47 rounds, empty grenade containers and squashed fruit.

The next day, LtCol Haring ordered the platoons of Echo Company on convoy security duty. Convoys of some sort went each day from base to base throughout Panama City. We loaded up in Amtracks spread out through the truck convoy with LAV's leading the way and bringing up the rear. As always, the squads of Marines were crowded and cramped in their Amtracks during the jarring ride. It was hot and the dust rose, filling the Amtracks with thick dust. We could sure have used a little of that rain now.

On Feb 21st, Echo Company was choppered back into the jungle to check out a suspected village hideout. After we landed, Lt Norton formed the entire company on line as we moved through the jungle toward the village. He halted the company and ordered me to check out a fence ahead of us. I sent Sgt Davis's 2nd squad up to check it out for booby traps. When he found it clear, the rest of the company moved forward crossing the fence. Beyond the fence we made our way across rough open pastures. Then the pastureland gave way to two high hills that were ringed by thorny brushes. It felt like Vietnam and I knew just how dangerous this mission could become as we searched for the PDF forces. And just like Vietnam, we first sealed off the village. Then Lt Norton and my platoon entered the village and talked to the village families one at a time as my men searched their houses.

Behind one house, Cpl Cunningham found a tunnel entrance. L/Cpl Conn checked the entrance for booby traps. Finding none Cpl Cunningham and L/Cpl Conn lowered L/Cpl Morris down by his boots head first through the one-foot by one-foot opening. L/Cpl Morris had a 9MM pistol in hand and a flashlight in the other.

Although he was spooked when the hole opened up into a bigger tunnel, he found nothing.

On Feb 26th, Echo Company was again rotated out of the jungle and back to the base, tired, dirty, but not as hungry as the last time. Again, we had failed to find PDF troops. But LtCol Haring had steaks and beer waiting for us. After eating, we cleaned our weapons, took hot showers and put on clean camouflage uniforms.

I lay down on my rack in the officer's tent and drifted off to sleep. It was after midnight when I woke up. I got up and walked out pushing the tent flap back out of the way.

Outside, clouds were drifting past the moon. I sat down in the dirt enjoying the quiet and cool night. After about an hour, I returned to my cot and instantly went back to sleep.

By Feb 28th, my platoon was back out on patrol. Sgt Davis's squad was out front on point when suddenly one shot rang out. Sgt Davis's head jerked back as he spun backwards to the ground. The 2nd squad opened fire as one, at the hill in front of them as they spread out. Sgt Ewing rushed forward past me to Sgt Davis's side as I grabbed the radio handset and ordered Sgt Huebner to bring his 1st squad up on our left flank. Sgt Ewing pulled Sgt Davis by the collar of his flak jacket back behind a tree as a corpsman joined them. Then I ran over to check on him and found Sgt Davis holding his head smiling. Sgt Ewing looked up at me smiling as he spoke, "Hit his helmet sir. He's fine, just a little headache. Lucky son-of-a-bitch."

Then with two squads on line, I had them sweep forward up over the hill from where the enemy fire had come, but we found nothing.

By March we learned that or battalion XO Maj George back in Camp Lejeune had been promoted to lieutenant colonel and had been transferred. A Maj Arguedos had replaced him.

On March 6th, a platoon from Hotel Company reported heavy enemy contact. Lt Norton gathered us platoon leaders around a map, studying the area were the fight was going on.

I was drinking MRE coffee from my canteen cup. As usual it wasn't very good, but it was hot.

He pointed to the map saying, "Here the platoon found a well-used hard packed dirt road just before dark yesterday. At 0200 this morning one of their squads ambushed a small enemy force killing one armed black shirted PDF. After sunup they swept the area, finding a large cache of weapons."

"This means we'll probably be sent out," I mumbled.

"Yes, we'll be on standby alert now. So, prepare your platoons gentlemen," he said looking right at me.

"How many weapons did they find sir?" asked GySgt O'Malley

"The report from Colonel Haring says the cache is a large one. There're light machineguns and RPG's, all brand new, still wrapped in cosmoline from the factory. We're talking twenty to thirty cases," answered Lt Norton.

"Christ," I said.

"The rest of Hotel Company is moving out to help their one platoon that's in contact. They want to search the area for more caches," said Lt Norton.

That night we slept with our gear ready. Early in the morning, Lt Norton received the mission to have Echo Company choppered into the area and sweep the area parallel with Hotel Company to look for weapons caches or any signs of enemy buildup and destroy anything we find. At the end of his briefing, Lt Norton rubbed his chin saying, "Gentlemen we just might run into some big shit this time. So be careful."

Later as the CH-46 choppers landed, Cpl Cunningham's 3rd squad and I ran out the back down the ramp and across the clearing as the squad spread out through the rotor blasted tangled grass. Then I dived into the thicker jungle and lay still listening as the rest of my platoon came in and spread out into a 360 circle as we secured the landing zone for the rest of Echo Company to land.

I rolled over behind a tree and looked back across the LZ. I pulled my map from my left leg cargo pocket.

Sgt Ewing knelt down beside me saying, "Well so far so good sir."

"Sergeant, I have a feeling we're gonna see some action this time," I said more to myself then him.

"The last time you said that all we got was rain," said Sgt Ewing laughing.

I looked at him as I said, "I hope we get rain then."

Soon the rest of Echo Company had landed and Lt Norton ordered my platoon to take the point. I had Sgt Huebner's 1st squad lead off, cutting a thin trail through the solid mass of jungle for the rest of the company to follow in a column. Like ants, we followed each other. The jungle closed in overhead cutting out the light. I hadn't seen anything like this since Vietnam.

Early in the afternoon, Echo and Hotel Companies joined forces. In the evening, each company dug in on different hills. LtCol Haring and his battalion CP group went with Hotel Company.

As my platoon dug in and cut fields of fire, Sgt Ewing and I walked along the platoon line studying the terrain and where the machineguns should be set in, until I was satisfied.

The night passed quietly. The next day both companies swept the jungle separately, but came together to dig in for the night.

I lay back on my poncho in my fighting hole. I looked up at the clear sky. The night air was cool after the heat of the day. I folded my hands behind my head looking at the twinkling stars.

A mosquito flew around my ear. I reached to the band around my helmet and pulled out the green plastic bottle of insect repellent. I twisted the greasy cap off, then squeezed the repellent on my hands and rubbed it in my ears, neck, face and the backs of my hands.

I pulled my dirty poncho liner up around me. As usual, in the field it was starting to smell like me. I closed my eyes as I began to drift off. Like so many other times I was once again far from home in a far-flung country on the outskirts of the world. Nearby, I could hear the radio humming, which was sitting between me and my radioman who was on watch.

First, I felt the sudden movement, and then I heard the radioman whisper into the radio handset. I opened my eyes as the radioman reached over and touched my shoulder and whispered, "Gunner the listening post from second squad's got movement!"

I sat upright blinking and whispered, "Let Lieutenant Norton know."

"Aye, Aye sir," he answered.

I looked at my watch. It was 2013 as I muttered to myself, "Damn they've found us early." Then I thought, "This must be the main PDF force if they are probing a Marine company."

Meanwhile my radioman radioed Lt Norton with what was going on and then got back with the listening post. Then he whispered, "They're closer, sir."

"Make sure first and third squads are on full alert," I ordered.

He radioed the rest of our platoon and then he radioed the listening post again. Then he whispered to me, "They're within twenty meters of the listening post sir."

"How many?" I asked.

"At least two men moving toward our lines."

"Are they sure they're men and not animals?"

"Men sir." Then he added, "The movement has stopped."

I reached for my rifle checking the magazine. I shuddered remembering what it was like to be on a listening post back in 1965 in Vietnam.

We waited for half an hour, but the listening post had heard nothing else.

I took a deep breath knowing it was going to be a long night.

It was 0012 the next morning when suddenly the WHAAMP of an explosion split the night. I came awake instantly throwing my poncho liner off me as I sat up.

"Grenade! Grenade!" someone yelled.

"Get on the hook and find out what happened," I whispered to my radioman. He made the call as I listened to the quiet around us.

Then my radioman whispered, "First squad sir."

"What happened?" I asked.

"One of the fighting holes had a man right in front of them and they threw a grenade at him."

"Call Lieutenant Norton and tell him what happened," I ordered my radioman. Then I looked at Sgt Ewing saying, "I'm going to check out first squad."

I crawled out of the hole and slowly and carefully moved up to 1st squad's positions and found Sgt Huebner.

"Did your man see a man?" I asked.

"No, they heard him. They were still shaking when I checked them," he answered.

"Did you hear anything?" I asked.

"No sir, but I wasn't in their hole when they were hearing it."

"Did they say what it sounded like?"

"Like a man low crawling through brush."

I listened again myself, but all I heard were the night sounds of the grass rustling in the breeze.

"I believe they heard something, Gunner. But these dark moonless nights are spooky," he whispered as I strained my eyes looking into the black night. Then he added, "They asked me to let them fire a flare, but I said no."

"Good thinking, sergeant. That would've just exposed our

positions."

"Gunner! Did 'ya hear that!" he whispered.

I bent forward listening to the night sounds, but then suddenly I heard a different sound. Adrenaline suddenly flowed through my veins as I heard again the sound of cloth being snagged by brush. Then came the sound of a shoe scrapping against stones. As the shuffling came closer, I nodded to Sgt Huebner. We both pulled grenades out of our flak jacket pockets. I carefully pulled the pin on my grenade with my left hand, as I held the spoon down firmly against the grenade with my right hand. Hearing the movement again, I released the spoon and it popped free. I counted to myself one, two, three as I cocked my arm back and tossed it toward the movement.

It exploded in the air with a WHUUMPFF followed by silence; even the night sounds had stopped. I felt my heart beating as we waited.

Fifteen minutes passed with nothing happening and the night sounds slowly returned and I returned to my fighting hole.

When morning came, I had Sgt Huebner take a fire team out and search the area in front of his squads fighting holes. I wasn't surprised that they found no bodies or blood. I had been through this before in Vietnam.

Throughout the day as Echo and Hotel Companies swept through the jungle, LtCol Haring was always on the move constantly checking not only the company CP groups, but the many platoons and at times even squads.

On March 11th, Echo Company was leading Hotel Company through the jungle with Lt Vie's 1st platoon on point followed by Lt Novak's 3rd platoon, and my platoon bringing up the rear.

Suddenly, the column stopped and the men of my platoon dropped to one knee facing outboard with weapons at the ready. Kneeling down myself, I looked back at my radioman who was listening to his radio. Then he looked over at me whispering, "They've found a dirt road. It's not on the map sir. It's been freshly graded. It even has guardrails made of bamboo."

At hearing this, Sgt Davis in front of me asked, "Why in hell would a road be out in the middle of this shit?"

"This could be big shit," whispered Cpl Cunningham behind the radioman.

"Oh shit!" said Sgt Davis and then added, "What 'a think Gunner?"

"I don't know," I whispered back.

Up ahead, Lt Norton was moving up along the column through the jungle, which seemed to close behind him. GySgt Simon followed him wiping the sweat from his face with a green towel. He couldn't help but remember how it was twenty some years ago in Vietnam when he, a young lance corporal walked point cutting his way with a machete through jungle. He shuddered thinking of it. But then he thought, "Rank does have its privileges."

Then up in front of them, they saw Lt Vie pointing forward saying, "There it is sir."

Lt Norton and GySgt Simon pushed past him and the jungle opened and there was the road. Again, GySgt Simon shuddered at the sight. Like a flash back he had seen well-maintained dirt roads like this before in the jungles of Vietnam. And just as back then, this one was hidden from air view because the jungle closed in overhead making the road more like a green tunnel.

Back with my platoon, I finally saw the column ahead of us stand up and begin to move forward. I stood up waving to Cpl Cunningham's 3rd squad behind me to move out.

Soon, my platoon had moved up to the road. There we split up into two staggered columns on each side of the road just inside the brush. As I crossed to the other side, I noticed tire tracks heading in the direction we were going.

"Big enough to be a six-by," whispered Sgt Ewing walking on the other side of the road.

My radioman crossed the road behind me listening to his radio as he walked.

I suddenly felt conscious of each step I took as sweat ran down the back of my neck. I drank from my canteen as I felt I was starting to drag. I found myself frightened and thought, "Maybe forty-two is too old to be doing this grunt shit."

As I looked around at my young Marines near me, they seemed to feel something too, because they all had their thumbs on the safety switches of their weapons.

Suddenly up ahead we heard Kak, Kak!

"AK forty-seven!" someone ahead of me yelled as all of us dropped for cover.

Then a Marine machinegun opened up returning fire.

I quickly looked up and down both sides of the road as far as I could see making sure my men were facing outboard.

I listened to the firing up ahead of M-16s, machineguns and AK-47s, which grew intense for a few seconds and then slowed down and stopped.

I looked behind me at my radioman listening to his radio. Then came the Kak, Kak, Kak sounds of Ak-47 fire closer this time along the left side of the road where I guessed Lt Novak's 3rd platoon was.

"What the shit is happening?" yelled Cpl Cunningham.

Up ahead I heard the bloop sound of a grenade launcher being fired followed by the explosion and more rifle fire.

I crawled back to my radioman and took the handset from him to listen myself. I could hear Lt Novak saying, "We saw black-shirted armed men moving off to our left and I gave the order to open fire."

Then I heard Lt Norton say, "Break, break, Echo two actual this is Echo six, over."

"Echo six this is Echo two actual," I answered over the radio.

"Echo two actual this is Echo six. Move your platoon up and sweep to your left. Copy?" asked Lt Norton.

"Echo six this is Echo two. I copy. Out," I answered. Then I handed the handset back to my radioman saying, "Call the squad leaders, have them bring the troops from the right side of the road to this side. Then call Hotel Company and ask them to move up and take our place in the column."

"Gunner, the skipper is calling Hotel now."

"Good," I said smiling.

"Come on let's go!" yelled Sgt Ewing as he moved the Marines over from the right side of the road.

Then by squads, I moved my platoon to the left. As one squad dropped to the ground another one moved forward.

"I wish I knew what is going on," said Cpl Cunningham.

As my platoon moved in squad rushes through the jungle I yelled, "Slow it up men! Gun teams be ready!" I realized I was bent over like an old man as I moved just behind Sgt Davis's squad. But I felt safer away from the road.

"Be careful of an ambush!" I yelled.

Then we heard the Pop, Pop, Pop sounds of mortars leaving a

tube in the distance. The whole platoon froze as one, listening.

"Incoming!" someone yelled and we dived for cover. I hit the ground, pushing my face into the dirt and leaves. I slapped my hands over the back of my neck with my elbows tight against my face. Seconds dragged by as I waited for the explosions. "Dear God don't let them hit us." Then came the crunching sounds of explosions one after another close by. Sweat ran in my eyes stinging them as the last shell exploded. I jumped up yelling, "Move out! Now! Before they adjust!"

My platoon ran forward with Sgt Ewing and I pushing and kicking the slower ones.

Then again, we heard the Pop, Pop, Pop of more mortar shells leaving the tube.

Again, we dived for cover as I prayed, "Dear God don't let them hit us."

But these exploded behind us.

I yelled, "Keep going second platoon!"

Forward they went with Sgt Ewing pushing them as we all listened for more sounds from the enemy mortar tube. But then a different sound caught the ear of Cpl Cunningham. Instantly in one motion, he dropped to one knee and raised his right fisted hand in the air to signal his squad to halt.

Over the radio my radioman learned and reported to me that 3rd squad had heard a man moaning ahead of them. I ordered the rest of my platoon to halt.

Cpl Cunningham felt that someone was very close up ahead. He whispered to L/Cpl Conn, "Take your team and check it out and we'll cover you."

Together L/Cpl Conn's fire team slowly crouched as they moved forward.

L/Cpl Morris stopped and began crawling silently twisting his way through the brush. Seeing this, L/Cpl Conn waved for the rest of his fire team to halt. As they waited, they watched L/Cpl Morris glide forward like a shadow through the brush. Suddenly, he heard a sound just ahead of him. He stopped and holding his rifle in one hand he used his other hand to part the brush slowly in front of him. He cursed this thick jungle to himself. Again, he heard the sound and then he saw the black-shirted man lying on his side, back to him in a pool of blood.

L/Cpl Morris looked around slowly but saw no weapon or any other PDF forces. Then he waved for the rest of the fire team to move up. L/Cpl Conn moved the rest of his fire team up in a wide circle around the wounded PDF as they checked for an ambush or booby traps. When he felt secure L/Cpl Conn stood up straight with his finger on the trigger and called out to the PDF. The PDF looked up suddenly in fear, but then uttered in plain English, "Corpsman."

"Son-of-a-bitch calling for our corpsman!" spat L/Cpl Conn as he waved back to Cpl Cunningham that he could bring up the rest of their squad. Then he said, "Lance Corporal Morris check him out for weapons."

Again, the PDF moaned and said, "Corpsman."

Cpl Cunningham then called me on the radio reporting the capture of a prisoner.

As L/Cpl Morris searched the PDF for a weapon, the wounded man motioned for water.

L/Cpl Morris unsnapped his canteen cover and pulled his canteen out. The PDF tried to sit up, but the movement caused him pain and he lay back down groaning. Cpl Cunningham could see blood shining through the black shirt as it spread. As L/Cpl Conn covered him, L/Cpl Morris laid his rifle down a few feet away and gave the PDF a drink. The man drank quickly as the water spilled down his chin.

Meanwhile, I moved up to 3rd squad to check on the prisoner myself. From behind me my radioman said, "Gunner, first platoon just reported finding a large cache of food. Before I could answer the enemy mortar, fire started up again.

Even though these shells weren't hitting close to us, my men began digging in.

I dropped to one knee reaching behind me for the radio handset and said, "Echo six this is Echo two actual, over."

"Echo two this is Echo six, over," answered Lt Norton.

"Echo six this is Echo two. Be advised we have a prisoner WIA. Hit in the left side, over," I said.

There was a long pause as I waited for a response. Then I heard Lt Norton say, "Echo two this is Echo six. Can the prisoner walk, over?"

"Echo six this Echo two. Negative on your last. Over."

"Echo two this is Echo six. Can he be moved? Over."

More mortar shells exploded in the distance as I looked over at the prisoner as the corpsman was bandaging his side as he trembled in pain and asked, “Can he be moved Doc?”

“He’ll be okay,” the corpsman said looking up at me and then added, “We can carry him in a poncho.”

The mortar explosions stopped except for the echoes.

Then over the radio Lt Norton said, “Echo two this is Echo six. If you have to, carry him with you until we can get him medivaced to the rear. Over.”

“Echo six this is Echo two. I copy your last and will do. Out,” I answered.

Later in the day, the prisoner and the captured food was choppered back to the base.

By March 13th, I was struggling as we continued the sweep through the jungle. My pack seemed to be getting heavier and heavier. It seemed it was taking all my strength to keep going. I wondered if it was my age of forty-two or what?

And Lt Norton kept calling me to speed my platoon up.

I wiped the sweat from my eyes as I looked through the brush. I moved up through my point squad until I was with Sgt Huebner who was directing his point fire team.

My mind felt numb from fatigue, as the whole platoon seemed to be struggling also. It was as if I had to will myself to concentrate.

I checked my map and compass again and again as I plodded along like a zombie as I grabbed at branches to pull myself along.

Then the column halted and the men dropped where they stood rolling back on their packs. I stood holding on to a tree making sure every other man was facing in a different direction and alert. I saw some of the men weren’t facing outboard and not seeing Sgt Ewing I started trudging back through my platoon to correct them myself. I ran my hand up along the pack straps to ease the pack on my shoulder.

My anger pushed out the fatigue as I cursed my men who were letting their guard down. I found Sgt Ewing sitting down with his head in his hands and through clenched teeth I said to him, “Get on your fucking feet sergeant and help me square this platoon away!”

He looked up at me sadly and stood up shrugging his shoulders as he began moving back along the column.

I stopped and pulled out one of my canteens. I unscrewed the cap and took a swallow of warm water. I shook my head and took another drink. Then I walked back up toward the front of the column, stopping from time to time to wake up a sleeping Marine.

By 1600, we were climbing the crest of a hill. Like the rest I was low on water and I was struggling to keep from drinking what little I had left.

Then the column halted again. Over the radio my radioman learned that a Marine in Hotel Company was down with heat exhaustion.

After looking up and down my column I took my helmet off and wiped my face with my green towel.

Suddenly up ahead AK-47 fire was heard. Then M-16's from Lt Novak's 3rd platoon returned fire as the firing from both sides grew.

Then my radioman told me that Lt Norton had ordered our platoon to sweep up on the right flank. I yelled for Sgt Ewing to swing our platoon around to the right flank as I felt my adrenaline start to pump.

"What's going on?" he asked.

"An enemy force bumped into third platoon," I answered.

"How many?"

"Don't know. Form the platoon in a skirmish line and move 'm out."

The firing suddenly stopped as I waved my platoon to move out.

Then the 3rd platoon opened fire again giving us a base of fire as we scrambled around their right flank.

Suddenly, I saw the flash of a black shirt moving through the brush toward us. "They're coming right at us!" I yelled as I opened fire with my rifle.

Sgt Huebner swung his rifle up smoothly aiming as he squeezed off three shots at a PDF in front of him who staggered and fell dead.

My platoon, as one, rushed forward firing and the PDF force broke and ran.

Sgt Ewing slowed our platoon down to a walk with weapons at the ready even though there was no PDFs in sight.

Then Cpl Cunningham yelled, "There they go!" He opened fire as nine PDFs ran through low grass toward thicker jungle. The whole platoon opened fire with M-16s, grenade launchers and machineguns. Then Lt Novak's 3rd platoon, moving up on our left, opened up on them, too. Even GySgt O'Malley of weapons platoon walked up holding a machinegun at the hip firing. He held the machinegun firm as his body absorbed the bucking and kicks as red tracers poured out the muzzle. All but one of the PDF's was knocked down as the firing slowed down and stopped.

GySgt O'Malley sat down exhausted from the pent-up tension of continued alertness and after being mortared and the urge to fight the unseen enemy.

Then, I ordered my platoon to halt, waiting for further orders. As Lt Norton moved up, LtCol Haring was on the radio asking what the body count was?

I had Cpl Cunningham's 3rd squad check the area and I was surprised to report to Lt Norton we had found sixteen PDF KIAs and no friendly casualties.

At dusk on the evening of March 14th, our two companies had set in around a hill. I lay back against my pack feeling the deep fatigue flow through me. I felt the total relief of just lying perfectly still. But I knew I should get up and check my men. Finally, I willed myself to get up and check my platoon positions. After that I walked up to our company CP and found Lt Norton and asked, "Lieutenant, you want to check my platoon positions?"

He looked up at me in silence. I could see the exhaustion in his eyes. I waited for an answer as he stared at me, seemingly in a daze until his eyes blinked and he said, "No Gunner, I'm sure your platoon is fine."

"Yes sir," I answered turning to go. But I stopped looking back and asked, "Sir, you all right?"

He glared at me, and then smiled saying, "I'm fine, Gunner."

I turned walking back to my platoon and found Sgt Ewing and gave him my final instructions for our platoon for the night. Then I sat down in my hole. I lay back against my pack for a long time unable to move. I knew I had to eat something. But instead I drifted off to sleep.

The next night at dusk as I had the rest of my platoon dig in for the night, I ordered Cpl Cunningham to send out one of his fire teams to be a listening post.

I had heard them bitching when he told L/Cpl Morris that his fire team had the LP duty.

"Why us?" asked L/Cpl Conn.

"Somebody has to do it and your team is the best I have,"

answered Cpl Cunningham.

Soon, I saw L/Cpl Morris leading L/Cpl Conn's fire team carefully down the path we had just made up this ridge. They were on their way to a position 300 meters in front of our platoon.

Later, L/Cpl Morris found a low spot in the thick waist high brush. He had his fire team settle in there for the night. In a few minutes, it was dark without even a star showing. He had the fire team quickly set out claymore mines and trip flares. This done, he set watches for the night with one Marine awake at all times, one hour at a time.

L/Cpl Conn took the first watch as the other three lay down trying to sleep. He sat up with his rifle across his lap. Exhaustion flooded over him as his aching muscles tried to relax. He radioed my platoon to make sure we had good communication.

Suddenly, he heard movement in the brush. He listened harder as he thought, "Could PDFs be here already?" A cold sweat broke out on his forehead as he waited for another movement or a step, but heard nothing. After about five minutes he began to relax. He sighed looking down at his other fire team members.

Three hours later, L/Cpl Morris was shaken awake for his watch. He opened his eyes sitting up at once. He had only been able to doze on and off and now felt tired. He made his radio check back to my platoon. Then he struggled to stay awake knowing the rest of his fire team was depending on him now just as he had them, when they were on watch. He closed his eyes as his head dropped. "Shit!" he thought shaking his head trying to clear his head. He looked back in the direction where he knew the rest of our platoon was. Suddenly, something moved. His back stiffened as he heard the sound of clothing snagged on brush. He was instantly full awake now as he stared into the night. Then he felt panic as he saw the shadow of a man. His hand fumbled around on the ground next to him as he searched for a grenade. Finding one he picked it up slowly with his right hand, straightened the pin with his left hand. He then pulled the pin letting the spoon fly and tossed it. His heart was racing as he heard the grenade hit the ground and then explode.

Around him, L/Cpl Conn and the rest of the fire team rolled up on their knees with weapons at the ready.

"Incoming or outgoing!" demanded L/Cpl Conn in a whisper.

"Outgoing. They're between us and the company," whispered

L/Cpl Morris.

"Did you get him?"

"Can't tell."

Then they heard clothing brushing against brush in front of them followed by the steps of several people.

Meanwhile, I was asleep when I heard Sgt Ewing say, "Gunner, wake up." Then he touched my shoulder.

"Yes," I said sitting up looking at my watch and finding it was just after midnight.

"The LPs got movement all around them, sir," said Sgt Ewing handing me the radio handset. I listened first to the quiet night, feeling tired. Then I spoke into the handset saying, "Three LP this is Echo two actual. I understand you have movement. How far away is the movement? Over."

"Echo two this is three LP. Fifty meters to our front, now. But it started behind us. Over," whispered L/Cpl Conn.

Hearing the fear in his voice I said, "Three LP this is Echo two. Keep your heads down. I'm calling in mortars. Out," then I said, "Break, break, Echo six this is Echo two actual. Over."

"Echo two this is Echo six. Got ya covered with the Mike Mike's. You make the corrections. Over," answered Lt Norton.

A few minutes later I heard the mortars firing behind us followed by the explosions down the ridge.

"Three LP this is Echo two actual. Give me corrections. Over," I asked.

Again, I heard the fear in L/Cpl Conn's voice as he whispered, "Echo two this is three LP. They're hitting too far. Over."

I took a deep breath to keep myself calm saying, "Three LP this is Echo two, you have to stay calm. Give me corrections in meters. Over."

"Echo two this is three LP. Be advised the shells are thirty meters to the left of the movement. Over."

"Three LP this is Echo two. Fine I got it. Now keep your heads down. Out."

With GySgt O'Malley listening on his radio he gave the corrections to the mortar crews and they were firing again.

"Three LP this is Echo two actual. How's that? Over."

"Echo two this is three LP. Right on target. Over." I could hear the relief in L/Cpl Conn's voice.

"Three LP this is Echo two. Stay low I'm going to fire one more salvo. After that you listen again. If you hear anything call me and we'll do it again. Over."

"Echo two this is three LP. I copy. Over."

"Three LP this is Echo two. Out," I said and tossed the radio handset back to my radioman. I lay back exhausted. Then I forced myself up and I climbed out of my hole. Bending low I walked along my platoon positions checking my men. Then I returned to my hole and allowed the exhaustion to flood over me again and I went to sleep.

The next night, mortars exploding in front of Lt Novak's 3rd platoon awakened me. I sat up asking, "What's going on?"

"LP from 3rd platoon had movement tonight," answered Sgt Ewing whispering.

"Pass the word to go to 100% watch until further word," I ordered.

"Aye, aye sir," he said reaching for the radio handset.

Soon, it began to rain as a fog moved in. All eyes were straining into the darkness.

Then my platoon's LP from Sgt Huebner's 1st squad reported hearing something, but they weren't sure what.

I knew that in this rain and fog the PDFs could walk right into the LP positions before either group knew it.

By 2100 the rain had slowed, but the fog had gotten worse.

Again, the LP from Lt Novak's 3rd platoon reported a lot of movement to their left.

I heard a grenade explode in front of 3rd platoon. A few minutes later another grenade exploded in the same area. I figured it was the LP tossing grenades to keep from giving away their positions.

Suddenly, rifle fire broke out toward the 3rd platoon lines. My stomach knotted up as 3rd platoon returned fire and the firefight increased. Then I heard grenades exploding.

Listening to the radio, Sgt Ewing whispered, "Lieutenant Novak is calling his LP back in."

"I hope it's not too late," I said.

Behind me I heard our mortar tubes being fired adding to the fight.

"LP is adjusting the mortar fire," whispered Sgt Ewing.

Then more mortar shells exploded in front of 3rd platoon. Flares were also being fired into the area in front of 3rd platoon. As the flares floated swaying toward the ground, they seemed yellow to me through the fog.

More mortar shells hit in front of 3rd platoon as I felt the ground around me tremble. But when the mortars stopped the rifle fire picked up again.

Then for a while the firing died down, but just past midnight it picked up again. And again, Lt Novak called in mortars in front of him. Then the firing stopped. Two hours later, Lt Norton ordered the whole Company back to 25% alert and I lay back down and went to sleep. In the morning a squad from 3rd platoon searched the area to their front and found some blood trails, bloody bandages, some flesh and bloody torn pieces of black clothes, but no bodies. It was just like fighting the NVA in Vietnam.

The night of March 19th, I was awakened by a blast in front of my platoon. As I sat up Sgt Ewing whispered, "The LP from 1st squad has movement. They tossed a grenade." He listened to the radio and then added, "Gunner, they hear a man moaning from the grenade explosion."

As the moans grew louder into screams, even I could hear them.

Then another grenade exploded.

"They had movement on the other side of them," whispered Sgt Ewing.

Then it became quiet. But just after midnight a long scream floated up from our LP area.

"Gunner, the LP is requesting to come in. They're pretty rattled out there," whispered Sgt Ewing.

"All right, but pass the word to the rest of the platoon that the LP's coming in," I said.

The night was dead silent as we waited. Finally, the LP entered our lines and safety. Like them I breathed a sigh of relief.

Sgt Huebner came back to my hole and whispered, "Sir that LP says they're sure they were followed."

"Thanks sergeant. Tell your men good work," and then I turned toward Sgt Ewing and added, "Report this to Lieutenant Norton and put the whole platoon on full alert."

Sgt Huebner crawled out of my hole heading back to his squad. I settled back deep in my hole. My bowels rumbled as I fought the feeling. This was not the time to have to shit. The last thing I wanted to do was leave this hole. I could almost feel the enemy coming.

As I sat waiting, I felt like I was back in Vietnam.

"What's going on sir?" asked Sgt Ewing.

"I think the PDF have been following us, building up strength. I think they may try us tonight," I answered.

"What do we do?"

"We wait. If they attack, we hold back the machineguns until they get close."

"Do you think they're strong enough to overrun us?"

"Well there's supposed to be a battalion of PDF forces out here. That's why we're out here to find its scattered units. If they can join together as one against our two companies it could be a hell of a fight."

"What do we do if they break through?"

"We stay in our holes and kill anything that moves outside."

"Then what?"

"We call in mortars on our own positions." I closed my eyes and prayed to myself, "Dear Lord keep me alive through this night and help me make the right decisions to keep my men alive."

Later I looked at my watch. It was 0420. I thought of Marty. I could almost feel her naked body against me, her lips kissing my face.

Then I heard the pop of mortar shells being fired in the distance. Sgt Ewing and I looked at each other as the mortars exploded just beyond Echo Company's perimeter. Then the PDF's adjusted their mortar tubes and they walked the explosions right in on top of us.

I felt the shock waves from the explosions. The blast slammed me, jarring my bones. The ground shook as shrapnel flew overhead.

I got on the radio and called my squad leaders and told them to be ready to fire as soon as the mortars stopped. But hold their machinegun fire.

Suddenly the mortars stopped, but then there were different explosions followed by the whistle and flash of RPG's.

"Get ready!" I yelled over the radio to my squad leaders. Then in front of us, the enemy started yelling as they fired. I could hear their leaders blowing whistles.

Sgt Ewing yelled, "Get up! Get ready! Here they come!"

Then like black ghosts from my past they rose up out of the smoke and fog coming toward us like a wave. They were running bent low firing wildly from the hip.

Then our mortar flares popped overhead lighting the night up like day. The whole Marine line seemed to open up at once.

"Fire the machineguns!" I yelled over the radio. With long machinegun bursts of orange tracers, the bullets hit along the human wave. The black shirted men fell, some slammed backward, others spinning sideways. Some grabbed their chest and stomachs and stumbled falling.

Grenades were tossed back and forth exploding.

The black wave staggered to a stop as more fell. Some tried to run to the sides, but bullets ripped into their sides and backs knocking them down too. Then the wave just stopped. I could see bodies lying in the brush and hear men moaning. Both sides were still firing, but at a much slower rate.

The men of my platoon stared out over the bloody ridge.

Sgt Ewing was looking at me with relief, but was still tense. I yelled at him, "Check the men. Get more grenades ready and ammo. There may be another wave coming!"

Even before he could move, we heard the whistles again.

"Here they come!" I yelled.

"I can't believe this shit," said Sgt Ewing as the second wave of black shirted PDF's came running bent low firing toward us. A man was out in front waving them on with a machete. A machinegun team from Sgt Davis's 2nd squad opened up as orange tracers ripped into the machete swinging man's body cutting him in two. I heard a Marine fire a LAAW from Sgt Huebner's 1st squad. I watched its white sizzling light as the rocket hit the wave exploding in a blinding flash, which opened up a huge hole in the wave of men. The rest of the wave dived for cover into the brush twenty meters away.

"My God!" cried Sgt Ewing as we watched another wave run right over the first wave as they gave them covering fire. I automatically pulled my K-bar knife out of its scabbard and stuck it into the side of my hole.

"Enemy in the perimeter!" someone yelled from Sgt Huebner's 1st squad's area.

Then over the radio Sgt Davis warned me that enemy troops had broken through between the 1st and 2nd squads.

Somehow, they must have probed and found a weak spot between the two squads. How in hell had I missed that?

Then I saw a man in black carrying a satchel charge running bent low, his head moving back and forth looking for something, probably a good target. As I raised my rifle the man in black saw me and turned running right at me. I flipped my M-16 rifle on full automatic without even thinking. It was like so many other times before, it was kill-or-be killed. I pulled the trigger firing a short burst.

The bullets hit him spinning him backward five feet. Sgt Ewing stood in our hole next to me staring as if amazed. I grabbed him by the shoulder pulling him down into the hole as the man in black exploded.

I grabbed the radio handset yelling, "Echo two one and Echo two two this is Echo two actual. You have to plug the gap between you now!" Then I stood back up looking around. The wave was still coming as another LAAW rocket exploded in a blinding flash among them. Marine bullets were hitting them as I saw machinegun fire rip off the head of a man dressed in black. Then the 2nd wave seemed to disappear.

We waited reloading weapons for the next wave. Marines on the line moved their weapons back and forth across their fronts searching for targets. But nobody else was coming at us. We could hear moaning out in front of us.

Then Marine mortars began falling all around our perimeter. As we sat in our holes Sgt Huebner radioed me saying the gap between the two squads had been plugged.

I could see the relief in Sgt Ewing's face as he whispered, "We're gonna make it."

"Thank God," I said.

Later I watched dawn break as tears filled my eyes. I had survived yet again. We had been lucky. I had only four men wounded.

As soon as it was light enough to see, the choppers came in to pick up our wounded and bring us more ammo and chow.

When the fog cleared, LtCol Haring had Echo Company sweep the area around the perimeter. As we carefully searched the bloody area, we found a few bodies close to the perimeter. I ordered my men to shoot the bodies. I didn't want to take any chances and they were in no mood to take prisoners anyway. Inch by inch we searched the area. I passed two dead PDF's shot in the face. The backs of their heads blown out. Most of the bodies had been dragged away by the enemy. The bodies we did find were all near the perimeter. Further out, all we found were bits of clothes, gear and flesh hanging in the brush. In the end we sent thirty-seven PDF bodies back to the rear. I figured we probably killed at least a hundred more.

Both companies swept through the jungle the rest of the day without enemy contact. At night we dug in for the night and waited, but had a quiet night.

The next morning, March 21st, two new companies were choppered out by Col Doyle to relieve us. Both Echo and Hotel Companies were flown to the rear for a rest.

In the rear, after cleaning our weapons, we got our first shower in fourteen days.

Four days later, Lt Norton was called to the battalion CP. When he returned, he had orders for Echo Company to be ready to return to the field within the next forty-eight hours.

But forty-eight hours later we were still waiting. But waiting with two hot meals a day, showers and a cot isn't bad.

The evening of March 28th, I was drinking a beer in the staff and officers club with GySgt Simon.

From the doorway I heard Lt North's voice, "Gunner Cord."

"Yes sir," I said turning around.

"Colonel Doyle is at the battalion CP. He wants to speak to all the officers of Hotel and Echo Company's. ASAP."

"All right, sir." I said following him out the door. I headed for the battalion as Lt North went in search of other Echo Company officers.

I walked into the battalion headquarters building and down the hall to the briefing room. There I found Col Doyle, LtCol Haring, Lt Norton and the captain from Hotel Company. They paid no attention to me as I took a seat.

"We've got to wrap this thing up," said Col Doyle

"I know. But the civilians are afraid to tell us where the PDF forces are. They're scared to death of them. They figure they'll still be here after we're gone," answered LtCol Haring.

"Listen Tim, both South America and our congress are watching us. They want results and fast. Congress wants us out of here by June. With the Berlin wall torn down and communism falling apart in Europe, they're already talking about major cut backs coming in the military and this show is costing big bucks down here."

"I know sir, we're doing the best we can with the Intel we have," said LtCol Haring.

Col Doyle stared at him with hard cold eyes.

I watched as both men stood staring at each other, then they heard the noise of the other officers entering the briefing room.

Then LtCol Haring faced us saying, "Take your seats gentlemen. Colonel Doyle is here to brief us on our upcoming operation." Then he sat down as Col Doyle walked over to a chart and map board. He began explaining how the operation had been going since we were in the rear. Just today eight PDF troops had been captured.

My mind drifted away because I had heard this kind of bullshit many times before.

By March 30th, we were back in the jungle. I watched the sun come up bright and clear. I looked around thinking, "Like the Nam this place was beautiful and green."

Then men of my platoon seemed bored as they began to eat MRE meals, write letters or clean their weapons. I sat back in my hole and started fixing myself a cup of coffee.

The morning of April 10th, I woke up blinking in the sunlight and feeling warm wrapped up in my poncho liner. I rolled the poncho liner back off me.

"Good morning Gunner," said Sgt Ewing.

I grunted at him smiling as he ate, spooning chow from an MRE bag.

I opened my pack, searched and pulled out my own MRE meal.

Holding out his canteen cup toward me he said, "Want some coffee sir?"

"Sure, thanks," I answered taking the canteen cup and sipping the hot coffee.

I noticed my radioman listening to the radio. Then he looked toward me saying, "Sir, Lieutenant Norton wants all platoon leaders on the hook." He then flipped the radio handset to me. Sgt Ewing leaned toward me wondering what was up because it was unusual for Lt Norton to call all of us first thing in the morning.

As I placed the handset to my ear, I heard Lt Novak say, "Three actual here."

Then I said, "Two actual here." Followed by Lt Vie's voice,

"One actual here."

"Echo one, two, and three this is Echo six. Battalion just called and Hotel Company had heavy contact last night south of us. Saddle up and be ready to be picked up by choppers in ten minutes. Over."

"Echo six this is Echo two. I copy. Out." I tossed the handset back to my radioman saying. "Call the squad leaders. Tell them to pack up and be ready to be choppered out of here in ten minutes. Expect to land in a hot LZ."

Sgt Ewing stared at me stunned. Then he tossed his coffee away and the three of us began throwing our packs together.

"Here we go again. I knew things were going too good," grumbled Sgt Ewing.

Soon, around us our platoon was rushing to pack and check their weapons. They were excited, but deadly serious in their preparations.

Right on time, the CH-46 choppers arrived picking up Lt Vie's 1st platoon first, followed by Lt Norton's Company's CP group, then my platoon followed by 3rd platoon.

When we landed, I was just as glad it was a cold landing (not under enemy fire). Then Lt Norton called us platoon leaders together. He told us Hotel Company had attacked PDF forces on a hill yesterday afternoon. This time they were well dug in and threw Hotel Company back. During the night the PDF's had attacked Hotel Company and even got into their lines. Now Echo Company was ordered to attack the hill.

I returned to my platoon and gathered my squad leaders together and passed the word to them. As the word was then passed to their squads, I could feel the tension rise, as the men grew quiet.

Soon Echo Company was moving through high grass on line.

"I don't like this Gunner. There's no cover here," said Sgt Ewing.

"Spread the men further out," I ordered worrying about enemy mortar fire as I looked at the hill in the distance.

Then Marine mortar fire opened up on the hill. I squinted in the bright sunlight as my mind raced thinking of the many things that could happen and how I would react. I took my glasses off quickly wiping the sweat from my eyes. I was thinking of the coming battle and of past battles.

Soon Echo Company was at the base of the hill as Marine

mortars exploded around its top.

Then we started up the hill, climbing and pulling ourselves forward.

"Move it! Keep going!" I yelled pushing my platoon up.

From the top of the hill the enemy opened fire and the whole company returned fire.

Behind me, I heard GySgt Simon and Lt North yelling at the other platoons, driving them forward. I looked back at GySgt Simon. His face now was the grizzled hard face of an old man with deep sun wrinkles around the eyes with a touch of gray hair at his temples. He had become old in uniform like me at forty-two.

Around me my platoon was screaming like wild Indians as they charged up the hill.

"Push on! Push on!" I yelled through sweat spraying lips. I could hear GySgt Simon's voice yelling, "Go! Get some! Get some Echo!"

Sweat was pouring down my face and off the tip of my nose and my legs were aching and we were only half way up the hill. The going was tough in the high grass.

But then suddenly we hit the top in a screaming mass firing. Marines jumped in the PDF's fighting holes fighting hand-to-hand. I was exhausted physically as I tried to keep control of my platoon. As the fighting ended, Lt Norton ordered my platoon to move down the other side of the hill.

I in turn yelled, "Sergeant Ewing get the platoon moving down the other side of the hill and be prepared for a counterattack."

Moving off the top of the hill the smoke from the mortar blast stung my eyes.

Suddenly a machinegun opened up as bullets flew everywhere.

Sgt Ewing and I grabbed and pushed our men into position.

"Take cover sir, before you get hit!" screamed GySgt Simon in concern behind us on the hill.

I then heard a thud nearby and then a grenade exploded. I dropped to the ground crawling around and talking on the radio moving my squads into even better positions. Around me my platoon crawled or moved in individual rushes into positions.

Marine machineguns opened up supporting us then.

I pulled a grenade out of my flak jacket pocket. I rose up on one knee pulling the pin. I tossed it down the hill yelling, "Get some!"

Standing up, I fired my M-16 rifle from the hip. My platoon rose up around me and charged down the hill screaming wildly and yelling, "Kill! Kill! Kill!"

They moved in fire team rushes, covering each other, firing and throwing grenades. They were doing with precision what they had been trained to do.

Further down the hill, through drifting smoke, I could see more men in black shirts moving up toward us.

I could hear Sgt Ewing yelling to a Marine machinegun team, "Get that fucking gun up here!"

On their stomachs the machinegun team crawled forward toward a better position.

Then he began crawling along the rear of Cpl Cunningham's 3rd squad. From the right he suddenly saw movement. Men in black shirts were running up on our right flank. Instantly he braced his elbows in the ground moving the rifle into his shoulder and braced his knees and toes of his boots into the ground. He fired a quick burst into them. One PDF's rifle seemed to explode as the bullet hit him.

Cpl Cunningham looked to his right seeing the PDFs coming. He spun around firing into them also.

L/Cpls Conn and Morris also turned firing. But the PDFs kept coming. Then the Marine machinegun team in their new position swung their machinegun around pouring bullets into the enemy.

Cpl Cunningham fired quick burst ripping a PDF in half.

"Hold your ground!" I yelled. Looking around and behind me I was glad to see more of Echo Company moving down to support us. Then I heard the pop of Marine mortars being fired behind us, and the shells started exploding twenty meters down the hill ahead of us.

I began crawling along my platoon line checking my men. They were holding their own as the battle grew in fierceness. Bullets cracked around me as I screamed a rebel yell turning it into a recon growl. Then the men around me started yelling curses and howls. The enemy firing seemed to slow.

"Kill the mother fuckers!" screamed Sgt Ewing.

"Let's go get some!" I yelled standing up firing.

As one, my platoon rose up charging forward, firing and throwing grenades. But the PDFs were still coming as both sides fired like mad.

To my right a Marine fell with blood squirting from his throat.

I screamed again as I ejected an empty magazine and rammed in a full one. I charged straight down the hill firing. A PDF stopped and turned to run as I shot him down.

Another PDF appeared right in front of me. I swung the rifle barrel slashing him across the face knocking him down. I stepped over the body firing into his chest. Then right next to me L/Cpl Morris fired calmly killing a PDF ten feet away from me.

I looked over at him. I had never seen his eyes so hard and defiant as he smiled.

"Slow up Gunner. You shouldn't be this far forward. We don't want to lose you," pleaded L/Cpl Morris looking me in the eyes as the battle raged around us. I thought, "I may die here, but I'll die with a band of brothers."

Now the rest of my platoon slammed into the PDFs like tigers.

"Kill the bastards!" yelled Sgt Ewing.

L/Cpl Morris covered me as I tossed a grenade. After the explosion he rushed forward firing from the hip knocking PDFs down.

A grenade exploded and shrapnel zinged against the side of my helmet as sweat ran down my face. I quickly wiped my eyes.

I heard a thud nearby as L/Cpl Conn yelled, "Grenade! Watch out!"

I dived away from where I had heard the thud sound; hit the ground rolling further away as it exploded sending shrapnel zipping through the brush. I looked up through the smoke with gritted teeth yelling, "Shit!"

I shook my head flipping sweat in all directions. Then a man in a black shirt appeared in front of me with wide-open eyes. I set up on my knees firing from the hip blasting the man backwards. Then I saw L/Cpl Morris searching for me and together we charged forward firing, covering each other as we tossed grenades.

My whole platoon worked in fire teams as all of Echo Company surged forward on line screaming as we killed everything in our path.

"Go! Go! Get some!" yelled GySgt Simon off to my right side.

"Kill the mother fuckers!" yelled Sgt Ewing.

I dived for cover behind the body of a dead PDF. I fired covering L/Cpl Morris as he jammed in a full magazine into his rifle. Then he covered me as I changed the magazine in my rifle. Then I pushed myself up with one hand and my feet kicked me up as I charged, bent low firing from the hip. I could see our bullets tearing through the brush. Then two PDFs appeared in front of me. I saw one PDF swing his rifle toward me just as a bullet from L/Cpl Morris's rifle entered his forehead blowing the back of his head out.

The other PDF was so close I jumped at him thrusting the barrel of my rifle into the man's mouth busting his teeth and then fired a burst of three rounds. His head exploded splattering me in the face with pieces of bone and brains.

Suddenly, we were at the top of the next hill. I kneeled down looking over the top of the hill and waved my platoon up, yelling, "Go on over! Take cover, but be prepared for counterattack!"

My men struggled over the top looking for something else to kill, firing down the hill or at the still warm PDF bodies.

Sgt Ewing jumped down beside me as his knee slipped in the blood of a headless PDF.

Together we slowly stood up looking at each other.

"We sure kicked their fucking ass," he said smiling with blazing eyes.

"Yeah we did Sergeant Ewing," I said as I felt the tension of combat slip away.

He shook my hand saying, "Gunner you're one fight'n mother fucker."

"You did good yourself, sergeant," I said smiling. I thought that maybe now he realized why I had been so hard on them.

Then I reached up, wiping the bits of bone and brains off my face.

From behind me I heard GySgt Simon say, "Gunner are you fucking crazy?"

I turned around smiling and answered, "A leader's job is to lead, Gunny."

"Bull shit and you know you're not supposed to be that far out front. What if you had gotten yourself killed?" he asked with true worry in his eyes.

"Then Sergeant Ewing would've taken over. You must have seen how well he did."

He took me by the arm and walked me away from Sgt Ewing to say, "Damn it, Gunner, they're not many of us old Nam vets left. And I don't want to lose anymore. So be careful. Let these young bucks be the heroes."

"All right Gunny, I'll be careful," I answered realizing maybe for the first time how much of an old friend Gunnery Sergeant Simon really was.

Then he turned to walk away and I said, "Gunny."

He stopped turning back toward me saying, "Sir."

"You be careful yourself," I said smiling.

He smiled and said, "You don't have to worry about me, Gunner. I gave up being a hero a long time ago. Just ain't no future in it."

Then I went around checking my platoon as they dug in for the night. Lt Norton radioed for choppers, which flew in to pick up our dead and wounded.

The night passed quietly. But in my corner of my hole where nobody could see me, my hands had begun to shake with the thought of what I had done this day and the stupid chances I had taken. It had been a long time since I had been in a battle this fierce.

But I felt better when the dawn broke clear and I could see down the hill.

Sgt Ewing was already up and I watched him trudging along the hill checking our platoon line. I smiled thinking he had come a long way in the last month. I knew, now, he could handle my platoon without me.

Soon our whole platoon was busy making coffee or cleaning weapons.

I was surprised when Lt Norton got orders from LtCol Haring for Echo Company to rest in place. But I agreed the troops needed the rest.

At noon, a chopper landed with our resupply of ammo, LAAWs, grenades and MRE's. Sgt Ewing sent Sgt Huebner and some of his men to pick up our supplies from GySgt Simon.

After the supplies were handed out, I walked along my platoon positions talking to each man.

Later by radio, Lt North let us platoon leaders know that LtCol Haring was checking Echo Company's lines with Lt Norton. I sent Sgt Ewing to let our platoon know they were coming.

Soon, I could see them walking along Lt Vie's 1st platoon line. My whole platoon seemed to be watching them come toward us.

I walked down toward the point where my platoon was tied in with Lt Vie's platoon.

"Good afternoon Colonel," I said shaking his hand.

"Good afternoon, Gunner. I take it your platoon is next," said LtCol Haring.

"Yes sir."

"Well Gunner, I understand your platoon took some losses, too. But Lieutenant Norton here tells me you did an outstanding job yesterday."

"Thank you, sir. But these men are the ones that did it, sir, not me," I said waving my arm back toward my platoon as I felt myself stand a little taller with pride.

Then we walked along my platoon positions as he asked me questions about my platoon's actions yesterday. Along the way he shook hands with Sgts Ewing, Huebner, Davis and Cpl Cunningham. He listened carefully as I explained my tactics. As we passed my men, they stood up in their holes watching the three of us walk by. I saw the pride in their eyes.

"Gunner, by the way, I got the word that all of our wounded are doing fine," he said

"Thank God, sir," I said smiling.

Near the end of my platoon I saw Lt Novak standing to take them along his platoon positions.

Once there, LtCol Haring shook my hand and walked on with Lt Novak.

Lt Norton hung back with me and said, "I hear this fight has made news all over Panama, we've got the largest body count so far in Panama of PDFs."

"I guess some things never change. It always seems to come down to the body count," I answered.

He looked at me kind of funny, and then he ran to catch up to LtCol Haring.

The next day, Echo Company was picked up by choppers and flown back to the rear for a rest. Five days later we were back in the bush searching for what was left of the PDF forces. But the rest of April passed quietly with no contact with the enemy. And as the month passed, I felt my platoon was the best ever. With what I had tried to teach them for months and now after weeks of real combat operations under their belts, they had become tough and ready. They were real Marine Infantry now moving as a platoon like clockwork. They moved through the jungle quietly, ate evening MRE meals silently, not smoking or talking. But not just my platoon, also all of

Echo Company had become hunters of men. That night after digging in and checking my platoon positions, I sat in my hole. It felt great being with these men.

The 3rd of May, Sgt Huebner's 1st squad was set in an ambush position. With patience and discipline, they waited silently with weapons at the ready as they had done before. He watched the clear places in the brush. First, he felt them before he actually saw them coming along the trail. He slid the safety off his rifle silently. He waited until the last second, then he blew the claymore mines and the whole squad opened fire. They fired at every moving thing in the kill zone as the enemy screamed, dying as they tried to return fire. Then it was quiet as the dust settled. Again, they lay and waited. Finally, Sgt Huebner sent a fire team forward to check the bodies. They found two dead PDFs.

On May 8th, Echo Company was picked up by choppers with orders to land near a village and search it. As we flew, I concentrated on the lush green jungle below us.

A little later Sgt Ewing tapped me on the shoulder as he pointed to the village coming up.

I pointed out the LZ on my map and then pointed to the ground as I felt the chopper tilt beneath me toward the LZ. Lt Vie's 1st platoon was already landing. I checked my rifle, tapping the magazine as Sgt Ewing waved for Sgt Davis's 2nd squad to get ready. As the chopper landed the 2nd squad and we ran out. Ahead, off to my right I could see Lt Norton with our Echo Company CP group. Sgt Ewing quickly gathered the platoon together on line with the rest of Echo Company, as we started moving toward the village.

My platoon moved up a small bank to the village, which seemed deserted. Lt Norton ordered out flank security as the rest of Echo Company searched the village. By fire teams, my men looked under fire pits, haystacks and in haystacks. From my days in Vietnam I looked for breathing reeds, in wells, false walls and floors. Echo Company found twelve women and five children hiding, but nothing else. When we asked them where their men where they said they had fled into the hills. Brave men, they had to run away and leave their women and children behind.

During the night of May 14, I suddenly heard firing in the distance. I reached for the radio handset and listened to a squad leader in Lt Vie's platoon report they had just ambushed an enemy unit carrying weapons and packs. We waited as the squad checked the bodies. Then he reported to Lt Vie over the radio that they had killed four PDFs, captured four rifles, four packs, but no documents.

On May 15th, Echo Company was picked up by choppers and landed near another village. This time as we advanced toward it, we came under fire.

Quickly, Lt Norton ordered my platoon to lay down a base of fire as Lt Vie's 1st platoon moved off to the right to hit the village from the flank. Once Lt Vie's platoon entered the village, it was over in five minutes. Then I moved my platoon up with 3rd platoon into the village. Sgt Ewing quickly broke our platoon down into fire teams to search the village. Sgt Davis was called over to a hut where his men had found seven dead and wounded PDFs. Being nearby, Lt Norton and Sgt Ewing entered the hut as Sgt Davis began searching the wounded. As he bent down to help a wounded PDF, a grenade rolled out from under him.

"Grenade!" yelled Lt Norton as he dove to the floor grabbing the grenade and as he rolled on his back tossed it out a window where it hit a tree bouncing along the ground exploding.

Sgt Ewing had dropped to the floor also and now looked up under his helmet saying, "Damn, sir, that was close!"

Lt Norton said nothing as he stood up brushing himself off as Sgt Davis stood, his finger on the trigger pointing his rifle at the enemy dead and wounded.

The rest of my platoon went on searching the village even more carefully as the wounded PDFs were made ready to be medivaced.

Echo Company started moving up a hill toward more huts. We were moving through shoulder high brush. We first knew there were enemy troops up there when they started rolling grenades down toward us. They exploded as we pushed up through the brush. Suddenly, GySgt Simon yelled, "Watch out!" as eleven PDFs charged out of a hole just in front of my platoon, firing at us. Sgt Ewing standing next to me fired a burst into them. One PDF swung his rifle toward Lt Norton. Lt Norton fired one round hitting the man in the face. As another one started running across our front, GySgt Simon yelled firing a burst hitting the man who fell rolling to a stop in front of me. Firing was growing all along the hill as the enemy tried to retreat up the hill. Now I could hear Lt Vie's 1st platoon hitting them from the flank.

Then Sgt Huebner's 1st squad moved up toward nine PDFs who had their hands up in surrender, some others were too wounded to raise their hands. Sgt Huebner's squad had the ones that could place their hands behind their heads walk down the hill as a fire team covered them. Other PDFs carried their wounded.

When it was over, Lt Vie's 1st platoon had found six more dead PDFs, three rifles, eight grenades, documents and ten medical kits.

On May 16th, we were on choppers again heading toward another village. As usual I studied my map and the area below.

Soon I felt the chopper bank to the side as it began to land. I checked my rifle, tapping the magazine and touched my K-bar knife. Lt Novak's 3rd platoon was already landing under fire. I felt my heart beat faster. Maybe I was getting too old for this. Too many battles. Then with Cpl Cunningham's 3rd squad, I ran out down the ramp as bullets cracked nearby. I dived for cover and then rolled up on one knee watching my platoon moving.

Off to our right, I saw Lt Vie's 1st platoon down on their stomachs and knees firing.

I saw GySgt O'Malley with one of his machinegun teams moving up as he shouted at them. Overhead, two Cobra gunships were firing covering fire for us from just above the treetops.

I moved my platoon toward a hut as I passed a dead PDF. I moved up closer to one corner of the hut. Then someone fired from the other side of the hut. I dropped to one knee with Sgt Ewing diving to the ground next to me. Sgt Huebner's squad began running around the east side of the hut. Then ten PDFs ran out. Sgt Ewing rolled up on one knee as we opened fire into them. One spun around firing at us as I fired a burst knocking him backwards. Some of the PDFs grabbed their wounded dragging them to cover disappearing into the brush.

Slowly, I moved my platoon forward as we covered each other. As Cpl Cunningham's 3rd squad entered the hut to search it, I noticed a black shirted body lying in the yard, a rifle lying just out of reach of his hands.

A little later, L/Cpl Morris stepped out of the hut and said, "It's clear Gunner."

"Good," I said, moving up, sliding along the wall of the hut. I came to a wooden cellar door. I fired a burst through the door. Then I pulled a grenade as Cpl Cunningham quickly opened it.

"I got it, sir," said L/Cpl Morris as he moved ahead of me with his rifle at the ready. Down into the cellar he went. When he came out, he had found a rifle, a grenade and some documents.

Then Lt Vie's 1st platoon came out of the brush with eleven PDF prisoners.

I then had my platoon search the brush around the hut and they found pieces of equipment, twelve grenades, four rifles and more documents.

The next day, Echo Company was searching another village. Suddenly someone yelled, "Grenade!" As the Marines near me dived for cover, I dropped down to one knee bending my head down on my chest. I saw a black shirted man run out of the brush toward us raising his arm to throw another grenade. I squeezed off a burst hitting him in the chest slamming him backwards into a tree, and then he slid off sideways into the brush. Quickly, I swung my rifle to the left and right, searching for another target.

I hadn't heard the grenade explode, but now I heard Sgt Davis yelling, "Corpsman up!" I turned seeing him bent over a wounded man.

Meanwhile L/Cpl Morris walked up and dragged the PDF I had killed out of the brush and began searching the body. The dead man had a radio on his back, documents in his chest pockets and a pouch containing seven grenades.

Again, someone yelled, "Grenade!" as it came out of a window. We all dropped flat as the grenade hit the ground rolling to a stop between Sgt Ewing and me as it exploded. I tasted dirt as shrapnel ricocheted overhead around us. I rose back up on one knee as Sgt Ewing looked up and around. Sgt Huebner's squad ran past us into the hut.

To my right, Sgt Davis's squad started searching the brush.

I ran up to the hut, moving around the side of it, going around a corner with Sgt Ewing right behind me. Then I heard firing inside followed by a grenade explosion. I slowly turned the next corner to see Sgt Huebner dragging a body from inside the hut. I stepped over the body leaving him in the dirt. Sgt Davis's squad captured three PDFs in the brush and I watched him bring them out with their hands tied behind them. I stopped to watch other Marines kicking at the brush still searching.

It was getting late in the afternoon when we finished searching the village. We moved off up a hill and dug in for the night.

On May 20th, Cpl Cunningham's squad had set in an ambush along a trail near a village. As the village settled down for the night, the Marines were close enough they could hear a woman's voice singing in Spanish, probably to her child. As the village became quiet the jungle became still.

The night became very cool. At 0212 in the morning, Cpl Cunningham noticed a patrol of four armed men coming down the trail toward the village. He had warned his squad not to fire until he did. He watched the PDF point man moving slowly checking the area. He stopped bending down placing his ear close to the ground like an Indian. Then he slowly stood up waving to the three men behind him. Cpl Cunningham flipped the safety off his rifle waiting until the patrol was right in front of his squad. Then he opened fire followed by the rest of the squad and the Marine machinegun team attached to him. All four PDFs dropped spinning to the ground dying.

But just as L/Cpl Morris started to go out and search the bodies, there was more movement up the trail as close to a dozen more armed men were now spreading out on both sides of the trail moving toward them. As Cpl Cunningham quickly shifted his squad around, an enemy machinegun opened fire. Cpl Cunningham radioed me for help, L/Cpls Conn and Morris threw grenades at the enemy machinegun. But it was the Marine machinegun team that silenced the enemy machinegun. Then with the machinegun team laying the base of fire, Cpl Cunningham moved his squad forward in a skirmish line, killing eleven PDFs in the second group, before they broke contact, leaving nine blood trails behind.

Not knowing just how many more PDF troops were out there and knowing he had been lucky, Cpl Cunningham quickly moved his patrol away from the ambush site about a hundred meters, set them in a tight 360 defensive position and waited out the night.

After daylight, when I arrived with the rest of my platoon, we followed the nine blood trails finding seven dead PDFs.

The evening of May 23rd, Sgt Huebner's 1st squad was moving through the jungle to their ambush site. They were moving slowly, watching the area and stopping to listen at times. Suddenly, word was whispered up to him that the rear guard said someone was following them. Quickly, he shifted the first two fire teams around.

As the last of the 3rd fire team passed through them, he saw movement coming through the brush. He waited until the enemy force was right on top of them and then both fire teams opened fire. He emptied his magazine and then tossed a grenade. After the explosion, there was a scream from one of about nine PDF bodies lying in front of them. He could hear voices beyond the bodies in the jungle as the 3rd fire team eased itself around on line with the rest of the squad. There was movement in the brush and then two PDFs crawled out and started dragging the bodies away. There were more voices and movement in the jungle behind the bodies as Sgt Huebner had his squad hold their fire and moved away about a hundred meters and then set in a tight 360. It was quiet for a while, but then they could hear men walking toward them again. Two PDFs walked right up to Sgt Huebner before he emptied another magazine into them. Then six more PDFs came around to hit the squad in the flank, but because of their circled position these men were cut down also. Someone screamed as a grenade exploded in the brush. When it was over, Sgt Huebner noticed his right arm was bleeding. He refused to be treated by his corpsman and instead, again quickly moved his squad a hundred meters and set them in another 360 circle. The rest of the night passed quietly. The next morning, Sgt Huebner was medivaced to the rear, weak from loss of blood. The 1st squad had no NCOs left and none of the lance corporals there, I felt were strong enough leaders to take his place. And with few corporals left in my platoon I moved L/Cpl Conn from 3rd squad to be the squad leader of 1st squad.

The night of May 24th, LtCol Haring was moving Echo and Hotel Companies from different directions to surround a large village. Echo Company crossed a small stream coming in from the north. Quietly, both companies tied in together surrounding the village at 2111. The two companies settled in to wait.

At 2208 firing broke out. Lt Novak's 3rd platoon opened fire when six PDFs leaving the village walked up to their positions. Then there was silence and then more firing broke out from 3rd platoon. And then there was silence again. Over the radio, Lt Novak reported to Lt Norton that 3rd platoon had killed five PDFs including a woman and had captured a wounded PDF, six weapons and some documents.

At 0700 in the morning, we began moving into the village. As soon as we stood up twelve men, women and children without weapons surrendered to Lt Novak's 3rd platoon.

Then L/Cpl Conn's 1st squad killed a black shirted man as he ran along a ditch carrying a rifle.

We swept on steadily searching huts and civilians. Within eighteen minutes my platoon killed eight more PDFs as we moved through the village. But I had two men wounded at the same time. One of my wounded Marines was crying like a baby as they carried him to a clearing to be medivaced.

On May 26th, LtCol Haring had both companies again surround another village during the night. The next day we moved in without a shot fired and captured twelve PDFs with weapons.

The 1st of June, LtCol Haring received the news from Col Doyle that the Department of Defense had decided to reduce the size of American forces in Panama back to its pre-1988 levels. 600 Marines would leave Panama on June 13th. And Echo and Hotel Companies would be part of this number. We also learned that BGen Colyne, our brigade commander back at Camp Lejeune had been transferred. Also, I had the pleasure of seeing Conn promoted to corporal.

But that night, Echo Company was again slipping in around a small village. At midnight we had crossed a river silently. Once we were set in around the village, we settled in to wait. I leaned back against a tree. Lt Norton had passed the order for 50% watch, which meant every other man could sleep.

We would be going home in a few days and as before I wondered if we weren't being withdrawn too soon, before the job was done. But I was proud to be here and of the job we had done.

As the night passed, two squads from Lt Novak's 3rd platoon ambushed two groups of armed men. In all, eleven PDFs were killed and four wounded were captured. Along with their weapons, they found two bags of grenades, wire cutters and demolition cord and fuses.

After dawn we entered the village. As Lt Vie's 1st platoon searched their section of the village one of his men saw an old lady starting a fire under a pot as if the Marines weren't even around. A Marine using his boot pushed the pot and sticks to the side and found a metal trapdoor. He opened the door firing a round down the hole. Suddenly a man in a black shirt with his hands up crawled out of the hole. In the hole they found a rifle and some documents.

On June 3rd, Echo Company landed by chopper north of a village and started sweeping toward it. As we searched the huts, all we found was thirteen old men, women and three young children.

The night of June 4th, Cpl Conn's squad was laying in ambush when he spotted two armed men moving up the trail toward them with packs on their backs.

Fifteen meters from the ambush site, the two men stopped and sat down taking a break. Finally, after about ten minutes they stood up and walked up the trail. But when they were only two meters outside of the kill zone, the point man suddenly dropped down on one knee looking right at where the first Marine in the ambush was laying. Fearing the man had somehow sensed their presence, Cpl Conn opened fire early. He dropped the point man dead, but the second man left the trail running off through the brush without firing a shot. When they checked the black shirted body still holding his rifle, they were surprised to find it was a pretty young girl.

The night of June 5th, a squad from Lt Vie's 1st platoon was moving to their ambush site when they were ambushed. But the ambush was sprung too early and the Marine squad was able to fight their way out of it losing one Marine killed just eight days before we were due to rotate home.

On June 6th, LtCol Haring alerted Echo Company in the morning to be ready to board choppers to go to a village where PDF forces had been sighted.

Later, I looked down from my chopper at the smoke in the LZ. Lt Novak's 3rd platoon had already landed and was in contact with the enemy. My platoon landed, running out of the choppers down the ramps. Marine Cobra gunships were firing at the enemy in front of 3rd platoon. I dropped down on one knee as Sgt Ewing formed our platoon into a skirmish line. One of the Cobra gunships flew low overhead firing into the brush ahead of my platoon. As we moved forward, Cpl Conn's 1st squad found two dead PDFs in the brush. As I moved on, a PDF raised up on one knee firing. As bullets hit around me Sgt Ewing shot him dead.

I yelled, "Into the village! Let's go!"

Another PDF stood up firing at us. Cpl Cunningham fired a burst knocking the man backward out of sight. The Cobra gunship just hung overhead firing at the enemy ahead of us. As my platoon broke out into the open, I saw Lt Novak's 3rd platoon off to my left passing two dead PDFs laying sprawled face down. As my platoon entered the village, I jumped to the side of a hut. Three old women and three young men walked out with their hands up. As Cpl Cunningham waved them to the rear under guard, L/Cpl Morris's fire team entered the hut, but found nothing.

As my platoon went on searching huts, I stepped over two dead PDFs, shooting them again just to make sure they were dead.

Suddenly, a grenade hit my shoulder bouncing off into the street. Instantly, I saw the PDF who had tossed it standing in a doorway. I fired a burst hitting the man in the chest driving him back inside. I then dropped flat hard as the grenade exploded. I rolled up on one knee and another grenade hit the ground next to me. Sgt Davis kicked it away and dived flat as I bent down low still on one knee. Several Marines threw grenades into the hut, from which the enemy grenades had come. I could hear people scrambling around inside. One PDF dived out a window into the street as the grenades started exploding inside behind him. He was shot dead on the ground. Another PDF trying to get out the doorway was blown out into the street, leaving a trail of blood and intestines behind him. As Sgt Davis stood up, I looked at him saying, "Get some people in there and clean it out."

As a Marine fire team ran toward the hut, I saw a rifle and face appear in the doorway. I squeezed off a burst blowing the face apart.

In the hut, my men found eleven documents and two rifles. When it was over, Echo Company had killed twenty-seven and captured twenty-two PDFs. Echo Company only had twelve men wounded.

That evening, Lt Norton received word from LtCol Haring over the radio that in the morning Echo Company would be picked up by choppers and flown to the rear to stand down and prepare to leave Panama for home in seven days. When Lt Norton called us platoon leaders together and passed this welcome news, he also aborted the planned ambush patrols for that night. Only listening posts would be sent out. When I returned to my platoon, I had Sgt Ewing gather the squad leaders, Sgt Davis, Cpls Conn and Cunningham together. They all smiled at the news, but none more than Sgt Ewing.

I don't believe any of us got much sleep that night. But the long night passed quietly.

The next morning Echo Company was flown back to the rear. I

had my platoon clean their weapons first, and then we took showers and got some hot chow and went to sleep.

On June 8th, I had my platoon again clean their equipment and weapons. In the afternoon I inspected my platoon.

On June 9th, Lt Norton inspected all of Echo Company's weapons and equipment.

On June 10th, LtCol Haring inspected both Echo and Hotel Companies.

On June 11th, again both companies stood at attention as Col Doyle passed quickly through our ranks and then told us how proud he was to have had us attached to his command for the last fifteen months. As I stood there, it hit me that this was the longest separation Marty and I had ever had. It was definitely time to go home. I just hoped she hadn't got too use to being without me.

June 12th was a day of liberty for both companies. But a few of us especially the old timers like GySgt Simon and I stayed back and just went to the staff and officers club on base, drinking a few beers, talking of old times and old friends.

On June 13th, Echo and Hotel Companies walked up the gangway aboard the USS Trenton to begin our five-day trip home.

First, I checked the berthing area that Sgt Ewing and the rest of my platoon had been assigned. As always, they would be crowded. But they were clean. Then I found my way to my room, which I shared with Lt Vie. After we put our gear away, we went to the wardroom and I drank three cups of good strong Navy coffee.

As the days passed, we rested eating good Navy chow. Sharing the same room, Lt Vie and I talked as we had never talked before. He was born in South Vietnam in 1966. I told him I had been fighting in Nam a year before he was even born. He was nine years old when his family fled Vietnam in 1975 when the country fell to communism. His father had been an officer in the South Vietnamese Marine Corps. I told him I had been an advisor to the South Vietnamese Marine Corps for two years. He asked me if I knew his father showing me an old faded picture of a young South Vietnamese Marine Corps officer. It brought back a flood of sad memories, but I didn't recognize him. I wondered if his father had known my old friend LtCol Hu and if he had made it out alive. I told him I felt that the South Vietnamese Marines were the best military force the South had had. He smiled and said his father had always said the same thing and that of course they were formed and trained by the US Marines in the fifties. He said from the time South Vietnam fell to the communist and after they left Vietnam his father had never smiled until they landed in the US. Once here his father had tried to join the US Marines with hopes we would yet return to free his country. But they wouldn't take him because of his age. Lt Vie had wanted to join the Marines right after high school. But his father insisted he go to college first, which he did. I told him he was smarter than I had been in my youth, for he had listened to his father as I should have listened to my grandmother and finished high school.

On June 18th, the USS Trenton docked at Moorehead City NC. We walked down the gangway to waiting civilian buses. We formed up into companies and waited to get the order to board the buses.

Finally, GySgt Simon returned with Echo Company's bus assignments. He pointed to the bus my platoon was assigned. Sgt Ewing moved our platoon in a column onto the bus. He and I were the last ones on and we sat down together behind the driver.

As we waited for the rest of the buses to be loaded, the bus driver turned around in his seat and asked, "Where are you guys coming from?"

"Panama," answered Sgt Ewing smiling.

"Panama! I thought that ended the first of the year," said the bus driver surprised.

Sgt Ewing's mouth dropped open as he looked over to me and said, "I guess the people here have no idea what we've been through during the last six months."

"Panama is old history already," I said remembering I had felt this way before.

But when our buses pulled into our battalion area at Camp Lejeune, we knew we hadn't been forgotten here. Maj Arguedos was standing in front of Fox and Gulf Companies formation to honor us. Also, Col Gagush our Regiment CO was there and he shook our hands welcoming us home as we climbed off the buses. And off to the side stood the people we really wanted to see, our wives and children.

As Marty and I walked toward each other smiling, Samantha ran to me, her red hair blowing in the wind and jumped into my arms saying, "Dad am I glad you're home."

"Me too, baby girl," I said hugging her. Of course, she was no baby girl anymore. I couldn't believe how much she had grown while I had been away. It was hard to believe she would be thirteen in a few weeks. Then Marty was there hugging both of us and kissing me. Together arm in arm the three of us walked to our car.

Later that night after making love, I lay back exhausted and glad to be home. Marty rolled over next to me kissing my neck saying, "It feels good to be your arms again."

"I love you," I said.

"I love you, too."

Feeling her naked body next to me I wanted her again, so I pulled her over on top of me.

"You're going to wear me out," said Marty smiling.

"I doubt that," I said kissing her neck.

Usually I would take thirty days leave after a deployment like this one and we would go home to visit with our families. But this time Nat, my oldest son, and his wife were expecting their third child in September. So, I decided to wait and take my thirty days leave in September. So instead, I put in for a ninety-six-hour pass to spend time with Marty and Samantha.

The next day I phoned Lance. From his letters to me and talking to Marty I was surprised and thankful that he had bounced back so well from his terrible wounds. He had been released from the hospital in February and transferred to Henderson Hall in Washington DC.

A GySgt Moser answered the phone.

"Gunner Cord here. Is Lance Corporal Cord there?" I asked.

There was a quiet pause before he said, "Yes sir, he's right here."

When Lance began to talk, I was surprised at how strong he sounded. He told me how the Corps wanted to medically discharge him. But he was fighting to stay in. I told him I was proud of him no matter what happened.

That night I called Nat. But his wife Donna answered. Nat was working the evening shift at the prison in Georgetown De. So, I talked to her instead, which was always a joy. I asked her how she was doing. She said, besides being hot and fat she was fine. I had always enjoyed her because I could kid her and she would kid me right back. I had come to love her as if she were my own daughter. I hoped all my children would marry people I could get along with so easily.

After we hung up, I phoned my father. We talked a little about Panama, but mostly about farming, how high the corn and soybeans were and how well his garden was looking and of course uncle Clark.

The morning of June 23rd, I drove back to Echo Company's area. There were very few men at muster because most of them were still on leave. We started each day with PT and a three-mile run. Then the troops went to classes or rifle drill, while I went to meetings to plan for the training Echo Company would need for our next deployment next year.

On July 2nd, Samantha became a teenager and we took her out to eat to the place of her choice.

On July 11th, Sgt Huebner returned to my platoon from the hospital. I put him back in command of 1st squad, which bumped Cpl Conn back to fire team leader.

On July 16th, I went to a 6th Regiment briefing given by Col Gagush. Among the things talked about was the fall of Russia. Few of us believed that Communism was truly dead yet. There was also talk of the military draw down that congress was talking about and how it would affect the Corps and us. As much as I'm not ready to retire after twenty-five years, at least I would get a retirement. But the thing that surprised me was when Col Gagush talked about the lack of real combat experience in the Corps. We now had the fewest combat veterans in the Corps since before WWII. In Officer ranks only 9% had combat experience, mostly warrant officers and colonels and up. Of the enlisted ranks there was only 14% of which most were gunnery sergeants and up.

By July 18th, most of our men on leave had returned. But also, as usual after a long deployment like this, many men were getting transferred or discharged. Six men from my platoon alone were transferred out. Lt North our company XO was transferred.

By Aug 1st, Lt Novak and twenty-four more Marines had been transferred from Echo Company, eight of which were from my platoon.

The evening of Aug 2nd, Marty, Samantha and I had just sat down to eat supper when the CBS news came on. My mouth dropped open in surprise as I listened to the news about the invasion of the peaceful country of Kuwait by its neighbor Iraq. Elite Republican

Guard armored units had poured across the northern and western borders without warning, quickly capturing Kuwait City and then rushed south toward the oil-rich and nearly defenseless Kingdom of Saudi Arabia. Suddenly, Saddam Hussein declared that Kuwait was Iraq's 19th Province. He was in control of 20% of the world's oil reserves and already was threatening 25% more of the oil fields in Saudi Arabia. This had already triggered nearly unanimous condemnation from the United Nations.

"What does this mean?" asked Marty looking at me.

"I'm not sure, but I have a bad feeling about this. I'm not sure we can let a man like Saddam Hussein get control of nearly 50% of the world's oil fields," I answered looking back at her. I felt those old butterflies in my stomach knowing this could lead to the biggest war since Vietnam.

The next morning when I reported in to Echo Company's area, everyone was talking about the invasion and whether we would go to war over oil and how soon we might be put on alert. As we trained, we waited for the word that didn't come.

On Aug 6th, the United Nations approved a total trade ban against Iraq.

That night I took Marty out to a movie and walked on the beach at midnight just like we had done fifteen years ago on our first date. As before we always talked about our future on such walks. But this time we were both quieter than usual. We both had our own worries about the possible coming big war. This could be a four-year war with us being separated longer than ever before. Not only was I concerned about surviving another big war, but also the last long war, Vietnam had cost me a marriage. And yet I couldn't consider retiring even though I could. Not now when my country might need men with real combat experience.

The next day Aug 7th, Saudi Arabia requested American support. By the evening CBS news, President Bush had ordered major deployments of US aircraft and troops to Saudi Arabia as part of a multinational force to defend that country against possible Iraqi invasion from overwhelming Iraqi forces, which had taken up positions along the Saudi-Kuwait border.

Later GySgt Simon phoned me with news. A friend of his assigned to the 1st Marine Division in Camp Pendleton, CA, told him that the 7th Marine Regiment, the only purely desert trained Marine regiment at 29 Palms CA had been put on alert.

On Aug 9th, the United Nations declared Iraqi's annexation of Kuwait to be "Null and void."

By now, we had begun to hear rumors that the US forces about to be committed would end up being a major deployment, the largest since Vietnam and the most demanding in terms of time since Korea with major units from all four services involved.

The morning of Aug 10th, Morris from Cpl Cunningham's 3rd squad was promoted to corporal.

Later in the day we heard that US Army Gen Schwarzkopf, the Commanding General of all allied forces in the Gulf had ordered the 7th Marine Regiment to begin deploying.

Within the hour, our 2nd Marine Division and the rest of the 1st Marine Division in CA had been put on alert. Not since Vietnam had a whole Marine Division been deployed overseas, let alone two of them.

The morning of Aug 11th all of the new men who had transferred into Echo Company since our return from Panama, suddenly received orders transferring them to other battalions within our 2nd Marine Division to beef them up.

Later in the day, Gen Gray, the Commandant of the Marine Corps, announced that elements of the 1st Marine Expeditionary Force from Camp Pendleton CA were deploying "East of the Suez" to the Gulf. These units would form up around the reinforced 7th Marine Regiment already in the area.

On Aug 15th, Gen Gray announced the 4th Marine Expeditionary Brigade would be committed to Saudi Arabia, comprised of units from the 2nd Marine Division.

Within forty-eight hours, the 4th MEB built around the 4th Marine Regiment began deploying from Camp Lejeune to the Gulf.

On Aug 19th, all the staff and officers of the 6th Marine regiment were ordered to a briefing at regimental headquarters given by Col Gagush. He started by saying that unless Saddam Hussein got out of Kuwait; our country would go to war. At least two Marine Divisions would be there. The powers to be believe this war is going to go one of two ways. One way is the Iraqi's would surrender in mass. The other is the Iraqis would fight tooth and nail using chemical and biological warfare. If this was the case, we expected 50,000 casualties the first two weeks.

At hearing this, I looked over at GySgt Simon who was looking at me. I knew he was thinking the same thing. We lost 58,000 killed in eight years of war in Vietnam. And now we could lose 50,000 in two weeks.

Then, Col Gagush went on to say he couldn't say when the 6th Regiment would leave. But don't expect to be home for Thanksgiving. But with so few combat veterans left in the Corps, those of us who were could get individual orders to units leaving soon.

Again, I looked over to GySgt Simon who was looking back at me smiling now.

After the briefing, I requested in writing a transfer to a unit that was going to the Gulf. Lt Norton walked my request and me to LtCol Haring's office.

LtCol Haring read my request, then looked up at me and said, "Gunner I can understand why you want to get over there. And I know any unit going over there could use your experience. But as Colonel Gagush said we're all going anyway. And I want you in my battalion when we go. So, I deny your request. Of course, you know you can request to speak to Colonel Gagush yourself."

"No sir, not at this time. But I may do that after my leave in September."

That night I talked to Marty about the briefing. Then almost holding my breath I told her about me volunteering to go to the Gulf. I had expected her to blow up.

But even with the worry in her eyes she said, "It doesn't surprise me. I just hope you stay until October after our leave home."

Later, I lay unable to sleep beside Marty. I feared this coming war, but yet I felt I should go. I love this lady beside me so much and I know she loves me enough to let me be me even when it hurts her. I had expected her to pressure me to retire with almost twenty-six years in while I could. But she hadn't and I respect and love her for it.

By Aug 21st, Saddam Hussein had taken foreigners as hostages calling them his guests, but at the same time placing them in areas likely to be targeted if the allies decided to retaliate against his country.

Already, US Air Force jets flying in Saudi airspace had been fired on by Iraqi Soviet made MIG-23's.

Saddam Hussein had ordered all foreign diplomats to abandon their embassies in Kuwait by Aug 24th.

On Friday Aug 24th, Iraqi troops surrounded nineteen foreign legations in Kuwait.

The same day the US Pentagon began the call up of 49,703 military Reservist. Of these were 3,000 Marine Reserves.

Meanwhile, an international force had begun moving toward Iraq. Canada was sending two destroyers and a supply ship. Britain was sending a flotilla made up of a destroyer, two frigates, three mine sweepers, four support ships and two squadrons of fighter-bombers. France was sending seven ships including an aircraft carrier and 180 paratroopers. Italy was sending two frigates, two corvettes and one supply ship. Belgium was sending two mine hunters and a supply ship. The Netherlands was sending two frigates. The Soviet Union had a destroyer and a support ship already in the area. Australia was sending two guided missile frigates and a supply ship. Bangladesh was sending 1,200 troops. Egypt was sending 4,000 troops. Morocco was sending 1,200 troops. Syria was sending 2,000 troops. The Gulf Cooperation Council made up of Bahrain, Oman, the United Arab Emirates and Qatar had 10,000 troops in the area. Saudi Arabia had a 65,000-military force.

Together they would face the fourth largest military force in the world with more than 1,000,000 troops. 200,000 of these troops were veterans of the eight-year war with Iran. It was estimated that Iraq had 160,000 troops in Kuwait backed up by 1,500 tanks, Soviet and French made aircraft, an assortment of weapons purchased from various world markets, Scud missiles and chemical weapons which they had used against Iran.

On Aug 26th, the 1st Marine Division headquarters began arriving in Saudi Arabia.

The 1st Marine Division was already short of personnel because of the normal attrition and personnel transferred to the 7th Regiment to bring it up to full strength as well as other units already deployed to Okinawa during the first half of this year. Again, throughout this month our battalion was still being stripped to help build up the 1st Marine Division.

Lt Vie was transferred to the 1st Marine Division along with seven more of my men leaving me with a nineteen-man platoon.

I thought about requesting mast to Col Gagush to ask for a transfer to the 1st Marine Division. But with me close to going on leave I decided to wait until I got back.

The morning of Sept 1st, Marty, Samantha and I left Camp Lejeune driving the nine hours north to Delaware. As usual we stayed with Marty's mother in Georgetown.

The next day we drove over to Atlanta to the farm and visited with my father and uncle Clark as they prepared to shell corn. Of course, they asked questions about the Gulf problem and whether I thought I would be going. I told them I thought I would. But I didn't tell them I was trying to be transferred over there. I could tell by my father's eyes that he was worried about me once again. I hadn't seen him this concerned about me since Vietnam.

Then we drove north to Greenwood to see my oldest son Nat, his wife Donna and their son and daughter. As we sat and talked, I could tell Donna was uncomfortable and she looked like she could have this baby any time. Again, the talk turned to the Gulf.

"Can't you retire now?" asked Nat.

"Yes, I could. But I can't do that with the country about to go to war," I answered surprised.

"But Dad haven't you done enough for this country. It's somebody else time," argued Nat.

I looked down at my hands thinking before I spoke. I felt like I was dealing with his mother. Then I looked up at him saying, "I can't get out, leaving the young Marines I've trained and fought with in Panama to go to the biggest war since Nam or worse. Before I went to Nam it was older men my age now, with combat experience from World War Two and Korea that helped me survive and learn the ropes. It's like your work at the prison. Even if you were home and you heard there was a riot at the prison, how would you feel?"

"I'd want to be right there helping out my friends," answered Nat quickly.

I threw up my hands smiling saying, "I rest my case."

Nat looked from me to Donna shaking his head. Then Donna frowning added, "Well you can't leave until this child is born."

"I'll try not," I said smiling.

It was after midnight when the phone rang and Marty jumped up to answer it. Then she ran back into the bedroom saying, "That was Nat, they're at the hospital."

I rolled out of bed and started dressing as she went and told Samantha.

Within forty-five minutes we arrived at the hospital in Seaford. In the waiting room we found the grandchildren Amber and little Nat lying between Donna's parents Mr. and Mrs. Seymour. Before I could ask anything, in walked Donna and Nat.

"This maybe a false alarm," grumbled Nat.

"I'm sorry," said Donna.

"Are you all right?" I asked placing my hand on her shoulder.

"Oh yeah, the pain is almost gone. But the doctor wants me to stay here a couple of hours and walk a lot," said Donna.

As we sat and waited, we watched TV. When news came on about the Gulf, Mrs. Seymour asked me if I thought I would have to go. It was the one question everybody back here kept asking me.

A few hours later Donna did give birth to their second son who they named Brock. He was just as beautiful as their first two. I told Donna that they do good work.

The rest of the month was great, filled with family dinners and get togethers. But in the back of my mind was always the Gulf news and how it was affecting the Corps. Marty and Samantha could sense my worry and frustration with not receiving orders. Every day I made a point to watch the CBS news. At family gatherings while the other men were watching sports, I would slip away to a quiet bedroom where there was a TV and watch the latest news. About every three days I would call Lt Norton down at Camp Lejeune to get the latest news or rumors.

On Sept 6th, the 1st Marine Division took command of all Marine ground combat elements in Saudi Arabia.

By now the 13th Marine Expeditionary Unit with 1st Bn 4th Reg was nearing the Gulf coming from the South Pacific.

All the remaining units at Camp Pendleton were put on alert to be prepared to deploy on short notice.

On Sept 11th, President Bush spoke at a joint session of Congress saying, "Our objectives in the Persian Gulf are clear, our goals defined and familiar. Iraq must withdraw from Kuwait completely, immediately and without condition. The Kuwait legitimate government must be restored. The security and stability of the Persian Gulf must be assured. And American citizens abroad must be protected."

By now, the Marines in SWA (South West Asia) had assembled the largest armored mechanized force in Marine history.

Our commandant Gen Gray went to SWA to visit his Marines.

On Sept 26th, he spoke to a large group of those Marines. One of the questions asked of him by a young Marine was when would they be going home?"

He answered, "You'll be going home when the job is done, not before. We're trying to work this crisis out diplomatically and with economic measures. You're providing that military might to back up these measures. If the diplomatic and economic measures don't work, then we'll do whatever is necessary. We're dealing with a very dangerous individual in Saddam Hussein. He's got good equipment and good units."

Our middle son Lance got home for two weekends while we were home. I was surprised with joy at how well he looked and how well he was doing after his terrible wounds in Panama. It seemed the wounds would keep him from duty in the Gulf. He seemed disappointed at not getting a chance to go. As a Marine I understand. But as a father I was glad he wasn't going. Now I truly understood my father's fears.

By the 1st of Oct we were back in Camp Lejeune. While I was gone Lt Norton received orders to the 1st Marine Division. With me being the only officer left in Echo Company I took over the duties of company commander of a company made up of only thirty-two Marines. There weren't enough men left to form a platoon.

I requested Mast in writing to Col Gagush, again asking for a transfer to the 1st Marine Division. But my request was turned down this time because of the shortage of officers left in the 6th Regiment. I couldn't believe it. Everybody was getting orders it seemed but me. I phoned Marty and talked to her about my frustration at being turned down again to go to the Gulf. She always made me feel better because of her total support. But I knew it had to be working on her and Samantha.

The 12th of October I turned forty-three years old. I was beginning to think the Corps was thinking I was too old to go to war.

By Nov 1st, Echo Company was down to twenty-eight men. But at least I still had some good men left like 1stSgt Bean, GySgts Simon and O'Malley, Sgts Ewing, Huebner and Davis, Cpls Conn, Cunningham and Morris.

On Nov 8th, President Bush announced that an additional 150,000 troops would be sent to the Persian Gulf.

I had heard rumors that the 3rd Marine Division on Okinawa had gone on alert for the Gulf. That night from home I phoned my old friend BGen Hester on Okinawa.

"Brigadier General Hester speaking," I heard him answer.

"Yes, general this is Gunner Cord."

"Nathan, how are you doing?"

"Fine, General. The reason I'm calling is I understand the 3rd Marine Division is going to the Gulf."

"Some units are going, but not the whole division, not yet anyway."

"General could you get me orders to one of those units that are going?"

There was a long silence, and then he said, "Nathan are you still with the 6th Marines?"

"Yes, General I am.'

"Are you with some good men?"

"Yes, General. I'm a company commander of a unit with only twenty-eight in it."

"Nathan, I could get you ordered to the Gulf with one of my units. But your unit needs you more than I do. And you'll get your chance and soon."

Now I was quiet before I spoke, "You sure, General?"

"Yes, I know it for a fact."

"Okay General. I'm sorry for bothering you."

"No bother, Nathan. I always enjoy hearing from you. And you be careful over there."

"Yes, General I will. Thank you and you be careful too."

"I will if I get there."

I hung the phone up feeling relieved and fearful at the same time. A man should be careful what he begs for.

On Nov 10th, the Corps 215th birthday, our battalion being so small had one Marine Corps Ball for all hands.

On Nov 14th, the Secretary of Defense authorized the Marine Corps to call up 15,000 reservists.

The next day, LtCol Haring called us company commanders to his office. After we had sat down, he began speaking, "Well gentlemen the First Battalion has been put on alert to be ready to deploy to the gulf by the first of the year. I know we are under strength. Especially Echo and Hotel Companies. This battalion is to be fleshed out by reservist who will be reporting in just after Thanksgiving."

I believe we were all stunned as our mouths dropped open.

"Sir how can these reservists be ready for combat in less than two months?" I asked.

"They'll be ready because we will make them ready. In fact, Gunner Cord, I want you to work with my S-3 and with them to put together a training package that will last thirty days to bring them up to speed."

"Okay Sir I'll do the best I can," I said.

When I returned to Echo Company, I gathered all twenty-eight men and told them the news. They weren't anymore happy with the news than I was. I told them if they wanted some leave, they better take it quick. Because when the reserves arrive, we'll be going balls to the wall for the next month. I also put GySgt O'Malley in charge of Echo Company while I'm working with the S-3 shop. I took GySgt Simon with me to help as my assistant.

The night of Nov 15th, I went to bed feeling uneasy about the state of the reserves readiness that we would get. I dreamed that when they reported in, they had hippie length hair. I woke up glad it was only a dream.

By thanksgiving the 5th Marine Regiment had deployed from Camp Pendleton CA as part of the 5th Brigade. With them was a reserve tank company, a reserve Amtrack company, a reserve LAI company, a reserve artillery battery, a reserve truck platoon, and their combat engineer company was heavily manned by reservist.

During the same time, two reserve battalions were processed through Camp Pendleton for duty on Okinawa. This would allow other units from the 3rd Marine Division to deploy to the gulf.

On the morning of Nov 26th, Echo Company finally had a few regular Marines transfer in. Two of them were old friends of mine. One was SSgt Higgins who had served with me from 1981 to 88. I assigned him as platoon leader of 3rd platoon. The other was SSgt Crew who I assigned as platoon leader of 1st platoon.

The same morning the first reserve units began to arrive at Camp Lejeune. Some of these units were quickly disbanded so they could be absorbed into regular units like ours

Late in the afternoon our reserve replacements drove into view in buses.

Standing next to me, GySgt Simon said, "Gunner did you ever think we'd be babysitting reserves and going to war with 'm?"

"No, I didn't Gunny. And I better not see any earrings. I'm not going to take any shit from these long-haired boy scouts," I grumbled.

The buses slowed down to a stop. And as the reserves started getting off, I was surprised at how close their haircuts were. Soon one of their staff sergeants began yelling orders, falling them into one big formation.

"At least they have good haircuts."

"Yeah, they look sharp, but can they fight?" grumbled GySgt Simon.

But then I saw five captains get out of a car and head toward me.

"Who are these guys, new staff officers?" I said wondering if we'd get many company officers.

As the group of captains neared us, GySgt Simon and I snapped to attention saluting them saying, "Good evening gentlemen."

All five captains returned our salutes as the one in the lead said, "You're Gunner Cord I take it?"

"Yes sir."

"Well I'm Captain Smith your new company commander. This is Captain Stordhal who'll be my XO." Then pointing to the tallest captain, he said, "This is Captain Drumbore who will be the First platoon leader. And this is Captain Johnson who will be the Third platoon leader. And Captain Bailey will be the weapons platoon leader. Of course, Gunner you will return to your Second platoon."

"Thank you, sir." I said clearly shocked at all these captains being placed in lieutenant billets.

Later I would find it wasn't because they were screwed up like I thought. The real reason was because in the Marine reserve 90% of the officers have already done at least three years on active duty. Because of this they come into the reserve usually as senior first lieutenants who then make captain soon after. Which means the reserve platoon leaders actually have more experience than our active duty platoon leaders.

Then Capt Smith said, "Gunner I intend to keep your first sergeant and company gunny. Have the gunny get these men into shelter for the night. Then you, the other platoon leaders and the first sergeant will sit down and figure out how best to combine our two units into one. Where I can I want to keep your men at least in the same platoon as they are now."

"Yes sir. This is Gunny Simon." I said pointing to him and added, "He will take charge of them now and get them shelter for the night."

"Very good. Gunny carry on," said Capt Smith.

"Aye, aye sir," said GySgt Simon saluting and walked off toward the reserves.

Together us officers and 1stSgt Bean worked late into the night going over the two rosters, active and reserve and formed them into one unit.

As far as my platoon, I got a new platoon sergeant, SSgt Adams, which I didn't want, but of course had to take. The reason being, this would bump Sgt Ewing back to platoon guide. I also had to take on Sgt Murphy, which I put in command of 3rd squad, which bumped Cpl Cunningham back to fire team leader. Among the reserves I got to fill out my platoon were also four corporals. Cpls Cook and Seth I sent to Sgt Davis's 2nd squad. Cpl Pusey went to Sgt Huebner's 1st squad. Cpl Short went to 3rd squad.

I slept in the company office after phoning Marty. I told her that suddenly our battalion was at full strength again. In the morning we would assign the reserves to their platoons and together we would start training in earnest.

And the next morning the training began. It was broken down in two courses. One course was for the enlisted men up to sergeant, which dealt with individual marksmanship, nuclear, biological, and chemical protection, minefield breaching of fortified positions, desert survival and navigation, briefings on Southwest Asia and Iraqi army organization and equipment.

The second course was for the Staff NCOs and officers, which covered much of the same material, but also included classes on fire support coordination, frag orders and exercises in the integrated combined arms staff training.

LtCol Haring had ordered us regulars not to talk down to the reserves and I had warned my men. And we were careful not to speak down to them. And soon I was happy to discover the reserves were highly motivated, skilled individuals who were proud to serve their country and asked only to be accepted as fellow Marines by us on the active duty side. They were devoted, enthusiastic, intelligent and I noted that the only operational difficulty was familiarizing themselves with our standard operating procedures. And slowly, the relationship between regular and reserve improved as friendships grew founded by our common bond of Marine brotherhood and the coming challenges and sacrifices.

Near the end of November, I jerked upright suddenly in bed next to Marty in a cold sweat.

"Are you all right, dear?" she asked.

"Yeah, I had a nightmare," I said laying back down.

She rolled over next to me putting her arm over me as she kissed me on the temple saying, "You sure you're all right?"

"Yes." I answered thinking about my dream. In it I had been trying to save a wounded Sgt Ewing. But each time I moved close to him, he seemed to drift out of my reach. I just couldn't help him.

With the coming of December, the training of our battalion continued at a quick pace.

I read in the Navy Times that my old friend BGen Hester had been promoted to Major General and was taking command of the 3rd Marine Division with most of it still on Okinawa.

I phoned him saying I couldn't believe my old captain from Hue City days in Vietnam was now a two star General.

On Dec 6th, our battalion started its Phase II training with its emphasis on night operations.

On Dec 10th, the rest of the 2nd Marine Division began deploying to Southwest Asia.

On Dec 11th, our battalion started live fire exercises, NBC defensive measures as our battalion staff ran command post exercises. And like before, the reserves to my surprise took to the challenge of the six days a week training in stride.

On Dec 15th, the rest of the 1st Marine Regiment of the 1st Marine Division was ordered to deploy to the Gulf.

The evening of Dec 16th I was just sitting down to the supper table with Marty and Samantha. Marty had fixed my favorite dinner, fried chicken. The phone started ringing and Samantha jumped up and answered it. Then she looked toward me saying, "It's for you Dad."

I stood up taking the phone saying, "Gunner Cord speaking, sir."

"Gunner this is Captain Smith. I just got the word from Colonel Haring. The battalion just went on alert for movement overseas. The Colonel wants all reserves notified tonight that after tonight all liberty will be cancelled until we leave."

"Do what, sir? You mean us regulars will get the weekend off?" I asked.

"That's the way I understand it," said Capt Smith.

"Okay sir, I'll pass the word. See you in the morning," I hung up saying more to myself, "I can't believe this shit!"

"What's the matter?" asked Marty.

"The battalion just went on alert to deploy to the gulf and Colonel Haring canceled the planned ninety-six hour passes this weekend for the reserves. Probably their last weekend before we leave."

Then I picked up the phone and dialed.

"Lieutenant Colonel Haring here."

"Sir, this is Gunner Cord. Forgive me for breaking the chain of command. But I just got the word about us going on alert. But sir, I think the reserves deserve this weekend off like the rest of us. Many of them have wives, kids or girlfriends down here for the ninety-six, in hotels or the hostess house."

There was a long silence before he spoke, "I know. But the closer we come to leaving, some of them may not come back."

"Sir, we were ordered by you to treat these reserves no different than the regulars. This is not fair to them and their families."

There was another long silence before he spoke again, "Gunner, I have a great deal of respect for you. But my order will stand."

"Okay sir. But my whole platoon, reserve and regular alike will not take liberty after tonight."

"That's your call."

When I hung up the phone, I phoned SSgt Adams at his hotel room with his wife and daughters.

"Say what!" he said hearing the news about the cancelled reserve ninety-six-hour passes. Then he hung up to call Sgt Ewing and our squad leaders.

I was again eating my fried chicken when Sgt Ewing phoned me. He was clearly upset with me canceling the regulars' ninety-six in our platoon like the reserves. After I explained my reasons he understood, but he still wasn't happy. And of course, Marty and

Samantha weren't too happy with me either, knowing this would be my last weekend home before I left for the gulf. But looking back on it, I still felt my decision brought my platoon even closer together.

While most of the regulars in our battalion enjoyed a long weekend, the reserves and my whole platoon spent the weekend training. I was again surprised at these reserves who took this lost weekend as a small price to pay to defend their country. Besides most of them seemed to realize they were about to embark on the greatest adventure of their lives.

In the next six days our battalion rapidly readied itself for deployment. Medical and dental records were updated, shots given, personal effects, allotments, will, and powers of attorney were arranged, every Marine fired a familiarization course with his weapon and went through the gas chamber, NBC training and other predeployment classes.

In the middle of all this on Dec 19th, LtCol Haring was issued orders from Col Gagush placing our battalion on twenty-four-hour alert to deployment. Which meant we were to be ready to leave within twenty-four hours.

LtCol Haring gave our battalion the day of Dec 23rd off and allowed our families to spend the day with us. But most of the reserve families had already left to go back home.

That evening I walked Marty and Samantha to our car. I kissed and hugged them both fighting back tears. As they drove away, I felt it would be a long time before I saw them again.

The next morning Christmas Eve, I was sleeping on a cot in the company office when I heard GySgt Simons voice say, before he touched me, "Gunner."

"Yes Gunny. What's up?" I asked.

"It's a go sir. We have to be ready to leave in an hour."

"Okay. Have you passed the word to the platoon sergeants?"

"Yes sir. I'm waking up the officers now."

"Very good gunny. I should've known. What time is it anyway?"

"A little pass 0030 sir," he said as he walked away.

I got up and went to the phone and called home. A sleepy Marty answered.

"Marty it's me. It's a go."

"Oh Lord, how soon," she cried suddenly sounding wide-awake.

"We leave within the hour."

"I can't believe you're leaving on Christmas Eve."

"I know. I love you girl."

"And I love you. You be careful now."

"I will. And you be careful."

"I will."

"I'll see you," I said with tears filling my eyes.

"Goodbye." And she was gone.

I hung the phone up and already I could hear movement in the company street as sergeant's yelled orders.

By 0400, our battalion had stacked our gear on Marine trucks and we had climbed aboard school buses. Throughout the morning the convoy of gear laden Marine trucks and buses rolled down the highway toward Moorehead City where Navy ships lay docked waiting for us.

Once there, our battalion joined up with other Marines of our regiment. Altogether 2,500 Marines climbed aboard five ships that would carry us to the Mediterranean.

After checking on my platoon, I put my gear into my room that I would share with Capt Johnson. He and I went to the wardroom and drank coffee and talked.

Later, we felt the ship move and walked up to the outer decks of the ship. We found many of the men standing in groups, all of them looking at the last American soil they would see in a while, maybe forever. The air was tense as they realized with fear that soon their lives could go in harm's way.

My own mind thought back eight days ago to my 15th wedding anniversary. It wasn't the first time I had missed it because of war or training. And tomorrow would not be the first Christmas away from home. But as usual, Marty being the good Marine wife was more concerned that I take good care of myself. She said to remember, she and Samantha would be waiting for me. I knew she was worried like never before, but she tried her best to keep her feelings inside so as not to worry me.

I wondered if all I had been through in my life; the Vietnam War and training had been leading up to this. Was Vietnam just a testing ground for this? Could this really turn out to be bigger and worse than Vietnam? But for some reason at least for now I wasn't worried. I was ready to do whatever I had to do to bring the men of my platoon back. I could almost say I felt great. This was what I had entered the Corps for and why I had stayed in for twenty-six years.

Christmas day we spent miles from home out at sea. I went to a church service in the morning and at lunch I ate turkey with all the trimmings in the wardroom.

New Year's Day 1991 was spent at sea as we neared the gulf.

A few days later in the morning I stood on the outer deck staring out at the beach of Saudi Arabia as our ship made its final approach. My mind flashed back in time to a similar landing in Vietnam almost twenty-six years ago. The temperature was 110 degrees back then, too. My emotions were very much the same as back then, apprehensive and uncertain mixed with a tingle of excitement, which I had found, was normal for men going to war.

Of course, the terrain here was very different from Vietnam. Here I found myself looking at a landscape with no points of reference, no people, no buildings, no trees, and no grass. This place looked even worse than 29 Palms, CA.

Thirty minutes after we landed, we climbed aboard shuttle buses, which took us to a base camp sixty miles away.

Arriving at the base camp, we rounded a bend in the road and we were stopped at a Marine sentry post bunker. A marine there led us into the main compound. This struck me like a flash back, it reminded me of Vietnam. I knew I had never been to this base camp before and yet I felt instantly at home, in this sea of brownish green tents, the sky filled with thick black smoke from burning sewage barrels from the heads. Even the salty look of the young Marines manning the post with their scuffed jungle boots and unshaven faces meant this was a combat unit. They had that look of being in country since August, holding the thin line waiting for the rest of us to get here. I smiled knowing we newcomers looked green to them in our new issue desert brown and tan camouflage uniforms and spit shinned boots.

Soon, the buses moved through the camp coming to a stop. As Echo Company stepped off the buses onto the fine sand of the Saudi desert, another Marine guide met us and took the officers and GySgt Simon and showed us to our company defensive positions.

That night after a meeting with LtCol Haring, Capt Smith briefed us platoon leaders. The 2nd Marine Division now numbered 20,000 men in country. Our regiment was ordered to conduct training exercises in preparation for offensive operations to begin by Jan 15th.

We quickly noticed there were no showers or hot chow to be found here. It wasn't long before my men started dreaming of rivers, snow and women. As Echo Company started training, like always through SSgt Adams, Sgt Ewing and the squad leaders my platoon became molded in my own image. These reservists were confident, cocky and arrogant. And I demanded perfection, chewing asses as well as beating their asses if need be. SSgt Adams thought I was too hard on our men. Sgt Ewing just smiled for he now understood I had only one motive. I wanted to bring as many of my men back home alive as I could.

Again, Echo Company's training included night patrols, calling in simulated artillery and close air support, use of night vision goggles, night defensive tactics and how to best acclimate to this sweltering all-encompassing heat. We were lucky because most of the reserves in Echo Company had participated in combined-arms exercises at 29 Palms last summer, so they were intimately familiar with the rigors of a desert environment. I noticed SSgt Adams ordered our squad leaders to make sure their men drank enough water at each break, which resulted in a minimum of heat casualties.

In the steel gray dusk, our desert camouflage uniforms clashed with the off-white color of the sand. The clear desert air enhanced the almost unnatural brightness of the moonlight and starlight.

During the day we stayed underneath the shelter of tents. Security was established on the perimeter of the camp and the Marines on guard were rotated every couple of hours.

While in the tents, Marines cleaned their weapons, ate MRE's and rested. We also conducted platoon-size chemical weapons drills.

As night came on, I stood with 1stSgt Bean as we watched the squads from my platoon moving out on patrols to become familiar with the terrain.

"You know Gunner, I think the night sky of Saudi Arabia seems brighter than it is in 29 Palms."

Later I took my platoon out on a tactical movement, which seemed to go on for endless miles. There were stretches of sand where I sank in past my ankles and other areas where the sand was hard like concrete. Maneuvering out there was tricky and even I needed to get used to it. When we finally did stop, everyone dropped to the sand exhausted, except for the corpsmen who dropped their packs and walked around checking the men.

We also trained in squad, platoon, company and battalion offensive and defensive tactics, a relief in place, passage of lines, obstacle breaching, movement to contact, infiltration, tank killer teams and trench clearing. I was glad to see my squad leaders making their men change into dry socks at each of our breaks.

Then we trained in heliborne operations.

During the day I gave classes that ranged from vehicle identification to actions in the assembly area. All this was done at times in 120-degree heat and humidity.

Sometimes in this searing sun, my Marines cursed under their breath. But they couldn't really complain because whether they were regular or reserve, they were all volunteers and I found them all to be professionals. And they were all confident in their ability to fight. By now the integration of the reserves was so successful that no one could tell us regulars from the reservist.

When my men were on guard duty, they kept their eyes on the desert watching for movement. We all spent every waking and sleeping moment with our weapons loaded and by our sides just like in Vietnam. Our weapons had become extensions of our bodies.

And as before when the shooting started, I knew I would lead men into combat and had to make critical life and death decisions. Each night I prayed to God to help me make the right decisions to keep my men alive. Lt Col Gagush and the generals worried about the big picture. Just give me my mission and my platoon of Marines to help me do it.

On Jan 10th, our regiment moved forward to new positions near the Saudi and Kuwait border. We relieved an Arab unit along this sector of the front.

Our mission here was to observe and report the activity across the berm to our front, which marked the international boundary between the two countries. But if war started, our mission would be to close with and destroy the Iraqi forces on the other side.

By now we had become adjusted to life in the desert, the sand, with hot days and freezing nights and worst of all the flies.

The evening of Jan 13th, Capt Smith called us officers and Staff NCOs together for a briefing. He told us about the Iraqi defensives and countermeasures. The 1st and 2nd Marine Divisions with the US

Army Tiger Brigade were facing eleven Iraqi Divisions behind two complex obstacle belts. The 1st Marine Division had begun slowly moving forward as well as westward.

On Jan 14th, Capt Johnson's 3rd platoon had watched thirteen Iraqi soldiers climb over the berm waving white flags and surrendered to them.

By now we had been on alert more times than I could count. We had been ordered to our fighting positions because the Iraqis were supposedly attacking. Then we would be told the Iraqis weren't attacking. Then we would be put on alert to standby to be attacked. Then we would be ordered to stand by for a gas attack. Then we would receive the all-clear sign.

During another briefing, Capt Smith told us our attack was set to kick off on Jan 25th. And there were now 86,000 Marines in country.

At 0230 on Jan 16th, Capt Stordhal shook me awake in my sleeping bag saying, "Gunner, Gunner."

"Yes sir," I said sitting up unzipping the bag.

"Put your platoon on full alert. The war is starting."

"What's happening?"

"Like I said the war is starting. At least the air war anyway."

"Okay sir." I turned toward SSgt Adams who had risen up in his sleeping bag. "Did you hear, Staff Sergeant Adams?"

"Yes sir. I'll wake them up."

Soon I could hear the men of my platoon in their fighting holes locking and loading their weapons. Then they quieted down to wait for orders to attack or for the threatened Iraqi scud missiles attacks or counterattack against us.

Suddenly after 163 days, Operation Desert Shield had become Desert Storm as the war began with US cruise missiles launched from Ships in the gulf and F-117 Stealth bombers attacking key Iraqi targets achieving complete tactical surprise. The coalition Air Forces of US, Britain, Italy, France, Saudi and Kuwait unleashed their attacks flying more than 1,000 sorties, dropping more than 2,200 tons of ordnance in the first fourteen hours and losing only four aircraft.

Initial targets on the first night were Iraqi command and control systems and its formidable air defense network. Meanwhile US Navy and Marine jets were attacking ground forces.

That evening Capt Smith gathered us officers together and briefed us on our 2nd Marine Division plan of attack. Together with the 1st Marine Division we would penetrate the forward Iraqi positions.

The battle was broken down into four phases. Phases I and II would be the air offensive period. Phase III would be air offensive and preparation of the battlefield as our 2nd Marine Division moved to our attack positions and conducted probes and artillery raids. Phase IV had four stages.

In stage A, the 1st Marine Division would attack to penetrate forward Iraqi positions, hold open the shoulders of the penetration, and help in the passage of our 2nd Marine Division.

Stage B, would be the movement to blocking positions along the main supply route southeast of the Burgan oil fields.

Stage C, the 1st Marine Division, after providing local security at the point of penetration, would move up along our 2nd Marine Division left flank. Together, both divisions would then attack northwest to seize key road junctions around the Burgan field.

Stage D, both divisions would continue attacking north while linking up with US Army units and coalition forces and help in the forward passage of Arab forces so they could advance into Kuwait City.

As I listened, I couldn't help but think that in my eight years in Vietnam, the biggest action I was in was regimental size. And here I would take part in an attack by two full Marine Divisions at once. This was the first time this had happened since WWII.

Later that night, both Marine Divisions moved north closer to the Kuwaiti border in preparation for the expected start of the ground war, which we all knew would start soon. Finally, after weeks of waiting, watching and worrying, it felt good to be on the move.

The morning of Jan 17th, US Army Gen Schwarzkopf reported that Iraqi rocket positions had been silenced by Marine jets. He also reported that three Iraqi patrol boats had been sunk or disabled.

Meanwhile, the Iraqis had started to probe our lines with artillery and mortar fire. Our regiment already was one of the first US forces that had been hit by Iraqi artillery, rocket and missile fire. We had found out the Iraqis didn't bracket their targets like we did. Instead they saturate an area.

Early in the evening, Marine artillery units were the first to trade artillery fire with Iraqi artillery units with one Marine being wounded.

Later during the night even though our air strikes had knocked out fixed Scud missile sites in western Iraq, some of Hussein's mobile launchers had escaped and fired seven to ten high explosive warheads into Israel hitting the coastal cities of Haifa and Tel Aviv. Casualties had been light and Israeli officials warned that they reserved the right to retaliate.

About the same time, a Scud missile was fired at Dhahran Saudi Arabia, which was destroyed in the air by US Army Patriot missiles.

By 2210, I was sick of the news reporters talking about how air power would win this war. There sure was no sign of Iraqi forces fleeing Kuwait yet. I crawled into my sleeping bag to get some sleep.

Five minutes later I was shaken awake by an artillery air burst followed quickly by three more. I sat up grabbing the radio handset and listened as different companies reported to LtCol Haring that they were receiving incoming, but so far, no casualties.

At 2245, Col Gagush ordered our regiment to 100% alert and to be ready to repel a ground attack. SSgt Adams and I went checking our platoon line making sure everyone was awake and ready. Then we returned to our hole and waited.

At 0220 the next morning, LtCol Haring radioed Capt Smith and the other company commanders and cancelled the alert.

I sent SSgt Adams out along our platoon line to put our squads on 50% watch the rest of the morning. Again, I crawled into my sleeping bag to get some sleep.

A half hour later, I was shaken awake by rocket explosions and artillery air bursts.

I climbed out of my sleeping bag to see what was going on. Within minutes Capt Smith called me on the radio yelling the alert, "Gas! Gas! Gas!"

I quickly radioed my squad leaders with the alert. Then I joined SSgt Adams as we scrambled to pull on our NBC uniforms out of our packs and put them on and test our gas masks to make sure they were on right. Again, we waited at 100% watch.

Finally, at 0340 Capt Smith radioed me telling me the gas alert was called off.

We pulled our NBC suites off after I had passed the word to my platoon to go on 50% watch. And again, I crawled into my sleeping bag to get some sleep.

A little after 0600, I woke up listening to GySgt Simons voice as he told SSgt Adams that hot chow had been brought up and the men could take turns going back to our battalion CP to get some. I waited until Sgt Ewing and the rest of our platoon had eaten and then SSgt Adam and I went to get some hot breakfast.

In the afternoon at 1545, Capt Smith called me on the radio telling me we were now put on air alert because Scud missiles had been launched toward us.

Fifteen minutes later he radioed me with the all clear order.

At 1640, Col Gagush placed the whole regiment on full alert to be ready to defeat an enemy attack.

A half hour later Capt Smith radioed me with the all clear order.

At 1830, Sgt Ewing had climbed out of his hole to piss when suddenly he yelled, “Incoming! Take cover!” As he dived back into his hole, I looked up seeing multiple rocket trails overhead and muttered, “Son of a bitch!” As I lowered myself down even deeper in my hole thirty some rockets hit exploding west of our battalion.

By 2100, it was quiet and with our company back at 50% watch I tried to get some sleep. But during the night I was awakened first for an air alert and then later for a Scud missile attack alert.

The morning of Jan 19th I ate an MRE.

At 0800, GySgt Simon walked up to my hole and handed our platoons mail to SSgt Adam. Then he handed two letters to me.

“Thank you,” I said looking up at him.

“No problem, Gunner,” answered GySgt Simon as he walked away.

I looked down at my letters, one from Marty and the other from my oldest son Nat. I opened both letters and read them quickly. Then I climbed out of the hole and walked along my platoon positions checking on my men. I then returned to my hole at 0900 and reread my letters slowly. Then I wrote a letter to each of them telling both pretty much the same thing,

“I sure am tired. It’s hard trying to get any sleep with all the different alerts we have about every two hours here. Everything from air alerts, Scud missile alerts, artillery incoming, terrorist attack and ground attack alerts.

But my men, regular and reserve alike are handling all this quite well. Like me they’re pretty scared at times, but they've responded well. Our battalion has taken some Iraqi artillery and rocket fire. So far none of my men have been hurt.

In your last letter you said the news reporters back home were wondering how it would affect us here if the Israelis should attack Iraq because of the Scud missile attacks that hit them. The other day I talked to some Saudi soldiers about this fear. And they weren't concerned about any Israeli reaction to Scud missile attacks.

Well, I better go. I'm okay and so are my men. I'll write again when I can. I love you.

Semper Fi."

During Jan 20th because of the growing Iraqi threat, Marine artillery began firing on Iraqi positions.

While we have been building up our forces here for six months, Iraqi troops had been busy constructing a network of fortifications along the Kuwaiti-Iraq border preparing for our offensive we all knew was coming.

We knew the Iraqi defensive lines stretched from Kuwait City south down the coast, then turned westward and followed the border of Kuwait and Saudi Arabia toward Iraq. In front of us were two minefields, 100 to 200 meters deep, bordered by large sand berms, concertina wire, overlooked by trenches, fighting ditches, bunkers and dug in tanks and anti-tank guns.

And behind these positions were artillery, already aimed at the places in the minefields where we would have to cross. And there may be fire ditches filled with oil, ready to be ignited by remotely detonated explosive charges.

In eight years of war in Vietnam I had never faced anything like this. The closest to it would have been Hue City. And at times there we had felt like bugs hitting windshields.

As we waited, LtCol Haring's Battalion staff, Col Gagush's Regimental staff and our 2nd Marine Division staff was constantly refining our technique to breach these berms and marking a pathway through these minefields while under fire.

For some reason the Iraqis had now set several hundred oil wells on fire. At times soot and smoke filled the air limiting our visibility down to only fifteen to twenty feet. At these times I put my platoon on full alert even without orders fearing the Iraqis might try a sneak attack under the cover of the smoke.

But even with the limited visibility, at times we were able to watch the air war and see the impacts of the B-52 bomb explosions on the enemy.

The morning of Jan 21st, Capt Johnson and SSgt Higgins of 3rd platoon put their platoons on full alert as they watched two Iraqi officers and three enlisted men walk toward their positions and surrendered. Later in the day fifty-one more Iraqis walked up to their platoon and surrendered.

On Jan 25th, Baghdad radio announced that captured POWs would be used as human shields to be placed near likely targets of coalition aircraft.

Meanwhile, the nearly round the clock air strikes on Iraqi targets continued averaging more than 2,000 sorties a day as we Marines, US Army and allied Infantry forces moved up closer to the Kuwaiti border.

By Jan 27th, our regiment had moved into new positions close to the Kuwaiti border.

With the night came the rain, which made the night even colder.

At 2359, Marine artillery began firing at Iraqi positions, logistics sites and truck parks inside Kuwait. The shelling lasted thirteen minutes with the Marines firing eighty rounds without any enemy return fire. Later, probably in retaliation for our artillery raids, the 5th Iraqi Mechanized Division attacked into Saudi Arabia with four battalions of tanks and Infantry in a three-pronged attack along a fifty-mile front.

At noon on Jan 29th, LtCol Haring ordered Echo Company to move up to stand OP (observation post) duty.

By late afternoon, our company had dug in at our OP around a castle-like building with two towers built of brown stone. To the north of the castle was a white one-story concrete building housing an electrical generator, which provided power to the complex. Here, there were small trees, a fenced in area and a water tower.

This station bisected the wall of sand fifteen feet high that extended the entire length of the Saudi-Kuwaiti border.

Capt Drumbore's 1st platoon was dug in along a bunker set in the berm 200 meters north of the complex. Capt Johnson's 3rd platoon was dug in along the berm 300 meters south of the complex. My platoon was dug in behind them as the reserve force.

As dusk fell, it looked like it was going to be another cold overcast winter night.

At 1926, LtCol Haring radioed Capt Smith to warn us that a Marine recon patrol had spotted thirty-five vehicles on the Kuwaiti side of the border moving southwest toward us. Capt Smith quickly put Echo Company on full alert.

Soon, Maj Arguedos updated the warning to fifty vehicles being led by tanks. Capt Smith requested assistance. Maj Arguedos answered that Marine tanks and LAV's were moving up to support us.

At 2000, SSgt Crew in 1st platoon, using a night vision scope, observed a column of thirty Iraqi armored vehicles moving toward us. Capt Drumbore reported this by radio to Capt Smith who in turn reported this situation to LtCol Haring requesting permission to engage. LtCol Haring quickly gave him permission to engage when he was ready.

By now, SSgt Crew could see five T-62 tanks followed by several Infantry fighting vehicles moving in our direction.

The Iraqi force was advancing slowly, feeling its way toward us. Capt Smith had requested air strikes. As the enemy tanks neared us the first jets arrived on station and attacked the Iraqi force, but failed to halt their advance. Soon the tanks entered small arms range and the 1st and 3rd platoons opened fire with M-203 grenades, LAAWs and heavy machineguns. Capt Smith radioed battalion telling Maj Arguedos that Echo Company was in contact. Two LAAW rockets hit a tank and it exploded. Marine tanks opened fire behind us destroying two tanks. Now we began receiving tank main gunfire blowing holes in the buildings near us. A platoon of LAVs attacked around our left, firing at the Iraqi forces. I saw four enemy tanks fire and a Marine LAV disappeared in flames. But at the same time, ten enemy tanks were quickly destroyed. As always, fighting at night was strange with tracers flying overhead in continuous lines and tanks silhouetted by their muzzle blast and shells impacting everywhere.

Now we began receiving Sagger missile fire. I couldn't see the missile being launched, just the missile coming at us. I watched a Sagger pass to the right of my platoon. The enemy's fire was as remarkably ineffective as our 25MM fire was remarkably accurate. Two enemy tank crews abandoned their tanks surrendering to Capt

Johnson's 3rd platoon. Capt Smith ordered me to send up a fire team to take the prisoners to the rear. I ordered Sgt Murphy to pick one of his teams. He in turn sent Cpl Cunningham's fire team. While the team was taking the prisoners to the rear, Cpl Cunningham was shot in the elbow becoming my first casualty of this war.

Meanwhile, the Iraqi forces attempted to push through us as another Marine platoon of LAVs and tanks moved up to support us.

More jets arrived on station and Capt Stordhal made radio contact with them. They started running air strikes on the enemy forces guiding in on the flames of the burning tanks. After three air strikes, three enemy tanks tried to go around our left flank, but Marine LAVs destroyed them. Iraqi tanks burst through the berms within the complex, firing. As rounds passed overhead or hit around us, my platoon opened fire on the Iraqi armor. The Iraqis seemed to pause and then suddenly began to disperse trying to flee the battlefield. This whole firefight had lasted only ten minutes.

During the same time, a Saudi unit shot apart an attempted ambush killing seven Iraqi soldiers.

Also, Marine Harrier jets had destroyed a convoy of twenty-four Iraqi tanks, armored personnel carriers and trucks. We could barely see the flames from this action across the desert.

At 2030, SSgt Crew of 1st platoon spotted Iraqi forces advancing toward us again. With Echo Company still on full alert from the first attack, Capt Smith radioed LtCol Haring that there were close to fifty enemy vehicles heading south. Once in range, the Marine LAVs opened fire and immediately an Iraqi tank exploded. Within seconds three Iraqi T-55 tanks emerged out of the darkness as the firefight between Iraqis and Marines grew furious.

By 2130 with the help of jets firing on the Iraqi forces, we fought them to a standstill. In the illumination of burning Iraqi tanks, I watched Iraqi crews from two damaged Iraqi tanks climb out and run away back into the dark night. By now, both the 1st and 3rd platoons were beginning to run out of LAAWs. Capt Smith fired a red star cluster, which was the signal for the two forward platoons to withdraw. As the 1st and 3rd platoon fell back past my platoon, we fired TOW missiles to cover them. An Iraqi tank exploded in a bright flash. But at the same time, a Marine LAV exploded after being struck by a missile disintegrating the LAV and its crew.

Then the Iraqi forces were again moving, this time around both flanks of my platoon as we fell back. The 1st and 3rd platoons fired volleys of TOW missiles to cover us. Then Echo Company, as one, fell back covered by air strikes.

The Iraqi attack halted again as Echo Company kept up a constant rate of fire. Both sides took casualties. Again, tracers flew overhead in continuous lines with tanks silhouetted by their muzzle blasts. Shells exploded around us as bullets flew everywhere.

Cpl Conn radioed me that Sgt Huebner had been hit in the arm and was heading back to the aid station and that he had taken command of 1st squad.

At 2230, a missile destroyed a Marine LAV carrying seven men.

In spite of our losses and shortage of ammo, with the combination of Marine LAVs, tanks and air support, we had stopped the Iraqi attack.

At 2351, LtCol Haring ordered Fox Company up to join Echo Company with a resupply of ammo.

Fox Company dug in next to Echo Company at 0055 the next morning. Capt Smith radioed LtCol Haring that Echo Company had suffered two killed and ten wounded during our two fights. We had destroyed twenty-five enemy tanks.

Suddenly, at 0110, Iraqi artillery began shelling Echo and Fox Companies with high explosives and illumination rounds. Thirty minutes later the Iraqi forces attacked us.

At 0144, LtCol Haring radioed Col Gagush to inform him that Echo and Fox Companies were involved in an intense small arms firefight with Iraqi units which were being backed up by a much larger force of around fifty-four vehicles.

Again, LtCol Haring called in air strikes to support us against this large Iraqi mechanized force. After being repeatedly hit, the Iraqis withdrew under the cover of antiaircraft fire.

I moved along my platoon line checking my men as I watched the tracers from the enemy antiaircraft fire.

At 0337, the Iraqi forces again attacked Echo Company with twenty vehicles. We opened fire with eleven TOW missiles destroying eleven vehicles before allied jets flew in making air strikes. The Iraqi survivors retreated back into the night.

As dawn broke, I looked ahead at our old OP site and saw only destroyed Iraqi vehicles.

Then LtCol Haring radioed Capt Smith and ordered Echo

Company to advance back to the OP site. As we moved forward, SSgt Higgins of 3rd platoon radioed Capt Smith that he had spotted two Soviet made armored personnel carriers and two tanks. Capt Smith requested air support and LtCol Haring ordered Cobra gunships forward and they destroyed both armored personnel carriers.

As the two tanks turned to flee, Capt Johnson's 3rd platoon began collecting enemy prisoners for transportation to the rear.

As we settled back into our old positions at the OP site, Capt Smith walked around checking Echo Company lines.

"How you doing sir?" I asked.

"Gunner I feel good, real good knowing that in our first real battle with Iraqi forces they have suffered heavy casualties from us."

"Sir, where is Gunny Simon. I haven't seen him this morning?"

He looked back at me saying, "He took a nasty shrapnel wound to his hand last night and I ordered him to the rear."

I looked away as my eyes filled with tears as I thought, "At least the old war horse is out of this shit and safe for a while."

Meanwhile, the USS Missouri and Wisconsin were shelling Iraqi positions on the Kuwaiti shore with their sixteen-inch guns.

I heard a report that near Khafji a column of eighty Iraqi tanks had advanced toward Saudi positions with their turrets pointing backwards in the universal sign of surrender. The Saudi forces prepared to accept the surrender when the Iraqi tankers suddenly turned their guns around and began firing on the Saudi troops. A Marine artillery unit opened up on the Iraqi tanks and Saudi M1A1 tanks rolled forward firing as air strikes were called in.

At 0411, Iraqi artillery fired shells in our direction for ten minutes, but they all fell short of our positions

Once the excitement of our first engagement was over, life returned to the familiar routine. I looked across almost featureless landscape except for the burned-out tanks and vehicles. I ate an MRE, brushed my teeth and shaved the best I could.

Later army Gen Schwarzkopf would say, "I've never doubted the ferocity of the Marines. They performed brilliantly in the face of overwhelming odds."

The first of February Gen Boomer the commanding General of the 1st MEF (Marine Expeditionary Force) ordered the 1st and 2nd Marine Divisions to prepare to conduct two separate simultaneous breaches of the Iraqi lines.

This new plan shifted the 1st Marine Division attack further west to a location near a border police station with a front covering sixty miles. They would make a deliberate attack to penetrate Iraqi defensive positions located between the Al Wafrah and Umm Gudair Oilfields. Our 2nd Marine Division would move around to our attack positions north of the police station.

After our division staff briefed Col Gagush, he gathered the officers of our regiment to brief us on the five phases of the coming attack.

Phase I, our regiment would move to its assembly area while engineers began reducing the bermed wall of sand that marks the Saudi-Arabia and Kuwaiti border.

In Phase II, we would breach the first obstacle belt. Infantry companies would infiltrate the obstacle belt on foot and establish blocking positions. This would be followed by mechanized forces breaching the first obstacle belt and then driving forward to the second obstacle belt.

Phase III, would be the breaching of the second obstacle belt.

In Phase IV, we would begin the capture of the oilfields to our front.

In Phase V, we would attack northward toward Kuwait City and link up with either the 4th MEB (Marine Expeditionary Brigade) or Arab coalition forces. Then we would prepare to attack into Kuwait City.

But first, I was worried about breaching the two obstacle belts. We officers and Staff NCOs gathered around sand tables studying the Iraqi obstacles. I realized the Iraqis had built strong defensive positions leaving little chance to surprise them. The only advantage we have is the selection of the exact time and place of the attack. Col Gagush told us that recon units had reported gaps along the boundary lines between Iraqi Divisions. But they were working slowly to close them up.

Meanwhile, an Iraqi armored force had been massing to attack through the narrow safe lanes of their own minefields. The column was stretching for miles when US and allied jets flew in and destroyed them.

I was surprised to learn from Col Gagush that our Marine strength in the Gulf had now reached 94,000. This was more Marines then we ever had at one time in Vietnam.

While we had been here, both the 1st and 2nd Marine Division had celebrated their 50th anniversary. And yet this was the first time that these two divisions had ever served together in combat.

By Feb 9th, our regiment had manned the same positions for eight days. The weather had turned cold and wet with the nights seemingly unbelievably long. When they were not on duty, I told my men to get some sleep. But as each day passed, they got more weathered looking and thinner.

I knew the long-anticipated attack was about to start. There was hardly a minute we didn't hear the noise of aircraft flying to or from bombing missions in Kuwait. All these aircraft overhead for some reason caused me concern. I had been unable to sleep for three days. Enemy activity had picked up as well as enemy soldiers crossing to our side to surrender during the day.

Sgt Ewing walked over and jumped down into my hole and asked, "Gunner are you all right?"

"Yeah why?"

"Well sir you've been awful quiet lately. Staff Sergeant Adams is concerned about you."

I looked at him hard saying, "What 'a mean?"

"Well sir, he doesn't know you like I do. That's why he asked me to speak to you. He says you haven't slept much the last couple of days."

Taking a deep breath, I said, "I know the largest ground offensive of my career is near. Like I told you men, I've got my personal gear in order and written my final letters to my wife and each of the children. But I seem to becoming more anxious each day." I shivered, but it was not only from the cold, then went on to say, "I keep going over it in my head asking myself what I can still do to better prepare these men for what's coming."

"Well sir, you've already done all you can. And we have learned a lot about these reserves in the last weeks as only combat could do. But hell, I'm still scared. But I'm ready and I'm ready because of you and so are these men."

"Thank you, Sergeant Ewing. I do feel better talking about it. But I'll tell you what; we're in this together. And as long as I have a breath in me, I'm going to do my best to take all these men back home."

"I know sir and we believe in you. But you have to take care of yourself too. You need to get some sleep too. Me and Staff Sergeant Adams can handle things for a while."

"All right," I said sitting back in my hole, feeling suddenly relaxed and went to sleep and slept the best I had in days.

By Feb 13th, the troop strength of our 2nd Marine Division had risen to almost 20,000. Our battalion had spent time in the rear repeating training drills and exercises, which prepared us to react quickly. Again, the officers and Staff NCOs studied sand table models of the area we would have to cross. We rehearsed assaulting and breaching bunkers. One morning we did the sand table walk-through of the control methods by which our battalion would be moved from our assembly area and through the lanes which would lead us to the breach sites. In the afternoon there was a full-scale regimental rehearsal.

Meanwhile, allied air forces had flown more than 65,000 sorties in Iraq and Kuwait losing twenty-eight planes, nineteen of which were US.

The air war shifted to tactical targets including dug in Iraqi troops, armor concentrations, artillery emplacement along the Kuwaiti and Saudi border, Iraqi fortifications, logistics supply lines both in Iraq and Kuwait and the Republican Guards along the northern Kuwait border.

By Feb 15th, it was estimated that 30% of Iraqi armor, 35% of their artillery and 27% of its armored vehicles had been destroyed in the Kuwaiti theater of operations.

LtGen Boomer sent a message to the 1st and 2nd Marine Division.

It read,

"After months of preparation, we are on the eve of liberating Kuwait, a small peaceful country that was brutally attacked and subsequently pillaged by Iraq. Now we will attack into Kuwait, not to conquer, but to drive out the invaders and restore the country to its citizens. In so doing, you not only return a nation to its people, but you will destroy the war machine of a ruthless dictator, who fully intended to control this part of the world, thereby endangering many other nations, including our own.

We will succeed in our mission because we are well

trained and well equipped, because we are US Marines, Sailors, Soldiers, and Airmen and because our course is just. Your children and grandchildren will read about our victory in the years to come and appreciate your sacrifice and courage. America will watch her sons and daughters and draw strength from your success.

May the spirit of your Marine forefathers ride with you and may God give you the strength to accomplish your mission.'

Semper Fi
Boomer

Later I gathered my platoon together. I talked to them trying to prepare them for the battles that lay ahead of us. I tried to pass on the things I had learned from my own experiences in combat. In a soft voice I said, "When I went to Nam nobody told me what it would be like." I told them of the terror, the noise and confusion. Fear is normal, but tolerable if you do what you have been trained to do. It will be kill or be killed. You must kill your enemy first. We regulars and reservists have trained together and played together and have fought as one and bled together. We are the band of brothers. We can depend on each other. It's that trust in one another that helps us stand our ground when every nerve wants to run. This trust will help us do the impossible.

Later as I sat in my hole, I was thinking I had seen this all before. Young Marines preparing for their big battle. They all acted differently now. Some of them showed their fear by bragging or horseplay. Some grew quiet thinking their own private thoughts. Some yawn a lot. Some speak with higher than normal voices. My own heart seemed to be beating faster. I saw some troops having trouble hyperventilating. I saw young sergeants and corporals acting differently too. The tyrants became gentle and kind. The laid-back leaders became intensely business-like.

Again, I lay awake going over and over in my mind the details, checking and rechecking equipment and tactics to make sure I hadn't forgotten anything. After all these years I still fear failure, letting my squad leaders down. These thoughts always haunted me just before a battle. The thought of failing my men was worse than my fear of death.

During Feb 17th, I counted eighteen different fires in the distance from burning oil wells.

Two days later upon orders from Col Gagush, LtCol Haring moved our battalion to the assembly area from which we would attack.

During Feb 20th, Marine engineers and Navy Seabee bulldozers started leveling the sand berms in eighteen places across the front of the 1st and 2nd Marine Divisions so the enemy wouldn't know which two routes we would use.

At 0236 on Feb 21st, I was awakened when Marine artillery began firing shells at Iraqi positions near the minefield in front of our battalion. The Iraqi artillery returned fire with only one volley, which hit, exploding 100 meters in front of us.

At 0330, I was awakened again when Marine artillery fired shells after a Marine recon team requested support during a probing action.

At dawn, Col Gagush drove up to the berm and got out walking along it among our battalion and his other forward battalions talking to us, wishing them all good luck. When he reached my platoon, he stopped and we talked about Vietnam back when he was a first lieutenant serving as an Infantry Company XO.

After he left, I spent the day resting, rechecking my equipment and my men.

During the day Gulf Company watched two Iraqi vehicles drive toward them. They fired a TOW missile, which slammed into the lead vehicle blowing it up. The second Iraqi vehicle quickly turned around speeding back the way it had come.

By now all the units of the 1st and 2nd Marine Divisions had finished moving up into our attack positions on the Saudi side of the berm.

After dark, like other platoons, I had Cpl Conn send out one of his fire teams from 1st squad to be a listening post in case Iraqi patrols should try to probe our lines. He sent Cpl Pusey's fire team out.

Marine recon teams were also sneaking out in front of us and soon were calling in artillery and air strikes on Iraqi units.

I knew the attack would be soon when Capt Smith ordered Echo Company to take anti-chemical and anti-biological pills.

Just after midnight, Marine recon teams again called in artillery and air strikes on Iraqi personnel and vehicles. It was hard to sleep with loudspeakers from outside broadcasting across the border asking the Iraqi soldiers to surrender before their camouflaged bunker complexes are hit by accurate air strikes.

At 1022, Iraqi artillery shells hit, exploding within our battalion. LtCol Haring quickly radioed Col Gagush and requested counter battery fire, which silenced the Iraqi guns.

At 1440, our battalion was hit again by artillery shells. Col Gagush this time called in air strikes against the Iraqi artillery.

LtCol Haring passed the word that President Bush had presented Saddam Hussein with his final ultimatum: be out of Kuwait by 2000 Saturday Feb 23rd or else.

At hearing this, Sgt Ewing looked at me saying, "What 'a think he means or else?"

I laughed saying, "We are the or else."

Just before dark, Col Gagush called in another air strike on the Iraqi forces in front of our regiment.

At 0141 on Feb 23rd, the Iraqi positions to our front were hit by air strikes.

Again, at 0830, jets roared in, bombing the bunker complexes to our battalion's front.

The day had started clear and warm with great visibility under a deep blue sky. But in the afternoon, this gave way to a great heavy black cloud of smoke as it moved over our area blocking out the sun. Of course, this smoke was coming from the burning oil wells in Kuwait.

At 1300, Capt Drumbore's 1st platoon watched two Iraqi T-55 tanks and four-scout vehicles drive into range. The 1st platoon opened fire with TOW missiles destroying all six vehicles. As we watched them burning, we saw several Iraqi soldiers start to run rearward. Marines from 1st platoon fired on them. One Iraqi soldier stopped and turned with his arms raised walking toward them. As he neared their lines, SSgt Crew and Capt Drumbore walked out to meet him. The Iraqi soldier dropped down to his knees as if to pray. SSgt Crew bent down and handed him an Arab pamphlet, which advised him he was now a prisoner of war.

SSgt Crew then took a cherry cake from a MRE bag, opened it, took a bite out of it and then handed the rest to the prisoner.

Then suddenly fourteen Iraqi soldiers appeared in the distance from behind the burning vehicles with raised hands and walked toward them to surrender.

SSgt Crew waved them to him. He searched them as Capt Drumbore covered him.

Twenty minutes later, thirty more Iraqi soldiers started walking toward Capt Johnson's 3rd platoon with their hands up. As SSgt Higgins searched them, he discovered one of them, a major was a battalion XO.

At 1645, ten more Iraqi soldiers surrendered to 3rd platoon. Meanwhile our loud speakers encouraged more to surrender.

Still for two hours, Col Gagush called in artillery trying to stop Iraqi reinforcements from moving up to the bunker complexes in front of our regiment.

As dusk fell, GySgt O'Malley came by, handing out extra grenades to each platoon. Meanwhile my men cleaned and oiled their weapons. Like many of my men, I wrote last letters home to Marty and each of my children. As I wrote I couldn't help thinking of the sand berms, minefields, and fighting positions we were facing. I knew we were outnumbered seven to one. I was expecting 10% to 50% of us would be killed in the coming attack. We would be trying to kill them and they would try and kill us. If the Iraqi's try to surrender, they would get a chance. If not, we would kill them.

At 1730, Iraqi artillery returned fire, but their shells hit the battalion next to us.

Ten minutes later, Hotel Company watched three trucks drive toward them through the minefield. Just out of range, they stopped and twenty-two Iraqi soldiers climbed down from the trucks and walked toward them through the obstacle belts and surrendered.

By evening, the wind shifted and the moon could be seen through light clouds.

I watched the lights of plane after plane flying overhead bombing Iraqi positions. Their identification lights would suddenly go off as they made their bombing runs in the distance. Bright flashes marked the bombs exploding and then the planes' lights would come back on as they returned flying over our heads.

After the air strikes were over it was quiet again.

I tried to get some sleep knowing we had a long night ahead of us.

During the night under a half moon with scattered rain showers and a biting wind, Marines all along the Kuwaiti border moved into their final attack positions and like us were waiting for the order to go. The deadline set by President Bush for Iraq to leave Kuwait had passed. Now it was time to force them out the old fashion way.

We put our chemical protective suits and boots on over our desert camouflaged uniforms, took our nerve agent pills as LAVs and tanks near us started up. Mine plows moved up ready to go as we tried to steady our nerves knowing soon, we would be riding into history. The ground offensive to liberate Kuwait would begin and us Marines would once again lead the way. As usual we had the worst job to do, fight through two bunker complexes while the Army got the glory of making a grand sweep around the Iraqi open flank.

With all this going through my mind, I rested the best I could as the hours slipped by and we waited for the order to advance. But there was little sleep to be had as each of us wondered what tomorrow would bring. Quietly my men kept rechecking their equipment. I knew what we were supposed to do, I knew how important our mission was. My men were calm and they were ready.

Capts Smith, Stordhal and our battalion Chaplain visited each of our platoons giving us last minute words of encouragement, inspiration and comfort.

The Chaplain read us a quote from Shakespeare's Henry V, "We few. We happy few. We band of brothers. For he who sheds his blood with me shall be my brother."

Then Capt Stordhal said, "We said get out of Kuwait or else. Well we are the or else. We are going to do great things tonight. Great things for our country and even greater things for this country."

Capt Smith said, "Let's go kick some ass!"

After they had left, I walked off into the darkness to be alone. I sat down in the sand and prayed:

"Dear Lord I pray for you to be with us in this fight. Keep me calm and help me make the right decisions to keep my men alive. If we must fight help us fight well. If it is my time to die, please let me die well. Please comfort Marty and my children when I'm gone. In Jesus name. Amen."

I stood up and walked back to my platoon. I had done all I knew to do. It was in God's hands now. I felt strangely calm.

At 1930 a missile roared into Echo Company's area exploding

next to a hummer followed by secondary explosions from ammo stored in the vehicle. Capt Drumbore, caught in the open was hit in the leg. He dropped to the ground holding the gaping wound as blood poured out onto the sand.

"Corpsman up!" yelled SSgt Crew as he ran up to help him.

As he was carried away it was again brought home to these young Marines that this was real war, not just another exercise.

Capt Smith moved Capt Bailey from weapons platoon to take command of 1st platoon.

At 2000 we were wearing our NBC suits when Col Gagush ordered LtCol Haring to move our battalion forward. Radios seemed to come alive; vehicles' engines started as we swung seventy-pound combat gear loaded packs on our backs and walked forward to infiltrate the first obstacle belt.

My platoon moved slowly and as carefully as they could under their fully loaded combat packs. I felt uneasy as we walked into the unknown across this dark desert. There was no concealment in this terrain; it was just so damn flat. I fully expected at any second for our battalion to be hit by artillery and small arms fire. And then there was what I feared most, land mines. Too soon I began to feel every ounce of my heavy pack as we moved through the cold and damp night. Even though I was sweating in my NBC suite, every time we halted, I shivered in the cold.

Once past the minefield, LtCol Haring formed our battalion into a wedge formation because he didn't know for sure what kind of Iraqi defenses were ahead of us.

Echo Company took the point of the wedge with Capt Bailey's 1st platoon at the point, Capt Johnson's 3rd platoon on the right rear and my platoon on the left rear. Fox Company was to the right rear of Echo and Hotel to our left rear. Col Gagush with 2nd Battalion was following us.

Suddenly, there were explosions to my far right as Marines of Fox Company ran into an unexpected minefield that was not on any of our maps. So much for surprise.

Carefully, Capt Bailey's 1st platoon entered an empty Iraqi bunker complex and an ammo storage site. They found booby-trapped explosive charges left by the hurried enemy withdrawal. They had fled so fast they had left their personal possessions. SSgt Crew found a radio with its frequency set and a safe wide open filled with documents.

By late evening our whole regiment had suffered few casualties as we met only light enemy resistance.

Both the 1st and 2nd Marine Divisions were advancing with 36,000 Marines. In all, there were 150,000 allied troops attacking across a 300-mile front into Kuwait and Iraq. US fighter-bombers, ships and artillery were hitting enemy concentrations behind the two Iraqi defensive barriers.

Just after midnight Capt Bailey's point fire team discovered another, but smaller minefield not on our maps. Capt Smith ordered Echo Company to halt in place as he radioed LtCol Haring requesting engineers to come up and deal with these mines.

As we waited, the clouds lowered again and the smoke returned reducing our visibility, which to me meant less close air support if the enemy did put up a better fight. To make it worse, a cold rain began to fall.

Our battalion was behind schedule by 0130 when Marine engineers showed up and used an Amtrack to fire a line charge to blow mines out of their positions. Then an old M-60 tank, like the ones I had seen in Vietnam, moved forward equipped with a track width mine plow moved through the minefield opening a lane by pushing the mines out of the way to the sides.

And still the enemy counterattack had failed to begin.

Finally, at 0325 our battalion started moving through the first obstacle belt. Echo Company led the way with the rest of our battalion now in a column behind us while under sporadic and inaccurate artillery fire.

At 0400 my platoon moved up near the barrier, still under the cover of the cold rain, darkness and the thick fog of oily smoke from burning Kuwaiti oil wells.

As sunlight began to filter through the darkness, the desert was filled with the sounds of combat.

At 0430 we heard the sounds of Marine artillery firing over our heads mixing with the explosions far out in front of us. The low-lying clouds were illuminated by the passage of flaming rockets and tracers of Iraqi anti-aircraft fire as allied aircraft hit the enemy north of the second obstacle belt.

At 0519 Marine Hummers with mounted antitank weapons skirmished with three Iraqi T-72 tanks. Both sides fired at each other quickly, then the Iraqi tanks retreated northward disappearing.

Suddenly, our battalion came under tank and small arms fire. As we returned fire, a volley of accurate artillery fire also hit us. As our battalion pushed forward, we were taking casualties as seven trucks and Amtracks were destroyed or damaged by the tank fire, killing and wounding thirteen Marines.

By 0600 the enemy had retreated as we entered the first main minefield. It seemed suddenly quiet. All I could hear was the growling of the Amtrack diesel engines behind us.

Echo Company took cover as I watched the Marine engineers ahead of us clear a lane for us through the minefield. I knew from our briefing that the 2nd Marine Division needed six lanes to enable it to get through this massive minefield.

So far, the breaching operation was looking like a training exercise. Cutting through concertina wire the engineers found British bar mines, Italian anti-tank and anti-personnel mines, Russian mines as well as daisy chain and chemical mines.

First, tanks and Amtracks fired line charges made of 1,750 pounds of plastic explosives attached to 100 meters of rope, which cleared a path about 16 meters by 100 meters. But these only destroyed pressure mines.

Next came M-60 tanks moving through the path pushing rakes, mine plows or rollers to get the remaining mines out of the way.

Meanwhile over our heads, Cobra gunships and Harrier jets gave us close air support as we began to push forward.

The engineers now left their vehicles to do a more thorough cleaning of the lane by using their hands.

My platoon quickly crossed a trench filled with oil. This first obstacle belt looked between 150 meters wide with 12 feet high sand berms.

I watched a tank plow push ahead of us through the lane. Suddenly the tank hit an Iraqi mine blowing the left track off.

At seeing the explosion, someone behind me screamed, “The tank hit a mine! Let’s get out ’a here!”

I looked around at the men of my platoon who were looking at me. I waved them down to take cover as we again came under light Iraqi artillery, small arms and mortar fire.

At 0615 Hotel Company, to our left rear, called in artillery on two Iraqi tanks.

At 0656 LtCol Haring ordered our whole battalion to chemical alert level four. I had heard over the radio that Fox Company had detected mustard gas on our right rear. With our NBC suites and boots already on we quickly put our gas masks and protective gloves on. Over the radio I heard a Marine Amtrack in Fox Company had hit a chemical mine. Three Marines had blisters on their hands, face and necks.

Just after 0700 LtCol Haring reduced the chemical alert for our battalion and we removed our gas mask and gloves.

Then Marine tanks punched through the sand berms and took up covering positions. Behind them, Echo Company rushed through and added to their covering positions. Then came Hotel Company in Amtracks roaring through the breach in the sand berms in clouds of dust as they moved up on our left. Fox Company did the same thing on our right. Then LtCol Haring ordered them to dismount and take the trench line. The ramps to the rear of their Amtracks clanked down and the rest of our battalion charged out into the desert joining Echo Company as all three companies charged forward. Never had I seen so much manpower and machinery in one area. To my right and left, as far as I could see stretching toward the horizon, were other Amtracks discharging Marines. The sounds of outgoing fire from our artillery and armored vehicles were overwhelming. But there was also incoming artillery fire with numerous airbursts over our heads. But as we advanced, Iraqi soldiers started popping up between the lines of armor to surrender. First, they surrendered as one or two, then tens and then by the hundreds.

Shocked, but happy LtCol Haring ordered our battalion back into our Amtracks to prepare to attack the second barrier as the prisoners were led to the rear. We had been told to expect only light enemy resistance at the first barrier. But now, when we attacked the second barrier, we would be more vulnerable to Iraqi artillery and armor counterattacks.

As we waited for the order to advance, again northeasterly thunderstorm winds plunged us into a choking black cloud from the oil well fires reducing our ground visibility down to 100 meters. This would mean little air support for us again. Even my night vision goggles wouldn't be of any good in this oily soup. It was like we had entered hell.

Then, over the radio, I heard LtCol Haring yell and then

repeated quickly to my men behind me, "Gas! Gas! Gas!"

Behind me I heard Sgt Ewing say, "Fuck me this is it."

For a second everyone seemed to freeze. Then suddenly gas masks and gloves were flying through the air. Putting my gas mask and hood on I looked back at my men, afraid I would see some of them twitching or coughing from poison gas. But they all seemed fine as they looked back at me. Cpl Conn even gave me the thumbs up sign.

Within minutes, LtCol Haring radioed to us the all-clear sign. I took my mask off and yelled back to my men, "Relax Marines, it's all clear."

Just as LtCol Haring radioed the order to advance again, as if by divine intervention, the wind changed from the south and the clouds disappeared and the sky cleared.

As before, the Marine engineers went first to mark the lanes through the minefields. Even though the mines had been buried in front of us, the wind had blown enough sand off most of them that even I could easily see them from inside the Amtrack. I watched the engineers marking each mine with brightly colored plastic garbage cans as they came under light Iraqi fire. This minefield looked to me to be about 200 meters wide.

Again, M-60 tanks fitted with mine plows and rollers pushed forward breaching the minefield. In doing so, two M-60 tanks were disabled from damage to their mine clearing equipment.

Amid the sounds of the tracked vehicles and artillery shells exploding, I suddenly heard the Marine Corps Hymn blaring from a loudspeaker somewhere in our area. Years before in Vietnam I remembered charging into battle singing the Marine Corps Hymn. Some things don't change.

As Echo Company led the way for our battalion, there wasn't time to look back to see where the loud speaker was. We were moving at a furious pace firing and hitting every available enemy target we saw.

Near the second defensive belt, we started receiving fire from Iraqi T-55 tanks dug in the sand up to their turrets. Capt Smith quickly ordered the Amtracks to halt so we could deploy on foot. No sooner had Echo Company charged out the back of our Amtracks and took cover in a skirmish line, the Iraqi T-62 tanks counterattacked us.

I watched as our Marine tanks fired hitting Iraqi tanks, which exploded in balls of fire as their turrets were blown off.

I couldn't help but think, "Lord if one of those Iraqi tank rounds had hit the aluminum hulled Amtracks of ours before we had gotten out, what would've happened to the twenty Marines inside?"

I could see enemy shells flying through Echo Company as we advanced and yet none of them were hitting us.

I wondered, "Can't these Iraqis shoot straight or what?"

I saw an enemy armor-piercing sabot round go bouncing harmlessly through our whole battalion without hitting anyone. It was as if God was protecting us, making our attack unstoppable.

In the middle of all this I watched in horror as a dog ran across the minefield. How he made it across alive I'll never know.

Then Capt Bailey's 1st platoon followed a tank as it punched its way through a sand berm. Next, my platoon followed another tank through the berm. Soon the rest of our battalion was pouring through and together we deployed on line attacking the enemy trench line. Again, I was pleasantly surprised as the Iraqi soldiers came running from their trenches toward us with their hands in the air to surrender. As we gathered the prisoners together, disarming them, I learned through interrogators that some of the Iraqi soldiers were saying they didn't want to be here. They had been forced to fight.

I couldn't help but smile in relief.

"What's so funny?" asked SSgt Adams.

"In my twenty-six years in the Corps this is the weirdest fight I've ever been in." And I was truly dumbfounded by these Iraqi soldiers surrendering in hordes, waving, smiling and flashing the 'V' sign for victory at us.

"These ass holes can't wait to surrender," added Sgt Ewing.

But at 0724, Capt Bailey's 1st platoon came under fire from a bunker. The platoon quickly returned fire, taking cover as he radioed for an antitank vehicle to support them. A hummer rolled up firing a TOW missile, which destroyed the bunker. This caused thirty more Iraqi soldiers nearby to surrender.

At 0730, a scout team from Capt Johnson's 3rd platoon fired at a suspected enemy position. Receiving no return fire, the rest of his platoon moved up to the position and discovered it empty. It seemed that the majority of the Iraqis between the two obstacle belts had withdrawn. As the time passed, the threat of an enemy counterattack was decreasing. This lack of major enemy activity was truly a relief to me and my men around me. But I still was afraid we were being drawn into a trap, even though there was still a constant stream of Iraqi troops surrendering. Capt Bailey still kept calling in artillery strikes on bunkers his point fire teams saw in the distance.

At 0745 our battalion began taking sporadic fire as we neared another trench line and enemy resistance stiffened. LtCol Haring radioed requesting artillery and air support. Soon Cobra gunships flew in, firing right down the Iraqi trenches.

At 0850 two Marine engineer vehicles ahead of us hit mines destroying both. Still two Marine engineers on foot entered the minefield and set live charges, then ignited them and ran back out of the minefield only seconds before they exploded.

As Echo Company moved through the minefield to within 300 meters of the enemy trenches, we started taking rocket-propelled grenade fire. A grenade exploded among Capt Bailey's 1st platoon. He looked back to see SSgt Crew on the ground withering in pain. A corpsman rushed to his side and found he had been hit by shrapnel in his left leg, hip, hand and arm, the same arm that was injured so bad years ago in Vietnam. Later when I talked with SgtMaj Burns about him he would say, "Staff Sergeant Crew sure doesn't have many parts left that doesn't have metal in them." And still later Marty would tell me of seeing the wounded SSgt Crew in the hospital in Camp Lejeune on the evening news.

Meanwhile, my platoon was moving forward in squad rushes under the cover of 50-cal machinegun fire and we were hit by volleys of RPGs. Cpl Morris one of my long-time regulars in 3rd Squad spun to the ground hit in the throat by shrapnel. Then at less than 100 meters from the trenches, my whole platoon was pinned down by automatic weapons fire. Over the radio I ordered Sgt Murphy's 3rd squad to crawl forward while the rest of my platoon laid down covering fire. I was shocked to see Sgt Murphy a reservist, stand up in full view under this enemy fire and walk among his men giving orders and encouraging them to move forward. He went on to maneuver his men to within 20 meters of the trench and then led them into the trench itself. And this was a Marine who didn't believe he was a very good sergeant. From the backside of the trench, shaken Iraqi troops climbed out running away across the desert as we shot them down.

At 0930 Capt Bailey saw a tower that the enemy could be using to call in the sporadic mortar fire Echo Company was receiving. He radioed, requesting artillery fire and the barrage destroyed the tower. But still the enemy fired mortars at us. And then Capt Bailey in turn called in artillery fire on the area from which he thought the mortars were being fired. After the next volley of Marine artillery shells exploded, the enemy mortar crew surrendered.

By 1020 our whole regiment was on line advancing under increasing enemy artillery and tank fire. My platoon was trying to stay behind a Marine tank as it led us forward through small arms and antitank fire. In a series of tank and infantry attacks made up of rapid fire and maneuver, we fought our way through the fortified trenches, bunkers, dug in tanks and artillery overwhelming the Iraqi forces. By using these quick, sharp engagements and outflanking the enemy, constantly destroying their heavy weapons with our air and artillery support, we were able to defeat the enemy. As our regiment overran an Iraqi brigade-size bunker complex destroying large numbers of enemy tanks and armored personnel carriers, we gave the Iraqi's a choice: surrender or die. Suddenly thousands of Iraqi troops threw their hands up in surrender.

Just before noon, Capt Bailey saw nine enemy vehicles stopped with over twenty infantry troops standing around them. He immediately radioed for artillery fire on them and they disappeared in flame, smoke and dust.

At 1200, hundreds of Iraqi soldiers were seen waving white flags as they crawled out of bunkers and trenches. Capt Bailey's 1st platoon discovered a cache of ammo containing RPGs, which Capt Smith ordered to be blown in place.

But first, Col Gagush drove over in his command Amtrack to look at the cache himself. As he prepared to leave, he walked up to me and said, "Gunner, these Iraqis could've put up one hell of a fight if they had wanted to. With all the ammo this regiment alone has found, this battle could've been Iwo Jima all over again."

A little later as my platoon searched some bunkers, they found TVs, home appliances, air conditioners, even fire alarms, carpet samples and beds.

Because of the overwhelming number of prisoners, our advance was being slowed down. Col Gagush ordered up support troops to relieve his infantry troops of stripping, searching and guarding the prisoners and marching them back south.

Many of the Iraqis who surrendered were waving, "Get Out of Kuwait Free" Cards. They reminded me of the old "Chiue Hoi" cards in Vietnam that we dropped over the enemy controlled area from planes.

One card pictured an Iraqi soldier thinking about his wife and children as he surrendered to an American soldier. On the reverse side of the card, it read in Arabic, instructions on how to surrender.

1. Remove the magazine from your weapon.
2. Sling your weapon over your left shoulder with the muzzle down.
3. Have both arms raised above your head.
4. Approach the Multi-National Forces positions slowly with the lead soldier holding this document above his head.
5. If you do this you will not die.

Some Iraqis waved white T-shirts that they had saved for just this occasion.

But a couple of Marines in Capt Bailey's 1st platoon were wounded when an Iraqi soldier pulled the pin to a grenade he was carrying under his shirt killing himself.

Capt Smith ordered Echo Company from now on to strip the prisoners down to their underwear.

Once we had passed this second obstacle belt, LtCol Haring halted our battalion long enough to get resupplied with fuel and ammo. As we waited, we formed up in a skirmish line in front of our Amtracks. Then we climbed back inside our Amtracks and moved north again.

Inside my Amtrack I could see my men breathing easier as more and more Iraqi soldiers continued to surrender. They knew that the Iraqis had missed their best chance at inflicting heavy casualties on us as we crossed those two barriers.

Now our 2nd Marine Division was advancing in six columns. At times our advance was slowed down by vehicles becoming bogged down in the sand.

About twenty miles beyond the second barrier I suddenly heard Capt Smith's voice over the radio yelling, "Expect enemy vehicles within 5,000 meters! Dismount!"

The Amtracks stopped quickly as Echo Company ran out the

back and down the ramps and started advancing on foot. As my platoon climbed over a small rise in the desert, Cpl Cook was the first to see three Iraqi T-55 tanks and eleven armored personnel carriers and dismounted Infantry.

We opened up with our small arms fire as our tanks fired over our heads. I could see our tank rounds hit the Iraqi armored personnel carriers as if they were peeling a tin can open, then the sides caved in followed by secondary explosions as they went up in flames. The Iraqis advanced to within 1,000 meters of us, which was point blank range for our M1A1 tanks. Our tanks rolled up on line and quickly destroyed six armored personnel carriers and two T-55 tanks. Then they fired on anything moving including a Toyota land cruiser moving at a speed close to 50 miles per hour.

Capt Smith ordered my platoon to move around in a flanking movement and we came upon four Iraqi officers and three enlisted men. They had no time to react when my men opened fire cutting them all down before they had a chance to surrender.

As I turned my platoon back northward, I saw a tree line containing bunkers, trenches with dug in tanks. Over the radio I requested artillery and air support. First, the artillery rounds roared overhead hitting the enemy positions and then Cobra gunships flew in firing missiles into the enemy positions.

On line, the rest of Echo Company swept toward the tree line. As the dust cleared from missile strikes, nearly 1200 Iraqi troops seemed only too happy to surrender.

Advancing again, I was awestruck by the great amount of smoke coming from over 50 nearby oil well heads on fire. There was no way to not inhale the fumes, which were making it hard to talk let alone breath. I began to cough so hard it hurt my chest.

At times the smoke was so thick I couldn't see my hand in front of my face. I thought maybe fighting a jungle war hadn't been so bad after all.

Suddenly, Cobra gunships flew overhead firing TOW missiles at enemy tanks trying to use the smoke to sneak up close to us.

Cpl Cook saw an Iraqi tank break through the smoke coming right at his fire team. But as they dived to the sand, a missile from a Marine Cobra destroyed the tank, ripping the turret off blowing it fifty meters in the air.

Then through the smoke, I saw a building. I quickly ordered Sgt

Murphy's 3rd squad to attack it. As Cpl Short's fire team moved around a corner of the house they ran into an Iraqi tank. An Iraqi captain standing up in the turret with his arms up said in plain English, "What took you guys so long. We've been waiting to surrender."

Over the radio Col Gagush told LtCol Haring and the other two-battalion commanders that our objective was now Kuwait City. And as our regiment advanced in that direction the Iraqi Army continued to surrender or retreat offering little resistance. We were finding a lot of abandoned enemy equipment, capturing tons of ammo. Most Iraqis that we met now were firing a few rounds, then quickly surrendering or falling back.

I noticed the Iraqi prisoners seemed surprised that we were treating them so well. It seemed the leaflets that we had dropped explaining the terms of surrender have helped even though their leaders had told them that if they surrendered, they would be brutally handled.

At 1245 Capt Johnson's 3rd platoon reported by radio that an enemy armor unit was moving toward us. LtCol Haring quickly called in artillery fire on them.

By 1252 one of our Marine tanks had destroyed six enemy tanks and our battalion had captured sixty-three Iraqi soldiers.

At 1300, over the radio, I listened to the report of a nearby Marine tank company making contact with two Iraqi T-62 tanks and quickly destroying one of them. Then the other Iraqi tank retreated under the covering fire of mortars.

Echo Company took cover in the sand as the tank battle raged around us and Marine tanks destroyed two Iraqi tanks and the rest fell back again under the cover of mortar fire.

Later in the afternoon, our battalion made contact with another enemy trench line. LtCol Haring ordered us to dismount and attack. Even as we were running out the back of our Amtracks, Iraqi soldiers were running toward us with their hands held high. My platoon alone quickly captured twenty prisoners as more came toward us. Sending them quickly rearward, Echo Company began making a flanking movement on the enemy position as our Marine Amtracks fired their machineguns giving us a base of fire. We were about 1700 meters away from the enemy positions when Marine mortar crews fired smoke shells to cover our movements.

"This is just too damn easy," I thought to myself as my platoon ran toward a group of frantic Iraqis begging on their knees to surrender. Sweating heavily in their NBC suits my platoon was quickly forced to slow down as they moved from bunker to bunker. Echo Company had captured over 200 prisoners.

By now our whole battalion was sweeping forward using the combination of tanks, machineguns, TOW missiles and supported by Cobra gunships firing missiles as we engaged more Iraqi bunkers, tanks, rocket launchers, trucks and armored personnel carriers.

By 1410, 500 Iraqi soldiers under the command of a colonel had surrendered to our battalion.

It seemed our two Marine Divisions alone had thrown back eleven Iraqi divisions. I thought to myself, "I'm just glad these aren't hard core NVA divisions like I faced in Vietnam."

Our 2nd Marine Division had covered thirty miles ripping our way through Kuwait devastating the Iraqi units and capturing over 5,000 prisoners.

I still had this fear that the Iraqis were just retreating deep into Kuwait, preparing one big corps size ambush.

Next, we ran into an Iraqi supply convoy. Quickly, by using speed and maneuverability, our battalion took them by surprise. They surrendered without firing a shot. Searching the trucks, we found tons of food and ammo. The ammo had Jordanian military markings on them. I thought Jordan was supposed to be neutral. LtCol Haring ordered the ammo blown in place. The food was loaded in our vehicles and we began passing it out to the Kuwaitis we were now beginning to see. It was plain the Kuwaitis were happy to see us as well as get the food.

By 1500, we had fought some determined Iraqi defenders; still thousands of enemy troops were trying to surrender. Again, the sheer number of prisoners was swamping our prisoner handling teams and was slowing our regiment down.

At times the Iraqis seemed to be surrendering from every direction at once. My platoon had captured over 350. They surrendered blowing us kisses, waving American flags, white flags and begging for food and water.

Finally, at 1539, Col Gagush ordered LtCol Haring by radio to halt our battalion and dig in for the night. I was surprised we weren't pushing on. But we were all exhausted from the lack of sleep and I could feel the great sense of relief in my men. All day they had quickly eliminated what resistance they encountered and best of all they had taken few casualties. After months of preparing for the worst some men began to hope the rest of this war might go as easy as today. I prayed to God it would be so.

As my platoon dug in, I kept looking ahead at four cone-shaped German-built bunkers in the distance capable of holding hundreds of enemy troops. Smoke was pouring from two of the bunkers, obviously the targets of the allied air strikes.

I also looked around at the dozens of burning oil wells, which are silhouetting our tanks, Amtracks and LAVs.

As darkness fell, the rest of the 2nd and 1st Marine Divisions had halted also. Col Gagush was called back to our division headquarters to plan and prepare for the morning attack.

After Echo Company had finished digging in and Capt Smith had inspected our lines, he ordered Capt Bailey to take his platoon out on patrol to check out those bunkers in front of us. I felt better knowing they would be checked out. But I was glad it wasn't my platoon doing it. Although I knew he and his platoon were just as tired as we were.

But after 1st platoon had sneaked up to the bunkers, they found them empty except for some candles still burning on tables with bowls of uneaten rice. The two smoking bunkers were mostly collapsed with corrugated metal tops. Few bunkers in this area were unscathed by the relentless allied air strikes of the previous weeks. In one bunker on a table was a deck of cards laid out in an unfinished hand of solitaire, left by its fleeing occupants. Outside, expended cluster bomb canisters lay around looking like broken eggshells.

I had just dozed off when at 1734 I was suddenly awakened by Cpl Short yelling, "We got tanks coming!"

I looked up to see two Iraqi tanks rumbling toward Capt Bailey's 1st platoon's section of the line. A Marine tank fired hitting one Iraqi tank and it exploded with its ammo cooking off with eleven secondary explosions. The other tank quickly turned around disappearing in the night.

I knew there was a threat of an enemy counterattack, but there just seemed to be nothing coming. Maybe it's because of the poor visibility from the smoke of the oil well fires drifting over us in clouds.

Every time I tried to get some sleep it seemed we had Iraqis coming to us to surrender.

By 1935, 3,000 more Iraqis had surrendered to our battalion.

By midnight the smoke was blocking out the moon. It was so dark I couldn't see past the end of my rifle.

At 0109 on Feb 25th, SSgt Adams shook me awake to tell me that our 2nd Marine Division had just ordered Col Gagush to place our whole regiment on full alert because of the possible counterattack by two Iraqi brigades. LtCol Haring was already moving tanks and anti-tank weapons up front to use their thermal and night vision devices to try and see through the darkness.

By 0315, Col Gagush returned from our division headquarters and gathered LtCol Haring and the other two battalion commanders together and issued his orders for this morning's attack.

At 0330 in the middle of this meeting, our regiment was hit with enemy tank and mortar fire. But by using the thermal sights, the battalion XOs like our Maj Arguedos radioed for air strikes on these forces and threw them back.

The smoke had shifted by first light and again I could look across the desert, right and left and see two Marine Divisions on line preparing to attack.

Soon Col Gagush received the order to advance from our 2nd Marine Division and the whole regiment was attacking another bunker complex. LtCol Haring ordered our battalion of tanks, Amtracks and Hummers to recon by fire as we advanced. We met moderate resistance as we destroyed Iraqi bunkers and vehicles over 2,000 meters away by using TOW missiles and 25MM cannons. Then the Infantry, like us, dismounted and moved forward on foot and began clearing the bunkers. 400 Iraqis led by a major quickly surrendered to our battalion.

At 0515 the smoke had shifted back toward us and under this cover an Iraqi tank force counterattacked our regiment. With a combination of TOW missiles and 25MM fire, Echo Company knocked out five enemy tanks coming at us.

Suddenly, there was a loud bang behind me and I felt a blast of heat. I quickly looked back over my shoulder to see Capt Stordhal tumbling across the sand. Near him 1stSgt Bean was down on his knees holding up his left hand. There was blood on his arm. Capt

Stordhal tried to stand, but his left leg gave way beneath him and he fell. My own ears were ringing, but I could still hear the vicious hail of automatic weapons fire around me. The ground shuddered with the impact of incoming mortar fire.

Capt Stordhal's leg was shattered as a hot wet sensation filled his pant leg. He began screaming, "Corpsman up! Please God somebody help me!"

Suddenly both of my platoon corpsmen ran to them despite the firefight raging around us. Both corpsmen dropped down next to Capt Stordhal and 1stSgt Bean. The eyes of the corpsman bending over Capt Stordhal grew wide at the sight of his wound. He immediately slapped a large battle dressing to the wounded leg. He yelled for help, but the rest of us were too busy fighting right then. Getting to his feet he grabbed hold of Capt Stordhal by his web gear harness and pulled him up and over his shoulder. Then the two corpsmen both started running as they carried the two wounded Marines toward a medivac vehicle, which was 100 meters away. As they were running Capt Stordhal was begging, "Please put me down!"

"Just hang on, we're almost there." The corpsman answered.

Finally, Capt Stordhal was laid down on the ramp of the LAV. As the corpsman carrying 1stSgt Bean arrived he noticed the back of the other corpsman's flak jacket and helmet was shredded from multiple shrapnel hits. But miraculously he was unhurt as he tried to replace the blood-soaked dressing on Capt Stordhal's leg. But the moment he removed the dressing, his hands and arms were showered in a fresh red spray. Capt Stordhal tried to sit up to see his wound, but before he could see, the corpsman pounded him in the chest with a bloody palm pushing him back down.

"Don't look at it!" ordered the corpsman.

As fast as he applied a new battle dressing it would become soaked with blood. By the fourth dressing he was ready to use a tourniquet. But he decided he would try one more dressing first. He placed it over the wound and pushed it in with both fists. Finally, the bleeding began to slow.

Meanwhile 1stSgt Bean and other wounded had been loaded and now Capt Stordhal was being placed on a stretcher. By now the morphine was starting to take hold as he was rapidly sliding into shock.

As the ramp to the Amtrack started to rise, Capt Stordhal yelled, "Thanks Doc!"

Grabbing his rifle, the corpsman looked back inside with eyes filling with tears and yelled, "I'll see ya in the states sir!" Then both corpsmen turned heading back to the fight. By the time they returned to my platoon the fighting had stopped.

At 0550 the smoke around us was still thick. Suddenly over the radio a Marine tank commander reported seeing something through the smoke like spots or heat sources at long range through his thermal imaging system. Capt Smith ordered Echo Company to dismount. As we ran out the back of our Amtracks, Cpl Cook heard rumblings out in front of us, but thought they were friendly tanks. Still he yelled to me, "Gunner there's something out there!"

He and his fire team dived for cover as he became alarmed as the sounds became louder, sounding like deep rumbles of diesel engines with the clanking of tracks.

As I ran around getting my platoon into position, the sounds didn't sound like the M-60 tanks I had heard for years or the new MIAI tanks either.

Suddenly I saw eleven enemy vehicles ahead of us through the smoke. I radioed Capt Smith telling him about the enemy vehicles. He in turn alerted our tanks.

Over the radio I listened to Capt Smith yelling at our tankers, "You gotta shoot these people!"

Meanwhile, Cpl Cook watched Iraqi tank gun barrels start traversing toward our direction.

Then I heard our tanks fire behind us and saw the shell hit a T-72 tank ahead of us blowing the turret clear off as more Marine tanks opened fire. Instantly, I saw three Iraqi tanks get blasted apart. Then two more enemy tanks were destroyed, all within eighty seconds.

For the next ten minutes as the smoke cleared, we watched Iraqi tanks trying to retreat eastward as our tanks picked more of them off at long range. It seemed every round our tanks fired was hitting an Iraqi target. I felt sorry for them in a way I never felt for the NVA or VC in Vietnam.

Over the radio Capt Smith ordered Echo Company to advance, but not to shoot any Iraqi's if they were moving away from a burning vehicle. Our company had soon captured ninety-three badly wounded enemy prisoners. These prisoners were shaky as they shivered in mismatched uniforms. We gave them MREs, which they devoured. An English-speaking Iraqi said this was their first complete meal in weeks.

As we passed the destroyed T-72 tanks, I could see the crews inside had been incinerated as the thin tank armor had melted down to nothing.

By 0600 we were back within our Amtracks when one filled with Marines of Capt Bailey's 1st platoon hit a mine.

Then over the radio I heard the dreaded words, "Gas! Gas! Gas!"

Quickly we put our gas masks on as the Amtracks hatch closed.

But soon Capt Smith radioed the all-clear sign.

At 0620 our battalion bumped into an Iraqi battalion of tanks and Infantry moving toward us. Both sides opened fire at once. We dismounted quickly to join the battle with our tanks. As LtCol Haring radioed in air support, Hummers with mounted TOW sections drove through us to the front. Within the first few minutes of battle even under heavy enemy fire the Marine TOW sections destroyed three Iraqi tanks. After losing thirty-four tanks and armored personnel carriers the enemy retreated.

At 0630 the same thing happened again as the oily smoke made it difficult to determine whether chemical agents were being used and we moved through these infernal oilfields. Like most of my platoon, I was beginning to get a headache as we passed through hundreds of oil fires, which at times turned day into night.

Over the radio I heard Capt Bailey say, "This is more like a training exercise than war. In fact, our training exercises in 29 Palms were harder than this."

Meanwhile, I was still surprised as thousands of Iraqis kept surrendering which still at times slowed us down. Sometimes we just pointed them to the rear and told them to walk in that direction because there were not enough trucks to carry all of them.

By 0730 our battalion was moving slowly through the thick black smoke mixed with fog, which had reduced visibility to 200 meters or less.

At 0753 I heard massed Marine artillery shells passing overhead and exploding in the distance in front of us. This shelling over our heads lasted until 0817. By now the fog had gotten even denser enveloping the area around us reducing visibility down to 100 meters. Still we pushed on groping through the fog and smoke. But

I figured this fog and smoke was just as big a problem for the Iraqis as it was for us.

Suddenly through the fog and smoke came an enemy unit of T-63 tanks and armored personnel carriers bumping into our regiment surprising both sides. A T-63 tank halted with its big gun pointing right at Col Gagush's command vehicle. I expected someone to fire, but no one did as the whole enemy force stopped too. Instead the hatch on the T-63 tank pointing at Col Gagush was pushed open. From this hatch climbed out the Iraqi brigade commander who walked up to Col Gagush's command vehicle and surrendered his whole brigade saying he no longer wished to fight. But that he couldn't speak for the units behind him in the fog.

Before Col Gagush could answer him, another Iraqi unit attacked out of the fog and smoke with tank and automatic weapons fire. As we ran from the back of our Amtracks, tank shells exploded among us, yellow rifle and machinegun tracer bullets passed by us. Looking around at my platoon, I saw Maj Arguedos diving to the sand as yellow tracers passed by him at knee high level.

Our regiment returned fire with tank, machinegun, rifle and antitank rounds. In a ten-minute free for all, my platoon alone using Dragons and LAAWs destroyed five enemy tanks and ten armored personnel carriers as our regiment forced the Iraqis to retreat into the fog and smoke.

Col Gagush radioed our division headquarters notifying them of our firefight with a brigade size force.

Our battalion moved forward and was again hit by enemy automatic weapons fire as bright yellow tracers cut through our ranks. Echo Company returned fire with Dragon and light antitank fire. As before, the Iraqi attack began to falter.

The deep rumbling of engines and the high-pitched squeaking of tank tracks mingled with the sounds of the enemy fire. Marine tanks and antitank Hummers halted only long enough to aim and fire on enemy vehicles. The TOWs, being the first to engage the enemy, had knocked out seven tanks as Echo Company destroyed thirteen vehicles.

I saw a Marine tank swing its turret toward a T-55 Tank to shoot, but it misfired. Luckily another nearby Marine tank fired destroying the same Iraqi tank.

As we fought, the fog and smoke suddenly lifted and Marine jets dived down, bombing Iraqi re-enforcements moving toward the battle. This seemed to break the enemy's back and they broke contact fleeing in retreat.

At 0915 our battalion ran into the flank of an enemy force when a platoon and antitank section from Gulf Company opened fire.

Fifteen minutes later, Echo Company joined the fight destroying six enemy armored personnel carriers and capturing nineteen enemy soldiers.

By 1000 the rest of our battalion had joined the battle with the Iraqi force. The extra TOW sections quickly swung into action. Firing even at great distances when they could see. They hit several Iraqi tanks and other vehicles before the Cobra gunships joined the attack as more enemy tanks and armored personnel carriers burst into flames.

A Marine LAV suddenly fired a 25MM round into the fog and smoke. I was looking to see what he had shot at. But over the radio I heard the LAV commander say it had been an accidental discharge. Capt Smith was screaming over the radio chewing him out. Then from the direction the 25MM round had entered the fog ninety-two Iraqi soldiers appeared surrendering.

As we sent them to the rear, I heard the low rumbling sounds of tanks and vehicles ahead of us in the fog and smoke. Suddenly the smoke and fog lifted revealing an enemy attacking force of twenty-six T-55 tanks and armored personnel carriers and dismounted infantry.

Our battalion was advancing with Fox Company on the left, Gulf Company in the center and our Echo Company on the right.

A vicious firefight erupted as Fox and Gulf Companies opened fire with TOWs, 25MM rounds and automatic weapons fire. Soon burning enemy vehicles were littering the desert.

Both Fox and Gulf Companies continued to fight several more company-size Iraqi units capturing four hundred and ten enemy prisoners including an Iraqi lieutenant colonel. With so many prisoners, again, they just ended up waving them to our rear.

Then our battalion entered more burning oil fields. At times this thick smoke reduced the visibility down to less than fifty meters.

Suddenly Cpl Conn felt a violent stinging sensation burning his left arm above the elbow. Then something thudded into his back knocking the breath out of him. On the ground he gasped for breath as he thought, 'Oh my God I'm hit in the back!'

He heard Cpl Pusey yelling, "Corpsman up!" as he rolled over on his side still gasping for breath and saw blood streaming down his arm. A corpsman ran over and dropped down beside him and ripped up his T-shirt sleeve and then started tying on a battle dressing.

"My back! My back! I've been hit in the back!" cried Cpl Conn.

The corpsman looked around at his back quickly, then whistled in amazement saying, "No you haven't" He then jerked a large piece of shrapnel out of the back of the flak jacket and dropped it instantly.

"Damn! It's still hot. But it didn't go through your flak jacket," said the corpsman shaking his hand violently.

"Am I going to be okay?" pleaded Cpl Conn.

"Sure, it's just a little thing," the corpsman answered.

The fear drained out of him as his body shuddered with relief as he almost laughed knowing he would be medivaced to the rear, out of this sand and smoke.

Hearing the yell for corpsman, I moved through the smoke in that direction until I saw the corpsman working over someone.

"Who's hit?" I yelled running over.

Seeing it was probably Cpl Conn, one of my best NCOs I blurted out, "Oh no it's not...." I stopped dropping down to my knees next to him.

Cpl Conn sat up staring me right in the eyes as I cried, "Are you okay?" I reached out with both hands grabbing Cpl Conn's shoulders squeezing tightly.

Cpl Conn looked down watching blood trickle down over his left hand.

"Are you all right Corporal Conn?" I asked again almost crying.

Tears rolled down Cpl Conn's face as he tried to speak.

I touched the bandage wet with blood, looking now at the corpsman saying, "Is he okay? Will he be all right?"

Finally, Cpl Conn spoke first, "Yeah, Gunner. I'm okay. Just a scratch."

"He's a tough one," said the corpsman.

"I know he is. Thank God," I mumbled, thankful.

"Come on Corporal Conn I gotta get you moving to the rear," said the corpsman as he lifted him to his feet and began walking him rearward. Over his shoulder Cpl Conn said, "Gunner, you be careful."

Nearby Cpl Pusey sat looking at me and I said, "Well Corporal Pusey you have first squad now. Get 'em moving."

"Yes sir." He answered looking around at the rest of the squad and waved them forward.

I didn't know it, but my other corpsman was working on my 3rd squad leader Sgt Murphy, cutting his shirt away as he tried to stop the blood, which was pouring out of a bullet wound in his right shoulder. By the time I found out, he was already safe in the rear with Cpl Conn. Cpl Short had taken over the 3rd squad.

Meanwhile, Cpl Cook, a fire team leader in 2nd squad, was hit in the neck. He's hands went up to his neck as he dropped to his knees, feeling a deep hole. Blood was pumping out against his fingers. He jerked his hands away, but then quickly put them back tightly to the side of his neck. Thick blood gushed out on his hand running down his forearm. His helmet rolled off as he laid back down dazed looking up into the smoke-filled sky. Then with one hand he searched his flak jacket for a bandage. He rolled on his side bringing the bandage up to his mouth. With his teeth he ripped open the green wax paper around it. The blood now ran across his face in streams. He placed it on the wound as he clumsily tied it under his opposite armpit.

Capt Smith, moving up behind Echo Company saw Cpl Cook in trouble and yelled, "Corpsman up! We got a Marine down!"

He ran diving to the sand next to Cpl Cook.

"Oh, corporal it's gonna be all right," said Capt Smith as he cradled Cpl Cook's head in his lap checking out the wound. He pulled out one of his bandages and added it to the first bloody one. Then he put one arm under Cpl Cook's shoulder and the other arm under his legs. Standing up, Capt Smith carried him stumbling rearward. Cpl Cook's face was white as his body sagged in his arms.

Suddenly a mortar exploded ten feet behind them. The blast slammed Capt Smith forward as he took the full blast of shrapnel. His helmet bounced rolling across the sand.

Meanwhile over the radio my radioman heard and told me that GySgt O'Malley is reporting to LtCol Haring that Capt Smith is badly wounded. LtCol Haring radioed 1st platoon to tell Capt Bailey to take command of Echo Company. But their radioman found Capt Bailey sprawled in the sand dead. As his men lifted his body to put it in a poncho his head fell apart.

So Capt Johnson the 3rd platoon leader and the only captain left in Echo Company took command.

Meanwhile our regiment was pushing ahead fighting amid this dense smoke. Again, because of this smoke, we were unable to call in close air support or artillery. Instead, as usual we used our TOW sections with their thermal sights. But still, within the last hour our regiment had destroyed seventy-two enemy vehicles and captured over 500 prisoners.

By 1100, our battalion was still heavily engaged even after destroying thirty Iraqi tanks, twenty-four armored personnel carriers and capturing thirty-one prisoners.

By this time, our 2nd Marine Division had had only six Marines killed and of course, three of them were in Echo Company.

In the early afternoon Fox Company made contact with an Iraqi mechanized unit. Rain now added to our poor visibility due to the smoke. We found ourselves facing two Iraqi brigades. Col Gagush radioed for division artillery, which unleashed a barrage on the enemy.

Near me a Marine TOW team fired missiles destroying two enemy tanks as Cobra gunships attacked the enemy from above. With all this firepower brought to bear against them, the Iraqi tanks scattered. In all, forty enemy tanks and 100 other vehicles were destroyed.

By 1315 the remnants of the two Iraqi Brigades were withering under the intense Marine fire and were surrendering or trying to withdraw through the burning oil wells. Still our regiment was hit by artillery fire and quickly Marine artillery returned the fire.

At 1341 our regiment was pushing on through the incoming artillery fire, tank engagements and small arms fire. The 3rd platoon now commanded by SSgt Higgins, with the support of tanks destroyed twelve Iraqi tanks and ten armored personnel carriers. As Echo Company pushed forward, the 1st platoon destroyed two more Iraqi tanks.

Then our regiment was fighting its way through a bunker complex clearing each bunker individually.

Col Gagush personally accepted the surrender of an Iraqi brigade commander.

At 1600 LtCol Haring halted our battalion because we had reached our objective line on the map for today. But Col Gagush ordered him to push on to the al-Jaber airfield, and at the same time warned him of a hasty laid minefield ahead of us that was reported by captured Iraqi prisoners. As they talked, the weather conditions suddenly deteriorated. What little sunlight there was disappeared under a completely overcast sky. Also, the wind was shifting and bringing with it more smoke from the burning oil fields further reducing visibility.

Two minutes later our battalion was moving forward again as night came and this darkness was the worst I had ever seen in my life, even in Vietnam. Even our night vision goggles were useless.

As our battalion neared the fence around the airfield, twelve Iraqi soldiers climbed out of the airfield's outer defenses and surrendered to 1st platoon. They said the airfield was abandoned and LtCol Haring reported this to Col Gagush. He ordered LtCol Haring to halt the battalion because he feared an ambush.

At 1645 Marine combat engineers came up and planted explosives that blew holes in the airport fences.

At 1722 Marine mortar rounds began raining down on the airfield defenses. At the same time Col Gagush had artillery fire on suspected command and control positions. The Iraqis fired back with their own artillery fire, which this time was unusually accurate. Hotel Company was bearing the brunt of the shelling, but so far had suffered no casualties. But our Echo Company quickly had eleven men wounded. Another volley of shells fell wounding Marines in both Fox and Gulf Companies. Then the shells began falling behind us.

Already this battle had cost our regiment the heaviest casualties so far in the war. Still, Col Gagush ordered LtCol Haring to advance.

At 1746 my platoon was following 1st platoon as they slipped through a hole blown in the perimeter fence. We quickly established a foothold within the airfields outer defenses and met no resistance. Looking through thermal sights and night vision goggles, I could see only a few Iraqis ahead.

LtCol Haring radioed in artillery illumination rounds as we crept forward. For the next four hours, our battalion searched the airfield capturing twenty-one Iraqi soldiers. We were forced to move slowly because of the blowing oil smoke, which at times reduced visibility down to a few yards.

By 2100 Sgt Davis's squad had reached the outermost buildings when, finally, Col Gagush ordered our regiment to halt. I was glad because I was afraid we were going to get into house-to-house fighting in the dark. My thoughts of Hue City still haunted me. Even though exhausted, we dug in for the night. For the next few hours the enemy fired mortar rounds at our regiment. It was midnight before I finally drifted off to sleep.

But at 0230 the next morning I was suddenly awakened when the darkness was pierced by red-hot streams of 50cal tracers being fired from machineguns and the orange flashes from the 120MM guns of the M1A1 Marine tanks. Our battalion was being hit by a two-pronged attack of Iraqi armored personnel carriers, tanks and Infantry.

Without thinking I grabbed a LAAW and rose up taking aim as Cpl Short fired his rifle covering me. I fired the rocket destroying a tank bearing down on my platoon. Then as the rest of 3rd squad opened fire to cover us, we both picked up LAAWs and fired them.

Meanwhile in the 2nd squad, Sgt Davis and another Marine fired M203 grenade launchers keeping Iraqi heads down. Cpl Seth and a dragon team closed in and destroyed an enemy machinegun position as they were setting up. Quickly, with the help of other Marine dragon teams, heavy weapons and tanks returning fire destroyed eight more Iraqi tanks silencing the enemy opposition. Droves of Iraqi soldiers began surrendering.

Again, our battalion began taking accurate artillery fire wounding eight. But with the support of tanks and dragon teams, our battalion beat the Iraqi forces back destroying six more enemy armored vehicles, some of them as close as 75 meters from our positions. Marine counter battery fire began to silence the enemy artillery fire. Still, the battle raged on for over an hour.

Finally, at 0400 it was quiet again. Capt Johnson asked me to go with him to check Echo Company lines. When we had finished, he invited me to have some coffee that he was going to prepare. But I said no because I wanted to get some sleep while I still could.

At first light, I was awakened by SSgt Adams who told me that Capt Johnson had passed the order to prepare to advance. I knew that all along the front, the Marines of 1st and 2nd Marine Divisions were doing the same thing. As I sat up, I noticed the fog of yesterday morning was gone. Ahead of us I could see the burned-out hulls of nine Iraqi T-62 tanks and thirty-six other enemy vehicles.

As we moved forward again, Cpl Seth's fire team was checking out a destroyed Iraqi tank. He stuck his hand inside a hole in the tank and started to look inside. Feeling something soft and wet, he pulled his hand out and found it covered with human brains.

Then our battalion began taking sporadic small arms fire. LtCol Haring ordered us to return fire. Within minutes, Marine artillery, mortar, machinegun, 40MM grenades and LAAW rockets were raining on the buildings in front of us. Tracers were hitting the buildings as explosions ripped them apart. As Echo Company advanced near the buildings, the smoke cleared and we found them in ruins with the Iraqis left inside, dead or dying.

As our battalion advanced beyond the buildings, we found nine abandoned T-62 tanks, large quantities of ammo and more enemy soldiers ready to surrender.

Col Gagush formed our regiment into a wedge formation as we advanced, encountering only scattered resistance, which we easily brushed aside.

At 0600 the 1st Marine Division launched its attack toward the Kuwaiti International Airport. By now our recon units and the Kuwaiti resistance was telling our division that the Iraqi forces were withdrawing to Iraq in long convoys, even now forming up in Kuwait City to escape the tightening noose. Hotel Company had reported encountering remnants of a retreating Iraqi Corps.

At 0615 Echo Company was suddenly hit by small arms fire from the right flank. We returned fire and they broke contact with us, fleeing.

Over the radio I heard that Iraqi units were not only surrendering in mass, but were now leaving their equipment abandoned in place. Soon our battalion was passing more abandoned Infantry positions and tanks. To be on the safe side we still fired at the abandoned tanks as we passed them.

By 0654 both the 1st and 2nd Marine Divisions were advancing on line. Our regiment was now passing through destroyed enemy tanks and vehicles, which showed the signs of being destroyed from air strikes. But more and more we found vehicles, which had been abandoned intact. There were a few Iraqi tank crews who stayed in their tanks and tried to ambush us. Fox Company destroyed six Iraqi tanks and killed 100 Iraqi soldiers. Soon we began firing at everything at long range with machineguns to see if the enemy was hiding there. If the enemy was there and responded, a Marine tank would fire a round or TOW missile at them. Our battalion was leading with point squads using TOW thermal sights to determine whether the enemy vehicles ahead were giving off a hot or cold signature. If the Iraqi vehicle had its system turned on, it would register hot and we would fire at it. These frequent firefights were stopping our rapid advance with many stops and starts.

Our battalion next encountered an abandoned bunker complex. We bypassed it only to run into a second bunker complex with seven dug in T-55 tanks. Marine tanks quickly raked the enemy tanks with machinegun fire, but got no response. These enemy tanks had been abandoned too, so we quickly bypassed them.

At 0904 our battalion spotted entrenched Iraqi Infantry. LtCol Haring called in Cobra gunships as Dragon sections quickly moved up. Together they began destroying enemy machinegun positions as we attacked under the cover of Amtrack 50cal machinegun fire clearing the enemy from their positions.

At 0939 our battalion got into a brief firefight with a T-62 tank, which was quickly destroyed.

Next our battalion ran into a T-72 Iraqi tank, the most lethal tank they have. But again, after a quick firefight a Marine antitank Hummer knocked it out of action with one missile hit.

Then our battalion encountered more tanks. I fired one LAAW destroying a tank and Cpl Seth fired a LAAW and destroyed another tank and the rest retreated.

By 1100 our battalion was again, like yesterday slowed down when the wind shifted bringing with it the clouds of black smoke residue from several hundred burning oil wells. It was literally raining oil, and the sun was so completely blocked out that even night vision goggles did not work. What had been only a black smudge on the horizon in the morning had become a total blackout.

Over the radio I heard that Marine aircraft were now attacking those Iraqi convoys heading toward Iraq.

The rest of the morning we pushed on as company after company of enemy troops surrendered. The heavy black smoke at times filled the sky, turning day into eerie night. Again, enemy tanks tried to use the smoke as cover to hide their attack against us. But dozens of these Soviet made tanks and armored personnel carriers were destroyed by Marine tanks and heavy weapons. Under orders, now we were destroying the abandoned Iraqi tanks and armored personnel carriers we found.

At noon our battalion encountered an Iraqi battalion-size defensive position. LtCol Haring ordered us to attack. As we assaulted this line, the Iraqis on the left surrendered. Gulf and Hotel Companies quickly moved through the enemy positions on the left outflanking the Iraqi bunkers and dug in tanks on the right. By using TOWs and Marine tanks, our battalion destroyed thirty-four Iraqi tanks and armored personnel carriers. Then our battalion pressed on northward encountering a minefield protecting another Iraqi bunker complex.

LtCol Haring quickly ordered Fox Company to breach the minefield by using mine plows and rollers attached to the front of old M-60 tanks. The rest of us provided fire support for Fox Company as they assaulted through the minefield. Of course, the breaching operation was done under fire from the enemy bunkers, which were quickly being destroyed. Once Fox Company was through, our Echo Company rushed in, followed by the rest of our battalion as we secured the bunker complex.

Soon we came across a hard-surface road. LtCol Haring ordered our battalion on this road and formed us into a column. Gulf Company led the way with our Echo Company next, followed by the other two companies. We began passing more Iraqi armor, which had been destroyed earlier by air strikes.

To our right, I watched an Iraqi armored force retreating parallel with us. I had heard of such things happening in France during WWII.

LtCol Haring ordered Hotel Company who was behind us to attack them. Quickly Hotel Company swung out from our column opening fire on the lead Iraqi tanks destroying eight of them. Then ten other Iraqi tanks stopped suddenly as their crews abandoned them to surrender.

Then Fox Company, also behind us, left the road to attack a building. The fighting here became room-to-room killing twenty-eight Iraqi soldiers and taking nine prisoners.

Then it was Echo Company who was ordered off the road. We found ourselves breaching a minefield and destroying two Iraqi tanks.

Our regiment as a whole was encountering dug-in Iraqi tanks.

Col Gagush called in Cobra gunships to engage them. The Cobras destroyed Iraqi self-propelled artillery pieces and tanks. Hotel Company, using TOW missiles, destroyed four Iraqi armored personnel carriers.

Our battalion moved north. We went around another minefield as we began encountering increasing armored resistance.

By 1300 our regiment was advancing over an area littered with tanks, antitank and antiaircraft guns and other vehicles of all types as Iraqi troops surrendered along the whole front.

At 1400 the 1st and 2nd Marine Divisions were pushing together on line through the fog and blowing smoke.

By 1500 the visibility was down to less than 200 meters. Still our battalion fought a series of brief engagements with enemy T-54 tanks.

So far this day our battalion had destroyed 114 Iraqi vehicles.

Many of these Iraqis acted like they had just been waiting for us to show up so they could surrender.

By 1530, the frequent wind changes at times covered us in clouds of black smoke, which blocked out the light. During one of these black outs a TOW team with Cpl Short's squad, using thermal sights, spotted two T-54 Iraqi tanks ninety meters away. The TOW team quickly sighted-in and destroyed both tanks with two missiles. Immediately, another TOW team with Sgt Davis's squad spotted a T-62 Iraqi tank and destroyed it with a TOW missile.

At 1545 our battalion encountered an obstacle belt of three bands of double strand concertina wire running east and west. LtCol Haring halted our battalion and radioed Col Gagush and asked him whether we should proceed through or go around it. As our battalion waited, we prepared to breach the defensive line when firefights broke out across the whole battalion front. The sounds of tank, machineguns and TOW missiles firing, was heard above the constant sound of the wind blowing sand and oil over us as we deployed out of our Amtracks.

By 1609 our battalion had destroyed nine Iraqi tanks.

Three minutes later, Col Gagush ordered LtCol Haring to push on through the minefield. With LtCol Haring's order, our Marine combat engineers who were prepared and waiting, immediately moved forward with M-60 tanks and Amtracks firing line charges to open three lanes for our battalion to advance. Suddenly 200 meters away, two Iraqi tanks appeared out of the smoke and opened fire at the engineers. But those old Marine M-60 tanks destroyed both enemy tanks.

Again, covered by a curtain of 50cal machinegun fire from Amtracks and tanks, the combat engineers successfully fired more line charges across the minefield. Three different times a line charge failed to explode by remote control. Each time a combat engineer had to run out and manually prime the line charge to make it go off. Still, within a short time, they had opened up the three lanes. LtCol Haring then ordered our battalion through the minefield, fighting our way into the enemy positions.

My platoon was fighting through enemy bunkers when a square package was tossed out near my platoon CP group. As I spun to fire at the unseen enemy, SSgt Adams sprang toward the package with incredible speed. Scooping it up he screamed, "Satchel charge!"

It left his hands as he tossed it sailing away from us. Suddenly, there was a great booming sound amid a great dazzling flash. SSgt Adams was blasted back into me knocking us both down with him on top of me. I struggled to get out from under the big man. SSgt Adams was moaning as the moans grew louder as he screamed, "My hands! My arms! Where are my hands! I can't feel my arms! Can you see my hands! Are they there?"

As I slid from under him, I saw his left arm was gone at the elbow and of his right arm, all that was left was his wrist with a lot of bone and frayed flesh hanging.

"Do something! Help me!" he screamed lying in the sand, the sand soaking up his blood. I sat there stunned as a corpsman started working on him. He may have been a reservist, but he was a damn good platoon sergeant and now he was maimed for life. Lucky for my platoon, Sgt Ewing quickly took charge until I was able to get my fears back under control.

Meanwhile as SSgt Higgins led 3rd platoon against other bunkers, an Iraqi with a grenade in hand broke from the back of a bunker running directly at him tossing a grenade at his feet. SSgt Higgins butt stroked the Iraqi with his rifle as the grenade exploded. Both he and the Iraqi soldier were peppered with shrapnel. SSgt Higgins fought on leading his platoon as he killed four more Iraqis. Quickly, the Iraqi defenses collapsed. When it was over, he was standing, bloody, angry and proud as he radioed Capt Johnson saying, "Sir my objectives are secure. But I'm wounded and feel weak. I think I should turn over my command."

As our battalion pushed on northward, LtCol Haring called in artillery on known enemy positions.

The constant wind gradually increased in intensity until it became a raging storm. Still our battalion pushed on through a combination of smoke and darkness. Artillery rounds were still hitting ahead of us as our battalion progress slowed down to a blind grope. LtCol Haring ordered us to dismount from our Amtracks and move in the pitch-black darkness and blowing sand.

At 1620 our battalion again became heavily engaged in clearing another obstacle belt.

And yet ten minutes later, Echo Company was fighting the environment as much as the enemy as we moved through an oilfield, which was a complex of burning oil wells belching thick black smoke, over ground pipes, and power lines. My platoon walked around these obstacles as the smoke, blowing sand and darkness hid the terrain features making our progress even slower. Behind us our battalion armor was being channeled into two columns by the burning wells and the above ground pipelines. I felt uneasy being this far ahead of our heavy armor.

Still, our regiment pushed on bypassing many abandoned Iraqi positions and pointing the surrendering Iraqi soldiers toward our rear.

At 1730 our battalion encountered yet another two sets of obstacle belts. But unopposed by the enemy, our Marine combat engineers quickly cleared lanes through both belts.

By 1800 our battalion had passed through the two belts and were assaulting the bunker complex of fighting positions supported by Amtracks, LAVs and tanks. But again, most of the Iraqis were choosing to surrender and what little resistance we met didn't slow our advance. Then suddenly our visibility dropped again to near zero as a sandstorm added to our problems, slowing us down to a crawl as we walked around the oil wells, pipelines, and lakes of oil.

Still Echo Company pushed on northward through harassing small arms and sniper fire. Our battalion then came upon a large number of what appeared to be abandoned Iraqi armored vehicles. Not wanting to take any chances, LtCol Haring ordered these vehicles to be destroyed by direct fire weapons.

At 1815 our battalion was advancing on a building as smoke hid everything. With the TOW crews looking through thermal sights, our battalion felt its way north, now against many Iraqi tanks and armored personnel carriers manned by determined crews who were willing to fight. Several firefights started as Marine and Iraqi vehicles opened fire on each other with tank and machinegun fire. Leaving destroyed and burning Iraqi vehicles behind, our battalion brushed aside this opposition and bypassing surrendering Iraqi soldiers, we pushed north against another obstacle belt.

No sooner was our battalion through this barbed wire and minefield than the TOW crews saw three enemy vehicles through their thermal sights. The enemy vehicles were trying to retreat westward across our front at high speed, but the TOW crews fired three TOW missiles, which slammed into all three destroying them. After these explosions, dazed and dying Iraqis surrendered. All of them turned out to be Iraqi officers. Later as our battalion neared the airport road, an enemy armored personnel carrier suddenly appeared from a concealed position and drove toward the highway. A missile from a TOW crew hit and destroyed the vehicle. As it stopped, the survivors ran out firing. The Marines of Gulf Company returned fire killing them all.

At 2100 our battalion reached the airport perimeter road.

By 2200 Echo Company was pushing on with my platoon on point. I was uneasy because even in the dark I could see on our left there was a thick orchard and to our right was an eight-foot berm. I radioed Capt Johnson and warned him, “Skipper this area is a perfect place for an ambush.”

His reply was, “Gunner my orders are to keep going.”

Over the radio I ordered my squad leaders Cpls Pusey, Short and Sgt Davis to take it slow and keep their eyes open.

Suddenly Sgt Davis yelled over the radio, “We got bunkers in the trees!”

I radioed a nearby Marine tank for help. He opened up with machinegun fire into the bunkers and one of them exploded and burned ferociously.

My platoon crept forward now. My men didn’t need me to tell them that we were at great risk here. They were tense, the worst I had seen them so far. None of us knew what was ahead of us in the dark or on our flanks in the orchard or behind that sand berm. We could really get hurt here in a hurry. Everything had just gone too well so far.

Suddenly there were two explosions, BOOM! BOOM! Followed by two bright flashes ahead of me where Cpl Pusey's 1st squad was. Then there were great secondary explosions lighting up the sky.

My heart was in my throat as I looked forward into the night where I knew 1st squad was.

"They've been ambushed! They've had it!" said Cpl Seth nearby.

Over the radio I heard, "What's going on up there? Speak to me! Speak to me!" screamed Capt Johnson trying to sound calm.

And I felt his concern as I moved forward to see just what had happened and heard only silence.

"Do ya think it was our tanks?" asked Sgt Ewing following behind me.

"Speak to me!" ordered Capt Johnson over the radio. But there was still only silence.

"God they all can't be dead! They'll hit us next," said Sgt Ewing.

I felt like throwing up. It was like a flash back to Vietnam.

And still there was only silence ahead of me.

Again, over the radio I heard, "Any point platoon element, any point element, this is Echo Six. What's going on up there?"

Then finally, over the radio, I heard Cpl Pusey say, "Roger Echo Six, this is Echo one, one. We have destroyed two enemy trucks. No friendly casualties."

"Thank you, Jesus!" I said as I looked back at Sgt Ewing and then added, "Trucks, just Iraqi trucks."

At 2250, our battalion had reached the perimeter of the airport.

By 2300 in the middle of a blowing sandstorm, our battalion had cut through the fence and had established a foothold inside. Finally, Col Gagush ordered LtCol Haring to halt our battalion here and dig in for the night.

It was hard to talk to each other outside of the vehicles in the blowing sand. The Amtracks moved into a circular defense position with the tanks outside this circle where their guns could give maximum coverage forming a protective ring around the Amtracks. We, the Infantry, dug in to add to the strong defense of tanks, heavy machineguns, with interlocking small arms fire.

I checked Echo Company's positions with Capt Johnson, and then he left to go to a battalion meeting with LtCol Haring and the other company commanders to be briefed on tomorrow's actions.

At 2340, the wind suddenly shifted direction, which improved our visibility, but now the flames from the nearby burning oil wells suddenly illuminated every vehicle in our battalion making them and us good targets.

When Capt Johnson returned from the briefing he walked along Echo Company's positions briefing us about the plans for tomorrow. Like me he was glad we could now see better, but didn't like being exposed like we were. Suddenly, mortars exploded among Echo Company instantly followed by RPG's and heavy machinegun fire pouring in on us. Marine Amtracks and tanks returned fire. As Capt Johnson ran toward his CP hole, Cpl Short, my 3rd squad leader, was hit in the face by shrapnel knocking him down. Dazed and bleeding he started to crawl out of his hole until a corpsman pushed him back inside.

A Marine tank fired over our heads destroying an Iraqi armored personnel carrier as it exploded in a flash.

Enemy mortar rounds continued to come in walking their way through the circle of Amtracks and then out the southwest side. RPG rounds were still flying into our positions. One of these grenades penetrated the rear ramp of an Amtrack. I could hear at least three heavy machineguns firing at us. This was definitely an unusually determined Iraqi unit as their fire-intensified bullets hit the sand around me and thudded into an Amtrack nearby.

For fifteen minutes the battle raged as orange tracers crisscrossed through the night until the Iraqis broke contact withdrawing as the wind again changed direction and darkened our battalion's position as if a door had closed on a lighted room. Checking my platoon lines, I shifted Cpl Seth from 2nd squad over to take charge of 3rd squad.

By 0005 Feb 27th, the 1st and 2nd Marine Divisions had achieved their primary objectives. It seemed enemy resistance had collapsed.

I managed to get an hour and half of sleep when at 0300 Col Gagush ordered our regiment to prepare to attack as our TOW sections watched the airport with thermal sights looking for enemy activity.

At 0330 Col Gagush ordered our regiment to advance and as we did Iraqis opened fire with rocket propelled grenades and machinegun fire making the darkness come alive with bright orange tracers and the flash of explosions. But we suffered no casualties and the enemy firing slowly lessened.

At 0430 LtCol Haring ordered Echo and Fox Companies to advance on line. In complete darkness we advanced. Fox Company immediately engaged an Iraqi armored personnel carrier destroying it and capturing three Iraqi soldiers. Then they encountered antipersonnel mines and halted. The wind had shifted the sand and the mines could be seen on top of the sand. Our visibility deteriorated as the wind shifted again bringing in clouds of black smoke from the oilfields.

Col Gagush ordered our regiment to halt because of the poor visibility, the minefield and the unknown enemy situation. He felt, with the enemy clearly routed, the risk now just wasn't worth the chance.

At 0615 Col Gagush received the welcome news from our 2nd Marine Division that the NBC threat level was zero. After LtCol Haring passed this word to our battalion, we took off the cumbersome, heavy and oil blackened NBC suits for the first time in days.

Still our regiment advanced carefully through the minefield.

At 0645 Marines from Gulf Company raised the US and Marine flags up flagpoles in front of the airport terminal.

Then our battalion quickly moved on past the airport. As we neared a farm complex, we received sniper and rocket fire. Reacting quickly, our battalion destroyed an Iraqi ammo truck and killed seven Iraqi soldiers.

Then our whole 2nd Marine Division was rushing toward our final objective, Kuwait City, which served as a major intersection for roads heading in all directions, including north into Iraq. We were ready to liberate Kuwait City.

By now the only contact we were having were some grateful Kuwaitis who ran up to us giving us little tins of tomato paste, which was all they had to give us.

As the sun rose through the limited visibility, Gulf Company discovered four fully functional, but lucky for us, abandoned antiaircraft guns.

As we entered the city, I could hear blowing horns from Kuwaiti cars as well as random shots being fired throughout the city. As we advanced, I saw a TOW missile streak across the landscape.

By 0900, it seemed the fighting had all but stopped across the whole 2nd Marine Division front.

By noon, Marine and coalition forces were sweeping everywhere through Kuwait City. Soon we were seeing hundreds of cheering men, women and children waving American, British and the green, white and red Kuwaiti flags in celebration of their liberation. Kuwaiti people were dancing on the rooftops. The women were tossing candy to us. Some people were standing on the top of destroyed or abandoned Iraqi tanks and other Iraqi equipment. Mothers were holding up their small children in the air yelling in broken English, "Thank you for coming."

Many of our Marine tanks and Amtracks were now flying American and Marine Corps flags. This reminded me of the pictures I had seen as a boy of the Army when they liberated Paris in WWII. This would probably be the happiest memory of my Marine career.

I saw SgtMaj Burns riding through the city on top of an Amtrack when a Kuwaiti tossed a Kuwaiti flag up to him.

At seeing this Sgt Davis looked at me saying, "Now tell me this was only about oil."

Maj Arguedos was all smiles too saying, "I've never seen people so happy. What a great feeling of accomplishment this is."

Still the rattle of small arms fire could be heard in parts of the city as allied troops mopped up what Iraqi forces were left. That was when GySgt O'Malley was struck by a stray bullet in the upper arm and was medivaced.

At times we found ourselves in the strange position of protecting our Iraqi prisoners from the Kuwaiti resistance forces who wanted to kill them.

Echo Company was making a sweep through the city streets when Cpl Seth's 3rd squad discovered six wounded Iraqi soldiers. As he was searching one of them, the Iraqi suddenly lunged at him, but was instantly shot dead by one of his Marines who were covering him.

By 1400, Kuwait City was declared secure. Around us we could see the horrible evidence of the Iraqi occupation. Every highway overpass had Iraqi constructed concrete sentry posts and antiaircraft gun emplacements. There were hundreds of stripped cars left as evidence that Iraq had intended to strip the country of anything of value. The Kuwaiti beautiful luxury hotels were completely gutted by fire and most shop windows were shattered and their contents taken away. And just a short distance away in the desert the oil wells still burned as the smoke rose from them creating an eerie black inferno making the sky a charcoal gray. It was midafternoon, but it seemed more like late evening.

Back home Marty would hear on the CBS news in his nightly briefing, Army Gen Schwarzkopf say,

"I can't say enough about the two Marine Divisions. If I use words like brilliant, it would really be an under description of the absolutely superb job that they did in breaching the so-called impenetrable barriers. It was a classic, absolutely classic military breaching of a very, very tough minefield, barbed wire, and fire trench-type barriers. They went through the first barrier like it was water. They went across into the second barrier line even though they were under artillery fire. They continued to open that breach. And then they brought both divisions streaming through that breach. It was an absolutely superb operation, a textbook and I think it'll be studied for many, many years to come as the way to do it."

Meanwhile I had heard there were 600 oil wells burning in the Kuwaiti Theater of Operation. It seemed the Iraqi Army was in full retreat. LtCol Haring had ordered our battalion to halt as he waited for further instructions. It was then that Col Gagush passed the word to him that a ceasefire had been agreed upon to begin at 0800 tomorrow by order of President Bush.

As I passed the word of the ceasefire to my platoon, I could tell they were still pumped up with adrenalin. They knew we had accomplished our mission, but they were ready to carry the war to Baghdad.

They almost seemed disappointed that the war had ended so soon and as much as I was glad it was almost over, I wondered if the job was really done.

The ground campaign had lasted only 100 hours. I couldn't help but laugh telling Sgt Ewing that I had been on patrols in Vietnam that lasted longer than this campaign. Even including the air campaign, the war lasted only forty-three days.

Our battalion held the same positions for the rest of the day and night. I was able to get my first good night's sleep in days.

At 0800 Feb 28th all American forces ceased offensive combat operations. But on the other hand, we were authorized to engage any Iraqi unit or individual that showed hostile intent or refused to honor the ceasefire agreement.

The 1st and 2nd Marine Divisions and the US Army Brigade attached to the Marines had destroyed 1,060 Iraqi tanks, 608 artillery pieces, two Scud missile launchers and captured 20,000 Iraqi soldiers.

There were 92,000 Marines in country, made up of twenty-four Infantry battalions, nineteen fix wing and twenty-one helicopter squadrons, which was 90% of the operational forces of the Marine Corps including 30,000 Marine reserves. I knew this was the largest Marine force assembled for combat since Vietnam. In the process of this buildup the Marines had met every deadline imposed by the President.

I was extremely proud of my platoon. To me they were everything the word Marine stood for. They had done everything I had asked of them and more. And they trusted me and that meant everything to me. I trained them, but it was the quality of the young Marines of today and their individual spirit and the Marine combined arms team organization and their confidence in each other, which drove them to victory. I just hoped that the people back home were as proud of what they had done as I was.

At 0847 Capt Johnson received more good news from LtCol Haring. We could now stop taking those NBC pills. I truly felt the war was over now. The threat of chemical and biological weapons, which I feared most since arriving, was over.

Through the day, I had my platoon work to improve their positions just in case and take turns cleaning their weapons. Nearby tank and Amtrack crews were performing maintenance on their vehicles too.

On March 1st our battalion was still in the same defensive positions. And our 2nd Marine Division continued to uncover Iraqi weapons, ammo and equipment in our area of operation and destroy them.

Heaps of Iraqi bodies were being buried in mass graves. In all 85,000 to 100,000 Iraqi soldiers had been killed. Still, groups of

Iraqi soldiers were found roaming the desert, dazed, hungry, thirsty and humbled, looking for anyone to surrender to. It was estimated the allies had captured 150,000 prisoners. Other Iraqi soldiers, after deserting their officers were walking north to home, having had enough of Saddam's military adventures.

The Iraqi Army had fought eight years of war with Iran and gained nothing. Now they had fought the allies and suffered six weeks of constant air bombardment and been defeated in four days of lightning quick war and lost everything including their pride and honor.

By March 5th the allies were talking about the problems of keeping a responsible peace. But my platoon had already started thinking of going home. We had already received the word that the units that had arrived here first would return first. Which meant we would not be leaving early.

Meanwhile, hoping to take advantage of the allies' victory over Iraq, dissident factions within Iraq launched an unsuccessful attempt to overthrow Saddam Hussein. But even after the defeat of his army, Hussein ordered an attack against the Kurdish population of northern Iraq, which started hundreds of thousands of desperate people fleeing toward Turkey, Iran and Syria.

As the days passed, the world grew outraged. By March 15th, GySgt Simon, Sgt Huebner and Cpl Cunningham had returned from the hospital. I sure was happy to see my old warhorse of a friend GySgt Simon return and take over the duties of acting company first sergeant. I placed Sgt Huebner back in command of 1st squad and Cpl Cunningham back in command of 3rd squad and let Cpl Seth return to his fire team in 2nd squad.

On April 7th Capt Drumbore returned from the hospital with the news that 1stSgt Bean had been transferred back to the states because of his wounds. Capt Drumbore, being the senior captain, took command of Echo Company and Capt Johnson returned to command the 3rd platoon.

On the same day, the allies started dropping supplies to the fleeing Kurd refugees. This operation became known as Provide Comfort. By now 500,000 Kurds had gathered in the mountains of southern Turkey. Another 1.3 million Kurds were huddled in camps along the Iranian border. The US 10th Army Special Forces Group had been sent into these camps. The camps were among snow-covered peaks. The many trails from Iraq were littered with abandoned, broken down cars, furniture, suitcases and frozen bodies.

The Green Berets were organizing and identifying the camps and drop zones as they provided medical assistance.

By April 9th our battalion was in its third month in the Gulf when Col Gagush ordered LtCol Haring to put us on standby to be prepared to be choppered into northern Iraq in response to that rapidly developing situation.

On April 13th, after being briefed by LtCol Haring, Capt Drumbore gathered his platoon leaders together to explain our new mission. Our battalion was to establish a forward support base at Silopi, Turkey from which choppers could begin to carry supplies to the refugee camps in the mountains of Iraq.

On April 14th, Cpl Morris returned from the hospital and I placed him in charge of a fire team in Cpl Cunningham's 3rd squad.

By April 15th Marine chopper units began flying out of Silopi, Turkey on humanitarian missions into Northern Iraq. In the next two weeks the Marine Squadron would deliver over 1,000,000 pounds of relief supplies to the Kurds in Northern Iraq.

Meanwhile, our battalion was flown into Silopi with orders to prepare to enter Northern Iraq.

On April 19th the 1st platoon provided security for US Army LtGen Shalikashvili who held a meeting with an Iraqi delegation at the Habur Bridge border crossing with Iraq. He informed the Iraqi representatives that coalition forces would enter Iraq tomorrow. Their mission will be humanitarian, there is no intent to engage Iraqi forces. But Iraqi forces should offer no resistance, there should be no Iraqi planes flying above the 39th parallel. All Iraqi troops are to be pulled back thirty kilometers south of the city of Zakho. A Military Coordination Committee will be formed for the purpose of maintaining direct communications with both Kurdish and Iraqi authorities.

Later, LtCol Haring briefed us platoon leaders of our orders for tomorrow. We were to join other allied coalition forces that would enter Northern Iraq and establish security zones to help with the safe transfer of 500,000 refugee Kurds from their mountain havens to the countryside they have fled from.

To start the operation, our battalion would conduct a chopper assault into a valley to the east of Zakho.

On April 20th I was in a chopper with Sgt Huebner's 1st squad and a machinegun team as we lifted off the ground. I could see US Air Force Jets as they flew cover for Echo Company as we headed toward the Iraqi border.

The first thing I saw of Northern Iraq was lush green pastures ready for spring planting. This brought back memories of my family's farm back in Delaware. It was hard to believe that somewhere down there people were starving.

Then our green camouflaged choppers banked left at the Tigris River and flew east along the Turkey-Iraq border. Below us now, I watched shepherds tending their sheep. But further on I saw the specks of plastic shelters reflecting the sunlight.

On the ridge to our left I saw Turkish soldiers manning lookout towers.

Then below us the lush green was replaced by gray and brown as the gentle rolling hills turn into jagged cliffs streaked with goat paths. The river gorge narrowed as the choppers weaved left and right. Suddenly, drafts of air blasted through the gorge and lifted and dropped the choppers. The air screamed through the crew chief's porthole and was becoming cold. I saw patches of snow still holding out under the mid-April sun.

The choppers climbed sharply over the crest of a ridge. Then I saw them, at first only as tiny orange, green and tan tents that dotted the river's edge below. As the choppers flew in closer, there was a steady stream of refugees pouring down from the higher trails. There must have been tens of thousands of tents and plastic shelters enveloping the surrounding ridges and shallow valleys beyond. There must have been 100,000 starving Kurdish refugees down there and they were all looking up at us.

I could see spots of freshly dug earth, which speckled the mountainside, where the dead had been buried. Other refugees were digging new ones. A small bundle filled with the body of a small child lay near one half-dug hole. For the first time I realized the urgency of our mission.

As the choppers began to land, I saw large groups of Iraqi soldiers watching us from the high ground surrounding the city of Zakho.

Our choppers landed on the outskirts of the town and I saw the nearby Iraqi military compound come alive with activity. Once on the ground Capt Drumbore quickly set Echo Company into a 360 defensive position as we waited for Fox Company to come in. Soon, Fox Company landed with LtCol Haring. Then he ordered both companies to advance up to the Iraqi compound. Once there, speaking through an interpreter, LtCol Haring ordered the Iraqi commander to have his unit withdraw from the region as well as the city of Zakho.

The Iraqi commander said he didn't know we were coming. But he didn't want any trouble with US Marines.

The Iraqis quickly slung their AK-47 rifles over their shoulders and started retreating.

Near me I heard, "That's a good move on their part," mumbled a tired Cpl Morris standing with a sixty-pound pack on his back including plenty of ammo.

Then both Marine companies moved on and began digging in for the night. Marines from Fox Company began setting up refugee tents. Twelve tents were set up by nightfall, which in time would become one of the largest resettlement camps ever built.

By the next day, the rest of our battalion arrived and occupied all of the surrounding ridges, the primary road intersections and landing zones. Meanwhile, Marine engineers also had started clearing the border crossing of mines and plastic explosives so our battalion armored vehicles could roll in to beef up our security.

On April 22nd, the 45th Commando of the British Royal Marines fresh from Northern Ireland, and the 1st Air Combat Group of the Royal Netherlands Marines choppered in to join us bringing our total force up to 3,400 Marines from three nations. As one British Marine captain liked to say, "There can never be enough Marines around."

We had found the city of Zakho, which usually had 150,000 people in it, now was a ghost town with fewer than 2,000 people in it. The houses had been looted and vandalized by the Iraqi Army who continued pillaging the local towns and villages as they retreated south. I would see this type of thing again six years later in Bosnia.

But despite agreeing to withdraw his army, Saddam did not surrender Zakho without a last effort to retain some control of the city. He ordered 300 policemen back into Zakho with the excuse to maintain law and order and protect coalition forces from Kurdish rebels. It was clear that Saddam's police were still terrorizing the few residents left in Zakho.

On April 24th, a resupply chopper also brought Capts Stordhal and Smith, Sgt Murphy, Cpls Conn and Cook back from the hospital. Capt Smith took command of Echo Company and Capt Drumbore took command of 1st platoon. Capt Stordhal became Echo Company's XO again. I put Sgt Murphy back in charge of 3rd squad. Cpl Conn went back to his fire team in 1st squad and Cpl Cook went back to his fire team in 2nd squad.

The same day US Army Col Noab again explained the coalition's intent to the local Iraqi commanders. He also ordered the Iraqi Army to continue to withdraw from Zakho to a point in all directions from which their artillery couldn't reach us.

All but fifty of the Iraqi police would immediately withdraw from Zakho. Iraq would be allowed no more than fifty uniformed policemen in Zakho at any time. They would carry only one pistol and would display coalition forces identification badges at all times.

Coalition forces would enter Zakho on April 26th for the purpose of verifying compliance and would begin to regularly patrol the city.

Coalition forces would establish a security zone complete with checkpoints around Zakho. No weapons other than those of the coalition forces would be permitted in the zone.

No members of the Iraqi Army would be permitted in this security zone, in or out of uniform, without approval from the Military Coordination Committee

It wasn't long after this statement was issued that Iraqi police were seen boarding buses heading south out of Zakho.

During the hours of darkness on April 25th, our battalion cordoned off the city from the south, east and north and dug in while Dutch Marines sealed off the western approaches and bridges at the border. Then the British Royal Marines moved in and started patrolling the streets of Zakho, sending what few Iraqis left fleeing south.

By nightfall of April 26th the people of Zakho were enjoying their first taste of freedom.

On the morning of April 27th, the 3rd battalion 325th US Army Airborne landed by choppers to beef up our force. Along with them came the last of our wounded that would be able to rejoin us, GySgt

O'Malley and SSgt Higgins. GySgt O'Malley took back the duties of company gunny and SSgt Higgins went back to being the platoon sergeant of 3rd platoon.

Then we waited as first only a trickle of refugees dared to leave the camps to begin the trip back to Zakho. But soon as the news spread many more former residents slowly began to return to their homes.

By May the French 8th Regiment Parachutist Infantry Marines had been choppered in to help us. Then the British and French Marines began probing eastward. The British Royal Marines pushed on to the town of Batufa and then onto the airfield at Sirsink and then on to the city of Al Amadiya, a fortress dating back 3,000 years.

In early May the 4th Brigade 3rd US Army Infantry Division joined us.

Every day at noon Marine explosive ordnance experts blew up large amounts of explosives and ammo, which had been abandoned by the Iraqi Army. They destroyed weapons made in China, Russia, America, Italy and Spain.

Along with their regular duties, our corpsmen of Echo Company also operated a temporary aid station and soon were treating eighty some Kurds every day. Most of them suffered from malnutrition and dehydration along with some burn cases.

By May 10th, the coalition security zone had been expanded east and west covering an area eighty miles in length.

The same day Echo Company advanced southward mounted in Amtracks. Each time we moved forward we forced an Iraqi Company ahead of us to retreat.

After we had reached an area northwest of Summoyle, Fox Company was choppered in to join us, followed by LtCol Haring, his battalion CP group and Gulf Company. He then ordered all three companies to push on toward Dohuk. Behind us choppers flew in the 29th British Commando, an Italian Special Forces Company and the 3rd Battalion US Army's 325th Regiment Airborne.

On May 12th our battalion advanced south establishing checkpoints to the west and east of the city of Dohuk as the Iraqi forces retreated from Dohuk only to take up new positions seven miles to the south of the city.

On May 20th a small convoy of coalition vehicles entered Dohuk and established a forward command post in an empty hotel in the heart of the city. By now the security Zone had been extended not only eighty miles east to west, but also now thirty miles north to south below the Turkish-Iraqi border.

LtCol Haring was ordered by Col Gagush to start planning for the phased retrograde of our battalion back to Iskenderun, Turkey.

The first of June, Gulf Company was choppered back to Turkey.

The next day the UN took over the administration of both refugee camps from the coalition forces, which now numbered 13,000 men.

It was clear the coalition objectives had been achieved. The Kurdish refugees were out of the mountains and either back in their villages or on their way there, or in camps built by the coalition forces.

Within a few days we learned that our Commandant Gen Gray had retired and had been replaced by Gen Munday who had been a major during Tet in Vietnam in 1968.

On June 12th Fox Company was choppered back to Turkey. During our remaining days, Echo and Hotel Companies and the rest of the coalition forces continued to stabilize the area as well as reassure the Kurd leaders that even though the Marines were leaving, this wouldn't change the resolve of the allied forces to support the Kurdish people.

Meanwhile the UN had also set new terms on Iraq, stating that Iraqi fixed and rotary wing aircraft were not to fly north of the 36th parallel, which was approximately thirty miles south of Dohuk.

The Iraqi Army and secret police were not to enter the security zone.

A coalition ground combat force composed of forces representing several nations would be maintained across the border in Silopi, Turkey.

Coalition aircraft, both fixed and rotary wing, will continue to patrol the skies above the security zone.

The military Coordination Committee will continue to monitor the security Zone and Iraqi compliance of the terms of the agreement.

On June 15th the responsibility for Echo and Hotel Companies area was transferred to the Italian forces.

But it was a month later, on July 15th, that Echo and Hotel Companies with the USA 3rd Battalion 325th Airborne Combat Team withdrew from northern Iraq.

Once in Turkey, LtCol Haring gave our battalion the word that we were scheduled to re-embark on ships in a few days to return stateside.

The night before we were to go aboard ship, GySgt Simon gathered the enlisted men of Echo Company together and said, “Men I’m a veteran of five deployments overseas, which includes such places as Vietnam and Panama. I have some advice for you married men. When you get back home you will be going back to her world now. Don’t be surprised if she doesn’t want to turn over the car to you. Don’t be surprised if she gives you ten dollars for pocket money. Don’t start leafing through the checkbook. Don’t complain about how the house looks. For a while you’ll be the guest in her home.”

Hearing about it later, I knew it was good advice as I thought of all the times I had returned to Marty after a deployment. I wished someone had talked to me about such things when I was a young Marine. And still I would hear a young Marine say, “When I get home, I’m going to get drunk as a skunk.” I just hoped his wife wouldn’t be expecting a romantic evening.

On July 19th our battalion was aboard ships watching as the city of Iskenderun and the Turkish horizon slipped into the sea. After seven months we were on our way home.

But the triumph of our quick victory had left me with an odd feeling. I kept wondering if it just hadn’t ended too easy. I feared our orders would be changed and the ships would turn around and take us back to the desert.

Back in the states, our battalion arrived by buses back to Camp Lejeune at 2300. I was amazed at how many people, plus our families were waiting for us on the parade field when our ten buses pulled into sight. We got off the buses still wearing desert-camouflaged uniforms as we formed up by platoons and companies. Everyone was cheering us and seemed to want to touch us. People were tossing us cans of beer. Young women were shouting, “I love you!”

Col Gagush was there and gave a ten-minute speech. Marines were drinking beer and eating hot dogs and hamburgers within the ranks. At seeing this, I gave the men of my platoon some hard looks, but I didn’t stop them. It was late and the last thing they or I wanted to hear was a speech, even from Col Gagush.

Finally, he had finished his speech and LtCol Haring dismissed our battalion and the Marines surged forward into the crowd. Somehow in this mass of people I found Marty and red headed Samantha. I hugged them both and we all cried with relief.

"Are you all right?" asked Marty.

"I am now. Man, you feel good. It's good to be home," I answered.

When we walked into our house, I found fried chicken waiting for me. I wolfed down four chicken breast and two glasses of ice tea. Samantha went to bed about 0300. Then Marty and I went to bed and made love and then talked long past sunup. As we lay in each other's arms exhausted from lovemaking, I was about to drift off to sleep when Marty said, "I need to talk to you about something."

Instantly awake I said, "Okay." Feeling frightened at what could be the matter after this great homecoming we had just had.

Marty then took a deep breath, which also frightened me as she spoke, "You know I've been doing Bible studies through the mail for several years now."

"Yes," I answered wondering where this was going. I was suddenly afraid she had somehow got us in debt.

Taking another deep breath, she said, "I have decided; that is, I feel God has called me to be a preacher."

I turned to look at her wondering if I'd really heard her right. I knew she had always been a good person; she knew the Bible well and I had seen her faith grow stronger through the years.

She looked up at me with pleading eyes as she asked, "Well, what do you think?"

"I don't mind you becoming a preacher. But how will this affect us? You know I may not always be stationed here. And I'm not ready to retire."

Marty smiled saying, "I'm not asking you to retire. This won't happen overnight. I have to go back to school first. And I don't want to be a full-time preacher until Samantha finishes high school. So, we're talking at least five more years."

"Well I'm glad of that and I might be retired by then. I've almost been in twenty-seven years now."

"I don't want my career to interfere with your career. There must be a way for me to be a preacher wherever you go. But when you do retire, I want to return to Delaware to preach there."

"So just when I'm preparing to retire, you will be beginning your career."

"Yes, I guess so. Can you live with that?"

"Yes, as long as you keep loving me."

She hugged me, raising her naked leg up over my naked waist saying, "I will always love you."

"And I love you dear lady."

Later as we were taking a shower together, I was still thinking through what Marty had talked to me about.

"What are you thinking?" she asked.

"For years since we met you have been prepared to follow me anywhere. Now I see the time coming when I'll be following you around."

She looked at me with a strange look. I would not know it for years just how upset she was over this statement of mine.

Later in the day, LtCol Haring phoned me at home to tell me that I was to take command of what would be left of Echo Company now that the reserves had been detached from our battalion and would report to the Reserve Support Unit here on base to be demobilized and sent home.

The next day July 25th, Sgt Ewing and I drove over to the RSU building to visit with the reserves and say goodbye. They were in the process of signing discharge forms, getting discharge physicals, getting pre-separation briefings about benefits and entitlements that were now due them. I spoke with Capts Smith, Stordhal, Drumbore, and Johnson, Cpls Pusey, Cook and Seth. And I saved Sgt Murphy for last. Although he had worried about everything including his own actions, he had never let me down. I told him it was an honor having a sergeant like him in my platoon.

Tears were in his eyes as he said, "Thank you sir. It has been a pleasure serving under you. Good luck to you."

"Good luck to you back on civy street."

As always, for days after returning from a combat zone I found myself more quiet than usual.

It seemed everywhere I turned there was a party or reception I was invited to. When I took a week's leave back home in Delaware, I was requested to speak at my home church and even my old high school in Bridgeville that I had quit at seventeen to join the Corps. I almost felt like a movie star. This was definitely not like returning from Vietnam. Maybe my country somehow was trying to make up for the way it had rejected us back then.

By August, woodland camouflage uniforms had taken the place of desert camouflage as new troops started reporting into Echo Company and we started settling back into a normal training routine.

One of the new people to arrive was Capt Peacock who took command of Echo Company forcing me back to the XO position. Ewing was promoted to staff sergeant. And Marty and I went to the retirement ceremony of our division SgtMaj Burns. I hated to see another of my old warhorse friends from Vietnam retire. I asked him why when he didn't even have thirty years in yet. He could have stayed in for four more years. But he said where could he go after being a division sergeant major. I said he could be a base sergeant major or maybe even the future Sergeant Major of the Marine Corps. He just laughed saying it wasn't worth it to have to live in DC.

The first of September, Huebner was promoted to staff sergeant and Capt Peacock moved him over to be the platoon sergeant of 1st platoon.

By the middle of September, the 2nd Marine Division was back to its usual business of deployments and rotation of units overseas. And I had received orders transferring me to the 1st Marine Division at Camp Pendleton Ca. The last time I was stationed at Camp Pendleton I was a master sergeant back in the 70's. I phoned Camp Pendleton and put my name on the base housing list. Then I phoned Marty and told her the news. She said she had always wanted to live in California. Bless her heart, but I knew this would be hard. We had been stationed here in one unit or another for many years, which enabled Samantha to be in school with the same friends. Now all that would change. And we would be 3,000 miles away from our sons and our families. This would be the first Christmas that Marty and Samantha wouldn't get home to visit the families. But hopefully we three would be together for Christmas.

I checked out of Echo Company the last day of September. Col Gagush and Lt Col Haring both came by to see me. They were both great officers that I enjoyed serving under. But I would be surprised years later to learn that they both retired at their present ranks. Cpl Conn also came to say goodbye to me. Years later after I retired from the Corps, I would join a veteran's group just for Marines called The

Marine Corps League and would meet Cpl Conn again to both our surprises. I found SSgt Ewing and said goodbye to him and I told him I hoped to serve with him again. Years later, to my surprise, I would learn he left the Corps after eleven years. Then I said goodbye to two old warhorses GySgts Simon and O'Malley. I would run into O'Malley two years later and he would be a warrant officer himself by then. Simon and I would stay in touch through the years and even after our retirements. He would make master gunnery sergeant in 1998 and be forced to retire in 2000.

I took thirty days leave and we drove up to Delaware for twenty days with our families and of course spent time with Nat and our grandchildren. Then we left for California with Marty driving our van and me driving the truck.

By Nov 1st, I had reported into the 1st Marine Division headquarters at Camp Pendleton. From there I was ordered to the 1st Regiment commanded by Col Hanson. I was surprised to learn that Col Hanson and Col Gagush had served together in Vietnam. From there I was ordered to the 1st battalion commanded by LtCol Lloyd. As I pulled into the battalion parking lot, I saw an old friend 1stSgt Cain who I had served with on the USS Hampton and the 2nd Marine Division. He saw me too as I parked my truck. As I got out, he walked over saluting me saying, "Gunner Cord what are you doing here?"

Returning his salute, I answered, "I'm reporting into this battalion. What are you doing here?"

As we shook hands he said, "I'm assigned to this battalion as First Sergeant of Alfa Company."

"No shit Top. Maybe I'll be assigned to Alfa Company too."

"That'd be great sir. But there's no officer billets open in Alfa. Unless someone's going to leave early that I don't know about."

"Well I'm glad to have at least one friendly face in this battalion. Well I better check in and find out which company I am going to."

"Okay Gunner I'll see you around."

After I reported into 1st Battalion, I was ordered to Delta Company. At Delta Company headquarters I introduced myself to GySgt Bruce. He took me to the CO's office and introduced me to Capt Gillette. He looked up from his desk and studied my over five rows of ribbons with four ribbons to a row and said, "I see you were in Vietnam."

"Yes sir," I answered.

"What years were you there?"

"March 65 to March 73."

"Shit," said Capt Gillette opening my record book. Looking through it he said, "I see you were in El Salvador, Beirut, Grenada, Panama and the Gulf War. I'm not sure if you're the unluckiest son-of-a-bitch I know or the luckiest."

"I would say I've been lucky."

"You know Gunner there's not many of you Nam vets left."

"Well sir there's still a few."

"As it stands now you will be only the second Nam vet in Delta Company."

This shocked me. In my twenty-seven years in the Corps this was the first unit I had served in, in which I would be one of only two Vietnam veterans in it.

"Gunner, I'm giving you command of third platoon. Gunny Bruce here will take you to meet your platoon sergeant."

"Thank you, sir," I said.

GySgt Bruce led me out of the office and found 3rd platoon. He introduced me to my platoon sergeant, SSgt McAdams. He was a big broad-shouldered black Marine who could still run three miles in seventeen minutes, I had only done that once in my career. He in turn called over our three squad leaders, Sgt Apriesing of 1st squad, Sgt Bowen of 2nd squad and Sgt Brown of 3rd squad. They all seemed surprised that their new platoon leader was a warrant officer. I asked them about their careers and told them about mine. Then I told them what I expected of them. Then I gathered the rest of our platoon together and talked with them.

In the afternoon after a company formation, Capt Gillette introduced me to our company XO Lt Smith, a tall thin officer, the 1st platoon leader Lt Connolly and his platoon sergeant, SSgt Biles, the other Vietnam veteran, and the 2nd platoon leader, Lt Shaw, another big broad-shouldered black Marine and his platoon sergeant SSgt Gavin.

On Nov 10th Marty and I went to the Marine Corps Birthday Ball with my new company.

On Nov 17th I went to the 1st Battalion briefing by LtCol Lloyd concerning cold weather training that was being planned for next year.

After the briefing I was walking to my truck when I again saw my old friend 1stSgt Cain who saluted me saying, "Well, Gunner you might get another promotion after all."

Returning his salute, I asked, "What are you talking about Top?"

"You haven't heard?"

"Heard what?"

"Congress has approved the new rank of Chief Warrant Officer Five."

"You're kidding."

"No sir. I read it this morning. Five percent of the total warrant officer force can be promoted to CWO-5 next year."

"Well that's good. But you'll probably need ten to twenty years in grade and I only have a little over five."

"You never know. Hell, I'm up for sergeant major. We might both reach to the top of our rank structures next year."

"I hope so. Good luck Top."

"Thank you, sir," he said as we parted.

December came and Marty, Samantha and I didn't go back home for Christmas. It seemed strange. But we still enjoyed the three of us being together unlike last year. Of course, we phoned home and received phone calls from our sons and families and talked with our grandchildren.

We three also spent New Year's at home together. Marty and I didn't even go out. And so, began the new year of 1992 and my twenty-eighth year in the Corps. I was also forty-four years old. It seemed funny to realize that this year I would reach the age my mother was when she died. And in Delta Company the only people older than me was the first sergeant and SSgt Biles.

On March 9th our battalion traveled to northern California to a Marine training area known as Pickle Meadows for cold weather training. In my twenty-eight years in the Corps, this was the first time I had trained here. SSgt McAdams told me this was actually late in the year to be doing cold weather training up here because it's colder and there is more snow in January and February. And it had rained the day we got there and there wasn't much snow around. Delta Company's sergeants and below were assigned to their own barracks. The Staff NCOs were assigned to a barracks with the other battalion Staff NCOs. I was assigned with the rest of the company grade officers of our battalion in a barracks.

The first few days we had classes indoors on surviving in snow and cold weather and how to treat wounds and cold weather injuries. Then we were issued skis. I was concerned about this because I had never been on skies before. I was used to taking the lead in things and teaching from my past experiences and setting the example. But here I was barely able to stand up on these things. Soon, I was being kidded by Sgt Brown and even SSgt Biles from 1st platoon. But by day's end, I could cross country ski with the best of them. I could even herring bone up hills as good as anyone. But once we started downhill, it was all over. It was so bad that I began to hear my young Marines whisper, "Look the Gunner is reaching the top of the hill. Watch this." And sure enough, I would fall before getting to the bottom.

That evening in the chow hall, SSgt Biles said, "Gunner I hear you're just like the little old man on Laugh In. You know the guy who's riding the tricycle, that just tips over."

"That's what I hear," I answered laughing with my embarrassment.

By March 13th we had had a heavy snow, which made the training and skiing for most people easier, but it didn't help me.

Each squad was issued an artic tent, which was the low wall design with a liner. We were given classes on how to set them up and take care of them.

Then it was another day of cross-country skiing. As I led my platoon to the top of one hill, I saw SSgt Biles preparing to take 1st platoon down the hill ahead of us.

I herring boned up next to him and asked, "Staff Sergeant Biles, could you take a picture of me skiing down this hill?"

"Sure Gunner," he answered.

I pulled my camera out of my inside pocket and handed it to him. He quickly and expertly skied about half way down the hill and stopped, watching his platoon as they passed by.

Then it was my platoon's turn. I started down first leading the way like a true leader of Marines. I didn't get many meters downhill before I fell. And as I slid down hill on my back head first, SSgt Biles took my picture as I slid by him.

Finally, at the bottom of the hill I managed to stand up as SSgt Biles skied up next to me and gave me back my camera, smiling.

I looked at him hard saying, "I thought I told you to take a picture of me skiing."

"But sir you weren't standing up long enough," he answered laughing. Then he skied away to join his platoon.

As I watched him go, I had to think, "Well I guess he was right."

The next day each squad was issued an Ahkio sled. The Ahkio sled was used to carry the artic tent and its equipment along with extra food, sleeping bags and equipment not needed to fight with. During field marches the fire teams would take turns pulling the sled. Three men would pull the sled, while the fourth man held a rope to the rear to guide it when going downhill.

The rest of the day we spent pulling Ahkio sleds across country.

Within a few days our battalion started its two weeks war game in the fields of snow the whole time. It got colder and snowed almost every day. We ate MRE meals for breakfast and lunch, but we had a hot meal trucked out to us each evening as well as fuel for our tent stoves.

The twelfth day in the field the Ahkio sleds and artic tents were taken from us. The next two nights we had to build squad shelters out of branches and leaves.

And as in the past, hard training such as this always made a platoon grow even closer and I had grown close to the men in my platoon.

On April 5th our battalion returned to Camp Pendleton.

On April 11th I looked at the just posted promotion list for Staff NCOs. I was sad to see 1stSgt Cain's name wasn't on it. But I was happy to see that my old friend Simon still with the 2nd Marine Division had been selected for master sergeant.

When I ran into 1stSgt Cain a few days later he told me he was going to retire in August.

I told him, "I'd hang in there. There's a good chance you'll get selected next year."

"I know you're right. But I've had enough. It's just not fun anymore. I'm starting to feel like a dinosaur in this Corps."

"Top you'll miss it when it's gone."

"You're probably right. If I talked to you much, you'd probably talk me into staying in longer."

"Then I'm going to talk to you every chance I get."

"Okay sir. I'll see ya around."

On the evening of April 26th LtCol Lloyd held an officers Mess

Night to welcome our new battalion XO Maj Grier to our battalion. Wearing my dress blues with over five rows of ribbons with four ribbons across, it was a good chance for me to meet the other officers of Alfa, Bravo and Charlie Companies.

On May 11th I received a letter from CMC telling me I was indeed up for promotion to the new rank of Chief Warrant Officer Five. I was surprised even though I had five and a half years in grade. I asked Capt Gillette, LtCol Lloyd and Col Hanson to write up a recommendation for me. I even phoned my old friend MajGen Hester on Okinawa and asked him to write something up for me. They all did and as I suspected MajGen Hester's letter was the best. I had my picture taken in green dress trousers and tan short sleeve shirt with my five rows of ribbons to go with my promotion package.

By June first I sent my package in to the promotion board in Washington DC and hoped for the best. But I knew there was just too many other warrant officer fours in the Corps like me with a lot more time in grade.

The next day LtCol Lloyd was transferred out and Maj Grier took command of our battalion. A Maj Dorset transferred in and took over the duties as our battalion XO.

During July, Col Hanson and Capt Gillette transferred out. Col McCarthy replaced Col Hanson. And a mustang Capt Mousier replaced Capt Gillette.

On Aug 12th I took Marty out to celebrate our first date as we did every year. We went to the movies and as usual walked on the beach at midnight. Except for the first time it was a beach on the Pacific coast in Oceanside California.

On Aug 19th Marty and I went over to Alfa Company's area and watched as 1stSgt Cain was ordered out front of the company formation to have his retirement orders read. As part of the ceremony, his wife was escorted out to his side and she was given a dozen red roses.

I hated to see him go. Another old friend retiring, leaving even fewer of us old Vietnam veterans still in active service.

On Sept 9th during a battalion field exercise, I was surprised to see Col McCarthy and our tall thin black regimental SgtMaj Hill drive up in a hummer. As they got out, I realized that Maj's Grier and Dorset were with them. I watched Capt Mousier run over to them saluting. After Col McCarthy returned his salute, Capt

Mousier turned and pointed in the direction of my platoon. As all five of them walked toward us SSgt McAdams asked, "What the hell do ya think is up sir?"

"I don't know staff sergeant, but keep the men in position and I'll go find out," I said standing up and walking toward them.

SgtMaj Hill had a big smile as I saluted the officers walking up to them.

I could tell Capt Mousier wasn't sure either why the colonel and majors were here.

After returning my salute Col McCarthy handed me a brown folder with stapled papers inside.

As I pulled the papers out Col McCarthy said, "Congratulations Gunner. This just came in."

As I looked at the papers, I found them to be the promotion list for warrant officers. About fifty warrant officers had been selected for Chief Warrant Officer Five. Of these, nineteen were Infantry Warrant Officers and my name was on the list. My mouth dropped opened in disbelief. Later, I would learn that thirteen out of the nineteen were fifty-nine years of age. And once promoted to CWO-5 they were guaranteed three more years in the Corps even beyond the age of sixty. But there was a catch for the rest of us. Before this new rank a CWO-4 could stay in the Corps until the age of sixty if he wanted to. Now all warrant officers were only guaranteed thirty total years in the Corps, which included their years of enlisted time. I would go over twenty-eight years next month. Of course, with this promotion I would have three more years. So, for the first time I knew I could be forced to retire in October of 1995 after thirty-one years' service.

Col McCarthy gave me the rest of the day off and SgtMaj Hill drove me back to Delta Company's area. There I got in my truck and drove home and told Marty and Samantha the news. I suddenly realized I might be in my last tour of duty in the Corps at my last duty station. That evening I phoned our sons back in Delaware and invited them to my promotion ceremony. But of course, it was too far for them to come. If only I had still been at Camp Lejeune NC.

On Sept 21st Marty and Samantha were my guests of honor sitting in chairs next to Col McCarthy, SgtMaj Hill and their wives.

With our battalion standing at attention Maj Grier ordered me to report to him, front and center.

As I stood at attention in front of him, he read the promotion warrant. I couldn't help but think of the past twenty-eight years. This was the second time I had reached the top of a rank structure. First, I had made Sergeant Major and now Chief Warrant Officer-5. I had been lucky and God had blessed me. That was why I requested Marty and Samantha to come up and pin the blood red bars surrounded by silver of my new rank on the collars of my tan shirt and the shoulders of my dress green blouse.

I thought my career was quickly coming to a close. I had no way of knowing it then, but there would be more campaigns ahead and my Corps would find use for me beyond three more years. But that is another story.

THE END

About the Author

Noble Callaway spent a combined 35 years in the Marine Corps and the Marine Corps Reserves. He served in Vietnam as a sergeant of infantry and in 15 years made master sergeant. After being appointed to the rank of Warrant Officer, he served in such places as Bosnia, Kosovo, Honduras and Iraq and retired as a chief warrant officer 5. He now lives with the love of his life, Martha on the farm he grew up on which has been in the family since 1777. They have 4 children, 11 grandchildren and 13 great-grandchildren.

Made in the USA
Middletown, DE
27 January 2022